LONE PLAYER

Lost Island
PRESS

LONE PLAYER

Your survival is their game.

JULIA ROSEMARY TURK

Lost Island
PRESS

Lone Player
Copyright © 2023 Julia Rosemary Turk

All rights reserved. No part of this book may be reproduced or used in any manner without written permission of the copyright owner except in the case of brief quotations embodied in critical articles and reviews.

Library of Congress Control Number: 2023910028

ISBN 979-8-9850102-8-2 (paperback)
ISBN 979-8-9850102-7-5 (ebook)

This book is a work of fiction. Names, characters, places, and incidents either are the product of the author's imagination or are used fictitiously. Any resemblance to actual events, businesses, companies, locales or persons, living or dead, is entirely coincidental.

Cover design by MAD Book Covers
Select interior illustrations by Gonzalo Mansilla

Lost Island Press LLC
Oro Valley, AZ
lostislandpress.com

LONE PLAYLIST

CURATED BY THE AUTHOR

♪ HERE'S YOUR FUTURE - THE THERMALS ♪

♪ SO HERE WE ARE - BLOC PARTY ♪

♪ ARE YOU - THE DELTA SAINTS ♪

♪ THREE DAY ROAD - BIRTH OF JOY ♪

♪ NEVER GROW OLD - AMERICAN PRINCES ♪

♪ IN THE SHADE OF THE SUN - KAPITAN KORSAKOV ♪

♪ MUSCLE MUSEUM - MUSE ♪

♪ RAINY DAY LOOP - SALES ♪

♪ NEW LOW - MIDDLE CLASS RUT ♪

♪ KILL OR BE KILLED - DIRTY SWEET ♪

♪ DEVIL YOU KNOW - PINBACK ♪

♪ NARROW MARGINS - HALF MOON RUN ♪

♪ YOU ARE A RUNNER AND I AM MY FATHER'S SON
- WOLF PARADE ♪

♪ INSINUATION - FOLK IMPLOSION ♪

♪ YEAR OF NO LIGHT - THREE MILE PILOT ♪

♪ WAITING - ALICE BOMAN ♪

♪ BLACK BEAR - BLACK BEAR ♪

♪ AFTER TIME - HIMALAYAS ♪

♪ FUTURE STARTS SLOW - THE KILLS ♪

♪ BLACK CREME - HRVRD ♪

♪ STUNTED - REMEMBER SPORTS ♪

♪ SILBURY SANDS - WOLF PEOPLE ♪

♪ SATURNINE - MYSTERY JETS ♪

♪ IMPLODE ALRIGHT - BUILT BY SNOW ♪

♪ THE LENGTHS - THE BLACK KEYS ♪

♪ IT'S SPRINGTIME AND THE APHIDS HAVE ARRIVED - SAY HI ♪

♪ LONGEST DAY - THREE MILE PILOT ♪

♪ FAREWELL TRANSMISSION - SONGS: OHIA ♪

To my brothers,
who I would go the lengths for.

Reaching, reaching, all around.

PROLOGUE

Sunday, December 31
The Pick

They are soaked in blood.

Both of them, eyes shut but sleepless, still as still can be.

Despite what most would think, I'm not familiar with blood. I can wield a Nightjade syringe like a pencil, but when my assignments are exterminated, they never bleed. I know the color of blood, its makeup, the way it flows through the body—but not its persistence. I've never had the chance to realize that when there's so much of it all at once, you can almost taste it.

Not until I find the Voclains.

Only five fleeting minutes ago, I made my way toward the scene like a lamb to a slaughter that wasn't mine. Rain was falling in whispering curtains that covered my white uniform in little glass beads. I readied my fist to knock on the door as my partner and I walked up the front steps, clenching my fingers and unfurling them over and over again. I fidgeted to the rhythm of the downpour, hoping it would soothe the nerves I'd been dizzy with all evening.

It did not.

The house was dreadfully silent as we entered in search of our target.

There was not a person in sight, but instincts and Chaser protocol urged us to search in caution, just in case our target was hiding nearby. I expected to hear the shuffle of evading sneakers, but the only audible sounds were the slow drum of our boots and the eerie percussion of rain. The same rain we carelessly tracked inside the house as though it belonged to strangers, and not a family I once knew so well.

The foyer showcased no evidence of the violence we would eventually find. Well-loved shoes lined the walls, all cloaked in the same thick coat of mud. If I didn't know any better, I would've believed they still had a purpose. My partner didn't pay any attention to the shoes as we walked inside, but to me, each one was a bleak symbol of a life once lived.

I couldn't bring myself to look him in the eye, but he seemed unaffected. Apathy allowed him to be separate, because it was a Chaser's job to be just that. Disconnected. You couldn't complete an assignment with guilt standing in the way.

But he didn't know the Voclains like I did.

The kitchen was cleaner, but it still displayed bits and pieces of the people the Voclains once were. A vague grocery list was scribbled on the back of a receipt left on the counter. Report cards and faded photographs of school athletic teams decorated the fridge like paintings. Grimy dishes were piled too high in the sink, a forgotten chore that no Voclain would ever be able to complete again.

I did not see their bodies until I entered the living room and found myself stepping in a thick pool of blood. It fanned behind Mr. and Mrs. Voclain like a crimson mirror, but it did not belong to them.

The Voclains were lucky. They got the syringe. But the two dead Chasers were the ones to suffer from knife wounds.

And now I stand here, looming over their still-warm bodies while I mentally replay the horrors that took place. There is so much blood. Its flavor rests on my tongue, sour and metallic, the seasoning of death. I wonder if its taste will ever leave.

I stare at the corpses, at the mutilated necks of the white-armored Officers, lifeless at my feet. I can tell they'd been punctured again and again by a hand that could have only belonged to our target. Who else could have done this but Eddie—the sole survivor of this occurrence?

She loves her family more than anything. She would have fought back, right?

My eyes flicker back to Eddie's parents. Mr. and Mrs. Voclain look so peaceful, so hollow. I assume her father, Mateo, was the first to go. Adele's body hovers over her husband's lifeless shell, somehow tending to him as she strokes his dark hair from beyond the grave.

I stare at Eddie's dead mother, whose eyes are still pried open. I watch her belly, waiting for it to rise and fall, waiting for some sign of life that never comes. *She really is dead.*

Dead because of people like me.

I reach out to close her eyes—but I can't.

The Voclains would still be breathing if it weren't for the system I devoted my life to when I became a Chaser, despite everything—*everyone*—it has taken away from me.

The same system Eddie cheated when she Ran away.

But of course she Ran. She couldn't have let this happen on purpose— I know Eddie better than that. After killing the Chasers for what they did to her parents, she must have fled.

My partner crouches down, running a finger through the blood of our fallen Officers. He inspects the stain on his gloved hand. "I know what happened."

My body trembles. I bite back a scream. *He doesn't know a damn thing.* But I can't open my mouth or peel my eyes away from the blood.

"It's written all over the scene." He stands up, wiping his finger on the back of the couch. "The Chasers came knocking, looking for Eddie, and when she tried to Run, they killed her family. Runner's penalty."

The Runner's penalty. It keeps us obedient, eager to accept our fates and let death come, because we all know the consequences of Running away. A Runner causes far more bloodshed than their own.

"Eddie didn't Run." I shake my head. My skull is filled with denial's cotton, my vision hazy. The frame of my sight lightens like someone has set the edges on fire. "She would never do that."

"It's the only explanation. They wouldn't have killed her parents for any other reason." He lets out a deep, frustrated sigh. "I don't care if you two had a history. She's your assignment now, and the evidence is all here."

He takes a few steps closer, walking over the dead Voclains without a second thought. He places a hand on my armored shoulder, gaze hollow. "You need to face the facts."

Face the facts.

Face the facts?

I can never face the facts, because these are not facts.

Something doesn't add up here. No one knows our target like I do. Although I can't verbalize my doubts without appearing disloyal to the Corps, I know that Eddie can't be at fault.

I need to find her. I need to save her, to figure out what really happened. Even though I'm expected to kill her.

My partner urges us to move forward and continue to look for our target. His words are like the call of some faraway train, distant and meaningless. I know I should cry, but grief is a luxury I can no longer afford. I sold that privilege for a white uniform.

Instead, I rise to my feet, remove my gloves, and wash the Voclains' dishes until the last plate is fully clean. But I can't stop. I keep scrubbing until the ceramic shatters under the pressure of my grip. I hold the shards as tightly as I can until more blood drips to the floor, staining the kitchen tile red.

But the sound of the drops is swallowed by the rain, and I can't bring myself to clean the mess. I fall to my knees and stare at the red dots until I can no longer keep my eyes open.

And before I know it, I am sobbing, and the sound of my cries is swallowed up too.

PART ONE
LIES

EDDIE

Wednesday, May 3
30 Days Until Graduation

♪ HERE'S YOUR FUTURE - THE THERMALS ♪

Margot and I are sprawled across what her dad likes to call grass, but I wouldn't call it that.

What might have been grass twenty years ago is now lifeless and dry, itchy like cheap carpet. Most of it is actually dirt.

I've never been able to figure out why Margot's father doesn't water his lawn. It's been decades since the last drought, and we live in one of the only countries in the world with constant access to water. In the only place able to have green lawns, the McLellans' is intentionally the color of wheat.

"Can you believe we're graduating soon?" I ask the question rhetorically, but Margot answers. The dead grass pokes through my sweater, but I don't mind. It's peaceful out here, and peace is a rarity for me these days.

"I believe it," Margot says, hands beneath her head as she stares at the sky. "Thirty days left."

"And you're not... unsure of anything?" I sit up and raise my eyebrows in her direction. I expect her to give me one of those Margot looks, but her eyes are fixed on the clouds.

"Unsure? No. I live a life of facts," she replies. "I'm sick, but at least I'm sure of it."

"Careful." I elbow Margot in warning of her word choice. *You never know who could be listening.*

"I think graduation only frightens you because you're scared of breaking the expectations everyone has set for you," she says, now turning to give me the look I expected earlier.

I scoff. "What expectations?"

"C'mon, Ed. Everyone thinks you're gonna be a Chaser. You're the top of the class," she says, lowering her voice. "Have you told anyone else you don't want to be one?"

"No." I look down at my grass-stained sneakers, opening my mouth to speak before taking a brief pause. *I never even took the exam.*

"See? I told you, you're afraid of breaking expectations."

But those expectations have already been broken.

I'm expected to become a killer when that's the last thing I want to be.

Either way, Margot has a point and I don't like it. I turn away from her and look at the clouds again, trying to soothe my thoughts by finding shapes and patterns in the sky with no luck.

Margot has always been the one with a good eye for things like that. I glance at her once more, and right away, I can see the gears spinning in that magnificent mind of hers.

I've always loved her knowledge and creativity, but I would be lying if I said I didn't envy her for it. Working hard to mimic intelligence is not the same as actually possessing it. While I've been academically successful, Margot has found success in other ways with *true* intelligence. Sure, her condition affects her grades, but her mind can never be quantified.

I wish I could understand her understanding—her love for the unloved, her ears for the unheard, her sight for the unseen. Life has been nothing close to easy for Margot, but despite it all, she seems to have a deeper appreciation for it than anyone else I've met. I would trade almost anything in the world to have a mind like hers. A mind that can truly see the similarities in all living things.

That is, after all, how we became friends as little girls. She noticed we were both unlucky enough to have matching Joker Cards on our wrists.

I've been called unlucky my whole life. Everyone knows there are two Jokers in a deck of cards, and having one inked on your skin is seen as a curse. I can't recollect every time a stranger warned my parents in the grocery store that I would bring them immense misfortune.

I suppose there are some logical origins to this belief. If there are two identical Joker cards in a deck, then I guess there is a slightly higher chance of a Joker card being pulled on New Year's—and being Picked is just about the unluckiest thing that can happen to a person.

And I was lucky enough to be born with a Joker on both of my wrists.

Part of me thinks my tattoos are what urged my father to push me so hard to take the Chaser's path of life. *Be the best you can be, and you can manipulate the odds to work in your favor.* I try not to laugh. If my old man had a motto, that would be it.

Until I met Margot, I didn't believe anyone else understood what it was like to be labeled as unlucky. And while she knows exactly how it feels— more than me, in fact—she has never treated me differently. Even with over a decade of friendship behind us, she still loves me just as much as she loves the rest of the world.

And that's why I love her too.

"Hey, that one looks like a Spade." Margot sits up and points at the vast expanse of blue.

Sure enough, a white streak in the sky paints the shape of a Spade to near perfection.

"If Ren held his left tattoo up to the sky, it would be an identical match." Margot brings her wrist closer to the cloud. "Now all we need is the letter *A*, and you have a perfect Ace of Spades."

Ren. The sound of her brother's name makes my stomach turn, and I grit my teeth in malice. I try my best to smile without clenching my jaw too much, but Margot notices and lets out an exhausted sigh.

"When are you two gonna learn to get along?" She laughs, but her tone is frustrated. "You guys are so much alike and neither of you have any idea."

"We won't, and we're not," I protest firmly. "We're *opposites*, Margot.

Night and day. Cold and warm. Mean guy and nice girl."

"Ren's a lot nicer than you are."

"Not true. There are plenty of people who would agree with me."

"Who, Duke Carmody?" Margot wiggles her eyebrows.

"Dear God, no." I shudder. "Look, my point is... Ren and I don't compute. I know he's your twin and all, but I'm sorry. Some people aren't meant to get along."

Margot doesn't say anything. She picks at a dried leaf instead, and I hear it crunch between her fingernails as she folds it, the material creasing until it breaks into little brown crumbs. I know her well enough to be patient, to not interrupt her train of thought.

But I ask the question anyway, because I want her to know she's seen.

"Is something wrong?"

There are no more leaves to pick at on this side of the front lawn, so she twirls her necklace around her finger instead. The chain is gold, delicate, and older than she is. I'm surprised it's remained in such good condition after all these years. While her mother's old locket has always had a few scratches, it hasn't changed since the day I met her—even with all the anxious fidgeting.

"We haven't gotten in a fight, if that's what you're wondering. Ren and I," Margot announces after a minute or two, reading my mind with ease.

"You can always talk to me, you know."

She nods.

"Even about Ren," I clarify with a smile.

There's a pause. "He's just been... distant, lately. I don't know." Margot holds the locket in her hands and stares at the pendant intently, avoiding my gaze.

"Isn't he always an emotionally distant shut-in?"

She nudges me teasingly. "Shut up."

"Have you guys been talking much recently?" I ask, dropping the humor from my tone. Ren is the last person I want to talk about, but Margot's peace of mind is a higher priority than any grudge.

"Not really," she answers, her voice heavy with concern. "I mean, we have small talk when he gets home from school. But after that, he just stays locked in his room or leaves the house without telling me where he's going. He doesn't even join Dad and me at the dinner table anymore—he just eats at his desk."

Margot continues to fidget, and I watch her unravel her thick double braids. Her hair is night black and characteristically neat, cut just past her shoulders, unlike my own impossible curls. They fall to my back and get in the way of everything, and there are days when I seriously consider shaving it all off to rid myself of the unruly mess.

Margot combs out the strands with her finger before re-braiding them as cleanly as possible. She only fidgets this much when her anxiety is about to peak. Even with the stress of hiding her illness—let alone the weight of dealing with her symptoms day after day—she only seems to focus on the well-being of those around her.

So I believe her when she tells me something's up with Ren.

"It's a long shot, but he probably has a girlfriend." I tease, but if his social skills magically improved overnight, it could very well be a justified answer.

"If he did, I'd know," Margot assures me. She looks away.

That weasel, I think, clenching my fists so tightly they pull tufts of dead grass from the ground. Does he see what this distance is doing to her? Lyme is lonely enough as it is.

"I don't know," Margot says firmly. "I honestly don't. I just know he's hiding *something*."

There's a pause. "Is there anything I can do to help?"

"No." Margot shakes her head, staring at the back of her hands. "I just hope we don't grow apart."

I don't know what to say, so we sit there in silence. A breeze loosens the braids Margot fixed only a moment ago. With her solemn expression and disrupted hair, I can't help but notice how tired she looks. Even with the weight of chronic fatigue bringing her down, she has always been a colorful soul. But now, she looks exhausted, as if the energy she's worked so hard to maintain has been completely drained from her.

"He's all I have, Eddie." Margot stares at the Spade in the sky, the once-clear shape now an undefined brush stroke against an endless blue canvas. "I love you, Ed, but I don't know who I am without him."

REN

Wednesday, May 3
45 Days Left of Being Human

The envelope is light, but it weighs heavy in my hands.

It feels like I've waited my entire life for this moment, and I can't even bring myself to open it. My hands shake, but other than that, I don't move. My whole body is frozen.

I stare at the seal to ensure this is the real thing. A black poker chip keeps the envelope closed, like a mouth promised to stay shut. Paper lips guard a secret kept by the Chaser Corps, as signified by the gold lettering that decorates the seal. My eyes remain glued to the insignia for two whole minutes, and though we are all too familiar with this symbol, it feels new to me. Foreign. Intimidating.

They told us when we would receive them and they kept that promise to perfection. Wednesday, the 3rd of May. Exactly a month before graduation.

I always knew when it was going to arrive, but now that it's here, I'm not sure if anything could have prepared me for this moment. Not even a date. I knew nothing before, and I still know just as much.

A timeline is nothing.

It's like knowing how you die. It's not better if there are thirty days between you and your demise instead of one; it's the waiting that hurts more than the fall itself.

My eyes trace the edges of the ivory envelope. There must be a mistake. It's simply too thin to carry the heavy news it holds inside. No one urges me to open it. No one places a hand on my shoulder, prepared to either congratulate or console me—though I'm unsure which reaction would be appropriate for either outcome.

It feels surreal that my family doesn't know about any of this. I almost expect my father to walk in and give me a pat on the back as he normally does when I achieve something important. But this is no achievement. He would never approve of this. How could he, considering all that has been taken from us?

How could anyone?

The seal cracks as it breaks, overwhelming me with the sharp scent of stale paper and printer ink. My hands won't stop shaking and I cut my finger on the envelope as I pull the documents out of hiding. The sliver of slit skin stings, but the burning goes completely over my head. All my focus is spent on the letter I've been waiting so long to receive.

All that's left is for the papers to unfold.

It's funny, really, how a few short moments can change your life so drastically.

I close my eyes, inhaling deeply, concentrating on the oxygen that fills my lungs. I think about what has been sacrificed to make this air clean in the first place. I think about how this air is the same air that fills all of our bodies, even though the rest of the world is not privileged enough to access clean air at all.

We as humans don't like to admit it, but we are all the same. We are all born with the same lungs and we are cursed with the same task of using them until the day we die. But as similar as we are at our core, the differences are also too significant to ignore.

And though I sit here, breathing like everyone else, I have a fifty-fifty chance of becoming a person whose sole purpose is to take away life, the one thing that makes all of us the same.

I could become a Chaser. An elite government soldier paid to kill. *A monster.*

And that's why I'm so terrified when I unfold the papers in my hands. I take a deep breath, count to three, and take a dive.

Dear Applicant,

It all feels too dreamlike. I read the two words again and again, and they ring in my ears like the echo of a bell.

Dear Applicant, Dear Applicant, Dear Applicant,

I could dwell on this simple phrase for hours in fear of reading on, but I know I can't.

You are receiving this letter in regards to your recent application and completion of the Chaser Corps Entrance Exam.

I read the words as slowly as I can, legs shaking. I chew the inside of my cheek so hard I taste iron, but it doesn't bother me. I welcome any distraction that will take me away from the truth I'm so afraid to uncover.

But the truth can't hide forever.

It always comes.

Congratulations, Ren McLellan.

Congratulations? What could that mean?

Does the word signify that I passed? Or does it mean that in my failure, I avoided something potentially destructive to myself and the people around me? Do I really deserve to be congratulated, even if I passed the exam? Is it right to receive praise for something like this?

You have passed. Through both the written and physical sections of the exam, you have proven yourself to be an excellent candidate for training this summer.

I forget how to breathe. Part of me wants to sigh with relief, but the guilty half is too heavy to let that happen.

The 17th of June awaits you with open arms.

I wish it didn't. I beg for June to disappear completely. Maybe I could tear the page right out of my calendar.

The rest of the letter goes on to explain logistics to me. Dates and expectations dance around in my mind, going completely over my head. I can't focus on anything but the very last sentence of the letter.

It's the last sentence that hits the hardest. Five simple words, and they nearly break me.

Welcome to the Chaser Corps.

Before the reality of it all sinks in, my father's voice pulls me back to Earth and calls me down for dinner. I shove the envelope in my backpack, because despite the contents of the letter, I still have to pretend to be Ren McLellan.

For my family's sake.

It's pasta again. I can smell it.

I walk down the stairs briskly, eager to grab a bowl and return to my business. But I stop dead in my tracks when I see the guest in our kitchen.

Lavender Voclain, again. The girl most people call Eddie, though I would rather call her a nuisance. And by the expression on my father's face, I can tell he expects me to stay.

She sits next to my sister at our scratched wooden table, her dark brown curls spilling over her shoulders in a way that makes me want to hand her a comb. She's not unattractive, just careless. Eddie pretends not to see me staring, but I know she does. Neither of us wants me to be here.

I'm bothered by her presence, perpetually frustrated by the confusing dynamic of her friendship with my sister. Margot is intelligent, sensible, and grounded. Eddie may be academically inclined, but she is unpredictable and reckless enough to be considered foolish. To put it simply, they don't match.

Eddie doesn't bother to greet me with a smile—let alone look at me—but I offer a synthetic one out of polite obligation. I try to make myself comfortable in the seat next to her, but being anywhere within a foot of her person makes me nauseous. Unfortunately, I don't have much of a choice.

She heaps piles of plain cassava penne into her bowl. I wonder if she's used to Margot's dietary restrictions by now or if she just pretends to be. There's a lot about her that seems pretend.

"So Eddie," Dad says between mouthfuls as he pokes around his bowl with a fork. "Don't acceptance letters come this time of year?"

I almost drop my fork.

"I think so," Eddie replies politely. Her quick smile seems as plastic as mine. Margot gives her a look I can't read from across the table.

"I mean, I don't know much about the process, but I'm assuming an acceptance letter means you go off to training this summer, correct? To become a Chaser and all that?" My dad helps himself to a second serving, while Eddie has barely touched her first.

"Yeah, that's right," the girl replies. "June, I think."

"Right after graduation then, huh?"

Eddie nods, as though confirming the question aloud will make it real. For once, I can't blame her.

"It'll be interesting to see this all play out," my father adds. "I mean, it feels like only yesterday you kids were pretending to be dragons or wizards out in the yard. It's strange how you're all growing up so quickly."

"Yeah." Eddie nods, staring at her bowl before shooting me a glare. "But people change, don't they?"

"They sure do." I take a sip of water as I keep my gaze fixed to the wall behind my father's head, not bothering to reciprocate Eddie's glare. I feel

Margot kick me from beneath the table. She knows who my response was targeting and gives me a sharp scowl to defend her friend, but I pretend not to see it.

Something's off with Eddie tonight, even more so than usual. I can't help but think she's hiding something. Her mind is in another place. I try to shake the thought out of my head because I know it's none of my business, but it's hard to ignore the signs of a liar when you're hiding something yourself.

Then it sinks in. If Eddie is becoming a Chaser too, there is no more hiding. I won't be able to keep my decision from my family anymore. I might be able to avoid Eddie at training this June, but I won't be able to escape seeing her every day that follows. I'm sure that she could never—*would* never—keep that kind of a secret from Margot.

Right?

Margot is strong in many ways, but fragile in others, and Lyme is to blame for that. Half of her symptoms are neurological. Her ravenous anxiety and depression are more than what most able-bodied people could handle in a lifetime. It would hurt Margot deeply if she discovered just what I was doing for her sake, but it would absolutely break her if Eddie kept that same secret from her as well. Surely Eddie is aware of that.

If Eddie really did pass the Chaser exam, I know she wouldn't let me hide it from my family.

"So Ren," my dad blurts. "What do you think? About Eddie becoming a Chaser?"

I almost choke on my pasta. I gulp several generous sips of water from my glass and set it back down, clearing my throat.

"I mean, we all expected it—with her grades and everything," I mutter. "There's no better candidate or career choice out there, if status is what you're after. Or Immunity."

It's a lie. If you're not as desperate as I am, there are plenty of choices out there. Choices that don't involve murder. Choices that wouldn't put a Nightjade syringe in the hands of the last two people I'd trust with that responsibility.

"I wouldn't say *that*." Dad looks over his shoulder cautiously before lowering his tone to a near whisper, just in case someone might be listening. "I mean, no offense, Eddie, we love you and all, but you know how we feel about the whole Chaser ordeal."

"*Dad*." Margot nudges our father in the shoulder.

"It's alright." Eddie chuckles. "In all honesty, I feel the same way."

The room goes dead quiet.

What could she possibly mean by that?

"Then why the hell are you going through with it, if being a Chaser isn't something you want to do?" Dad laughs through a mouthful of pasta.

"Well, like Ren said..." Eddie looks down at her bowl again and pokes pieces of cold penne with her fork. "Expectations."

"It's okay to break expectations sometimes." Margot gives Eddie a reassuring smile from across the table. Like clockwork, it's returned.

When you decide to become a liar, the best thing you can do is to read other liars. Make note of the way people consciously or unconsciously break. Recognize when you can actually *tell* that someone is lying, and do what you must to avoid following the footsteps of a person too easily read. That's where truth-keeping becomes a tricky skill to master, because most people are open books. Lavender Voclain is certainly no exception to this rule.

Eddie is an open book, but her words are written in code.

I know she's lying, but about what?

I'm robotic through dinner's closing. The apathy continues as I begin to tackle Margot's nightly medication routine while my father collects the dishes. Eddie has left the room, and I feel slightly less paranoid with the absence of her hidden glares and darting eyes. She makes me nervous. Dizzyingly so. Like a timer about to go off, or a spark snaking closer to a stick of dynamite.

I drop the capsules into a ceramic dish, careful not to spill any. Waste leads to a quicker decrease of her stock, and I know how much of a hassle it is to obtain these supplements. Olive leaf, grapefruit seed, reishi, garlic, turkey tail, dandelion, green tea—the list is an extensive one, and Underground orders are not easy to fulfill.

Margot and I have known about our father's connection to the Undergrounders for as long as we can remember, but even when we were younger, we never questioned it. In a world where asking the wrong thing gets you killed, you learn to keep your mouth shut at a young age. But that doesn't mean we don't worry.

Every time he leaves, we fear he won't come back. We know he drives hours away to restock these supplements with cash, often crossing state boundaries to avoid detection. This is how the Undergrounders work. Always on the move, always relocating transaction points, always hiding from the system that has made illness and a thousand other things a crime.

I hold a little brown capsule in my hands and wonder how much it cost him. Enough of his paycheck to cause those stress lines on his face, that's for sure. *Or maybe he bargained with a different kind of currency?*

I'm careful because I know these priceless gems are absolutely necessary for Margot's survival. The few herbal supplements we have access to on rare occasions are not enough to rid her of this disease, but they are enough to lessen her symptoms just enough to hide her illness from the rest of the world. A world where being chronically ill deems you undeserving of the resources that could easily go to a person who is healthy and has the physical and mental capabilities to better our society.

A world where Margot could be killed in an instant.

Her protection comes at a cost too deep to fill any wallet. But she can never be allowed to know, because she would break if she did.

I hand the capsules to my sister with a glass of filtered water so she can start gulping them down. The color drains from her face as the liquid touches her tongue, and her expression twists with nausea and disgust.

"It tastes like soap. Soap and metal," she mumbles.

"I know." I lie, because I don't know. To everyone else, water is tasteless. Water is a refreshing and essential element that gives life to all things. Access to it is what makes us so lucky—and keeps our borders closed to *protect resources*—yet Margot cannot stand it. More than a glass at a time will make her vomit. She says she can taste the pipes it came from.

And if I have to devote my life to being a pawn in this system, even if it means losing myself in the process, I will. Because I want my sister to get better. I want her to wake up without a migraine. I want her to be able to walk reasonable distances without collapsing. I want to rid her of the novel-sized list of symptoms that torture her nonstop, day after day. I don't want to hear her crying to herself in the middle of the night when she thinks we're asleep, when her spine is burning or her leg is burning or her brain is burning and her entire body feels like it's on fire. I pray for quiet nights that have never come to pass.

But most of all, I want her to drink water.

So if this awful system is in place to give water to all, let water be given to all.

I will Chase to earn her the saving grace of Immunity, no matter the cost.

EDDIE

Wednesday, May 3
30 Days Until Graduation

The silence that follows after Asa's questions makes me uncomfortable.

I know he's just trying to make conversation, but I can't help but feel exposed. Like everyone knows what I've done. Or haven't done, I should say. My gut is ridden with the guilt of pretending to be something I despise so much.

Asa is more than just the father of Ren and Margot, more than a car mechanic, more than a widower, more than a reader and a lover of the outdoors. The twins and I both know Asa has some unspoken connection to the Undergrounders, and in my false pursuit of becoming a Chaser, I have disappointed him.

He hates Chasers more than anyone. Chasers are killers, and they go against everything the Undergrounders stand for.

None of them know I want to be an Undergrounder too. I bite the inside of my cheek as I look around the dinner table. *But I'd like to keep it that way.*

I feel the burning of Ren's stare, but his eyes dart away as soon as I try to match his glare. He walks over to the counter and begins to sort out Margot's vast collection of herbal supplements—bottles filled with desperate attempts to fix something unfixable in a world where chronic Lyme disease might as well be a death sentence.

When he's not looking, I shift my gaze to watch Ren work. As he concentrates on preparing Margot's medication, I try to find something behind his eyes, though I can't see much of them from my distance. Loose strands of feathery black hair fall over his forehead and shield his gaze. But there is a contortion to his face I cannot ignore, and it looks a lot like guilt.

Something is definitely up. I try to keep my expression as natural as possible as I set down my fork. He's hiding something big from Margot, and I'm going to find it. *For her.*

"Restroom, be right back." I say the words to Margot, but I speak them just loud enough to signal a natural exit from the room. Ren doesn't even notice.

I make my way up the stairs, craning my neck once I reach the landing to ensure that everyone is preoccupied. I don't want them to see me turn the handle to enter Ren's room, or to watch me slip inside and intrude upon a space that is not my own.

I close the door behind me, keeping the knob turned as I do so to prevent it from clicking too loudly. I feel like an idiot, but that's not new. Deep down, I know this will most likely come back to bite me later. Things usually do. But right now, I don't give a damn. I just need to find something— *anything*—to ease Margot's stress. And if I don't find anything, that's something too.

Ren's room is too neat to belong to a boy who spends so much time locked away within its walls. There is no surface clutter, no trinkets lining the carefully organized bookshelf. No memories perched upon his desk. No school work spread across the tabletop, no mountain of dirty laundry, no electronic cords twisting around his furniture. There is no mess, but everything still feels out of place.

I start searching the bookcase, grabbing novel after novel and flipping through their worn pages to see what information might fall out. A letter, a photograph, money—anything worth hiding in the binding of a book.

It's a mismatched collection of nonfiction works and sci-fi novels. There are so many books about the stars—where they come from and how they work, or what they would be like if blue people in spaceships were to live among them. Ren has the library of both a realist and a dreamer, and I'm stumped, because I cannot tell which category fits the boy I used to know. My recollection of the Ren from my childhood does not match the Ren of today. There is simply no way of deciphering which version of him is synthetic.

One book catches my eye, and I pause to crouch to its level. It looks forgotten as it rests on the bottom shelf, begging me to reach out and grab the bright yellow spine that seems so out of place in this dark room.

I stare at the cover for a moment until, with a gasp, I finally recognize it. It's an old botanical encyclopedia from the Yesterdays, and I remember it fondly.

As a child, I spent countless hours pouring over the McLellans' vast library of books. While most valuable Yesterday titles were banned and put out of print, some people were lucky to have a large enough collection by the time Nightjade laws came around that they had no need to purchase a book again. The only way to get a decent, uncensored book these days is to inherit one, or find someone else who has.

Fortunately, Asa reads just about as much as he breathes. He holds onto every book he stumbles across, keeping his shelves full of unfamiliar titles I never knew until I met Margot. He must have access to countless Yesterday heirlooms, given the unspoken connections that his children and I pretend to know nothing about. We're not stupid enough to believe it doesn't exist, but we're not stupid enough to acknowledge its existence aloud either.

But this book topped them all. Out of every book I had access to growing up with the McLellans, something about the beauty of vintage illustrations and the detailed descriptions of so many plants captivated me. When Margot was having a bad health day and couldn't go outside, I'd sprawl out on her floor to keep her company while she napped, absolutely mesmerized by the encyclopedia until it was time to head home.

The book got old after a while, but my love for plants did not waver. It sowed a passion for growth, for learning things—especially the things I'm not supposed to know. This book is the reason why I succeed academically. Without its influence I doubt I would have ever dreamed of becoming an Undergrounder someday—instead of the Chaser my father wants me to be.

As much as I want to stay here and read, I know I can't. I close the book and give up on the shelves when my search yields no results. My eyes scan the room for anything worth noting, but as usual, I have no luck. *Damn Joker Cards.*

A constellation map is plastered near his bed, but other than that, his navy walls are completely bare. His closet is the home of nothing but clothes, his hardwood planks hold not even a single speck of dust, his desk drawers hide only pencils and worn-down erasers. Everything in this room signifies that it belongs to a perfectionist, but I know Ren can't possibly be as perfect as he pretends to be.

The weight of passing time and a lack of success pushes me closer to forgetting about this whole ordeal. I'm just about to give up on my efforts when I spot it.

Ren's backpack hides under his desk, blending in with the shadows so well I almost miss it.

I crouch down, kneeling on the floor to reach out and grab it. It's heavy, and I can tell it's filled to the brim with books long before I manage to open the zipper. The sound is louder than I expect it to be, but I don't care. I'll be quick.

The aroma of fresh paper and wood pencil shavings floods my nose as its contents reveal themselves before me. At a first glance, I don't notice anything that's not academic. I pull out the textbooks and workbooks one by one.

Calculus Made Easy
Nightjade Economics
Climate Change History
Literature of the Yesterdays: A Time Before Nightjade
Modern Botany for a New Society

I'm not sure what I expected, but I'm disappointed when I don't find anything suspicious. As cruel as it is, part of me wanted to—if only to prove how justified I am in my hatred for Ren. Forcing Margot to view her brother in a negative light would not benefit her. I start to shove the school books back inside the bag with a heavy sigh.

And then it falls out.

An envelope of crisp ivory, sealed with the wax black poker chip insignia of the Chaser Corps. It floats to the ground like a feather, delicate and without sound.

I stop breathing. I let go of the letter like it's cursed, afraid to even touch something so sinister, so infectiously evil. I wipe my hands on my shirt like I've been corrupted, tainted by this horrible thing I can barely comprehend. In my irrationality, I almost wonder if it's for me, even though I know that's impossible. Though I told everyone I did, I never even took the entrance exam in the first place.

This is not my acceptance letter, but it can't be Ren's.

This doesn't belong here. This is an impossibility.

I blink a dozen times to make sure I'm not mistaken, but the image in front of me doesn't change.

Maybe there's been some mistake. Maybe he grabbed the wrong bag at school, and this letter isn't his. *That's probably it,* I tell myself. The seal is already cracked. I could read the letter and find out who it really belongs to.

I take a deep breath. I remove the neatly folded paper. I unfold it, and I read.

I deny it.

I shake my head.

It takes reading over the letter three times for me to realize that it truly does belong to Ren McLellan.

This is what he's been hiding, I think to myself, lungs strained, trying to breathe through the white-hot shock hollowing out my chest and seeping into my bones. I put the paper back inside its envelope and stare at the wall until my eyes cross. But the image is still burned into my mind, like I faced the sun for too long and now there's a rectangular white spot in my vision, making it far too difficult to see anything else clearly.

Ren is becoming a Chaser.

Ren, of all people.

The paranoid moral perfectionist. The germaphobe health nut who hates blood. The pacifist son of a secret anti-Chaser, interested in the art of murder.

"If you wanted help with your homework, you should have just said so."

I jump as a mocking voice interrupts my thoughts. I whip my head around to find Ren standing in the doorway, arms crossed as he glares intently in my direction, his narrow chin raised in an above-all way that makes my blood boil. His inky hair is parted down the middle, a handful of disobedient strands falling over his forehead, tracing the skin just above his sharp stare like little curtains.

He is grinning falsely until his mouth falls into a thin, unamused line. "What are you doing?"

I freeze. The color drains from my body, churning my stomach. I swallow the lump in my throat, hands seizing vigorously as I turn around with *Modern Botany* close to my chest like a shield. I suddenly want nothing more than to be invisible.

"Lavender Voclain is struggling with botany." Ren scoffs, looking at me as a lion might eye a mouse. To him, I am weaker, smaller, and certainly not worth his time. "Who would have guessed?"

Annoyance brings the color back to my complexion. My face floods with heat.

"Sure, yeah. *I* need help from *you*." I roll my eyes. I feel irrationally angry at him, as though *he* looked through *my* room and not the other way around.

But I know my anger is justified. Maybe I put my nose where it doesn't belong, but people have done far worse things.

And nothing is worse than becoming a Chaser.

Nothing.

"No one told you I'm number two?" Ren folds his arms as he leans against the doorway, tilting his head to the side. His face is plagued with a hubristic smirk that makes me gag. "One little slip-up on your end and I'll be top of the class."

"Second best is still second best," I spit. "But I guess it's enough to become a Chaser."

Ren's eyes widen, and when they flicker to the envelope in my hands, he turns ghastly. Frantic, he shuts the door like I've just confessed to killing a man. "What did you just say?"

I reply at an obnoxious volume. "I said, second best is still second best, but it's enough to become a Chase—"

"For once in your life, would you shut up?" Ren seethes. He walks over to where I stand before snatching the envelope and putting it back in its place.

"Why should I?" I keep my arms crossed against my chest as I hug the textbook. "Like hell I'd ever do anything for your sake."

Ren grits his teeth. *"Because this is bigger than me."*

I've known Ren as long as I've known Margot, and he's always been a boy of quiet hatred. But I've never seen him this angry before.

Ren's tone softens, but he doesn't speak gently. "This is bigger than me, and it's certainly bigger than you."

"How?" I whisper. Not for him, but for Margot. Something tells me I don't want her overhearing this. "How can this be bigger than you?"

Ren freezes.

"You were the one who decided to take the Chaser exam." I shake my head in disbelief. "You know, even after that day—*especially* after that day —I never expected *you* of all people to do such a thing. Not after all they've done to Margot. Not after all they've done to your father. To *you*, even."

"You can't be angry at the way I'm rowing when we're in the exact same boat."

I blink, puzzled until I realize what he means. "Oh. That."

He still thinks I'm becoming a Chaser too.

"Yeah, *that*." He gives me a condescending look.

"Bold of you to assume I even took the exam," I mumble under my breath.

He pauses. "What?"

"I'm not..." I let out a sigh instead of finishing the sentence.

I haven't said the words aloud to anyone but Margot. She doesn't know

I lied about taking the exam—that's a secret only I know—but she's certainly aware of how I truly feel about Chasing.

My secret has been well-kept up to this point, but there's no way I can keep it any longer with Ren's new involvement. Who knows what he'll say when he goes off to training and doesn't see me there? There's no way he'd ever lie for my sake. He'd never protect me.

I have a good reason for keeping the truth from everyone. Not even Margot can know. But for Ren, I might have to make an exception.

"I'm not becoming a Chaser."

I always thought those would be proud words. I imagined they would escape my lips in another argument between my father and me. He would be speechless. He'd pause one of his lectures on why it's so important to be the best and he would freeze, because for once, he wouldn't know what to say. But I would.

I would tell him how undeniably twisted it is to worship a flawed system that runs on murder—and to try to raise his daughter to do the same thing.

But now, the words are shameful. They feel like a coward's confession, not a noble statement of my pride, of the morality I thought I had.

"I'm just—how the hell can you support something like this? How can you be so *selfish*?" I swallow the shame and toss Ren's *Modern Botany* workbook on the neatly made bed where it lands with a muted thud. "Don't you realize what they've done? Don't you realize what *you've* done?"

"*Of course I know what I'm doing!*" Ren hisses, so enraged that it should be impossible to keep his voice low. "This is all for her."

He speaks softer than he has all evening. "Don't you get it?"

I don't know what to say, so I don't say anything at all.

"Everything I do is for her." He shakes his head. "*Everything.*"

His words feel like a brick to the head or a punch to the gut, and I bite my lip. I could never feel sorry for Ren, but I feel like an idiot for not realizing it sooner.

Of course he's becoming a Chaser. Is there a better way to save Margot than with Immunity, a privilege most wallets can't afford? A privilege Chasers earn for themselves and their families without financial sacrifice?

Even though Margot has access to simple treatment through her father's connection to the Undergrounders, her illness is chronic, and her secret is still at risk of being exposed. *This is why Ren wants Immunity for her*, I realize. He wants to protect her.

If they find out she's sick, she could be killed—or worse. They could send her to work at the Tombs if they determine the debt of her unsatisfactory existence must be paid with labor before death. She'd spend the rest of her life digging graves and working crematoriums in conditions that kill most able-bodied people in a heartbeat.

Immunity would save her from the Nightjade Order and its laws. Immunity would allow her to be sick, freely, without the threat of extermination. We could focus on finding her better Underground treatment instead of spending all energy on hiding the fact that she's sick to begin with.

The absence of noise thickens the air and weighs down on my tongue. I struggle to overcome it, but I do. Because there are elephants running amuck, and the room is getting full.

"I know."

I whisper so low I can barely hear myself, and I can't look Ren in the eye.

He's silent for a moment, looking up at me though I try to avert his gaze. His head falls lower and he stares at his hands instead.

"All Chasers are automatically given Immunity for themselves and their immediate families," he states quietly. "It's the only way."

"I know."

"Look." Ren sighs and sits on the bed, running his hands along the sides of his face in a clear state of distress. "I know it's a lot to ask, but you can't tell Margot. You owe me that much."

"I don't owe you anything."

"For sneaking around in my room," he points out sharply and I glare. I know it's fair, but I can't come to terms with the idea of being indebted to *him*.

"It's not my place to decide which secrets you can keep from Margot, but I can't lie to her," I confess. "She would never speak to me again if she figured out I was hiding this from her."

"Well you made it your place when you decided to invade my privacy," Ren snaps. My lips stretch into a thin line, and as much as I would love to argue with him, I know he's right.

"I'm sorry for snooping, but I can't do that for you." I fold my arms. "Margot is more important to me than protecting your secret."

"You really are daft, aren't you?" Ren glares, his anger true and potent. The question hits me with another blow to the gut, and my jaw drops in disbelief.

My mouth moves quicker than my mind, and before I know it I'm mocking his words. "You really are an ass, aren't you?"

"I'm not asking for me. I'm asking for her," Ren claims, his tone somber. "I know my sister better than anyone. Better than you, better than our father, better than any other person on the planet. Alright?"

I clench my jaw in stubborn annoyance, but I nod to let him continue.

"If she found out just what I was doing for her sake, it would break her," Ren says, and for once, the words coming out of his mouth make sense.

There's a pause. "Have you ever seen Margot with a mosquito?"

"No," I reply, refusing to look him in the eye.

"She just sits there and lets the bug suck her blood. I can't tell you how many times she's cried because I swatted one off of her," Ren explains. "But you know what she asks me every time?"

"Yeah?"

"She asks me how her life is any different from that mosquito's." He chuckles bitterly. "She asks how a bite-free arm could possibly be worth the cost of another life."

I smile at the thought of Margot's gentle nature, but then I realize something. How would she feel if she discovered that Ren took the Chaser exam? How would she feel if she learned her own brother would rather kill another human being than watch her suffer?

How would she feel if she learned the true cost of surviving in a world that wants you dead?

Margot's life is difficult enough as is. Every day is spent justifying her existence, questioning her purpose. She tries so hard to smile but I know it's difficult to do so when smiling feels wrong. There's no telling how she would react to Ren's idea of Chasing for Immunity—especially *her* Immunity.

And if she found out what I was going to do instead of Chase, what I was risking, she would crumble.

The truth is what would really take her away from me, not the lies I know I must tell.

"Can I ask you something?" Ren says, but I know he'll ask his question with or without my approval, so I nod.

"If you're not becoming a Chaser," he continues. "Then what are you doing?"

I pause, unsure of how to continue without triggering the mics. No one is safe from being heard, from disappearing for saying the wrong thing.

"I'm going to help her," I whisper as softly as I can.

I feel like I should say more, but I don't need to. Ren immediately understands what I mean.

We both know about his father's mysterious tie to the Undergrounders, and we both know how stupid it would be to question the subject aloud.

"You're going to try to heal her, aren't you?" Ren whispers, wrapping himself in his arms and staring at the wall behind me. I nod, because it's true.

I cannot Chase, because a healer is the only thing I can see myself becoming.

Margot's current treatment is simple. Her few herbal supplements are enough to keep her symptoms manageable, but not enough to treat her fully. They're not consistent enough, and if Asa can't make a trip or swing a bargain, we don't always have them on hand. She needs regular access to a doctor who can give her stronger doses, an Underground healer who can communicate with her frequently and study her case in person, not through exchanged letters.

If I were a healer, I could be that person. She would get the help she needs.

And I could help others like her too.

"You should talk to my father." Ren clears his throat, keeping his voice low. "He knows people."

My eyes widen at the mention of Asa's connections. It's such a risky thing to talk about, even at such an inaudible level. I always knew about his ties, but hearing them verbally confirmed gives me a strange feeling. Excitement. Anxiety. Fear, perhaps.

Ren shifts his gaze to meet mine, coming to a realization I have yet to understand.

"This could work, you know." He looks up at me with brightened eyes, the corner of his lips tugging into the slightest mimicry of a smile.

"I don't think I'm catching on."

The smile fades, and he rolls his eyes in frustration. "You're gonna need more than just my father's word to vouch for you. You need to have something to offer."

"Something to offer?" I question.

"I'll feed you information," Ren explains quietly. "If you tell them you have a contact on the inside, it might earn you some credit. A bit of trust. I assume that'll be enough for them to teach you a thing or two about... helping her."

As much as I hate to admit it, it's a solid idea. Buying my place among the Undergrounders with insider information sourced directly from the Chaser Corps would be risky for the both of us, but it could work.

He feeds me information, and I provide him with an alibi to help keep his secret.

Ren will Chase. I will heal. Illegally, but carefully.

This could work.

Margot has lived enough of her life in hiding, just barely getting by with the simple treatment her father manages to provide. She needs more. She needs someone who can truly understand how to help her, someone who has access to the knowledge and resources necessary to do so.

This partnership is exactly what we need to save Margot.

"I won't say a word." Ren pulls me out of my thoughts as he stands up to offer me a handshake.

"I won't say a word," I repeat, accepting the shake reluctantly. His hands are so soft I almost tease, but I bite my tongue.

I wait for something to happen, though I'm not sure what I'm waiting for. Ren doesn't say anything either. The words don't escape his mouth and all he seems capable of doing is standing there, helpless and wide-eyed like a child lost in a crowd. We're both stuck with so much to say and no way to say it.

For an impossible moment, I'm reminded of the way things used to be. But we're different now. Changed. So close to being adults, and so far from the ignorant children we once were.

Now we're beings of hatred. Beings of secrets, beings of lies, beings of whispers. Hiding things from the people who matter to us.

I don't want to be in this room anymore, so I turn around and make my way toward the door. I entered with frivolous expectations and now I must exit with heavier shoulders. I haven't even left the room and the guilt of hiding this from Margot is already too much to bear.

I've successfully confirmed her suspicions. I found what has been eating away at Ren, but I can never let her know.

"Wait," Ren calls, and I pause, turning around to see him offer me his *Modern Botany* workbook. "Just in case you need an excuse. For being in here."

"Thanks." I tuck it beneath my arm.

"Eddie," Ren threatens grimly, a firm reminder of where we still stand. "Never tell a soul."

"Not a soul," I promise as I leave.

My mother is a tattoo artist. She says she comes from a long line of them, but I'm not so sure the craft is something to be proud of anymore.

Although Mom is an artist at heart, these days, her career has nothing to do with art. What was once an occupation filled with creative leaps and artistic expression is now a highly esteemed government position in which a person is tasked with tattooing Cards onto the wrists of every healthy baby born in our country. Every design is the same. Every gig is brief and simple, assigned to you by a computer. A thousand pairs of wrists and a thousand inky copies of cards from a standard playing deck, the same deck the Presidency uses for the Pick. The event that determines the fate of an entire group of people each year.

The thing that causes so many people to die.

Tattoos used to make people happy, Mom often reminds me, but it always feels like a reminder to herself. *Now they're forms of government-issued identification, not artistic expressions. I can never get used to the fact that people get killed for these tattoos.*

That's usually when she shudders and says, *My tattoos.*

She claims I too have an artist's soul, even though I will never be able to truly continue the work of the people who came before me. Card identification is not art, she says, but a way to control a population of people and make it easy to publicly randomize death orders.

"Do you know what art is, Eddie?" she asked me once.

"Yes."

"Then explain it to me."

To this day, I'm still stumped by that question. I don't think I gave her much of an answer back then, not one worth noting, anyway. The question was too broad, too interrogative.

"Well, I think I know what it is," she said some time after my answer. *"It's a lot of things, really. The biggest part—well, in my opinion—is the way it connects us all."*

"What do you mean?"

"It's the connection between mind and heart and soul, the connection between humankind and the earth we came from. The same earth we will all go back to when we die."

"How does it connect us?"

"In more ways than you could possibly imagine."

"Like how Margot and I became friends?"

"How you noticed your matching Cards?"

"Yeah."

"I guess so," she said. *"You both saw the art, after all. Not what they symbolize."*

I've learned to hate her answer.

We humans choose what we want to see. When something is just bad enough to make comprehension dangerous, our brains will filter things out. We feed ourselves concoctions of lies and separate realities. We satisfy the appetite of our guilt with false things, thriving on the diet of our own biases. We tell ourselves that things are fine. We convince ourselves it's for the good of the world because that is what we are taught.

We see a murder weapon, and instead of seeing that weapon for what it is, we connect over its beauty. We see a Chaser and we see status, success, and loyalty to a system so broken we cannot find the flaws.

In Ren I see desperation, maybe foolishness. He doesn't want to be a weapon.

But that's exactly what he's chosen to become.

REN

Thursday, May 4
44 Days Left of Being Human

My head hits the desk with a soft thud.

I am jolted awake. I sit up, rubbing my skull tenderly. A moment ago my chin was in my hand. I blink a few times before I realize I must have dozed off.

The room begins to reintroduce itself as I'm pulled away from my temporary slumber. The girl sitting next to me snickers, but I don't care. Sleep was fleeting last night. My exhaustion is justifiable.

"Did anyone actually do the homework assignment?" Mr. Aguilar looks up from his laptop as he takes his attendance. He scans the room for a response, a wide grin plastered below his dark brown mustache.

White tile floors, bright rectangular lights, a neat grid of synthetic wood desks. It's not much to look at, but Aguilar studies us all carefully, waiting for a response. Not many students even bother to look.

"I did," someone finally says sarcastically, and I frown when I realize it's Duke Carmody. We all know he's full of it, and Aguilar knows it too.

"Thank you, Duke. I appreciate it."

A few unfocused laughs escape the lips of some of the students across the room. I'm surprised they manage to laugh at all, because most of them are not paying attention to anything but their rushed attempts to complete the assignment before it's time to submit.

The nearing end of our school career has certainly taken its toll on us all. Every student is hunched over, pencil in hand, working hard to produce effortless chicken scratch and finish just in time. I wonder if any of them know how pathetic they look.

Eddie seems to be the outlier. Rather than scrambling to complete the assignment, she's completely still. She slouches with her eyes fixated on the empty plastic desk in front of her, head resting heavily in her right hand, a mess of dark brown curls spilling over her shoulders. For a moment, I can't tell if she's bored or exhausted, but when I see the bags under her eyes and the emptiness in her gaze, I assume it's a mix of both.

She's a mess.

She is weighed down by something. I almost expect to see some parasitic creature perched on her shoulders, sucking the life right out of her veins, but the weight remains hidden to the eye. Visible or not, she's still carrying something heavy, and I don't feel responsible.

She's the reason why I'm not the only one bearing my secret anymore.

"Wait a minute," Aguilar blurts, squinting at his laptop. "None of you saw the new seating chart I sent out? I'm pretty sure I emailed it to all of you."

Students around me groan in mutual levels of annoyance, and our instructor shakes his head in disappointment.

"You know the drill. New unit, new seats."

I couldn't care less about something as pointless as a seating chart, but it would be nice to sit in the back for a change. Away from prying eyes and unwanted attention. Unlike most students, I would rather stay unseen.

I pull out my phone and open my email to check Aguilar's new arrangements. I notice that my wish has been fulfilled, but I'm not so quick to be relieved. Not when I see who I'm stuck with for the rest of the year.

"What?" As usual, Eddie's mouth moves quicker than her brain and she covers her lips with her hands. The girl next to her chuckles and wishes her luck before getting up to find her own seat. I suppose I wouldn't want to sit next to me either. I have quite the resting glare, though I have to admit, it's intentional most of the time. But it's not like sitting next to Eddie would be any better.

Luck. I shake my head. *Like she needs it.*

For a Joker, Eddie is unusually lucky.

The stigma around Joker Cards is one that has always bothered me. Not because it's true, but because it's quite the opposite in Eddie's case. Margot really is unlucky, but any other Joker who is fortunate enough to have a functioning body is lucky by my standards—especially Eddie.

I wouldn't call her rich. Though they can't afford to be Immune, the Voclains are definitely more financially privileged than most. Aside from that, Eddie has not one, but two parents. Her family has been completely unscathed by the Pick, even without Immunity.

She doesn't realize how lucky she is, and that's why I can't stand her.

"Hey," Eddie mutters aggressively as I walk over to the back corner of the room.

"Hey," I reply dully, setting my bag on the desk and taking a seat to her left. To my dismay, Duke Carmody takes the chair directly in front of Eddie, diagonal to me.

The other students chatter as they settle down in their new seats, but neither of us says a word as the room rearranges itself. We are both angry for our own reasons.

While Eddie's snooping last night can't be justified, I do understand it. I know how close she and Margot are, and I know my sister is no idiot. We haven't been talking as much as we normally do, and I'm sure Eddie took it upon herself to soothe Margot's nerves by recklessly invading my space.

But now, she's caught up in something I wanted to handle in solitude, a situation that eats at me constantly. I don't sleep. I hardly eat. I can barely look Margot in the eye without feeling overwhelmed with a rotting sort of guilt.

My sister would hate me if she knew I was becoming a Chaser to protect her. And now, my secret lies vulnerable within the untrustworthy mouth of Lavender Voclain, the one person who hates me more than anyone.

"Thanks for lending me your workbook," Eddie says robotically, and I glance to my right to see her holding my copy of *Modern Botany*, offering it to me like a gift. I'm not surprised to see the corners folded and torn, no longer as crisp as they were in my care.

I take the workbook with a scowl and flip through the pages to check for last night's assignment, only to find blank lines.

"Really? You couldn't take an extra five minutes to fill this out?"

"No, I couldn't." She flashes a false grin and retrieves her own workbook from her bag, its pages somehow more tattered than mine.

"Typical."

"Aren't you top of the class? I'm sorry—*second best*?" she questions with inauthentic confusion. "Can't *you* take an extra five minutes to fill it out?"

I shoot her my coldest glare and join the rest of the class in their desperate attempts to finish the assignment.

"Your handwriting is disgusting, by the way," she adds without looking at me, and I don't spare her a glance either.

"Good. That's what I was going for."

"I can tell. Your attempts were very effective."

"Thanks."

"My pleasure."

"How neat are my circles? Do they meet your standards?"

"There's no way those are circles."

"Damn. I'll try harder next time."

"I recommend that."

"Should I have borrowed *your* work, perhaps?"

"Look." She breaks the banter, shooting me a frigid glare. "If you're gonna be such a goddamn baby about it, then give me that."

I open my mouth to protest, but I'm interrupted when she reaches over to snatch the workbook from my hands. Before I can stop it from happening, she's filling out the answers with a dull stub of a pencil, not bothering to refer back to her own work. She writes too fast to ponder the questions or answer them accurately.

"Filling it out with random answers won't help," I mutter.

"Statistically, random answers are better than none at all." She scowls at me before continuing.

"It's still not as good as—"

"I remember the answers, dimwit," she snaps.

I want to argue back, but I can't without making an idiot of myself. Through all these years of separation and rivalry, I seem to have forgotten about her memory.

There's a reason why Eddie is at the top of our class, and it isn't because she's a genius. She's too reckless for that, too lacking in caution and logic to be classified under such a label.

Eddie remembers things better than most people. She can look at a menu once and remember every dish, every beverage, every price. In our mandatory elementary school music class, it took her one sight-read to memorize sheet music. She can hear a date and remember the outfits people wore, according to Margot's rambling adoration.

It's not perfect enough to be called a photographic memory, but it comes pretty close, and Eddie knows how to use common sense to fill in the gaps.

Maybe it is genius, maybe it isn't. Whatever it is, Eddie uses it to fill out my worksheet in a heartbeat, just in time for Aguilar's announcement that it's time to submit. She tears out the page and passes it forward, and before I have time to thank her, our teacher speaks. But I would have decided against boosting her ego anyway.

"So, as you all know, we're starting the last unit of the year." Aguilar walks up to the whiteboard that decorates the front wall and uncaps his black pen. He turns around to stare at the class, expecting a response.

"Oh come on." He chuckles. "No one's excited about that? The last unit of the year?"

"I am, Mr. Aguilar." Duke Carmody pipes up again, but no one laughs this time. The class is too preoccupied with the thought of graduation being just around the corner.

Chasing is just around the corner.

In forty-four days, I will become the one thing I fear the most.

"Thanks, Duke," Aguilar says for the second time today. The instructor turns around to face the board again, pen in hand.

"You're welcome, Mr. Aguilar."

Duke's commentary is so idiotic it's almost entertaining, I'll give him that much—but I'm bothered by his inexplicable need to be seen as something he's not. What he sees as charming and hilarious can be interpreted as slimy and arrogant to people who see past the mask.

I've seen the way he acts when no one's looking, and I've heard snippets of the sort of things he says. He's disgusting. Duke is not a clown, but a rat.

And the rat turns to face Eddie, who sits behind him. She is too preoccupied with her own thoughts to see him. He grins as if to ask, *Did you hear what I said? I'm funny, right?*

I can't help but feel uneasy at the thought of his interest in Eddie. His locker room chatter and hushed cafeteria snickers would make anyone in their right mind agree with me. If she suddenly found herself associated with a guy like Duke Carmody, there's no telling what he'd eventually learn.

If he somehow stumbled across what Eddie knows, my secret would spread like wildfire.

How strange that the quiet kid is becoming a Chaser. Or fitting.

Now, it's not enough to be careful about the people I choose to be around. I have to be mindful of the people Eddie associates herself with as well.

My unease doesn't subside naturally, so I try to force it out of me. I open my notebook and click my pen and get ready to absorb the lecture as Aguilar writes the name of the new unit on the board.

NIGHTJADE AND ITS ROLE IN MODERN POLICY

Shit.

The one topic we all dread more than anything else. The topic none of us wants to discuss, no matter how tightly woven into our lives it might be.

"Okay, you guys." Mr. Aguilar closes his dry-erase pen and leans against the whiteboard. "As you know, I'm a pretty lenient guy. I let a lot of things slide in this classroom."

The class listens closely, because the smallest drop of seriousness in this man's tone is a rarity. I look around the room to see people sitting on the edge of their seats, anxiously anticipating what's to come.

"But as we discuss this month's unit," he continues, "I want something to be clear. This time, there are some things that I *won't* let slide."

Some students nod, but others are too uncomfortable to move at all. I find myself fitting in the latter category.

"I'm sure you're all familiar with Slander," Aguilar warns. "I know you all have your own opinions, but I encourage you to keep them to yourself for the next few weeks, alright? Say the wrong thing and it could mean a lot of trouble for both you and me."

Nobody moves a muscle this time, but even without the nods, Aguilar knows we understand perfectly.

Slander. The term nobody wants to talk about, ironically, because talking is a dangerous game. We all know how strict the rules are. We're all aware of the mics planted within the walls of every public and private facility.

We all know that no matter where you turn, you can't escape the feeling of being heard. Watched. Studied, like a rodent in a maze with no way out. Even wrong words spoken in whispers are a risk.

"You know the rules, so follow them," Aguilar states cautiously. "Remember, we live in a just society—a fair society. We all have our part to play, and right now, your job is to remember that fairness."

Fair. Flawed probability is not fair. Forcing people to either play or pay for Immunity is not fair. Killing innocent people is not fair. But we all must pretend that it is.

When he gets the sense we understand, Aguilar uncaps the pen once again before writing something else on the board in black ink.

NIGHTJADE + THE PICK

Of course, I think as I clench my jaw. Of course we're starting with the worst part of it all.

I fidget with the paper in my notebook. The neat blue college-ruled lines are blurred, and I crinkle the corners of the page before flipping it over and folding the same corner. Back and forth, turn after turn. The page is worn thin, and the lecture hasn't even begun. I wonder how many folds it can take before it tears.

"I'm assuming you all know what the Pick is by now," Aguilar says rhetorically, but the class nods silently nonetheless. "Regardless, I still have to cover the subject."

He sets his pen down on the metal tray beneath the whiteboard, folding his arms across his chest in a manner so uncharacteristically solemn it makes me uneasy.

"The world was dying," he says, clearing his throat. "Climate change, war, natural disasters, drought, famine, and a global shortage of resources, to name a few. Overpopulation ruined everything."

Normally, Aguilar expects us to take notes during his lectures. Today, no one moves a muscle. We know this all too well.

"When an American botanist developed Nightjade as a personal research project, the government was quick to seize an opportunity to take modern warfare to the next level. How could they not? This new hybrid of nightshade and a handful of other toxic plants could be farmed quickly, easily, and cheaply. It required minimal water to grow, and it was a resource far more attainable than metal. Guns, bullets, and violent machinery became a thing of the past. While the rest of the world struggled to reclaim the power they once had, we didn't need to. We had the world's most easily accessible poison on our side."

I gulp, adjusting the collar of my sweater.

"Nightjade bullets are more inexpensive than metal. Cheap plastic guns married perfect poison and the result was a country buzzing with rumors of war and death. American leadership was suddenly feared by not only enemy territory, but by the country's own citizens as well. Nightjade became a symbol of fear, and the Presidency uses that fear to their advantage."

Fear. I think about the word—how poisonous it is.

It's ironic, really, how terrifying it is to admit you are afraid. And when I glance around the room, watching my classmates pick at their curling notebook corners or chew their nails to the quick, I can tell we are all in the same formidable boat.

"While everyone initially thought Nightjade would be used to initiate another world war in a desperate attempt to obtain more resources by force, the Presidency had other ideas in mind. Sure, they were going to use this new and easily accessible poison as a weapon. But not against opposing forces. They'd turn against their own people."

He trails off, staring at his feet. No one takes another breath until he clears his throat.

"So, the Nightjade Order," Aguilar continues, rubbing his hands together like we're discussing the structure of plant cells instead of our collective nightmare. "Can anyone briefly explain this to me?"

The instructor scans the room, and his eyes fix on Eddie. But she's not raising her hand as usual. I can tell this surprises him—it surprises *me*—but I understand why she doesn't want to talk about it. None of us do.

Aguilar notices me staring at her and taps on the whiteboard with his pen. "How about Ren?"

I can't breathe.

I slouch in my seat as my pulse comes to a halt. I don't open my mouth, because I'm too afraid my heart will leap out of my throat and make a run for it. *I can't talk about this.*

But what will people think when they see that? *What assumptions will they make if I avoid this question?*

I can't act like my sister is sick. I can't act like I hate the system more than anything else in the world, even when that's exactly what I think.

"Alright, Ren doesn't want to talk about it," Aguilar says, and my face heats up. "Eddie, then?"

I blurt out before Eddie can speak.

"The idea was to implement control in ways that would positively affect the country as a whole."

There's a pause, and Mr. Aguilar turns to look at me once again. "Go on."

"By enforcing fatal penalties for crime, for example, you would simultaneously be lowering crime rates and decreasing the population. It's quite literally killing two birds with one stone," I say, as low in my seat as possible, pretending to view the subject far too casually for my liking. I feel like I'm going to be sick.

Don't let them see your hatred.

"Perfect explanation, Ren. And what are some of the other policies put in place by the Nightjade Order?" Aguilar asks, and if I had managed to eat something for lunch, I'm sure my anxiety would have tossed it back up by now. All I can do is pray it doesn't go after my breakfast next.

"Well, there's the houselessness policy. You're allowed three months to get yourself back on track before you're exterminated." I mutter so softly I wonder how Aguilar manages to hear me at all.

"Good, good. But you're forgetting one."

"Am I?" I tremble. My mouth tastes bitter, and I bite my cheek so hard I can taste the sharp flavor of iron. All eyes are on me.

Unlike Eddie, staying quiet has always been a skill of mine. But I can't help but be afraid of letting my true anger show, because I know for a fact that if I open my mouth again, they'll have me killed for Slander.

Stay focused.

"People were starving to death." To my relief, Aguilar speaks for me. "There wasn't enough food or water to go around. This is why the government needed an immediate solution to yield immediate results, or our country would not have survived for much longer. Our own species was endangered.

"So the Nightjade Order was put in place. Crimes, chronic illnesses, and disabilities result in immediate extermination or a sentence to labor their life away by working the Tombs, where the bodies that can't afford a very costly tombstone are burned in mass quantities. If you aren't able to improve society, you aren't worth the resources. Even in death. That was—and still is—the government's mindset.

"However, it wasn't enough to eliminate the unworthies. The population was still too high. While the Nightjade Order as a whole has done an excellent job of strengthening our society, strict penalties weren't enough to be the only solution. The government was in dire need of something much more massive in scale. This is where the Pick comes into play."

He pauses before questioning us. "Who wants to tell me what this is?"

Nobody raises a hand. Nobody offers a single word, because we're all afraid of saying the wrong thing. We've all been touched by the Pick in some way; we all have a reason to hate it, but articulating this hatred is a death wish.

"No one?"

Every face in the room remains blank.

I don't know if I can stand much more of this, I think, twirling my thumbs as my leg begins to shake. I don't know if I can take this.

"The Pick. At the start of every year, two cards are publicly drawn from a standard playing deck on national television. And every citizen in the country with a matching pair of these"—he pauses and gestures to the Cards tattooed to both of his wrists—"is exterminated."

He hesitates, and I can't resist the shiver that slithers up my spine. The class seems to be trembling in unison.

Instinctively, we all stare at our own tattoos. Although I hide them with long sleeves, the top inch of an Ace of Spades Card peeks out anyway, reminding me of everything I want to forget. Of this black ink branding I can never remove. I don't have to look to know that a Queen of Hearts hides behind my right sleeve as the other half of my curse.

"Two Card tattoos are given to you at birth. But the moment you turn eighteen, there is a chance that your Cards will be drawn for extermination when New Year's comes around—all for the sake of decreasing numbers and increasing resource availability. It's the fairest way to save us all."

His words are followed by a silence so potent that a dropped pin could echo with a trembling thud. *Exterminated*.

"And this is why the Chaser Corps was developed," Aguilar says. "Military and police forces were replaced with a corps whose sole purpose is to support Nightjade laws and the Pick. These Chasers are the ones who execute exterminations. They are the backbone of the Pick, and every policy the Nightjade Order protects.

"An Officer of the Chaser Corps is an elite soldier trained to carry out these penalties with Nightjade weaponry. They complete assignments in exchange for a desirable stipend and Immunity for themselves and their immediate families. With this Immunity, your name is specially registered in the Chaser database and exempt from extermination."

He pauses for a moment, but just as he opens his mouth to continue, Mae Soto shocks us all and raises her hand.

She is a quiet girl, almost as small as Margot, and I've only heard her speak once or twice in the entirety of my school career. None of us expected anyone to willingly say a word during this lecture, let alone Mae.

"Question, Mae?" Aguilar pauses and points to her raised arm.

Her voice is delicate, like down feathers. "Yes."

"Ask away." Aguilar smiles, folding his arms and waiting for her to speak.

"Isn't this whole Chaser thing... I don't know. Wrong?"

Everything stops.

Jaws are dropped, frozen in this position of awe and stuck to the floor. A thousand questions are asked by everyone at once, yet no one says a word. Our stunned expressions say it all.

Did she really just say that?

Did someone really just openly oppose this? This questionable thing we're taught to never question?

"Well..." Aguilar laughs nervously, looking at the clock and the door and then back at Mae in a clear state of panic, afraid of who might be listening. "What do you mean?"

"I don't know." Mae's face is red, and she looks down at her shoes. Her hands retreat to the safety of her oversized sweatshirt sleeves. "It just doesn't seem right to me, that's all."

The class is petrified. Too nervous to move a muscle. Too nervous to even fidget, or exchange nervous glances. Nobody knows how to react.

"Well, if you look at this whole thing scientifically—at statistics and such —you can clearly see how this system is what makes our country livable." Aguilar is quick to change the subject, transitioning from questioning the system to praising it.

"We're one of the only places in the world where green lawns still exist. We have clean water, plenty of food, lower poverty rates, and significantly low pollution levels compared to what people of the Yesterdays had to deal with—and what others across the globe are still dealing with today. Starvation, dehydration, poverty, sickness, violence, incredibly high crime rates, civil wars, etcetera.

"You see, today, we're the only place in the world with quality of life levels this high, and this is all thanks to the fair policies that have been put in place by our leaders. This past century has been our best. Our fairest."

Aguilar laces his hands together, and you can tell that he takes pride in keeping things pleasing to the listeners behind the mics. He opens his mouth to move on from this detour and continue with his lecture, but Mae speaks first.

"I'm still a bit confused."

Silence.

"It just—I don't know. That didn't really answer my question," she mutters.

The room is filled with more of that dreadful, painful absence of sound.

"Well, Mae, I can't answer that question." Aguilar folds his arms.

"So you don't know the answer?"

Aguilar is thrown off, confusion spelled out in the smile he wears and the crease in his brow.

"There's a difference, I guess. Between not knowing the answer and not knowing what to say." Mae's not wrong in her confusion. If anything, she's *right*.

"You see, Mae, unfortunately this is the kind of conversation I can't allow in this unit. We're really not supposed to discuss political views here—"

"It's not politics, Mr. Aguilar." Tension grows with Mae's interruption. "It's just morality, that's all."

The professor's grin morphs into one of doubtful genuineness. He strokes his chin with clear anxiety, and a bead of sweat grows prominent on his forehead. He's scared of something. It's the same fear we all know too well, a fear so potent the act of articulating it alone is enough to make you tremble with dread.

He's afraid of saying the wrong thing, and the consequences it might bring.

"Mae." Aguilar addresses her in a soft tone, but his words are stern and solid. "There's a reason why ethics classes have been expelled from the curriculum. It's an outdated subject, and it's just not something we talk about anymore."

"Why not?"

"The discussion of ethics isn't something we can have. Not only because of school policies but for the sake of our society as a whole. Putting so much weight into right versus wrong could cause our system to crumble. Do you get that?"

Mae doesn't say a word.

"We can't question a system that is undoubtedly right. It works. It's fair, and we know it is. But it won't work anymore if we lose faith in it."

Mae is silent once more, and this seems to make Aguilar content. He's satisfied by the act of bringing closure to this conversation, saving his job and his own skin by neatly wrapping up this discussion and securing it with a ribbon. It has become a parcel he can place on the top shelf of some storage closet to forget about entirely, never to open again.

But Mae isn't finished. She stands up, clutching her book with all the bravery she can muster. She stares at the desk in front of her, too afraid to make eye contact with anyone or anything but scratched artificial wood.

"You still haven't answered my question." Her words are audible and clear. She doesn't yell, but this is the loudest anyone has heard her speak. "It's wrong, Mr. Aguilar. It's all so wrong and no one ever talks about it."

"Mae, sit down."

"Isn't it?" Her voice is louder now. She lifts her chin and looks Aguilar in the eye, staring at him directly and intently. The action is so out-of-character that someone gasps.

Some past wound is reopened, and before we know it she's sobbing, showing more emotion than she's ever displayed in school. Her gaze doesn't waver.

"I think you should take a break. I can phone up your counselor and write you a pass—"

"I'm fine," she interrupts.

"You seem a bit unwell."

"I said I'm fine."

"Then please, sit down."

Mae stands still, her stance as firm as her gaze.

"Mae—"

"*Why won't you answer me?*" Her cry is nearly a scream. "Isn't this all so wrong?"

Now it's Aguilar who remains silent.

"Killing people for resources? We destroyed our own planet for the same reason, and now we're destroying ourselves too? Haven't we learned from our past? *Haven't we done enough?*"

"Mae, please. I'm calling your counselor—"

"*They killed my brother!*"

The room goes quiet. Not a single person takes a breath, like all the air was vacuumed out.

We know hatred far too well to be shocked by Mae's. It's her bravery that pinches our lungs shut. She's treading over ice so thin it could be paper.

No one speaks out against the system and gets away with it.

"What wrong could he have done to deserve a Nightjade injection?" Cracks web through her voice. "Was existence the crime? Or was it bearing a pair of tattoos he didn't even consent to having in the first place?"

Aguilar is pale.

I'm pale too. The color drains from my skin and I'm sick to my stomach. *We all are.*

"Answer me." This time, she doesn't yell. But in her stillness, in her quiet, shaking rage, she commands the entire room.

"No, okay?" Mr. Aguilar finally shouts. In an instant, all the air in the room is vacuumed up. There is no sound. No breathing. Not a single flinch. His face is crimson, no longer belonging to the relaxed Modern Botany teacher the class knows and adores. "It's not right."

We all watch in horror as Mae leaves the room. The door slams shut behind her. Aguilar adjusts the collar of his shirt, resuming his lecture as if nothing happened. He continues to talk about the symbolism behind the Card system and other topics I couldn't care less about.

I'm not paying attention. My mind is humming with a swarm of inescapable fears and preoccupations I just can't seem to shake. Mae's outburst. Eddie's recent involvement in my personal life. My newly noticed perception of Duke's interest in the only person who knows my secret, the triggering concepts we're covering in class, Margot, always. *Everything.*

And then the swarming becomes a million dive bombs and I'm hit by everything all at once. I'm slammed by this invisible force that knocks the breath out of me, and I'm suddenly too nauseous to stay here. My legs are shaky and weak, making decisions without my approval. Before I know it, I'm standing. All eyes are glued to me now. Not to Mr. Aguilar or Mae Soto's empty seat or the floor littered with paper clips and gum wrappers —but to me.

I cover my mouth and hurry over to the wastebasket. The class groans with disgust as I fall to my knees and regurgitate my last meal. I don't stay long enough to see the looks on their faces; I'm out the door before I can blink. I turn too many corridors to count, and by the time I reach the bathroom, I no longer know how to breathe.

I stand there in front of a sink, gripping the grimy sides so tight my knuckles burn white, matching the color of the ceramic I hold too tight.

Exterminated. The word that hasn't left my mind since it escaped Aguilar's lips.

The same word we use when ridding our homes of pests. The same word we use when referring to diseased insects and rodents. The same word Chasers used when they murdered Mae's brother. The same word they used when they murdered Mom. The same word they will use if Margot's secret gets out before I get the chance to earn her Immunity.

The same word I will use someday, because there is no other way to keep my sister alive.

EDDIE

Thursday, May 4
29 Days Left Until Graduation

I'm disturbed.

I think we're all a bit shaken up as we exit Mr. Aguilar's classroom, but amidst the whispers of Ren's sudden departure, I'm the only one who knows why he couldn't stand to be in that room any longer. Why it was breaking him to hear Mae Soto's public display of hatred for Chasers and the system as a whole.

And I'm bearing that burden with him, as much as I hate to admit it.

Routine keeps my legs walking toward my locker, but my movements are robotic. Everything feels subconscious and habitual because my mind is too busy to focus on where I'm going. I can't say why I wonder where Ren ran off to or why I have the urge to go follow him.

For our secret's sake, I tell myself. *Not for his.*

"Eddie," someone calls, yanking me out of my thoughts. "Eddie Eddie Eddie."

I jump, startled by this sudden yet expected address. A figure jogs up to my side, and I don't have to look up to know exactly who it is.

"Duke." I acknowledge him dryly. I'm never in the mood for his pestering, but he chose the wrong day to continue his habits.

"What, you're not excited to see me?" He shifts from walking next to me to walking in front of me, his back facing my path, gray eyes glued to mine.

"You're an idiot," I mutter.

I can smell the gel he uses to style his short brown hair. Combined with the strong stench of laundry detergent seeping from his light jeans and black jacket, it gives me a killer headache. He alone is enough to make me nauseous, but the fragrance is almost as artificial as his ego and I'm too bothered by it to be polite. Not that I would ever be polite to a person like him.

"That's not very nice." He pouts.

"Being nice has nothing to do with it. You're literally walking backwards."

I reach my locker and tinker with the padlock. My hands know the combination better than my brain does, and I rely on muscle memory to do the work for me. I can't think right now, not about passcodes or Duke's insistent pestering or any of it—just Ren.

I need to talk to him. I need to remind him not to lose sight of what really matters, despite everything that happened during class. He can't back out of becoming a Chaser. Not now. Because as much as we both hate this system, Margot needs him to become a part of it. She won't survive without Immunity.

We both need to work to make her survival a possibility. Maybe his method is different from mine, but we still have the same goal, and we would both do anything to achieve it.

Backing out is not an option. Chasing is something he has to do.

It wouldn't hurt to smack some sense into him either. People will catch on if he keeps throwing up every time someone brings up the word *Chaser*.

"Someone's in a bad mood today." Duke leans against the locker to my right, hands in his pockets.

"Gee, I wonder why."

"Damn, Voclain. You really don't like me, do you?"

"I can't say I'm very fond of you."

"Ouch."

I shove my materials in my locker and pull out the items I need for tonight's homework. The textbooks are tightly packed in my bag, like one too many sardines in a small tin can. I struggle to cram in the last book.

"Need help with that?"

"I'm fine, thanks."

"Again with the rudeness, wow. You really *aren't* very fond of me."

"Like I've told you repeatedly, I'm not." The books in my bag won't budge, but I don't want to spend any more time talking to Duke when finding Ren is my priority. I grab the zipper and pull the backpack closed, holding the extra book in my arms as I close my locker and walk away.

"I think I can change that." Duke jogs to catch up, and I can practically hear the smirk he wears through his voice.

"I highly doubt that."

"Look"—he grins mischievously—"there's gonna be a party at my house after grad. You should come."

"Parties aren't really my thing," I turn a corner sharply, but Duke still follows close behind.

"Only because you've never been to one," he claims.

"Because I think they're stupid. And boring."

"C'mon, Ed. Lighten up a bit, will you?" He nudges my arm like he knows me well, and I don't like it. I exit the hallway and walk into a stream of early evening sunlight that seeps in through the sides of an outdoor corridor. The outside air is refreshing, but I'm too worried to feel its effects.

"I'm not exactly interested in doing anything illegal for the time being," I mutter, which I find ironic when I remember who I want to become— and what I agreed to become a part of last night.

But if I'm going to be doing something illegal, it might as well be worthwhile, and wasting that by partying with a bunch of rich kids like Duke would be foolish. We all know alcohol is a privilege reserved for those who can afford to pay for Immunity from Nightjade policies. For the rest of us, *toxic substances* that could weaken the physical and mental state of the existing population are outlawed.

"What, you don't wanna ruin that spotless record of yours with a little fun?" He teases, but I'm not laughing. Any law is a broken law to a Chaser.

"Everyone has a spotless record."

"Unless you're Immune. Or tomb scum," Duke scoffs.

I clench my jaw. "Not everyone's as privileged as you are, okay? I can't exactly afford to buy Immunity."

"What are you on about?" he chuckles. "Chasers get free Immunity."

I nearly stop in my tracks.

"Yeah," I reply, not knowing what else to say. "They do." *That was too close.*

"So you're Immune. Temporarily, at least, until you get your results back."

I pause. "Look, Duke, I'm not really interested in a *party*, alright? I have better things to do with my time." I give him a humorless smile and shove past him, walking faster to leave this boy behind me. I can't say I'm surprised when he jogs to catch up.

"You wanna know what I think?"

"I don't, actually."

"I think you're stuck up."

Duke is flashed with a particular finger.

"You think you're smarter than everyone else. Above everyone else," he argues. "You're too good for a little fun."

I've had it.

I stop walking and he stops too, standing in front of me and looking down with a smirk that tests my personal restraint. I'd love to kick him in the shins right now. Or a variety of other sensitive places.

"Look, Duke." I plaster on my fakest smile and look him dead in the eye. "You wanna know what *I* think? It's not *fun* that I'm uninterested in. It's you. I think you're entitled and desperate and yes, you're right—*beneath me*. Great observation, truly. Now if you'll excuse me, I have to go."

He lets out a descending whistle.

I turn around to walk away. Over my shoulder, I can see him stand still for a few moments, until he finally turns around to take his exit, disappearing from my sight. *Good,* I think to myself. *He's gone.*

I find my favorite bench and pull out my phone. I notice a notification from Margot, and I click on the banner to open our messages.

MARGOT

> did your class end late or something? i'm waiting for
> my ride but i don't see ren anywhere…

I close my eyes and exhale in frustration. If Margot goes looking for Ren and finds him in his current state, she'll know something's up. Our secrets will be compromised.

I have to be the one to go after him—wherever he's run off to.

EDDIE

> yeah, class ended a bit late. i saw him stay after class
> to talk about an upcoming assignment, he'll be out
> soon. don't worry :)

I sigh, suddenly just as nauseous as I was in class. Even a lie this small makes me sick because it's Margot I'm relaying it to. My best friend. The one person in the world who trusts me more than anyone, and I don't even deserve it.

Think about it later, I tell myself. *You need to find Ren.*

I move my fingers to text him for his whereabouts, but I pause. This isn't something I've really done before. I'm disgusted that I even have Ren's number in my phone to begin with, but Margot insisted on giving it to me for emergencies a few years back.

My thumb hovers over his contact page, waiting to press on the little message icon next to his name.

You have to, I remind myself. *If this is part of the price for Margot's safety, you must pay it.*

I take a deep breath and press the button.

EDDIE

> hey.

No response.

EDDIE
where are you?

I set my phone down and tap my foot, looking up at the tree that looms above this bench and me. The tree is old, an oak so aged and arthritic I'm positive it was here to see the Yesterdays. I wonder if it's judgmental or pitiful of the mistakes we humans have made over the years.

I think about my mistakes and all the mistakes I'm sure I'll make from this point on.

A few minutes pass, and I still get no text back from Ren. I stand up, walking away from the bench and back beneath the overhang of these outdoor hallways, hoping Margot doesn't show up and see me leaving our spot. I glance behind my shoulder as I turn the corner alone.

As I walk, I check my phone again. Still no response from Ren. I bite my lip, thinking about the places he could be. *Maybe he left for home already*, I wonder before correcting myself. He wouldn't leave without Margot.

But where else could he be?

The library. I've run into him in the library before on multiple occasions. Our campus library doesn't have the greatest selection—only Presidency approved material and censored school resources—but it's the only quiet place on campus, and I wouldn't be surprised to find Ren waiting within its walls.

I quicken my pace, walking faster and turning corners mindlessly until I approach the large brick building. A handful of students file in and out, but for the most part, this fraction of campus is vacant. School is out for the day, and most students would prefer to avoid a library at this hour.

I open the glass door and take a step inside, immediately overwhelmed by the scent of crisp paper and stale coffee. The white tile flooring is pristine, almost nauseating as it mirrors the bright lights that line the ceiling. I hurry past the entryway and crane my neck to observe the rectangular wood tables spread throughout the center of the room. One girl sits with her nose buried in a school project, while a boy sits at the table behind her, reading something on a tablet. I don't see Ren anywhere, and my heart sinks.

I turn to my right, walking past aisles of clean white bookshelves, each row featuring neat stacks of books, but no Ren. I start to wonder if this is a waste of time as I scan the second half of the room.

But when I search the very last row, I come to a pause. There, sitting on the ground in a secluded corner, his back leaning against a shelf and eyes glued to an open book, is none other than Ren McLellan.

He doesn't look up from his book, but I know he's aware of my arrival. I roll my eyes, opening my mouth and readying myself for a rude remark, but I stop myself when I notice exactly what book he's observing.

It's a school yearbook, decades old, by the looks of it. Its hardcover corners are dulled and tattered, its pages yellowed with age. I squint to read the year on the cover. That has to be his father's graduating year.

I set my bag down and take a seat to his right, legs stretched out, back against the shelf. Ren doesn't look at me; he doesn't even blink. I lean over to investigate what holds his attention so firmly.

When I see the image his gaze is angled toward, I stifle a gasp.

There's a photo of a young girl about our age. The image has been blurred by time, but I can still see her long raven hair, her wide grin, and the dimples in her cheeks that look far too familiar to be coincidental. *Noriko Teshima*, I read, studying the name under the photo.

"That's her, isn't it?" I ask.

Ren keeps his eyes glued to the page, trembling. "I don't know what you're talking about."

I hesitate, lowering my voice to a whisper. "Your mother."

He's silent for a moment, and I wonder if I've done something wrong by being here. Maybe I should have left him alone. He would have composed himself eventually.

And then he nods, so subtly I wonder if he really moved at all. I shift my focus from the photo to Ren, seeing something unfamiliar in his eyes. For a boy who pretends to be far better off than he is, finding this kind of sadness is a rarity I'm not used to.

"I don't know why we have no photos of her at home," Ren mutters, "but we don't."

All is quiet until he clears his throat and stands up, ashamed of this moment of weakness. I stand up too and watch as he tucks the yearbook under his arm and shoves his hands in his pockets, gaze fixed to his shoes.

I give him the smallest of grins. "She has Margot's smile."

He looks at me, trying so hard to be angry and finding nothing to say. He relaxes his shoulders, staring back at his shoes. "I know."

And then he looks up at me again, and the two of us stand there with nothing and everything to say, unsure of how to proceed. He clears his throat for a second time and slings his bag over his shoulder.

"I'm gonna go put this back." He turns to walk away.

"Wait," I call out, and he pauses. I walk over to him and take the yearbook from his hands.

I flip to the right page—and I tear it out.

He yanks the book back, eyes wide. "*What are you doing*?"

"You won't have access to this library forever," I mutter, reaching out my hand to offer him the page. "Take it."

He doesn't budge.

"Look—I know what you and your family have lost." I bite the inside of my cheek, looking down at the paper and back at Ren again, speaking softly. "That's something no one should ever go through."

He can't look me in the eye.

I shove the paper into his hand. When he grabs it, I let go. "I think you should keep this. Let it remind you what you're fighting for." I allow myself to smile. "She reminds you of Margot, doesn't she?"

"I'm not backing out," he states, so quietly I almost miss it.

"Good."

"I can't back out," he mumbles. "You know that."

I nod. "I do."

All is silent once again. He continues to glare at me for a moment longer before shoving the folded page into his pocket, but he doesn't walk away. Not yet.

I can't get the photograph out of my mind. Every time I blink, I see Margot's mother—Ren's mother—trapped in time, stuck in a little box on a page in a book that does nothing but gather dust.

There's something so eerie about photographs of people who are long gone. They are fragments of a life once lived, pieces of a person who no longer walks the earth. Reminders of what the Presidency has taken from all of us.

"So Ed... was that little speech of yours a *no*?"

I'm yanked out of my thoughts when a voice materializes down the aisle. Ren and I whip our heads to the right, flinching to face this intervening figure.

I shouldn't be surprised by Duke's persistence, but I am.

"What are you doing here?" Ren says.

Duke shrugs. "Returning some textbooks. Year's almost over, you know."

"Piss off, Duke," I tell him, clenching my fists.

I bring my textbook closer to my chest, hugging it tightly. It takes all I have not to go off on him, but I need to keep my voice low. We can't afford to draw any unnecessary attention.

I've heard plenty of cautionary tales about school conflicts getting out of hand—and they always lead to extermination. I can't draw in a crowd. Not with this loose cannon in our proximity.

Duke may have Immunity, but Ren doesn't. Not until he's an official trainee. If Duke pushes Ren too close to the edge, there's no telling how either one of them will retaliate.

"Let's go," I mutter to Ren. We shove past Duke, making our way toward the end of the aisle, but we're followed.

"Need me to hold that book for you?" Duke says from behind us. "It looks heavy."

"That's pathetic." Ren pauses, turning around to face him. I do the same. "It's like, what, two pounds?"

Before I can blink, Duke takes the textbook from my arms.

It takes a moment for me to register what's happening, but when I do, I can feel rage boiling over. I would be shocked if steam wasn't pouring out of my ears, like the old Yesterday cartoons you learn about in history class.

I've had enough of Duke for one day. A lifetime too.

"What the hell is your problem?" I glare, arms crossed.

Smugly, Duke grins. "I don't have a problem. Do you have a problem?" He shoves one hand in the pocket of his black jacket as the other holds up my book.

"Oh wow, would you look at that!" I turn to Ren with a faux smile before facing Duke again. "He's learning."

I reach out to grab the book, but he holds it up higher than I can reach. "You're gonna have to try a little harder than that."

"What are you, five?" Ren says under his breath.

Duke raises it up even higher. "Don't these things cost a lot of money to replace?"

"Yes, which is exactly why I'd like it back," I spit.

Duke holds the book as high as he can, standing on the tips of his sneakers, as though he doesn't already have a height advantage over me.

He opens the textbook and flips to a random page. "What would happen if I"—his fingers wrap around the corner, tearing the paper ever so slightly —"tore out a page?"

"I'd beat the shit out of you."

He gently rips the page further, growing the paper's tear by an inch.

"This isn't as hilarious as you think it is." I seethe through clenched teeth.

"Seeing you get all worked up over a little book? Yeah, it's pretty entertaining." He conceals the textbook behind his back with both hands. "I'll give it back to you if you agree to come to the party with me."

"Fine, I'll go," I lie quickly. "Now hand it over."

"That didn't sound very genuine."

"Oh it was very genuine."

"Then how about you do something else for me?"

I scoff. "No."

"Not even a little kiss?"

He takes a step forward. He's so close now I can smell the lunch lingering behind that smug grin of his. I want to take a step back, but I don't. I look him in the eye and stand still, refusing to budge.

"Okay, this is getting ridiculous—" Ren begins, but I interrupt him.

"Back off. I got this." I avert Ren's gaze, keeping my eyes fixed on Duke's mischievous sneer.

"Are you sure?" Duke adds.

I nod. "Positive."

Ren rolls his eyes and takes a step forward, putting himself between Duke and me. "Look man, just give her the book, alright? We don't have the time for this."

"Wait." Duke pauses for a moment, taking a step back to study us both with a laugh. "You two aren't a thing, right? No. No way!"

Oh my God.

I grit my teeth together. "We're not."

Duke laughs again.

"C'mon, Eddie. He's not gonna do anything. Let's go." Ren nods toward the exit.

"No." I feel myself nearing an edge. "I want my book back."

I know it's the attention Duke wants. Feeding into the conflict is the same as fanning a flame, but I can't bring myself to brush it off and walk away. My anger is boiling over, and I'm on the brink of combustion.

"What if I don't feel like giving it back just yet?" Duke asks, taking a step closer.

"Eddie..." Ren touches my shoulder, and I lift my palm up to let him know I'm not finished here.

Duke is as close as he can get without touching me, and I can *taste* my hatred. My hatred for this day, for this school, for Ren, for this system that gives Immunity to the privileged and impossible decisions to those who happen to be any less fortunate. I despise the way I can see our country's flaws in Duke's entitlement, and I've just about had enough of it all.

And then, he's even closer, so close his jacket touches mine, neither of us blinking. He leans forward and reaches out to tuck a loose curl behind my ear.

"Don't." I snatch his wrist before his hand touches my hair, gripping it so tightly he struggles to shake free.

"Or what?"

"You'll find out."

I almost jump when Ren takes advantage of Duke's distraction, grabbing the book from his free hand. He passes it to me and I tuck it under my arm, holding it close as though it could be taken away again in an instant.

"What the hell, man?" Duke's focus is on Ren now, ashamed of the small blow to his unnecessarily bountiful supply of self-esteem.

"What? I don't have a problem. Do you have a problem?" Ren mocks.

Duke is silent, glaring at Ren so intensely I wonder if he'll retaliate physically. I've seen the brawls this kid gets himself into—and out of, with the help of his Immunity. If he wanted to, he'd fight over something as frivolous as a stolen pencil.

But to my surprise, Ren chuckles, shaking his head before turning to face me. "Let's go."

"You're scared of me, aren't you?" Duke laughs in a desperate attempt to patch the control he no longer has.

"I don't think anyone's scared of you." Ren turns around and gestures with his chin to let me know it's time to leave.

We exit the building, leaving Duke to sulk. We cut across the front lawn in silence, pausing to stand beneath a tree when we're far enough from the library. The two of us stand in our quietude until Ren leans over to whisper in my ear.

"I'm not backing out," he reassures me. "And my lips are sealed, alright? No one will know about the test."

The test, I repeat in my head. Vague enough to mean just about anything, specific enough to apply to both of our secrets.

"Alright," I reply.

"I can promise you that much."

He gives me a look I've never seen before. Not his angry look. Not his sister's look. No—this is something else entirely. For the first time in years, there is a small part of it that I find myself trusting.

I hope that he can find it within himself to trust me too. For Margot.

The house is warm as I lock my car and step inside, but not from the heat of summer's nearing approach.

Something sweet is in the air as I kick off my shoes and add to the foyer's mountain of footwear. It's a smell I recognize instantly, a scent that brings me back to the joyous happenings of my childhood. Nostalgic notes of cinnamon and cloves make my mouth water, and for a brief moment, I'm happy to think that Dad is making cookies again. But bliss instantly turns into panic when I realize just what that means.

Dad is making cookies.

He can't be home from work this early, not on a weekday, at least. For a dentist with a relatively flexible schedule, he insists on working long hours, taking pride in knowing that he's the closest thing our country has to Yesterday's definition of a *doctor*. But today, perfect teeth are nothing more than a symbol of status afforded by the upper class. People will always crave luxury—no matter what state the world is in.

A lump forms in my throat, hands shaking as I brace myself for his confrontation. There's no way he didn't hear me walk through the door, but I pray for the unlikely and embark on a desperate attempt to sneak into my room as silently as possible. I can't take one of his lectures right now. Not today.

I scold myself for not deciding to hide away at the McLellans for another evening. Spending time away from home ensures maximum avoidance of my father and his constant suspicion. But after everything that's happened within the last twenty-four hours, all I want is some time alone. I couldn't face Margot any more than I had to, and I broke my routine because of it. But I didn't know Dad would be home so early.

I hear crisp pings of silverware and the soft hiss of a faucet at work. *Good,* I think. He's doing the dishes. Maybe he won't hear me.

I know my mother will appreciate a clean kitchen and a freshly baked batch of spiced cookies, but I'm bothered by it. He does everything for a purpose. Nothing is straightforward with him, nothing is ever what it seems. He is not a man of kind gestures but a man of image and maintaining a personal agenda. When he does manage to do something nice, you can't help but feel like you owe him something. And I think that's the point.

To me, spiced cookies are not a pleasant surprise, but rather the culinary embodiment of a guilt trip.

To him, it means that I've disappointed him, despite *everything* he does for me.

"You can't avoid me forever, you know."

I freeze, rotating my neck to view the man in the kitchen.

He's changed out of his work attire and is now wearing Mateo Voclain's definition of *casual*—a dark polo paired with jeans that must be twice as expensive as the textbook I fought to save not so long ago, promoting the inaccurate assumption that we are the kind of family who can afford such a luxury.

My father's arms are folded neatly, his deep golden skin glistening with beads of sweat and soap suds. His glare is as stoic as freshly cured concrete. He says nothing as I turn the rest of my body around to face him, shoulders tense and thumbs in my pockets.

"You made cookies." I point out the obvious in an attempt to change the subject, but he doesn't reply. I purse my lips and look down at my tattered sneakers.

"I got an email from your school today," Dad finally says, walking back to the sink to busy himself with the dishes once more. "About sixth period."

"Botany?" I ask, and he nods.

"Someone had a *meltdown* in class?"

"I wouldn't call it a meltdown," I say, annoyed by his insensitivity and constant need to exaggerate. "There's nothing wrong with showing a little emotion."

"Not when that emotion could potentially compromise the mindset of a whole classroom." He scoffs as he scrubs at a plate. "I heard your teacher didn't handle it well. He should have sent that girl out as soon as she said anything questionable."

"Dad, it's fine. It wasn't that big of a deal."

"I'm just checking in with you, that's all," he says, still scrubbing the same plate. He looks up at me. "Am I not allowed to check in with my own daughter? To have a conversation with her before she sneaks off to God knows where to do God knows what?"

"I haven't been *sneaking off*. I've been at Margot's." I cross my arms, no longer paranoid but frustrated. I can feel an argument brewing, even though I know there isn't really anything to argue about. Not anything my father knows about, anyway. I brace myself for words to be taken out of context and minuscule things to be blown out of proportion.

"I wasn't born yesterday, you know." He's still smothering that plate with a sponge, though the dish is spotless. "You're hiding something, Lavender."

I wince at his accusation. I hate it when he calls me by my full name. Only strangers do that. But I guess it perfectly describes our relationship.

"Dad, I'm—"

"Is it drugs?" He interrupts me before I can say anything.

"Yes, Dad, I'm on drugs." I laugh because his suggestion is so comically out of character for me, but I quickly correct myself when he doesn't get the joke. "No."

"Are you dating someone? Someone you don't think your family would approve of?"

"No."

"Are you in some kind of trouble?"

"Can you stop with this—*interrogation*? I literally just walked through the door and right away you started accusing me of all these ridiculous things."

"Lavender—"

"Has it ever occurred to you that *this*"—I pause to gesture with my hands —"is the reason why I don't like being home? Why I would rather spend my time around people who aren't always accusing me of doing something wrong?"

He doesn't say anything. I know his tactics; let the interviewee lead the interview. Use silence to push me to talk. But I can't *not* say anything. The words just tumble out and I can't keep them from doing so.

"If you always accuse people of lying to you, they're gonna start lying to avoid the accusations. You create problems out of thin air and it drives me mad."

"So you are lying to me?" He shuts off the faucet and turns to face me, anger brewing.

"No!" I throw my hands up in frustration, though I know he's correct. "That's not what I meant."

"It doesn't seem that way to me."

"Dad." I sigh, slowly forcing myself to inhale and exhale as deeply as I can. But my breathing is shaky, and I can't calm down.

"You can talk to me, you know," he says, lowering his voice until it's uncharacteristically soft. "About anything."

I look down at my feet because I know that's not true. If he ever found out just what I'm doing for Margot's sake—if he knew I'm refusing to become a Chaser to pursue the illegal art of healing—her life would be in even more danger than it already is.

My dad is a smart man and he would surely connect the dots. He would turn his disappointment into bitterness toward Margot and her family, and I wouldn't put it past the man to report them to the authorities for alleged treason—the one thing Immunity cannot save you from. Even Chasers can be killed for treason, and their families are always subjected to the same fate as punishment.

He would turn the McLellans over to the Presidency without hesitating if he thought they had tainted me in some way.

Because the eldest daughter of Mateo Voclain must be perfect. She will be flawless, a mirror image of the man himself. Being anything less than perfect will spark assumptions of failure on his part, and he could never allow his daughter's name to be associated with the Undergrounders.

He can never know, I decide. *Who knows how he'll retaliate?*

"Why aren't you saying anything?" he questions. I can't tell if he's disappointed or angry.

I can't look at him. "What if I don't have anything to say?"

"There's always something to say."

"You know what I have to say?" I swallow the aching lump in my throat. "Absolutely nothing. Because I'm not hiding anything from you."

As I turn around to walk away, I can hear him grab a cookie and begin to devour it in solitude. While I don't trust my father's nature, part of me feels guilty for lying to him.

"Eddie," he calls before I disappear down the hall. "Remember to tell me as soon as you get your letter. It should be here in the next few days."

I ignore him.

Sometimes I wish things were different. I wish I could tell him everything, and I wish he had the ability to listen.

REN

Friday, May 4
43 Days Left of Being Human

Mae Soto has disappeared.

She doesn't show up to sixth period, and after analyzing pieces of hushed gossip, I discover that she was absent from her other classes as well. She simply never showed up for school.

I overhear a few of her friends expressing their concern for her. No one has heard a peep from Mae since her breakdown yesterday. Not one phone call, not one text—nothing.

Mr. Aguilar has vanished too.

And then *she* walks in—a woman none of us have seen before. We hear her heels clicking down the glossy white hallway before she enters, drawing our eyes to the direction of the door before her fingers have time to grip the handle. Her lips are drawn in an emotionless line, an expression as tidy as her strict bun and crease-free business attire. She is the embodiment of order and I can't help but feel intimidated when she sits down at Mr. Aguilar's desk.

"Good morning." Her voice is dark and smooth as she sets her bag on the ground. She pulls out a metal name card and sets it where Aguilar's used to rest, and I wonder why it's not here anymore.

And then I notice that nothing is here anymore. Every poster, every decoration, every colorful writing utensil has vanished into thin air. No more photos of him and past students. No more framed certifications. No more of his collection of favorite student essays that used to reside on the wall behind his desk. Every reminder of Aguilar's presence has been removed, and something tells me that the man himself has been subjected to the same fate.

It's like he was never here to begin with.

"Open your textbooks to page 337, please," the woman says. None of us follow her instructions, and she repeats herself robotically. "Open your textbooks to page 337, please."

"Wait," Duke blurts out, raising his hand. "Where's Mr. Aguilar?"

"As of right now, I will be teaching this class," she states firmly, avoiding the question.

"Like a substitute?"

"More like a replacement." She opens her laptop and clicks on the attendance software like she has done this every day for the entirety of the school year. She acts as though Aguilar was nothing but a bad dream, and she is the reality we have all woken up to. The scary thing is—her act is almost believable.

"Did he get sick or something?" another student asks aloud.

"Yeah, where did he go?" another one blurts, and the room erupts with a concerned cacophony of chatter.

"I can already tell that this previous teacher of yours was ex—is no longer here—for a reason." Her fumble makes my heart drop, and I wonder about the word she almost let escape. "It is clear to me that this classroom has not been run the way a modern classroom should be run."

The chatter decrescendos, and so does our curiosity. We sink into our seats in silence.

Deep down, in some shadowed, cobwebbed corner of ourselves, we all know exactly what happened.

"In my classroom, you will raise your hands. No more of this unsolicited conversation." She crosses her arms and stares into the sea of students intently, displaying a drastic level of seriousness that intimidates us all. We're terrified of this stranger, of the system, of the chilling thought that we could be next.

"And not one of you will utter a single word about Mr. Aguilar or Mae Soto ever again."

For the rest of the day, no one stops thinking about the vanishing of sweet Mae and the beloved botany teacher. But no one is brave enough to talk about it. We keep our heads down and speak about the subject exclusively through nervous glances and unsaid words.

No one wants to say the wrong thing, because we all know the same alarming and unspoken truth:

Saying the wrong thing gets you killed.

Margot and I don't say a word on the way home from school.

Our lips are sealed by the fear of what we have discovered, and the fear that we will meet similar fates if we are heard by the wrong people. The presence of the mics hangs heavier than ever, and for now, it feels safer not to say anything at all.

I press my foot on the brakes and put the car in park, seatbelts clicking as Margot and I step out of the vehicle. Today is a day of rare warmth, and I feel the sun scorch the exposed skin on the back of my neck with its burning rays of golden light. I find it odd that the sun chose today of all days to make itself known.

But even with the light, the day is still gloomy, even more so for Margot. I see it in the way she holds herself. Her shoulders sink a bit lower, her steps a bit heavier, her gaze a bit hazier. By the way my sister keeps obsessively checking her phone, I doubt Eddie is answering her texts. I can't help but wonder what Eddie could be up to, now that it's my responsibility to worry about such things.

The silence still lingers on as we walk through the front door. Our father hasn't come home from work yet, and the house greets us with emptiness. Margot keeps her head down and walks upstairs, quiet, absorbed in the happenings of her own mind. It hurts a little, because once, we were never quiet around each other. We always had something to say. And now, there are no words that feel right.

I take off my shoes and trudge upstairs, feet dragging against the carpeted platforms as I make my way toward my room. I open the door and sit down at my desk, pulling out my books for an evening of assignments, but I pause.

Something needs mending, and I intend on doing just that.

Forcing a grin, I stand up, toss my books on my bed, and walk out of my room. I make my way across the hall and open my sister's bedroom door.

Margot is sprawled across her cream and pink rose quilt, head perched in her hands as she reads a book. Light seeps in through white wooden blinds, which she insists on keeping open to brighten up the space—unlike me, who thrives behind blackout curtains.

There are similarities in everything Margot and I do, but we have our differences too. Like mine, her space is similarly neat and organized, thanks to Eddie helping her keep it that way, which I find rather hilarious as Eddie is not a characteristically neat person. I suppose she puts all of that energy into helping Margot instead.

While Margot's room is clean, it's not decluttered like mine. Her walls are painted a warm light green so pale it's almost white, and covered in just about everything she loves. Thrifted frames filled with paintings, photos of her and Eddie in various stages of life, letters, vintage movie posters from the Yesterdays, pressed leaves and flowers glued to pages ripped out of yellowed old books.

There are plants everywhere, decorating the floating bookshelves that line the entirety of her room. The greenery is all Eddie's doing. Her father doesn't like dirt in the house so she brings plants here instead, caring for them herself when she comes over, as Margot cannot. But Margot loves them too. The whole room looks as though it could belong to both Eddie and my sister, and when I think about it, I'm pretty sure it does.

"Hey," I nod, knocking on the white molding that trims the entryway. Margot seems startled by my presence, head turning quickly to meet the intruder leaning against her door frame.

"Hey," she says, confused by the smile I somehow manage to maintain. Today is not a day for smiling, but I do so anyway. For her.

I walk over to the velvet green swivel chair tucked into her desk and take a seat. "Would you be up for visiting the river this weekend? Like we used to? You, me and Dad?"

"God, yes." Margot's grin pokes deep dimples in the side of her face. "It's been forever."

"It has." Seeing my sister smile makes my own expression feel less forced.

It's quiet for a moment, and I hesitate before clearing my throat. "Eddie can come too, if you want."

Margot sits up, closing her book. She observes me with a puzzled expression, eyes wide, brow arched in suspicion as she chuckles. "What did you just say?"

I blush stupidly. "You heard me."

"Incorrectly, probably." She smirks.

"I'm mature enough to handle an outing with Eddie," I argue defensively, straightening my back, trying to convince myself more than Margot.

"Whatever."

"Milo can come too. If you really want it to be like the old days," I add, hoping she takes a liking to the idea. We used to get along quite well, all those years ago. Unlike his older sister, Milo Voclain is a lot more bearable. I've always liked him; he's a year younger than I am, but more grounded than half the adults I've met. Maybe his presence will dull some of Eddie's edges.

"That would be nice." Margot nods.

She pauses, grin fading, studying me for a moment as if to question my motives. "Why do you wanna go to the river all of a sudden?"

I shrug, though I know the answer. *There are no mics out there*, I think to myself. You can't say the wrong thing when no one is listening.

Eddie and I can move forward with our plan.

"I don't know. Just thought you could use a little... lightening up, I guess."

It's the truth too, but it feels like a lie.

She smiles again, softly. "I think we could both use some lightening up."

I mirror her expression to the best of my ability. "I think you're right."

I hold off on my school assignments for now and head downstairs to do the dishes because my sister cannot, and my father is still at the shop. I dust, I do laundry, I run to the store and stock up on produce to prep Margot's meals for the week. When my father gets home, exhausted, I make dinner, and I handle my sister's evening meds.

While my family sleeps, I do the dishes all over again. I'm worn to near shreds, but I do so bittersweetly, thankful I have the ability to do any of it at all. It's early in the morning by the time I finish my homework.

There are many weights resting on my shoulders. Days are heavy now and then, but if I can spare my family the weight, I will carry it any day, even if my back must break in the process.

And maybe—just maybe—it will kill the guilt too.

EDDIE

Sunday, May 7
26 Days Left Until Graduation

"This is stupid."

My brother stands by the front door in a black hoodie and swim trunks of the same color. His curls are messy and uncombed, dark to match his clothes, framing a face whose glare seems to be angled in my direction.

It's obvious the boy doesn't spend enough time outside from appearance alone. Milo is naturally pale like our mother, but unhealthily so, constantly neglecting himself from sunlight by spending every waking hour locked inside his room. Sure, he insists on being homeschooled, but he could benefit from some exposure to the outside world. If it weren't for the shared inheritance of our mother's unruly curls, it would be difficult to tell that Milo is related to me at all; I would rather be outside soaking up whatever sun I can find than spending all my time confined within four walls.

My brother is a hermit, in both appearance and attitude.

"*You're* stupid," I retort, keeping my eyes fixed to my book as I lay upside down on the couch with my feet hanging over the back. It's a Yesterday fantasy novel Margot lent me, a rare find these days. I finish up my sentence and shut it closed before sitting upright and shoving the book in my backpack. Margot and I have plans to spend most of our time by the river reading; she's excited for me to finish so she can rant about her new imaginary half-human lovers.

"I don't understand why you need me to come with you," Milo mumbles, slinging a gray drawstring bag over his shoulder.

"Because we all want you to." I zip my backpack shut before giving him a look. "Come on, it'll be fun."

"Your definition of *fun* is severely warped," he mutters, walking out the front door. I take my bag and follow him out to the car.

The past few days have been getting an unusual amount of sun, and that light is still present today. There's barely a cloud in the sky, a rarity for our area, even in the summertime. I squint as I open the door to my vehicle, a refurbished red sedan from the Yesterdays, suited with a CD player and everything—though I have yet to come across a CD in good enough shape to play.

Milo climbs in the passenger's seat and buckles up with a tired sigh as I start the car. I pull out of the driveway carefully, glancing to my right to see him rummaging through his bag. As if to read my mind, he pulls out a small square case, opening it to retrieve a shiny round disc that he inserts in the player.

"Where did you get that?" My jaw drops, and I stare at my brother with wide eyes for a moment before shifting my focus back to the road. "Must have been worth a fortune."

"I have my ways." He smirks. I forget how sly he can be with his resourcefulness.

My brother is a genius, though he doesn't spend his intelligence pursuing academics in the same way I do. Sure, he does online homeschooling, but most days, he finishes his assignments within the first couple of hours. He spends most of his time building things, experimenting with old Yesterday gadgets and contraptions that have been replaced by the digital world we know today. Repairing old-fashioned radios and CD players, fixing ancient video game consoles, taking the bus to search pawn shops and consignment stores for whatever he can get his hands on. Probably dumpsters too, because for a genius, he's dumb like that. And he hides it all from our father, of course.

I think back to the loose floorboards in my brother's closet, where he conceals anything our modern father would disapprove of. Milo is much more clever than a seventeen-year-old should be, and I would be lying if I said I wasn't a little bit jealous.

Out of the corner of my eye, I can see him mess with the car buttons, skipping around until he gets to the song he wants. He leans back in his seat with his hands behind his head.

A mellow song begins to play, but there is no song at first—only talking. Two muted voices converse in a language I don't understand, and when the song finally starts, I'm pleasantly surprised. It's oddly calming, and there's a sadness to it I can't place.

"It's a band from the Yesterdays," Milo says, answering my question before it escapes my lips. "Voxtrot."

"The song—what's it about?"

"I'm not sure, but I think it's about a couple during wartime," Milo explains with a shrug.

"Makes sense," I reply as I listen to the lyrics.

We sit in silence for a few minutes, absorbing the song as we drive out of town, past modern buildings and suburbs and down a road that cuts through an endless expanse of pine.

The song plays on, and there's something eerie about it. I'm not surprised Milo likes it so much. It's artistic, and there's so much to analyze.

I can't help but picture the two people in the story, who are drawn to each other because they're stuck in the same circumstances. They're not sure if they're in love or if they're just connecting over some shared experience.

It talks about how love doesn't always make sense. Sometimes nothing makes sense, and as the world keeps spinning around you, accepting that as truth is all you can do.

It gives me the chills.

In less than an hour, we find Asa McLellan's car parked in a clearing in the woods, right on the edge of the river.

Through the windows of my car and gaps in the trees, I can see the water, each side surrounded by round gray river stones and tufts of wild grass that grow between the crevices. It's not the largest river, only a few yards across, but it's still a sight that makes me grin. The creeks we have in the city—the ones that merge together and feed this very river—just can't compare to this.

Milo and I file out of the car, greeting the McLellans with a wave as Asa and Ren unload coolers and chairs from the trunk of their vehicle. Margot sits in the dirt, eyes fixed on the sequel of the book she's been urging me to read. She looks up when she hears my brother and me approaching and flashes me a grin. I walk over to help her rise to her feet.

Folded chair in one arm and Margot's hand in the other, Asa helps his daughter walk down the dirt slope to get to the river, steadying the girl as her weakened legs tremble. Milo and I head back to our car to begin carrying our belongings down, but to my surprise, Ren follows.

"I can help you with that," he mutters blankly, nodding in the direction of the cooler I struggle to hold. I glare at him, but he gives me a look, and I wonder if he has something to say.

I turn to Milo. "You go on ahead. We'll catch up."

My brother raises an eyebrow in suspicion, and I resist the urge to kick him in the shin, as I often find myself doing in his presence.

Ren waits for Milo to walk down to the shore, looking over his shoulder to make sure we're alone as we stand by my car. I fold my arms, waiting for him to speak.

Instead, he walks forward, stepping so close to me I almost step back. He leans forward to whisper in my ear.

"We can speak freely out here," Ren mutters, keeping his voice low. My brows crease in confusion, and he rolls his eyes. "No one should be listening. There are no mics."

"Oh," I reply, feeling a bit stupid. *So that's the real reason why we're here.*

Not that I expected anything else, deep down. When Ren messaged me about this weekend, I thought he might have had some other motive.

"If helping Margot by becoming a healer for the Undergrounders is really something you're interested in..." Ren looks over his shoulder again. "Now's your chance to do something about it."

"What?"

"You have to talk to my father," he explains, taking a step backward to look me in the eye. "You and I both know he's involved in some way."

I nod, staring down at my shoes, because it's true. How else would he get Margot's supplements, without at least *some* connection? Even if he's only a customer, it's still a tie, and any tie is a good enough lead for me.

As much as I hate to admit it, Ren is right. This might be my best chance—maybe even my only chance—to talk to Asa about the Undergrounders.

But I can't help but feel a little nervous. What if he refuses to tell me what he knows? What if he pretends not to know what I'm talking about and tells my father, out of concern for my own safety? What if he doesn't have a connection at all?

The crunching of shoes against dirt and dead pine needles spins Ren's attention backward, and I look over his shoulder to see Asa approaching, finished helping Margot, and ready to help us unload the car. Ren takes my backpack and gives me a nod so subtle I almost miss it. Before I have time to plan what to say to Asa, Ren is gone.

"You and Milo brought some pretty lousy chairs." Asa chuckles humorously, grabbing the last chair from the back of my car. "They're practically falling apart."

"I know." I grin, shaking my head. "We need to replace them."

I'm quiet for a moment, watching in silence as Asa takes the item, turning to walk down the slope to meet the others at the shore.

"Wait," I say, and he turns around, raising a gray eyebrow.

I blink slowly, hands shaking ever so slightly as my heart begins to race. I let out a sigh. It feels strange, being this nervous speaking to a man I've known my whole life. The McLellans are family to me; it makes no sense to feel so anxious.

You can't be nervous about this anymore, I tell myself. *Not if you want to be an Undergrounder.*

"I want in," I state bluntly.

There's a pause, almost eerie in the way it holds itself, as though something supernatural is keeping it in place. In the distance, I can hear Margot laughing at something Milo said. I am suddenly all too aware of white rapids dancing far down the river, a woodpecker's persistence, and the call of a knowing crow.

Asa looks at me like I've just spoken in tongues. "What?"

I hesitate, but my voice is firm. "I want in."

He looks at me for a moment, humorously at first, until the humor is replaced with confusion. "I'm not sure I know what you're talking about."

I stare at Asa carefully, trying my best to seem braver than I am. To speak with my eyes, to let him know how serious I am about this.

"We both know that's a lie," I reply.

Asa is silent, his face growing paler by the second. He is a tall man, but now, he seems smaller than ever.

"You know the supplements won't work forever," I mutter. "They help, but they're not consistent or strong enough. She needs access to a healer. Someone she can trust, who has the time and will to study her, to develop a more advanced treatment plan."

I pause. "Someone like me."

Asa is horrified. He looks at me like a fatal countdown. I might as well be standing on a cliff, back facing the edge, threatening to spread open my arms and fall. He speaks so frantically I wonder if that's actually what he sees.

"She has a healer. He's competent; I know him personally."

I shake my head. "Not one who can communicate with her. Not one that's around her all the time and knows her symptoms in and out. Not one who loves her as much as I do."

He shakes his head too. "We shouldn't be talking about this."

"There are no mics out here."

"Mics or no mics, I don't care," Asa snaps, and I'm taken aback. He's the most carefree man I know, and to hear his voice so stern is like a slap to the face. "This is dangerous, Eddie."

"You think I don't know that?"

"It's so much more than danger," he replies, his voice dark as he glares protectively. "Are you willing to give your entire life to this cause? Your entire existence? To sacrifice your future?"

I don't say anything, and he continues.

"Are you willing to give up the ignorance that keeps you safe? The safety of your present and future family? To throw away everything you once thought you knew and trade it for a world gone upside down?"

My heart races. "I know the cost."

"*Costs*," he corrects firmly. "There are many."

I lift my chin. "Then I will pay them."

"Margot is my responsibility. Keeping her safe is my burden to bear, not yours." Asa points a slender finger to his own chest. His hair was a red-brown once, but now, it looks grayer than ever. I can see the exhaustion circling his eyes, the lines cutting through his face. He has paid many tolls.

His words feel like a stab in the heart. He knows how much Margot means to me, how much of my life I dedicate to making hers better. He knows how far I would go to save her from her hauntings. And yet here he is, telling me none of that matters.

"Look." Asa sighs, tucking the folded chair beneath one arm and rubbing his temples with the other. "I appreciate everything you do for Margot. You're part of our family, and you know that."

I nod, and I can't help but stare down at my shoes. They're worn and stained more green than white, but still bright in comparison to the floor of the woods around me. I wonder how long it'll take for them to be coated in a thick layer of dirt.

"Which is exactly why I can't let you know what I know. Why I *won't* let you know what I know," Margot's father claims. "It's for your own good."

"I'm not a child anymore," I snap, meeting Asa's gaze. His eyes are green and sad. "I know the risks. I know the costs. I know all of that.

"But this isn't just for her, you know." I shake my head, crossing my arms against my chest. "I'm doing this for my brother. For my parents. Because I want a better world for them."

Asa doesn't say a word, so I go on.

"A world where my mother doesn't spend her every waking hour regretting the tattoos she creates to earn a living. A world where my father doesn't feel obligated to pressure his children to become killers for their own safety. A world where my brother can be whoever the hell he wants to be without hiding.

"But I'm also doing this for me." I lower my voice, dropping my arms to my sides. "For the little girl who spent hours and hours pouring over every botanical encyclopedia and herbalism resource she could get her hands on. For this inescapable longing I have for something more. Something more than following my father's expectations and becoming a Chaser. Something more than what this system has to offer, because what it has to offer will never be enough. Not until it's fixed. Not until someone decides to do something about it.

"And I'll find a way to do something, whether you help me or not. Because I already decided I'm becoming an Undergrounder long ago."

I pause, choking on my words. "No matter the costs."

Asa places his free hand in the pocket of his brown jacket. He looks up at the sky, at the towering evergreens that guard the blue with sharp emerald teeth. He closes his eyes, letting out a weary sigh.

"I'm sure you've already guessed what I do when I leave town," he says, his voice quiet. He shifts his gaze to look at me once again.

"I can't tell you everything right now, and I can't tell you why. But this is far bigger than it seems. This is more than a small ring of smugglers selling medicinal herbs and stolen Yesterday goods on the black market," Asa explains. "And I'm more than just a customer."

My eyes widen, and I stare at him in awe. More than just a customer?

Could he be a smuggler himself?

"There's a saying they tell us every now and then that I often forget," he continues. "They tell us not to pick and choose our players."

They? I question. *Us?*

The realization hits me like a ton of bricks. I feel as though I've swallowed a handful of gravel, and I can feel my pulse beat faster by the second.

I always thought Asa knew the right people. That he had a tie with someone who would give him medicine in the dark in exchange for money or other valuables. But now, I realize how wrong I was. He is deeper in this rebel quicksand than I thought.

Because how can there be an *us* if Asa McLellan isn't an Undergrounder himself?

"There's something to be said about loyalty, no matter how young you are." Asa sighs, giving me a smile that feels more bitter than sweet, as though he's remembering something from long ago.

"In my eyes, you kids are still just that. Kids." He gestures over to the shore, where I can hear more echoes of Milo laughing with Margot and Ren. That laughter feels so far away, so distant, so unfamiliar. It all sounds too much like a memory.

"But if this is the path you wish to take, and if it's a path I can't stop you from taking," he continues, "then I can't have you knocking on all the wrong doors. I'll guide you to the right one if you promise me one thing."

"Anything," I agree.

"You can never tell a soul about any of this. For the sake of many lives, including your own."

"Never." I nod, ashamed of the quiet words that follow. "Not even Margot."

"Not even Ren," Asa adds, and I feel my face grow increasingly warm.

"Not even Ren."

Asa looks over his shoulder as if to check whether or not his children can hear the conversation. They are too far from where we stand to hear anything, even an argument, if one were to arise.

"If you want to grow ties with them, you have to prove you're trustworthy," Asa claims. Another stab to the heart.

I frown. "You've known me my whole life."

"I trust you, but they won't. Not all of them, at least," he states. "You have to prove your loyalty. That you're capable of helping the cause."

The cause. The words ring in my ears, their echo almost surreal. "What cause?"

"Change, Eddie. This is change in play." For a moment, the worry drains away, and Asa shows me a grin. A true, heartfelt grin I haven't seen him display in a long time.

And I can't help but show him one right back.

This is what I want, I think to myself. Change.

"I'll ask you one more time." Asa's expression is serious once again. "Is this really something you want?"

I pause, and he speaks again. "This isn't an answer you have to give me right away."

I ignore his disclaimer and nod. "What can I do?"

Asa gives me a look, and I suddenly get the feeling that I've already bitten off more than I can chew.

"There's a contact of mine I think you should meet."

REN

Sunday, May 7
41 Days Left of Being Human

♪ SO HERE WE ARE - BLOC PARTY ♪

It's a bit tricky to breathe.

I'm on edge as I walk down the dirt slope with Eddie's bag in hand, looking over my shoulder to see her standing in hushed conversation with my father. I bite the inside of my cheek nervously, wishing I could overhear their discussion.

I pray Eddie knows how to keep a secret. Because if things go as planned, pretty soon, she'll be keeping more than one.

The air smells like algae and filth, and I don't like it. The child I used to be would have been ecstatic over any opportunity to be closer to the outdoors, but after learning the truth about the world I live in, I now gain more excitement staying locked indoors.

I learned about germs. I learned that dirt is another word for dead things. I learned about the mites that permanently reside on your skin. I learned that parasites, bacteria, and mold can make someone ill beyond an outsider's comprehension, and that more people are this ill than you'd think. I learned that even the most unnoticeable bite from the smallest, nearly invisible juvenile tick can change a life forever.

I learned that this world is simply a cycle of death and decay, with or without humans to make it all worse.

I see Milo and Margot spreading beach towels and chairs on the rocks a few yards ahead of me next to our mound of coolers and bags. My shoes crunch against the dirt and the rocks, which are round, grapefruit-sized, and tricky to navigate. I'm glad Margot had assistance walking down here; she's too unstable to manage this terrain on her own.

I set Eddie's bag down on one of the white and pink striped towels, printed with strange tropical flowers I've only seen in books. We haven't brought out this towel since our last river trip. It feels odd seeing it again, considering all that happened.

"You shouldn't be barefoot," I mutter to my sister, mindful of the dangers. Lack of protection will lead to cuts, and Margot's immune system can't afford the infection bacteria exposure will bring.

"And you shouldn't be such a stickler for wearing shoes," Margot claims, sitting in her chair with an open book as Milo sets up the umbrella. I walk over to help him. "Being barefoot is good for the soul."

I can't see her eyes through her sunglasses—she's extremely sensitive to the sun—but I know she doesn't bother to look up at me from the page. I don't argue with her. It's not like she'll be doing much walking, after all.

Milo and I are quiet as we both work together to set up the umbrella. We do it quickly, but the silence makes it take longer in my head. We haven't spoken a word to each other in a long time.

"Aren't you hot in that?" he says, nodding toward the forest green crewneck sweatshirt draped around my torso.

"Aren't you?" I add, eyeing his black hoodie.

He makes a fair point. I would rather stay in the sweatshirt, but the sun is shining too brightly to make anything comfortable. I pull it off, the bare skin of my back soaking up the light. I take the sweater and toss it over to Margot, and she steals it happily. She's always cold.

"Maybe," Milo says, taking a seat next to Margot in his own cloth chair. "I just hate the sun."

I shrug and set up my own chair to his left, looking over my shoulder once again. I squint to make out their shapes in the blinding sunlight, but I can still see Eddie and my father talking between the trees in the distance. It must be going well if it's taking this long, right?

Unless she's telling him more than she should. I gulp nervously and try to shake the thought out of my head. She knows he can't be allowed to know about my letter.

I'm quiet as we wait. Milo has pulled a book out of Eddie's bag for the sake of being a pest—which I very much support—and is now quite ironically invested in the first chapter. He and Margot converse about the contents, but their voices are fuzzy; my thoughts are elsewhere.

After what feels like ages, I hear the crunching of shoes against dirt and gravel. I turn around to see my father helping Eddie carry the last of the Voclain's belongings down the slope.

"Alright, where's the food?" Eddie announces, pulling off her shoes as she walks, throwing them to the side.

A light breeze tangles her charcoal-brown hair, and she takes steps as though she's not bothered by the sunlight heating the rocks below her, or the sharp edges of little stones pressing into her feet. Of course she doesn't care about the dangers. She walks as though she's been barefoot her whole life. I don't think that would be very surprising.

"Over here," Margot says, pointing to the cooler without peeling her eyes away from her book.

"Great." Eddie rummages through the cooler and pulls out a container full of watermelon, stuffing her face with a few dripping chunks before putting it back. I watch as she walks to the shore and rinses her hands in the water, which is green, murky, and not something I would like to touch —let alone use to wash my hands. She jogs back and takes a seat on the rocks next to my chair.

My father sets up his chair far enough down the river to be completely out of earshot from his children and the Voclains, and he pulls out his own book, enjoying the silence and separation.

For a moment, we all sit and enjoy the quiet. Everyone has a book but Eddie and me, who are too busy studying our surroundings to care.

While I'm not exactly fond of being out in the woods, I have always appreciated the beauty of the natural world. The river is the color of my abandoned sweatshirt, snaking in both directions as far as the eye can see. It's less of a river and more like a large creek, with shallow water and only a few yards' worth of width. The deepest points can only be about twelve feet, one below the jumping rock and the other below the bridge.

Farther down the river, the banks on either side rise higher and higher, shifting into sloping walls of mud and gnarled roots. At the tallest points, an old wooden bridge stretches across the river's width at a good enough distance to seem small from our position.

We are surrounded by an endless expanse of evergreen, a blanket of pine that drapes over nearby hills and mountains in the distance. I close my eyes and inhale as deeply as I can, and for once, I don't smell the stench of pollution. My lungs fill up all the way, and I gulp the air desperately, for I know air like this is scarce. Rich, clean, addictive air.

An illusion.

"Is anyone gonna go in the water with me or what?"

I look to my left to see Eddie standing up, wiping dust off her black athletic shorts, which are almost hidden beneath the edge of the oversized gray tee she wears.

"Thanks for the invite, but no," I grumble, staring at the boulder that lies across from where we sit, trying not to think about what happened all those years ago.

"In my head, I was leaving you out of the question." She gives me a false grin and shifts her glance to her brother. "Milo?"

"I'm good," he mutters, comedically invested in the book Eddie intended to read. I don't think her attention span would have let her do much reading, anyway, not with the temptations of the river.

"Fine." Eddie shakes her head, looking at my sister. She softens her voice. "Margot?"

Margot looks up from her book for the first time this afternoon, and she gives Eddie a sad smile. "You know I would love to."

To most people, that's a yes, but it's really a no coming from Margot. Because it's true. There are many things she would love to do, but cannot.

Eddie smiles at my sister, letting her know she understands. I'm thankful she doesn't push her.

"Milo." Eddie looks at her brother again, walking over and kicking him playfully in the shin. "Swim with me."

"Not happening."

"Come on. You have to," she begs. "I'll threaten you. Creatively."

"I agreed to come with you. Not to get in the water," Milo argues.

"Go by yourself then," I add, hoping the suggestion will inspire her to stop talking. I glue a fake smile to my face and stare up at Eddie, who shoots me a glare.

"Why aren't *you* swimming?" she questions, ignoring my statement and gesturing to my shorts. "You wore swim trunks."

It's true. I didn't think much about my clothing today, but I did choose to wear these old black swimming shorts, even though I intend on staying right where I am for the entirety of the afternoon. Habit, I suppose.

"Because the water's gross. Especially with you in it."

"I'm glad you're scared of water." She folds her arms against her chest. "Didn't want you joining me anyway."

I scoff. "Scared? Of dead fish floating around? Or the possible presence of brain-eating algae? Why the hell would anyone ever be afraid of something so fantastic?"

"So you *are* scared."

"Maybe I will go in the water, then." I cross my arms too. "If it'll bother you so much, it's worth it."

"I hate you."

"Thanks."

"Hey, you two," Milo calls, looking up from Eddie's fantasy book as he reads next to Margot. It would be an entertaining sight if Eddie wasn't so infuriating.

"Do the both of us a favor and jump off the bridge. The far away one over there." He holds up the book for effect, pointing to a passage. "Your lover's quarrel is ruining mine."

Eddie's face pinches with annoyance and she readies a fist, but I stand up, and she pauses.

"Fine," I say, glaring at Eddie. "You coming? Or are you too *scared*?"

That does something to her. She stares at me, and for a moment, I see the smallest spark of fear flickering behind her eyes. It's a rarity in Eddie, but an understandable one. I know why she wouldn't want to jump, and that makes me want to do the same more than anything.

Because Eddie is like a wild creature, unable to back down when challenged, willing to bash her head against another and chip her horns if it means she can prove people wrong.

She will jump with me, though she doesn't want to. And maybe that's exactly what I want.

I turn to the left and walk in the direction of the bridge, not bothering to look behind me. She follows me, and for a rare, impossible moment, she doesn't say a word.

The bridge is from the Yesterdays, with wood that peels in damp splinters and big round iron nail heads that feel cold against the bottom of my bare feet. My shoes lie on the top step of the stairs that lead up to the bridge, far to my right, out of reach. We stand in the middle, out of reach from them too.

Our shoulders are so close they nearly touch. We look down at the water below, unable to see the bottom or know how deep the water falls. It is a pool of dark black in a river of murky mud green, and it lies directly below our feet, far from where Milo and Margot sit, even farther from my father's distant solitude.

Everything looks so quiet from where we stand. But I know that if you get closer, if you walk a bit farther into the trees or stand next to the reading people, you will hear things you can't hear from far away. Birds chirping, pages turning, twigs snapping, wings scraping against the sky. Termites viciously chewing away at ripe wood, spiders spinning silk catastrophes, honeybees humming to the tune of clover pollen.

But from up here, we know none of it. Only the quiet place of distance.

"We're both scared, aren't we?"

I turn to my left and crane my neck down to look at Eddie, who stares up at me with questioning eyes the color of green river water. For a moment, I search for a witty remark, but then I see it again. The fear.

"I think so," I say, looking down at the water again. It seems farther away than it did a moment ago.

It's silent again, and a cloud moves over our heads, shading us in a circle of dark, lingering while the rest of the world is light. We are separate from the places touched by the sun.

"How many days left until training?" Eddie asks quietly. She knows I'm counting.

I pause before regretfully swallowing my hesitation. "Forty-one."

"That's soon," Eddie mumbles, shaking her head in disbelief. "Really soon."

I know, I say in silence. I know all too well.

"You know that feeling?" She speaks softly. "When you're somewhere between consciousness and sleep and you can't stop thinking about something horrible? And you know you'll lose your grip and it'll turn into a nightmare?"

I nod. I'm too familiar with the gnawing fear that everything good could collapse in an instant.

"That's what all of this feels like," she whispers.

"You don't have to jump if you don't want to," I say, though I know it's not the river she's talking about.

"Neither of us wants to." I can feel Eddie look up at me, and I meet her gaze again. "But I think we should."

There's a blink, a fraction of a second. For a moment, I catch a glimpse of the girl I used to know so well. Like plucking a dandelion seed out of the air and opening your pinched fingers, only to watch the little white umbrella fly away again.

For a moment, I forget to try so hard to hate her. For a moment, I forget I hate her at all, and I wonder what it would be like to fall.

Without thinking, I climb onto the railing, cautious as I support myself with my arms and swing my legs over. The railing is wider than I thought it would be, and there's enough room for me to stand, as stable as I can be from such heights. I reach out a hand, but Eddie doesn't take it. She hops up on the railing in a much more agile fashion, and she flashes me an arrogant grin.

I don't ask her if she's ready. There is no such thing as ready, because you can never be ready for anything. Not when anything is not a constant, but rather something fragile, something unstable that can change in the blink of an eye.

"Don't be an idiot," I say, turning to look at her one last time.

She smirks. "I can't make any promises."

We jump.

We fall.

We close our eyes.

It feels like the end of a simulation, like a switch has turned off and all of a sudden we're enveloped in cold nothingness. I am not in the presence of water, but absent in emptiness, overwhelmed by the sudden disappearance of light. I fleet away too.

We are so far below the surface. I open my eyes, adjusting to the darkness around me. For a moment, I panic. I can only see nothingness. A shiver traces its long fingernails up and down my back, and I worry about the things that could be lurking below my feet. I turn around, cheeks puffed, lungs paused, waiting for the appetite of some unknown freshwater monster of a fish to take me.

Something grabs my ankles.

Bubbles of air escape my lips as I hold back a scream that wouldn't be heard. I'm too afraid to look down, but I don't have to. The something lets go, and in a moment, I am face to face with a girl, foolish and intimidating, but no monster.

As it gets harder and harder to hold my breath, my shoulders relax. Now that I see her, I wish I had a little more time down here, alone in the darkness with Eddie.

Because this is the Eddie I remember. This is the Eddie I forgot.

Her eyes are open too. She looks at me, hair reaching above her like arms of kelp, and she disappears.

I follow her, arms sweeping through the water as I stare above me, watching the surface dance as shards of broken sunlight grow closer, watching Eddie as she reaches them. I meet her there.

I break through the surface, gasping for air. I gulp the oxygen ravenously, using my legs to stay above water as I flip my shaggy hair back. Eddie does the same, parting through the curtain of brown turned shiny black, blinking the water out of her eyes. She looks so unfamiliar as we float, her once curly hair now straightened and soaked, sticking to her head and her neck, falling to the water in fans.

We stay there, treading water, trying our best to breathe. I watch her.

She notices me staring and shoots me a glare, her thick brows angled. She splashes water in my direction, but as I glare back and try to do the same, she swims away. Pretty soon, she's swimming to the other side of the river, in the opposite direction of where Margot, Milo, and my father reside.

The bridge is attached to two small cliffs of bare earth sprinkled with ferns. On either side is a naturally steep, sloped embankment of dirt and greenery. But there is a shallow, water-soaked shore of river clay, bullfrog tadpoles, and rocks so small you could almost call them sand. To my displeasure, that is exactly where Eddie is headed.

She wades out of the river, long hair, gray tee, and shorts pressed against her small frame as she shivers and steps right into the mud.

And from where I stand in the water, I finally splash her back.

She gasps in annoyance, wiping water from her face. She huffs, glaring at me once again, and before I know it, she bends over, digging her hand straight into the earth to scoop a handful of mud.

She holds it up like she wants to throw it in my direction, and my pulse quickens.

"Wait, *wait*," I call out frantically, holding up both hands innocently. "Eddie... you don't have to do this."

This can't be happening, I repeat to myself, over and over and over.

It can't be.

We couldn't have jumped off the bridge. We couldn't have done it together either. I didn't enjoy our moment of peace. Our darkness wasn't ours. It was a river, and we were simply there.

I can't be in the water. Amidst the tadpoles, the frogs, the animal waste, the algae. The mud.

The world spins a second faster. *This can't be happening.*

"Do what?" she says synthetically, inspecting the mud like it's a baby bunny and not a handful of oozing filth. "It's just a little mud. It doesn't bite."

"Eddie..."

Before I have the chance to prevent it from happening, she takes the handful and tosses it in my direction. I close my eyes in the nick of time, but it hits my face, the leftovers sliding down my skin like slime and falling into the water with a gentle splash.

I'm horrified. Speechless. Disgusted beyond description.

My pulse pounds and the blood rushes heavier in my ears, and suddenly, everything feels quiet. Like the world has been put on pause to let me soak in this filth. It takes everything I have not to start scrubbing the skin right off my bones.

"That's for the time you tripped me in fourth grade. During that race." Eddie pulls me out of my shock as she speaks, lifting up her elbow and pointing to a mark in her skin where a little piece of gravel sits, trapped in a scar.

I stare at the scar, and despite the mud painting my skin, I chuckle at the memory.

I'll never let her know it wasn't on purpose. In fact, I remember stumbling myself. It was my own clumsy tripping that caused her to fall.

I wade out of the water, letting my feet meet the muddy shore. Soft clay oozes between my toes as I walk toward Eddie, but I try not to think about it.

I stand directly in front of her. We're so close I can hear her breathing. I can see the flecks of gold in the hazel of her eyes. I can smell faint remnants of her shampoo, the natural lemon and tea tree variety she uses because Margot can't be around the chemicals put in artificial fragrance. It's overpowered by the river, but I notice the familiarity of its ghost.

Without thinking, I take a handful of mud, and I put it right in her hair.

She gasps, eyes open as wide as her jaw as she stands there, frozen.

"Do you have any idea how long it will take to comb this out?" Eddie seethes.

She gestures to her damp, mud-caked hair, which is already curling as it dries. "How difficult it is to untangle *this*?"

I smirk. "That's for the time you put a millipede in my hair. Fifth grade."

If this is the game she wants to play, then I'll play it better.

"Oh yeah? Well the millipede was revenge for pouring out my juice box because it was filled with *chemicals*."

Eddie takes another handful of mud, standing on her toes to put it in my own hair. It drips down in soft pieces, weighing down every lock.

I step closer. "That's because it was."

"Obviously." Eddie steps forward too. We'll touch if we get any closer. "But I didn't care."

I take more mud, and this time, it meets her face. "That's for not caring."

She spits out mouthfuls of the brown river clay, so angry I almost expect steam to pour from her ears. But then her face softens, and now, she seems more sad than angry, and it confuses me. I watch as Eddie takes more mud and tosses it at my chest.

"That's for not caring either."

For a moment, it feels like we're underwater again, and I think about the way things used to be. Before this river divided us.

I look at her. She and I are covered in mud. She looks as though she's been living with the tadpoles for the past decade. Bits of twigs, leaves, and other goodies from the clay stick out of her hair, braiding with the curls that are now starting to come back to life as the sun dries them even frizzier than they were before. She stares at me with a mix of fury, sadness, and confusion that twists her face into a puzzled knot of glaring distaste.

And then, to my own surprise, I begin to laugh. Eddie looks as though she's seen a ghost. I guess she's hearing one, in a way.

"I'm sorry—you look ridiculous."

She glares, crossing her arms. "Thanks to you."

"Hey, you started it." I raise my hands in innocence.

Oddly enough, when she wipes the mud away and I can see her face again, there's a beauty to her I wish I didn't see. It's not elegant, but it's there, dirt and all.

And even odder still, she looks at me, and she laughs too.

I walk through the mud and find a rock surrounded by greenery on either side. It sits in the earth, perched above the water, where a small drop-off awaits.

Eddie takes a seat on the rock, dangling her feet in the river. I wade through the water, the murky liquid already rising to the bottom of my torso. I stand in front of Eddie, and for once, our eyes are level.

She dives in for a moment, rinsing out the mud and combing out the filth before rising again, hopping on the rock once more. She sits there, running fingernails through her hair, trying to work through the tangles the mud had introduced.

"Here. Let me help." I move closer, stepping around the rock until I'm standing at her side. "You're a mess."

To my surprise, she doesn't protest as I reach forward, helping comb out the tangles by hand. I don't mind doing it. I'm the one who made this mess, and the last thing I want is to be indebted to Eddie. To owe her something.

That's why I'm helping her.

"Thanks," she mutters quietly, kicking her legs gently. Her feet create ripples in the water. "It's hard to reach the back sometimes."

Her hair is a matted disaster, but it's soft, almost meditative to work with. I untangle it quicker than I expected to, but my hand lingers longer than it should.

"Hey idiots."

Our chins lift up in a simultaneous start, looking for the owner of the voice. To my surprise, I see Milo standing with Margot on the nearer side of the bridge, leaning over the railing. They wave in our direction, and Eddie waves back. I drop my hands like I had been touching hot coals a moment ago, not Eddie's hair.

His sister gasps excitedly as Milo climbs onto the railing. He helps Margot do the same, and before any of us can question it, they jump together.

Eddie cheers, and my heart races as I wait for their heads to pop up. I see Milo resurface, but no sign of Margot. My blood feels hot, and the clouds above me begin to whirl. I'm dizzy and far lighter than I should be, aching for a sign of life.

But the panic subsides when I see her, breaking through the shards, smiling with a grin I haven't seen for a very long time. *Today must be one of her good days*, I think to myself, as rare as they can be.

The two swim over to meet us by our rock, and before I know it, we are all covered in mud again. We laugh until our cheeks are sore, we swim until we can't, we drench each other in green-brown river clay like no days have passed at all.

For the first time in a long time, we are children in a world that never wanted us to grow up.

Night has fallen by the time Margot and Eddie come back from dropping Milo off at the Voclain household. They waved him goodbye, but Margot stole away Eddie for the night, per my sister's desperate request.

The two are still chattering incessantly as they climb out of Eddie's car in tandem, talking nonstop, forgetting how exhausted they must be. My father and I are still in the driveway, unloading the last of our belongings as Margot and Eddie head upstairs.

I help my father finish unpacking everything and get started with our nightly routine as he lumbers off to bed. I wash today's dishes, I prepare Margot a quick snack, and I get started on arranging her capsules and a glass of water.

I knock on Margot's door with a little ceramic dish of pills and apple slices in one hand, and the cup of water in the other. No one answers, so I open it myself, only to find Eddie inside, with Margot nowhere in sight.

I stand there by the doorframe, watching as Eddie tackles the basket of clean laundry in the corner of Margot's room, putting away my sister's clothes.

It's not out of the ordinary for Eddie to help out around the house when she comes over; she likes helping Margot in whatever way she can. In fact, it's almost expected. Regardless, I watch her with a curiosity I can't explain.

She looks up at me, eyes widening just a little, startled by my presence.

"Sorry," I mumble.

Eddie looks at the meds in my hands before turning back to her task. "She's taking a salt bath. Her muscles are sore."

As always. One of her symptoms is muscle pain. Not just a general soreness—but a constant burning, a perpetual aching that tortures every muscle in her body and never goes away. Some days are worse than others, especially after physical exertion. But she's never been one to complain.

If Margot says she's in pain, that means she's *really* in pain.

"Good." I nod. "The river must have been a lot for her."

"Yeah." Eddie studies the sweater she's hanging up.

I walk into the room, setting the glass of water and the tray of food and capsules on the nightstand. I pause.

"Thank you," I say, placing my hands in my pockets and clearing my throat.

"I do this all the time. It's no big deal." Eddie shrugs, still focused on the clothes. Her own outfit has changed since we got home. She wears an oversized brown flannel and black lounging shorts, her curls frizzy thanks to the river. She looks so peaceful it almost feels out of place.

I hesitate. "I'm not talking about the laundry."

Eddie freezes, clutching a plastic hanger and one of Margot's pale blue hoodies. I walk closer, looking over my shoulder to make sure we're truly alone.

"Don't thank me. This isn't something you made me do." She almost sounds angry, and I wonder if I said the wrong thing.

"Sorry."

"I want to do... more," she says vaguely, mindful of who might be listening. "And it has nothing to do with you. It's something I've wanted to do for a long time."

"So he agreed to let you help?" I ask hopefully, quietly.

Eddie nods, staring at her feet. "There's someone I'm meeting. Tomorrow."

Tomorrow? I feel a bit queasy all of a sudden.

"You don't have to go through with it, you know."

"I know." Eddie snaps before softening her voice. I forget how little she likes being told what to do. "But I will. And I am."

I understand why she looks so upset, why she looks at the laundry in her hands so sadly. It takes familiarity with guilt to recognize it in other people too. Liars know how liars look.

"I should get going," she says, clearing her throat. Her tone is less defensive, and she puts away the last of Margot's shirts before closing my sister's closet doors.

"I thought you were staying the night."

"I can't." Eddie looks at me, and I see the guilt again. I watch as she turns to walk away.

"Don't be an idiot," I tell her, but I can't say why. Eddie pauses, rotating her head to look at me again. She knows I'm not talking about her drive home.

Eddie smiles. "Can't make any promises."

EDDIE

Monday, May 8
25 Days Left Until Graduation

My stomach churns as I steer my way out of the school parking lot, hands trembling, gripping the wheel so tightly my knuckles pale. It's been like this all day. The nausea, the dizziness, the persistent feeling of someone removing chunks of my chest with an ice cream scooper. Anxiety is a good name for it, but agony is a better synonym.

I'm not used to feeling so scared, helpless, and confused. The comfort of knowing what to expect is something I've taken for granted all these years. The Pick certainly keeps us all on our toes, but at least I know what to fear by the time New Year's comes around.

Now, I'm not sure what to fear. But I fear it anyway.

I keep my left hand on the wheel and use the other to dig into the pocket of my hoodie. I wore all black today because I don't want to stand out. Now I'm wondering if my outfit is suspicious enough to make me stand out more than a comfortable olive green sweater would.

The paper crinkles as I fish it from my pocket. My brows crease again as I study the note for the thousandth time today, absorbing what little information Asa gave me and hoping I know what I'm doing.

His instructions were vague during our conversation at the river, but this is even worse. At the river, at least he told me I would be taking his place at a scheduled meet-up with another smuggler. He told me that's the only way to get in contact with the Undergrounders; they can't use phones, which are too traceable. They can't exactly travel in a way that would allow them to be noticed by the public either, according to Asa, for reasons I have yet to uncover. They are easily identifiable and like to stay as hidden as possible.

The note tells me where to turn and where to stop, but not what to look for, and certainly not what to expect upon my arrival.

I'm well past the city limits by the time I reach the destination. I followed Asa's instructions almost obsessively. I made every windy turn, drove past every crooked tree, parked by the truck-sized boulder draped in sheets of moss. I climbed out of my car, hiked along the stream, and reached the large rotting log that could swallow me whole. Now, all I can do is hope I did everything right.

I use a branch to hoist myself onto the log, sitting on top so my legs dangle over the side. The bark is damp and uncomfortable. I take a deep breath, trying my best to soothe these nerves and failing miserably.

The air smells like cedarwood and pine, of dusty stones and river grass and fallen leaves. Yesterday, these same woods pleased us with good weather, but today the gray is back for its regularly scheduled programming. The sky floats down in little droplets of cold mist, and I shiver as the fog tickles my skin and excites my hair.

I pull out my phone to check the hour. I've been sitting here for quite some time, but as far as I know, I'm completely alone. I look at the device in my hands and wonder if it was smart to bring something traceable.

My thumbs fidget perpetually as I observe my surroundings in solitude. I begin to wonder if the contact will be a no-show. Or maybe they did show up, and they saw me instead of Asa and ran for it.

I reach inside my pocket, digging past the crumpled note of directions and pulling out the envelope the McLellans' father gave me. It's cream-colored and sealed with a red wax symbol of a rabbit with deer antlers. The symbol is bizarre, and I wonder about Asa's many vintage collectibles from the Yesterdays. The seal must be one of them.

This will explain everything, he said. The words inside this letter are the goods I'm supposed to exchange. For what, I don't know.

And then, I hear a twig snap. I shove the envelope back in its place.

My eyes widen and my heartbeat picks up its pace as I slide down the log. I take a few steps forward, cautiously scanning my surroundings, terrified of this stranger I have yet to meet.

I don't see anyone. Surprised, I study every bush, every rock, every tree trunk thick enough to hide a person. Nothing. The sound either belonged to an animal or no one at all. I let out a sigh as I turn around to climb back onto the log.

But to my horror, someone has already taken my spot.

I am frozen. I can feel every joint lock in place, my whole body painfully rigid. A chill traces my spine and my eyes peel wide open as I study the stranger in pure, unadulterated fear.

Because in this moment, standing face to face with this Undergrounder I have never met, I realize how little I know about what I've gotten myself into.

The Undergrounder wears a black long-sleeve shirt and a pair of brown utility pants that are torn in three places and patched in five others. He's narrow-framed and tall, with warm brown skin and feet that nearly touch the ground as he sits on the log, arms crossed. His jaw is sharp and stubbled, his dark hair wavy and lazily combed back, every strand disobedient. Though his eyes hide behind a pair of shaded glasses, I know he glares at me; I can feel its burn in my bones.

I watch as he slides off the log, stepping closer with slow, suspecting strides. A satchel is slung over his shoulder, contents clinking together while he walks. My heart beats faster and I swallow a nervous lump in the back of my throat. I urge my mouth to open, to say *something*—anything at all —but my tongue only stills.

He pauses two feet away from me. "You're not supposed to be here."

When I hear him speak, I realize how young he must be. He can't be much older than I am, more boy than man.

Boy or not, he still radiates a knowing I cannot understand. He walks with the air of a person who has seen the worst this world has to offer—and expects the worst in return.

This is what it's like to meet a true Undergrounder, I think to myself. Even Asa is no Undergrounder. He has connections, but he still lives among those ensnared by the Presidency, not off the grid and separate—traits assigned to the rebels by rumors I have yet to verify.

I feel the stranger observing me through a dissecting scowl I can't even see. I try and fail to blink away the nerves. *Speak*, I tell myself. *Now.*

"And here I am." My voice is weaker than I hoped it would be.

I squint to read the scowl beneath his glasses, and I'm surprised to see a jagged pink scar, cutting vertically through the skin around his left eye like a serpent made of flesh.

The stranger shoves his hands in his pockets, studying me. After a moment, he shifts to cross his arms once again, pacing in a circle around me. He is slow in his shark-like revolutions, so predatorily observant I can feel his stare pricking the back of my neck like a needle.

"You lost?" he questions rudely, as though I'm doing him a great disservice by simply being here.

I shake my head no. If I weren't so afraid, I'd probably give this guy a substantial piece of my mind.

Eyes closed, I force myself to take a deep breath that I can't seem to down all the way. It's like trying to gulp three sips of water at once. *Don't be afraid*, I tell myself. *Don't appear weak.* I'll give him the illusion that I think I'm in control, and maybe, I'll get my way.

Coyly, I copy his stance and fold my arms. "Do I look lost? I've just been found, haven't I?"

Even as he circles around me, I keep my feet planted.

"What is it then, if you're not lost? Coincidence? Wrong place, wrong time?" Now, standing directly behind me, he stops his circling. Something sharp presses against my throat, so gently I nearly miss its sting. "Or are you exactly where you're supposed to be?"

The knife is cold, but it's not the chill of the blade that sends shivers down my back.

I freeze, heart pounding. It takes all my strength to keep still and pretend

I am not afraid...

Deep breaths, I tell myself. *You are in control.*

I am in control.

"I'm here to meet you, actually. Unless you're the one in the wrong place at the wrong time, not me." I ignore the knife positioned against my neck and turn my head back to meet his gaze. "Coincidence, maybe?"

His glower intensifies when he presses the blade firmer into my skin. "Tell me why you're here and maybe we'll find out."

You are in control. Show him how you handle your fear.

Deep breaths.

"Why don't we start with names, like well-mannered people?" I try to swat the knife away, but he only presses it deeper. If it moves a millimeter farther, I will be cut.

I know I could probably break free, but something about the way this guy holds a blade makes me think that if he really wanted me dead, I'd know. I won't risk an escape attempt—not yet.

"Manners are overrated," he finally says. "But I'll take a name."

"Lavender. Lavender Voclain," I say. He doesn't seem like the kind of person I can get away with lying to.

There is a lengthy pause. I watch as he looks around, gaze bouncing between trees, checking to see if I'm alone. Defeated, he lowers the knife with a sigh. I wonder if my brief moment of honesty actually helped.

"Yours?" I ask, remaining still. "*Pal?*"

There's another pause. "Cedar."

Why the hesitation? I spin around to look him in the eye. "That's not your real name, is it?"

He shrugs. "Identity is powerful. Gotta protect it."

That explains the shades.

Cedar makes a fair point, but I don't like missing puzzle pieces. I like seeing the bigger picture. I like having the answers.

"From who?" I ask, more curious now than afraid.

He gives me a bitter look. *From people like me*, it says. I am no Undergrounder. Not yet, at least.

"So why are you here, Lavender Voclain?" Cedar says, twirling the knife as he takes a step closer. "I'm expecting someone and it certainly isn't you."

He leans against a tree, still inspecting the tool, as though I am simply not interesting enough to hold his attention. *He's not threatened by me*, I note. I'll have to work on that.

I study the weapon he holds. Its wooden handle is dark and polished, its blade long and clean. Even with my limited experience with knives, I can tell it's worn with use—but still sharp enough to slice me to ribbons.

I take a deep breath. "I'm here on Asa's behalf. He wanted me to give you this."

Cedar's brows furrow at the mention of Asa's name. Even through the tint of his glasses, I can see him question me with his gaze, blinking to the hum of turning gears. I pull the envelope from my pocket and offer it to him.

The Undergrounder pauses, eyeing me up and down before snatching the envelope from my hands. I watch as he flips it over, studying the wax jackalope seal. His arms reach inside a leather satchel slung over his shoulder, and the envelope disappears inside the depths of the bag.

I can't help but wonder why he doesn't read it—slightly annoyed that I went through so much trouble to deliver something he clearly doesn't care about. *Maybe he's supposed to deliver it somewhere himself.*

"Why isn't Asa here himself?" Cedar asks, hands in his pockets. "Is she okay?"

"She?"

"His daughter."

I blink, stunned for a moment until I shake my head. "Margot's fine."

He nods. "Good."

How could he possibly know Margot? I think to myself. *He must know Asa better than I thought.*

There are a thousand questions I want to ask, but I shove them all aside. "Asa wanted me to take his place today." I try to keep my voice strong, but it trembles, just a little. "Thinks I show promise."

"Promise?" Cedar chuckles cynically, raising a doubtful brow. I nod and he scoffs.

"There is no such thing as promise. You're either suitable for something or you're not."

"I disagree." I lift my chin. "You can't be ready for anything. You learn. You adapt. And that's what I intend to do."

"Good for you, kid," he says, and I grit my teeth as he steps away from the tree and closer to where I stand. *If I'm a kid, then so is he.* "But I know for a fact Asa wouldn't send some random Chip in his place for no reason."

Chip?

"So what is it, then?" He pauses his pacing but still twirls the knife. "His reason for sending you, if that's really the case?"

"Read the letter." I nod in the direction of his satchel, sliding my hands into the pockets of my dark jeans. "It should all be in there."

"I'm only a messenger, pal. Even I don't have clearance to read his letters." He glares.

Even I. I try not to laugh at the phrase. Surely a guy like this can't be as important as he claims to be.

"Well, he said you can read this one." I return the expression, growing more impatient with the Undergrounder by the minute. Asa did mention including a note somewhere in the letter, specifically for him.

I watch as he cracks the seal with reluctance and reads the letter.

Cedar strokes his chin in contemplation, confused by the words on the page in front of him. I have no idea what the letter contains, but I imagine it must have some answers. Enough to make this contact of Asa's trust me, at least a little bit. I hope.

He places the letter back in his bag when he finishes reading, observing me with a furrowed brow. I know I should say something.

It seems I've waited my whole life for this very moment. But now that it's finally here, my tongue feels tied, like anything I say could turn into a jumbled mess in a heartbeat.

Deep breaths, I tell myself. The inhalation is shaky.

"I want in."

There's a pause. It's dreadful, spreading thin in the air like taffy stretched too far until Cedar finally laughs.

"In? There is nothing to be *in*." He continues to chuckle for a moment until his expression turns grim. "Whatever game you're playing is all in your head."

To my disappointment, he turns to walk away, stepping deeper into the woods.

He can't go, not yet. Not when I have so much to say. So much to do. So much to fight for.

He can't go.

"I know you're part of the Undergrounders," I yell, and Cedar pauses. For a moment, I can't help but feel frightened. Have I said the wrong thing? Maybe.

He turns to look at me. I wait for him to retaliate, to dispose of me in the name of protecting the secrecy of the Undergrounders before getting on with his business.

But then, he speaks. Slowly, darkly, sharp like thorns. "You know nothing."

He tries to walk away, but I follow.

"I know this is bigger than you," I state, struggling to keep up with his strides.

"You're annoying me and I have things to do."

"Let me help, then."

"I'm a smuggler," Cedar continues. "I work alone, I trust no one."

"I don't think that last part is true."

"Truth is a funny word." He chuckles, refusing to look back at me as I follow him. "Subjective. Abstract."

He halts briefly. "You're better off putting your energy into something real."

Cedar walks faster this time, so quickly I almost have to jog to keep up, clumsily crunching twigs and leaves beneath my steps while he navigates the woods in perfect silence.

"Stop following me," he orders.

I balance myself when I almost trip over a root. "Not until you tell me who you work for."

"You're real entitled, you know that?" Cedar scoffs. "Like I owe you an explanation."

"You don't. But if I'm gonna be working with you, I would prefer one."

He stops dead in his tracks, whipping around to face me. "I've said it already, and I'll say it again. I'll say it a thousand times if it gets you to leave."

He leans forward, pointing the knife in my face like it's a toy, not a weapon. I stare at the point with wide eyes. "I work for no one. I don't work *with* anyone. I work, but I do it alone."

He walks away again, but this time, I don't follow. I don't know how to get through to him. I can't bribe him; I have nothing to offer. I can't threaten a person I can't defeat. I'm sure he's had far greater experiences with conflict than my few elementary school fistfights.

But maybe, just maybe, I can do what I do best—and lie.

I take a deep, trembling breath. I have no idea who this guy is or what he's capable of, but I know one thing. Joining the Undergrounders is something I have to do, because healing is what I'm meant for, if I believed in that sort of thing.

Being a healer for the Undergrounders is one step closer to bringing change for my family. For Margot. A small step, sure, but any step is better than none at all.

I take a deep breath and suppress a grin.

"What do you think they'll give me for turning in a rebel smuggler?"

Cedar freezes like his blood has suddenly gone cold, turning his head around slowly. For a moment I think I see him tremble with anger, but when I blink, I realize I'm wrong. He's so perfectly still it feels flawed.

I lean against the nearest tree casually, pulling my phone out of my pocket, suddenly glad I decided to bring it. I pretend to turn it on and stare down at the dark screen. "What's the number for the nearest Chaser headquarters again?"

Before I can duck, a blade is flying in my direction. I close my eyes, waiting for the sting of steel to puncture my throat, maybe even my heart. But the knife hits the tree with a dizzying thud, pinning the fabric of my hood to the bark. I'm unscathed—but stuck.

"You missed," I spit.

Right as the words escape my lips, another knife flies, and before I know it, my right sleeve is nailed to the tree too. I drop my phone. The device shatters against a small rock, spraying glass shards around my feet.

He walks closer until he's near enough to step on the phone for good measure. "I never miss."

"That was unnecessary."

"I disagree."

His glare burns through the shades, so hot with rage I can feel it. I begin to doubt my odds of returning home in one piece. How ironic it would be to be killed by an Undergrounder rather than the punishing injection of a Chaser—or a slow traitor's death at the tombs, laboring away to the smell of burning flesh.

"You have no idea what you're dealing with here, do you?" His words form a question, but his tone turns it into a statement far firmer than the grip of his knives.

"Maybe I don't, but I don't give a damn." I glower. "I already told you, I want in. And I'm not taking no for an answer."

"Sorry, I'm not exactly taking applications at the moment."

"I'm serious."

"Why would you ever want such a thing?" Cedar raises his hands in frustration before they fall to his side. "You live an easy life. Protected by your comforts, your ignorance." He takes a step closer. "Your fear."

"How dare you ask me a question like that," I snarl. "Why wouldn't I want things to be different?"

Cedar's frown intensifies.

"I don't want to kill. But I don't want to be killed either." My throat tightens. "I want a world where my brother can speak his mind without looking over his shoulder. I want a world that gives people like Margot the ability to live." I pause, lowering my voice. "I want a world where you don't have to pay to afford the right to exist."

Cedar hesitates, loosening his glare, but not yet the knives. I remain attached to the tree by the fabric of my clothes, even after he backs away. I could easily break free if I wanted to, but I don't.

"Why should I trust you?" he asks, crossing his arms.

"Let me in and I'll keep my mouth shut." I raise my chin. "I'm a pretty good liar, you know. Could be useful."

"What an *excellent* way to establish trust." There's another pause.

"And if I don't? Trust you enough to let you in, that is?"

"I'll turn in the paranoid Undergrounder with the ridiculous shades."

"Blackmail?" He scoffs, almost entertained by my answer. "Your phone is useless. You're not calling anyone."

"I still have a mouth, you know. I can talk."

He whips around. In less than a second he yanks the first knife from the tree, pointing it at my neck. The tip of the blade is so close to my skin that I almost feel its sting.

"And I still have a knife. Two, actually. And plenty more hidden in various places I can definitely reveal if you're curious." Cedar smirks darkly, crooked and inauthentic. "One wrong word and you can say goodbye to your tongue."

I hold my breath.

He leans closer. "They dispose of people without tongues where you come from, right?"

"Asa trusts me," I argue. "He sent me. He's vouching for me, you know. Thinks I would make a solid Undergrounder. Maybe not the best, but good enough to deserve at least an ounce of your trust."

I pull the second knife out of the tree, tossing it in Cedar's direction. He catches it by the handle without breaking his stare away from mine.

"If you don't believe me," I say, "then why don't you reread that letter of yours?"

Cedar stares at me for a moment until he closes his eyes, placing both hands on his hips with a slow and painful sigh. Absorbed in thought, he leans over before finally succumbing. He swears under his breath and tears out Asa's envelope.

I watch as Cedar scans the letter again, eyes flickering from side to side until its contents are fully digested. He's a quick reader.

He pauses before sliding the letter in its place and shoving the envelope back into the satchel. Cedar looks at me, so clearly tormented—like he doesn't want to trust me, even if something else is telling him he should.

"It's dangerous," he finally says.

"I know."

We're both quiet for a moment, stilled by contemplation. And then he stands up straight, sheathing both knives and sliding them into his boots, visibly displeased. "You have any skills?"

I blink, doubtful that I heard him correctly. "Excuse me?"

"Skills?" He raises an eyebrow, crossing his arms. "Knives? Lock picking? Thievery? General trouble-making?"

I shake my head no, and he continues. "Herbalism or healing? Familiarity with Yesterday contraband or weaponry?"

I pause, glaring when I realize that we both know I have no experience in any of these fields. But I wipe the scowl away, straightening my back. "I'd like to be a healer."

He chuckles in disbelief. "*You?*"

I glare at him. "I'm serious."

"I'm not laughing at you. I just—didn't expect it, that's all." He smirks. "So you're a healer then, huh?"

I look down at my shoes. "Not yet."

"Then what are you?"

I pause. "I'm not sure."

Cedar looks at me. He turns his head to the side to stare at the trees, then at me once again.

It's quiet for a long time. Somewhere far, birds chirp unknowingly. Listening insects buzz to the tune of summer. The air smells cool and clean, and I find it hard to trust that a place this peaceful could still exist.

I meet Cedar's gaze, and when I do, something in it has changed—just a little.

"Look. Let me get something out of the way here, okay?" He sighs. "The only reason I'm agreeing to do this is because I trust Command. Command trusts Asa McLellan, and I'm not keen on pissing off my superiors. Alright?"

My jaw burns as I hold back a grin, unable to believe I'm hearing the words at all.

So I was right about him having superiors, I want to say, but I don't. I nod instead, though I can't hide the smirk that tugs at the corner of my lips. "Alright."

"Here." He opens his satchel and digs inside, fishing out a little cloth sack.

He hands it to me, and the contents inside clink together.

I peer inside to find a jar filled with little brown capsules I recognize, and then a tincture jar with more capsules. I close the bag and fold my arms.

So this is where Margot's medicine comes from. I wonder what information must have been inside Asa's letter to be worthy of an exchange like this.

Or maybe this is a long-term arrangement—something he already paid the price for.

"I'm delivering a package tomorrow night. If you're serious about this, meet me here at 11:00," Cedar explains, closing his satchel. I open my mouth to speak, but I don't have time to question his words before he continues. "Oh, and Voclain?"

"Yeah?"

"Tell anyone about this and you'll die peacefully in your sleep."

"Peacefully in my sleep?" I grin. "Not a bad way to go."

He unsheathes one of his knives. "Would you prefer *Death by Crazed Knife Murderer* to be the headline instead?"

"Fine, fine." I raise my hands. "I won't tell a soul."

And with that, Cedar leaves—and I can't stop smiling.

Tuesday, May 9
24 Days Left Until Graduation

It's a trade. Herbal tinctures and medicinal alcohol in exchange for Yesterday guns.

Most of these weapons were confiscated by the Presidency after the Nightjade Order was put in place, but some found ways to keep them safe just in case they would have a use for them. The Undergrounders know exactly how to locate these civilian outliers, and Cedar has found one who is desperate for a remedy.

The woods feel louder at night. Quieter than the city, of course, but in the dark, I can hear every cricket, every frog croak, every snapping twig. There is something so eerie about a symphony I cannot see, and in our absence of conversation, it's almost maddening. I'd never survive in the woods alone.

"Are we close?" I ask for the third time this evening. Unlike my previous attempts to get an answer, to my surprise, Cedar responds.

"Stop talking."

I furrow my brows, shoving my hands in the pockets of my black hoodie. I shiver, and though I can't see my breath materialize in front of me, I know it must be doing just that. Cedar didn't bother to tell me I should bring a jacket and I get the feeling he did it on purpose.

It's hard to see much in this absence of light, but I can tell that he isn't wearing one either, which makes me feel at least a little bit better.

But if the cold is bothering him, he doesn't show it. In fact, he isn't really doing or saying much at all, like he's used to wandering the woods alone at night. *Or maybe he's from somewhere colder.*

"As your partner in this particular crime, I think I deserve to know if we're close or not," I claim, growing impatient with the lack of conversation.

My footsteps let the whole forest know exactly where I am, but Cedar doesn't make a sound. He is so inexplicably silent I can barely tell whether he's still beside me or not. His response is the only thing that lets me know I haven't lost him. "If you keep talking, I can't listen."

I scoff. "Listen for what?"

It takes me a moment to notice that Cedar's stopped walking, but when I do, my left foot is no longer touching solid ground.

And I slip.

I let out a startled shriek as I close my eyes, balance lost, legs scraping against branches and rocks as I start to slide down a steep muddy slope. My throat burns like I've swallowed my own bloody heart, and I can taste the metallic flavor of adrenaline on my tongue. I have no idea where I am falling to.

But I only slide for a second, because a pair of arms have looped firmly underneath my own, and I still.

I have been caught by Cedar.

Arms under mine, he pulls me up the slope with ease until my back meets his chest. My pulse hammers, and there is a prickly sensation in every single one of my pores that tells me I just might have plummeted to my death. He steadies me, hands on my shoulders, and all I can do is stand there, blinking.

Cedar leans closer to whisper in my ear. "You hear that?"

I blink. Though it's hard to hear anything at all now over the sound of my throbbing heartbeat, I try to shift my focus past the blood rushing in my ears.

It takes me a moment to realize it is not the course of my blood that I am hearing, but the white rapid rush of water, dozens of feet below.

"Beyond this slope? That's a waterfall, sweetheart," Cedar says, clearly entertained by my stumble. He removes his hands from my shoulders and gives me a pat on the back, turning right to walk along the slope's edge. I don't hesitate to follow close behind.

He looks over his shoulder. "I'd do a lot less talking and a lot more listening if I were—"

He doesn't have the chance to finish his sentence, because now, Cedar is the one who has slipped—and I have caught his arm.

"Be careful." I give him a faux smile. "That's a waterfall, sweetheart."

He steadies himself, jerking his arm away. When he's walked a good distance ahead of me, my grin feels a lot less synthetic.

But I'm careful not to say another word.

We reach the edge of the woods and walk to a nearby abandoned parking garage, located about a mile away from our meeting spot in the forest. The garage is closed off by rusted chain link fences that stand to protect the building until its scheduled demolition, which, by the looks of it, appears to have been completely forgotten.

The sidewalk is overrun with sprouting ferns and little tufts of grass growing in the cracks, and mice tickle empty tin cans as they sprint past our feet. I envy their boldness, their ability to slip through shadows unnoticed.

Cedar stops walking when we reach the metal fence, an overstuffed backpack slung over his right shoulder. I pause too, looking to my left to await his instruction.

In the faint citrine glow of a dying street lamp, I can see that he wears the same black and brown attire, and even in the dark, he is still sporting those awful shades. I can't help but wonder what his eyes look like.

He bends over and pulls a sheathed blade from his boot, tossing it in my direction. He really wasn't lying about the knife thing. I catch it, surprised I manage to do so, inspecting the weapon with equal parts confusion and curiosity.

I pause, momentarily trapped in my own little bubble of something I can't name. I feel a surge of something inexplicable run through my veins as I unsheathe the knife. Maybe not power, but excitement, perhaps. Confidence, even.

This one is different from the wood-handled weapon Cedar seems to favor. It's a glistening hunting dagger with a handle of the same smooth steel as the blade. It mirrors the flicker of distant lights, harboring a warped image of my reflection. It feels surreal to hold in a place where weapons have been completely outlawed, where the defense of oneself or one's beliefs may as well be a one-way ticket to the tombs. I feel as though simply holding the knife is a little rebellion in itself. Like I'm playing my own game, not theirs.

"What do you want me to do with this?" I question, inspecting the knife carefully.

"Stab me," Cedar responds plainly, setting his satchel on the ground before kneeling down to rummage through his backpack, double-checking that every good is in place.

"Gladly." I attach the sheath to the belt loop of my pants and slip the knife inside.

"Alright." Cedar clears his throat, zipping up his bag when he deems the contents satisfactory. "You're on watch duty."

"*Watch duty*?" I scoff. "I thought you agreed to let me help you."

"Staying out of the way is helping."

"What am I supposed to do, then? If someone shows up?" I fold my arms tightly across my chest, glaring.

"Stall them."

"So I'm *bait*?"

"Hmm... yes. Bait *and* watch duty, don't forget." He begins to climb over the fence, not looking over his shoulder. When he reaches the top, he jumps without hesitation, sticking the landing with perfection. He's familiar with this kind of thing.

Now, Cedar looks over his shoulder. "I'll try to come back in one piece."

He walks away, heading toward the empty parking garage, no longer focused on me but on the task at hand.

"Wait!" I call out. He doesn't flinch, and all I can do is stand here helplessly, watching him disappear into the dark of the hour.

He's left me with far too many unanswered questions. He didn't even tell me how long he'll be gone. What if someone does interrupt, and I can't fend them off? What if we're caught by Chasers?

What if he doesn't come back?

I nearly choke on my saliva. *What if this is how I go?*

I bite my lip, pressing my forehead against the fence until there is a hexagonal imprint in my flesh. I squint into the distance. No matter how hard I try, I can't locate Cedar in the darkness. I have no flashlight, no phone—nothing but a knife I cannot wield and my own skin, which is not as thick as I'd like it to be. I just hope that's enough.

I sigh, blowing loose curls away from my eyes and turning around to rest my back against the chain links. I slide down the fence until I'm sitting on the ground, hugging my knees to my chest. My fingers trace patterns in the dirt, and I can already feel my attention wandering.

Goosebumps prickle my skin and I shiver, looking up at the sky. I regret not bringing a warmer jacket, though I don't think I have a decent coat for this kind of cold, anyway. Maybe I'll get one someday. *If I make it out of this alive, that is.*

It's hard to make out the stars with so much smog, but I can see the moon just fine as it perches above all else. It watches, waiting like it knows something is bound to happen—any moment now.

Unless nothing happens, and the moon and I are stuck waiting here forever.

I pull the knife out of its sheath again, comforted by its presence. The blade is a great distraction, because if I leave myself alone with my thoughts, I'll realize how frightened I really am, and that won't do me any good.

Minutes slip through my fingers, but it feels more like hours. Days. Lifetimes. All is quiet as I stand guard, and I still haven't heard anything from Cedar. No signs of life, no movement, no sounds. He is the epitome of radio silence, an embodiment of absolutely nothing at all. I stand there in solitude for so long that I begin to wonder if I could have imagined this whole thing.

A twig snaps after a nauseating stretch of silence. I'm dragged back to earth as I whip my head around, scrambling to my feet. Frantic, my eyes switch from side to side, scanning the area for any unwanted visitors. *Stay calm*, I try to tell myself, but it's hard to hear my own reassurances over the pounding of my pulse.

I let out a sigh of relief when I realize there is not a single person in sight. There is only me, the moon, and this knife of mine. Maybe a mouse too.

You're on too sharp of an edge, I tell myself, closing my eyes and taking deep breaths. *You need to keep your head clear if you want to make it out of this alive.*

And then, I hear it.

Something explodes.

The bang is thunderous and all-encompassing, like some faraway deity took the cloth of the sky and ripped it open with their bare hands. My eyes shut so tightly I see stars, and my hands cover my ears protectively, but it does nothing to calm the whining ring that persists.

I've never heard a gunshot before, but I always paid attention in history class, and I would bet every book I love on what my instincts are currently screaming.

I can feel the color drain from my face. If I am inflatable, something has taken a needle to my skin. I am deflating. My heart races at an impossible speed, and while I've never been a nail biter in the past, I find myself gnawing so intensely I taste blood. My legs tremble, and I wait for Cedar to return. It was he who pulled the trigger, right? I know about his proficiency with knives. Cedar is one to overpower, not to submit. He has to come back. *He has to.*

He doesn't.

Seconds melt into minutes, and before I know it, so much time has passed that I have bitten each of my nails to little ragged stubs that sting when touched. Every second that Cedar doesn't return is another moment I fear he never will.

After waiting for far too long, there's a sound in the distance and a bright light that grows stronger and stronger as the seconds roll by. I bring a palm to cover my eyes, but it does little to shield them. Wheels crunch against crumbling asphalt, and before I realize what's happening, a white patrol car slows to a halt in front of me. I am a deer in literal headlights. Two figures dressed from head to toe in sleek white armor step out of the car and slam the doors closed, headed right toward me.

I'm standing face to face with two Officers of the American Chaser Corps. *Breathe, Eddie*, I beg. Breathe. *Breathe.*

I cannot.

"Is everything okay over here?" One of the Officers questions as she and her partner step closer. "Someone reported hearing something suspicious in this general vicinity."

"I'm alright. Thanks for asking." I swallow my fear painfully and force myself to respond. *Let them know you're unafraid. Let them know you have nothing to hide. Be casual.*

"Something suspicious, huh?" I chuckle when it gets too quiet. "That's kind of vague, isn't it?"

"Yeah, not really much to go off of." The other Officer chuckles too. He scans the scene, studying our surroundings with a raised brow. "Are you sure you're alright, ma'am? It's rather late."

"Oh yeah, I'm fine." I try to wave it off, but they stare me down. With suspicion, concern, or maybe even both. I cannot tell.

"You're waiting for someone, aren't you?" the woman questions, and my heart stops.

My face pales. They give me a look, and I panic. "I—no, I'm just—"

To my surprise, one of the Chasers chuckles, his laughter echoing. "It's alright, we were all young once. There's a lover's lane around here some-where, isn't there?"

"Want us to wait with you? Or we can escort you back home, if you want." The woman says. "It's dangerous in the dark."

"What?" The color comes back, but this time, my face is beet red. "No, I…"

I pause, because all of a sudden, this feels like the perfect cover. *You are hiding nothing.*

"It's fine, I'll head home in a few minutes if they don't show."

I smile nervously as the female Officer pats me on the shoulder, too friendly for my own comfort. I wonder if they know how the world fears them.

"I've been stood up before. It sucks." Her lips stretch into a thin line. "You're better than this punk."

The male Officer laughs, turning to his partner. "By who?"

"Shut up," she snarls before turning to me once again. "Well, get home safely."

The two turn to walk away, but before they do, she pauses, rotating her body to face me once again. "Oh, and find yourself a fling who won't ask you to trespass next time. Consider yourself lucky that we have more pressing matters to tend to."

I blink foolishly, barely processing her words before giving the Chasers a frantic nod. Before I can truly absorb the encounter, they drive off, leaving me alone to wallow in my worries once again.

Lucky.

I shudder when I think about it, because deep down, I know they could have exterminated me for this if they wanted to. They wouldn't need much of a reason to give me a Nightjade injection. They never do. But this time, I am one of the guilty ones. They could justify it on claims of trespassing, definitely. Loitering, perhaps, or maybe even suspicious behavior alone.

Anything can be the death of anyone.

It doesn't matter if these two Officers treated me with a rare glimpse of kindness, if sparing me from death can be called kindness at all. They are Chasers through and through, and no matter who they were before they gave their life to the system, they have transformed into monsters of the worst sort.

I can't help but think of Ren, and how soon, he will be no different.

I fall to the ground, trying so hard to keep it together, to put an end to this uncoiling before I am nothing but a tangled mess of threads. The moon rises. The night ages.

I wait for Cedar to come back, but he never does.

EDDIE

Wednesday, May 10
23 Days Left Until Graduation

I don't say a word to anyone at school.

The anxiety is back, and as I drift from class to class, I can't focus. It takes all the concentration I have to breathe, to function, to keep myself from throwing up every time I think about what could have happened last night.

Because Cedar is dead. He has to be.

And I was one of the last people to see him alive.

I wonder if his family will ever have an answer—if he has a family at all. *Had*, I correct myself. Not has.

I wonder, if they do exist, whether they'll spend the rest of their lives thinking about where he went, or if some part of their conscious depths will instinctively know he's gone. I can't imagine what it would feel like to not know the answer. For a moment, I decide it would be better to know the details of a death than to live out a life wondering what happened, but then I'm not so sure. Sometimes truth is a certainty best left unconfirmed.

I can't stop thinking about the dagger in my room either. The blade is tucked away in my sock drawer, protected for now, but I know it won't be forever.

I can't get rid of it. If I disposed of it, the authorities could easily use fingerprinting or public surveillance to trace the weapon back to me. I would be exterminated for possessing an illegal weapon, and perhaps treason, if they wanted to get creative about their suspicions and tie me to rebel terrorists. Keeping it seems to be my worst and only option.

No one can ever find it.

It's not my own potential downfall that frightens me. We are all raised with expectations of death. The Pick is a horror you can train yourself to fear enough to get used to its existence. It's not my inevitable end that scares me, but the danger I've put my family in.

I just hope they know that if worse comes to worst, they'll realize I'm doing this for them too. Not just Margot. Not just myself.

They deserve a better world—a difference. And I will pay every price to give them just that.

When I come across Ren in sixth period, I'm filled with guilt. I want to tell him everything that happened. I feel like I *should* tell him, like I have this unspoken obligation to let him know. We've both agreed to keep each other's secrets. He deserves to be in the loop.

But I can't bring myself to tell him anything. In fact, I don't even look at him, even when I feel his stare burning into the back of my neck. Even when I feel him trying to catch my gaze, prying curiously with knowing eyes, trying to get some sense of what happened through facial expressions I cannot give him. He knew exactly what I was getting into. Now that I'm in it, he has questions.

I think back to the river, and for a brief moment, I wonder what it would be like to speak as friends might. To confide in him, even with my secrets, because as little as I can endure his stubborn arrogance, he is the only person who could truly understand.

And then I decide against it. That was a one time thing. An isolated incident. We are not friends, and I do not trust him enough to burden him with what I carry.

He has enough on his plate, and he is becoming a Chaser, after all. Knowing anything about the Undergrounders could be seen as treason, and as a Chaser trainee, Ren would be under far too much scrutiny for this information to be safe.

I will keep my own secrets. For all of our sakes.

Upon my homeward evening return, I manage to avoid my family quite effectively.

Somewhat effectively.

Almost effectively.

When I come home from school, the house is still lingering with the aftertaste of cinnamon cookies. I walk through the foyer and notice Milo hunched over at the dining table, both feet planted on his chair, dissecting what looks like a Yesterday cassette player. I'm not even sure where he acquired such a rare find. He uses the table when his desk is crowded with other projects, and only when my father isn't around to see him do so.

Good, I tell myself. I'm glad he's not around. I can't handle an interrogation right now. I give my younger brother a quick wave as I exit and make my way down the hall, but he's too busy to give more than a nod.

I run upstairs, turn down another hall, and almost make it to my room before I'm stopped by my mother.

"Hey, you."

I pause, bag slung over my shoulder, heart racing. "Hey."

She stands in the hallway, chewing an apple with her hands on her hips, the corner of an old Queen of Diamonds tattoo sticking out through the right sleeve of her mauve hoodie. The 4 of Spades on her left remains concealed. I notice that her walnut ringlets are tied in a messy updo, letting me know she's been home from work for quite some time. I must have stalled my return from school a little longer than I should have.

"What are you up to?" Mom asks, and my heart skips a beat.

Checking to see if the knife given to me by a dead rebel smuggler is still safely hidden in my room.

"Nothing," I say instead. The word falls out swiftly, sharper than I expected.

My mother raises an eyebrow. She knows my body language better than anyone. "That's not suspicious at all, kid." She chuckles.

Shit.

Mom must notice my newly obtained ghost-like complexion, because she gives me a pat on the shoulder. "I'm only teasing."

I roll my eyes, stepping past her. "You're the worst."

"*You're* the worst."

"Thanks."

"Any time, kiddo."

We don't mean it, of course. We're just close like that.

You were *close*, I correct myself. Now, I'm a liar—a daughter who hides terrible things from her mother and distances herself on purpose.

"Oh, and Eddie?"

I pause, turning around to face her again. She stands still, the humor drained from her face. "Yeah?"

"Your dad's getting anxious," she says quietly. Her mouth opens to continue, but then she bites her lip in careful analysis, unsure of how to word the things she wants to say. "He's worried about the results. Make sure you show him the letter as soon as you get it, alright?"

I feel like I've swallowed a handful of rusty nails, and I clear my burning throat. "Alright."

"I know he's tough on you, but..." She pauses, noticing my nerves. "He's proud of you, Ed. For all you're doing for this family."

Mom gives me a soft smile. "*I'm* proud of you. For choosing what you think is best."

Her words are not meant to be a stab to the heart, but I acquire puncture wounds.

"Thanks, Mom." I force my best grin, turning around again before she sees just how I'm breaking.

As I walk down the hall, away from my mother, the guilt weighs heavier than ever. Every new, horrible thing I hide feels like another betrayal.

Because that's exactly what I'm doing. I am betraying them, and they have no idea.

Fighting for the right thing is something I do with my family in mind.

But by refusing to Chase, I am also taking away their only chance of Immunity—and my treasonous Undergrounder connections are putting them in the worst sort of danger.

I'm certain that if I had it in me to tell Mom all of my truths, she would be the only person to truly get it. She's my mother, the one person on the planet who's more like me than anyone else.

Milo would call me an idiot for risking my life, or try to get involved to prevent me from doing something stupid. He's a year younger than me in age, but decades older in his intelligence and resourcefulness. He'd probably join the Undergrounders himself in secret.

My father is the last person I could tell. I wouldn't be surprised if he dropped me off at the nearest Chaser headquarters holding a sign labeled *I COMMITTED TREASON.*

But Mom? Although she loves my father with incredible ferocity, deep down, I know we're on the same page about Chasing. She is well-aware of its cruelty. She would understand.

I lock myself in my room and finish my assignments before washing up. I slip out of my school clothes and into a brown oversized crewneck and black athletic shorts. The clothes are comfortable, but I am not.

Gray sunlight leaks in through the window. A stretch of desaturated rays reaches out to touch my dresser, almost as though it knows what I'm hiding. *Look here*, it says. *Find the traitor's blade.*

I bite my lip and open the drawer, irrationally expecting the knife to be gone. Maybe I was imagining everything that happened with Cedar. Maybe I'm going mad, and I never met him at all. I hallucinated my reception of this knife, the gunshot, and the Chaser confrontation. His death was a construct of my decaying grip on reality.

But sure enough, when I rummage through my socks and underthings, the knife is there, mocking me beneath a pile of fabric.

I'm still here, I imagine it saying with a laugh.

I close the drawer louder than I want to, and my dresser trembles. I can't focus on the knife. I have to pretend it's not here, or its presence and all it represents will be the only thing I think about—and I have more pressing worries.

Dad is expecting to see an acceptance letter, and I will never receive one.

I walk over to my desk chair and fall into it with a sigh, setting both arms on either rest. I spin in a circle, arching my neck backward to watch the ceiling fan do the same thing, spinning slowly until I'm too dizzy to be anything but still. The fan moves on without me, and I feel more stuck than ever.

I look at my desk, studying its contents. It's a light bamboo board with white legs and a lot messier than I'd like, holding loose paper and enough pencil shavings to fill a litter box. My closed and probably dead laptop is surrounded by crumpled balls of returned homework assignments I fished from the bottom of my bag two weeks ago. I think about how nice it would be if I were to pull a black poker chip envelope from the bottom of my bag, as I did with Ren's.

How am I supposed to reinforce this lie of mine without a letter? There's no way my father will believe I'm a Chaser if I don't have solid proof that I've been invited to become a trainee, and his belief is critical if I want the fact that I'm actively committing treason to stay a secret.

My thoughts are interrupted when I hear my laptop chime, and I nearly jump out of my chair. It's been forever since I've checked my school email. I open the barely charged device and log in, praying there isn't some big project I forgot about.

But when I click on the mail icon, it is not a classwork notification I see, but a message from Ren.

This can't be good. Ren never emails me. In fact, I'm not even sure how he got the address; the only way I can think of is through Margot.

My heart drops. Through all my sneaking around and paranoia, I forgot to tell Margot about the destruction of my phone. She must think something's wrong.

I take a deep breath and click on the message.

SUBJECT: PHONE DEAD?

You're an idiot. Charge your phone. Not safe to let it drop so low.

> – Ren
>
> PS: Ringer on, please.
>
> *Sent from phone*

My lungs deflate like an air mattress as I let out a sigh, relieved to hear that nothing's wrong with Margot. I click the reply button and type my message quickly, pressing send as soon as I do.

SUBJECT: PHONE DESTROYED.

> Piss off, I'm busy.
>
> Best wishes,
> Eddie
>
> PS: Apologize to Margot for me. My phone really was crushed.

I check the timestamp on Ren's message, noticing he sent it almost forty minutes ago. He must be preoccupied with other things by now. I reach my hand out to close the laptop, but just as I do, I'm flashed with another notification.

SUBJECT: DESTROYED?

> You need a new phone. Soon. Just in case.
>
> Additionally, screw you.
>
> – Ren
>
> PS: Done and forgiven. She says to be more careful next time.

> PPS: We need to talk.
>
> *Sent from phone*

Talk about what? The rendezvous? How I may have been the last person to see Cedar alive? How I'm stuck with this goddamn knife in my sock drawer with no safe way to dispose of it? How my father is closing in on my Chaser lies and I need to find a way to prove my lesser falsities if I want to protect my darker secrets?

I press my forehead against the desk. After enough time passes, the edge forms a line in my skin. I remain in this position for so long my eyes start to blur, the room spinning in a pinwheel of colors and textures as blood rushes to my head.

Maybe I should climb my way out of this pit while I still can, before I dig myself too deep. Maybe if I tell my father I never took the exam, he'll understand. I close my eyes and try to picture how the conversation would go.

And I can't imagine anything but anger.

If he heard the truth, he'd tell me to take the exam next year instead. He'd kick me out if I refused. I know he would. Maybe living with the McLellans wouldn't be so bad. I already kind of do.

No. That's not an option. My father needs to believe I'm a Chaser, otherwise, he'll switch targets. If he realizes that I will never meet his expectations, those expectations will fall on Milo. He's already hard enough on my brother for his homeschooling and hermitry, and I know for a fact that Milo would break as a Chaser.

And then it hits me.

The answer is so unbelievably simple I can't help but chuckle.

I've read Ren's acceptance letter. I could make a copy of my own. A replica of the real thing, with my name instead of Ren's. Maybe I have no way of making it look official, but didn't Asa use a wax seal on that letter I gave to Cedar? And a non-Presidency-issued envelope? Couldn't Ren help me figure out how to make my forgery look legit?

Just as I click the reply arrow and begin to type my response, the screen turns black and the device shuts down, officially out of power. I curse under my breath, looking for a charger, but I seem to have misplaced it.

I slam the laptop shut and shove it in my desk drawer. I can't exactly create my replica without a computer.

Unless there's something else I can use to write the letter.

I rise to my feet quickly, eager to exit the room, bare feet stomping against the cold floorboards as I make my way down the stairs and out into the kitchen. But to my dismay, Milo is nowhere to be seen, and neither is his project.

Dad must be coming home soon, I think to myself, muttering a substantial number of detailed profanities under my breath yet again.

I turn around, walking back up the stairs and through the hall, pausing once I approach his door. Not bothering to knock, I burst it open, closing the white slab of wood behind me.

Milo jumps two inches out of his chair, almost hitting his head on the loft bed that stands above his desk. When he sees me, his shock immediately forms a glare. "What the hell, Ed?"

He grips some intricate tool I don't recognize so tightly I wonder how it doesn't break, spinning away from his tinkering to face me.

"What do you want? I'm busy," he groans, frowning.

"I need your advice."

He scoffs, raising a brow. "*You* want advice? For what?"

"You know how to find... things, right?"

My brother gives me a strange look. "Things?"

"You know." I change my voice to a whisper, just in case someone might overhear—and not the mics. I picture my father coming home from work and hearing our conversation and suddenly having the urge to hurl up my breakfast. "Yesterday things."

"Uh, yeah? I guess."

"Alright. Suppose I'm looking for—one of those clanky things. With the buttons."

"A cash register?" he jokes.

"Actually, kind of. You use it to type things."

Milo displays a tired expression, although the answer is painfully obvious.

"Well?"

"You mean a typewriter?"

"Yes! That." I point excitedly in his direction. "Is there a place that sells them?"

"Not anymore," Milo explains, leaning back in his chair and resting his head in his hands. "They're a rare find, you know. But you might be able to track one down at a consignment store if you know where to look."

"Do you know of any good spots?"

"Yes, but you shouldn't go."

I scrunch my nose. "Why?"

"Because..." Milo stands up with a sigh, walking over to his closet. I watch as he slides open the door, brushing back a collection of dark, muted hanging shirts so he can access the shelf behind them. He pulls out a dusty cardboard box that clunks when he sets it on his wooden desk. "I made one."

My eyes peel, clawed open by awe as he removes a dented red machine from the box, placing it gently on the table. He puffs his cheek and blows a thick layer of dust from its surface, using the sleeve of his sweatshirt to remove the rest.

"You... made this?" I reach out to touch the machine, tracing the keys curiously. The sides of the strange object are scratched and the paint is chipped, but other than that, it looks pristine. I knew Milo was good with Yesterday machinery, but not *this* good.

"Not from scratch or anything." Milo pats the typewriter with a proud smirk. "But let's just say it took a lot of work to get this thing functional. And books. And dozens of thrifting trips and under-the-table exchanges."

I blink, surprised to hear about this side of Milo. I always knew he was a genius—and quite resourceful—but not like this. This is a far greater skill than I could ever expect from a boy his age.

"Why go through so much trouble for this?" I question. "I mean, it's amazing and all, but you do have a computer. You use it every day for school."

"Sometimes... I don't know." There's a pause as Milo bites his lip, craning his neck to stare at the closed door behind me, making sure it's closed. He looks around the room before softening his voice. "Sometimes it's nice to write without being monitored. Or censored."

I look down at my feet. I know the feeling all too well. I can't count how many school essays I tried to write on my computer that were blocked by writing programs for containing certain word combinations deemed *unsuitable* or *unfair* by the Presidency. I've heard about worse cases where the AI grammar checks detected *treasonous thought patterns*. That'll surely warrant a visit from a Chaser or two.

"You could always write by hand, you know," I point out.

"Really? I've never thought about that before." He gives me a look, mouth stretched into a thin, disappointed line, a characteristic reaction to my statement of the obvious.

Milo stands up, walking to the center of his room where he kneels down. He grabs the small screwdriver he always keeps in his pocket and, to my surprise, begins twisting away at a screw hidden within the wood. Once loosened, he plucks the screw from its hiding place and removes the floorboard. My jaw sinks when I take a look inside the hidden compartment.

Beneath the absent floorboard rests a vast collection of tattered journals and loose sheets of paper. There are dozens of thick journals, each one with more pages sticking out than the last. Milo reaches inside, grabs one of the notebooks, and flips to a random page. He lifts it up so I can see.

"Oh." I squint to read the tangled mess of chicken scratch scrawled across the page, so twisted and woven into itself that I feel guilty calling it handwriting. It's written in pencil—as a lefty, Milo hates pen and ink—and as a result, graphite dust has stained a significant portion of the paper a polluted gray. "I see why you need the typewriter now."

Milo closes the journal and tosses it carelessly into the hidden compartment, concealing it with the floorboard once again before screwing it back in place.

"I didn't know you were so keen on writing," I tell my brother with a grin.

He stands up, shoving his hands in his pockets and mirroring the expression with a shrug. "There are plenty of things you don't know about me."

Though I know it isn't meant to, the sentence stings. I've spent too much time in the past focusing on school and Margot, and now, with my new involvement with Ren and the Undergrounders, I spend even less time with my brother.

I wish I could change that.

"Oh really?" I swallow the negative thoughts and raise a teasing brow. "Name one thing."

"I'm gonna write a book," Milo says proudly. Quietly, undetected, but proud all the same. "Not the unfinished garbage I've written in the past. But an actual book, real, raw, and haunting."

"What kind of book?"

"Something evil. Wicked and horrible, even, like thought-provoking fiction." He chuckles. "Maybe some classic Yesterday fantasy. Forbidden romance. Rebellion."

A crooked smirk creeps through the bottom half of his face like a faultline in fracture. "Something the Presidency will hate."

I nudge him aggressively in the stomach, sharpening my gaze into a glare. "Shut up, they'll hear you."

"I don't care." Milo shrugs, taking a seat in his desk chair again. He reaches into his drawer, pulling out a fresh stack of clean white paper before feeding it into the typewriter. He flexes his fingers, joints cracking before he leans his head back to face me. "Now let me show you how to use this thing."

I remove the paper from the typewriter. The ink is still fresh, and I am careful not to smear it as I set it on my desk to dry.

Forgery complete, I hurry down the hall with the machine, returning the typewriter to Milo before racing back to my room. The paper is dry enough to fold, and I tuck the end of it behind the waistband of my jeans, hiding it behind my sweatshirt. My father will be home any minute, and if he catches me trying to leave the house holding this letter, he'll know I'm up to no good.

My hand dives into my knife drawer to retrieve a pair of long plaid socks.

I stand on one leg to pull the sock over the other foot, but just as I switch to the other leg, the door flies open, and I fall back.

My eyes come to a close. *Please don't be my dad*, I repeat internally until I'm sick of the phrase.

And when they open again, I nearly choke on my own breath, because I'm staring face to face with Ren. Milo stands behind him, hands in his pockets.

Though I am glad it isn't my father, the relief is quick to morph into confusion, and a healthy amount of frustration. He hasn't been to our house in ages, and I'd prefer it if he never set foot within its walls at all. Ren being here is too bizarre to not draw harmful attention to our hidden partnership.

Ren stands in the doorway, leaning against the white molding, arms crossed loosely over his chest. "I never knew you were so bad at putting on socks."

Scowling, I pull the last sock on and use my hands to push myself to a standing position, folding my own arms. "I never knew you were so bad at knocking."

"You two are ridiculous." Milo rolls his eyes, turning around to walk down the hall and back to his tinkering.

We wait in silence for a painful stretch of a moment before Ren looks over his shoulder, closing the door behind him as he walks inside the room. But the quiet continues. It's prickly and uncomfortable, like hugging a cactus or standing with a pebble in your shoe.

"Going somewhere?" Ren finally says, and I give him an odd look. "What?"

"The socks." He nods his chin in my direction. "Where are you heading off to in such a hurry?"

"To see you, actually."

"Oh." His brows crease together in puzzlement. "Is something wrong?"

From the way he looks at me, eyes wide and glossed over with a rare kind of worry, I know exactly what he's talking about. *He's talking about the rendezvous.*

But I know that I can't tell him what he really wants to know. It's too dangerous for the both of us—and our families.

Cedar's death and my involvement is a secret I have to bear on my own.

"It's nothing." I shrug, deciding to ask him about his father's wax seal later. "But you're here for a reason, right?"

"Yeah. Here." Ren pulls a small object out of his pocket to offer in my direction. When he turns over his palm, I realize it's a prepaid flip phone, white and sleek, glistening without age.

"What's this?" I reach out to take it, observing the item closely. I spin it over in my hands, eyeing it carefully, realizing just how light it is.

Ren scoffs at my question. "A phone."

"I know it's a phone, genius."

"Good," he says, and there's another pause.

"It wasn't too expensive or anything. But I thought since we're... you know." Ren looks down at his shoes, shuffling his feet before looking back up at me, face stern. "Being able to contact you is more convenient for me. And with your... new interests... I assumed this would fit your style."

I crease my eyebrows after hearing his last sentence, puzzled by his strange wording until I realize what he's trying to say.

Since he and I are working together to protect our secrets—for Margot, of course—he needs to be able to contact me.

And now that I'm associating myself with the Undergrounders, I could use a phone that's harder to trace. It's better for records to show he bought something potentially suspicious like that and not me, since he'll have Immunity and I won't—just in case anybody watching or listening finds the behavior questionable.

But he can't say any of that aloud. Not outright. Not with the threat of listening mics.

"Thank you." I raise my chin a little higher, shoving the device into the pocket of my shorts. "This will be helpful."

"I already put Margot's number in there. And my father's, if you ever need it." Ren nods. "And mine."

I nod too, and after a few slow seconds of standing in a horribly uncomfortable silence, Ren takes the pause as his signal to leave.

"Wait," I call.

He halts, turning around, hand wrapped around the doorknob.

"There's something I need to talk to you about. Something that concerns both of our... interests."

His hand falls from the doorknob. I stare him in the eye, forcing myself to articulate the words I most definitely do not want to say.

"I need your help."

REN

Wednesday, May 10
38 Days Left of Being Human

"I'm telling you, it's fine. We could get this over with a lot quicker if you would just trust me."

Eddie stands on the sidewalk in front of my house with her arms folded across her chest, glowering at me through the rolled-down window of my car as I try to parallel park.

My father thought it would be a great idea to occupy my usual parking spot in the driveway with a Yesterday car he wants to flip. I know we need the money. Margot's running low on her supplements, and it'd do us good to stock up for the next few months. But now, I am forced to park between the neighboring vehicles lined up in front of my house.

It would be a lot easier to focus on straightening out the car if Eddie would just keep quiet.

"You're really bad at this and I hate it."

"Taking my time to get something right is not *bad*."

I readjust the positioning of the vehicle. The cars in front and behind me are a little too close for comfort, and I'd rather not settle for a crooked parking job, as Eddie has been suggesting for the last five minutes.

She closes her eyes and leans her head back, groaning impatiently. "Oh my God."

"Would you cut that out? It's getting obnoxious."

"Your perfectionism is more obnoxious," she snaps. "You said you wanted my help parking, and I'm telling you, it's literally fine."

I spin the wheel, observing the side-view mirror to make sure I don't hit the SUV behind me. "By your standards."

"I'm the one standing outside of the car, here. Your perspective is limited."

"*Your* perspective would see a car sticking out in the middle of the road and call it fine. *My* perspective would rather not risk adding another dent to the collection."

"I thought we were over the parking meter thing!"

"You hit it with your door."

"You act like I did it on purpose." She rolls her eyes. "It was a tight spot. The store was crowded."

"You're the one who needed black candle wax, of all things. That's uncomfortably specific."

"You're the one who agreed to take me."

"And I still don't know why you needed my help with something so incredibly simple."

"I take it back. I'm glad I hit the parking meter. You could use a few good car dents."

"You're careless."

"And you're annoying." Eddie spins around until I see the back of her brown crewneck. I expect her to walk inside without me, but she doesn't. Either way, I decide to take advantage of the silence.

Not seconds after she shuts up, I park. Perfectly.

I hop out of the car, walking past where Eddie stands so I can hurry up and get inside. Whatever reason Eddie has for insisting on coming back to my place, I'm sure it involves Margot—not me.

But before I can get too far, Eddie tugs on the back of my shirt, spinning me back around.

I glare. "Would you cut that out?"

She shushes me aggressively, putting a finger up to her lips. "I don't want Margot to know I'm here."

I don't have time to question her sentence—or the fact that she is lifting up her shirt to pluck a neatly folded sheet of paper from the waistline of her jeans.

"You couldn't have just kept that in your pocket?"

"What?" she says. "I didn't want it to get wrinkled."

I frown and consider the unfortunate state of the botany workbook she borrowed.

"And I couldn't let anyone see me leave the house holding it," she mutters, and right away, I know she's referring to her father. I don't remember much about Mateo Voclain, but I can recall how strict he was when Margot and I would visit their home as kids.

"I need your help making this look official," Eddie explains, handing me the paper. The moment I unfold it, I know exactly what lies inside, and my heart skips a beat. "Your father gave me a letter to... mail. To people. It had a wax seal." She swallows nervously. "You think you can help me find the tools he used?"

I look over my shoulder before leaning down to whisper. "You want to forge an acceptance letter?"

She nods. "It doesn't have to be perfect. Just similar enough to the one I found in your room, with the black seal. We only need to trick my father."

Now the black table candle she made me purchase at the grocery store makes sense.

I get why she wants so badly for her family to believe she's a Chaser. Again, Mateo Voclain is a strict man, and if he found out her interests occupied other places, I wouldn't put it past him to do some digging—and perhaps come across Eddie's desire to be a rebel healer.

Eddie wants to close the letter with a wax seal, a practice reserved for the Chaser corps. Everyone else has to send their mail in resealable envelopes so they can be checked by the system and censored if need be.

But for the hand-delivered letters my father uses to correspond with the Undergrounders, his seals are useful for ensuring that the information isn't compromised.

And Eddie is right about my father having the right tools; I've used them myself.

I'm just not sure how we'll be able to sneak past my family.

"Is your dad home?" Eddie asks, and I nod.

"His car is here."

"Doesn't mean he's home. You know how old-fashioned he is. Doesn't he like walking places?"

She makes a fair point.

I pull out my phone, dialing Margot's number before holding the device up to my ear. Eddie panics, scrambling to yank the device from my grip, but my height advantage serves me well and I swat her hands away.

"Where are you?" Margot asks when she picks up.

"I'm almost home. Do we need any groceries?"

"*She'll hear us through her window, idiot*," Eddie hisses quietly, but I ignore her, listening for Margot's reply.

"No, Dad just left. He's walking to the store," my sister states.

Perfect.

"Alright, then I'll see you in a bit."

"Okay?"

"Love you." I end the call and shove my phone in my pocket, staring down at Eddie, who has given up trying to take it from me. "See? I can lie too."

She glares. "Let's just get this over with so I can go home."

"You mean so *I* can take you home," I mutter bitterly. "You don't exactly have a ride."

"Whatever."

I lead Eddie to the side of the house, reaching over the wooden gate to unhook the lock. I don't bother holding the door open for her, and she scrambles to keep it from slamming shut, locking it behind us once it's closed.

Ducking to make sure we can't be seen through the kitchen windows, we walk around the side of the house and into the backyard. Dead leaves crunch beneath our feet as we weave between overgrown planter boxes and stone birdbaths, stopping in front of the sliding glass door. It's blocked by the layer of red velvet curtains that shields us from the inside.

We move to crouch beneath the kitchen sink's window instead, which is distinguishable by the small planter box of flowers Eddie planted for us last year. They're quite annoying, really. With Margot's forgetful brain-fog and my father's busy schedule, I'm the one who waters them every morning. For my sister, who enjoys seeing them bloom—not for Eddie.

"Check to see if she's in the kitchen," Eddie whispers into my ear, hiding next to me.

"That's what I'm doing." My eyes roll as I slowly raise my head above the planter box, peeking up above the flowers. "She's probably upstairs, anyway."

But as soon as I peek inside the kitchen, I freeze.

Margot stands with her arms crossed, glaring at me through the glass. My pulse pounds as she slides the window open, leaving nothing but a screen barrier between outside and in. "I can see you, you know."

I should have held my tongue.

Eddie panics, crawling to hide behind a large round pot filled with boxwood that needs a good trimming. My mind races, trying to come up with a good excuse for my private association with Eddie in case my sister notices—and I cannot.

"If you're trying to scare me, it's not going to work," Margot glares, hands on her hips.

Good. I sigh. *She thinks I'm alone.*

I rise to my feet with a sigh, briefly scanning over my shoulder to make sure Eddie remains unseen. If I can't see her behind the planter, I doubt Margot can.

"What are you looking at?"

"I'm not looking at anything."

"You're so weird." My sister shakes her head through the screen, taking a sip from a glass of orange juice. She glares at me, puzzled. "Why are you still standing outside? It's freezing."

I shrug.

She observes me for a moment, reading me as my heart races. Margot is no idiot; she knows I'm hiding something. She just can't seem to tell what.

"Whatever," she finally concludes with a sigh. "I'm going upstairs."

And with that, Margot disappears, her footsteps tapping against the floorboards until they vanish completely.

When I deem it somewhat safe, I turn back to the boxwood just as Eddie peeks her head out from behind the planter. I nod to let her know the path is clear, and when we're certain Margot is upstairs, we open the sliding glass door and walk inside.

Swiftly, quietly, we head upstairs, slowing our pace once we reach the corridor that leads to all three bedrooms in the house. I can hear Margot shuffling around in her room behind a closed door, opening and shutting drawers, a clear sign of preoccupation.

"Stay quiet," I whisper to Eddie as we tiptoe delicately past her room.

"See, I would have been quiet, but now I have to respond and tell you what a stupid thing that is to say. Obviously we need to be quiet." Her whisper is sharp, a yell encased in quietude.

"It's not my fault you've displayed patterns in the past that tell me you don't know when to shut up."

"Oh, I'm very good at knowing when to shut up. How about *right now*?"

We approach my father's room, stepping closer to the door handle, carefully but quietly.

That is, until my foot presses against a creaky floorboard.

"Who's the loud one now, genius?"

I put a finger over Eddie's lips, widening my eyes and hoping she'll understand the gesture without an explanation. She swats my hand away and glares, opening her mouth to speak, and deciding against it when she realizes that I'm trying to listen.

The movement in Margot's room has stopped, and I can no longer hear the persistent roll of dresser drawers. For a moment, I wonder if Margot heard, terrified of what she'll think if she takes a step out of her room—but nothing happens. The rummaging continues, and a sigh of relief escapes my lips.

I wrap my hand around the doorknob, twisting it slowly, cautiously. The door creaks as it opens, but Margot doesn't seem to hear it. I stick my head in just to make sure my father really is running an errand, and sure enough, the bedroom is vacant. I gesture for Eddie to follow me inside, closing the door behind her.

My father's bedroom is smaller than mine and Margot's, although it certainly holds more. It smells like cedarwood and something earthy, laced with the sour smell of old leather and paper. Light seeps in through sheer white curtains that have been around for as long as I can remember. Stacks and stacks of Yesterday books line the pale yellow walls. Some of the mountains are tall as Eddie—though that isn't saying much.

Aside from what's stored within his two bookshelves, there is also a stack on either side of his bedposts, a stack sprawled across the cream linen sheets, and a stack in a lamp's place on his oak nightstand. Three piles line the top of his dresser, covering the large, vintage brass mirror that rests above it. I assume the only thing left uncontaminated by the touch of books is his closet.

The funny thing about my father's personal library is that none of the titles are covered in dust. Each one is cleaner than the last, worn to near shreds but free of any signs of extended periods of disuse. I wouldn't be surprised if he's read each of these books a dozen times.

"He keeps his letter-writing tools in the closet I think." I keep my voice low as I walk toward the closet. "I haven't seen them in a while so I'm not exactly sure. We might have to dig around a bit, so try not to mess anything up."

Eddie frowns. "What makes you think I'm gonna mess something up?"

Right as the words escape her lips, she trips over a stack of books, managing to regain her balance quickly—though the novels aren't so lucky.

I stop walking to give her a glare. "Lucky guess."

She scrambles to pick up the pile, scanning the mess to analyze what went where.

"You better put those back in order or he'll know we were snooping."

"Good thing you teamed up with me and not some bubble-headed halfwit."

I raise a brow. "Bubble-headed halfwit?"

She doesn't avert her gaze from the mess.

"I didn't exactly *team up* with you on purpose, you know," I remind her.

"Trust me, neither did I."

I watch as she finishes reconstructing the pile of books. I notice she put the top one back in its exact place, and the second title as well—before I realize she's managed to place every single book back where it had been before she toppled it over, at least from my own limited understanding of the picture. I don't tell her I'm impressed.

She rises to her feet, crossing her arms over her chest. "Let's just get this over with, alright?"

I roll my eyes and step closer to the closet, gripping the black metal knob to slide open the door. It's cold beneath my fingertips, and to my own surprise, I tremble. I'm not exactly thrilled to find what we're looking for. But if this is a step we have to take to keep Mateo off Eddie's back, it's a step I'll take anyway.

I open the door.

Unlike the rest of his room, my father's closet is filled with dust. He keeps most of his clothing in his dresser drawers, though he doesn't have much to begin with. A handful of winter coats, outdoor gear, an old suit, and a couple of nice pants are the only things that hang on the rack, and the rest of the space is filled by two built-in shelves secured to the back wall. It's a mess in here, storing everything from blankets and pillows to boxes of mine and Margot's old elementary school artwork. Some of his seasonal jackets were hung up sloppily and have fallen to the floor, along with a few extra blankets we bring out during the holidays.

With the mess, I could never step inside, but I can reach just enough to rummage—barely. I scour through cardboard boxes of documents and old work uniforms, filled journals, and even more books, to my surprise. But no matter how hard I search, I cannot seem to find the little tin I remember my father using to store his wax seal supplies.

I don't remember much about the tools—it's been forever since I've written any kind of letter. But I do remember my dad hiding the tin when it wasn't in use.

It's not that having letter seals is illegal; plenty of households are filled with all sorts of family heirlooms and Yesterday finds. It's their usage that is banned. That kind of secrecy is for the Presidency and the Chaser Corps alone. Everyone else's mail is triple-checked and edited, if necessary, censored under the inaccurate claims of fairness for all. The public use of wax seals, as opposed to the standard Presidency-issued resealable envelopes, would be an inconvenience to the government workers who process mail. The fine is significant.

I don't know much about the rebels or even what my father does for them, but I am aware that he can't let anyone know he uses this jackalope seal to write his letters to the Undergrounders. Not that his kind of letters would be sent through the postal system, anyway.

Still—it's strange to me that he's so keen on hiding it this obsessively. I wonder if there's more behind the symbol on his seal than I realize.

"Would you hurry up?" Eddie says, growing increasingly impatient as she watches me search. "Your dad will be back any minute now."

"Telling someone who's already in a hurry to *hurry up* doesn't make things go any faster."

"Well I wish it did."

I open my mouth to reply, but just as I do, someone else speaks instead. It's Margot.

"They're not in the living room."

Her voice echoes down the hall, conversing with someone on the phone. Eddie and I freeze as my sister's footsteps grow louder and louder. Before I can tell my unfortunate choice of a partner in crime to hide under the bed, I'm being shoved into the closet.

"*What are you doing?*" I hiss, pulse pounding furiously as Eddie puts her hands on my shoulders, pushing me into a closet we cannot fit inside. She ignores me.

There's barely enough room for my father's possessions in here, and there is certainly not enough space for Eddie and me. But neither of us can move now because the footsteps grow louder, and so does Margot's voice.

"Dad, I'm telling you, they're not in the living room, I checked," she claims to the other line. "They're in your room somewhere."

"Would you hurry up and close the door already?" I whisper frantically.

"I'm trying," Eddie says, though she's having a hard time doing so. We're as far right inside the closet as we can go, and with her back pressed against the door and such little space to move, she can't rotate her arm in a way that will allow her to slide the left half closed.

She doesn't have time to shut it all the way before Margot walks in.

Since Eddie cannot close the closet without my sister seeing, she has no choice but to move closer—until we are standing face to face without an inch of space between us, praying that Margot won't decide to look through the left-side gap.

"Two words," I seethe through clenched teeth, glaring down at Eddie as her palms press against my chest. "Bubble-headed. Halfwit."

"You mention this to anyone and I'll kill you."

"Trust me, being stuck in a closet with you is nothing to brag about."

"I hate you, you know. *Severely.*"

"You're not exactly tolerable either."

Eddie opens her mouth to reply, but I cut her off, holding a finger to my lips. She glares, but the scowl melts away when she hears Margot's footsteps growing closer to the closet.

In my panic, I realize all of the ways we could have avoided this situation. I could have had Eddie hide in the car. Margot potentially spotting her out there would have been a lot better than uncovering us like this. Or even better—Eddie could have distracted my sister while I handled this in secret.

I blame Eddie for my lack of focus. If she wasn't so infectiously infuriating, maybe I could have thought this through after parking.

"You clearly don't know where these books are so I'm hanging up now," Margot says to our father over the phone. Her voice is a lot louder than I expected it to be; she must be right outside the closet door.

Before I have the chance to resist, Eddie is holding me by the shoulders again, but this time, she presses down, forcing the two of us into a seated position, knees touching. She grabs one of the fallen coats and drapes it over our heads. I grimace as my back presses painfully against the overstuffed shelves, shoulder blades digging into some object I cannot see.

Neither of us can see a thing under the cloak, but we've swallowed our breath, hearts pounding, lungs put on a gut-knotting pause as we listen closely. I can hear Margot put her hand through the gap and slide the left side of the closet door open.

We're done for.

Eddie and I exchange frantic looks, holding our breath as Margot begins to rummage through the closet, so focused on finding whatever books she's looking for she doesn't seem to notice us—yet. Although we're pressed against the far right wall of the closet, hidden by mounds of clutter, surely she'll notice the person-shaped lump in the back. Or hear our heartbeats.

I look to Eddie again, ready to combat her wordless glaring assaults, but to my surprise, her face is ridden with something other than anger. It is no longer contorted by her intolerance for me, but soothed in a somber kind of way that leads me to wonder if it is guilt she's feeling, not annoyance or even fear. She looks in Margot's direction, and although a thick layer of fabric shields her view, she watches anyway, so close to her friend in theory, yet so separate in more ways than one.

Eddie notices me watching and turns her head to face me. Our eyes lock, and for a moment, we share the same guilt, the same sadness.

No matter our cause, no matter how different our methods may be, we are both deceiving Margot—and it hurts more than anything.

A few more seconds pass until the rummaging comes to a halt. Our eyes widen as we brace ourselves for the inevitable exposure we will surely face.

But the jacket is never lifted, and we are never confronted. Slowly, I pull the jacket away from my eyes.

To my horror, Margot is still searching through the closet, though she is too preoccupied to see me. *Stay still*, I tell myself. *Don't blink.*

I watch as Margot accidentally knocks down a file folder from one of the shelves, spilling documents all over a pile of clothes. She scrambles to stack them all together again, picking up one of the pages before freezing completely.

Her eyes peel open wide. She is a statue for a long time, until she puts the rest of the pages back in their folder. She takes the file and a pair of books and rolls the closet shut. Her footsteps grow softer as they drift away, and she closes the bedroom door on her way out.

I pull the jacket fully away from our heads. Although Margot is long gone, Eddie and I don't budge. Neither of us says a word, too absorbed in what just happened to do anything but sit there in our silence—until she clears her throat.

"I think she's gone now," Eddie whispers. She looks up at me, so close I can see the grains of her eyes, even in the dark.

"I think so too," I whisper back. We still don't move.

I notice a round boxwood leaf stuck in her hair, a souvenir from sneaking around in the backyard. I consider letting Eddie walk around like that, but it bothers me too much to see that leaf so out of place. Slowly, I reach out my hand.

"What are you doing?" She glares.

My right hand combs through her hair, and I use the left one to pluck away the debris. I turn over my palm to show her the leaf.

"Oh." She clears her throat. "Thank you."

My right hand lingers and I don't know why. Slower than before, I brush my fingers through, looking for another leaf, another sign of something out of place. I find nothing. And still, my hand stays.

I clear my throat and pull it away. "You're a mess."

She flicks me on the forehead.

"*Ow*." I shoot her a glare. "What if that was a compliment?"

"Yeah right. A compliment from you?" She laughs. "Nice try."

I get the feeling she would have flicked me either way.

My shoulder burns, and I'm reminded of the sharp object digging into my back. I reach behind me to grab the mystery item from the shelf.

Of course. The hidden tin.

The tin is square-shaped with sharp, dented edges. Rusted hinges testify its age. It's heavy, but stuffed so full the objects don't have enough space to clank together when it moves.

"Is that it?" Eddie questions.

I nod. "It is."

"We should get started." Eddie uses my shoulders to propel herself to a standing position, extending a hand to help me do the same. I take it, though I don't need it. Her hands are small, dimpled, and softer than I remember.

Eddie is quick to drop my hand as we emerge from the closet, stretching now that we're not in such a cramped space. I feel dizzy and I'm not exactly sure why.

I walk over to the foot of my father's bed, sit cross-legged on cold floor-boards, and lean my back against the end of the frame. Eddie sits across from me, observing curiously as I set the tin down in the space between us, flip the latch, and open the container.

As soon as the lid opens and I find myself staring at the contents inside, I freeze, eyes wide, suddenly injected with a wave of something between nostalgia and an absence I cannot place. I stare at the wooden wax furnace and a set of two boards held together by decorated pillars with a hole in the top for the matching brass spoon to rest. I eye the used scraps of crimson sealing wax rectangles, the nearly empty tea light, the book of matches, and the little wood-handled palette knife my father always used to cut the red blocks. There are envelopes at the bottom of the tin, beneath every tool, yellowed with age, lacking the resealable strip that government-issued envelopes have.

This is Yesterday stationery, meant for illegal, uncensored hand-to-hand exchange.

These are tools for treason.

And that peculiar seal, an engraving of a side-profile rabbit head, with antlers branching from its head like that of a deer. I know a creature like this could never exist, even in the Yesterdays, when oddities like elephants and rhinos and spiny fish of every color imaginable were still around. And yet, here it is, a symbol I've only ever seen on the signet ring my father hides away in this tin.

There is something so chilling about it, familiar and foreign all at once.

Eddie reaches out to grab the silver signet ring, turning it over beneath her fingertips, tracing the odd engraving, and studying it with creased brows. Curious, she slips it on her finger. "This is the symbol he used on the letter."

"What letter?" I ask, and she looks up at me with an expression that says it all.

Right. The letter she delivered to the Undergrounder contact, an event I still know nothing about.

I clear my throat, grabbing the small wood furnace from the tin. It's lighter than I remember, the result of time and larger hands, I suppose. "I've been meaning to ask you about that."

"Oh." Eddie fidgets with the matches. "That's what you wanted to talk to me about."

I nod, and a wave of silence overcomes us both. I'm asking out of curiosity, not concern, of course. I obviously must care about Eddie, to a small extent, because we just happen to rely on each other to keep both of our covers stable enough for our families to believe. But mostly, I want to know what kind of people my father associates himself with—and exactly what he's trading for Margot's medicine. For my family's sake. Not Eddie's.

Maybe, if my father is giving up more than he should, I can help him lighten the load. I'll be making a decent living as a Chaser. I could certainly spare some coin.

Or information.

"The contact didn't show," Eddie says, soft and vaguely enough for her words to remain undetected by any unwanted listeners.

"That's odd," I reply, but I can't help the sigh that escapes my lips, or the sense of relief that floods through me. Maybe it's best Eddie doesn't join the Undergrounders. Not yet, at least. She is reckless and I am not yet a Chaser.

But what if something happened to Dad's contact? Was he discovered by the Corps, perhaps? Would that compromise our family?

Don't think like that, I tell myself. *You need to keep your head screwed on straight if you want this Chasing thing to turn out in your favor.* I tell myself there is no use worrying.

Still, I find the situation odd. My father's contacts have been reliable for years, from my understanding. Perhaps the insertion of Eddie as a variable into the Undergrounder equation didn't compute with Dad's higher-ups.

"How do we use this?" Eddie asks after clearing her throat. "I should be getting home soon."

"Right. Here." I shake my head and shift my focus to the task at hand, speaking with gestures. "We need to ignite the tea light and place it in this furnace here. Then you set the spoon above the flame and melt the wax inside."

Eddie reaches into her pocket and retrieves the black decorative table candle we grabbed from the grocery store. "And then you can pour the wax on the envelope?"

I nod my chin in the direction of the signet ring on her finger. "And seal it with that."

For the second time, Eddie retrieves the folded letter from within her sweatshirt, its edges still uncharacteristically crisp. *Convincing her father this letter is real must mean a lot to her.*

I can't help but wonder if there's more to this than maintaining a cover. Through remembrance of previous interactions with Mateo Voclain—and reading between certain lines—I've gathered enough information to understand the relationship between the man and his daughter.

Perhaps there is a part of her—a small part, but a present one nonetheless —that wants to please him. A part that feels guilty for not meeting his expectations, even if they go against everything she believes in.

Eddie hands me the letter, still holding onto the matchbook as I take the piece of paper and find an envelope to enclose it within. Through the corner of my eye, I watch her light a match, studying the flame as it creeps closer and closer to her finger. I worry she'll burn herself until she blinks out of it, grabbing the well-used tea light and transferring the flame to the small candle. She shakes out the match and sets it to the side.

Carefully, I slip the letter inside the envelope as Eddie places the tea light in the little wooden furnace. She takes the palette knife from the tin, observing it with the same playful curiosity she's displayed with every item.

"Do you know anything about these?" Eddie questions, eyes still fixed to the sharp metal object. I raise a brow, and she mouths the word *knives* in silence.

"Only as much as you do." I give her an odd look. "You mean like... how they're made or something? What they were used for back in the Yesterdays?"

"Not information, Ren. I'm not looking for facts." She takes the black candle and cuts off the end with the tool, placing the piece inside the metal spoon and setting it on the furnace. "I wanna know how to use one."

"There's not much to it. You just... stab."

"There has to be more to it than that. I wanna be *skilled*. Strategic."

I pause, thinking about the Undergrounder association she desires to have. Perhaps she has another correspondence rescheduled.

"I might learn something during training," I say. "I could teach you a thing or two if I do."

"Quite the generous offer."

"And one I might revoke after a second thought. I'm not sure how I feel about *you* wielding a *knife*." I whisper the last word.

She shifts her gaze to the flame, watching the tea light burn. "I suppose you're right to have your reservations."

I look down at the furnace. I observe the wax melting inside the spoon, slowly transforming into something else entirely, a glistening goo that is now more of a liquid than a solid. It's odd to me, how a thing can turn into a completely different substance when exposed to fire. *Even people can shift like wax.*

When it's the right consistency, I lick my fingertips and pinch the flame, a line of smoke streaming into my nose.

My heart drops.

"The smoke." I exchange a worried glance with Eddie as she comes to the same realization.

"Maybe we can open a window?" Eddie suggests, but I shake my head.

"He'll still smell it. He's too observant."

"Can't we just... tell him the truth?" She lowers her voice to a whisper. "That I'm making this? To trick my dad? He knows I'm not actually *Chasing*." She mouths the last word in silence.

"Forgery requires reference. Where will he think you got a real acceptance letter from?" I give her a glare. "If I'm the person helping you, he'll definitely connect those dots."

She doesn't respond.

I stare at the tea light, watching the smoke disappear. I let out a sigh. *I know what I have to do to excuse the scent.*

I pour a glob of wax on the envelope, handing it over to Eddie once it dries just enough. She stamps it with the signet ring she still wears on her right index finger. We set the letter aside to dry.

I take the palette knife, cut myself a healthy chunk of red wax, and set up the furnace to melt my own seal.

"What are you doing?" Eddie raises a single brow in my direction.

"Writing a letter. So I can excuse the candle smoke."

She scrunches her nose, puzzled. "I don't get it."

"He used to make Margot and I write letters. To..."

For some inexplicable reason, I can't say her name aloud. My words drift out of reach, and I search Eddie's eyes for an understanding I'm surprised to find. Somehow, she knows exactly who I'm talking about.

Mom.

I let out a sigh. "My dad thought that writing to her would let us... I don't know. Feel connected to her in some way, I guess. That writing letters to someone who could never write back would help us understand our grief or heal or something like that. If I tell him I was just writing another letter he won't question the smoke."

Eddie and I watch the red wax melt, struggling to find the right words.

"I think he was right to have you guys do that." She shifts her gaze, eyeing me with a knowing glance.

I shrug. "It's hard to have a relationship with a person you don't know."

Eddie gives me a sorry smile.

"I do feel connected to her, of course. She's half of my whole no matter what. I just... I wish I knew what parts of her I keep alive. I want to know her voice, not its absence." I look down at the back of my hands, lowering my voice. "Letters don't make her any less dead."

It's quiet for a moment, and Eddie bites her lip. "I know it's not the same at all, but I used to write angry letters to my dad. And it helped. A lot, actually." She shakes her head. "I never gave them to him, of course. I'd burn them."

"Smart move."

She chuckles emptily before continuing. "He's always so... I don't know. He makes me feel crazy sometimes. Like I'm always in the wrong. Like I don't have the right to any voice but his." She shakes her head, gaze hollow as she watches the candle flame once again. "Writing letters and throwing them away was the only way I could spare my sanity."

Eddie looks up at me, something alarmingly similar to sympathy flickering in her gaze. "What I'm trying to say is that maybe it's good we're doing this. That you're... you know. Writing another one."

"I think they did help. Only a little bit." I pinch the tea light out and let the smoke fade into nothing. "But it made her absence tangible. Something I could acknowledge, accept, and grieve. Otherwise, I'm sure I'd be living in some permanent state of denial—on autopilot, so to speak."

"I get that." Eddie smiles.

"So…" I look up at her, locking my vision with hers. "Why did you stop?"

"It made his disappointment too real." She stretches her lips into a thin line. "I guess I eventually just accepted it all as okay."

I turn to the wax, pouring the crimson substance onto an empty envelope.

"You're not going to write a letter?"

I shake my head. "Not today."

Eddie uses the ring to seal it when it's ready.

The red is darker than normal, mixed with the leftover black from Eddie's candle. It looks too much like blood. For a moment—with the viscosity of the wax, the smell of metal from the furnace, ring, and spoon—I think it really is.

"Hey Eddie?" I lift my chin to look at her again, and she does the same. "It's not okay. The way he treats you."

Eddie glances down, spinning the signet ring in circles around her finger.

Instinctively, I reach out to put a comforting hand on her knee—but I stop myself, and it rests on the floor near her leg instead. "You're allowed to expect better from people."

Our gazes don't meet, and I begin to wonder if I've crossed a line I shouldn't have—until she smiles to herself, finding my stare once again. "Thank you."

We sit there in a silence that is unexpectedly comforting. In our quietude, I notice her eyes are not as uncomplicated as hazel. They are an intricate mix of deep olive and bronze, like someone poured a hot vat of melted gold into a murky pond and didn't stir.

There are times when her glare is the most infuriating thing I know. But for a moment, I swear there is a light behind her eyes, and I wonder if—in some horrible, impossible way—we might share a fraction of understanding after all.

"Address it." Eddie nods to the empty envelope I've sealed, pulling the signet ring from her finger and handing it to me. "You should write *something*, at least."

I scoff, taking the ring and putting it away. "What's the point? My dad will know who the envelope is for. He's not gonna look inside."

She crosses her arms. "Do it."

I clench my jaw as I return the rest of the tools to the tin and close the latch. While I would love to refuse Eddie's command, I know how difficult it is to win an argument with someone as stubborn as her. *Choose your battles wisely.*

I let out a long sigh. I think about it for a minute, and I cannot find a good reason not to. "Fine."

I rise to my feet, walk over to my father's nightstand, and open the drawer to fish out a pen. I turn my envelope over and stare at the blank space, its ivory emptiness so mocking and cold. I hesitate before scribbling on the back of the envelope. I'm quick to turn it over, letting it rest on the surface of the nightstand, its odd blood seal waiting to be broken by a hand that will never move again.

I can hear Eddie put the tin back inside my father's closet before sliding the door closed. I am still staring at the envelope when Eddie makes her way to my side, looking up at me with a burning I can feel like candlelight.

"What did you write?"

I am not lucky enough to have a memory like Eddie's, but without looking, I can still see the words scrawled across the envelope. I can hear their echoes in my head too, because they are haunting, etched into all fibers of my being, woven into my very sinking soul.

I meet Eddie's stare, holding it like the only piece of driftwood in a sea that will not let me float. My voice cracks when I whisper the words.

"I miss you."

They feel different when I'm looking at her.

We make our exit unseen, and we don't say another word all evening.

EDDIE

Wednesday, May 10
23 Days Left Until Graduation

By the time I get home for the evening—for good—my father is finally home.

As exhausted as I am, I feel equipped. Nervous, but armed with a piece of newly forged evidence I think he will appreciate.

I just hope he believes me.

Deep breaths, I tell myself, shutting my eyes as I close the front door behind me. I slide off my shoes and clutch the fake letter close to my chest. *You are in control.*

The house is filled with the faint echo of running water, letting me know he's in the kitchen, probably cleaning up the messes made by the dinner I missed. And by the way his sponge aggressively scratches against ceramic, I can tell he's pissed that I didn't call.

I am in control.

Or at least, I can pretend to be.

"Hey Dad," I call out as I walk out of the foyer and into the kitchen, concealing the letter behind my back. "I'm home."

"As you should have been hours ago," he mutters, focused on the plate he's scrubbing.

"I know, and I'm sorry. But..." I force a grin, swallowing the disgust that brews inside me. "I have great news."

There's a pause, and for a moment, I wonder if he's going to drop the plate. Or maybe even throw it. I'm not exactly familiar with the way he expresses excitement.

He stares at the sink in silence, eyes wide, trembling until a thick arm reaches out to shut off the faucet. Slowly, his neck turns, his face angled in my direction. "No. It didn't..."

You need to pretend, Eddie.

This isn't how you really feel.

Nodding, I force my smile to expand until my cheeks hurt. "It did."

My father's face lights up in a way I haven't seen in years. "You passed?"

"I passed!"

Before I know it, he's walking away from the sink, and suddenly his arms are wrapped around me, still coated in a layer of suds that soaks the back of my shirt. "I can't believe it!"

I'm stunned, not used to this amount of affection. I can't remember the last time I hugged anyone but Margot. I'm not sure I even remember my father ever hugging me at all, and it feels like I'm trapped in some alternate universe.

There's a Yesterday book that the twins really loved as a kid, where this girl climbs through some closet and meets these evil clones of her parents who try to trick her into letting them sew buttons into her eyes by displaying more affection than her real parents. Maybe this is my other father, because he certainly isn't the cold one I remember.

For the first time in a long time, my father is proud of me.

"I'm so proud of you, Lavender." Dad tightens his embrace, patting me on the back and giving me a kiss on the top of my head before pulling away. He places his hands on my shoulders and looks down at me with a bright smile, his dark brown eyes glittering with delight.

"Am I allowed to see it?" he asks. "The letter?"

"You mean, this letter?" I pull the envelope into view, smiling falsely. He hesitates for a moment before taking the item gingerly, as though it might spontaneously vanish in the presence of haste.

Seeing that the wax has already been cracked, to my relief, he pays no attention to the unconventional seal, and I suppress a sigh as he removes the letter quickly.

I bite the inside of my cheek as he reads, so sure he will realize that it's false. The content of the letter is almost identical to Ren's—I made certain of it—but I also took the liberty of making a few changes.

The location of the training center is confidential. In Ren's letter, an address is given, and trainees are instructed to share it sparingly, only when necessary for rides and other similar scenarios.

According to this forgery of mine, for my training days, I will rendezvous at a certain community college bus stop, where all Chasers from the city carpool to the training location together.

I figured it'd be easy to lie about Ren taking some college course over the summer. That way, no one would suspect anything if we allegedly drove there together. I can spend my days searching for a way into the Underground, and no one will think a thing because I'm supposed to be gone at training anyway, and Ren will have an excuse for leaving every day. We'd both have a pretty solid alibi, and I could even store his Chaser uniform at my house if he needs to. It's a good scam.

Logistically, it might not make much sense to carpool with Ren on his way to training. We could just tell our lies, take two cars, and go our separate ways. But we are both neck deep in this mess, and something about lying as a pair feels a lot less horrible than lying as one. The weight is easier to bear when spread across two shoulders. Maybe it's a bit complicated, but so are we.

At this point, as much as I can't stand the guy, I think I need Ren. For what, exactly, I'm not sure, but it's definitely something.

And if I were him, I don't think I could stay human for very long if I went to training alone every day.

I study my father closely as he reads. I watch the way his face remains completely still, free of any emotion at all, until his expression changes. It morphs from this proud stranger back to the stoic face of the dad I'm used to, and my heart is quick to cease its beating.

"Dad?" I mutter. He remains frozen, like a rigid sculpture of ice. "Is something wrong?"

"No." He shakes his head, and I realize that his eyes are wet. "Nothing's wrong."

He finishes reading the letter and hands it back to me. I take it gladly before he changes his mind and notices the errors I'm sure Milo and I made, but I'm left more puzzled than ever as I slowly slide it back into the envelope.

"It's just—you're already so grown up, and it happened so damn fast. Sometimes I feel like I never got the chance to..."

We're both thinking it, I say to myself.

Just let me hear the words. Please. Say it so I know I'm not crazy.

"Nevermind, Lavender." The glossiness fades, and the grinning pride returns. He gives me another pat on the back before exiting the kitchen. "Your mother is going to be so proud when she hears the news."

He leaves, walking down the hall and disappearing around the corner. I hear my parents laughing in another room, celebrating my faux achievements. And I share none of the joy.

I wish you said it, Dad.

I know the words he was going to say, but when I think about it, it's not that he never got the chance to know me.

I realize now that the problem is that I have changed. In my secrecy, I have pushed him away. I pushed them all away and I will keep doing exactly that if that's the price I have to pay to do what's right. But it doesn't change the fact that I am a liar and a fraud, and my father is too blind to see my forgery for what it really is.

I was made of bricks once, solid and true. Now, like a house made of straw, I am composed completely of flimsy things, too weak to avoid bending with the breeze.

I cannot shake the fear that someday, the wind will be too much, and I will collapse.

You feel like you don't know me anymore.

When I finally make it to my room for the night, I am restless.

I check on the knife. I cover it with green socks. I cover it with purple socks. I close the drawer, turn out the lights, and tuck myself into bed early.

I check on the knife again and move it under my mattress instead. *Maybe this will be a better hiding spot.* I close my eyes.

I move it back to the drawer. I cover it with green and purple socks. I toss and I turn and I toss again.

By the time I manage to still, my brother and my parents have already put themselves to bed. My eyes flutter to a final close at such a late hour it no longer matters that I called it an early night.

I wonder if this is what all my nights will feel like from now on. *Sleep is another price*, I tell myself. *That's all it is.*

But before I get the chance to drift away, there's a knock on my window.

I freeze, my pulse a jackhammer. My gaze shifts to the right. Sheer white curtains protect the panes, allowing only the faintest moonlight to filter through, warping prickly shadows that belong to the pine tree outside. When I see the shadows sway, I know the wind is my only visitor.

The tree is always there, right outside my window, and I've never had a problem with the shadows before. But tonight, they look far too similar to arms for me to remain fearless. Or teeth. Long, sharp, nightmarish teeth. I'm about to close my eyes again when a second knock cracks against the glass.

I sit up slowly, careful not to make a sound, heart pounding in my ears and throat. Childishly, I pull my comforter closer, clutching the fabric with knuckles so tight the skin burns. Telling myself to breathe doesn't make it happen. My lungs are on pause and I can't do anything to get them functioning again.

What if someone is out there?

What if, through some fluke in my short and simple connection to Cedar —who is now *dead*—I made an enemy with the Undergrounders? Have they sent someone to get rid of me?

If that unpleasant smuggler was intense, I can only imagine what his higher-ups would be like. More paranoid than he was, probably. Unless making angry knifepoint threats was a Cedar-specific feature.

Before I have time to blink, something clicks.

I clutch the covers tighter as the window begins to rise, so slowly it barely makes a sound at all. My heartbeat hammers as a gut-knotting chill courses through my veins. When the window is fully open, I suddenly regret not sleeping with my dagger beneath the mattress.

This is the end, isn't it?

A boot. A leg. Two boots. Two legs. One shadowy figure, sliding into my room and parting the curtains. Too tall to be my brother, too able to be Margot, too impossible to be Ren. There is no one else I know.

I tremble as the figure takes a step into the moonlight, and before I know it I'm tossing the comforter to the side and grabbing the lamp right off my bedside table, clutching it as tightly as I can. My arms shake. The chattering of my teeth intensifies. I can taste the metallic flavor of fear as if a coin were resting on my tongue.

If this Undergrounder is here to kill me, to take my life for allegedly causing Cedar's demise, what will they do with my family when they're done?

I've heard stories about how ruthless the Undergrounders can be. They will kill failed contacts, slit the throats of traitors, and plunge blades into the hearts of backstabbers. There are rumors that if the wrong person stumbles across the right secret, even the most innocent individuals are swiftly handled—because the Undergrounders will do anything to back their cause.

I just hope this stranger makes an exception tonight.

"Come any closer and you're dead," I threaten, jaw seizing, my voice an angered whisper. I clutch the lamp the way I would hold my knife.

The figure raises their hands. "Calm down, alright? It's me."

Me? I don't know who *me* is. I hold the lamp tighter, ready to throw it in their direction.

But then I stop myself. This figure's voice sounds so familiar, enough to make me lower the lamp, just for a moment. I squint, trying to make out their shape in the dark. There's barely enough moonlight for me to see anything at all.

And then I see it. Dark hair, helplessly slicked back, too many unruly strands going this way and that. His face is compromised by shadows, but if I squint hard enough, I can see the tail end of a gnarled scar, creeping out beneath the left lens of a tinted pair of glasses.

Cedar.

So he is alive after all.

I drop the lamp. It lands on the bed, rolling near the edge until I snap out of it and grab the object, placing it back on the nightstand. I know it would have woken my father if it fell.

For a moment, I am stilled by my shock. I can't tell if I should be relieved or angry or terrified. I grieved him, of course, even though he was and still is a complete stranger. Death is an awful, permanent thing, and I don't get to choose who should or shouldn't be mourned.

But if Cedar is here, breathing and alive...

I don't want to think about what he must have done to get away, and I don't know enough to jump to any conclusions. But I do know enough to realize what he did to *me.*

He left me.

I can't believe he actually left me alone, in the dark, in front of some terrifying abandoned parking garage, ready to be obtained and skinned alive by whatever horrible people lurk in the night in wait for such easy prey.

Or exterminated by the Chasers I ran into while waiting for him to reappear.

I fold my arms across my chest, blood boiling. I try to contain my fury for the sake of my sleeping family, but my whispering is still aggressive.

"You shouldn't be here. You *can't* be here." My head shakes. "And I really, *really* don't want you to be."

"And here I am," he spits, crossing his arms too.

I bite my tongue. What could Cedar possibly be upset about? He's the one who abandoned *me*, not the other way around. There is little I truly know about him, but I can confidently say he'd feel the same if he were in my position—probably even angrier.

I glare, though it's useless in the dark. "I never told you where I live."

"You're easy to follow."

"*You were following me?*"

He shrugs.

I shake my head. "And I thought you were dead, by the way. Thanks for abandoning me last night. A *very* trustworthy move on your part."

"You're one to talk about trust," he seethes. "I should have known you were nothing but a backstabbing rat."

"What are you talking about?" I scoff. I also want to ask him why he's still wearing shades past midnight, but I don't.

He ignores the second question, and I can practically hear him glaring as he takes a few angry steps closer. "You really thought I wouldn't see you talking to those..." He pauses, remembering the mics. "Other people?"

So he did see me talking to the Chasers.

"I was covering for you," I explain. "Someone reported the... sound."

Cedar freezes at the mention of the gunshot, and I look down at my hands.

In his hesitation to reply, I begin to understand. Something happened that night. Something he doesn't want to talk about.

"He turned on you, didn't he?" I ask, voice soft. "The contact."

The smuggler doesn't say a word, but he nods, so subtly I nearly miss it. Now that he's closer, I can see his entire body shift from furious to grim. His shoulders tense and he looks the other way. I wonder what could have possibly happened during that rendezvous to rattle him so badly.

And then it hits me. He's an Undergrounder. Cedar wouldn't have let that man live, would he?

He turns to leave, walking back toward the window with his hands in his pockets.

"We're not done here," I tell him.

He turns back around, still shaken by whatever memories I've stirred. His voice is both annoyed and hollow at once. "I got my answers. You're alive. Not a spy. That's all I need."

I open my mouth to protest, but before I get the chance, a door creaks down the hall, followed by a pause—and then the soft thud of footsteps. My heart pounds faster, and I can taste my fear again, only this time, it is much more potent. The sound grows louder with each passing second.

I would know those angered footsteps anywhere.

"Hide."

Cedar's brows crease. "What?"

"Just trust me, alright?" I seethe. "It's my dad."

In the moonlight, I can see his frown disappear. He ducks and rolls under the bed quickly, just as terrified as I am.

In a matter of seconds, the door opens, and my father walks in. I can feel his glare burning as he stands against the doorframe, arms crossed.

"I heard voices," he says, posing it like a question.

"Sorry. I was talking to Margot on the phone," I lie, praying my father won't see me tremble.

"Didn't sound like Margot."

"Okay? What do you want me to do, call her up again and have her apologize to you?"

His scowl only intensifies. He walks over, lifting the covers like he's looking for something.

"There's no one in here." I laugh like it's a ridiculous accusation, feeling disheartened when I realize how right my father is to be suspicious. For the wrong reasons, sure, but right nonetheless.

The man ignores me, walking to my left to open the closet doors instead. I watch as he shifts through hanging clothes and folded blankets, but out of the corner of my eye, I can see Cedar roll out from under the bed. I look in his direction, eyes wide, praying he knows how to read lips.

What are you doing? I mouth. Cedar simply places a finger over his lips.

Dad turns back around, and Cedar freezes, still planted on his back. My pulse races as my father kneels down to check under the bed. *This is it*, I tell myself. *There's no lying my way out of this one.*

Just as my father's face disappears beneath the bedframe, Cedar climbs out the window and hangs on with two hands. He waits for my father to finish the inspection, postponing his drop to avoid making a ruckus by landing in the bushes below.

"Dad, this is ridiculous." I roll my eyes, praying the man will come to the same realization quickly so Cedar can escape. My father doesn't say a word.

Out of the corner of my eye, I can see one hand slip. My eyes widen and I try so hard not to gasp. Cedar is hanging on by one hand, ready to fall in an instant.

Finally, my father stands up, wiping dust off his hands with an annoyed sigh, bothered he woke up for nothing. "Keep it down next time, alright? And no phone calls past 11:00. I have work in the morning."

I nod as my dad exits, closing the door behind him. For a moment I sit there blinking in silence, until I remember that Cedar is still hanging.

But when I look over to the right, I don't see either of his hands.

I climb out of bed and rush over to the window. I stick my head into the night and angle my neck down, examining the bushes below. To my disappointment, I don't see him. *He's already gone.*

"Over here, Voclain."

I scan my surroundings. *He can't be in my room,* I think. *I would have seen him climb back in.*

"The tree, genius."

Sure enough, when I shift my gaze, I see none other than Cedar, seated on a large branch. He leans against the trunk so casually that I can't help but wonder how being dozens of feet in the air doesn't phase him. I can only assume he's used to worse perils.

"What do you want?" Cedar mutters, still irritated.

"You know what I want," I say. *I still want in.*

My response incites a chuckle. "It's too dangerous."

"I'm serious," I argue. "And you already agreed."

"That was before I almost got you killed," he snaps before lowering his voice. "Like I said, kid. It's too dangerous."

I glare. "Look. I know how to make my own decisions, alright? And I already made this choice a long time ago."

I watch as Cedar leans his head back. I can't see his eyes through the shades, but I can tell they must be rolling. He sighs, studying the sky momentarily before fixing his stare back on me.

"If you want this to continue, you need to prove your loyalty. Your worth," he says, and I can't help but grin. "So I know that next time we run into a pair of... armored shitheads... I won't have to worry about you ratting us out."

I nod. "I can do that."

"How?"

I pause. I don't have much to give. I can't offer him Yesterday weaponry, except for the dagger in the sock drawer. I can't offer him money or medicine, because I don't have any. I can't offer him my time, because that means nothing to him until I can prove that it does.

But I have Ren.

"I have a Ch—" I stop myself, remembering the mics. "I have a you-know-what on the inside."

Cedar is silent, dead still, quiet and stoic as the tree he sits in. For a moment I wonder if I've shot myself in the foot, if my connection to Ren has only worsened my chance to earn his trust.

But then, to my surprise and puzzlement, Cedar laughs. He laughs a belly-aching kind of chuckle that leads me to believe my proposed contribution isn't as significant as I thought.

"*Shut up!*" I whisper-yell, drawing my lips into a thin, frustrated line. "You're gonna wake up my family. My dad will literally kill you."

His laugh subsides with a sigh, and his expression turns blank, almost grim. "You really don't think we've thought of recruiting Doubles before?"

He speaks swiftly, so arrogant I consider throwing the lamp at him after all. Although, I can't help but pause, flustered by my own ignorance. I never really thought about that before. To my disappointment, he makes a solid argument.

By the sound of Cedar's claims, there must be more than one Chaser working under their influence.

I always knew the rumored rebels are real, that they are masters of stealth and wanted things, that they knew how to move beneath the overlook of prying eyes completely unnoticed. But I never knew their numbers are large enough to manage not one, but *multiple* Double Agents in the Corps. Are the Undergrounders really powerful enough to execute an operation like that successfully?

"You have... Doubles?" I ask.

Cedar nods proudly. "I even know a few personally."

I look down at my shoes, suddenly more hopeless than I've felt in a long time. Feeding information from Ren to the Undergrounders was supposed to be my ticket to earning their trust.

Before, I thought the connection alone would be more than enough to buy me not only trust but training as a healer too. And now, knowing Ren will get me nothing, I feel as useless as ever. It's probably best he doesn't get involved, anyway. I'd be putting him in a lot of danger.

Just as I consider telling Cedar I don't have anything to contribute, ashamed of my inadequacy, an idea pops into my head. I certainly don't have the right skills yet, so my last option has to involve goods.

Maybe I don't have any medicine to offer—but my father certainly does.

"My dad's a dentist. He does oral surgery and stuff," I suggest. "If you have the need for mild anesthetics, I can get you some."

"Seriously?" Cedar leans forward eagerly, pine needles spraying the ground below. He reminds me of a child, excited to open a gift.

"Would that help?"

Cedar nods.

I don't ask what the drugs will be used for, but I assume they will make good bargaining chips. We sketch up a vague plan using whispers as pens, indistinct enough to throw off any unwanted listeners, if anyone is listening at all. The idea is solid enough for Cedar to agree to let me help with a few additional missions until he can make time for this new one, and I hope he doesn't see me grinning stupidly under the cover of darkness.

"I'll see you around." Cedar waves, readying himself to climb down the tree. But he pauses before he takes his exit.

"Oh, and Voclain?"

"Yeah?"

"There's no such thing as the *Undergrounders*." Though I cannot see his face, even beneath the shadows, I know he must be smirking. "We call ourselves the Unseen."

And with that, Cedar disappears into the night, truly and completely as unseen as he claims to be.

Monday, May 29
4 Days Left Until Graduation

On Monday of the last week of school, Dad insists on giving me a ride to class.

I'm not very fond of the idea, so I walk out the front door without saying another word to him, happy to avoid another lecture. Though I can't help but question his sudden involvement.

I've always taken myself to school. While my father can't afford something as pricey as Immunity for the family, he makes enough through his occupation to afford the simple luxury of a car for himself and his oldest child.

My car isn't new. New cars are rare these days, and much more expensive than they used to be. But my family can afford recycled cars, vehicles from the Yesterdays that have been retrofitted with modern technology. Mine doesn't look too great, though I can't complain. The machine has helped me spend as much time away from my father as possible and I love it for that.

But it's not in the driveway.

My pulse drums. My shivers intensify. I look around frantically, praying that I parked it on the street in front of our house without thinking. Maybe it's just hidden behind a tree or a curl of fog, and if I look from the right angle, I'll be able to see my car clearly, present and not stolen.

To my usual luck, the car is simply gone.

I whip around to walk back toward the house and stop when I see my father standing on the front porch, locking the door behind him.

"Is something wrong?" he asks, twisting the key with a click.

"My car's been stolen. It's—*gone*. I don't know what happened to it. I swear I locked it, it's just—"

"Stop panicking. You stutter when you panic," he talks plainly, as though all he heard was the flaw in my speaking and not the problem itself. He puts his keys in his pocket and walks down the porch steps. "It's in the shop. You haven't taken it in for a while, so I took it for some routine maintenance yesterday. Turns out it needs a few fixes."

"My car was fine, Dad." I cross my arms. "I take good care of it."

"The alignment was outrageous. I'm surprised you haven't killed anyone yet." He shakes his head disapprovingly and walks past me, stopping in front of his own car. "Are you coming or not?"

"I'm not," I say, desperate to avoid him at all costs. A car ride with him sounds more like hell to me.

"Then how are you getting to school?"

"I already made plans with Margot. We're gonna get coffee before class," I lie, biting my lip and hoping that if he sees right through me, he doesn't care.

"I thought Margot can't drive," he questions, and the skin on my face turns beet red in an instant. *Shit.*

"She can't," I mutter. For once, it's the truth.

"Then who's driving you?" My father looks at me in a way that leads me to believe he's fully aware of how hard I'm trying to avoid this car ride with him—and disappointed that I'm trying to avoid it at all.

"Ren."

His name materializes out of nowhere. I almost cover my own mouth with my hands.

Am I really this desperate to escape my father's disapproval? Desperate enough to suggest that *Ren* would be giving me a ride, of all people? The boy whose name I haven't mentioned to my father since I was a child?

"Ren?" Dad looks just as surprised as I am, but I give him a sure nod. "McLellan?"

"Yes. There's only one Ren."

My father leans against his car, checking his watch. "I'll wait for him to get here then. I've got time."

I curse under my breath and turn around, pulling my flip phone out of my pocket. I open my messages and click on Margot's name.

EDDIE

> I need help

I tap my foot against the concrete anxiously, feeling my father's knowing gaze burn my neck. If Ren doesn't show, I know I'll never hear the end of this. He'll ask me why I was lying and he'll accuse me of a thousand things that are nowhere near the truth—the truth I'll never be able to tell him.

Or worse, he'll believe me and get angry at Ren for bailing. He knows the McLellan address. He'd give him a good talking to. I'd laugh at the idea if I wasn't freaking out, because he probably deserves it.

I wait and wait, but Margot doesn't answer, and I know what I must do to get out of this situation alive. I bite the inside of my cheek and reluctantly tap on a different name in the messages app.

EDDIE

need a favor

I shove my phone in my pocket, eagerly anticipating his response. My foot taps faster and I pray that Margot sees her phone before Ren does.

I'm surprised to hear the device beep in the back of my jeans, and I take it out once again. *Please be Margot, please be Margot.*

REN

a favor?

I swear inaudibly and reply.

EDDIE

yes

REN

why

EDDIE

idk

REN

Not an answer

EDDIE

i'm an idiot and i need a ride to school

REN

Much better.

What's in it for me?

EDDIE

that's a great thing to say to a girl keeping a secret

REN

That's a great thing to say to a guy who's also
keeping a secret

EDDIE

i'll buy you coffee?

REN

Coffee is bad for your immune system.

EDDIE

i'll buy you and margot a really fancy health food
smoothie

REN

You're maddening.

I can picture his glare so clearly.

REN

wait outside

I lock my phone, and a heavy sigh of relief escapes my lips. I turn around
and face my father again, trying to hide the smug look on my face as I wait
for Ren and Margot to arrive.

I find comfort in knowing that I've secured a ride, but at the same time,
I feel ridiculous. I can't blame Ren for our bad blood but that doesn't mean
I like the guy. Not enough to ask *him* for a favor, that's for sure.

But what other choice do I have? Mom carpools with her coworkers, and it's not like Milo can drive either.

Sure, Ren and I have our grudges. But our mutual distaste is nothing compared to the constant accusations I receive from my father. I can't see a car ride with Mateo Voclain going well any time soon.

I can't risk that. Not now. Not with the secrets I have to keep. I'll let something slip for sure.

My father and I continue to wait in silence. I hug my torso and shiver as morning air paints goosebumps up and down my exposed arms. It's an alarmingly gray day for the beginning of summer, but this region has always been fond of gray days.

"You forgot a jacket," my father says when he notices me shivering. He shakes his head, almost humorously. "Remember it next time. It's cold."

"She can borrow mine."

I whip my head to the left when I hear someone shout. A car door slams, and the owner of the voice walks up the driveway to approach us.

"Ren. Long time no see." Dad gives the boy a stoic nod.

I look around for Margot and frown when I see her waiting in the back seat of the car. While I can't blame her for wanting to save her energy, anything is bearable with her by my side. Even this.

"Hey, Mr. Voclain." Ren nods. He turns to me and points at his sweatshirt. "You need this?"

"I'm good," I respond plainly, resisting the urge to frown again.

There's no way I'm taking any additional help from Ren. I'm already uncomfortable enough as it is after asking him for a ride. Besides, there has to be a catch, right? He despises me, and that feeling is far from one-sided.

Yet here he is, agreeing to take me to school and save me from the wrath of my father's criticism. I should be thanking him, but the idea has a bad aftertaste.

"You sure you don't need a jacket? You're blue," my dad says. He removes his black wool work coat. "Here, take mine."

Funny, how he offers it to me now.

"I can just go back inside and get my own," I say. "Yours is too big."

"You're already out here, what's the point?" My father argues, using his facial expressions to signal that I'm being rude.

This is getting ridiculous. "Dad, it's fine."

My father shrugs and puts the jacket back on. I'm surprised he didn't threaten to ground me for being an embarrassment.

"Well, I'm running late for work." My dad checks his watch and climbs into the driver's seat of his SUV. He pauses before closing the door and driving off. "I'll see you kids later."

Ren and I stand there awkwardly as my father backs out of the driveway, leaving the two of us alone. I can't bring myself to look him in the eye, so I stare at my old running shoes instead.

"What was that about?" Ren asks. It's refreshing to know I'm not the only one who's uncomfortable around my strict father.

"Who cares?" I shrug apathetically. "It's nothing new, anyway."

I kick a stray chip of bark as I turn around to walk down the driveway. Ren follows me, catching up to my footsteps as we begin our trek down to the sidewalk. Our feet synchronize in silence, our breath simultaneously materializing in the form of clouds. The walk is a short one, but the absence of conversation makes it stretch on for decades.

I'm confused when Ren comes to a pause. I stop walking and raise a questioning eyebrow.

"Here."

Ren takes off his sweatshirt. It's a deep forest color, like the vast sea of evergreen this city was built around. My face warms foolishly as he pulls the crewneck over his torso, slightly lifting his white tee along with it. He extends a hand and waits for me to grab the sweatshirt. I don't know what to say.

"We don't have all day," Ren grumbles.

"I don't want it."

"Oh, don't give me that. You're shaking." He glares.

It's not that I don't want the sweatshirt. In fact, borrowing a warm sweater sounds a lot more appealing than spending the rest of the day with chattering teeth. I just don't want *his*.

I frown, untrusting. I keep trying to find some ulterior motive, some hidden agenda resting beneath his surface, but I cannot for the life of me find anything but kindness—and it freaks me out.

"Why?" I blurt. The question is vague, but Ren seems to understand what I'm asking.

"Because you're cold." His expression is momentarily plain, maybe even a little annoyed, but then I see the corner of his lips twitch into a grin. For a split second, it almost seems genuine, and part of me wishes he would smile like that more often. *Like he used to.*

"Thank you." I smile too.

I grab the sweatshirt from Ren's reach and slip it on. While the fabric is warm and relieves me from the morning's unforgiving elements, it's baggy on me. Ren may be thin, but he's a lot taller than I am and it shows now more than ever. The sweater drops to my knees but I have no complaints. It's comfortable and it holds the safe scent of the McLellan's all-natural laundry detergent. I pick up the soothing aroma of eucalyptus, peppermint, cedarwood, and other familiar notes I can't put my finger on.

And for some reason, it makes me feel safe.

He opens the door for me when we reach his old sedan. I hop into the passenger's seat and turn around to greet Margot, eager to communicate with her using silent facial expressions. But I turn right back around when I see her wiggle her eyebrows at me, and I flip her off as subtly as I can before Ren climbs in.

The car ride is not a memorable one. Ren and Margot exchange their typical chatter, but I'm quiet the entire time. I know it's unlikely, but I wonder if my dad was trying to be kind by taking my car to the shop last night and offering me a ride this morning. *There's no way Dad was just trying to be nice*, I conclude. He always has an agenda.

But Ren is surprising too.

He greets me at the house again the next morning with car keys in hand, ready to walk me down the driveway.

And the morning after that, and the morning after that, and the morning after that.

EDDIE

Friday, June 2
15 Days Until Training

"I can't believe it's all over," I tell Margot, taking a healthy gulp from my latte as I stare at the wall behind her.

"For you, not for me." She takes a sip of her tea and stares just as blankly as I do.

While we should be in the same grade, Margot was held back last year. She's the smartest person I know, but her brain fog gets in the way of academic achievement, and her attendance has never been the best—for obvious reasons.

I smile at her empathetically, but I know I will never truly understand what it feels like to have a brain like hers. A brain that's always on fire, a head that's always aching, a mind that always feels like it's slipping away. Her Lyme makes every day an unimaginable challenge, and that's exactly what I want to change.

"Are you scared?" Margot smirks, setting her teacup on the table.

I nearly choke, praying to whatever god will listen that she doesn't bring up my acceptance letter. "Of what?"

Dad is adjusting to his new role of proud father quite well. So well in fact, that he felt obligated to mail an Acceptance Card to everyone in his address book. It's a common custom, like a wedding announcement or a graduation photo, but I couldn't hate it more. He hired a photographer for a shoot and everything, and if the miserable look in my eye doesn't give away my secret, I don't know what will.

But the photograph on the card is the least of my worries. Now, everyone I know is involved in this lie that Ren and I have concocted.

It isn't just my lie anymore. It is both of ours. He is becoming a Chaser, and I am not, and we need each other to keep our truths a secret. If Margot confronts me about my acceptance, I don't know how well I'll be able to maintain my act.

"Graduation's tonight," she finally says, and I let out a sigh of relief.

"Oh. That." I pause. *Of course I'm scared.* "A little."

Margot and I come to Moon & Ground every Friday, but I feel out of place, like I am no longer myself. I'm more afraid than I used to be, more unsure than I've ever been. Chaser training starts in two weeks, and as it approaches, I have to start working extra hard to hide the fact that despite what everyone thinks, I didn't take the Chaser exam—but Ren did.

I have no idea what tomorrow will bring. Missions with Cedar, maybe. Diving deeper into the world of the Unseen, perhaps. Or maybe none of that at all.

My future is foggy because it's relying on maybes. Tonight is nothing but a bridge made of popsicle sticks, ready to collapse the second I take a step.

Once, I had everything planned out. I would conform to my father's expectations and exceed at school to have grades high enough to qualify for the Chaser exam. I would aim for the best so I could become the best. I was going to take the test and live a long life with a high-paying career, and my position would earn me Immunity for my immediate family. They would be protected from the Pick and every other Nightjade Order nightmare, and I would become a killer to make it all happen. I'd be a monster, but I'd have the closest possible thing to the white picket dream.

And then I grew up, and I realized how skewed my perspective was. How wrong it was to play God, to decide who gets to live and who doesn't.

The Chaser exam application deadline kept growing closer and closer, but I knew I couldn't take that mindless written test or undergo that stupid physical examination. I couldn't apply for the Chaser Corps. I couldn't become a killer. I still can't.

So I never took the test, and now Ren's name is listed in the applicant database instead of mine.

But what am I supposed to tell people when they ask me what I want to do instead? What career plan do I have to propose to my parents, to my brother and sister and classmates, and every other person who might ask? It's not like I can tell them I want to be part of the Unseen, or even a healer. That'll kill me for sure.

As I sit here in this familiar coffee shop with Margot, I feel like a stranger to myself. I'm an unlucky wolf in sheep's skin just waiting to be exposed, and the school year ending is nothing but a reality check I didn't ask for. I can feel myself crumbling, and I hope Margot doesn't notice.

"Eddie."

I'm pulled out of my thoughts when Margot tugs on my sleeve, eyes wide. I almost articulate my confusion verbally until she places a finger over her lips, gesturing toward the cash register with her chin. I turn around, unsure of what I'm looking for until I finally see it.

Not *it*, but *who*.

Standing at the cash register, dressed in white clothing from head to toe, is none other than Patrick Hale. The barista hands him a coffee without even asking him to pay.

"You're kidding," I mutter in disbelief, whipping my head back around to meet Margot's eyes. We exchange glances, speaking without speaking.

I remember Patrick, the freckled boy from my freshman English class. We were never friends or anything—he was too timid for my taste—but he always seemed like such a nice kid.

And now here he is, wearing white.

"You should go say hi," Margot encourages, forcing an unbelievable smile with the best intentions.

"Why would I do that?" I crinkle my nose.

"Because," she whispers, widening her eyes like I should already know the answer. "You'll see him at training, won't you? Maybe it'll be nice to have a friend."

I shake my head. I can tell she's trying so hard to be okay with what I claim to be doing and it hurts in a way I never expected.

"You seem too afraid for a person who claims to be so fearless."

I shrug. "I'm not afraid of him. He's a nice kid. Or, was. I guess." I shrug. "I just don't want to."

"It's okay. I get it." This time, the corners of her mouth lift naturally. She shrugs too and changes the subject. "Hey, why aren't *you* wearing white?"

When a Chaser or a trainee is out and about off duty, they have the choice to wear all white attire, a privilege no one else but a member of the Corps has access to.

Wearing the color as a civilian may as well be the equivalent of impersonating an Officer. So I wear a brown knit sweater and jeans because I'd rather avoid working to death at the tombs. But I can't tell Margot this, of course.

"Same concept as before," I reply, leaning back in my chair and picking at the tears in my jeans. "I don't want to."

"I thought you had to." Margot creases her brows.

I shake my head. "It's optional."

A Chaser doesn't have to wear white in public, but it lets people know about their authority, and they are given services they wouldn't otherwise receive. Like free coffee.

Margot holds her mother's old locket close to her chest. We watch Patrick as he makes his way toward the exit, coffee in hand. He pauses when he notices our stares. Margot's gaze flickers to her locket, but for a moment, mine remains. He sees my quiet questioning and he looks away.

Patrick walks out the door, vanishing into the gray evening air.

Margot lets out a sigh, staring off at something I cannot see. "Isn't it strange how people can turn so upside down?"

"Yeah." I glance at the door, and then study my cup of coffee. "Strange."

"What's with the face?" Margot asks as she takes another sip of tea, blinking herself out of the funk. I stir my coffee and avoid her gaze.

"I'm just—stressed. That's all." It's the truth, but it still feels like a lie.

"I get it," she says. "The future is daunting. Especially for you."

"Yeah." I give her an empty smile and chew on my straw.

"Is there something else going on?" she questions. "Something you haven't told me?"

"I tell you everything."

"We both know that's a lie," she says, and my heart skips a beat. "I don't tell you everything, and I know you leave things out too."

"What could you possibly have to hide from me?" I laugh.

"Lots of things," she teases. "There's something you're not telling me though."

"Oh *really*?" I lower my eyebrows. "Like what?"

"You're running away with Duke Carmody, aren't you?"

I burst out laughing. "I'd rather drop dead."

"You two are always talking though."

"*He's* always talking to *me*," I correct with crossed arms. "You of all people know how much I hate him."

"Well for someone who hates my brother so much, you sure have been fond of Ren recently."

I almost spit out my mouthful of coffee, and a bit of the iced beverage drips out of the corner of my mouth. I wipe it with the back of my sleeve and swallow the rest.

I can't say I'm surprised she picked up on our newfound interest in each other, but she can't know the truth behind it. Margot can never know what Ren and I are sacrificing for her; the guilt would be too much for her to handle. She would break.

It's not that Margot is weak, because she is not. In fact, she's the strongest person I know.

But for a person who already feels like she doesn't deserve to be alive, our secrets would only worsen her guilt. And if I can do anything to lighten the load off her shoulders, I will—even if it means I have to lie.

"Looks like I've hit a sore spot," Margot teases.

I shake my head. "You just surprised me, that's all."

"You guys aren't secretly in love or anything, right?" She winks at me, and the suggestion makes me laugh yet again.

"Margot." I set down my coffee. "I love you and all, but sometimes I have no idea what you're talking about."

"Oh please." She rolls her eyes and fidgets with her necklace, but she's not anxious. This is intriguing to her. "You know exactly what I'm talking about."

"I don't."

"You most definitely do."

"I think your tea was spiked."

I'm confused when she picks up my backpack and hauls it onto her lap, struggling to zip open the overstuffed bag but managing anyway. My face is beet red when she pulls out Ren's sweatshirt and throws it at me.

"Okay, I—" I stutter, internally praying that she doesn't mistake my reaction for a different kind of blush.

"Ed, you've been carrying this around for days. Ever since he gave it to you." She folds her arms and gives me a look, that same knowing look she always gives me whenever we both know she's right. But for once, she's got it all wrong.

"Well, I just haven't found the right time to give it back to him yet. That's all." I look down at my coffee and swirl the spoon in circles.

"You're so dumb."

"What?" I laugh. "I haven't. It's the truth."

"You're not sneaky, you know." She rolls her eyes. "You can't hide things from me. You're the worst liar."

"Thanks."

"You realize that you could have given it to me ages ago and it wouldn't have been awkward at all, right? 'Cause I could have just handed it over to him. We borrow things from each other all the time anyway. He probably wouldn't have even noticed it was the one he gave you." She gives me the look again. The mind-reading, all-knowing look that makes me feel guiltier than ever.

"Well..." I can't finish my sentence. I keep stirring my coffee, watching the spoon dance with the milky foam.

"You wanna know what I think?"

"Probably not."

"Hush, this is what I'm here for." She gulps the rest of her tea before setting the cup down. "I think you've been planning on using this sweatshirt as an excuse to talk to him, and possibly discuss the absurd grudge you've both been holding for so long."

"It's not like he doesn't have a grudge against me either!" I argue. "He's not as perfect as he pretends to be."

"So I was right?" Margot smirks, and I sigh. She can't be right, but for some reason, her words feel more accurate than ever.

It's not like the plan she mentioned is entirely out of the question, but it's not something I've been entirely conscious of either. Using the sweatshirt as a conversational excuse is simply a strategy, nothing more. But there's a reason why I never followed through with it. A reason why I kept the sweatshirt and still keep it close.

"What's keeping you from giving it back?" Margot asks.

"I don't know."

"Are you scared of rejection?"

"Rejection?" I scoff. "Do clarify."

"I don't know—of him not being receptive to what you have to say, I guess. We both know how hard it is for him to open up to people."

I shrug.

"Are you scared of ruining things between you and him? I mean they seem pretty ruined already, but they could be a lot worse."

I nod, because she's not wrong. Whether we like it or not, Ren and I need to work together if we truly want to help Margot, and we can't do that effectively without addressing this bad blood between us.

But I'm terrified of reopening old wounds. I've spent all these years trying to forget what happened that day, and Ren has spent every moment since then making sure we both remember it well. He saw what really happened. He knows what I did, and he still hasn't forgiven me for it.

"Hey." Margot's words are soft now. "I love you Eddie, okay? I would never lie to you or tell you anything that isn't true."

Her words are sweet, but they conjure up a kind of guilt that leaves a sour taste in my mouth. She reaches out and holds my hand across the table. Her fingers are always so cold.

"Ren is... smart. Capable. He's cautious and reserved and suspicious of people. And you?" She lifts my chin with her finger. "You're smart and capable too, but you're also reckless. You're lovably outgoing and outrageously irrational and so many things all at once. And I think... well, Ren isn't usually drawn to people like that."

I'm not sure where she's going with the conversation and I feel my heart sink. I know she's right to think these things about me. She knows what I did too—she was there, and she paid for it. She lied and defended my name, even after everything that happened. But Ren was not so quick to forgive. He still hasn't forgiven me, and I doubt he ever will.

I know we need to get over our past for the sake of Margot's future. But how can I ask him to forgive me? How can things go back to the way they used to be when all I do is take and take and take without giving anything in return?

"You're too much." Ren's old words echo in my head. *"You just love falling off that ledge, but you never stop to think about who is taken with you."*

"But you're different, Ed," Margot continues, and my train of thought is put on pause. "You're all the things he's not, and—I don't know. I think he likes that about you."

"*Like* isn't a word I would have chosen." I let out a dry laugh. "Try something like *hate*."

"He doesn't hate you, Eddie."

I shake my head, chuckling bitterly. "You don't know that side of him like I do. The side that's so"—I choke on the words, flashed with a memory of my old betrayal—"ashamed of me."

It's quiet for a moment until Margot speaks again.

"Even after everything, he doesn't hate you," she repeats softly. "Maybe he knows it and maybe he doesn't, but he forgave you a long time ago. I think part of him now just feels guilty for holding you to such impossible standards."

She pauses. "He's ashamed of himself, not you."

I stare at the refurbished wood table where my elbows rest, noticing its grain. Although the material has changed so much from its original state, the pattern is still the same as the inside of any old tree. It's so different from what it used to be, but it's still the same at its core. It's still wood.

Ren is still Ren, and I am still Eddie.

I raise my head to look at Margot, resting my chin on the top of my palms. She mirrors me and we sit in a knowing kind of silence. We smile at each other, and I think about just how valuable she is. Margot has been a part of my world for as long as I can remember, bearing these unlucky Joker Cards by my side with no complaints. I would do everything and anything for her all at once if I had to.

It's in this magical coffee shop of ours that I come to realize my fundamental truth: I never want to imagine a life without Margot McLellan in it, because I cannot survive without her.

"Thank you." I give her a soft smile.

"Always." Margot grins too.

"We should head back." I rise to my feet and offer Margot a hand. "I have a big day ahead of me. You know, with this sweatshirt I have to return."

There was a river only a few minutes out of town. Once, it was nothing but bones, a dry bed of rocks rounded by time, a sleeping ground for things that once were. But the water came back eventually.

It was not as powerful as it was during the Yesterdays, but it was still a river nonetheless, a mirror of vibrant emeralds and the coveted cerulean of a summer sky. Once, Margot and I did not crane our necks to watch the clouds. We were children who found them in the water's reflection, too young to be afraid of the faces that stared right back.

"It's so hot today," Ren complained as we walked. He was usually the one to point out problems, but I didn't care about the heat.

We were barefoot, though we didn't mind the pine needles and dirt; Asa made sure we were all used to the outdoors. He often told us stories about his own childhood. He was born after the Yesterdays, but before people truly gave up on seeking out nature. He spent his younger years playing in the river as we did. He often mentioned how he and the twins' mother used to go camping all the time before they had children, and this is what sparked the McLellans' interest in the world outside. Being such close friends with Ren and Margot, I was bound to fall in love with nature too.

"I'm so glad school is out for the year. We could go to the river every day." I giggled, holding Margot's hand as we carefully walked down the rocky slope from the parking lot to the river bank. The stones were smooth and sturdy, like a bunch of oversized gray chicken eggs. I remember how they felt beneath our toes—and how it seemed like we could slip any moment.

"Every day?" Asa chuckled. "That would be a lot of swimming."

"Exactly!" I exclaimed, and Ren and I exchanged enthusiastic glances. Margot smiled too.

"I guess your parents made a wrong turn, Ed," Asa announced, checking his phone. "So you big kids have some time to play before the little one joins you."

"Yes!" I exclaimed. "Does that mean we can jump off the rock? Just once?"

"Just once." Asa chuckled. "You three better be careful though. Remember the rules we talked about last time?"

"Jump one at a time, wait for your turn, and no pushing." Ren beamed, proud of his memory.

"Good job, buddy." Asa ruffled Ren's hair before the boy swatted the hand away.

"Are you gonna jump with me and Ren?" I questioned with excitement, turning to Margot as we stopped at an adequate spot by the shore. She shrugged sadly.

"Margot's feeling a little carsick. I think she'll sit out this time," Asa mentioned with an apologetic smile.

"Aw, what? That's no fun."

"Can I just go swimming, Dad?" Margot looked up at her father. "I won't go on the rock, I promise."

Asa blinked, like Margot said something funny.

"Are you sure you're feeling up for that, hon?" Asa asked, concern growing on his face as he spread out a beach towel. He set our bags on the soft surface and sat down.

"Yes. I'm not feeling carsick anymore, I swear."

Asa paused for a moment, staring at his daughter before letting out a sigh.

"I guess that's okay. No rock for you though, just swimming. Got it?"

"Yes!" Margot and I cheered in unison, but Ren and Asa seemed to be a bit uneasy.

"Hey Eddie!" Ren piped up as we waded into the water. The liquid was icy against our little legs, but it felt nice to be in the river again. "Wanna have a contest? Margot will stay behind and judge."

"For what?"

"To see who can do the coolest jump." Ren grinned from ear to ear. "I bet it'll be me."

"No way! It'll be me for sure."

"Prove it!"

The three of us giggled as Ren and I swam to the rock. It was less of a rock and more like a small cliff, but it was just small enough for us to climb. Dips in the rock served as a convenient staircase that made our climb to the top easy. Ren was already taller than me and finished the climb first, and he offered his hand out to help once I approached the top.

"I don't need your help!" I completed the task without assistance.

"Okay then." Ren laughed. He turned around and approached the edge, staring down at the deep water below. I pulled myself up and stood behind him to wait. Jump one at a time, wait for your turn, and no pushing. *Ren's voice echoed in my head, but I shoved the thought aside. The world had too many rules as it was, and they took all the fun away.*

"Are you guys ready?" I nearly fell over when I heard Margot's voice—right as Ren made his jump and landed safely with a splash.

I whipped my head around to my left to see that she had climbed up the rock against her father's wishes. She put a finger to her lip to tell me to keep quiet, and she pointed to the shore to show me that Asa was distracted by his book.

"Margot!" Ren hissed from below. It was loud enough for us to hear, but soft enough to not draw Asa's attention. "You're not supposed to be up there!"

"Shh!" She hushed her brother silently. He swam around the side, struggling to quickly make his way toward the cliff to climb up and meet us.

My gaze switched from Ren to Margot when I heard a strange noise escape her lips. She was breathing heavily, and her face was a ghastly green. The color had completely drained from her lips, and she looked as though she just ran a marathon. What's wrong with her?

"*You don't look too well,*" *I noticed.*

"*I'm okay,*" *Margot replied, and I shrugged it off.* If she says she's okay, she's okay. Right?

"*You have to jump! Before your dad sees. Quick!*" *I giggled, holding her hand and leading her to the edge.*

"*Okay!*" *she exclaimed, her breathing still so heavy.* "*Just a second. Let me catch my breath.*"

But her breath was never caught. No matter how long she stood there with her eyes shut and her hands on her knees, she could not put an end to the battle between her and her own lungs. She looked miserable. Nothing a little fun can't fix, right? *That will make her feel better for sure.*

"*Aren't you gonna jump?*" *I asked. Margot stared at the dark water below and took a few steps back.*

"*I want to, but I don't know. Now that I'm up here I'm not so sure I can,*" *she said with a nervous smile.* I've never seen her like this.

"*Of course you can,*" *I encouraged.*

She shook her head no.

"*What happened to the fun, Margot?*" *I pestered teasingly, but I was frustrated. I thought we came to the river to escape all the rules and restrictive things at home—not to be scared and boring. I was always scared. I needed a break.*

She didn't say anything, so I kept going. "*You never do anything fun with me anymore. You used to be so brave.*"

That seemed to hurt Margot, but she reacted with a forced smile. "*I'll try to be brave.*"

She approached the edge again, getting as close as she possibly could without tumbling over. She stared at the water as if it were a gaping monster jaw waiting to gobble her up. The smaller rocks near the base of our perch looked like little teeth, and Margot was frightened of the beast.

But it wasn't a beast. It was just water, and she needed to get over her fear. Maybe that's what this is about, *I thought.* Maybe she just needs to push through the scary parts and believe in herself. That will help her, right?

And with that, I pushed her off the edge.

She didn't scream as she fell, and I peered over the ledge with a grin. I knew she could do it! She's swimming back to shore now.

But something was wrong. She wasn't swimming at all. She was struggling to come back up to the surface; she was struggling to breathe, struggling to overcome this new weakness that I would not understand until later.

She was going to drown.

"Margot!" *Ren called. He was already halfway up the cliff, but he jumped off the side as soon as he saw her struggling, breaking the rules he was so proud of keeping. He swam as fast as he could, but it wasn't fast enough. Margot was not moving by the time he reached her.*

I wanted to scream. I wanted to jump into the water and help Ren save her, but I couldn't move a muscle. I was frozen by my guilt and struck dumb with a feeling I had never felt so strongly before: fear.

Not the fear I felt whenever my dad yelled at me, whenever he told me to shut up for simply trying to explain how I was feeling, whenever he talked about what I needed to do when I grew up and made Mom cry.

This was something else entirely.

A moment before, I was angry at Margot for being so scared. But then I felt that fear myself.

I was afraid of the guilt gnawing at my insides. I was afraid of the instant regret I felt for breaking Asa's rules, for pushing Margot past her limits and straight off the edge. I was afraid of losing the one person I loved more than anything else in the world.

I was still on the rock long after Ren dragged Margot to shore. I was still when she coughed up water and explained to her father that she jumped, and I was still when Ren tried to argue that I pushed her. I could barely hear the conversation from where I was, but it was just audible enough. I could hear Margot defending me.

I don't remember when I climbed down. I swam back to shore without saying a word, and I was still devoured by terror when I reached dry land. Asa pulled Ren and me aside. He explained that no one was there to listen to what he had to say; there were no mics in the woods. I was confused, but then he told me something I could never say to anyone. It was the first secret I ever kept.

He told me I couldn't mention this accident to a single person, not even my parents. I could never say a word about Margot's inexplicable weakness—about how the heat made her too sick to function correctly. How she was too weakened by the climb to save herself from the fall.

Asa took his daughter to meet a healer in the woods, a man who knew about sicknesses like hers.

Margot had chronic Lyme disease and two co-infections, and her life depended on that fact remaining a secret. We deserved to know the truth, he said, and we needed to help him protect her. He instructed us to pretend like we forgot it all, to never speak of it again.

But Ren could not forget, and he realized a different truth on that important day.

"You're not good enough for Margot anymore. You're too much," Ren whispered to me as my family arrived in my dad's car. We all pretended like nothing happened. Margot was simply carsick.

"You just love falling off that ledge, but you never stop to think about who is taken with you."

REN

Friday, June 2
15 Days Left of Being Human

♪ ARE YOU - THE DELTA SAINTS ♪

I'm blinded.

The lights are stronger than I am, and I'm weakened by their crippling glare. For a moment, I see nothing at all, and then suddenly I'm shaking someone's hand and walking down the steps with a rolled-up piece of paper in my grasp. I'm back in that icy metal chair before I can blink. And when I do blink, the crowd is screaming and throwing things in the air, and I can't bring myself to follow their footsteps.

I hate that I'm here. But even more, I hate that Margot's not.

It feels wrong to graduate without her by my side. I know the event would have been too much for her to handle—the sitting, the standing, the lights, the smells, the sounds—everything. It would all make her symptoms so much worse, and she would have been vomiting all night if she didn't faint during the event itself.

I know she would much rather stay at home with Dad, but I still feel empty. Like I'm cheating somehow because I wasn't the one who got sick.

As I stand here beneath these blinding football lights, I miss my other half. This night feels more like a betrayal than a victory.

The world does cartwheels around me. I'm not sure where to turn or what to look at. The air is thick with a heavy coat of toxic cologne, laundry soap poison, and cheap perfume, and I resist the urge to cover my nose with my red gown. How inconsiderate to drench yourself in things that make the people around you sick. *This is why Margot cannot be here.*

And then someone grabs my arm. The hand leads me through the commotion and I'm pulled out of my apathetic trance, squinting to make out the face in the bright shadow of the football lights. And then I see her.

Heart-shaped cheeks, button nose, well-defined dimples that crease her skin every time she grins. I don't want to smile, especially now, and especially not with her. But for some reason, it's hard to keep the corner of my mouth from twitching into a small grin. In this claustrophobic crowd of strangers, I'm saved by her familiarity. *I can exhale.*

Eddie looks up at me, her gaze tired. "Can we get out of here?"

I nod, widening my eyes to let her know just how much I agree with the proposed escape. She grins and leads me through the chaos.

We abandon the crowd and make our way to the edge of the football field, dodging hugging families and rowdy students as we head away from the designated exits, away from the immobilizing lights and sounds that haunt the lawn we leave behind. The only illumination at the back edge of the field is provided by the moon, the same silver haze that traces Eddie's shape in the dark.

She drops my hand, studying her sneakers as we walk along the asphalt track that curves toward the fence. "You're in shock too, huh?"

I shrug. "It feels weird doing this without her."

"You're acting as if she's like—I don't know, dead or something."

"Sorry."

"You never actually do anything *without her*, dummy." She nudges my shoulder. "She's just not standing right next to you, that's all."

Dummy. She hasn't called me that since we were little, and while it disgusts me, the insult feels familiar. It's a warmth too pleasant for my liking.

I notice that her other hand is curled in a fist, like she's holding something.

Curious, I stop walking. "What's that?"

"This?" Eddie opens her fist. A delicate gold chain pools in her palm, decorated with a few small charms I can't see from my distance. I nod. "Oh, it's nothing, really. My dad gave me this bracelet and I couldn't figure out how to put it on."

I take a step closer, pointing to the bracelet. "Mind if I..."

She nods. "Sure. Go ahead."

I pluck the bracelet from her palm and immediately wish I hadn't. The charms are green, like little emeralds. "This looks expensive."

"I'm sure it was," Eddie mutters.

I raise a brow as I wrap the chain around her wrist. "You don't sound too happy about it."

"I don't know. It just feels a little showy to me, that's all." She chuckles bitterly. "Like it's less for me and more for him, you know?"

I nod, struggling to open the bracelet's claw with my gnawed-down fingernails. "Maybe he was just trying to be nice."

"My dad? Nice?"

I nod again, still struggling with the bracelet. "He is your dad, after all. And you just graduated. It's an important night."

"He wouldn't have given me this if he didn't think I was becoming"— Eddie stops herself—"one of them."

A Chaser, I finish for her without speaking.

Eddie lets out a sigh. "He's only proud of me because he thinks I'm meeting his expectations."

"You really don't think—"

"You don't know him like I do, okay?" Eddie snaps, shooting me a cold glare.

"Okay fine, maybe I don't." I scowl right back. "I'm just making conversation, alright?"

"Stupid conversation."

"Hey, I'm trying to do you a favor here."

"Sorry."

I hesitate. "Sorry. I'm being an ass."

"It's fine."

I finally manage to clasp one end of the chain to the other. But I do it wrong somehow and the bracelet falls to the ground. "Shit. Sorry." We keep saying so many sorries that it's starting to get on my nerves.

Eddie grins falsely, clearly amused by my mistake. "Good job."

I don't bother rolling my eyes as I pick up the bracelet and attempt to clasp it together once more. This time, it works. I pull my hand away and clear my throat.

We start walking again. Eddie fidgets with the fabric of her gown. She doesn't seem to be looking at anything in particular, and I can tell she's just avoiding my gaze. She always acts so foolishly unafraid of everything, but she can't bring herself to look me in the eye.

And then she does, and now I'm the one who can't seem to hold contact.

"I forgot to congratulate you," I blurt awkwardly to put an end to the silence, clearing my throat.

She scoffs. "For what?"

"What do you think?" I glare.

"Oh. The speech."

"Yeah. *That.*"

She shrugs, as though being valedictorian is nothing but a task she can check off her to-do list, like making her bed or pouring herself a cup of coffee. It's like she's wired to be unfazed by her accomplishments and I cannot understand it.

"It was good," I mutter, looking off to the side. If I wasn't wearing this awful blood-red gown, I would shove my hands in my pockets.

"Thanks."

"You don't seem to agree with me."

"My dad did some... heavy editing." Eddie chuckles bitterly as we walk along the track. "And by that, I mean he pretty much had complete creative control."

"Yeah?"

"It's okay though. I didn't really put much effort into the whole thing anyway."

"Why not?"

"Well..." She sighs, her breath forming tendrils of moonlit smoke. "I just

—I don't know. I knew I could never say what I really wanted to say, for obvious reasons."

I nod.

Eddie kicks a stray pebble out of her path, and then she sighs. "I would have talked about her."

I bite my lip. "I know."

We reach the fence at the other end of the football field. It's dark over here, almost peaceful, save for the pestering echoes of some nearby house party. I turn to look at Eddie, but to my surprise, she's already climbed halfway up the wooden structure.

"What?" she says when she notices me staring. "Too scared?"

"Don't you have somewhere to be?"

"Told my dad I was invited to a party or something." Eddie chuckles and drops to the other side. Her sneakers land softly on the sidewalk that lines the normally quiet neighborhood next to our school. I can still hear her voice, but now we're separated by slabs of lumber.

"Well, were you?" I walk closer to the fence so I can hear her speak.

"Technically, yes." I can tell she's rolling her eyes by the sound of her voice alone.

"Let me guess—Duke Carmody?" I tease, but I'm just as disgusted by the guy as she is.

She taps a triplet into the fence with her fingers. "Ding ding ding."

"Well, are you planning on attending said party?" I ask, taking an additional step.

"I don't think so." Eddie's voice sounds closer. I wonder if she's nearing the fence too.

"Any other plans for the evening? Adventures to embark upon? People to meet?"

There's a pause.

"Nope," Eddie finally says. "None at all."

She's smiling—I can tell.

I'm touching the fence now, palms and forehead pressed against the panels. I know she's doing the same. I can hear her breathing.

The night traces my skin with cold fingers. Somewhere there is laughter, the clinking of glasses, the snapping of cameras, the cry of a songbird, the falling of a leaf so quiet no one can hear it happen at all. A serpentine breeze filters between us, past us, through us, wrapping around my neck before slithering over the fence and away for good. I can smell red cedarwood lumber and the lemon in her hair.

It's strange to think about how close we are, how she could be standing right in front of me and still feel so far away.

I lost her. Not when she climbed over the fence, not even when she stumbled across my acceptance letter and discovered who I'll soon become. I won't lose her two weeks from now when training knocks on our doorstep like the Grim Reaper himself, because I lost her long before that.

I pushed her away.

But here we are, touching through rotten and splintered wood. And with it, I am reconnected with something so painfully familiar. Blinded by the fence, I see the same girl I used to know—and she's hidden in the girl who stands before me.

There is a new guilt tying my gut in knots. A guilt for not seeing her sooner. For growing so distant, for losing hope in the person I used to believe in so fiercely. A moment ago I thought she was lost, but maybe she's been here all along.

I can't see her at all—and I see her clearer than ever.

"I'm sorry."

I speak to the dark, my voice soft, almost a whisper. I wonder if Eddie can hear me and part of me prays that she can't.

A response doesn't arrive, and for a moment I wonder if she walked away. *Have I said something wrong?* Could two words ever carry such a weight?

And then Eddie replies, her voice even softer than mine. "Me too."

"You were just a kid, Ed." I'm whispering now. "You were just a kid."

A silence lingers in the air around us. I can feel it weighing down on my shoulders and I want to curl up and hide. But I know I can't hide anymore. If I want Eddie to trust me enough to keep my secret, I have to trust her too.

Part of me wants to climb over the fence. I want to look at her, to actually see her standing in front of me. I want to apologize for every wrong thing. I want to explain my actions and explain this secret of mine and let her know that I'm not a Chaser at heart, and I never will be—even if I must step into that role out of obligation alone.

I'm not a monster, I promise. I just have to pretend to be one.

But the other part of me wants time to stop. I want to remain here behind this divide, hidden just a little longer.

So I don't climb to meet her. I stay put, forehead touching hers through the fence, closing my eyes to inhale, exhale, and be present in this rare moment of peace that—for some reason beyond my own understanding—I never want to end.

"I knew you were sorry the second Margot fell," I say, and Eddie listens. "I saw it in your eyes. I still see it."

She doesn't say a word.

I choke as the sentence falls out. "You love her more than anything, and I was too ignorant to see that."

"Ren, I—" She pauses, like she's trying to find the words.

No, please don't say anything, I think, eyes closed. *Just let this be. Let me hide for a little bit longer.*

For a piece of time, I believe my wish is granted. I inhale the cedarwood and the lemon of her hair and pray that for once, the world has been put on pause. And then Eddie whispers.

"Can you come here?"

I hesitate, not wanting to move, but I do. I hoist my feet on the lower wood bar and bring the rest of my body over the top. A splinter stabs its way into the flesh of my palm, and I grimace when I land.

"Splinter?" she questions, staring at my hand.

"Yeah."

"I got one too."

Eddie shows me her own in the moonlight, a careless smile curling her lips.

Without thinking, I reach out. Slowly. Softly. My fingers meet hers and I pull her hand close, turning it over to inspect the wound. But I don't see it, not in this darkness. So I trace the lines of her palm until I feel it. Her skin is smooth, and to my own confusion, I'm almost disappointed when I find the splinter easily.

I'm mindfully gentle as I remove the piece of wood, but she winces anyway. "Sorry."

"It's okay." Her hand remains in mine.

Disgustingly, I can't bring myself to let go.

Wordless, we stand still for a moment until she turns my hand over. I feel her trace my palm the same way I traced hers, searching for a splinter in the dark.

"Found it." She's not as gentle as I was and I cringe as she yanks it out of my skin. I give her a glare. "Sorry."

"You should be." I sigh. "I'll never forgive you."

I can feel her smiling up at me, though she tries to hide it.

She doesn't let go either. Instead, her grin transforms into a mischievous smirk, and I'm taken by surprise as she leads me by the hand again. "Follow me."

I stumble down the sidewalk in the wake of her footsteps, trying not to trip. She's a lot shorter than I am, but it's still difficult to keep up with her confident pace.

Aside from the shuffling of our shoes against the concrete, the only sound is the distant hum of that party and the lost echo of creek frogs calling out into the night. I open my mouth to ask where she's taking me, but I pause when I see it.

Concrete turns into grass and grass turns into sand, and we find ourselves approaching the neighborhood's playground. A rusty dome breaks through the center of the sand, so much smaller than I remember it to be. In the back there is a swing set, and off to the side, a castle-like structure equipped with a scuffed yellow slide, flat and wide like the tongue of a beast.

"Remember this place?" She beams at me, answering my internalized questions with a grin.

My lips twitch. "Of course I do."

"This thing!" Eddie walks up to the climbing dome and touches its chipped metal bars. I follow her as she explores the places we used to know so well, like she's meeting it all for the first time. "And this thing and this thing and this thing and—"

"What?"

"The slide." She points at the tallest structure, her finger drawing over its shape in the air.

I shake my head as she begins to climb the structure's twisting stairs. I'm not sure why I want to join her on this strange little adventure of hers, but my height poses an issue, so I watch instead. I couldn't climb the steps without hitting my head on something.

But Eddie is suitably unafraid. Only a few inches above five feet, she's the perfect fit for her escapade's size requirements, and makes her way to the top with ease.

"Are you coming?" she asks impatiently.

"No."

"Come on."

"No," I repeat robotically.

She's perched at the top of the slide, hugging her knees and smiling down at me. She's taken off her cap and gown and now she's sporting a familiar forest green sweatshirt and black jeans. I don't follow her up the stairs of the structure, but I walk under the slide and hold onto its grimy plastic side to look at her. I take off my cap and gown too, watching the silky red cloth fall to the sand like blood.

"This is your sweatshirt, you know." She pulls at the fabric with a nervous laugh. "Sorry for being so—forgetful. I was gonna give it back to you today but I got cold."

"I don't mind," I say. "Keep it."

"No."

"It suits you better."

"It does not."

"Really." I lower my voice. I want to look at my shoes, but I keep my eyes fixed on her instead. "It looks good on you."

Everything is black and white in the lateness of the hour, but I can tell her cheeks are flushed with color.

But I meant what I said. She makes me want to pull my hair out, but I've seen her wearing it before, and I'm not that blind. I've noticed the way she keeps her arms tucked within its baggy sleeves, the way the green brings out the best of her eyes. She makes it seem as though it's been hers all along, like she's known it for longer than she has. She's like that with people too.

It's in the way she holds herself, the way she looks at you with such familiarity it feels a bit like home, no matter how maddening she can be.

In all she is, Eddie has a way of traveling back in time to meet people far before they meet themselves.

"I have a question for you," she says out of the blue, pulling me from my thoughts.

"Okay."

She hesitates, fidgeting with her thumbs. Something flutters above our heads, and she eyes the bat's flickering appearance before it weaves between the arms of a distant redwood, disappearing within its branches. Eddie stares at the empty space above her head that the creature left behind for a long time before she finally opens her mouth again.

"Why did Margot defend me that day?"

I'm taken aback by the inquiry, and I blink a few times to register the question. Why did Margot defend her that day?

It's a question I've asked myself so many times over the years. Eddie was the one who pushed her off the rock, and even after nearly drowning, Margot swore she had jumped herself, loyal beyond all limits.

"Well, I'm not entirely sure," I say, struggling to find an answer. "We never really talked about it."

Eddie sighs with disappointment, and it hurts me a little.

"I have a guess though," I add.

"Yeah?"

"Somehow, she's figured out how to understand Lavender Voclain," I explain. "She knows how much she means to you because you mean just that much to her."

I can barely make out her face in the moonlight, but I think Eddie smiles.

"So what about you?" she asks.

"What?"

"Don't you have a question for me?"

"No."

"Seriously? You don't have a single thing to ask? Not even one?"

"Nope," I tease, but it's a lie. I'm full of questions I can't pinpoint.

"There's no time like the present, Ren. It's quiet. No one's around. There are many questions one could ask." Eddie spreads her arms out wide, gesturing to the emptiness of the playground where we reside.

"Oh really?" I give her a doubtful look. "Like what?"

"Aren't you curious about my favorite color? My deepest darkest secret?"

"I already know both of those."

She throws a stray twig in my direction.

"Okay, fine." I shake my head. *I'll ask something dumb.* "Why do you go by Eddie and not Lavender?"

She glares.

"I mean, Lavender's a solid name," I continue. "It's unique. It's a suitably beautiful flower and I've never understood why you refuse to use it."

Eddie shrugs. "I don't know."

"We both know you know."

"Fine. But it's nothing meaningful, really." Her eyes roll. "It's just what Milo used to call me when he was learning to talk. It stuck for everyone else too, I guess." She looks at her feet as she sits on the top of the slide, preoccupied with other thoughts. "Except for my dad."

"Oh."

"He only calls me Lavender and I hate it," she says, staring at her fidgeting hands before looking up at me with the smallest hint of a grin. "I don't mind when you call me Lavender, though."

I suppress a grin as I watch Eddie straighten out her legs, gliding down the slide like she did when we were children. I stare at her in disbelief, wondering how she manages to keep such an energetic disposition, even in a situation like ours.

Even without the weight of our secrets bringing her down, her life is not an easy one. Yeah, she's not sick. Her parents are both alive and well. But she's expected to prove her own validity to her father constantly, and I know his mistreatment affects Eddie more than she'll ever admit.

And yet here she is, sliding down a children's playground structure like there's no wrong in the world. I assume she wants me to meet her at the end.

But I never get to meet her there—because a new voice calls out from across the playground.

"Is that Lavender Voclain?" the voice shouts in the dark.

I freeze when I realize that the words belong to the one and only Duke Carmody.

I smell a cigarette and I can tell he's walked closer. I can see him from here, but I remain hidden behind the slide.

"So you did decide to come to my party after all." He stops when he's close enough and blows a puff of smoke into the crisp night air, bragging his Immunity with every breath. Nightjade laws banned cigarettes long ago, but not for those who pay to be exceptions to the rule. And what is Duke Carmody if not that?

"You're delusional," Eddie spits as she sits at the end of the slide.

"I'm serious. My house is right around the corner." He pauses and points to his ear. "You hear that?"

He's not lying. We're just far enough from the graduation scene to enjoy a bit of peace and quiet, but the atmosphere would be a lot calmer without the obnoxious murmur of music and laughter in the distance.

"What are you doing here, Duke?" Eddie says.

"Just taking a walk, that's all." He tosses his cigarette in the sand and stomps it out, wiping his hands and placing them in his pockets with a sense of informality that makes me uncomfortable.

"Can you take your walk somewhere else, please? Thanks." Eddie's tone is bland and flavorless. She's quickly running out of patience, and I am too.

"So, what brings you out here all alone?" Duke questions, ignoring her request. My brows crease with confusion. *Does he really not see me?*

"Like that's any of your business." She scoffs.

"Can I make it my business?"

"No."

"Oh, c'mon, Ed." Duke throws his hands up in the air before letting them drop back down. "You're so—"

"Don't call me *Ed*."

"—that."

"I'm so *what*?"

"Bitter. Rude. Aggressive."

"Wow, that's a fantastic way to approach a conversation. Just keep calling me names and I'm sure your presence will become substantially more tolerable."

"What's your problem?"

"You." Eddie crosses her arms tightly against her chest. "Now can you please go? I'm kind of in the middle of something."

"What? Sitting here, moping all by yourself? Is that what you're so eager to get back to?" Duke snickers.

"Sure. Whatever. See you later." She waves sarcastically.

"Couldn't you use a little company?" the boy says, sitting down next to her at the edge of the slide. His words sound insincere. "I don't know—someone to talk to?"

"I'm fine."

"You sure about that?"

"I'm very sure."

Duke inches closer, and I can tell it makes Eddie uncomfortable. I almost come out of hiding to put an end to this, but I catch myself because I know it would only cause some sort of conflict. Duke would provide us with some of his wonderful commentary, Eddie would articulate her rejection —it would all push him even closer to some reactionary edge and I would rather avoid that at all costs.

I've seen him get into fights at school, sometimes over something as frivolous as a dirty look. And the other kids can't fight back, of course, unless they're Immune too. He fights brutally, limitless in his drive to get what he wants. And he does. He gets what he wants because he respects no boundaries.

And I know Eddie will be offended if I underestimate her. She can handle herself, right?

"Have I ever told you how beautiful you are?" Duke asks, and Eddie glares. His tone is softer, but not kinder. "Because you are. You know, beautiful."

"Does it look like I give a damn?"

My legs twitch. I'm so close to walking out from behind this slide, to put an end to this increasingly uncomfortable conversation and give Duke a piece of my mind. But I know Eddie can take care of herself. I want her to know I'm aware of just how capable she is.

Regardless, I don't like the way he's looking at her. I shove my hands in my pockets, fidgeting with my thumbs.

"I've always had a thing for you, ya know," Duke claims. "You're smart. Pretty. Bold."

This is getting pathetic.

"I don't care what you think of me, I want you to go." Eddie's voice doesn't quake.

"Admit it." Duke leans closer and chuckles. "You've had a thing for me too."

She's silent again. Eddie has run out of things to say, and I can practically feel her impatience growing stronger. He inches closer, she inches away.

"Duke—"

"I'm not wrong, am I?" he says. He leans his face closer to Eddie's, slowly moving his lips toward her own.

"Duke," Eddie says through clenched teeth. The boy pauses, puzzled by the idea of someone being uninterested in his false charm.

"I need you to go."

Now Duke is the one who doesn't say anything. I exhale, relieved by how unintimidated Eddie is. He'll leave soon because he can't stay for too long with a broken ego.

But then the atmosphere changes, and it sends shivers down my spine.

"You know..." Duke laughs in a way that makes the air around us grow colder. "There's something so—interesting, about growing up in an Immune household."

There's a pause for a moment. While the party is still going on somewhere in the background, it somehow feels quiet, as though everything has been put on pause.

"At a young age, you learn to take advantage of your privilege—the privilege you pay a whole lot of money to deserve. You can say things other people can't. You can do things other people couldn't dream of. You're almost untouchable by the law. And it's all because"—he leans to whisper into Eddie's ear—"there are no consequences for people like me. I can sit here for as long as I want, and I can say whatever I want."

"Go," Eddie seethes. "I swear I'll slap you in the face if you don't leave right now."

"You see..." Duke lets out another cold laugh. "I don't really want to."

I feel my sense of calm slipping away. Who the hell does this guy think he is, talking about Immunity and privilege as if he could possibly understand what they mean?

How can someone like Duke Carmody deserve Immunity and not Margot? She needs it to *survive*, while people like Duke only pay for the privilege to abuse it.

My hands melt into frustrated fists as Duke leans even closer.

And when he does, Eddie slaps him in the face.

He's stunned as the sound of her palm against his skin echoes through the empty park. He clenches his jaw so tightly I can practically hear his teeth grinding together like angry bone gears. The rage brews hotter inside him, and I wait for the embarrassment and frustration to boil over enough to make him storm off.

I imagine it stung for a bit, but I doubt it hurt all that much because Eddie was holding back. I remember the way she used to interact with other kids at school, how she was always the one to win races or climb the highest play structures or emerge victorious from every frivolous schoolyard fistfight. She's one of the strongest people I know.

But Duke clearly doesn't see her that way—because he hits her right back.

The force of his punch knocks her backward, and I watch in horror as she pinches her bloody nose in disbelief. *I should have intervened earlier.*

That's it.

Duke and I are both startled when I lunge at him. He falls against the ground in an explosion of sand that sends grains of tiny rocks flying in every direction, too shocked to struggle as I hold him down. Rage curls my hand into a fist so tight I can feel my fingernails draw bloody lines in my skin, and I punch him once—twice, three times. My knuckles burn.

In my mind, I am yelling at myself to stop. I'm almost Immune, but not yet. If he wanted to, he could call a Chaser and have me exterminated.

But I lost all control the moment he hit her.

Duke is stronger than I am, and he quickly turns the table in his own favor. He pushes me back and my mouth fills with cutting granules of sand and dust. I feel his fists slam into my face with a force that blurs my vision and makes my ears ring.

"What the hell are you doing here, huh? A little weird to be hiding under a slide, don't you think?" He grunts as we struggle in the sand. How ironic that I'm the creep in this situation, not him.

Unlike Eddie, he doesn't hold back. He hits me like a stuck record. His fists meet my face again and again, over and over and over for what feels like an eternity of burning. Eddie is yelling something inaudible in the background but I can't make out the words, soft and broken like the static of a Yesterday vinyl. The party drones on in faded echoes, and the croaking of frogs seems more alarming than it had before.

My senses blur, all the colors, sounds, and shapes blending together into one foggy mess. Every inch of my body seems to be in pain, but I'm not done yet.

I roll to the side. I dodge a heavy blow to the face, stumbling as I manage to bring myself to my feet again. Duke does the same.

"You know, for a second there, I thought you followed Eddie here or something." He pants, out of breath. He lunges at me and I dodge. "But I think I get it now."

"Get what?" I spit a mouthful of bloody saliva into the sand. He swings at me again, and he manages to reach my face this time. I stand my ground and wipe my sleeve against the stream of red liquid trickling down my nose.

"Why you're here," Duke says between offenses. This little dance of ours is getting old. I'm the one to make a move this time, but he slips out of my reach. "You're seeing her, aren't you?"

My fist meets his jaw.

He grabs his most recent wound and bends over, the other hand on his knee. We're both out of breath, but I know this altercation has only begun.

"It all makes so much sense now." Duke chuckles, shaking his head like he suddenly understands some complex mathematical principle.

"You're out of your damn mind."

"You're the one out of your mind." He stands up straight, wiping blood off his hands and onto his expensive jeans.

I laugh a hollow laugh, amused by the creativity of his comeback.

He approaches me again and presses his palms against my chest. I want to stay calm, but I push him too. He retaliates with a shove more forceful than mine and it sends me stumbling back a few steps.

"There's something I've been dying to know," Duke says as he steps forward. He's so close to my face that I can smell the stench of iron and stale nicotine. Blood oozes from his split lip, and it stains his teeth a grotesque crimson. He licks his mouth and I cringe. "On a scale of one to ten, how good is she at kissing? I mean, I'd find the answer to that question myself, but she appears to be taken already."

I snap.

I dive at Duke with an unfamiliar fury, a tempest so forceful it scares me more than it scares him. My body moves with a mind of its own, pushing him against the side of the play structure and pinning him by the throat with my forearm. My free hand presses so hard against the metal I feel its pattern forming an indent in my skin.

Duke is taller than me—stronger than me—but I make sure he forgets all about that. He's slouched, and my strike has the boy buried in cold sand from the ankle down.

"Look man, I don't know what the hell your problem is, but you need to drop it," I seethe.

Duke struggles to breathe as the force against his throat keeps him silent. He doesn't want to waste precious breath by speaking, so I take advantage and continue.

"You're an entitled piece of misogynistic shit," I say through gritted teeth. "You don't respect people, you most certainly don't respect Eddie, and no one respects you either—because you're nothing."

I shake him a bit as he chokes, starved for oxygen as I withhold the vital substance just a little bit longer.

Duke's face darkens with a thirst for air. "You will not touch her. You will not breathe near her. And you know what, you won't even look at her ever again. Because if you give her as much as a millisecond of a glance"—

I lean closer, slowly—"you'll be dead before you look away. She gives a mean punch, man, but I'm sure you already know that."

I let him go and he drops to the ground, sliding his back along the structure before falling into the sand. He grabs his throat and takes gulps of air so pathetically I almost pity his coughs.

Eddie stands by the slide, frozen in dismay. Her stillness is not unlike what I displayed during the ceremony. She's in shock, and her hands cover her mouth as I rush over to her.

"You okay?" I ask quietly. She nods, despite the bruise beginning to form across the right half of her face. Of course she is.

"We should go," Eddie mumbles, and I couldn't agree more.

We hurry across the sand, heading back toward the school in the direction of that fence of ours. She refuses to look me in the eye, but it's not the same avoidance as before. What was once innocent and awkward is now a thing of shame.

We don't make it halfway across the sand before Duke tackles me from behind.

I'm taken aback by his persistence. I thought that going for so long without air would frighten him into leaving us alone, but I should have known better.

Eddie yells, defending me with words that are too fuzzy for my brain to comprehend as Duke's beating makes the world around me inaudible again. I can't feel a thing, but at the same time, I feel everything. His punches seem to hit harder than they did before, and it makes my ears ring. The ringing escalates, crescendoing into an aching dog-whistle of a sound that makes my eyes cross. His fists bombard my face like a group of carnivorous birds competing for the same target with dozens of downward attacks. *And I am the prey.*

I feel my consciousness slipping away from me, and I know that if I shut my eyes, they won't open again. Every second I'm unconscious is a second where Duke will focus on Eddie instead, and I can't let that happen. I have to stay awake.

But my eyes come to a close on their own, just as someone screams.

EDDIE

Friday, June 2
15 Days Until Training

I t's past midnight when he wakes up.

He is clothed in the polished nickel glow of a moon that brushes his skin with confetti. The light filters through the tiny circular gaps of the play structure platform we hide beneath, dotting his skin like freckles. The back of his head rests on a sand pillow, raven hair spilling to the side in a matted tangle of blood, sweat, and tiny little rocks.

I stare down at him with my back pressed against a plastic wall, legs stretched out in front of me, speckled in too much sand to notice its presence anymore. He looks peaceful until his eyes open, and in them I find no peace, but the piano delay of stale memories rushing back to his head like blood.

"Are you okay?" I'm quick to ask, just as shocked by his awakening as I am embarrassed by the level of concern in my voice.

"Never been better." He winces as he sits up slowly, rubbing the front of his forehead to soothe what I imagine to be a pounding headache so obvious I can feel it myself, just by seeing him this way.

His face is bruised, swollen, and stained, each mark a symbol of what he went through for my sake, every cut a surge of guilt like boiling water.

While I'm thankful for his interference, I know I didn't deserve it. Why go through something so painful for me, out of all people?

He could have left me alone with Duke to save his own skin. But instead, he stayed and he fought and put himself through too much trouble for a girl who hasn't exactly been kind to him in the past.

"Are you sure you wanna sit up? You're hurt," I say. It takes me a moment to realize that my hand is on his shoulder, retracting it as soon as I do. He notices and gives me a soft grin.

"No, I'm fine," Ren lies. I can tell his body aches, and I can see how he yearns to collapse in the sand once again.

"You don't look very fine," I point out as he scoots to sit next to me. He sighs and rests his back against the same play structure wall as mine. He's so close our shoulders touch, but I don't think he notices.

"Ed." He turns his neck to look me in the eye, and the visual contact makes me nervous. "I'm okay."

"I don't know about that. You took a pretty awful beating back there." I shake my head and look at my shoes. Ren looks away too. My white sneakers are drenched in sand and so are we. But I can't complain, because I am indebted to the sand.

"Wait, what happened back there?" Ren questions, expressing his confusion with creased brows and a flicker of panic behind the eyes.

"You blacked out."

"Wow." Ren is sarcastic in his reply. "I had no idea."

"Shut up." I'm not in the mood for banter.

"Really though." He adjusts his neck to look at me, and I look back—not because I want to, but because I care. "What happened?"

I'm not sure how to answer his question. I know exactly what happened, but I don't want to relive it. I close my eyes and all I can see is Duke hitting Ren over and over again.

Ren's expression darkens, and his eyes widen. "Did he hit you again while I was out? I swear to God, I'm gonna kill that self-righteous—"

"He didn't hurt me."

"But he did." Ren's voice lowers grimly, and he stares at me with a concern that seems so out of character. A few weeks ago, he never even bothered to look at me unless it was a glare.

But this Ren is different, and I can't say why. He reaches out to trace the mark on my face so lightly I can barely feel his touch. "He did hurt you."

"It's nothing."

"A bruise doesn't just appear out of thin air. It's not *nothing*." He lowers his hand and stares at the spot where Duke hit me. "You should be icing that."

"Okay, let me just get a frozen steak out of the freezer real quick. I'll be right back," I tease, but he's not amused. "You should be worried about *you* right now. Not me. You're the one who got attacked."

"I'm the one who attacked him, Ed. Not the other way around," Ren says. He looks away from me and stares at his sandy shoes instead, and oddly enough, his tone is stained with shame.

"Hey." I tap on his shoulder. "You did what you had to."

Ren's lips remain sealed.

"I don't know what would have happened if you didn't intervene," I mutter, and the thought sends chills up and down my back. Ren senses my discomfort and looks at me once again. "He could have turned me in. For hitting him. He still might, after what I did."

"I don't think he wants anyone else to know he got a good beating tonight." Ren offers me a soft smile, and I try my best to return it before looking away. I don't want him to know how frightened I was during the fight.

"Hey," he says, sensing the fear in me. "It's okay to be afraid, you know. I was afraid too."

No, I tell myself. Fear will only weaken me.

"You're brave, you know," Ren continues. "But brave people are allowed to be scared. I actually think that deep down, they're more scared than any of us."

He pauses, his tone so gentle it could belong to someone else. "It's okay to be small sometimes."

The last thing I want is to be seen as a coward. But the reality of it is that I am, in fact, a coward. Tonight has proved that fact to be true.

Maybe this is why I can't become a Chaser. Maybe I have no pride, no love, no morality. Maybe I'm just afraid.

How can he call me brave? Is it brave to defy the system by refusing to Chase? Or is it braver to get past my own illusions of pride and devote myself to the system, providing my family with Immunity in the process?

What is bravery, really, if not a concept we created to allow ourselves to play pretend and believe—if only for a moment—that we are something bigger than our fear?

But we can't be bigger than our fear. Humans are built from fear; it's the one thing that drives all we do. So I can't be the kind of person to be frightened. I have to be brave, even if it's all make believe.

And for some inexplicable reason, I want to be brave around Ren more than anyone else.

"Eddie?" he asks, shattering the silence like glass.

"Yeah?"

He hesitates. "You never told me what happened."

"Oh."

I pause, unsure of how to avoid the conversation—because this is the last thing I want to talk about.

"How did you..." Ren asks, trying to arrange the words in his mind.

"Get him to stop?"

"Yeah."

I bite my lip and draw swirls in the sand with my finger. "He wouldn't stop, remember?"

Ren nods solemnly, and I continue.

"He was consumed by this anger and forgot all about me. Like he lost track of why he was even mad in the first place."

Ren looks down at the sand too, perfectly still.

"It was..." I stop myself from saying it. *Frightening. Terrifying. Surreal and horrific and upsetting.* "Strange."

There's a pause, and Ren speaks. "So what made him stop?"

"I threw sand in his eyes."

I laugh at first, but then I stop myself. It wasn't funny. Not even a little bit.

"And that made him stop? A little bit of sand?" Ren is doubtful of my story, and he smirks. "You gave him a beating too, didn't you?"

"No. Really, it was just—sand. All the sand."

"How did you go about doing that?"

I hesitate again. "I didn't throw much because I was worried about hurting you too, but you know, your eyes were closed. So you were spared."

"Glad to hear that."

"He was thrown off guard and started rubbing his eyes a bit."

"Understandable."

"But as he was standing there and just blinking and trying to get the sand out, I realized he was gonna snap out of it and redirect his anger at me." I choke on my words. Ren doesn't reply.

"So I grabbed more sand. But this time it was like—" I gesture with my hands, scooping up a substantial handful of the material as we speak. It falls through my fingers and hits my lap with a soft hiss. "—a lot of sand. In each hand."

Ren nods.

"I walked up from behind and just... dug it into his eyes." The words taste sour. "And it wasn't just a light toss. I actually felt his eyes beneath my fingers."

Ren nods again, and I continue with a whisper. My breath is shaky, and while I know I acted out of defense to protect Ren and me, I'm ashamed of what I did to Duke. I'm ashamed of the desperation. Of the violence. *The fear.*

"It was a lot of sand, Ren. A lot. Enough to send him away."

"Damn." Ren lets out a low whistle. "That's—"

"Brutal, I know." I laugh again, but I'm far from amused.

"I was gonna say badass, but brutal works too."

There's a pause in the discussion, and we stare at the sand in silence until he speaks up again.

"I guess we all have a dark side, huh?" he says softly.

I nod, slowly. "I guess so."

"Man." A deep sigh escapes from Ren's lips. "The lengths we go for the people we care about."

I wonder if he's referring to Margot, and I feel pained by the thought of the burden he carries. For someone so obsessed with moral correctness, it must be breaking him to know he'll have to betray everything he believes in to become a Chaser.

Ren leans his head back to view the stars through the small circular openings of the structure's low ceiling. I adjust my head to do the same thing, and the right side of my forehead comes into contact with his silky black hair. It's usually jumbled in a casual mess, but now, the strands are unintentionally tangled, filled with so much sand it almost looks like the sky itself.

My heart stops for a second when I realize that our heads are touching, but the shock is short-lived, and after it passes, I let it be. Because right now, with the help of this subtle touch, I'm overwhelmed with the cooling rarity that is relief.

Something has changed between Ren and me. I feel safe with him, untouchable and vulnerable at the same time. This boy I used to hate with every fiber of my being has completely transformed. He's a person I would protect if I had to. Whether we like it or not, we're now tied together by these burdens we share, connected by the all-encompassing fear of losing Margot.

Then I look at him and realize that maybe he hasn't changed at all. He's the same Ren he's always been, loyal and emotional and pained by being so pure at heart. I wonder if he's been here all along.

I think back to what Margot said earlier today. Maybe Ren hasn't turned upside down.

"I'm sorry," he says after our shared period of silence. His voice is bitterly sincere, almost disgusted.

"For what?"

He gives me a sad look. "You know."

"I don't."

"For not intervening sooner. For letting that dipshit lay a hand on you." He pulls one knee closer to rest his left arm upon, and he keeps the other leg straight like a board. His right arm fidgets with the sand. Now he's the one who can't look at me.

"Hey." I turn my body to face him, shifting to sit cross-legged. He looks away.

"You did more than enough. And for me, of all people." I smile sadly at the thought of him going to such lengths for the sake of my undeserved protection.

"He hit you, Eddie. He hit you. And I was standing right there." He looks at the sky through the grated metal again, trying so hard to avoid my gaze at all costs.

"Ren—"

"I lost control."

"Ren."

"There was probably a better way to solve it. Without—without *fighting* him."

"Ren. There was no other way, and you know it," I state firmly. "We both know the kind of person Duke is. Things would have ended up a lot worse if you didn't do what you did. I know it."

I wait for Ren to say something, but his lips remain sealed. He closes his eyes and sighs, his breath tainted with regret and exhaustion. I wonder if he has trouble sleeping too.

"Ren, listen to me. You helped me. You protected me and somehow simultaneously let me know that I didn't need protecting." I reach out and touch his chin, redirecting his gaze. For once, I want him to look at me. I want him to see the genuineness in my eyes. "Do you have any idea just how honorable that is?"

He swallows a lump in his throat. His eyes are watery, and I envy the courage he has—the strength he possesses to express such visible vulnerability, to let himself actually feel his emotions instead of suppressing them.

Margot was right, I think to myself. He really is everything I'm not.

"You said it yourself. We all have a dark side." My hand drops from his chin, slowly. "It's only human to want to protect the people we care about."

I know that for Ren, deep down, this has to be about Margot. I want him to know that I understand his drive to save his sister because I'm powered by that same burning flame. She's the world to me, and I would do anything to save the world.

Ren looks me in the eye, and I think about what he must be seeing. I wonder what hazel eyes look like in the dark. Not bad, I hope.

But I know that his eyes are beautiful. They're the all-encompassing kind of dark and soulful that draws people in and leads them exactly where they need to be. You don't get lost in his eyes. You get found.

"You're right, you know," Ren says. "I'll do anything to protect the people I care about."

He stares at me with a gaze so soft and careful that I question whether or not that acceptance letter was just a fragment of my imagination. Chasers are monsters, and he is far from that.

"You know," he says, "I don't hate you, Eddie. I don't think I ever did, and I'm not sure I ever could."

I smile softly. "I don't completely despise you either."

He chuckles. "I said hate, not *completely despise*."

I mirror his laugh and before I know it we're quiet again. He looks at me with an intensity I feel ashamed of being drawn to. You hate the moth, not the light. I wonder if I ever really knew him at all.

"I care about you, Eddie. Even your dark side." Ren whispers in a way that sends a shiver down my spine and an eclipse of moths into the pit of my stomach.

I don't know what to say, but when I find the words, I keep them. I don't want to spoil this moment by questioning it. I don't want to ruin something with the right words at the wrong time.

Instead, I scoot closer to him. I lean my head against his shoulder and we stare at the stars through the metal ceiling until we drift into a well-earned sleep.

We get to Ren's car before the first wave of parents and children arrive at the park.

I thank the universe for sparing me from waking up to a toddler's curious pokes, but I would prefer the wrath of a toddler over that of an angry parent —especially my dad. *If he's even awake this early on a Saturday.*

I'm frantic as I hurry into the passenger's seat, swearing under my breath in a way that would make my mother proud. Mom works a lot of weekends, but I hope she's home. She'd understand if I explained what happened. Even without an explanation, I can picture her nudging me in the arm and congratulating me for *being young* and doing the stupid social things she thinks kids like me should be doing. Like going to parties and falling asleep at parks.

But I don't even want to think about what my father would say. Or do.

The sunlight feels sticky on my skin, and it does nothing to soothe the ache in my head. My brain pulses painfully to the berserk rhythm of my heartbeat. There's a dry taste in my mouth, like I swallowed a mouthful of sand. Maybe I did in my sleep.

Oh God, I think as I buckle up. I fell asleep with *Ren.*

If he is panicking, I cannot tell. I watch as he climbs into the seat to my left. He seems calm—relaxed, even—and I marvel at his ability to appear unaffected by our accidental slumber.

Maybe he feels guilty, not worried for his own sake. He spent one of the most important nights of his life without Margot, and I'm sure he's tearing himself apart for doing so.

This is the first time I've spent the night away from my house without letting my parents know where I'm going. Sure, I avoid them as often as I can. I stay over at Margot's all the time and I always send my family a text to let them know when I'm at Margot's. But last night was different.

I spent the night with the wrong McLellan.

I try not to think about it too much as Ren drives away. There wasn't much I could've done differently after that fight except stay awake. My old cell shattered and I left my flip phone at home, so I wouldn't have been able to call my dad anyway. I brace myself for the tornado of accusations I'll have to face.

The car ride is quiet. I can't tell if it's because we don't want to talk about last night or if we're just too focused on our fear of the aftermath.

In the silence of it all, I wonder if Ren blames me for the bruises covering his face and the rest of his body. It was partially my fault—perhaps wholly my fault. I was the one who found him after the ceremony. I was the one who took him to the park.

I was the one who couldn't defend myself.

Ren's aged sedan seems a whole lot smaller as we drive up the hill of my street and reach my house. The building looks so much larger, like it somehow doubled in size overnight. Or maybe I just feel smaller. Either way, the white walls and black door look like they could swallow me whole, and the little potted trees look more like jagged teeth.

From the bottom of the driveway, I can see Dad's SUV perched in front of the garage like a hawk. I pray that my father is still asleep. It's a Saturday morning, so he won't be needed at work. I cross my fingers desperately and hope that for once in his life he decided to go to bed early and sleep in late.

I wince at the high volume of slamming metal doors as we get out of the car. It echoes up and down the street and I wonder if the sound made it within the walls of my house.

"Want me to walk you in?" Ren asks softly. He gives me a look of concern that makes me feel a little better about where we stand, but not much. He is too bruised for me to feel okay.

"No, no." I shake my head and fold one arm, chewing the end of my other sleeve. "I don't..."

I don't want them to know I was with you.

"I get it." Ren gives me the slightest hint of a smile, just enough of a twitch to let me know that he means what he's saying. "But I'm walking you up."

"Why?" I ask, almost irritated. This was my fault—not his.

"Someone has to explain what happened to your dad, and I doubt you want it to be you," he argues.

"That doesn't mean I want it to be *you*. You've done enough for me already."

"Exactly." He chuckles darkly. "I've done enough already."

"That's not what I meant."

"I know." He averts his gaze. "But it's what *I* meant."

Before I can object, Ren starts to walk and I have no choice but to follow. I feel even smaller as we walk. The trek up the driveway takes ages, and it feels like an eternity before we reach the front door. I'm out of breath but

I can't tell if it's from physical exhaustion or anxiety.

The door is standing right in front of me, tall, ominous, and threatening. My hand reaches out to grab the handle but my fingers never reach the surface, like similar ends of a magnet trying and failing to meet.

"I can't do this," I mutter.

I turn around and step down the porch, eyeballing the quickest route to the gate that leads to the side yard. Maybe I can slip through Milo's window. He would keep his mouth shut. Or maybe, if I'm really this desperate, I can take Cedar's route and use the tree. Or run off to wherever he's at, for that matter.

"Where do you think you're going?"

The sound of my father's voice freezes the blood in my veins. It feels like every functioning part of my body has come to an unexpected halt, like each of my organs are shutting off one by one. I somehow manage to turn around, and when I do, I see the man standing on the porch, expression filled with an anger as dark as the polished car I'm now so close to.

"What the hell happened to you two?" Dad's face wrinkles with both agitation and confusion. His focus switches from me to Ren and back to me again like a ping pong ball. "And what did *you* have to do with it?"

My father glares at Ren like he's just committed a crime. He looks him up and down, eyeing the collection of bruises that paints so much of his skin blue and green.

"I'm sorry, Mateo. I—"

"Mr. Voclain."

"I'm sorry, Mr. Voclain." Ren lowers his tone and matches the expression with his hands, like he's talking through a hostage situation you might see in a Yesterday movie. "I kept Eddie up too late and we ended up falling asleep."

"Oh please." My dad scoffs. "You expect me to believe a story like that when you're covered from head to toe in bruises?"

"It's the truth, sir," Ren states respectfully. "I take full responsibility for what happened. It wasn't Eddie's fault."

"You don't have to tell me twice. I'm not surprised you had something to do with this—with that carefree father of yours. Maybe you don't have any structure at home, but that doesn't mean you can ruin ours."

I open my mouth to combat my father's words but he keeps going.

"In my home, we have rules. Expectations. Those were both broken last night when my daughter didn't come home."

Ren doesn't say anything, and I can see the unjustified guilt in his eyes. He stares at his shoes and shoves his hands in his pockets.

"I know there's more to this than you're telling me, but I don't wanna hear another word." He curses fiercely under his breath, hands on his hips. "I can't even look at you anymore. Just leave."

"It wasn't her fault, sir. Please just remember that."

"*Leave.*"

Ren nods in silence and turns around to walk down the driveway, facing the trek alone this time. I watch him open the car door and stare at me one last time before getting into the vehicle and driving away. The sedan grows smaller before it disappears over the curve of the hill, and I'm alone.

Dad whips his head around to glare at me. "Inside. *Now.*"

I walk past my father and into the warmth of the house. He follows close behind, but I don't feel like talking to him right now. Especially not about last night. I make my way through the entryway and into the kitchen in hopes of reaching my room, but I'm stopped by my dad's voice.

"Don't walk away from me," he barks, following me inside and closing the door. I'm surprised he didn't slam it shut. He must be a lot angrier than I think if he feels the need to suppress it.

"I thought we were finished talking."

"Oh, the conversation hasn't even started yet." He chuckles bitterly. "You didn't come home last night, Lavender."

"I know."

I walk over to the fridge and grab a bottle of water, not because I'm thirsty but because I need something to keep me busy enough to stay sane in the argument that's about to be born.

"Where were you?" He puts his hands on his hips as I twist the cap off my bottle.

"With the McLellans," I say, taking a gulp of water. It's easy to say because it's not a lie. I was with a McLellan; I was with Ren.

"Asa called," he comments, and I choke on my water. Asa and our parents never talk—not after my father found out he was anti-Nightjade. "He wanted to know if we had any idea where Ren was. I guess he never came home either."

He speaks like he knows exactly what happened, like he truly believes he has the perfect understanding of last night's occurrences. He looks at me, urging me to say something, but I don't. I'm not sure how to lie my way out of this one.

"Lavender."

"Eddie," I correct, my tone sharp.

"Lavender," he says slowly. He gave me my name, and he acts as though I'm privileged to have it. Like I'm lucky to have been born and named anything at all. "Why aren't you saying anything?"

I shrug.

"Did he do this to you?"

"Do what, Dad?"

"What do you think?" He leans over and slams his fist on the kitchen island. "You were gone all night with that McLellan boy and came home with a black eye!"

I shrug again, and he expresses his offense with a loud *tsk*.

"For a second, I saw both of your bruises and thought you might have gotten in an accident or something—which I worried about *all night*, mind you—but his car was perfectly fine."

"It's nothing."

"A black eye isn't nothing," he snaps. "It's a big deal, and so is not coming home. You could have been dead for all we..." He pauses, staring at my wrist. "Where's your bracelet?"

"What do you mean? It's right..." I feel my bare wrist and come to a pause, eyes wide. *The bracelet is gone.* I remember the way Ren struggled to figure out the bracelet clasps and realize it must have fallen off in the sand last night. *He must have put it on incorrectly.*

"You lost it?" To my surprise, my father sounds hurt.

In spite of myself, a pang of guilt twists in my gut. "I'm sorry, okay? It's not like I did it on purpose." I look down at my empty, unadorned wrist.

"Are you sure about that?"

I glare at the accusation in his expression. "Yes, I'm sure." I shake my head, playing with the plastic bottle cap because I don't know what else to say. But I don't want him to know that, so I take another sip of water.

"I want you to be honest with me here, okay?" My dad lets out a sigh, lowering his voice to a near whisper. He almost sounds worried. "Did Ren hurt you?"

"How could you even suggest that? Or think that?" I shout. Ren is a concoction of many unbearable things, but he would never hurt me. Not ever.

"What else am I supposed to think? That you got in some fistfight or something?" He's sarcastic in his response, but he doesn't know how close he is to the truth.

"What, you don't think I can get into fights?"

"Lavender." He scoffs and rolls his eyes. I hate when he does this—when he acts as though nothing I'm saying has any value to him. As though his intelligence is superior to mine and he knows it, and that I'm idiotic for opening my mouth to verbally challenge anything he says.

"Ren *protected* me, okay?" I raise my voice. "If it weren't for him I would have suffered a lot more than just a hit to the face." *Extermination, probably,* I want to say. I keep my mouth shut.

But I know it's true. I let my temper get the best of me. I hit Carmody first. If Ren hadn't given Carmody such a shameful beating—one his pride would never let him report—we'd both be in the tombs by now. As corpses, not workers.

My father doesn't have anything to say, so he keeps his mouth shut. I let out a weary sigh

"Look, Dad, I made a mistake, alright? I should have called to let you know that I wasn't coming home, but my phone is broken. I'm sorry. Now can we move on?"

"No, we can't." The man folds his arms and I'm reminded of Canadian geese. I've seen them at the lake I used to run around, back when I was doing track. I've seen how the males like to puff out their chests when they get territorial to appear bigger than they actually are.

"You should have come home, Lavender. I *expected* you to come home, and I would have been just as upset if you called me to let me know that you were completely disregarding those expectations."

"I'm sorry, okay?"

"And you still won't tell me who gave you that black eye."

"Dad—"

"*Who hit you?*" His voice echoes as he pounds both his hands on the granite counter tops, and for a moment, I'm frightened of him. I've always been afraid of confrontation with my father, of the yelling and the gaslighting and the manipulation, but never of him. This is different.

"It wasn't Ren, okay?" I shout, feeling so unbearably cornered. "I already told you that. Ren would never hurt me."

"Who did it then? If it wasn't Ren?"

"It doesn't matter." I close the lid on my water bottle and place it back in the fridge. *I can't do this anymore.*

"Of course it matters, Lavender. If someone hit you I'm obligated to know who it was. It's my right as your parent."

I close the door to the refrigerator and turn to face my dad. "I'm eighteen, remember? I don't have to tell you everything. Or anything at all, actually."

"As long as you're living under my roof, you're going to abide by my rules."

"It's Mom's roof too," I say, eager to reject his words.

"You're right. It's *our* roof because we're the ones paying for it. I don't see you paying for anything."

"You want me to start paying rent? Fine. I'll get a job. I'll do whatever I have to do to get you off my back."

"What do you mean, get a job? You got your letter."

Shit. I close my eyes. *I forgot about that.*

I wait for him to question me further, to notice my grimace and find the secret I want so badly to spill, but he blinks away the suspicion and shakes his head.

"Well if that's how you feel, once training's over and you start going on calls, maybe you can go find another roof to live under. One where you don't have to follow my rules anymore."

His words punch more than Carmody's strike. I almost lift a hand up to touch my bruise, as though my father's words are what left it and not a fist.

Is he really so disappointed in who I've turned out to be that he wants me gone?

No, I think to myself. I'm tired of being punched.

"Wow, what a great suggestion." I'm sarcastic as I throw my hands up, laughing like he's come across some groundbreaking discovery. "It's not like I've spent *every waking day* for the past eighteen years hating my life and just begging for a way to leave it all behind someday, or anything. No. It's not like that at all."

My dad is stunned, and the part of me that is kind is swarmed with a cold kind of guilt that almost aches. But the kind part of me needs a rest. The kind part of me lets herself get punched.

I exit the room robotically. The argument's memory fades into background noise, because all I can think about is Ren.

After last night, nothing feels right anymore, like something vital in the cords weaving my world together has snapped. The earth must have shifted off balance, because in spite of myself, in spite of our history, I'm ashamed of the mess I've dragged Ren into.

Asa is a good father. When Ren explains what happened, there will be no anger, no accusations—nothing but relief and understanding. But I know he must be feeling so guilty for causing his dad to worry in the first place.

On that playground, Ren saw sides of me that I never wanted him to see. He saw a deplorable blend of darkness and weakness that will not be easily forgotten.

You forget the strong people, eventually. There are plenty of strong people. It's the weak people you hold onto in the back of your mind, the ones you're pitiful of or disgusted by.

But it's the darkness in people you remember more than anything else. Because once you see it, it casts an everlasting shadow that can never be rid from its keeper.

I will remember Ren's darkness. And no matter what happens, I know he will remember mine too.

REN

Saturday, June 17
2 Hours Left of Being Human

♪ THREE DAY ROAD - BIRTH OF JOY ♪

The day arrives quicker than I expect.

I'm not sure what to expect, or if I should expect anything at all. The first day of training has finally arrived, and by showing up today, I'm agreeing to hand my life over to the Chaser Corps.

I decide to expect the absolute worst.

I'm mindless as I get ready, too unsure of everything to be conscious of the shower I take or the clothes I wear or the shoes I slip on my feet. And at the same time, I'm far too aware of everything, hyper-focused not on the shower itself, but on the fact that this will be the last time I shower as Ren McLellan. Like I am washing myself away, scrubbing the skin off my bones to become a pawn for the Presidency and their games. My skeleton will be a chess piece.

I walk out of the shower apathetically, my face empty when I stare at my reflection in the clouded mirror. The reality is, I'm far from emotionless. I'm completely absorbed with the fear of losing sight of who I am. I can't see my reflection through the steam.

I dry myself off and slip into a black tee and a pair of dark jeans before sitting on the edge of my bed. I should be taking advantage of this time, enjoying these last moments of being myself. But instead, I sit here and reread the acceptance letter for the thousandth time. It's crinkled and torn at the edge, as though it belonged to Eddie once and not me. It's strange how we've swapped places in so many ways.

> Based on your exam results, you have been selected to participate in the Chaser Corps training program.

My heart pounds just a little bit faster.

> The training program will take place over the summer. Please check the end of this letter for all designated dates, times, and other vital information regarding the location of the training center and our expectations from you as a cadet.

I jump to the end of the letter and triple-check the dates. I open my phone and make sure it truly is June 17th and not some other day, though I hope for the latter. But sure enough, the date on my device matches with the date listed as *TRAINING DAY ONE* on the chart at the end of the letter.

> You will be trained for exactly six weeks in preparation for your first field assignments. Upon arrival, you will receive your uniforms and more information about the structure of the training program.

> On your first day, please come clothed in casual or athletic attire. The articles of clothing listed below are approved by the Corps and recommended for maximum comfort and efficiency through the duration of your first day.

> After the first day, you will arrive at training with the clothing we provide you. This will be worn beneath your uniforms.

I read the rest of the letter and scan the lists, checking to see whether my attire is adequate enough for their standards. I know it's foolish of me to overthink something as frivolous as clothing, but if I'm not prepared in an area as simple as attire, how can I be ready for the horrors I will surely face?

I don't think I ever will be.

Please do not bring your own food or drink into the building. Nourishment will be provided as needed. Additionally, we invite you to leave all personal belongings (cellular devices, bags, etc.) at home or in your car. Any foreign items will be confiscated and disposed of. Bring only yourself.

The last sentence echoes in my head. *Bring only yourself.* It feels strange that they would say such a thing. Won't we all be leaving ourselves behind? The moment I walk through those doors, I will no longer be myself. I will enter as Ren McLellan and exit as his empty shell.

This will be the last time I walk in these shoes as a human, and not as a monster of the worst possible sorts—the kind that will give his life to the same system that has taken so much from him.

I check the time on my phone and see that Eddie has texted me. It's a quarter before 9:00 in the morning, and I remember how I instructed her to wait for me to pick her up in a few minutes.

EDDIE

change of plans. i'm here.

REN

?

EDDIE

decided it would be best if my dad didn't see me with you.

he still knows about our lie. the carpooling thing. but you get it.

The words sting a bit, but I have no time to dwell on them. All I can be is thankful that Eddie came up with the carpooling idea so I didn't have to. Maybe it's inconvenient for her, but I'm glad I won't be going to training alone. I'd never admit this to her, but if she didn't think of it first, I'd probably ask her to tag along myself.

She's my most comforting annoyance.

I shove my phone in my back pocket and exit my room, walking down the hall and past Margot's door. I'm glad the lights are off in her room; she's still asleep, so it will be easier to say goodbye. I jog downstairs and pause when I see Eddie and my father discussing something quietly in the kitchen.

"Ah, there he is." Dad turns around when he spots me. He gives me a pat on the back as I walk past him and head toward the fridge. "Eddie tells me you two are carpooling to class today."

"Yup." I flash a synthetic grin as I grab the jar of almond butter from the fridge and down a few rushed spoonfuls.

"So..." My father leans forward, whispering just audible enough for Eddie and me to hear, but too quiet to wake Margot. "Eddie told me she never took the exam."

My face goes pale. *I thought that was supposed to stay a secret.*

"Yeah, she didn't." I give Eddie a questioning look.

"Yep." Eddie smiles. "So I thought I'd take a summer class too. You know, to give me a cover while I muster up the courage to tell my dad."

"Advanced Botany." My father beams, giving her a look. "Good choice."

So this is our lie, I think. I give Eddie a small smile to thank her.

While I initially told my dad about the class, I never mentioned Eddie to him. The plan was to leave for *class* and drive over to the Voclain's to pick her up. We would carpool so there would be one more person to vouch for Eddie's supposed Chaser training attendance, just in case her father became suspicious. It gives us both an alibi, and neither of us wants to do any of this alone.

However, I know my own father isn't the one we have to worry about most. Keeping Mateo Voclain at bay is crucial to reaching our goals. If he discovered that Eddie has been lying to him about becoming a Chaser, it would jeopardize her plans, and perhaps my own secrets—not to mention the integrity of the entire Undergrounder operation.

Today, both of our plans are unfolding. I'm diving deeper into the system and Eddie is pulling herself farther away from it. I'll become a killer for the Presidency, and she'll become an illegal healer.

But we both have the same objective. We both want to save Margot more than anything else.

"Good luck, Eddie," my dad says in regards to her previous statement about her father. "I know he's a tough man to please but he'll come around eventually. He is your father after all."

Eddie shrugs, and he reaches out to ruffle my hair playfully before turning around to walk upstairs. "You kids be careful now, alright? I'll see ya later. Gotta finish getting ready for work. Those cars won't fix themselves, as fancy as they've been getting lately."

I finish off the almond butter and grab an apple as he exits the room. Eddie rises to her feet, slinging a worn mustard backpack over her shoulder.

"Ready to go?"

"Yeah," I lie, taking a bite out of the apple.

We walk out the door. Eddie pulls out her keys just as I retrieve my own.

"We're taking my car. I finally got it back from the shop yesterday," she states, not looking back as she heads toward her vehicle and hops in the passenger's seat. I don't comment on the fact that her father stopped using mine as his chosen mechanic. I suppose it makes sense.

"But you're driving," Eddie orders. "I'm exhausted."

Exhausted, I think to myself, wondering what could be haunting her. At this point, it could be anything.

Eddie tosses me her keys, and I have no time to respond before she shuts the car door. I shake my head and climb into the unfamiliar metal machine.

"Why your car?" I ask once I'm inside.

"It'd be risky if someone spotted your car in whatever parking lot we're headed to, right?"

"Fair enough." I shrug.

I turn on the car, but I don't drive away quite yet. Part of me wants to look back at my home, but I'm afraid of what I might see. I'm afraid of seeing two faces staring out the window, torn apart by illness, and grief, and the trauma this system shoved down their throats and forced them to digest. I'm terrified of seeing that and forgetting why I'm doing this, because no matter what, I can't lose sight of what I'm dying for.

I'm becoming a monster for her sake.

I drive away not because I want to, but because I have to. I clench the steering wheel so tightly my knuckles burn. I can tell that Eddie senses just how tense I am.

"I'm gonna drive around a bit and try to find a coffee shop once you're there." She says it like she's changing the subject, but there is no subject to change. She just can't stand this silence.

I nod. I want to ask what she's really doing, but we both know she can't tell me much.

For a while, I thought it was brave to become a Chaser. I'm sacrificing my beliefs and my humanity to save my sister, and I thought that doing so would make me a selfless person. But what if my choice is not as *right* as I initially thought? What if I'm not as selfless as I pretend to be?

The price of Margot's survival is deeper than I can comprehend. Every person I exterminate under the command of the Corps is a direct trade for her Immunity. Life is now a currency, and I'll give it all to ensure that my sister stays alive. But is that really selfless of me?

Am I doing this for Margot's sake, or for mine?

As I drive, I start to think that Eddie's the braver one of us both. She'd rather skip out on the Immunity she'd earn as a Chaser than contribute to the Presidency's brutal system.

While Eddie is sacrificing the safety of herself to help others, I'm sacrificing others to protect the people I care about. And I can't for the life of me figure out which one of us is doing the right thing.

Our car ride is uneventful, silent except for the occasional sighting of cows that Eddie feels the need to point out with childish excitement. We've exited the city limits and have now entered a rural sea of lush green dairy fields, surrounded by distant evergreen statues that are so out of reach they seem unreal. Like these meadows are all trapped in some big box, and the interior walls are painted with fantastical pine forests and furling twists of fog.

But the surrealism of the pine starts to fade away as background becomes foreground. The cow-scattered fields are now far behind us as we make our way through the windy curves and inclines that seem to stretch on for an eternity.

With the absence of farm animals to point out, Eddie is quiet. Something about these woods feels wrong, almost eerie, and I can tell she bears that same feeling as the car slithers deeper within the seclusion of this evergreen cloak.

It's strange to think that places like this still exist—places that seem unbelievably untouched by humankind. If not for the road, I would believe it if someone told me that Eddie and I were winding through an uncharted wood. But the road is here, too bumpy and present to be a figment of my imagination.

"My dad told me something interesting about the woods once," I say quietly, eyes fixed straight ahead.

"Really?" she adds. Through the corner of my eye, I can see her gaze move away from the window and trace me instead.

"There are quite a few abandoned structures out in these woods. And other places all over the country too."

She pauses, studying me. "Like old ones? From the Yesterdays?"

I nod.

"Why's that?" Eddie asks.

I hesitate, trying to remember.

"I guess when things started to get really bad—before Nightjade and the Pick and everything—people who lived in rural areas stopped having access to water. People who were really far out from all the cities, not just a few minutes out of town, you know." Now Eddie's the one who nods.

For a moment, all is silent but the hum of the engine. The trees outside our window blend together in emerald green water rapids as I continue.

"Eventually they got so desperate they just packed up and left their houses to move to more populated areas because that's where all the water was being focused."

"What did they call this again? I heard about this in a history class once."

"The Wandering Pandemic or something like that. I don't really remember." I shrug. "That's not even the worst of it though."

The light in her gaze dims. "Yeah?"

"Some people believed bigger cities would have less water because of how populated they were. So they would go farther out into whatever wilderness they were close to and try to find natural sources of water like creeks."

She nods.

"But the thing is, it was all dried up. All of it."

Eddie looks out the window now. She eyes the forest with some kind of sadness I can't trace.

"So what happened?" she asks quietly.

"People got lost. Died of dehydration," I answer, a chill running down my spine. "They just... disappeared."

I can hear Eddie swallow a lump in her throat as she stares at the dashboard. "That's awful."

"It is," I say, and she turns to look at me again.

"That's why no one lives in such remote areas these days," she concludes, and I nod my head in agreement.

"It's all a graveyard, really." I shudder at the thought. "Abandoned houses, decaying structures. Skeletons under old bridges."

"Makes sense then," Eddie mutters.

"What does?"

"That they'd put a Training Center where no one would ever go." Eddie stares out the window again.

"It's kind of scary." She speaks up after a pause in the conversation. "I wonder what they're trying to hide."

"Try not to think about it." I shoot her a quick and empty grin before my eyes fix on the road again, but she doesn't see it.

"I can't just not think about it." Eddie laughs a humorless chuckle.

"Why not?"

"'Cause you're going in there." She picks at the ripped fabric of her jeans, and suddenly it's all quiet again.

In the absence of Eddie's voice, I think about the woods. I can't imagine what it must have been like to not have access to the things we take for granted today—plenty of food, little to no pollution, an abundance of water. But then I realize that more people have died by the cruel hands of the Pick than nature's reaction to overpopulation.

Nature is forgiving. She works in an endless loop of cycles. What she takes, she pays back in full. Fires burn to make room for more growth and the forests come back healthier than before.

It's the people who are unforgiving, not nature.

There are rumors of those who run away to live in the woods, now that they've been abandoned. They're ghost stories, but I wonder whether there's any truth to the exaggerated whispers.

If someone were to run back into nature's arms and get lost in these woods, I doubt they would have an easy time being found. But would it be such a bad thing to never be found? To leave it all behind and remain lost for good, becoming a part of one of those cycles? To live without cruelty for just a moment before becoming a part of the earth again?

I don't think it would.

The training center sneaks up on us.

The winding road leads us to a clearing in the forest that seems to come out of nowhere, so sudden that I almost gasp as we approach the parking lot.

The building looks massive in its setting, but it can't be more than ten stories tall. It's a giant cube as sleek as the Chaser Corps itself, with white concrete walls and reflective windows that mirror pine trees and a slate-colored sky.

It's the kind of structure that makes you feel unworthy, like your entrance will taint the cleanliness of it all and leave people angered by the dirt that you are.

"Ren," Eddie grabs my hand before I make my exit, looking at me with wide eyes. She seems more terrified than I am, but gives me a comforting smile.

I expect her to tell me something about how I'm doing the right thing, but neither of us says a word. We're both haunted by the same doubts.

"Thank you," I mutter after the silence becomes too much to bear. Her words are unspoken, but I feel as though I've been grounded by her worry. I feel human—though I know I won't be human for much longer.

I study the parking lot as I get out of the car, nodding a quick goodbye to Eddie. She climbs over to the steering wheel before driving off, and before I know it, I'm left alone in this intimidating sea of asphalt.

My hands and pockets are empty, but I spot others exiting their vehicles with backpacks or books in hand that make me regret not bringing something to hold. Something to busy my hands with. We were told not to bring anything but ourselves, and although I did just that, I feel unprepared nonetheless. I am unqualified and fraudulent.

The walk from the parking lot seems to stretch on forever, but I eventually approach a clean sidewalk and a perfectly trimmed hedge that wraps around the entirety of the building's exterior, except for the front doors.

The only visible entrance to the building is a heavy pair of doors made from the same reflective glass as the windows. I keep my head down, unsure if I can manage to see my own shameful reflection right now. It feels strange to open them without seeing what's inside, but it's even stranger when I walk inside the building.

I'm nearly swept off my feet.

I inhale so sharply it hurts. I feel so insignificantly microscopic under these high ceilings, ancient in comparison to the state-of-the-art technology and breathtaking architecture that infects even the most basic of the building's features.

Bright lights are installed in sections of both the ceilings and the walls, and waves of early morning light stream in through the windows. Despite their reflective exterior, the glass panels are as clear as crystal from the inside. The light bounces off seamless white flooring that's so polished it could almost be a collection of reflective windows itself, illuminating three standing devices that block me from walking deeper into the lobby. Metal detectors, maybe? Scanners of some sort?

The machines are circular in shape and constructed from the same sterilized white that floods nearly every square inch of the building, save for the blue lights that flash with a high-pitched beep as people walk through. No government-employed attendee is present to guide the wandering cadets through, and everyone seems just as confused as I am as they wait in line. Invisible speakers convey the same message every thirty seconds or so, the voice belonging to some robotic individual I cannot see.

Please wait in line to be checked in. We thank you for your patience.

The line moves quickly and smoothly. One after another, the anxious stream of future Chasers filters through the scanners, each one relieved when the light flashes blue like it does for everyone else.

But with that relief, I see a mix of other emotions as well. Confusion furrows several sets of brows, and I notice a few people pausing to blink for a few moments before moving on. It's bizarre, but I don't think much of it.

I'm startled when the man in front of me triggers a red light instead of blue. It's accompanied by a loud and mechanical expression of rejection, like a card being declined at a cash register. The beep makes him jump back a bit and the lines seem to slow as people turn their heads to see what's causing the commotion.

Cellular device detected. Please place your item in the designated box.

The machine speaks, and part of its wall unfolds to make way for a robotic arm with a small phone-sized box at the end. It reaches out and waits, and the man hesitates before reluctantly placing his device into the small metal container.

Device detected. Thank you for playing your part.

The box closes and compresses to crush the phone. The arm then retracts back to its place inside the wall of the machine, and his compliance is rewarded with a happy blue light.

All eyes peel away from the cadet as he makes his way through the machine to the next section of the process, and a few people step out of line and exit out the front door to put their personal items back in the car.

It's my turn to move through the scanner now. I look to my left and right and see other cadets walking past with ease, some visibly more anxious than others yet still going through nonetheless. I inhale deeply to calm my nerves and take a leap—or step—of faith.

Sure enough, the light flashes the right color. But for the briefest of moments, my eyes are blinded by the light, so much so they ache. I blink in an attempt to clear my presumably faulted vision. *Did something just shock me?*

I look behind me to see all the other cadets in scanners reacting strangely too. There has to be more to these machines than I initially thought.

I walk past the scanners and into what looks like the lobby of some sophisticated hotel. There's a long reception desk that curves around the entire back wall, with two gleaming elevators on both of the side walls. This time, there are three employees working the desk and handing tablets to the cadets in line.

Their clothes, the tablets, the desk itself—everything is a blinding white. It's all so sleek, so electronic and technologically advanced it's almost nauseating.

"Sign this waiver, please."

A woman hands me a tablet when it's my turn, her voice just as robotic as the machine I just walked through. Her eyes remain glued to her large desktop computer, and I already feel less human than the boy who walked through these doors only a moment ago.

"What for?" I ask, desperate for some clarity, some kind of explanation to hold on to, because I feel like I'm falling.

"It's all there, Mr. McLellan," she replies, sparing me not even the slightest of glances.

How does she know my name?

The tablet is almost weightless, and probably more expensive than anything I own. As I hold it, I wonder how a place like this has so much money to throw around on things like scanners, tablets, and desktop computers.

And then I freeze, my breath snagging on the realization. *Immunity.* This tablet was brought to my hands by people paying for the right to stay alive. All of this.

Every white light, every blinding tile, every pane of glass. It's all funded by the same currency. We pay for life with death, and we pay for death with life.

Is this something I really want to be a part of? If I sign this waiver right now, what am I signing away? My life, perhaps? My rights?

My humanity?

"Please, Mr. McLellan. Time is of the essence here," the woman says in the same monotonous tone as before.

There's no time to read it all. Others have already moved on to the next step and I feel an imaginary clock progress inside of me, each tick cutting slices out of the last minute of my life. I skim over the contract and its collection of tiny words that are almost impossible to see. I'm afraid of what I might miss, and then the last section is caught by my vision.

You must complete the entire training course to earn a passing grade. Cadets who fail to complete the training course or neglect to do so with a passing grade will be exterminated for security purposes, as requested by the Presidency.

By signing below, you are stating that you understand and agree to these terms.

Thank you for playing your part.

Exterminated?

Suddenly, I can't remember how to breathe. The room around me transforms into a blurred swirl so bright it makes my head pound. It feels like I'm back in Mr. Aguilar's classroom, but this time, there's no wastebasket to vomit into. There's no bathroom to run to, no Eddie to understand why I ache or remind me why I'm doing any of this at all. There's nowhere for me to hide.

There is only plain white uncertainty, and it's so intense it takes everything I have not to collapse.

You can't turn back, I remind myself. Not now, not ever. Because I need this. Margot needs this, and she needs me.

No one can help her but you.

When I place my fingertip on the tablet and sign my name on the line, I know that Ren McLellan has finally fallen.

But no one is here to catch him.

EDDIE

Friday, June 16
The Day Before Training

♪ NEVER GROW OLD - AMERICAN PRINCES ♪

I can't fall asleep.

I kick off my cover for the second time tonight. I had pulled it back around my body when I started shivering, but now, it feels too warm again. The summer air is thick and so hot I can almost hear it buzzing.

But I know the heat isn't truly why I'm so miserable.

I lie on my back with my arms folded across my chest. If it weren't for my open eyes and missing funeral bouquet, I bet I could be mistaken for a corpse. The tossing and turning has faded into stillness as I try my best to think through the nerves.

This year's round of Chaser training starts tomorrow, and I'm terrified. Ren and I have a plan to help each other keep our secrets, but no matter how good we grow at lying, our success will never be guaranteed. I could slip up, and if my family found out I haven't been telling the truth, my real plan could be exposed. They have to believe I'm a Chaser, and the only way I can do that is with Ren's help.

And the only way he can keep his secret safe is with mine.

But for some inexplicable reason, it is not me, but Ren who I worry about the most. He's the last person anyone would expect to become a Chaser. His whole life, he's been so focused on the idea of doing the right thing, almost to the point of obsession. And now, the rightest thing he can do is so wrong it tears him apart like shark teeth to flesh—and I am the only one who knows he's being ripped to shreds.

No matter how I've felt about Ren over the years—no matter our past—isn't it my obligation to worry about him? Because if I don't, then who will?

I break the corpse position and turn on my right side, hoping the change will be more comfortable. But when I do, I gasp.

There's a person standing in the corner of my room.

My heart stops beating and I scramble to sit up straight, back pressed against my wooden headboard so firmly I can feel a line begin to form against my skin. I reach forward, frantic as I yank the covers back on—like that could protect me from the shadowy figure standing next to my window.

But my panic subsides when I smell pine needles and dirt, and recognize the familiar silhouette of a shadow that looks too much like Cedar to be a coincidence.

Fuming, I grab my pillow and throw it in his direction.

"*What the hell, Cedar?*" I whisper as loudly as I can, but it feels more like a scream.

"Relax, Voclain. It's me." He holds his hands up in innocence, blocking the blow.

"I thought you were an ax murderer," I seethe. "You can't startle me like that. I could have thrown a knife instead."

"Sorry to disappoint, but my ax-murdering days are over," Cedar says, taking a step into the moonlight that streams in through my open window. "Just a guy and his plants."

He picks up the pillow and tosses it back to me, and I catch it with a glare I'm not sure he can see. "Thanks for the warm welcome."

"My pleasure," I mumble. "Wait, what plants?"

He slides his hands in his pockets and uses his chin to nod in the direction of my desk. I squint to make out the shapes in the dark, and when I do, I can see the outlines of three small potted plants. My eyes dart back to Cedar, and I see a black backpack leaning against the wall. *That must have been how he carried them up here.*

I give him a confused look, and to my surprise, he reads it, like he can see me just fine in the dark. His eyes must be more adjusted to working in the shadows than my own, even with his shaded glasses.

"The Unseen relies primarily on phytotherapy for our medicinal needs. We're big naturopaths, you know." He folds his arms across his chest as he explains, voice dragging like he's annoyed to be doing so. "If you do well tomorrow and I decide to actually take you under my wing, I'd like to get a sense of how quickly you can kill plants. If you still wanna be a healer, that is."

"I can take care of plants just fine." I scowl. But my frustration melts into worry when I realize what he's talking about.

I've been so caught up in Ren and our lies that I almost forgot what I've been lying for. During his last visit, Cedar and I planned everything out.

I'm meeting up at some isolated coffee shop tomorrow so I can help him run a few jobs for Command before nightfall. The cover of darkness will allow us to sneak into my father's office quite literally unseen. *He must be here to remind me.*

"I'll believe it when I see it." Cedar's expression is hidden by the dark, but I can tell he gives me a look.

"You will," I insist.

"Calendula, peppermint, lavender." He points to all three plants, ignoring my statement. "It would be pretty sad if you couldn't keep that last one alive, at least."

"I told you, I know how to water a plant. It's not that difficult," I snap, quickly losing my patience. I need sleep, and none of this is helping.

"Oh, it's much more complicated than that, sweetheart." He chuckles arrogantly.

"Don't call me sweetheart."

"Sunshine?"

"Don't call me sunshine either."

"Pal?"

"That's criminal."

"What should I call you then? Sour... I don't know, liver? That's the opposite of sweetheart, right? Bitterbrain might make more sense but I'm kind of liking the liver one better."

"Shut up."

"If not sunshine, what about Your Darkness? Lord of All Things Sad and Gloomy?" He says it like *I'm* the ridiculous one.

"You know what? Your Darkness has a nice ring to it." I give him a glare and change the subject. "Why do you care so much about these plants anyway?"

"Unfortunately, as the head botanist and son of our group's lead healer, you'll be my responsibility," he replies unenthusiastically, and I put my head in my hands.

Of course Cedar, of all people, just so happens to be one of the most important healers for the Unseen. That's just my luck, isn't it?

Sometimes I forget I'm cursed by double Jokers.

Cedar continues. "If you pull your weight tomorrow, that is."

"And if I don't?" I cross my arms.

"We'll talk about it when we get there, then."

"Alright," I reply, swallowing painfully, trying to be discreet.

I don't want Cedar to know how nervous I am. Because deep down, I know that if I fail—if I slip up and make some unredeemable mistake that will prevent me from joining the Unseen—these rebels wouldn't let me live. I know so little, and even that is knowing too much.

"Be ready tomorrow at the location we discussed." Cedar picks up his backpack and slings it over one shoulder. "I'll brief you on our to-do list from there."

I nod, and Cedar does the same.

"Oh, and Voclain?" he says.

"Yeah?"

"I'd get used to sleeping with your knife under your mattress, if I were you. Not the sock drawer." I can't see him smirking, but I can certainly hear it. "It's a good habit to practice."

My brows crease. "How did you—"

"I have a feeling you would've threatened me with a blade rather than a pillow if you had one near you." He lifts his shades to wink, though it feels more patronizing than humorous.

Cedar lets the shades fall back on his face before walking over to the window, holding it open with his hands while hauling both of his legs over the edge.

"Wait," I call out, gesturing toward the plants. "How long do I need to take care of these?"

"Until you die."

"I'm serious."

"For all of eternity, then."

"Cedar."

He turns his head around to face me, sighing with a combination of exhaustion and annoyance.

"Until we meet again, Your Darkness."

All I can do is watch as he drops out of the window, catching a branch before slipping out of sight.

I'm too tired to move the knife under my mattress.

Saturday, June 17
Day 1

You would never guess that a Chaser training center is only a few miles east of Port Keys.

The coastal town is uncomfortably small with hidden eyes that watch from sheer curtains and rotting blinds, refusing to greet visitors with anything but a glare. Because people move here to get away, to escape the watchful eye of the Presidency and its people, if only just a little bit.

Main Street seems to stretch on for an empty eternity. It runs along the rocky coast to my left and the expanse of evergreen to my right, and if I wasn't so preoccupied I would stop the car to enjoy either view.

The words *PORT KEYS COFFEE CO.* snag my line of sight and I slow down. The building stands to my left, clean and bright against the dark coastline behind it. The exterior displays a fresh coat of white paint that tells me the establishment must have been redone recently. The new wooden paneling on the outside has yet to rot like the rest of the town, and it gives me a little bit of comfort as I pull into the parking lot.

Sprinkles of mist tickle my face like grains of cold sand as I step out of the vehicle. I lock the door behind me and shove my keys in my pocket, hugging my arms around my torso in a desperate effort to stay warm. A breeze that reeks of salted seaweed tangles my hair, stinging my eyes and painting my nose red as I walk up to the door.

A neon sign in the window says *OPEN* in twitching red letters, but the setting doesn't match the light display. It's empty, almost entirely vacant save for a single employee and two silent individuals sitting at tables on either side of the room.

I'm comforted by the building's warm shelter and the earthy aroma of freshly brewed coffee. It's nice to be out of the cold, but I feel like a stranger. A coffee shop in a town this small will certainly have regulars, and I'm just as irregular as they come.

"Welcome in," a woman behind the counter says, but she doesn't look up at me. She has dark amber hair and warm brown skin, her slender hands and focused eyes glued to the large black book she reads.

"What can I get started for you today?" The woman speaks up again, uninterested. She's not rude, but she's not exactly welcoming either.

"I'll have a latte, please," I reply as politely as I can, but the words come out nervous.

She closes the large book and types my order into the tablet in front of her. She spins it around and the price shows up in bold letters. I pull my dad's card out to pay. I almost tap the card against the reader before I stop myself.

I pay with cash instead, thankful that for once I caught a mistake before it was made. *I don't want to be traced—not by him.*

I take a seat at the bar.

"Latte," the woman says plainly as she walks over with my drink, placing a stout mug on the counter in front of me before walking back to her spot.

I take a sip from the beverage and steal a glance at the book she's so entranced by, realizing that the object is no book, but a photo album. It's filled with photographs of a little girl and a little boy who I assume are her children, but the photos look aged. They're at least a decade old, if not older.

She's been staring at one page this entire time, her eyes tracing the same few photographs with a tragic kind of sadness. I take a closer look at the name badge pinned to her blouse. *Esmerelda.*

"I have a daughter your age," she blurts out of nowhere. I offer a smile and a nod.

There's a pause. "She's gonna be a Chaser," Esmerelda continues, and I almost spit out my drink.

She hesitates, reaching out to touch the album. "I had no idea until last night."

When I see the sadness in this stranger's eyes, something ignites inside me, and I can feel a flicker of internal fury grow stronger the more I think about what I'm witnessing. Because the system tears people apart, not only from the inside but from their families too.

Everything I'm doing is for them—for every person out there who has been broken by the brutal hands of the laws we suffer through. *For all of them.*

I know I am fighting for my own family too, but for some reason, deep down, I can't help but wonder if they'll end up suffering for it.

Esmerelda takes out one of the photos to study it closely. She smiles at the image of a little girl standing in the ocean, laughing as a boy not much older than her splashes her with gray saltwater.

But it's not a happy grin. I can tell the woman and I are both filled with the same kind of sadness. We both grieve lost innocence, we both mourn over the way things change.

After a while, Esmerelda puts the photo back in the album and disappears into the back room. I hear footsteps against old wood and assume she's taking it upstairs to the apartment above the cafe.

Just then, the bell above the door rings, and someone else enters the coffee shop. Part of me wants to turn around, but I don't want to draw attention to myself, because I know exactly why I'm here.

The footsteps pause for a moment before continuing slowly, growing closer and closer until they stop completely, right behind me. My heart picks up its pace, and I pray it isn't someone I know. A nosy neighbor who knows my alleged training timeline would definitely turn me in to my father.

"You were supposed to meet me outside," the person seethes right into my ear, and I let out a sigh of relief.

"Sorry." I shrug, not bothering to look up at Cedar as I take a sip from my coffee.

"You're a pain," he grumbles, turning around to exit. "We're leaving."

I take one last hurried sip of my drink before setting the mug down, scrambling to catch up with Cedar as he holds the door open impatiently. I walk through and he follows, closing it behind him.

His dark hair is messier than usual today, almost curled by the morning's light rain, with a few loose locks falling over his eyes. His shades are there too—an accessory he always seems to be wearing. I can't help but wonder if it has something to do with that scar of his.

"What's our mission, again?" I ask as we walk across the gravel parking lot in front of the shop. The wind tangles my hair, and I can taste the salt in the sky.

Cedar stops, turning back around to face me and swatting a hand in my general direction. "Keep your voice down."

"Sorry," I whisper.

"And don't call them missions."

"Why?"

"Because it sounds dumb."

"What else am I supposed to call them?" I scoff.

"Tasks. Jobs, maybe."

"Fine," I grumble, crossing my arms. "Our job. What's our job?"

"Before we do anything else, we're gathering intel from a watcher of ours," he responds plainly, walking back toward the shop. "Stay put."

I roll my eyes, trudging over to my car to take a seat on the hood, frustrated that he still doesn't trust me enough to let me be more involved.

Of course he's doing this without me.

I watch Cedar through the tinted shop windows, squinting to make out his shape through the glass. Esmerelda is back at the counter, and as soon as she notices him, she announces something to the remaining customers, who take their leave with audible frustration. I avert my gaze as they exit the shop, climbing into their cars and driving away. Out of the corner of my eye, I can see the *OPEN* sign flicker until the illumination disappears.

Once the shop is emptied, I can see Cedar and Esmerelda talking face to face behind the counter. His back is to me, but I watch as he takes off his shades before giving the woman a warm hug.

I furrow my brows together, puzzled. I never would have expected Cedar of all people to participate in displays of affection of any kind. I still can't see his face—I've never really seen the whole thing at all, actually, because he keeps it hidden—but by the way he holds himself, I wonder if he could possibly be smiling. Could this be a relative, perhaps? An aunt or a cousin or something? An old family friend?

I glare as Cedar sips from a mug that looks a lot like the nearly untouched latte I left behind. They chat for a few minutes until they hug again, and Cedar turns around to take his leave, shades and mask already back in place.

"What was that about?" I question with a grin as he walks out the door, gravel crunching beneath his footsteps as he grows closer.

Cedar clears his throat. "That's confidential."

"Of course it is." I roll my eyes. "And thanks for drinking my coffee, by the way."

"So you were watching."

My face heats up. "No."

"If you really have to know..." He sighs, turning his head to look at me. I wait for a response, wondering if I was right about that woman being some relative of his. "I was drinking tea."

Of course. "You're a monster. Coffee is a blessing."

"Oh trust me, Your Darkness, I very much agree and I'll happily die on that hill with you. But you see..." He winces like he's about to say something controversial. "Tea is just so much better."

"Right." My eyes roll again. With Cedar, it's second nature. "Herbalist."

"So," he says, changing the subject, "we have a few runs to complete before tonight."

Tonight, I remind myself, stomach churning. "Alright."

He carries his brown leather satchel over one shoulder and his black backpack over both, and I watch as he double-checks the contents of both bags. "We're trading medicine today."

I look around nervously, taking in my surroundings and wondering whether or not someone or something could be listening. I doubt it—we're practically in the middle of nowhere, and the town has yet to fully wake up—but in a world like this, you can never be too sure where a mic might be.

"For what?" I ask, equal parts anxious and curious.

Cedar hesitates, lowering his voice, almost like he fears what he's about to say. "Yesterday guns."

I nod, though I can't understand what the Unseen could possibly need so many weapons for. Defense, perhaps. Maybe even trading for more valuable items, like Yesterday electronics untraceable by the government, or old radios. The possibilities are extensive.

Still, I feel uneasy, and I'm haunted by the feeling that I've bitten off more than I can chew.

I look up at Cedar when I hear his footsteps, giving him a questioning glare when I see that he's walking away. "Where are you going?"

"Away," he replies, annoyed. "You coming or what?"

"We don't have to walk, you know." I hop off my vehicle and pat the hood. "I brought my car."

Cedar stops dead in his tracks and turns around to face me as though I've just spoken in tongues. "Are you kidding me? I'm not getting into that *thing*." He gestures to the car.

"Asa's a mechanic, you know. He wouldn't let me drive his kids around in something that could explode."

"These explode?" Cedar's eyes widen, panicked.

"I mean, when you throw fire at them or something, then yeah. Or when you hit a tree," I reply, but my response only worsens the smuggler's glare.

"Look." I sigh. "If you're so scared of my driving abilities, you can take these, alright?" I fish my car keys out of my pocket as he runs his hands through his hair.

"Wait," I chuckle, "you don't know how to drive, do you?"

"No, I don't, okay?" Cedar hisses. He looks at the car like it's some fantastical beast that could swallow him whole.

I smirk. "You've never been in a car before."

He scoffs, grumbling. "They don't exactly have cars where I come from, alright? And we never had one when I was younger."

I give him a look. What could he mean by that? Where else could he be from?

"How do you get around, then?" I ask.

"I walk. I hike. Backpack. Camp. Whatever you wanna call it," he mumbles. "I'd trust my own two legs over a car any day."

"Well there's no way we're walking to my dad's office back in Port City."

"Fine. Then drive over there yourself." Cedar turns around again. "I'll handle these runs on my own and meet you there when you're done."

"I'm not breaking in alone! Especially not in broad daylight," I whisper as aggressively as I can. "Just because I know what we're looking for doesn't mean I have the skills to get it that easily. Which is why I agreed to join you and the Unseen or whatever you call yourselves in the first place. So I can learn how to do things like this myself."

He pauses, turning back around. I can tell he's glaring through his shades.

"I'm helping you with these jobs, but I'm not walking," I state firmly.

There's a pause, and for a moment, I wonder if I've overstepped my boundaries. I want him to trust me, after all, and I'm not sure I can accomplish that without establishing respect.

But to my surprise, he simply sighs. "If you crash the car, I'm killing you in hell, pal."

"Sounds good." I grin, making my way toward the driver's seat.

I climb into the car, waiting for Cedar to do the same. He hesitates, but eventually, he opens the door and takes a seat, struggling to fit his long legs in the space between the chair and the glove box. I forgot that I'd been sitting there earlier this morning when Ren was driving.

"Close quarters," Cedar grumbles, closing the door.

"You can move your seat back, you know," I tell him. "There's a lever down there."

He studies me for a moment, perhaps suspecting me of plotting some unspoken tomfoolery to get back at him for his perpetual cynicism. But as much as I love to mess with people like him, to his eventual relief, I have nothing mischievous in mind.

Reluctantly, Cedar reaches his arm and torso down, not finding the bar that moves the seat forward, but instead, the lever that folds the seat. I stifle a laugh as it hits him in the head, the impact triggering an obscene response whispered between clenched teeth.

"I should put an end to this right here, shouldn't I?" he threatens, fixing the seat and rubbing the back of his skull.

"Stab me," I mimic. All he can do is glare as I pull out of the parking lot and back down that long stretch of road.

We do a few odd jobs Cedar tells me absolutely nothing about. The only information I receive is where to turn, where to park, and when to follow him down to old trailheads or hidden boulders or abandoned buildings, and the occasional backyard or two. Like clockwork, he keeps his shades on at all times, his face truly unseen.

As we work, I can't help but wonder what his eyes look like. Sure, he lifted them up once last night, but it was far too dark to see anything but the motion of his wink. It feels strange to trust someone who doesn't trust me the same way, and there are times when I question whether or not I should trust him at all.

But I always correct myself, because even though this strange smuggler boy is absolutely infuriating at times, I would trust Asa with my life. In a way, I already have. Because Asa would never lie, and he would never associate with bad people. Right?

Of course he wouldn't, I correct myself, and I refuse to dwell on the subject again.

At an abandoned warehouse, we deliver a box of herbal salves and tinctures to a man who looks as frail as Margot in exchange for a hefty wad of cash and a generous tip. When Cedar thinks neither the man nor myself are looking, he slips in an extra jar.

And then the cash meets the hand of a hurried woman who finds us at a decaying bridge a few minutes into the woods, and then the cash turns into what looks like a Yesterday gun and a box of ammo.

After that, Cedar leaves a box of more herbal medicine in the hollowed out trunk of a tree on the edge of someone's property, and another in an empty parking garage nearby.

And when it's time for me to leave Cedar at Port Keys Coffee Co. for now and head back to the training center to take Ren home, I think about the people I've seen. The desperation. The pain behind their eyes. They all had the look of a person who has been devoured by the system. In one way or another, we have all had pieces of us torn away by the sharp teeth of Nightjade laws.

As I drive, I realize that now more than ever, I understand the McLellans' hatred for Chasers. Theirs is a hatred that only grows more potent with every year that passes over the Pick that took the twins' mother away.

Though I certainly notice the cracks in the Presidency's rule, I also see the risk of acknowledging those flaws. Any one of the people we met today, no matter how desperate they are—*especially* because of their desperation —could rat out the Unseen at the drop of a hat. Maybe the authorities would have a hard time tracking them down at first, but if any of those people gave them as much as a clue, they would find us eventually.

This is no longer just avoidance. This is no longer just a lie about me refusing to meet my father's expectations and become a Chaser.

This is risk, and as addictive as it is, it is like quicksand, and it's only a matter of time before I'm completely suffocated.

As much as Ren hates this system, he's learned to open his eyes and see what needs to be done—as disagreeable as it is—and do it because he knows that someone must. He's becoming a Chaser because he has the courage to do it, despite everything. Why am I not following in his footsteps?

If I were to Chase, I would be fighting for the protection of my entire family. I would have a well-paying job and enough Immunity to let them all live the natural life they're supposed to live.

But I would be lost as a Chaser. I would lose my sense of what's right and what's wrong. I would become a part of the system that's taken everything from so many people, and I would eventually become jaded to the core belief that every life matters. My mother would succumb to the mourning and spend the rest of her life grieving the little girl in her own photo albums.

While I can't become a part of the system, it's not enough to simply refuse to play my part.

I have to do more than just defy it, because I'm not defying it out of bravery. I'm defying it out of fear.

And I have a feeling that the Unseen hold more power than the Presidency wants us all to believe. They have to be bigger than a hushed rumor.

No one can ever really know what it means to do right. But if the Unseen has the hidden drive and influence I hope they do, then I think I could be very close to the right side—even if it's the riskier one.

And if I get killed for treason in the process, so be it.

REN

Saturday, June 17
Day 1

I'm surprisingly calm for a person who just signed their life away.

The woman at the desk takes the tablet from my hands and points a manicured finger at the elevator to my right. "Wait your turn and go down alone."

Down? I nod mindlessly, not able to do much else but obey.

When it's my turn to walk inside the elevator, I notice that it doesn't have any buttons, not even an emergency lever. Whoever designed it must have had high expectations that excluded any foreseeable malfunction. It was created to work just so and it will continue to work just so until the day it no longer stands. *Just like everything else in this building—and everyone.*

Every surface of the elevator is the same as the lobby's pristine and patternless flooring. It's seamless. No tile lines, no marble swirls, no sparkling granite texture, just white stone so polished I see reflections of myself wherever I turn. It sickens me, seeing myself as part of that colorless surface. I've only just begun and I'm already blending in.

The elevator comes to a soundless halt, and the doors open quickly and efficiently to release their cargo. They close just as swiftly the moment my foot exits the platform, letting me know how eager they are to be rid of such an annoyingly inquisitive passenger. I don't hear the machine make any movements, but I know it's silently departing to the lobby again to lure more prey within its jaws.

I spare a moment to take in the setting around me. The underground room is enormous, like an award-winning school gymnasium named after some long-forgotten physical education instructor. But the only similarity this has to a gym is the size alone. Everything else is unlike anything I've ever seen. The walls are that same nauseating white as before, but this time, the floor and ceiling are completely black. The atmosphere is different down here; it somehow manages to be more intimidating than the lobby.

The midnight floors are completely empty. Nothing decorates their surface, save for the rows of cadets in various shapes and ages lined up in a neat grid. A small oak podium at the front stands out against the monotony of the building's color palette—or lack thereof—and behind it is an older woman with dark sepia skin and glaring eyes, who is dressed in a glossy white uniform that looks more like protective armor than anything else. I assume it's some kind of metal, but the material is so lustrous and shiny that I find it hard to believe it's not plastic. The only thing left uncovered by this armor is her head, which is decorated by a tidy bun of thick black hair that seems just as orderly as the woman wearing it.

All of us could recognize the uniform from a mile away if we had to.

She is a Chaser.

I feel painfully out of place in my casual attire, but everyone around me seems to be in the same boat. We're a sea of approximately 150 trainees, each one more out of place than the next.

In this ocean of nervous expressions, I don't see a group of future Chasers. I don't see a group of monsters. Instead, I see a mass of peers who seem just as desperate as me.

I wonder what must transpire in order to transform a group of seemingly innocent people into an army of mindless, bloodthirsty beasts.

"I think we have to get in line."

Someone comes up behind me and whispers into my ear. I'm startled at first, but when I turn to look at the speaker I'm calmed.

She's a small, broad-shouldered girl with golden brown skin and kind eyes. Her bobbed black hair falls like shining curtains, straight as a board and neat as her composure. I know she must be just as scared as I am, but she succeeds at maintaining an illusion of calm.

"Do we have to be in some kind of order?" I lean over to whisper back to her, but she's already walking to an open spot in the line of cadets before me. The idea of walking out there alone intimidates me, so I take a deep breath before following her footsteps.

I stand next to the girl as more and more cadets file in from the elevator. One after the other, they all seem frightened and confused. We're all thrown off by the lack of instructions from the Chaser at the podium and the one who stands next to her in the same uniform, a brown-haired freckled man I did not initially notice.

We stand in this line for what feels like an eternity. We stand as straight as we can, trying to mirror the emotionless expressions of the two figures at the podium. But eventually, the elevator stops letting people out.

"I assume you are all arranged in check-in order," the woman in charge shouts to the crowd.

We are stilled by shock for a moment before the shuffling commences. Confusion reigns as we all struggle to remember where we stood in line. The girl and I switch places, and a handful of other trainees do the same thing.

I feel the weight of our group's mistake, and I can't shake the gut-wrenching understanding that mistakes are a thing of the past. Any misstep from here on out has the potential to contribute to my own execution.

"I expected more from you, cadets." The woman steps down from the podium and begins to slowly pace up and down the front row. "You're supposed to be the best of the best. The finest our society has to offer. And yet here you are, relearning skills you should have learned in kindergarten."

No one says a word, and the Chaser continues.

"Well, let me tell you one thing." She pauses her pacing for emphasis. "I will not tolerate that. Not anymore. From this day forward, you will be perfect. You will use the brain you were given—and selected for—and leave any forms of idiocy behind you for good. Is that clear?"

More silence fills the room. Everyone is too afraid to respond, terrified of saying the wrong thing.

I'm brought back to Mr. Aguilar's classroom again. The fear I felt after Mae Soto disappeared is no different from the fear that is currently making me sweat.

"Is that clear?" she barks, louder and angrier this time.

"Yes," we shout in unison. Terrified of being heard, I mouth the words.

"Is that clear?" she shouts again, and I assume she means for all of us to answer.

"Yes!" This time, I manage to let out a whisper.

"Good," the woman says, commanding our attention by beginning to pace once more. She speaks slowly and firmly. "Now, we don't have time for anything but the point, so I'll get straight to it."

She pauses, clearing her throat.

"You are all here for the exact same reason: to join the Corps and become a Chaser," she explains. "I don't care what brought you here. Despite how different you think you are, you are all the same. I want to make this very clear. You. Are. All. The. Same. You are nothing but Chasers from this day forward."

A few cadets exchange nervous glances, so subtle they are missed.

"By taking that entrance exam, checking in, and signing that waiver this morning, you have forfeited the right to be anything *but* a Chaser," the woman continues. "This is your life now, and I want that to sink in. We can't afford to deal with shock today, understand?"

"Yes," the crowd replies in unison.

"The first item on today's agenda is to get you all ready for your uniforms," she says. "Every day, you will show up to training wearing your Chaser uniform. Failure to do so will result in failure of the course. Your uniform is a fundamental part of your new identity.

"But, if you attempt to abuse this gift of power from the Presidency and wear your armor outside of training, the consequences that follow could be fatal. I promise you—the Chaser Corps will know if you attempt to use it outside of this building. Is this clear?"

"Yes."

"You might be wondering just how we'll know," the Chaser says.

There's a pause, but we know she wants us to stay silent this time.

"You all walked through those scanners while checking in, yes?" she says. There is no verbal response, but we all nod.

"And I assume you all have come to the same conclusion about those scanners, yes?"

Some of us nod, but most of us are statues, puzzled by her words.

"Good," the Chaser lifts her chin slightly higher. "I would be disappointed if you didn't figure it out by now, but we are all microchipped—and those scanners are there to confirm your identity and enter you into our database as an official Chaser trainee."

It is far too easy to forget how to breathe.

My heart stops completely. The liquid that once rushed through my veins turns cold, gray, and lifeless.

This is more than blood-curdling. This is marrow melting. Bile boiling. My cerebrospinal fluid solidifies.

Microchipped?

No. There's no way. This must be some kind of test, some mind game or clever puzzle we're supposed to unravel and put back together. Because I would know if I was microchipped. Wouldn't we all?

Wouldn't we feel it inside of us? Wouldn't we see it happen to our children? Wouldn't someone say something? Surely no one can keep a truth like this concealed from the public. There are hundreds of thousands of Chasers and Presidency workers dotted all throughout the country. If it is true, and all of them know, why hasn't anyone slipped up?

I think about how Eddie and I can barely keep our lips sealed about something as small-scale as our own lies. The human mind is weak.

And then I think about it.

If this is your career—if you sign your life away to them—a slip-up is a death sentence. The system kills families for punishment. Surely they'd kill for secrecy too.

Maybe the reason why no one hears about it is really as grim as I expect it to be. Maybe that is how no one knows.

The people who know are scared into silence. The people who find out are forced to be quiet forever.

The cadets turn to each other in confusion, exchanging glances as the air in the room thickens. A hiss of disoriented whispers surges through the crowd, confirming that the woman should, in fact, be disappointed in all of us.

Because not a single soul in this room had any idea.

"Now, I'll explain it simply for the purpose of investing in your efficiency." The woman shouts. "I cannot risk having a group of shocked and muddled cadets handle priceless Chaser technology today."

The whispering comes to an instant halt. We all want to know more. We all *need* to know more. Each one of us craves an answer to a thousand different questions, but I have a feeling that every answer will only cause the number of questions to grow.

"We all know that our Cards are an integral part of our identity."

This time, no one nods.

"We are all randomly assigned two playing Card tattoos at birth to signify the part we play in this system of ours. These tattoos serve as symbols for a system that is just, and odds that are fairer than all." She points to her arm for effect, though we cannot see her Cards beneath her uniform.

"But before the tattoos are given, we are microchipped by a member of one of the Chaser Corps' classified divisions—informally known as Chippers or NIM to most, and the Department of Nightjade Internal Microchipping on paper. For safety, NIM workers are the only ones who know the exact location of these microchips."

She pauses to let us take it all in, but I know she's not finished scratching the surface. There has to be more to the world of the Chaser Corps than meets the eye. My hands grow clammier by the minute, and I am terrified of what's to come.

It's not the unknown itself that frightens me, but the fact that there is an unknown to begin with. An unknown that must be explained.

I'm fearful of what I don't know. What I haven't known. What's been kept from me—from all of us—for our entire lives.

"This is highly classified information exclusive to the Chaser Corps and the Presidency alone," the Chaser begins again. "No tattoo artist or birth attendee or even parent is aware of this, because nobody is. Let's just say we take extreme precautionary measures to ensure that this information does not become public knowledge."

I attempt to swallow a lump in my throat.

She pauses. "We are always there. Always listening, always knowing."

The contents of my stomach begin to return to my throat. I can practically taste the sourness of bile. The room starts to spin, and everything is suddenly too overwhelming. Too nauseating. I know I can't stand here any longer.

But I must, and it takes all I have to remember that.

"We will know if this information gets out. We will always know exactly what you are doing, both in training and out," the Chaser threatens. "Keep that in mind as you proceed to take part in the training course, because there is much for you to learn, and just as much for you to keep to yourself."

So this is how they do it all.

I know this is only the tip of the iceberg, but I'm still so afraid of falling off the edge and plummeting below the surface, of seeing what truly lies beneath the darkness of this Arctic ocean I'm stranded in.

But from my perch on this small block of frozen water, I can see just enough to know there must be something massive beneath me.

This is how the Pick is possible. This is how the Presidency manages to dictate an entire country and maintain that control through whatever means necessary. This is how people are murdered on such a massive scale.

And this is why it's impossible to escape the synthetic, man-made fate we are all given from the very moment we come into this world.

We are all born to die. But some of us are born to kill too.

The woman tells us her name is Amelia, but we are to address her only by her last name: Pittman. She says that we cadets are to address each other the same way. The importance of this is stressed between lines.

Her partner—or her Second, as Pittman says—is Perry Price. He's a mousy man, so thin and quiet I find it hard to believe that he's a Chaser at all. But he commands with authority nonetheless, holding a palm out in front of the crowd and motioning for us to stand still as Pittman exits through doors that seem to appear out of nowhere. The wall opens for a moment and devours Pittman before closing just as quickly, becoming that seamless white wall once again.

My legs grow weary from standing for such an extended period of time, but I tell myself to get familiar with the ache. I doubt there will be much sitting in the career that lies ahead of me—but I imagine there to be quite a bit of waiting nonetheless.

After what feels like hours, something finally moves. To my left, the entire wall begins to unfold like a garage door. Two horizontal halves disappear into the floor and the ceiling until there is no longer evidence that a wall was ever there to begin with.

The wall's absence reveals an expansion of the room we're in, but unlike the one we occupy, it's not empty. Instead, it's filled with dozens of white pumpkin-sized boxes that make me feel like an insect eyeing a pile of sugar cubes. Pittman stands next to the mound with a tablet in her hands.

"When I call your name, you will come up and make your way into the dressing room over there," Pittman shouts.

"Once you are in the proper attire, you will retrieve your box. You will then go back to where you were standing and set this box by your feet.

"After that, you will not touch it. You will not mess with it, fidget with it, or even look at it. Got it?"

"Yes."

"Good."

I zone out as Pittman begins to announce an extensive list of names. My mind is too busy to pay attention, although I know I should.

I assume it must be important to learn the names of my fellow cadets, to see just who I'm working with. But now, I'm too focused on thinking, too focused on being in shock from the information that was unearthed, as I imagine the rest of us are.

"McLellan, Ren."

My pulse comes to a halt, snapping out of it as soon as my name is called.

I do as I am told and make my way up to the pile of boxes, swallowing the nervous lump in my throat. I've never been so close to a Chaser before.

As far as I can remember, anyway.

I tread to an opening in the wall where she said the dressing room was located. As soon as I walk through the threshold, automatic doors encase me in a glossy white coffin.

The room is cramped—only the size of a small closet—but just roomy enough to change. A large touch-screen tablet is mounted to the back of the wall, and beneath it is an installation of what seems to be a mini version of the scanners upstairs.

I wait for some recorded voice to tell me what to do, but nothing happens. I furrow my brow and try inserting my hand, and sure enough, I'm rewarded with a happy blue light that seems to trigger the tablet. I want to tell myself this is fingerprint technology, but I cannot shake the thought of microchips.

I wait patiently for something to move before a robotic voice reads the words that appear in front of me.

McLellan, Ren
Size: Medium

My name and what I assume to be my clothing size flash on the screen, along with two small images of my Cards. My eyes dart to my wrists, to my tattoos, and then to the cards on the screen. Ace of Spades, Queen of Hearts. I try not to think too hard about how they know.

I jump when I hear some machine start to hiss, and my eyes dart to the left to see a small opening appear in the wall next to me.

I look inside the opening and see a stack of neatly folded clothing. I'm hesitant to grab it—afraid of touching the wrong thing and losing a hand or two—but the fabric is warm when I do, a small comfort in a cold place.

Black shirt, black pants, black socks, black undergarments. Everything is uniform and made of the same soft, flexible fabric, silky to the touch and presumably very expensive. As I get dressed, the new clothes stick to my skin perfectly. I remember how they took my measurements during the physical I received as part of the Chaser exam. Now I understand why.

The clothing makes me sick to my stomach. It reeks with a chemical stench of artificial material, cleaning solution, and a laundry soap I cannot bear. I've gotten so used to using clean fragrances and soaps for Margot that I can no longer handle the stink myself, and I feel lightheaded—though there is more to the nausea and headache than toxins alone.

There's something dehumanizing about being forced to wear the exact same thing as everyone else. As Pittman said, we are all the same. We no longer have the legal right to be individuals. From this day forward, I am the one thing I hate the most in this world: a Chaser.

But I know these clothes are only the beginning. I know this isn't the real Chaser uniform; these are only the clothes we're supposed to wear underneath the white suits of armor displayed on Pittman and Price and every other Chaser in the country.

This is only the beginning, but somehow, it feels more like an end.

> **Please place your old clothing inside the designated compartment. This will be returned to you at the lobby when you exit the facility.**

The opening to my left comes to a close, only for a new compartment to appear to my right. I listen to the tablet's instructions and feed the wall my old attire.

I turn to where the entryway used to be. The hidden automated doors slide open to release me from the cramped dressing room. It feels strange to walk out in this outfit, and I already feel different from the person I was up in the lobby.

Pittman hands me my assigned box, and I'm surprised by how weightless it feels in my hands as I walk back to my spot. It's smooth on the outside, and I wonder if it's the same white material as the Chaser uniforms and everything else in this building. I'm too afraid to observe it any further and I set it down the moment my feet stop moving, like it's a bomb my curiosity will only trigger.

After the last name is called, Pittman walks back to the podium and the wall returns to its original place. She sets the tablet down on the oak stand and addresses the crowd of cadets once again, pacing slowly and authoritatively as she speaks.

"These boxes are extremely valuable assets to your career in the Chaser Corps. They do not contain your uniforms." She pauses. "They *are* your uniforms."

The trainees around me twitch with the urge to look at their feet and study the strange objects, but nobody touches them.

"Your uniform serves many purposes," Pittman announces. "It's more than just a uniform; it's an extremely useful and equally as expensive state-of-the-art solar-powered suit of armor.

"It's a communication tool. A GPS. A way to ask questions to a built-in artificial intelligence system. A translator. A camera. A device to help you track your assignments, even and especially Runners. And—"

Pittman presses some sort of button on her forearm and—not unlike the disappearing wall—pieces of the uniform fold away to reveal a hidden compartment. A white pistol rests within, round, simple, and small in its design.

The Chaser's movements are too quick for my brain to register, and before I know what's happening, she grabs the gun and shoots it directly at us cadets. The bullet hits the back wall, and we all turn around to see oozing, violet black Nightjade dripping down the colorless surface like blood.

"—a weapon." She puts the gun back in the compartment. In an instant, it disappears once more.

Pittman might as well have shot each and every one of us, because we are all breathless, quieted by our awe and soothed by relief. Before a few moments ago, I had never seen a Nightjade gun in person before. I had only seen such a deadly tool in textbooks and through words spun by exaggerating classmates.

Now I know just how frightening weapons can be—especially guns—and why no one is allowed to have them anymore. *Except for Chasers.*

"So, now you know the worth of the boxes sitting next to your feet," Pittman says. "They all hold a personalized uniform designed specifically for you, based on what was gathered from the physical examination you all went through a few weeks ago."

A few of us dare to look down at our feet, some cadets boasting their eagerness with grins and others expressing their nervousness with sweaty brows.

I can't tell where I stand; I'm apathetic, past the point of being afraid yet nowhere near a place where I can look forward with ambition. Or maybe it's the fear that's driving me. Maybe I'm too afraid to feel anything at all.

I'm scared of investing my energy into one emotion, only to lose control and watch it spill over—and I can't let that happen. I can't lose myself in the anger.

As much as I detest this system, I must distance myself from this burning hatred inside me. I can't let my pride get in the way of my one and only goal. In fact, I can't let *any* feeling get in the way.

I shouldn't let myself feel anything at all.

"I need each and every one of you to pay close attention as I demonstrate how this works," Pittman announces to the group, all eyes averting from the boxes to the Chaser standing in front of us.

I try to keep my mind from wandering as she begins to cover all of the uniform's uses. She uses Price as a model and goes from head to fingertips to torso to toes, thoroughly explaining the functionality of each piece.

I have to admit, the technology is intriguing. But I'm ashamed to be a part of this, ashamed to become a tool for these people to expend and exploit, just like the uniform I'll soon adopt as my own. I am no longer human but a monster with purpose, maybe even lesser than sentience and nothing but a purpose itself.

"It's important that you all know how to properly remove and store your uniform," Pittman says. "Price will demonstrate, pay close attention."

"Suit, right arm," Price orders, and the armor begins to fold instantly and automatically. It stops when it reaches his shoulder, revealing an arm covered by the same black long-sleeve shirt we all wear in unison.

"The uniform folds section by section—two arms, two legs, one torso," Pittman explains. "This function was designed for first aid purposes in case you need to access one part of the body and still cover the rest. Though I doubt you will ever have to use this function in your career.

"First aid is taught, but its usage is practically unheard of in this line of work. No one challenges a Chaser."

No one challenges a Chaser. My ear rings with the echo of her words, spoken with such menace it almost feels like a warning.

"But for convenience, there's another way to remove your uniform," she says.

"Suit, right arm," Price commands, reversing his previous command. The armor moves like he pressed some hidden rewind button and unfolds back over his arm, covering everything once again.

"Suit, unsuit," he adds.

The uniform folds faster than a blink, removing itself from the entirety of the man's body until it becomes one of the white cubes we were all given just a moment ago. It stands at Price's feet as if it were never a suit of armor to begin with.

"Now this is how you put it on," Pittman shouts. Price steps over the cube and stands so both of his feet are touching the sides.

"Suit," he says. And just as fast as it had disappeared, the uniform reappears on his body once again.

"Both of your feet have to be touching the box for it to work, understand?" Pittman says.

"Yes."

"Now, I want you all to try it when I give the word. You will say the command in unison," Pittman pauses. "Suit."

"Suit," the cadets bark, all in one voice.

The uniforms roll over the crowd like a wave of white sea foam, trapping each recruit within its powerful surge. In a matter of seconds, every single trainee is now dressed like a proper Chaser—including myself.

The material of the armor is more weightless than I expected, almost comfortable. I can barely feel its presence and wonder if it weighs anything at all.

I look down at the body below me and see something I can't recognize. I lift my hand up in front of my face as if to confirm how real I am, and sure enough, my fingers wiggle before my eyes—but they are trapped in a white metal glove. I cannot feel whole anymore. I am made of pieces.

Something feels different. The uniform doesn't feel like an addition to my person, but a replacement for some part of myself that I lost by agreeing to wear it. It adds no weight yet I am heavier than ever before.

Even after we're instructed to unsuit and our uniforms go back to their cubic form, it doesn't feel like I really took the armor off. While Pittman drones on about logistics for the rest of the day, it feels like I'm still wearing it—like I'm still carrying that invisible weightless weight. Even when we're released to go home, the feeling never leaves.

I retrieve the clothes I brought with me from the lobby and exit the heavy glass doors. These clothes should feel familiar, but they don't. They belong to a stranger now. They belong to Ren McLellan, not a Chaser. As I walk through the parking lot and reach my car, I worry that Eddie won't recognize me.

It's only the first day and I already feel so lost.

"What's that?" Eddie questions as I climb into the passenger's seat, grateful she's driving this time because I cannot. *Not like this.*

"Uniform," I respond.

I can't look at her, but I can tell that she's disheartened by my emotionless demeanor. It pains me to feel her energy deplete like that, but there is nothing I can do about it. She'll survive.

"Oh," she says. I can tell she knows how little I want to talk about what happened. That I *can't* talk about what happened. She shrugs. "Doesn't look like a uniform to me."

I don't say a word as we drive back home, but Eddie still remembers to point out all the cows.

EDDIE

Saturday, June 17
Day 1

When I come home holding Ren's uniform cube and the wad of black Chaser clothes, my brother spits out his cereal.

"What the hell is that?" Milo raises his eyebrows suspiciously, wiping sugar-infused milk from his chin as he stares at the alien box in confusion.

"Uniform." The lie comes easily because it holds an ounce of truth. It is a uniform, just not mine.

"No way." He laughs dryly. "You're full of it."

"I'm not, but okay." I shrug and make my way to my bedroom, closing the door behind me. My privacy efforts are immediately reversed as Milo follows me inside.

"How was it?" he questions, taking a seat at the edge of my bed.

"It was... good, I guess? I don't know." The words taste bitter in my mouth. Nothing about Chasing can ever be good.

"Seriously, what is that?" Milo points to the cube again.

"I'm telling you, it's my uniform."

"It's literally not."

"And you're *literally* dumb."

"Says you."

"Hey, at least I can own up to it. Idiocy is one of my best traits."

I set the cube and wad of black clothing onto my desk before taking a seat, turning the chair to face my younger brother.

"If that really is your uniform," Milo says with crossed arms, "then how does it work?"

"That's... classified."

"You don't know how it works, do you?" He laughs, and I can't help but grin. His laugh is contagious. "I will never understand how you ended up being the top of your class."

"Mean."

"I'm obviously the smart one here. And you're a year older."

I roll my eyes. "You're brutal."

"Thank you." My brother holds his chin high.

"Well, I don't know how it works. I just know that it does," I say. "We push a button or something and it turns into a uniform or whatever."

"That's actually really cool." Milo stands up to study the box, and I swat his hand away when he reaches out to touch the foreign object.

I know the way my brother's mind works. While he's always had a love for Yesterday trinkets in particular—gadgets that have been surpassed by the advancements of current technology—I know he'd be happy to investigate Chaser tech as well. His intelligence makes him curious, and I don't blame him for his interest. I just don't want him to be interested in *this*.

I want Milo to hate Chasers just as much as I do, no matter how much our father wants me to become one.

"Are you not allowed to show anyone what it does?" Milo guesses.

"We can't wear it at home, at least during training. So no," I explain. "And we can't tell anyone anything we learn, so don't expect any cool stories. And don't ask questions."

"That's annoying."

"I know. But hey, at least I don't have homework anymore. Once training's over I'll get to spend more time with you." I give my brother a pestering grin.

"Oh no."

"*Oh no* is right," I say. "Expect lots of—I don't know, making fun of old movies or going out to eat or whatever it is you kids do these days."

"You're so weird." Milo chuckles, but then his tone softens, all humor replaced with concern he tried his best to hide. "So how was it, really?"

By the look on his face, I can tell he knows that being a Chaser is the last thing I want to do. Even if school and avoiding my father's verbal attacks has gotten in the way of spending time with my brother, I'm certain Milo understands me as much as Margot does. He always has. I suddenly feel a dull, shameful ache in my ribcage, because I wish I could tell him everything.

Milo has helped me keep secrets from my father my whole life. If he knew the truth behind my lies, I know for a fact that he would keep his mouth shut. While I worry about him wanting to intervene, to help me with all of this Unseen activity and potentially put himself in danger, he could probably help me maintain my secret. Right?

Wouldn't it be useful to have someone else cover for me? To have someone know at least some of the truth, in case worse comes to worst and my father grows even more suspicious of me than he already is?

Can I tell him that I never even took the exam?

Can I tell him all I'm doing instead?

No, I think to myself, my voice of reason making a rare appearance. It's like I said. *That would only put him in danger.*

"It was alright," I finally whisper. The guilt of lying to Milo nearly brings tears to my eyes. I've never withheld the truth from him before—not like this.

I just hope he can find it in him to forgive me when he finds out the truth, because I know this can't continue forever, even if it all must stay hidden for now.

"Well, I better get some sleep." I clear my throat, unable to bear this heartbreak for a minute longer. "Early day tomorrow."

I stand up to open my door, shooing the visitor through the entryway. I begin to close the door but pause as he's halfway down the hall.

"I love you, loser," I call from where I stand, choking on the words.

"Yeah, yeah." Milo swats the air, not looking back as he approaches the corner.

But he pauses before he turns, rotating his neck to look back at me with a grin. "We have our whole lives to watch old movies and eat good food, Ed. Do what you need to do and don't worry about me, alright?"

And with that, he turns the corner and walks out of sight.

I am sinking in falsities, and I know it's only a matter of time before I drown.

I've seen the building in the daylight, back when I used to spend my summers working the receptionist desk for my father.

But at night, there is nothing familiar about Mateo Voclain's dental office.

After dropping Ren off at home and storing his uniform in my room, I met Cedar at our spot in the woods. There's been a lot of driving around on my part, but it's important that Ren has a place to hide his Chaser things, and that I can use them to strengthen my lie at home. And I cannot let him go to training fully alone.

Night had fallen by the time we reached our destination. The office is a cube, crisp, white, and far cleaner than I remember. I squint to make out two stories of reflective windows, but without the sun, this soft lunar haze is not enough light to reflect, and the glass panes remain as empty as the building itself. In an eerie way, it reminds me of a smaller version of the training center.

From where I sit, I can see pots of neatly trimmed shrubbery wrapping around the front and the side, guarding the entryway, where two glass doors stand tall, waiting to be unlocked.

I trace the key card that rests in my pocket next to the knife attached to my belt loop, trying to suppress the guilt that's been haunting me ever since I stole it from my father's wallet. I'm thankful I didn't wake him or my mother in the process, of course, but there's a small part of me that can't help but wish they caught me.

I'm trying to do the right thing. I just don't know if I like the liar I've become.

"You Chips really have a type," Cedar mutters to himself from the passenger's seat, shaking his head with folded arms.

"What are you on about?" I glare. *Chips?*

Cedar folds down to rummage through his backpack, pulling out a small cloth bag. "All the buildings in cities like yours are the same."

"I guess," I shrug. "Never really paid much attention to it."

"So modern, so sleek. High tech. Expensive." He raises his voice mockingly, lowering it back to normal when he continues, scoffing. "It's gross."

"What would you prefer, something from the Yesterdays? Nearly a hundred years old and rotting to bits?" I question.

Cedar shakes his head and removes his shades to wipe a smudge on his black long-sleeve shirt. I catch another glimpse of the scar running through his left socket, but he puts the glasses back on before I can get a good look. I am still left wondering what his eyes look like.

"Without the guaranteed exposure to mold toxicity? Yes, I would," Cedar grumbles, closing his backpack. "Buildings from the Yesterdays are easy to break into. *This*, however"—Cedar gestures to the building with his chin —"will be protected with alarms. Access codes. All sorts of inconveniences."

I pause, biting my lip. I didn't even think about that.

"I have my dad's key card. It should disable most alarms." I pull it out of my pocket temporarily for effect.

"What are we looking for, again?" Cedar asks. "I'm not exactly familiar with dental offices."

"Wherever they keep the anesthetics," I reply. "Also, gross."

"I have cleaner teeth than all of you Chips." He glares. "Charcoal? Sage? Coconut oil pulling? I do it all. I even floss. *Floss*, Voclain."

"Great," I mumble, but really, I can't help but be a little interested in what he has to say. He said he was a healer, after all, and I wonder about his natural remedies. *Another time*, I tell myself.

"Do you know what kind of anesthetics your old man uses? Names? Specifics?" Cedar questions.

"He's the professional, not me."

"Anything else that could be valuable?"

"My dad's wallet, perhaps?" I snap, briefly filled with anger and I don't know why. Cedar is completely silent.

As accusatory and verbally aggressive as my father might be, my stomach churns with guilt. This is his livelihood. He grew up with nothing, married my mother who also grew up with less, and did all he could to earn an education and build a business in a world where the less fortunate rarely have the chance to do so, let alone survive.

He is successful because he wanted to be, and while his methods of loving are cruel, all he ever wanted was for me to turn out just the same.

And here I am, completely invalidating all he's worked for.

"I don't know if I wanna do this," I mutter, turning to Cedar with a panic I wish would go away.

"Dear *God*, Voclain." He groans in frustration, leaning back in his seat as he covers his face with his hands.

I've ruined it, haven't I? All I've ever wanted was to be a healer. I wanted to help people like Margot, who can't always help themselves.

And now here I am, throwing it all away. Every lie, every job with Cedar, everything I've done to earn my place in the Unseen—all of it.

How could this smuggler—this scarred rebel of a young man, who has clearly done more for this movement than I could ever imagine—trust someone like me?

I don't know what I want. I don't know what I'm good at, if I'm good at anything at all. I'm not even sure I know who I am anymore, and I'm certainly uncertain of who I am becoming.

"Hey," Cedar says calmly.

His tone surprises me, and I am yanked away from my own thoughts. He studies me carefully. I wonder how long he's been watching me panic like this.

"Look." He sighs, pausing to glance out the window before turning to stare back at me. "I know you're smart. I mean, I've seen the books on your shelves. So you've probably figured a bit of this out already."

I focus on the shape of the steering wheel and shake my head no, but he continues.

"You were right, okay?" Cedar states. "I'm not just a smuggler, or a healer or a botanist. I mean, I am all of those things, but I..." He pauses, sighing again. "This is bigger than the both of us, alright? So much bigger."

My gaze shifts to look at Cedar instead. What could he possibly mean by that?

"Everything we do to help the Unseen matters," Cedar continues. "Every trade we complete, the supplies we gather, the people we help—all of it is for a greater purpose."

A chill runs up and down my spine, because I get the sense that this *we* is not him and me, but something far more significant. I know it is. *It has to be.*

"Where I'm from, we don't have access to anesthetics unless people like me can manage to find them. And while we prefer naturopathy, sometimes we need them, for reasons I'm sure you'll come to understand." He explains cautiously, mindful of what he reveals to me. "I know you and your people don't have access to medical equipment either—because, you know, it's been outlawed and all—but your father's supplies are the closest things we got."

I nod, forcing a small smile.

"Maybe it's stealing." The boy pauses, and even in the dark, I can tell he's smirking. "But we're also doing something good."

"Alright." This time, the grin doesn't feel false. But the feeling doesn't last, because in a moment, it's replaced with a different kind of panic.

I look around frantically, as though identifying the location of the mics would keep the Presidency from listening, if they are at all. "We really shouldn't talk about this here."

"Relax. I don't know much about cars, but I do know the government doesn't bug them. Buildings, yes, but not cars." Cedar chuckles, opening the door and stepping out as he slings his leather satchel over his shoulder, leaving the backpack in the vehicle.

"How do you know that?" I give him a look, climbing out of the car as well.

Cedar shrugs. "I just do."

We cut across the parking lot and approach the building carefully, holding our breath as I swipe the key card in the reader attached to the glass doors that protect the entrance. We stand in silence, watching, waiting, until we hear a quiet beeping sound followed by a little green light. The doors open with ease, and I allow myself to exhale, just a little bit.

I lock them behind us for good measure as we enter the lobby of my father's office. It smells like cleaning solution and artificial mint, a stench so strong and sharp I nearly pinch my nose. I get so used to using the McLellans' non-toxic alternatives to keep Margot from getting nauseous around me that I forget how harsh their opposites can be, and the smell burns my throat.

"This place reeks," Cedar complains under his breath. I get the feeling that things are very different from wherever he comes from.

"We don't have to whisper, you know. We're completely alone," I say, dodging clean white lounge chairs and acrylic coffee tables.

"You can never be too careful," Cedar replies, still whispering.

I shake my head as we turn the corner. "Why would anyone come here at night?"

"We're here."

"And we're not supposed to be."

"Fair point," Cedar says, sighing before raising his voice back to normal and flashing me a forced grin. "Fine. Whatever you say, boss."

I can't remember the last time I stepped foot inside my dad's workplace. Things got busier as my high school career progressed, overwhelming me with increasing expectations from my father. But even though I haven't worked here in quite a long time, I still remember bits and pieces of the building's layout—though I still wish I spent more time here.

The synthetic wood floors make muffled clicking sounds as our shoes collide with the surface, filling the narrow hallway with echoes of our careful footsteps. One of the doors to my left is open just a crack, and I stick my head in to investigate, only to find an empty break room. It's strange to think that this is where my father spends so much of his time, and even stranger how little I know the man.

I close the door and lead Cedar to the room on the right, which ends up being a cleaning closet, not a room. The scent is strong, so we close it immediately. But the next door to our left leads to something of significance.

The room is very small, wrapped within the hug of sleek white counters and cabinetry. Every surface shines when Cedar fishes a flashlight from his bag to observe our surroundings. Little sterilization machines of various shapes and sizes rest upon the countertops, as well as a bunch of other unidentifiable objects I couldn't name if I tried.

"My father called this the sterilization room," I explain. "It's where they clean their tools or something, I don't know."

"Tools?" Cedar raises an eyebrow, and I nod.

Before I can protest, the flashlight is positioned between his teeth, and the smuggler is rummaging through doors, removing plastic wrappings from sterilized dental and surgical equipment to investigate them.

I start to open cabinets myself, but nothing in here seems like it would be useful.

"Let's just go," I mutter. Cedar shrugs, closing drawers and following me as I lead him back through the door.

As we explore more rooms, the familiarity of my father's workplace begins to come back to me, and after snooping in a few more closets and small office areas, we finally stumble across a treatment room.

"Woah," Cedar says, jaw dropped. His brows crease, his expression puzzled. "What is this place?"

"Treatment room," I explain, pointing to the sleek white and state-of-the-art patient's chair in the center of the room.

There are more cabinets on both walls, and next to the chair lies an eggshell-colored rolling cart with a work surface and a little shelf sticking up from the back, where plastic compartments store fresh syringes and dozens of tiny glass jars, each one containing an unidentifiable liquid.

"This is it." I turn to Cedar and smirk. "Anesthesia cart."

"Wow. You really were telling the truth," he replies, and for what might just be the first time, I see him grin from ear to ear.

"They don't need to be refrigerated or anything?" he asks.

"Some do, but not all. Local anesthetic injections hurt more when it's cold, I think." I shrug. "My dad tried explaining this all to me but I tend to tune him out."

Cedar sucks on his teeth. "Yikes. He's a talker, isn't he? Nitpicky?"

"That's one way to put it." I chuckle. "How'd you know?"

"Lucky guess. And I mean, I was there when he barged into your room, you know."

"Right." I shake my head. "Forgot about that."

"I mean, do you have a habit of hiding visitors in your closet, or is he just a little..." I stand back as Cedar picks up a few of the bottles, reading the label before shoving them all into compartments within his satchel.

"Paranoid? Fond of jumping to conclusions? A man whose favorite pastime is gaslighting the people around him?" I finish his sentence.

Cedar gives me a sympathetic smile. "Yeah."

I nod. "You're the only person I hid in a closet. Though if I remember correctly, you jumped out the window."

"Wow, Voclain. I'm honored." Cedar takes his fair share of syringes too, and some extra bottles and alcohol swabs from the drawers below. "To be fair, you were harboring a dangerous criminal."

I look down at my shoes. "I know."

"Hey, that's brave stuff. Makes you a dangerous criminal too, doesn't it?"

I roll my eyes. "It's not like I gave you an invitation or anything."

He takes the last bit of supplies before closing his bag and shoving his hands in his pockets. "I have to say, I'm surprised you managed to be this helpful."

I glare, putting my hands on my hips. "Gee, thanks."

"Take the compliment, Voclain. Savor it."

"Oh, I definitely will." I flash him a false grin and he shakes his head.

"No, I'm serious. Look at all of this."

He flips open his satchel to reveal the stolen anesthetics, but I notice a hoard of scalpels and swappable blades of various shapes and sizes, comparable to the stash of a hungry raccoon.

"You stole those? Back in the sanitation room?" I look up at him with a glare.

"Uh, no?"

"You didn't even ask!"

He sighs, giving me a look that tells me he's losing his patience. "You were the one who suggested this whole thing, alright? I wouldn't be breaking in and stealing your dad's stuff without your help."

Now, his words don't sound so much like a compliment. They feel like a guilty punch to the gut instead.

"And I don't steal random shit, you got that?" He glares angrily before lowering his voice with a sigh. "I may be... you know... but I still have morals. I only take what I need, and nothing else."

"What could you possibly need so many surgical scalpels for anyway?" I say, and Cedar looks at me as though it's obvious. "I'm starting to think you have an obsession with knives."

I can tell he rolls his eyes behind the shades. "I'm a healer. I do heal-y things, and sometimes that includes cutting people open. Or into pieces."

"Ew, fine." I shudder, holding up a hand. "It's whatever. Let's just go."

I walk toward the door, but I turn around and press my finger into his chest. "Don't steal any more knives, *you got that*?"

"Your wish is my command, Your Darkness."

I walk toward the exit, but I pause, tracing the knife attached to my belt loop, feeling its gravitational pull at the mention of blades. I can feel its shape behind the sheath, and I cannot help but feel a little curious. I unsheathe the knife and face Cedar again.

"Jeez, Voclain, what the hell?" He raises his hands in innocence.

I lift my chin, trying to sound firm. "Teach me how to use this."

For the next half hour, Cedar introduces me to the world of blade combat.

He shows me how to properly hold a knife, how to hone my concentration and see it as a tool, not a weapon, an extension of my own arm.

But more importantly, he shows me how to use it for defense.

"Okay. Let's say a person is running at you, right?" he says, positioning himself in front of me.

"If you wanna escape, you can totally do that. It doesn't feel good to hurt people. But if you can't see yourself doing so without inflicting some damage—" He walks behind me to adjust my stance and the blade. I hold it with both hands. "—don't extend the knife. Let them meet it themselves."

He walks in front of me again. "If your stance is right and your grip is firm enough, they'll fall right into it."

For effect, he uses a shoe to push against my shin, and I don't budge.

I look at the knife, studying its point. I turn it over in my hands. "Can you teach me something offensive?"

Cedar gives me a look, hesitating before letting out a sigh. "Alright."

I watch as he pulls a knife out of his pocket, resisting the urge to grin. "Is there a corkboard anywhere?"

I lead him into the closest room, shutting the door behind us as quietly as I can, taking Cedar's flashlight and turning it on. It's an office space, one that looks awfully similar to my father's, presumably used for business needs and patient consultations. I remember it belongs to a man named Carl, and I can see him posing with his wife and two daughters in various frames scattered throughout the room.

There's more white cabinetry, with a desk in the center that has two drawer units on either side and an expensive looking desktop computer. I notice a window cut through the back wall with blinds pinched shut, and moonlight filters in through the slats, filling the room with thin silver lines.

And sure enough, on the back wall by the window, there is a corkboard.

"You can shift the defensive moves I taught you to work for offense too," he says, going on to show me how to swing the knife at a person. He even shows me how to properly stab, with one hand and both, and the best places on the body to target if you want to injure a person without killing them. But he shows me the fatal points too, just in case I ever find myself in a situation where it's necessary.

The nape of the neck.

The armpit.

The liver and other abdominal organs.

The carotid and femoral arteries.

Between the ribs. You can pick the heart or lungs.

"But there's a strategy I prefer to getting up close and personal," Cedar says, holding up his own blade. Before I can blink, he spins around and throws it across the room, where it lands in the corkboard's center with a thud. "And that's throwing."

I laugh emptily. "I can't do that."

"Why not?"

"Trust me, my dad made me try softball when I was a kid." I give Cedar a look. "I can't throw."

"It's more than arm strength alone. There are all sorts of factors involved. And it's different when you're throwing a *ball* in a general direction versus, I don't know, a *knife*?"

Cedar shakes his head before walking up behind me, gently positioning my arms to hold up the blade. He uses his shoe to nudge my legs in the right stance, resting his arms on my shoulder. "You hold it like this."

I nod.

"When you throw, you want your dominant leg forward. Remember what I said about thinking of it as an extension of your arm?" he asks, and I nod again. "Good."

He takes my hand in his, slowly moving it in a throwing motion. "You want to let go when it's about right here. Don't flick your wrist or try anything clever like that alright? You just... let it go. As smooth as you can, you just let it go."

Let it go, I repeat in my head.

He removes his hands and takes a few steps back. "This isn't a throwing knife, so it might be a little tricky. But once you find the right flow, just—"

I don't let him finish before I throw the knife.

To both of our surprise, it hits the edge of the corkboard, and it sticks.

"—stick with it." Cedar smirks, walking over to pull the knife from the board and handing it back. "You've got some eye, Voclain."

I can't pretend I don't want to smile.

But before either of us can say another word, a small, high-pitched sound echoes from the lobby, carrying over to where we stand. It's faint, so quiet we almost miss it, but I've learned much from Cedar's keen senses, and we both freeze in tandem. He turns to me in panic as we realize the same thing.

That's the key card reader.

"I thought you said no one comes here at night," he whispers frantically.

I elbow him in the shoulder, placing a finger over my lips. Cedar catches the signal and does the same to show he understands.

Cedar turns the flashlight back off for the sake of staying hidden and shoves it in his bag. It's so dark, even with the glow of the moon leaking in through the glass.

"Wait." Cedar grabs my shoulder to draw my attention. "Did you hear that?"

"Hear wh—"

He covers my mouth with his hand, and before I get the chance to swat his arm away, I hear the echo of slow, heavy footsteps down the hall and my heart stops. Cedar and I exchange glances in the shadows, and before I know it, we're both scrambling to climb under the desk.

The space is far too cramped for one person, let alone two. I press my back against one of the drawer units, and Cedar does the same as he struggles to fold his long legs as close to his chest as possible. Our feet touch, and I hate feeling so confined—especially with him.

With the door closed, we can no longer hear the footsteps down the hall. We wait in silence for what feels like ages, but we hear nothing.

"Are you sure we heard footsteps?" I whisper.

"Positive," Cedar whispers back. "Unless we're experiencing shared hallucinations, there were definitely footsteps."

There's a pause as we wait a little more. "What if they grabbed something real quick and left?"

He shrugs. "Then I guess—"

Cedar doesn't have time to finish his sentence before the door creaks open.

My heart pounds a thousand miles per hour, so viciously I can hear the coursing river of blood rushing through my veins, like I'm holding my ear to a seashell. I cover my mouth with my hands to keep my gasp contained as we both exchange frantic glances.

The footsteps are slow and heavy, and I can hear the man crouch down to open a cabinet. *This must be Carl*, I think to myself, praying to anything and everything that whatever he's looking for is nowhere near his desk— and that he doesn't spot our feet sticking out.

Through the backboard on my left, I notice there's a small circular cutout in the wood for electronic cords. I lean my head against it and look through the cutout, squinting to see Carl clearly enough to comprehend his movements.

I watch as he pulls something out of a locked refrigerated cabinet, and when I look closer, my eyes grow wide when I realize it's a bottle of what can only be smuggled alcohol.

I know this man can't be Immune. And even if he earned enough on this salary to pay for Immunity, it would certainly go to his children and spouse first, not to himself—and unless you're filthy rich, there's no way a person can afford that privilege for two children.

Carl pops off the cap and takes a long, grateful sip of the substance before closing the cabinet again, locking it with a key. He shoves the key in his pocket.

He can't find us. If he does, I know he wouldn't hesitate to report it to my father.

And if my dad knew his daughter was stealing anesthetics from his work, surely, he would find a way to shift the blame to that rebellious anti-Chaser family she spends so much time with.

Suddenly, Carl is walking toward his desk, getting closer by the second. There's no time to escape. If he's going to find us, he can't think we're here to steal. Anything but that.

Without thinking, I pull off Cedar's shades.

"What are you doing?" Cedar whispers angrily, reaching for the sunglasses. I still can't see his eyes.

The man is closer.

"It's suspicious to be wearing this in here. We can't have him think you're hiding any part of your identity. And we need a cover, alright?" I hiss. "We're two kids who snuck in here to... do stuff."

Cedar suppresses a chuckle.

"Is that really so unbelievable to you?" I glare.

It's hard to see his features in the dark, but I can tell he smirks. "Not entirely."

My glare intensifies and I open my mouth to whisper back, but the man is closer.

Closer.

Closer.

I blink away the sudden flood of light as Carl turns his desk lamp on, pulling his swivel chair out to take a seat.

"What the hell?" Carl shouts when he sees us, his plump, mustached face turning red with equal parts surprise and frustration. The bottle falls to the ground, glass shattering around his feet. He swears under his breath and kneels down to pick up the larger pieces of glass as Cedar and I gasp in synthetic surprise.

"What are you doing here?" I exclaim, putting on my best act. The desk lamp is dim, but out of the corner of my eye, I can see Cedar puckering his lips tauntingly in my direction. I elbow him as discreetly as I can, ignoring his audible expression of discomfort.

"I should be asking you kids the same thing." The man grumbles, standing up and walking toward the cabinets as Cedar and I scramble to our feet. He rummages through one of the lower shelves, pulling out a dustpan before kneeling down to sweep up the smaller shards that remain.

"You shouldn't be here," Carl mutters. "Just wait until your father hears about this."

"I'm sorry, sir. Breaking into this office was all my idea," Cedar pipes up, and I whip my head around to look at him. It's still quite dark, even with the soft glow of the desk lamp, but I can see the smirk on his face. "I just couldn't help myself."

He wraps an arm around my waist, and I express my disgust by wriggling out of his grip, trying not to shoot an obvious scowl in his direction.

"I'm so sorry, Carl." I take a pleading step forward, attempting to sound as believably naive as possible. "We weren't thinking straight. This won't happen again."

"You bet it won't. You kids don't belong in my office."

"Please don't tell my dad," I beg, but it doesn't sound as forced as I thought it would.

"If you were anyone else, I'd have you apprehended by Chasers," he snaps. "Telling your father instead of reporting you for breaking and entering would be a favor."

I glare at Carl as he brushes the last crumbs of drenched glass into the dustpan. My legs move with a mind of their own, and before I know it, I'm standing up with crossed arms, looking down at the man with clenched teeth.

We all know alcohol was banned after Nightjade, just like the prohibition that took place in the early 20th century. And right now, there's only one way to tell if this man is Immune or not.

"Just to be clear, when you tell him, you won't leave out any important details, right?" I threaten. My voice slows, lowering from high-pitched and naive back to its normal tone. "Hiding illegal goods here at work? Sneaking off in the middle of the night to get drunk because you're unhappy with your marriage? What would Chasers think of that?" I pause, grinning. "I'm sure they would view you as the criminal here, not me."

I look down at my nails. "After all, my father's the one who owns this place. You're the one breaking and entering, aren't you?"

He stands up, returning my glare. I expected him to be tall, but he couldn't be more than two inches above me. He's a pathetic sight to behold, and he doesn't intimidate me.

But he doesn't try to either, and I get the feeling that if he had Immunity from the law, he would have said something by now.

"I heard all about your wife's affair when I worked the desk last summer," I explain with fake sympathy. "It's a real pity. You seem like such a good man."

Carl doesn't say a word. He stews in anger, clenching his jaw as I continue.

"You know, her number's in your file. For emergencies." I cross my arms, taking a step closer. "What would she think if she found out her husband was a criminal?"

I plaster on a fake smile. "Or even better, if you were allegedly sneaking off with someone else to pay her back for the affair? You know, to make it even?"

The man doesn't say a word.

"Who would she believe? The daughter of your employer, with no reason to lie? Or the husband she's unhappy with?"

"You wouldn't dare," Carl seethes, taking a series of threatening steps forward.

But Cedar's feet move before the man can get any closer, catching Carl's thick arm with ease. Carl is just as startled as I am, and he shakes free of Cedar's grip with a scowl so intense I wonder if his eyes might pop right out of his skull.

"Watch it, pal," Cedar spits. His glasses are still beneath the desk, and it's too dark for me to see all of his features. But judging by Carl's expression, I bet the man can see Cedar's scarred face and threatening glare just fine up close.

"It's my word against yours," I state plainly.

"He's not gonna say anything to anyone," Cedar smirks, chuckling. "Let's go."

He retrieves his glasses and moves toward the exit as I give Carl one last look. The man stares at us like the criminals we are, and I swallow a helping of guilt as we walk out the door and down the hallway, exiting the building with exactly what we came here to retrieve.

When we climb into the car, Cedar chuckles, and I assume I know why. I open my mouth to excuse the cover suggestion from earlier—which just so happened to be our most believable option—but he speaks before I can.

"I know what your thing is."

"What?" I ask unenthusiastically, pulling out of the parking lot. What *thing*?

"What you're good at," he says. "You're a talker."

"Oh," I reply, puzzled.

Cedar leans back in his chair, resting his head in his hands. "You can lie on the spot—quite well, in fact." He chuckles, undoubtedly referencing the lie I wanted him to tell. "I guess it should make me trust you less but I'm kind of impressed."

"Shut up." I give him a look as he puckers his lips again. If I weren't driving, I'd punch him in the shoulder.

But as much as I hate to admit it, I wonder if he could be right. They say practice makes perfect. Perhaps with every lie I spin, I'm only becoming a better liar. It's certainly getting easier, that's for sure, and it frightens me.

"You have a way with words," Cedar adds, grinning crookedly. "Just your mouth in general."

I can no longer resist removing a hand from the wheel to give him that shoulder punch, scowling. "I never actually kissed you."

"Hey." Cedar raises his hands in innocence. "It's your word against mine."

Throughout the car ride, his teasing persists, even as we pull into the gravel parking lot of Port Keys Coffee Co., where he told me to drop him off. The lights are dark, and I wonder if this could be where he's been staying, for now at least. I know he doesn't live in the city, and I cannot help but question why he trusts this location so much.

"Are you sure this is where you want me to drop you off?" I ask as I put the car in park.

"Yes." He gives me a look. "I'm positive."

"Is this where you're staying?"

He doesn't say anything. Instead, he slings his satchel over his shoulder, grabbing his backpack as well.

"That woman in there," I say, and he freezes. "Who is she?"

I look up at Cedar, trying to read his expression but failing miserably. Because I still cannot see his eyes.

"You're smart," he says quietly. "You'll figure it out."

He pulls a key out of his pocket and tosses it in the air playfully, climbing out of the car and walking backwards. "I'll see you around, dear lover of mine."

"I'll hurt you."

He reaches the entrance and slides the key into the lock. The door opens, and he gives me one last look before taking his leave, placing a hand over his wounded heart. "You're killing me, Voclain."

With that, he disappears inside that quiet coffee shop, and as I drive away, all I can do is pray tonight's happenings will remain a secret—for both of our sakes.

And I think about the boy in the photo album who knew nothing about scars, or knives, or leaving what must have been a home behind.

I wonder if I'll ever know what happened to him.

REN

Sunday, June 18
Day 2

When I wake up for my second day of training, Margot is waiting downstairs.

"Hey."

Her voice sets off an alarm in my head, and I have to steady myself to keep from tumbling down the last few steps. If I expected her to be awake this early, I would have woken up even earlier.

She sits cross-legged on the living room couch, hair braided neatly with a book and a thickly knitted gray blanket on her lap. It's summer, but in addition to the company of the warm blanket, she wears a pair of fuzzy white and pink socks to help her circulation and keep her toes from turning purple, as they often are. Fresh logs burn in the fireplace across from her, and the TV screensaver flashes mountain colors in her direction.

"Hey," I reply, watching her carefully as I walk toward the kitchen. The first level of our house is annoyingly open-concept, and I can still see her as I open the fridge to fill a glass with water.

She closes her book and drapes her blanket over her shoulder, letting out a small cough as she walks toward the kitchen island. She reaches a barstool and takes a seat.

God dammit. I close my eyes and inhale slowly. *She has another cold again.*

"You're up early." Forcing a grin, I set the glass down on the island and make my way to the stove, turning on the kettle.

"That's what I was gonna say."

"I have"—I bite my lip—"school."

I almost said it. Without thinking, I almost told her exactly where I was going.

I open the glassware cabinet and grab a mug, setting it on the counter before walking over to the pantry to locate a box of turmeric and ginger tea.

"That doesn't sound suspicious at all." She chuckles with another cough. "You sure you and Eddie are really carpooling to school?"

The cardboard box of tea falls from my hands.

Could she know?

My pulse quickens, racing at a speed that's almost painful. I bend over to pick up the tea box, unable to find an answer. *She can't know.*

"I see I've hit a soft spot." Margot wiggles her eyebrows, and I let out a sigh, setting the tea on the counter. She doesn't know.

And then my face turns red because she has it all wrong.

The kettle whistles. I unwrap a tea bag and set it into the mug before pouring a steady stream of boiling hot water over the pouch of herbs. I can't meet Margot's gaze as I hand her the tea.

My mouth is uncomfortably dry as I think about what my sister insinuates. I grab the glass I prepared and take a long, generous gulp. The water is cool and soothing, but my nerves only seem to escalate. With Margot's subtle interrogation, I can suddenly relate to the frogs my class dissected in fourth grade. She knows exactly how to cut me open.

Margot blows on her cup of tea before sipping it slowly. "You and Eddie sure are spending a lot of time together recently."

I nearly spit out my water. My eyes widen as I turn to Margot, face warm. The liquid dribbles from the corners of my mouth and I wipe it with my sleeve before swallowing the rest. "What?"

"Look, I'm not blind," she teases. "I think I know what's going on."

I glare. "There's nothing going on."

That part is easy to say, because in this context, it isn't a lie.

"Ren," she presses. Her tone is still humorous in nature, but something about it feels strained, maybe even frustrated. "You would tell me if there *was* something going on, right? With anyone, not just Eddie?"

I force myself to roll my eyes, offering her a small, synthetic grin. "You know I couldn't have any luck in that department without your help."

"So you *want* my help?"

"No," I say, a little too aggressively. She raises an eyebrow and I clear my throat. "No, thank you."

Margot takes another sip of her tea. She sets the mug down, staring at the amber liquid inside for a long moment before looking up at me again.

"I want you to talk to me about these things, alright? I don't like that we've..." She struggles to find the words. "I don't like it when you don't talk to me, okay? That's all."

"Hey." I walk over to the counter, folding my arms. "I promise that if for some inexplicable reason I ever find myself romantically involved with another human being, you'll be the first to know. Alright?"

I'm not sure why my fingers are crossed.

"Okay." Margot smiles, but I still feel like a liar.

My phone beeps, and I don't need to check it to know it's Eddie. Before I can take my exit, Margot holds out her pinky. "No secrets?"

"No secrets." I extend my own, and we swear. She cannot see that beneath the counter, my fingers cross again.

"Eat two oranges today," I tell her on my way out of the kitchen, walking backwards to give her a smile. "And make some more tea with lunch while I'm gone, alright?"

She rolls her eyes. "Fine. Have fun at school."

I cannot say anything more as I head through the door. I don't think it's good luck to cross my fingers for three promises in a row.

Eddie arrives surprisingly on time, the passenger's seat occupied by my Chaser clothing and uniform cube, as planned.

"Thanks for holding onto those for me."

"Yeah, no problem." Eddie nods. "And thanks for, you know, letting me. I doubt my dad would have believed me for much longer without some form of proof like this."

"Even with the letter?"

"Trust me, if I started acting weird and *didn't* have the uniform, my dad would definitely suspect forgery."

She drives down the street and parks near a hedge between houses, secluded enough for me to change without my father or Margot watching through the window of my home.

Eddie looks down at her jeans as I change, picking at the strings along the rips again. I appreciate the gesture and the privacy. Not because I'm uncomfortable around her, but because I'm uncomfortable in *this*.

Chaser attire is so foreign to me, and it's not just about the clothes. It's about the principle. I'm being forced to transform into a being so different from who I used to be that it's becoming harder and harder to recognize my own reflection in the mirror.

I am no longer myself, but an unfamiliar boy with faded bruises and a strange new outfit funded by the Immunity tax.

I toss my old clothes in the back seat once I'm finished changing, and I'm surprised when Eddie begins to laugh.

"What?" Confused, I smile, even though I don't deserve to be doing so.

As difficult as the girl can be, her laugh is something else.

"You look ridiculous." She eyes me up and down and covers her mouth with her hand, face painted red. I observe my tight black clothing and then look at her.

And for the first time in days, I laugh. An honest, belly-aching laugh with a person I keep forgetting to hate.

And for some reason, beyond me, I don't want the laughter to end.

Whatever joy I felt during the car ride here has disappeared, now that I'm standing inside this scanner for the second time.

That same uncomfortable buzz appears again as I step through, and I'm not sure why, but it feels stronger today. I assume the gut-wrenching truth about the microchips has something to do with that.

**All cadets must suit up immediately after being scanned.
We thank you for playing your part.**

A robotic voice echoes throughout the lobby, and I see the other trainees following its instructions.

The machine recognizes the uniform cube in my arms and lets me pass through. I listen to the invisible speakers and pause to suit up before making my way to the elevator, cringing as I walk. It feels strange to wear a uniform so expensive and technologically advanced, like I'm wearing a bomb that's bound to go off any minute.

I don't feel like a person wearing a machine; I feel like I am the machine itself.

The cadets are quicker today. We line up more efficiently, mindful to organize ourselves in check-in order as we wait for the rest of the trainees to walk through the elevator. Coincidentally, I find myself standing next to the same girl I met the day before.

"So you figured it out today, huh?" She leans over and whispers to me.

"Yeah, I guess I did." I smile politely as I respond, but I'm too cautious of being reprimanded for chatter to look at her.

"I'm Loretta. You can call me Lori. Or—Salazar, I guess," she mumbles.

"Ren."

"That's your last name, right?"

"Oh, no. It's McLellan."

"Oh no, it's McLellan," she teases, and I grin. It's a pretty solid comma placement joke. But the grin disappears as soon as Pittman steps off the podium to face the crowd.

"Alright, cadets," she announces. "We have a busy day ahead of us, so let's get to it."

Lori—or, Salazar—wipes the humor off her face as we all become statues once again. We stand tall and still, slabs of raw marble waiting to be sculpted by what Pittman has in store.

"As I explained yesterday, Price here is my Second, and I am his One." Pittman begins her habitual pace across the front row. "As an Officer in the Chaser Corps, you will always be working with a Second or a One as a group of two."

She pauses, and we all nod.

"As trained up as you will be by the end of this course, this is still a relatively difficult field and it is customary for all Chasers to work in pairs for maximum efficiency," she states. "And although each pair must work as a team, Ones are superior in rank to their designated Second, and they will always have the final say when it comes to decision-making.

"For the sake of the training course, you will be paired to get a feel for the kind of collaboration that is absolutely crucial for the career ahead of you. Now, keep in mind that your partner for this course will not necessarily be your partner in the field. Who you are assigned to today has been determined by entrance exam performance, with Ones ranking higher than their Seconds."

She pauses.

"However, your true groups will be decided after the completion of this course. Your eventual pairing will not depend on your entrance exam performance but rather on your performance throughout the next six weeks. Is that clear?"

"Yes." Our response is unified, less foggy than it was yesterday. We are more alert today because we are frightened.

"Good. Now, I'll be calling up the Ones shortly," Pittman explains. "When you hear your name, please line up against the back wall. Seconds, stay in place. Your name will not be called until the Ones are all lined up."

I tune out as Pittman grabs her tablet and begins to list off the names, because I know my name won't be called. Our scores were never revealed to us but I get the feeling that I did poorly.

Even if I did do well, it's not exactly something I want to be enthusiastic about.

But I'm pulled out of it when Salazar nudges my arm.

"Go," she whispers aggressively, gesturing for me to leave.

Was I the first one called? I give her a confused look. *No, that can't be true.*

"McLellan, Ren," Pittman announces, and by the tone of her voice I can tell she's not happy to be repeating herself.

All eyes are on me as I journey toward the back wall. I can feel my face heat up like a stove burner, and I wonder just how crimson the embarrassment must be turning my cheeks.

"Eyes forward, cadets. He knows his mistake," Pittman shouts. "This won't happen again."

I stand in my spot against the back wall, soaking in my solitude and shame. But it's not my zoning-out that I'm ashamed of; it's the fact that I'm a One. Not just any One, but the first. My gut twists in pretzel knots when I think about what this means.

What if this turns into more than just an obligation? This career might be something I could learn to be *good* at, and that frightens me more than anything else.

"Alright, moving on," Pittman calls out.

I pay attention this time, curious to see which one of the recruits has the second-highest potential to become a good Chaser. Part of me wonders if I'll be able to sense that potential in the cadet. Does a person always carry a monster inside them, or is an internal beast something that must be earned? How can you detect its presence?

But when Pittman calls the name of the next One, all of my questions are thrown out the window.

"Carmody, Duke."

No.

It can't be.

I choke on my own saliva, interrupting the silence with a coughing fit brought on by my surprise.

My heartbeat halts and my blood cells freeze in their tracks. Terror, anger, confusion, and every negative emotion possible seem to course through my veins like river rapids, replacing the blood and spreading something unexpectedly dark through every part of my body and mind.

Duke Carmody?

His name wasn't called. It couldn't have been. I'm just hearing things, because this cannot be possible. I won't believe it. I *can't* believe it.

Aren't his parents paying for Immunity? And if he was truly planning on becoming a Chaser this entire time, how could I have not known? Surely he would have bragged about it to some extent, right?

How could I have missed this?

And then I see him walk toward me. Tall, somewhere between muscular and thin, heavily greased short brown hair from an age that took place decades before his time. But above all, I see the faint shadow of a fading black eye that matches mine.

When he stands next to me, I can tell he's already past the point of being shocked by my presence. He looks at me with a hollow smirk, and it takes all I have not to punch it right off that smug face of his.

But I know what that smirk means. He saw me yesterday. He knew that I was here, and he's known the entire time.

"What the hell are you doing here, Duke?" I whisper, trying my best to stay calm in fear of being heard.

"It's Carmody." He turns away from me and stares straight ahead. "Shouldn't I be asking you the same thing?"

"It's none of your business."

"And my business is yours somehow?" He scoffs before changing the subject. "Where's Eddie?"

I freeze.

"I've been looking for her but I haven't seen her." Carmody smirks. "What's that about?"

I snap, whipping my head around to face him until my face is inches away from his.

"I'd be careful if I were you," I whisper, my tone grim. "You're on some pretty thin ice."

"*I'm* on thin ice?" He chuckles. "I hate to break it to you, but you were the one who attacked me. Not the other way around. And that crazy girlfriend of yours hit me first."

My fist flinches instinctively but I calm myself when I see the third One making her way over to the wall where we stand. I shoot him a threatening look and he eats it right up with a satisfied grin.

I'm disgusted. After graduation, I thought I would never have to face the bastard again. Now here he is, as real as real can be, standing two feet to my right. I dig my nails into the flesh of my palms, hoping it will distract me from the scalding resentment I have for this sickening excuse for a human being.

But mostly, I'm petrified with fear. Because how can a person like *him* become a Chaser? How can the lives of so many people be carelessly discarded and tossed into the talons of a beast like Duke Carmody, when there's no telling just what sort of evil will emerge from within him?

I can't imagine it. Or maybe I just don't want to, because I know exactly what kind of a person he is. And it's getting harder and harder to see him as a person at all.

"Alright, cadets. I'll be listing the Seconds next." Pittman announces once the wall is filled with a line of confused recruits. "Seconds, when your names are called, I want you to line up in front of your Ones and face them. You will line up in the same order as the Ones, starting with McLellan."

It feels strange to hear my name, and I try to snap out of my state of internalized rage but it feels impossible.

"Salazar, Loretta," Pitman says, and I let out a sigh of relief.

It takes her a while to walk across the vast black floor and stand in front of me. She's one of the shortest cadets in the group, but I doubt she's one to be messed with. What she lacks in leg length she makes up for with an athletic build, with muscles more toned than my own—which doesn't say much, but still. She looks too experienced to be a new recruit.

"Looks like we're just destined to work together, huh?" she whispers teasingly. "I'm surprised that the roles aren't reversed."

"Hey, I'm surprised too." I shrug as the next name is called.

"Hale, Patrick," Pittman calls, and a scrawny red-headed boy makes his way to where Carmody stands. I can tell Carmody is frustrated by how small his partner is in comparison to himself, and he expresses it with rudeness.

I squint to observe his face. There's something familiar about him, but I can't place it.

"I'm Patrick. Or, Hale," he says.

"I heard." Carmody's tone is bitter and he folds his arms, refusing to look at the kid standing in front of him.

"McLellan," I whisper and offer Hale a polite smile.

"I remember. I remember both of you." Hale chuckles, eyeing Carmody and me nervously while he twirls his thumbs together. "We went to school together."

My face warms, and I instantly remember a quiet boy who sat in the back of a science class I took in eighth grade. Hale and I were never around each other too much, but he was always such a nice kid, so timid and kind. I think about the pressure Eddie faced to become a Chaser and wonder if he's here by his own accord—and how he'll make it out of the next six weeks alive.

I'd feel bad for anyone stuck with Carmody as a partner, but I feel especially pitiful of Hale. He seems so intimidated by the height difference alone, and I sense that the rude remark only made his anxiety more intense. I wouldn't be surprised if he was even picked on by Carmody at school. My fading black eye throbs and I shudder at the thought.

"Salazar," my partner introduces herself to Hale, and I'm encouraged by her kindness. *At least I don't have to work with the person standing next to me.*

When everyone is lined up in their proper place and introduced, Pittman and Price walk to the back wall to address us where we stand.

"Now that you're all paired up, we'll be starting our first day of physical conditioning," Pittman begins. "However, today's tasks will be mild ones. I expect positive attitudes and an effortless performance."

I gulp nervously, afraid of what her definition of *mild* might be.

While I did well during the written exam and displayed good health during the physical checkup, I know I'm no match for some of the other cadets.

I may have my father's height and lankiness, but I'm nowhere near as muscular as the majority of trainees. My build is slender and thin, and I wouldn't call myself strong. But I can't show my weakness. Weakness in the Chaser Corps means death, and I have too much to lose.

I sense a lot of challenging work ahead of me.

"Seconds, you will run two laps around the track with your Ones on your back," Pittman explains, chin held high. "After those three laps, the roles will be reversed, and Ones will be the ones running."

Pittman looks down at her tablet and presses a few buttons. In a matter of seconds, the floor begins to change from black to white in the shape of a ring around the entirety of the room. The ring couldn't be any less than a quarter mile long, and I find myself astounded by the sheer size of the building once again. The transformation is followed by whispers of awe and groans of dread for the task ahead. Pittman then silences the crowd with a whistle.

"You speak when spoken to, understand?" Pittman shouts.

"Yes."

"Understand?"

"*Yes!*"

"Good. I'll have none of that when we begin this exercise."

We're told to line up on the track, and we all do so without a drop of hesitation. I'm worried about what the future might hold for my teammate and me. As strong as Salazar appears, I doubt my height will make this an easy task for either of us. But I barely have time to process it all before Pittman's whistle blows again.

"You got this?" I ask as Salazar holds me on her back. It takes a lot of physical strain to hold up my legs and keep them from dragging on the ground, and I wonder if I'll be able to keep them like that for very long.

"Don't worry about it, McLellan." I hear a smirk in her voice and we're off.

We start off strong. Salazar jogs just fast enough to maintain her lead without losing an ounce of steadiness, but we are still so slow. I look to my right and see that Carmody is nowhere to be found, as expected. I would be surprised if Hale could carry him a couple of steps, let alone an entire three laps. But a few other pairs start to gain momentum, and before I know it, we're passed by three different partner sets.

They look ridiculous—as I imagine we do—but their physical capabilities are astonishing. Salazar doesn't seem to care that we're being passed, and I remember that Pittman never mentioned anything about a race. *But could it still be one?* I wonder. She never mentioned how she would be grading us either. I can only hope that completing the task is enough to pass.

The first lap is over the quickest, but it's the third one that seems to take ages. I watch as pairs struggle all around us. Some of the Ones let go, and some of them fall over entirely. Everyone moves in jagged, staggered motions, swaying to the weight of their partners and weakness. Salazar pants with exhaustion, jogging slower than the pace of my own walking speed. My legs burn as I try to hold them above ground, and I doubt I'll be able to do so for much longer.

We're not the only ones who seem to be completely drained of strength. In fact, everyone around us is struggling to move forward. The muscles in my legs feel like they're on fire, and I consider the physical toll this must be having on Salazar. I imagine a burning more fiery than my own.

We tumble past the finish line fifth to last. Salazar sits on the floor and rubs her calves, and I shake out my arms in an attempt to get the feeling back. My limbs feel weakened beyond a point of return, and I know I won't be able to do as well as my partner had done. I doubt I'll make it past the first lap.

"That was pathetic to watch," Pittman states once we've all finished the first half of the task. "I didn't expect a mild conditioning exercise to take so much out of you cadets."

I was smart to be afraid—her definition of *mild* is completely skewed. But now, it's my turn.

We line up the same way we did before, except this time, Salazar is on my back. I'm relieved by how light she is and thankful I was paired with someone so short—though I feel guilty for thinking so, after what she just endured.

The whistle blows and we're off again. I expected this assignment to be difficult, but not this much. Salazar is light, but I am simply too weak. I'm exhausted from the previous exercise, and the lack of physical strength in my stature makes things more difficult than they should be. I curse my past self for being so idle, for taking my time for granted and for not working harder to reach my one goal.

Reaching that goal should have been my only priority. Training. Exercising more. Preparing myself for the physical obstacles ahead of me, not just the emotional ones.

I wish I could have done more to prepare.

My speed begins to slow sooner than it did for Salazar. I put everything I have into each step, worried that I might collapse if I don't. But my everything still isn't enough. I can't seem to go any faster than this, and my run is starting to look more like a collection of pitiful missteps.

Miraculously, after what feels like centuries, I manage to reach the finish line. But I don't feel victorious. I don't even feel the slightest bit of accomplishment.

Instead, I'm overwhelmed by this dark cloud of dread—and I can't seem to shake the feeling that I won't be making it out of the training course alive.

I'll fail, and it'll cost me my life.

EDDIE

Friday, June 23
Day 7

I have a new routine, and as illegal as it may be, I find it quite enjoyable. After I drop Ren off at training, I meet Cedar at the coffee shop at Port Keys, where I'm sure he must be staying. We drive around, do odd jobs here and there, and when we're done, I drop him off again and drive over to pick up Ren.

While I suspect Cedar must be staying in that apartment above the coffee shop, and I have my suspicions about the boy in Esmerelda's photo album, I don't question it any further than that. By now, I know that if I want Cedar to trust me enough to keep allowing me to be involved with the Unseen, I have to let him have his secrets. Surely he must have a reason for hiding his relation to her.

But today, our routine has changed.

We're driving back from a successful trade with a man who gave Cedar a nice collection of vintage Yesterday hunting knives for a box of herbal tinctures. But when I signal to turn on Main, Cedar corrects me.

"We're not turning here," he states.

I furrow my brows in confusion. "What? Why?"

"'Cause we're not going to the coffee shop, that's why," he answers plainly, and I give him a strange look.

He directs me down a road that curves deep into the woods, and I recognize it as the road I took when I first met up with Cedar, weeks ago. We park, and we walk toward the meeting spot with the moss-covered boulder.

The sun is setting, and the trees leave barcode shadows, with white stripes of light streaming in through the gaps. Everything feels gold, but it darkens by the minute.

Cedar stops walking, pausing once we approach the boulder. He turns around to look at me, bags slung over his shoulder.

His dark hair is slightly messier today, and as always, he still wears those shades. I've learned to stop wondering what his eyes look like. As with all of his secrets, I know there is a reason for them.

It's not often we stand across from each other, staring. I'm used to walking by his side, to meeting contacts in the dark. Even in the lightness of this hour, the shadows of this forest still make it difficult to see him fully, though I can see enough of him to come to the realization that he's surprisingly not horrible to look at. Angular jawline, crooked smile, sharp nose, a scruffy bit of stubble decorating his chin. If I wasn't so bothered by the guy, I might even say he's handsome.

But there is something off about the way he's looking at me. Today is different. There are many things left unsaid.

"I'm heading back to camp," he finally says, patting his bags as he refers to the anesthetics I helped him collect. "I'll see what we can do with these."

"Camp?" I question. What is he talking about?

And then the realization hits.

"Wait, you're leaving?"

I didn't expect to feel this disappointed. Cedar is grumpy and cynical and difficult, but I've enjoyed my time helping him. The thrill, the adrenaline, the risk—and the knowledge that what I'm doing is actually making a difference. I'm defying the system, and Cedar has helped me do just that.

"Not for good," Cedar corrects, recognizing my disappointment.

"Are you coming back?" I ask quietly, trying not to sound discouraged.

"If Command wants it," he answers.

I bite my lip. "When?"

He smiles sympathetically. "I'm not sure."

I look down at my shoes, trying so hard to keep it together. What am I going to do without him? Without this purpose I've grown so accustomed to loving?

How am I going to be a part of the Unseen?

"Hey," Cedar says. "This isn't the end."

I look up, questioning him with creased brows.

"You wanted in, right?" he asks, and I nod.

"Well you got what you wanted," Cedar says. "Once you're in, you're in for good." He chuckles. "Unless you betray us. Then I'll have no choice but to silence you."

"Oh really?" I give him a look.

"Any special requests?"

"Poison," I tell him. "Or maybe a quick stab to the heart."

"Very Shakespeare of you," he replies, and I suppress a grin. "I guess I shouldn't expect anything less from a helpless romantic like yourself."

"You're impossible."

"But seriously, Voclain." He gives me a small smile. "I have some things to take care of back home, so it'll be a while before I can stay in town for this long again."

I look down at my shoes, stretching my lips into a thin line.

"But I am a messenger, and I'll be back with information for Asa. Soon." My eyes drift upward again. "And I'm sure I can give you some assignments of your own someday."

"My own assignments?" I repeat. His words are like flint to steel, and I can feel something flicker within me.

I try to hold back my excitement and tame my fear at the same time. Does he really think I have it in me to work without him by my side? To complete jobs without his guidance?

Maybe Unseen trust is more dangerous than I thought it would be.

"Don't worry. I'm sure you don't need me to tell you what you're capable of," he says. I take the compliment and hold it close. "And they'll be minor, anyway. You won't be handling weapons or smuggling goods or anything like that—mostly delivering letters and collecting payments. Maybe even some information gathering of your own, depending on the needs of Command."

All of this thrills me more than it should. To finally have a purpose, to do something beyond myself, is addictive. "How soon?"

"Wait for a message," he says. "There's a lot going on right now so it might take a while, but we'll find a way to reach you."

I frown. "That's very vague."

Cedar pauses to think, closing his eyes. He strokes his chin for a moment before opening them again, meeting my gaze through his dark glasses. "The bulletin board at Port Keys Coffee Co. I'll put up an ad for something. Take that as a sign to meet me here."

"How will I know?"

"You'll know."

I roll my eyes, but I nod, content with his answer.

"And make sure to check it every now and then," he says. "My mom could use a bit of company."

"*Your mom*?" I suspected this answer, but hearing it spoken aloud is not what I expected.

He gives me a sad grin and a nod, and I understand what he means. There is more to his story than I am able to know at this moment, more than he can tell me. I don't ask why they live so separately.

With his occupation and wherever else he goes, I realize that these smuggling trips might be the only time he gets to see her. I wonder if my future will look the same way.

I set the thought aside. If Cedar has told me a truth this significant, he must really be coming back.

"Well..." Cedar sighs. "It's time for us to part, my dearest Juliet. Stay away from any friars or apothecaries or whatever."

"Wasn't Romeo the one who drank the poison?"

His eyes roll behind the shades. "Whatever."

I watch as Cedar weaves his shoulder through the second backpack strap, crossing his satchel over his neck before shoving his hands in his pockets.

"Farewell, Romeo. God knows when we shall meet again," I state in my most flowery tone.

He walks backwards, giving me one last wave, speaking just as ridiculously. "I'm sure we'll meet again someday, Voclain."

And with that, he disappears into the thick of the woods, weaving between trees until he's completely out of sight.

Every time Ren comes back to the car from training, I can tell he's leaving little pieces of himself behind.

It wasn't much at first. Besides a bit of physical exhaustion and minor shock, he seemed to be doing relatively okay. I was actually concerned by how apathetic he was, given the situation. I expected him to be a lot more emotional than he had been for the past couple of days.

But today—the last day of his first week—he doesn't even wave to me as I pull into the parking lot. Even as he climbs into the passenger's seat and closes the door, he refuses to greet me, and I know something must be wrong.

"Someone didn't miss me," I tease in a weak effort to lighten the mood. He doesn't say anything, and I don't know if he's refusing to respond or if he simply didn't hear me.

"Is everything okay?" I say, though I feel stupid for asking the question.

Of course he's not okay. Nothing about becoming a Chaser is okay.

"Hey," I soften my tone and reach out to touch his shoulder to let him know I'm here, that I'm real and alive and breathing as I should be—and that he is too. But when he finally looks at me, I realize that he is truly so far from okay.

He's empty.

"I want you to say something," I whisper.

I've never been any good at expressing my emotions. Hypothetically, I should be the best. I remember every word I've ever heard, and even still, I can never find the right ones.

But I'm trying my best to do so without the words. Not just for Ren's sake, but for Margot's too. Because he needs to be okay—for the both of them. *I want to reach him.* I can show him that I want nothing more than to understand.

He says nothing, and without thinking, I reach out a hand, so painfully slow—and I touch his cheek.

When my hand reaches his face, the emotionless shell melts away like candle wax and reveals a boy so broken I barely recognize him. He stares at nothing at all, with so much to say and no way to say it.

It feels strange with Ren, to be so close to him. To feel him beneath my fingertips, to move my thumb across his skin like I'm wiping a tear that hasn't yet arrived.

When did things become so upside down between us? When I think back to where we stood a few months ago, all I can remember is the hatred. But I cannot for the life of me remember the day that hatred switched off. I wonder if it was ever really there to begin with.

Ren's lips are sealed. He says nothing, but his eyes say everything. They are glossed over and glistening.

And then, his hand extends to meet my own.

He holds it firmly while I trace my thumb across his cheek, wrapping his fingers around mine as though they'll disappear if he lets go. Like he wants them to stay. He bows his head in a state of dreadful, quiet agony. He touches his forehead to mine, and he slowly begins to sob.

And all I can do is sit there and let him cry.

I should say something—but I don't. Instead, I pull him closer, into an unfamiliar position that almost feels like an embrace. I hold him, one hand on the back of his neck and the other in his mess of thick black hair. It feels the way it did on that night at the park, when the sand made it look like the night sky. His neck cranes downward to reach my shoulder.

He's so much taller than I am and I can feel it in the way our hug is structured, yet he still manages to feel small in my arms. I feel his posture relax as I hold him close, like he's waking up from a bad dream.

I don't want to picture the nightmares he must be facing in that awful building, but I feel them as he cries into my shoulder. The guilt, the unknown, the lies, the truth—all of it. With every tear, he attempts to rid himself of things he can never shake, each drop a little nightmare I wish I could carry for him.

There is so much I want to tell him and so much I want him to hear. He is not the monster he thinks he is. He is Ren. His Ren. Margot's Ren. *My Ren.*

"It's okay to be small sometimes," I whisper.

It goes quiet. For a moment I worry that I've silenced him entirely, that my words were wrong and I will never hear him speak again. In my arms, he feels shattered. He feels like he will never be put back together.

He pulls me closer, and he continues to sob. He holds me in a way that makes me wonder if I am in his arms, and not the other way around.

"Thank you," he finally says, so quietly I wonder if he said anything at all.

The sun is setting as we drive past the dairy fields.

On most days, Ren is out before six, and if I'm lucky, I can make it home in time just before my father does. I like having the time to spend hiding away in my room before his arrival.

But we were kept late by what happened in the parking lot, and the drive home is a long one. The evening is disappearing, and soon, night will fall. I worry about what my dad will think, and then I remember the confidentiality excuse I've been fond of pulling. It keeps him from asking about my day—usually.

I swallow the worries and study the cows instead, watching them, observing the way they hold themselves, seeing the melancholy woven into their composure. They always graze like there will be no grass left for them tomorrow, even though their presence seems to be one of the only constants I know.

It's humorous to me how we humans often act the same way—even though tomorrow always comes. Usually.

I've grown fond of the creatures after driving by them every morning for the last few days, but I love them even more on the way home. Cows against a cold gray sky means we're heading toward the Chaser training center, and it's dreadful. But cows against a setting sun signifies that we're going in the opposite direction of that awful place, that when the evening comes to a close, it is finally time to go home. It reminds me that my home really isn't so bad, at least in comparison to a Chaser facility.

"Cows." I announce my findings like clockwork.

To my surprise, in the corner of my eye, I can see Ren's mouth twitch. I turn to look at him and almost gasp when I see that his lips are curled. He shakes his head and nearly smiles.

Ren still hasn't said a word since his moment of vulnerability, even as he wiped his tears, and even after we drove away. I eventually accepted the fact that he probably won't say much for the rest of the day, but his reaction to my cow-centered admiration gives me an idea.

"I'm pulling over," I say.

"What?" Ren looks at me like I've just spoken seven foreign languages at once. I smile, because while I don't want to admit it, it's nice to hear his voice again.

"I said, I'm pulling over."

Ren gives me a strange look as I navigate toward a small patch of dirt on the side of the road. I park my car and Ren unbuckles when he sees me doing the same thing.

"What are you doing?" He holds out his arms and shouts over the rough breeze as we exit the vehicle.

"You'll see." I look behind me and flash him a smile.

The car is parked right next to an aged barbed-wire fence that looks as though it's been here since the Yesterdays, and when I'm close enough to touch it, I assume that it has. Three horizontal wires seem to stretch for miles, separated by rotting wood posts that look just as dead as they are against the dark green liveliness of the grass. I walk up to the fence and observe the field beyond, a sea of rich green posed in the foreground of a distant forest backdrop.

"Carsick?" Ren walks over and stands next to me.

"No." I shake my head before looking over at him. "I wanted to see the cows."

"We see them every morning."

"No, we drive past them every morning. That's different from seeing them," I explain.

"Well, are you seeing any right now?"

"Yeah, but they're so far away. I wanna see them up close."

"Oh really?" He gives me a look. "And how are you gonna do that?"

I step forward, so close to the fence that my skin brushes against the wood post. I turn around and give Ren a grin. "Like this."

The fence is low enough for me to use the post and hoist myself over, avoiding barbed wire with swiftness. The sweet aroma of freshly grazed grass fills my nose as I breathe it all in. I spread my arms out wide and inhale freely, exhaling just the same. Truly breathing is a feat I have not been able to accomplish in a long time.

This nearly empty field is so far from the city, so far from the poisonous touch of mankind, a touch that has already caused so much to rot away. But away from the smog and the lying and the hiding, I feel like I can take in the oxygen around me without restraint.

There is something odd about the way Ren makes me feel like I can breathe.

When I turn around to see what's taking him so long, I see that he's back in the car, quickly changing out of those strange black clothes Chasers wear underneath their uniforms. He tosses the outfit aside and begins to change into the casual attire he keeps in the back seat. I didn't mean to look, but strangely, it's hard not to.

He's a lot less unbearable than I give him credit for. Tall, beautiful facial structure, slender but fit and well-defined—if it weren't Ren, I might even call him handsome.

Then his eyes meet mine, and before either of us can blink I whip back around. I want to feel embarrassed or ashamed, but I cannot find it in me. The more time I spend with Ren, the more comfortable I find myself around him. He grounds me. He keeps my secrets, and I keep his. He puts my tempests at ease and talks me down from every metaphorical ledge by simply being near me. He reminds me of what I'm fighting for.

In spite of the past we guard, I need Ren to balance me out. I might even say we work well together.

I might even say I need him, just a little.

"I can't believe you climbed over that so easily." I hear his voice and I turn around. Ren jogs up behind me, his fresh clothes already caked in dirt from head to toe.

"And you didn't?" I tease.

"No." He wipes some of the dirt from his hands onto his jeans. "I climbed under."

He is drenched in the warm citrine glow of an evening melting into dark. In the shadows that fall upon his face, his features are sharp and contrasted, everything saturated by the setting sun.

The closest cow is a football field away. Although the sun still falls, night nears, and in the growing dark, beyond the screen of my wind-tossed curls, I can see her shape in the distance.

I don't have to announce what I'm thinking for Ren to know. He complies in silence, though I can tell he doesn't want to as we walk forward. The grass is soft beneath our feet, like we're stepping on spongy beds of peat moss.

I imagine what it would be like to be one of these dairy cows. To have such limited fear. To have access to so much emptiness. To sleep in a field under the stars every single night, and to rest with the comfort of knowing that you'll be doing the same thing tomorrow and forever.

"Sorry for—you know. What happened back there." Ren breaks the absence of sound, and my face turns red. *Is he talking about what I saw in the car?*

"Oh. That." My face grows warmer with every step we take, despite the cold. "Wait, why are you apologizing? I'm the one who saw you."

"Exactly," Ren says. "I was—I don't know. I didn't want you to see me like that."

He pauses. "I don't think *anyone's* seen me like that. Not for a long time, at least."

I chuckle teasingly and raise an eyebrow at him. "No one's seen you undress before?"

"Wait, what?" He stops walking. "What are you talking about?"

I pause and look up at him. "What are *you* talking about?"

"I'm talking about the car."

"Me too."

"What?"

"When you were—ya know. Just a second ago."

"When I was crying?"

"Oh."

I chew on my lip, unsure if I should change the subject or hole up underground and commit to a life of hermitry.

But to my surprise, Ren starts to laugh. It's slow, at first, like the light trickle of stream water. And then it grows exponentially. He leans his head back into the sky and laughs so brightly it could challenge the setting sun.

Just a few moments ago, I thought I would never see him smile again. And now here he is, not only smiling, but laughing too.

I don't want to question it. I join in while it lasts, and before I know it, I'm laughing right by his side.

"You're something else, Ed." He chuckles as we start walking again.

"What?" I pester.

"Nothing." He shakes his head.

"Oh c'mon."

"It's just—you're the smartest person I've met, but sometimes you surprise me with how much you don't know."

"What's that supposed to mean?" I'm about to bother him for a better answer, but something else grabs my attention instead.

"Ren!" I whisper, tugging at his shirt. "Look!"

She stands tall and regal, much larger than what I expected from my limited car window perspective. Her hide is a beautiful mix of rich chestnut and milky ivory, and it takes all I have to resist the urge to touch. And those eyes. Those inky, soulful eyes that I could float within for an eternity. A cow's majesty is breathtaking, and this specimen is no exception.

Ren sits down cross-legged and I do the same. I'm not sure why, but he takes off his shoes to rub his feet. We didn't walk very far, but he must be sore from training.

We sit close together, but not close enough for our shoulders to meet.

We watch the cow graze from a safe distance, though part of me wishes I could reach out to her—at least to make sure that she's real.

The sun has finished its journey below the horizon. Nothing but the faintest orange glow remains, tucked behind a wall of evergreen. The sky is muted by gray weather, its vibrancy less saturated than it would have been on a clear day, but I don't mind. There is just enough color to rest on Ren, the cow, the field and me to create something worthy of an oil painting.

"She's beautiful." I state the obvious, studying the animal with intensity.

There's a pause, and Ren answers softly.

"She is," he says, though he's not looking at the cow. He's looking at me.

I pick at a tuft of grass, trying to avoid his gaze as I stare at my feet, but I'm distracted when I see a patch of red on his socks.

I lean forward swiftly. "Is that blood?"

My hand reaches out to point, not to touch, but Ren yanks his foot away, eyes wide as though I might pull out a knife and slice it off. I look at him, more concerned than I need to be, and he blinks the odd burst of fear away.

"I have blisters," he says, clearing his throat and sliding his shoes back on. For whatever reason, he can't look at me anymore. "We do a lot of running."

"Oh." I can tell he doesn't want to talk about training, so I don't say anything else.

It's quiet again as the last bit of light slips away, tucking itself beneath the cover of darkness. The only thing illuminating the field is the moon, and a clear map of stars above us that I don't have the privilege of meeting within city lines. Away from the smog, they glow through the gray of the weather, persistent in the way they insist to shine in spite of all that unfolds below them. A satellite flickers as it travels by. I wonder what it sees.

"Orion's Belt." Ren changes the subject, folding to rest on his back, a slender finger directed toward the sky.

I turn my head to face him, brows furrowed. "What?"

"Come here."

I squint suspiciously and lay back to join him, hands laced together like I'm holding some invisible funeral bouquet. He turns his head to look at me, and points at the sky again.

"You see those three stars?" Ren asks, and I nod. "That's Orion's Belt."

I still don't know what he's talking about.

"I know it's a pretty cliche constellation to point out, but... I don't know. I've always found it so interesting," he explains.

Constellations. I think back to some of the old McLellan bookshelf texts I stumbled upon in my youth. People used to have a fondness for the sky. We named patterns and studied movements and knew how to navigate with no map, only the glimpses of light we knew in the dark.

"Ren?"

"Yes?" he replies. I turn my head to look at him, but he keeps his eyes fixed above.

"Do you ever think about what life would be like? Without Chasing?"

"All the time."

"No Presidency, no group of nameless leaders anonymously deciding the fate of an entire population. No Nightjade. A country so... not closed off. Open to free travel. You can go anywhere and do anything and be anything you wanna be."

"So the Yesterdays." Ren chuckles, but not tauntingly.

"I guess so."

It's quiet again, and I finish my question.

"If you could be anything—anything at all..." I look at the sky again. "What would you be?"

He hesitates in a way that leads me to believe he's known the answer to that question for an eternity. "I'd study the stars."

"What did they call that?" I ask.

"Astronomy." He pauses. "Not really a thing anymore. At least not where we live."

"Why is that?"

Ren shrugs. "It's like healing, in a way. Apparently, there were entire schools and other institutions completely dedicated to studying what lies out there. But funds were cut and redistributed to other more *necessary* things."

He plucks a strand of grass from the earth, twisting it around his finger before it snaps. "I guess people stopped needing it. Or at least that's what they want us to think."

"So tell me about this Orion's Belt," I say, eyeing the three stars Ren pointed out. "What does it mean?"

"It's the belt of Orion. The hunter," Ren explains. "He was a character in Greek mythology."

"That's interesting."

"Some believe the constellation represents a kind of spiritual rebirth, in a way. Renewal." He lets out a sigh. "Others believe it can give light to warnings."

It's silent again as we both ponder Ren's words. With every passing second, the sky seems to grow deeper, all encompassing, a void so inescapably vast I cannot keep myself from sinking in its emptiness. It reminds me how hollow I really am.

"Show me how to use the stars," I ask. "Like a map."

"Demanding, but okay," he chuckles, pointing at the sky again. "You see that star? The bright one?"

"Yeah."

"That's Polaris. The North Star." I can hear him smile to himself. "No matter what time of year it is or where you are, or how the world keeps spinning around you"—he turns to look at me—"you can always rely on that star to lead you forward."

"North?" I ask, and he nods.

"Always north," Ren says. "All the other constellations move, but Polaris is the only star that really stands still."

"I don't think that's true, by the way. About people not needing this kind of thing anymore," I point out. "There's more to needing than survival. More to living."

I turn to look at him again. "I think there are lots of things we pretend we don't need. That we've forgotten about."

Ren's gaze shifts in my direction. "Like astronomy."

Our eyes lock, and for a moment, all we can manage to do is stare. There is an addictive quality to his eyes. It's maddening, really, and I'd have it any other way if I could. I hate that I cannot turn away, and I hate that hating him feels so incredibly wrong. Like a puzzle piece you were so set on placing that just doesn't fit, no matter how many times it is rotated or forced between the corners.

Something about looking at him twists my stomach in knots. I don't like that it is Ren who invites this internal moth eclipse.

I think about Ren's response to my statement and I want to say yes. But his answer feels so separate from all the things we say in silence.

I think there are lots of things we pretend we don't need. That we've forgotten about.

"These things you're talking about," Ren says. "How can you be so sure they're forgotten?"

I keep my eyes fixed to his. *Because they're not good enough anymore*, I want to say, but I don't.

"There are definitely things we pretend we don't need," Ren mutters. "But it's just as you say." He swallows, as though trying to gulp down a lump in his throat. "It's all pretend."

My voice falls lower, softer, beyond my intent. "Don't you ever get tired of pretending?"

He whispers. "More than you could ever know."

I cannot bear to look at him anymore, so I shift my stare ahead, studying the cow. She is no longer grazing and is now resting in the grass, arms tucked within herself, watching us with glossy black eyes. I'm sure there is somewhere she should be, but for some reason she stays, observing us with reciprocal curiosity.

"What did you mean earlier?" I ask, eyes still glued to the creature ahead of us. "When you said there's a lot I don't know?"

"Well, it's okay to not know things sometimes." Ren looks at me again, but I'm still watching the cow. "Sometimes there are truths that are best left unsaid."

I can't tell what he's referring to. His words could apply to so many things—to our own lies, to what he's learning in training, to whatever this horrible need, this inexplicable connection between us might be. Anything.

I know what Asa said about keeping my Unseen involvement a secret from his children—including Ren—but I can't shake the guilt. I don't know if it's fair or unfair to keep him away from the truth. *I am lying to everyone I know.*

"You know that what you're saying could apply to just about a million different truths, right?" I say.

"I know." There's another pause.

"What truth were you talking about then?" I ask. He looks down at the dirt coating his jeans.

"Quite a bit of truths, actually."

"Are you going to tell me? All these said *truths* you're surprised I don't know?" Our voices are softer now, like the arrival of the sky's darkness somehow signifies that we should whisper.

"Well for starters, you didn't know that I was talking about my crying incident earlier and *not* the fact that you saw me undress—which is something I think you've seen already," Ren teases.

"Okay, well, it's not my fault that you left out some pretty critical details. And besides, I usually look away."

"And that's another thing you don't know."

"What?"

"That I don't care whether you look or not."

"Ouch."

"No—I meant that I don't mind. I care." He chuckles, but then his tone soothes into one of a more serious nature. "I'm comfortable around you, that's all I'm trying to say."

"Unintelligent move on your part. I am a dirty, lying criminal, after all. Dangerous," I say.

"You make a solid point," he replies, but he knows what I really mean.

"Oh, and another truth," Ren adds. "It's okay to be small sometimes."

"I'm the one who told you that."

"I know," he hesitates, forming the words in his head. "But I don't think you set the same rules for yourself as you do for other people."

"That's not true." I place my hands beneath the back of my head. "If you think I'm difficult, imagine what it must be like to live in my head."

"Eddie." He gives me a look. "You're strong as hell, and I think that's something you *do* know, but—you don't have to be strong all the time."

I don't know what to say, so I let the silence do the speaking for a moment.

"At least not around me," Ren continues, softly. "You can let yourself be vulnerable too."

I give him a small grin. "Mind if I share a truth too?"

"Not at all."

I pause, looking him in the eye. "You're not as horrible as you were in my head, Ren."

He smiles, so subtly I almost miss it. "You're not so bad yourself."

Something about his words washes me in a wave of tranquility. For the first time in a long time, I feel truly relaxed. I feel at home out here in the middle of nowhere with Ren.

I glance over at the cow, who is still there in her position of rest, staring at something beyond our backs. Her presence set aside, the two of us are completely and utterly alone. The field is so empty and yet the dark is so full. I look at the sky and I worry that if I stare too long at the constellations, I'll become a part of the night too, joining an eternal parade of lonely stars.

I move my arms to the side, turning my head to the left to look at Ren. It's hard to make out his shape in the dark, but with the faint glow of the moon, I manage. I'll admit it this time; he really is beautiful. The reflection in his eyes is an astrology book, and his hair almost gives off a navy glow.

He turns his head, and he stares at me too. And suddenly there is so much I want to tell him. But I decide to let the silence remain, just for a little longer.

God, I could drown in his eyes. In his stare I am brought back to the river, to being underwater with Ren and sharing that murky darkness together. We are so close it almost feels dangerous. Like in the blink of an eye, we could inch closer and do something we would both regret.

Who have I become? The Eddie of before would be livid if she knew I would be here, side by side with the one boy I'm supposed to hate more than anything else. My enemy. My rival. My grudge, always.

But he reaches out, so slowly, and I am lost. With one arm he pulls himself closer, and with the other, he places a gentle hand on my cheek. His touch is warm. It is soothing and infuriating all at once, and I don't fight it.

We stare in silence, because speaking requires thinking, and thinking can be overdone, and if we thought about our nearness for even just a little bit, we would pull apart.

We are so close. *He* is so close. Ren, who couldn't be farther away, is nearer than all else.

And then his phone rings.

The interruption makes my heart plummet to my stomach. Ren mutters something under his breath as we sit up simultaneously. He grabs the device to see who's calling before turning to me, eyes wide. "It's Margot."

"Answer," I urge. My pulse quickens its pace.

"Hey," Ren says into the phone. I can hear Margot's voice, clouded and far, and then a pause. "She's right here."

He turns to me, covering the speaker with his hands. "She wants to talk to you."

I gulp nervously, grabbing the phone and holding it up to my ear.

"Hey," I answer. It feels like I'm talking with a sore throat.

"Don't *hey* me, where are you guys?"

Her agitation strikes my chest with a pang of guilt, but I lie anyway. "We're—in the car."

Just as my unlucky curse would allow, something—or someone—moos. The cow that rests in front of us has risen to its feet. She stares at us with glassy black eyes, chewing one last mouthful of grass before turning around to go wherever she belongs.

"Did something just moo?" Margot exclaims.

"No."

"Who was that?" She chuckles, but she's not amused. "Was that actually a cow?"

"No," I lie again, and the silence tells me that Margot doesn't buy it. I let out a painful sigh. "Maybe?"

"What the hell, Ed?" I can't see her over the phone, but I can clearly picture her frustrated scowl. "It's so late, I've been calling you for hours thinking you two crashed your car or something, and you're *literally* next to a cow right now. Great."

"I'm sorry," I mutter. "I don't have my phone on me right now."

"What could you *possibly* be doing alone with my brother in a cow field right now?" She pauses to jump to irrational conclusions. "No... you weren't—"

"*No*! Of course not."

"Like I'm supposed to believe you guys pulled over and walked all the way into an empty field just to see a cow."

"That's exactly what happened."

She sighs. "I can't believe this right now."

"Margot, you're being ridiculous." I roll my eyes, but the guilt doesn't budge. "We're a little late. It's not that big of a deal."

"I don't care that you're late. I care that you *don't* care." I can hear her swallow anxiously over the phone, voice strained as she tries to hold back her frustration. "You were too busy doing whatever it is you were doing to tell me. I thought that something was wrong. A crash. Maybe you two got hurt or something. I don't know."

"Margot—"

"Honestly, what is *with* you two lately? All this sneaking around, these detours?" She scoffs. "You and Ren didn't talk at all for the last *decade*, and now it seems like the only words you have are for him and him alone."

"I—"

"I don't care that you two are seeing each other, Eddie." Her voice softens, and her frustration transforms into sadness. My face turns bright red at the accusation. "I just wish you would stop lying to me about it."

My tongue is knotted. Ren places a hand on my shoulder, and I turn to him. He bites his lower lip and gives me a look.

He wants me to go along with it.

I shake my head.

"Eddie—"

"No," I interrupt him, blocking the speaker with my hand.

"It would be easier, wouldn't it?"

I open my mouth to reply, but my words are blocked by thought. It would be easier if this was our lie, if we could explain it all away with such a simple excuse.

And yet, something about that lie doesn't sit right. During the anesthetic job, I was fine playing pretend with Cedar because he is a stranger. I know next to nothing about him, and no one was around to witness the lie but him and my father's rude employee.

But Ren and I have a history; our past is too complex, and we couldn't pretend to be together forever. When the truth comes out or when we stop needing this partnership, even a staged separation would place an uncomfortable distance between Margot and me.

"Well?" Margot says through the phone.

"Margot," I finally say, letting out an exhausted sigh. "We're not."

"*Stop*! Okay? Just—stop," she exclaims. "Stop with the lying, because it's making me lose my mind. Even more than I already have."

Her voice cracks as she speaks, and I'm at a loss for words.

"Are you gonna tell me what's actually going on?" Margot's tone is almost a whisper now, and her question makes the weight of my lies burn more than it ever has before.

I wish I could, Margot. My vision is clouded. I wipe the tears before they have the chance to fall.

I wish I could tell you everything. I wish I could tell you everything the way I used to tell you everything before. Because you are my everything, so you deserve that much.

"Margot..." I am burning. "I can't."

It's quiet for the longest moment of my life until the other end clicks. It is followed by an angry, repetitive beep. Its echo is a haunting reminder of what my lies are costing me.

But Margot can never know what Ren and I are betraying for her sake.

Ren doesn't say a word, and neither do I. My stomach knots with shame. Margot and I have had our fights in the past, but nothing like this, and not with her brother involved.

And I know Ren heard every word. Her anger, her accusations, her assumptions, my lies—all of it. I can see how uncomfortable he is as he expresses a strong interest in his shoes.

"We should get going." He stands up, wiping the dirt from his jeans. I expect him to at least hold out a hand and help me up, but he doesn't.

"Yeah." I agree, standing up all on my own.

I think about the phone call as we walk back to the car. But the walk feels heavier this time around because we are walking away, not toward something. We move slowly, like we're trudging through the last stretch of a challenging hike. I cannot help but wonder about the true weight of what we are leaving behind.

I hate that I have to lie to Margot like this.

She can't know the lengths Ren and I are going to protect her. The weight of that guilt would crush her; her mental state is unstable enough as it is with Lyme. The illness can cause so many neurological symptoms, and for Margot, her mind is her heaviest burden. I do not want her to be crushed.

Ren and I both hold forbidden truths. She can never know that Ren is willing to kill in exchange for her Immunity, or what I am risking my life to become in her name. We are neck deep in both of our lies. At this point, the discovery could expose my own, and if word got out that we are working together, we could both be killed for treason.

I just wish I could let Margot know how much her brother cares about her. Ren is doing so much for her sake. But he is sacrificing more than his humanity. He is sacrificing the most treasured relationship he has, and it is breaking him. She is his everything, and she is mine too. I know how far we would both go for her sake.

As we walk, I turn to look at Ren. For a moment I wonder if he cannot see me, but in a blink, his eyes meet mine, and they fall away just as quickly. He refuses to spare me another glance and I look down at the grass. His avoidance hurts more than I thought it would.

Because he is becoming a person I would sacrifice something for, and it is perhaps the most horrifying truth of them all.

I don't know how much longer I can keep my secrets from Margot.

But I don't know how much longer I can keep my truths from Ren either.

REN

Friday, June 23
Day 7

There is a white room that I never leave behind, no matter how many times I limp through its door.

REN

Saturday, July 29
Day 43

♪ MUSCLE MUSEUM - MUSE ♪

On the last day of my sixth week of training, the only item on our agenda is learning how to kill.

Extermination, they call it, is the last thing we will learn before our final test.

Before Pittman told us today's objective, I thought I knew it all. I memorized every division, learned every lesson, watched every demonstration. I ran until I thought my lungs would pop. I punched bags until my knuckles bled. I filled myself with more information than I could ever have the strength to bear.

Now I know how wrong I was to think I knew anything at all.

"Alright, Cadets," Pittman shouts from her podium. "Before we begin, let's review what we've covered over the past six weeks. Price?"

She shifts her head in the direction of her Second, who nods without meeting her eye. He turns to the screen on the wrist of his armor and presses a few buttons.

In a blink, the floor behind our instructors opens, and a familiar whiteboard rises behind them, as tall as the back wall of a regular classroom back in school.

The sight of the board makes my head pound. My pulse begins to race as I try to blink away the things I've seen written in erasable marker ink, but my memory is unforgiving, flashing me with words from previous lectures.

Nightjade.

Uniform.

Injections. Illness. Assignments.

The Pick. Cards. Fairness.

Extermination.

You. Are. All. The. Same.

I feel like I'm drowning in black ink.

"After a week of conditioning," Price begins, "our first day of the second week covered the structure of the Chaser Corps. We learned about the different divisions within the Corps, like NIM, and the tasks that each division covers."

Price uncaps a pen and begins to write every division on the board.

"Whales—those who work at the Weaponry Application and Launching Sites, or WALS—are in charge of all aspects of the development of Nightjade weapons, specifically with Chasers in mind."

The word is seared into my mind.

"Sitters," he continues, "do all the office work and handle the business side of the Corps, NOT covers Nightjade Operations and Tech, FAD is a First Aid Division trained in basic legalized healing and trauma surgery for the more difficult Chaser missions."

He turns around to face the crowd. "Cleaners?"

Price awaits a response, but the cadets are chirping crickets.

"Come on, people," Price sighs, closing the cap of the pen and leaning against the whiteboard. "These are the basics. I know you know these things inside and out."

I cannot meet his eyes, but I keep my gaze fixed forward. I know where you go when your chin slips, when you look the other way. When you move out of line. When you speak out of turn. When you are not good enough. It takes so much strength to stand still that I end up trembling anyway.

"I need an answer or you're all walking coals."

My stomach flips inside out. The soles of my feet throb within the confines of my uniform, and I can feel a bead of sweat form above my brow. I cannot stop shaking.

I am not surprised when Carmody raises his hand. He didn't care enough to jump on the opportunity to answer earlier or to earn the favor of his superiors, but it is because he doesn't care that he is the only one able to speak now.

"Cleaners," Carmody answers smugly, "are the janitorial service."

Price stares the cadet in the eye. For a moment, I wonder if the joke will have him sent away. I try not to feel sick, but my efforts are hopeless. Even I wouldn't wish the coals on Carmody.

And then, Price chuckles, smirking in the trainee's direction. "Well put, Carmody."

Price turns around to write on the board again as he speaks. "Cleaners are the janitorial service of the Corps—not for spilled drinks and bathrooms, but for the bodies. They are the individuals who keep track of deaths in our database, and ensure that the bodies they collect are truly still."

Price writes a few more words on the board before capping the pen and shifting to face us once again. "It's the Officers who handle the grunt work: extermination, investigations, security tasks, and odd jobs like the training of cadets.

"But Agents hold the most power of them all. They have special clearance, Immunity, and work in high classification directly under the Presidency."

Pittman takes her turn now, stepping off the podium to pace as she speaks.

"Your second week was designed to familiarize you cadets with discipline, and with pain." She pauses briefly, hands behind her back, before continuing. "You all remember your first coal walk."

I wish I could forget.

"For the third week, guest speakers from each division—save for Agents

—came to perform demonstrations on dummies. Whales taught you how to use various Nightjade weapons, and the next week, *you* were the ones inflicting harm upon those training dummies."

I still have nightmares about Carmody beheading a rubber mannequin with a blade.

"The fourth week combined Whale attack tactics with self-defense and more physical conditioning."

This week is a blur. My memories brim with pain, with exhaustion, with that white room. They split at the seams. I try to suppress the things I don't want to think about, but I am putting out fires that will not extinguish.

"For the fifth week, we toned down the physical activity and learned more about Nightjade laws and Chaser Corps policies," Pittman continues to explain.

Until I thought my brain would explode, I think, but I do not dare say the words aloud.

She finishes our review by covering our sixth week, the string of days that taught us almost everything we need to know about the skillful art of murder. We learned about anatomy and the many different ways there are to kill a human being—and how the act is made so much easier with Nightjade injections. At the beginning of the week, we were shown an informational film. I broke line to run to the restroom and vomit all over the floor. Of course, it was my job to clean it—and to walk, for the second time that day, to bear the weight of my mistake.

"As you all know, this is your last day of the training course," Pittman says. "Final results will be posted at the end of the day, as well as your designated division and/or your official partner for the rest of this year as well as the next, if you are an Officer.

"After this course is complete, you will be given the location of one of the headquarters for your assigned division and given duty-specific training relevant to your given field—except for Officers. Officers will be going straight out into the field. Understand?"

"Yes," the crowd replies.

"If you have any questions, now would be the right time to ask them, as this is the only window of opportunity for you to do so. Is this clear?"

"Yes."

Nobody raises a hand, and Pittman looks pleased.

"Now today, we will be learning the most important skill you can have as a member of the Chaser Corps. No matter your eventual division, this is still a skill you must learn, because your division can always be reassigned as the Presidency sees fit." Pittman comes to a pause.

I know what she's going to say before the words escape her lips, but I don't want her to say it. I *can't* hear her say it, because it wasn't supposed to arrive so quickly. None of this was supposed to become so undeniably real so fast.

"This skill is extermination."

It feels like every one of my vital organs has decided to stop working at once.

My body is on strike. My lungs refuse to let in more oxygen. My brain goes blank, a white page with burning edges. My heart ceases to beat as the word repeats in my head for the thousandth time.

Extermination. That grim, horrendous word. Like saying *murder* a different way will make it *not* murder. *Dehumanize the human and kill a pest instead.*

This is the demonstration I've been dreading from day one.

"But before we get into that, you know what to do. Warm up, everyone," Pittman says. The track materializes before us, along with an intense pain in my chest I can't seem to ignore—no matter how hard I try.

It's not required to run alongside your partner during warm-ups, but Salazar and I have made an unspoken agreement to do so every morning. She is one of the only people in the room who feels like a good person, although it's difficult to be a good person and a Chaser at the same time. She is an open book, and I trust her.

"What's your least favorite part of the day?" She asks this every morning during warmups. We both know the answer by now, but she jokes anyway, because we both know how necessary it can be to pretend things are normal when they are not.

"This," I say, afraid to make too much of a sound. *I am pretending.*

"Wow, I see how it is," Salazar teases. Her tone is humorous, but I can tell it masks the same anxiety we are all haunted by.

"You're fine," I respond plainly. "It's the running I don't like."

"Because you're not faster than everyone else? You seem like a competitive person."

"I don't think I'm competitive."

"You showed up on your first day with a fading black eye that just so happened to match that of Prince Charming over there. Coincidence?"

She gestures to Carmody, who is already far ahead of us.

If I weren't afraid of the repercussions, I would have stopped dead in my tracks, but I keep going, surprised not by the fact that she noticed, but that it's taken her so long to point it out.

I really couldn't care less about Carmody, other than the fact that a person like him is becoming a Chaser at all. He excels physically, mostly during warmups, but not tactically.

And a good grade is something I want nothing to do with. A passing one would suffice, but I want to stay separate from excellence.

"There's a difference between competition and sticking up for someone," I mutter.

Salazar chuckles, out of breath but steadily keeping up with my pace. "Fighting over or sticking up for?"

I furrow my brows, giving her a look as we jog. "Sticking up for."

"Sure."

"She—the person..." I stutter before stopping myself. "Look, I don't give a damn about Carmody. I just want to make it out of this alive."

The words come out harsher than I mean them to. I force a grin in her direction. "But I will say, sharp eye, Salazar. You seem smarter than all of..." I use my chin to gesture toward the warm-up scene in front of us. I choose my next word carefully. "... this."

"Thanks." She beams, out of breath. "I wanted to be a technical analyst before—before I decided to Chase."

Before what? I want to question her stutter, but I don't.

"So you gotta be good at noticing things, right?"

"Yep," she says. "So what about you?"

"What about me?"

"After all this time, you've never told me what you're Chasing for."

I pause, unsure of how to answer without giving too much away. "My sister."

Salazar nods. I want to stay quiet, to stop talking, but for some reason, I feel obligated to explain to her that I have a reason for being here. That I'm not a monster by choice.

"I want the Immunity for my family," I state simply.

Salazar nods.

"My mother was Picked right after I was born. So I want to make sure that nothing happens to anyone else." I nearly choke on the words. "We can't handle more death."

"I'm sorry to hear that," Salazar says quietly. "But that's very noble of you."

It's silent for a moment, and then she continues. "What's your sister's name?"

"Margot."

To my surprise, Salazar stumbles to a halt. She looks at me as though I said something horrendous, like I yelled at her or cursed her family or spoke Slander against the Corps. But before I question her strange reaction, or urge her to keep going or risk the walk, I realize that we've finished our last lap. I shrug it off because there are greater things to worry about.

After all recruits are warmed up and hydrated, the track disappears and the floor is back to its usual black setting. We line up in front of the podium and wait for further instructions from Pittman and Price.

Our advisers go over the basics of the typical extermination process for an Officer. What to say to your assignments, how to handle potential conflicts. A dozen standard procedures, rules, and tactics to ensure that this country is free of all illness—including the disease that is crime.

Make no exceptions, they say, or pay the price.

"Alright, cadets." Pittman begins to introduce our task. "Today marks the last day of training and the beginning of your career in the Chaser Corps.

My heart beats faster. I cannot be sick this time. *I will not be sick this time.*

"You will face one final test. You will either pass or fail," she says. "Grades will not be determined by performance but rather by your completion of the given task. Passing will allow you to continue on your journey as a Chaser and receive your scores, division assignments, and potential partners." She stops pacing. "Failing this test, however, will negate everything you've done so far."

Pittman pauses her speech, staring us all down with the eyes of a hungry hawk as I feel smaller than I ever have before. "If you fail, you will lose everything."

I show no outward reaction because I cannot bear to walk coal today.

I've known all along what the training course entails, but Pittman's description of our concluding duty as trainees hits me like a freight train I never saw coming. There is so much dread and I am no longer treading water but drowning beneath it. I cannot keep my hands from trembling.

I know exactly what we must do, but I don't want to believe it. I don't want to think about it.

Still, this day was bound to come eventually. I knew what I was getting into when I signed my life away.

I can't be weak anymore.

There is a corner, and around it, a menacing evil lurks. I wait to walk around that edge. I wait for her to say the words.

"Today, you will complete your first extermination."

For a moment, there is a pause, as though the entire world is rewinding around me and I am left standing still.

I thought we would be watching another demonstration. That we would learn with our eyes, not our hands.

But this?

I know the risk of closing my eyes, of breaking my attention, but my lids fall nonetheless. I try to inhale but my breathing is tremorous, and I cannot keep myself from wavering.

In my mind, there is an echo as Pittman shoots the wall with Nightjade on day one. And there is so much more than that.

I open my eyes and stare at the floor, eyeing a uniform reflection I cannot recognize. In the back of my head, I can hear Patrick Hale sobbing after his first mandatory coal walk. I feel the fire burning beneath me, always. I smell the charcoal. I flinch every time an order is barked. I see the blood I scrubbed off the hallway rug at home when a blister broke. I feel the wrist of a uniform crack into the back of my head to punish me for staring off. I am burned by a backhand slap to the face. I see horrible words written on an endless whiteboard.

I am told I am nothing but what they want me to become. I watch Carmody behead the test dummy that looked so unbelievably real. I witness the autopsy of a human corpse, and I watch a live recording of an extermination behind the barrier of a screen.

The memories fade, and I realize where I stand, what I will leave behind, and all I will never forget.

Extermination.

Pittman's commands sound monotonous in my mind, lifeless and empty. We are instructed to wait in a single file line near the elevators, where cadets will be taken one by one to the floor beneath our feet. Further instruction will be provided at the destination on a turn-by-turn basis.

This is all we're told before Pittman wishes us luck, and the first cadet is devoured by the elevator.

None of us say a word as we wait, not even Salazar and me, because there is nothing to say. Nothing right, at least.

Verbally expressing any ounce of dread for the upcoming task could be interpreted as Slander—but even without the risk of potentially being killed for speaking ill of the Presidency, articulating our anxiety would make us all hypocrites. We all signed up for this, and right now, each and every cadet is more aware of that fact than ever.

Our mouths are locked shut by the same invisible key. The silence is thick and acidic, and I decay in the wait until it is my turn to leave.

The elevator opens, and I walk inside willingly. I turn around and lock eyes with Salazar. I am desperate as I reach for her in the crowd. I beg for help I cannot receive. I watch her until the very end until I am devoured too.

I count a lifetime in sixty seconds.

When I exit the elevator, a dark hallway awaits me. There are a few lights, but the glow feels more greenish than white. The floor is constructed with the same material as the story above me, but down here, the walls and ceiling are covered with polished black tiles. Something in the air feels more sinister than anything I've ever felt before. I can't shake the feeling that many wicked happenings have taken place right where I stand.

I step forward. A ring glows around my feet, like something in the floor is reading my uniform with a pale blue light. Somewhere, I hear a beep that sounds similar to the scanners upstairs, but there is no machinery in sight other than my own reflection.

Subject identified: McLellan, Ren.

A hidden computer speaks to me. I turn, spinning in a slow, aching circle, waiting for further instruction from the voice I cannot see. I jump when it arrives.

Please walk forward and wait at the end of the hall. You will be tested shortly. We thank you for playing your part.

Unable to do anything else, I obey the voice's command and begin my walk down the hallway.

There is a door at the end of my path. With every step I grow closer, but all I want is to be farther away. I walk slowly on purpose.

But my speed is irrelevant. It cannot save me from approaching my dimly lit destiny with every step I take. There is a gnawing ache in my chest as something unseen tells me that I won't walk out of this building unchanged. *Nothing can save me now.*

As I grow nearer and nearer to the door, I start to hear something. It's barely audible at first, but its volume increases with every reluctant footstep. I listen carefully as I walk forward. Laughing maybe?

No, I correct myself, halting not five feet ahead of my destination. *Crying.*

There is a person behind that door, and they are sobbing.

The sound is unlike anything I've ever heard before, a grim symphony of heartbreak and misery and longing that is sewn into me with every line of score. The singer begs for something, but I cannot make out what they beg for, or to who.

The words *please* and *I'm sorry* play on repeat, over and over again. It takes all I have not to crumble right now, to shield my ears with my palms, to curl up into a ball and forget I ever agreed to do any of this.

> We are ready for you, Ren. Please open the door and await further instruction. We thank you for playing your part.

My heart leaps at an uncontrollable tempo, my ears ringing to the rhythm of the unseen sobs. My hands are so clammy beneath the protection of my uniform that I wonder what it would be like to drown in my own sweat. Better than this, I decide.

The tremor in my arms is almost painful as I reach out to grasp the door knob. The metal is somewhere between cold and less cold, warmed up by the line of trainee hands who turned it before me.

I notice that this is the first manually opened door I've encountered inside the training center. I hesitate, gripped by a lifelike fear that wraps around my throat and chills every piece of my spine. It is a fear of the unknown, and everything it entails.

I wonder if I have to do this. I ask myself if this is necessary, if I can turn back around and go back to the elevator and face the consequences that follow. If I can give up my life and my family's Immunity, all for the sake of never having to open this door—of never seeing what waits for me inside this room.

I have to do this.

I open the door.

I shield my eyes with my hand. For a moment I am blinded by the appearance of so much light, but my sight returns. Everything is hazy as I try to make sense of what I'm seeing.

The room is small, every surface trademarked with the same bright, faultless material that decorates the majority of the building. There are no black tiles anymore, just the sterile glare of white.

I nearly tumble over when I see the man strapped to a white chair. He is older than me, in his late twenties, at least, but still far too young. His dark brown hair falls to his shoulders, and it is tangled with sweat and distress. His unshaven face tells me he should be used to captivity by now.

I assume that he was the source of the sobs I heard earlier, but now, he cries in silence. He seems just as confused as I am. Though he is older than I am, the terror in his eyes reminds me of a child.

"Please don't hurt me." He lets out a broken plea, and I feel sick to my stomach.

Hurt him?

The computer addresses my presence once again.

> Subject: McLellan, Ren.

I wish it would stop saying my name. This would all be so much easier if I could pretend to be someone else, just for a moment.

> Life is a gift. It is a gift allowed by the Presidency, but gifts can be taken away when it is deserved.

> This citizen has knowingly abused that gift. They have been accused of: Slander, Robbery, Murder, and Treason.

> This citizen is now your Assignment. In accordance with the Nightjade Order, by the authority of the Presidency, you have been given clearance to exterminate the subject.

A section of the wall parts. A robotic arm reaches out, offering a small dish that holds a syringe filled with dark Nightjade serum, just like the one the Whale brought for the demos.

> How will you proceed, Ren McLellan? Will you play your part?

The lifeless machine stops speaking to me, but its words echo over and over again in my mind. I'm completely still.

I blink. I rub my eyes. I pinch myself and I look around me, waiting for the room to disappear, waiting for some sleeping version of myself to wake up and remove me from this nightmare. If any of this is real, I don't want it to be.

I don't wake up.

I stare at the man. The moment my eyes meet his, he begins to sob uncontrollably. His cries turn into screams, and his fear has escalated to the point of hysterics.

"You can't do this. Please. I'm begging you." His voice cracks. "My name is Horace. Horace Randall Greer."

No, I beg in silence. *Please. Don't tell me your name.*

"I have a little girl at home," he sobs. "She needs me."

Please. No more.

"I wasn't perfect," the man chokes, "but I loved her. I still love her."

Stop it. "Please," he begs, "let me have the chance to be better. To see her again."

This is all too much.

I fall to the ground and before I know it, there is a pool of vomit below me. I cough up what little food I managed to eat this morning. The sour taste of bile burns my gums and throat.

He thinks I'm choosing to do this. That I have the power to make the decision to let him go.

And then it hits me: I *am* choosing this.

Becoming a Chaser isn't something I was forced into doing. I paved the path that has led me to this moment, each stepping stone placed by my hand and mine alone.

I chose to look over my family's past, to consider the possibility of becoming the very thing I hate most.

I chose to apply for the entrance exam in secret.

I chose to drive over to the testing facility so long ago, and I chose to put in the effort needed to pass.

I chose to open that letter.

I chose to rely on Eddie to maintain my lies and carry their burdens with me.

I chose to find the training center, and I chose to sign my life away to the Presidency.

I chose to sell my humanity for my sister's life.

I made a thousand awful decisions in Margot's name because I cannot bear to live in a world without her.

I look at the man again—this life I'm expected to take away, the act of which is treated like an undeserved privilege by the Corps. It's disguised as noble, but it is nothing less than evil. Pure, unadulterated evil.

How is this man any different from Margot? They are both human. They are both breathing. Where do they differ?

But Margot is my sister. She is my sister, and she needs me.

And more than all else, I need her.

I wipe the vomit from my lips and I think about how often Margot is in the same position. I think about how sick she is, and how sick she has been her whole life. I picture her clearly in my mind, withering away with each setting sun.

She often tells me how it feels like she's getting eaten alive.

For the past seventeen years, she's been feeling the spirochetes drill their way into every inch of her body, mind, and soul, leaving no part of her existence untainted. Lyme has declared war against her body, and it's only a matter of time before she realizes that she can't keep fighting anymore, and fades away for good.

And that is when I shatter.

Before I know it, I am sobbing like the hysteric man in front of me, because I know I can't live without her. I will never deserve to have her in my life, but I am not strong enough to be better than this. There is not enough good in this world for me to have hope in anything else but Margot. There is one last choice I need to make.

I can lose my humanity to save my sister, or I can save my humanity and lose both of our lives.

I have to choose the former.

I have to choose my sister.

I choose Margot.

Something within me snaps. A switch flips, and only now do I realize how hollow I've become. I have been emptied, like a tree punctured by a dripping tap, pouring its blood, its life, its soul, all into the cold hands of a metal bucket.

I am drained. I feel no different from the robotic voice that said my name far too much.

What is a name, anyway?

Who is Ren McLellan? Lavender Voclain? Duke Carmody?

Horace Greer?

A name is no longer anything less than a collection of words.

I stand up and grab the syringe from the tray. I walk closer to the man, who is screaming more than ever but I cannot hear him. I can't smell the fear in the air or taste the iron in my mouth or spare a moment to think, because there is nothing left of me to feel anything at all.

He stops screaming the moment I stab his neck.

After the last cadet finishes their test, Pittman announces that our final scores are posted.

Everyone is too shaken up to speak, but we all have to pretend that we're okay. We must settle into our role as machines, programmed for one lethal purpose. It comes easier than I thought it would be. I am too vacant to be okay or not okay.

Ren is dead. I am Officer McLellan, because a name means nothing anymore.

Pittman points to the back wall, where the usual glossy white has been replaced with a massive TV screen. We're told to check our scores as well as our official partners and assigned Corps divisions. I squint to make out the information on the screen, but Salazar comes up to me and startles me with a question before I have a chance to take it in.

"Where's Carmody's partner?" she whispers. She sees confusion paint my face and expands upon her initial sentence. "Hale?"

I shrug, unable to care about his whereabouts at the moment, or anything else, for that matter. The room is coated in a thick, translucent haze.

My ears will not stop ringing. From the corner of my eye, I can see Salazar crane her neck to scan the room with no luck.

"He'll turn up in a bit," she mutters in a desperate attempt to reassure herself.

Hale is the last one to exit. Someone groans when he vomits all over the floor. The Cleaners are too quick to expel the mess from existence.

I step away from Salazar, joining the flock of blank-faced recruits to check the screen for its contents. Maybe my mind has left my body; I cannot tell. An invisible set of strings is the only thing preventing my collapse, tying my pieces together, my every action only the wish of some unseen puppeteer. I am painted, crafted, emotionless.

I wonder if I'll be this separate forever.

Regrettably, I find my name on the screen. It still exists, blinking between pixels, shifting in place as new names are registered and displayed. I refuse to stop pretending I left it behind in that room, because the illusion of that loss is perhaps the only thing I am truly grounded to.

But am I grounded to anything at all? Maybe I am falling.

I cannot put off reading the score. Trying my best to breathe, I look at the name on the screen and brace myself for what is to come.

McLellan, Ren

With an inhale, I scan the surface for my results.

Score: B
Division: Officer

In spite of everything, I somehow manage to sigh with relief. Because if I didn't earn a perfect score, a part of me that is still human must remain. Lost within me, but there nonetheless. Maybe I will find it someday. *I hope.*

But relief immediately transforms into fear when I see who my assigned partner is. The words on the screen reach out with long, pixelated arms to pull the rug out from beneath my feet, forcing me to come back to life with a violent blow of dismay. I remember the weight of names.

I have been assigned my official partner.

Eddie was wrong about Joker Cards. They cannot mean a thing, because all the bad luck in the world seems to reside within me.

While I stare at the board, glued to the name I'd do anything to forget, someone comes up behind me. I pay little attention when Price pats me on the back, putting a friendly arm around my shoulder.

"You're lucky, my friend. I trained with his older brother Ian back when I was a cadet a couple years back."

I don't say anything.

Price chuckles at my lack of response, turning around one last time before walking away.

"Don't worry, Ren," he shouts behind him. "Duke Carmody will make a great partner."

EDDIE

Saturday, July 29
Day 43

♪ RAINY DAY LOOP - SALES ♪

I'm uneasy, and I think my mother can sense that as I walk through the door.

The car ride home from Ren's last day of training was uncomfortable, to say the least. He was quiet again, but this silence was different from our cow field evening. The air was heavier, but he didn't shed a single tear.

This silence was dark. Angry, almost. It loomed over Ren like a bitter storm cloud, and I got the feeling that there was nothing in my power to make it go away. I was terrified of provoking him, of saying the wrong thing, or making inaccurate assumptions about what had taken place during training. I stayed silent because I didn't want to make things worse, which always seems to happen when I try to fix something.

"What's going on with you?"

My mom sits on an island barstool, accompanied by a box of frosted wheat cereal and a bowl to match. She looks up from her meal and raises an eyebrow as I make my way into the kitchen.

"Nothing," I reply. I wonder how sour my expression must be. My jaw aches, and I realize I've been grinding my teeth.

I open the fridge to pour myself a glass of milk—my comfort drink. But the beverage is flavorless when I take a gulp and set the cup down on the counter. Every muscle in my body is on fire. Feet planted on the ground, I shift my torso to the left, cracking my shoulder before stretching to the right.

When Cedar asked me to check in at Port Keys Coffee Co., I didn't realize he'd set me up with a job. I wouldn't have willingly signed up for this kind of back pain.

I still haven't met her daughter, the Chaser, but Esmerelda is a gem. A lot like Cedar in her cynical commentary and sarcasm, unfortunately, but she tells a good story and keeps me on my toes, alert and proactive enough to help her out at the shop every day after I drop Ren off at training.

The job isn't bad for my physical shape either. She has me do all the heavy milk-crate lifting, and most of my days aren't complete until I've delivered at least a handful of online orders around Port Keys—by bike, to keep my father off my back for using so much gas.

Sometimes she has me deliver letters too.

The givers and recipients of these letters are from and for city-limit contacts, people like Asa, though they seem to have less status. None of the letters use his jackalope seal.

And I still haven't heard a word from Cedar.

"Ew," my mom says with a mouthful of cereal, watching me as I crack my own back. "What are you, eighty? They must be working you to death."

"Yeah, they really are." I guess coming home this exhausted every day isn't too bad for my lie, after all.

I sigh, turning to give my mother a forced grin. "Cereal for dinner?"

"It's one of those nights, I guess. Your dad's in a mood, moping in his office upstairs. So tonight's a free for all."

"Good," I mutter, pulling a bowl from the cabinet. "I don't think I can handle another altercation with Dad. Not today."

I take a seat on the stool next to hers. I place my glass and empty dish on the breakfast bar, and I try not to meet her stare.

"Why?" she asks plainly. "Did the two of you get in another fight or something?"

"No." I take another generous sip and set my glass down. "But I don't wanna have another one."

"Rough day?"

"Yeah." I sigh as she pours me a bowl, and I nod in thanks before chugging the remainder of my drink.

"When's your last day?"

"It was today."

"What?" Mom's eyes widen. "You're getting so old, love. Stop it."

"I'll try." I force another smile. "But I'm already eighty, remember?"

She smiles too, and I realize how much I've missed talking with my mother.

In all my recent endeavors, I haven't been setting aside much time for anyone in my family. I can barely spare a visit with Margot, let alone my mother.

My lies have turned everyone I love into strangers.

"I can't imagine what you must be going through in there." Mom shakes her head. I can tell she wants to say more, but we both know that Slander gets you killed.

But I can't imagine it either—and that's part of what has me so on edge. I have no idea what horrors Ren must be facing within the walls of the training center. I picture what I saw on Ren's feet back at the cow field, the bursting blisters. I think about the blood until the curiosity hurts and I have to shove the thought away.

"Well, it's over now." I clear my throat. "Things will only get easier from here—I suppose," I say with a shrug.

"I doubt that," my mom adds. "But let's hope so. For your sake." She reaches out to rub my back with a pale hand. I've missed her touch.

"I know it's hard, but you're doing the right thing." She smiles. "Providing your family with Immunity is honorable."

Her words are sweet, but they feel like a stab in the gut. She really has no idea that I've been lying to my entire family for weeks. Months.

We consume our food without speaking for a few minutes, and then she changes the subject.

"Something else is bothering you too. I can tell."

I scoff. "You can't just *tell*."

"Oh yes I can. Mother's Instinct, you ever heard of it?" She chuckles for a moment before her expression turns serious. "You can talk to me, love. I might be bad at giving advice but I sure as hell can listen."

Somehow her kindness manages to bring a small grin to my face, and she gives one in return.

Unlike my relationship with my father, the one I hold with my mother has always been a good one. Although she calls her counsel useless, it's helped me solve many conflicts in the past. Arguments with Dad, petty fights with Margot, bickering with Milo—you name it. I've always felt as though I can tell her anything.

But now, when I need her advice more than ever, my lips are bound by a fatal kind of secrecy.

"I'm just..." I exhale, not knowing how to construct my thoughts in a way that will protect the lies that Ren and I have been spinning. "There's something that I've been keeping from someone. For good reasons, but it's still lying. And I know I shouldn't tell this person the truth, because it could really hurt them. But the lying hurts too. And I..." I sigh. "I don't know what to do."

I place my elbows on the counter and hold my head in my hands. "It's tearing me apart, Mom."

She doesn't say anything for a moment, and I worry that I slipped up. Did I say something I shouldn't have? Did I reveal too much?

"I think I know what this is about," my mother says.

My heart stops dead in its tracks.

She knows I've been lying. She'll ask where I've been going instead if I'm not going to training. She'll search my things. She'll find my knife. She'll see the footprints on my window sill. She'll follow me to Port Keys.

"This is about you and Ren, right?" she asks.

I feel like I've swallowed an entire bowl of dry cereal without chewing. My gut is filled with river stones, and everything suddenly feels so heavy. My eyes widen, and I look down at my bowl in shame.

How did she find out? What will she say? Does my father know what she knows?

Does my whole family know that Ren is Chasing, and I'm not?

"You're not a very good liar, Ed," my mom says. "You try to push people and feelings away by keeping the truth from yourself and those you love, but you're not as good at hiding as you think you are."

"Trust me." She places a hand on my shoulder. I wait for her to say the words. "We all know you and Ren are dating."

I almost spit out a mouthful of milk.

Thank God, I think to myself, closing my eyes and trying not to exhale too deeply. I don't want my relief to be too obvious, but it's impossible to hide completely.

She's totally wrong, and I'm thankful for it. I open my mouth to deny the idea, but she speaks before I have the chance.

"If you think your secret is doing more harm than good, let it out," my mom states. "But if you think it would hurt Margot more if she figured out the truth, then don't tell her. Or at least wait to tell her until the timing is right."

She gives me a smile. "It's up to you to make that decision, though there's something you should keep in mind."

"Yeah?"

"You can lie all you want, but every lie will come back to bite you someday. They always do."

My mother winks, but in the context she cannot see, the context I am drowning in, her words feel too dark for a wink to be appropriate. She stands up to set her dirty dishes in the sink before walking away, leaving me more confused than I was before.

Am I really doing the right thing? Is Margot better off not knowing the truth?

Ren is Margot's brother. She will always love him, no matter what he's doing. I worry that if Margot finds out just what *I've* been keeping from her, she'll never talk to me again.

But as much as it would kill me to lose the friendship between Margot and me, I know I could never stop loving her. I could never stop fighting to save her. And if the cost of her survival is our relationship, and potentially my life, then so be it.

I need to become truly Unseen.

I need to keep up the lies. I need to risk everything because Margot is my everything. I need to fight for change, for a world where my family can live in peace—McLellans included.

But I can't shake the guilt, and I cannot rid myself of the doubt and fear I am haunted by.

All my lies will surely come back to bite me someday. I just don't know when.

Suddenly, I can't stand being alone. Ren is with Margot, and I can't be around either of them right now. But there is someone I can turn to.

I knock on my brother's door, but I open it before he does. The lights are off and he's tinkering with an old Yesterday radio in the dark, illuminated by the faint glow of an old flashlight.

He swipes it all to the side, hiding it beneath his sleeves, turning off the flashlight as he whips around to stare at the intruder in his room.

"*Shit.*" Milo lets out an annoyed sigh of relief. "You could have killed me. I thought you were Dad."

"Save the heart attacks for another day," I reply as Milo gathers his supplies from his desk, walking over to the loose floorboard by his closet he uses for storage.

"What do you want?" he mutters in frustration, hiding away his vintage contraptions before putting the board back in place. He stands up and wipes the dust from his hands.

"We're going out."

I force my brother to accompany me on a car ride. We listen to a scratched Yesterday CD called *Apologies to the Queen Mary*. We drive to a high-tech but retro-themed diner, and we eat cherry pie and sip vanilla ice cream sodas until we can feel the chemicals coursing through our veins, our bellies full of delectable sugar and fat we couldn't care less about. We order fries too, because why not? I am ridiculous, Milo says, though he eats more of them than I do.

We eat until the diner closes. We laugh until our stomachs might burst.

We drive home, and the CD plays an old track about hearts catching fire until we pull into the driveway. We walk to the porch, we laugh our goodnights, and my brother walks through the door and into his bedroom.

I walk through after he does, turning around to twist the lock and hanging my jacket on the coat rack by the window.

But when I turn around, my father is sitting across the room at the breakfast bar, reading the empty white countertops like a book.

"You two were out late," my dad mutters.

I hesitate, unable to tell if we've done something wrong or not. "It's summer."

"Fair enough," he grumbles. I remember what my mother said. He really must be in a bad mood if he doesn't have the energy for a lecture opportunity.

And then I remember the worry on Mom's face, the crease in her brow, the concern for her husband she pretended to hide for my sake.

So I walk over to the kitchen for hers.

I open the fridge and pour myself a glass of milk. "Is something wrong?" I ask without looking. For my mother and my own curiosity, not for him.

My father pauses. "Do you remember Carl, from my work?"

I freeze, feeling my pulse slow to a syrupy halt. I wrap my hands around the cold glass so tightly I worry it might break beneath my grasp. My whole body trembles, but I try to force my way to stillness. *You can't let him know,* I tell myself. *Keep it together.*

But how can I keep it together when I know something bad must have happened? Did he really rat out Cedar and me after all? If he did, I swear I'll—

"He's dead."

The glass falls to the ground, shattering on my foot, thousands of icy shards scattered across the floor. The milk flows through the grout of the tile, streaked with veins of pink. I must have cut my foot, but I can't feel it.

It takes a moment of mindless blinking for me to realize what I've done. I mutter something vulgar under my breath, tearing off a paper towel and crouching down to soak up the blood and milk.

My father stands up, shaking his head. He grabs a rag from a hook on the wall. "I'll get it."

"No Dad, I got it."

He doesn't say a word, and instead, he drops the rag on the ground, letting the soft white fabric soak up the liquid on the floor. I watch as he takes a paper grocery bag and dustpan from under the sink before sweeping the shards of glass into the pan. I reach out to help him pick up the bigger pieces by hand.

He visits the sink again, but this time, he pulls out a bandaid. I take it gingerly, unwrapping the little cloth sticker and wrapping it around the red line of broken skin.

When the floor and my foot are both clean, he stands up and washes his hands in the sink. But when he turns the water off, he pauses. His head hangs low as he regrets something, or maybe several things, perhaps everything.

I walk over to stand by his side, unsure of what to do or say. I can't hug him. I can't comfort him.

"I'm sorry." These are the only words I can muster up the courage to say before a long, quiet pause. "But... how? And when?"

He couldn't have been Picked in the summer. Maybe he got in an accident. A car crash. A collapsed bridge. Something freakish and random, not precise and planned. Not the result of a foolish girl's inability to predict the consequences of her actions.

Anything but that.

"The silent alarm was triggered at work one night, weeks ago," my father states, and I can feel my whole body go numb. Silent alarm?

What have I done?

"The alarm triggers a response from the authorities, and when the Chasers arrived on scene, they found him with a stash of smuggled alcohol he was storing at work to keep it out of his home." My father shakes his head. "The man didn't even have Immunity."

My blood feels like fire.

"The Chasers visited me at work the next morning to deliver the news and to ask if anything was missing. He stole enough anesthesia to supply his black market trading for months." My father scoffs. "And to think I once saw that man as a friend."

I see his pain, and I want to ask him why he kept it inside for so long. But I don't.

And then he turns to look at me, wiping all remnants of grief from his face. "You'll be doing good work as a Chaser, Lavender." He puts an arm around me, and I am a statue. "You'll be keeping people like him off the streets. Protecting good citizens like our family."

He smiles, a sweet, loving smile that most parents wear like nothing. But on Mateo Voclain, smiles like this are rare, and they are never for the right reasons. It makes my stomach churn like butter.

And with that, he walks away to take out the trash, disappearing into the night.

I throw up in the sink. I rinse it out and vanish to my room before he gets back.

I curl up under my covers and try my best to forget about what happened at my father's work and breathe, to close my eyes and get some rest because I desperately need it. Exhaustion has become a friend I would rather keep as an enemy.

I wait for a knock on my window because I want it to arrive. Cedar would understand. He's gone through this before, hasn't he? Surely his work for the Unseen has come with consequences like this.

But Cedar is gone, and I don't deserve understanding. I deserve to feel this—all of it. Because this is what I signed up for, and I need to realize the cost.

It is a necessary pain, I tell myself, *to bear the burden of this head I hold.*

I miss Ren, and I think about his touch. About what would have happened if Margot never called. About all the things I would give to have him beside me again, because he understands.

But I crave sympathy I will never deserve.

Even still, I wait for someone, anyone. Irrationally. Helplessly. Cowardly.

No one climbs the tree in my yard, and when I realize just how alone I truly am, I cover my mouth with my hands. The sobs lull my eyes closed, and I fall asleep to the muffled sound of my own slow, pathetic weeping.

REN

Monday, August 7
146 Days Left Until the Pick

It's strange, really, how people transform when they're staring death in the eyes.

It's not something I understand. There's no logic to it—like constellations that don't connect just right, and you're left with some unrecognizable shape you can't name.

Why change now? Why not years ago? What's the point of living your whole life as something mediocre—or worse—and completely turning around only moments before your demise?

We rarely get to be who we want to be. So why waste your last breath pretending to be something you're not?

The house is neatly tucked within a row of large suburban hideaways that reminds me of a tray of sugar cookies, copied and pasted and ready to be baked. It looks like every other house in the neighborhood. To an outsider, it is a desirable symbol of status and advantage.

The man thinks we have come to take his children away from him. He has two—a daughter and a son with the same brown hair and the same green eyes and the same sad look. Neither of them has done anything wrong, yet he still shields them with his own body as they sob on the kitchen floor. Brother and sister, holding each other close as they have done their whole life. Brother and sister, wanting nothing else but to protect the other from harm.

Our first assignment in the Corps is to terminate the life of a man who has done wrong. A criminal, a liar, a fraud. The very plague that the Nightjade Order seeks to eradicate. Chasers have become what the Yesterdays knew as doctors, and painless, highly concentrated poison has become the only vaccine. There is simply no room for the wrongdoers anymore. No space, no time, no resources.

This is why—after mic evidence was found supporting claims of parental neglect and the smuggling of illegal goods—this man's life must come to a bitter end.

Yet here he is in his final moments, following subconscious biological orders and instinctively shielding his offspring from the two young adults standing in the family's clean kitchen.

I think he knows he is going to die. I just don't know what's making him act so differently, now that his end has come.

"Todd Birch," Carmody begins. His tone is jaded and monotone, like an experienced engineer reading from a furniture assembly manual. "By the instruction of the Presidency and in accordance with the Nightjade Order, the Chaser Corps is obligated to terminate your life. We thank you for playing your part."

Carmody and I have spent the last week reading those same words to ourselves, trying to carve them into memory. It's odd how they sound no different now that they're being read to a real person. He reads the man his charges, and Todd's face turns green.

"Please," the son begs, his voice staccato as he cries and gasps for breath. "You're lying. You're all lying. You can't take him away."

There are bruises on his skin. I do not ask where they came from.

"Todd Birch, do you have any last words or reasonable requests?" Carmody says. His face is stone, his words cold and robotic.

"Dad, please." The daughter shakes her father's arm between sobs. "Don't let them do this. This has to be a mistake."

She has dark bags under her eyes, circles so deeply rooted their absence would appear out of place. Her sadness is completely visible.

"I don't want them in here," Todd Birch says. His tone is firm and agonizing. "Do what you must, but take them away first."

Carmody nods, gesturing to me that it will be my job to take the children away from their father before the execution takes place, even though I am the One and he is my Second. As complicated as our past has been, I appreciate his initiative. I don't care that it was probably a power grab of sorts, because I'm not in the mood to murder anyone today.

I feel my heart drop to my feet as I approach the children. Are they really much younger than I am? Two years below me, at most? I get closer and my heart plummets when I recognize the daughter from school. She had a class with Margot once.

They don't cooperate. The son and the daughter hold on to their father, grabbing his shirt like their lives are being taken away from them, not his, and if they hold onto him for a little longer then they will all be saved. Just a little longer.

I hold them by the arms and drag them into the living room. I make sure not to hurt them, but I hold on tight, because I know that if they break free from my grip, they'll find a pain that will never fade. They are too weak with tears to resist, though they could easily put up a fight.

I am weak, even without tears.

I try not to think about it all because I know that I will snap in half if I do. I have to pretend that I'm unaffected by this. My job depends on it. My life depends on it. *Margot depends on it.*

I hold them close. They kick and scream but their struggles feel more like a toddler's hopeless tantrum. There is a clicking noise as Carmody removes a Nightjade syringe from the designated compartment in his uniform. It will be filled with the dark purple poison I have come to know so well during training.

There is a sound too, and I realize it is the soft thud of a hard-hearted man falling to his death. He is gone before he hits the floor.

Carmody and I walk out of the house when the Cleaners arrive.

We use their front door, walk on their porch, and step on their lawn, every footstep killing years of manicuring in an instant.

I stop walking and Carmody chuckles as I feel my lunch come back up to me. I vomit on the freshly mowed sea of green. I wonder if Todd Birch was the one who cut the grass this morning, and I think about that for a long time.

Do you ever really know when you're going to die, consciously or not? Do you feel death when it's about to reach you?

Did Todd Birch have that feeling in his gut this morning, when he woke up and yelled at his children and lost his temper and bruised his son with those dirty hands of his, the same hands that mowed the lawn that I have now ruined?

If he had known, then why do those things? And why spend precious time cutting a lawn you will never get to enjoy?

Maybe he did know. Maybe he knew he was going to die and mowed this grass anyway, because it wouldn't matter whether he did or did not cut his lawn because nothing should really matter to a dead man.

Then why protect his children moments before his death, when it was him they needed protection from their whole lives? Why change then and not years before? *He couldn't have known.*

Hands on my knees, face to the ground, mouth bitter with vomit and shame. Just moments ago I was the most terrifying thing in the world to that family, and here I am now, succumbing to the weakness I've always had. The weakness we all have in us. I can't breathe and I can't close my eyes either, because I know I will only see the faces of the Birch kids.

Who was I when I was their age? What would I think of who I've become?

Will I change too, before I die? Or will I remain a monster for the rest of my pathetic life?

Carmody gives me a condescending pat on the back. "You'll get used to this."

If I were Ren, I would retaliate accordingly. I would ask my partner how he could say such a thing, how he could possibly have it in him to articulate or even think such nonsense. But I am not Ren anymore, and I cannot deny the truth in his sentence.

I know I will get used to this. That is the price I paid.

Carmody lets out a sigh, grabbing the back of my uniform and pulling me to my feet. An August sun sets on the lawn, on the neighborhood, layering all things with a covetous gold glow. White uniforms glisten.

Somewhere, an evening set of sprinklers is triggered by a timer no one can see, and then another, and then another, until the whole street is clicking and hissing and drowning every green lawn in water. The Birch sprinklers go off too, cleaning the grass we've tainted.

But Carmody doesn't move, and neither do I. I watch the sprinklers distort a white boot reflection with beads of glass. They gather on my shoes, like somehow, the water knows that I need to be cleansed too.

Carmody clears his throat. I turn to look at him, and he tosses me a plastic evidence bag holding a little orange bottle. It rattles as I catch it, and when I take a closer look, I can see that it holds a dozen little capsules. The label holds a name I do not recognize.

"Painkillers," Carmody says with a sigh, hands on his hips. "Our country doesn't even make those anymore. This was smuggled in from the outside."

He shakes his head and stares at the house across the street, the first sprinkler set to die out. We are both quiet for a long time as the other sprinklers die out too, and everything is silent once again.

A bluebird hops on the Birch family's white picket fence. I find it odd since a bluebird is supposed to be a symbol of happiness, not death. It chirps in our direction before it flies away.

"Poor guy." Carmody turns to face me. "You know, Todd Birch is the perfect example of why our job is so important. This"—he grabs the evidence bag and waves it in the air—"is why."

He studies it for a moment, observing the bottle before opening a compartment in the torso of his uniform, placing the evidence inside. He doesn't mention the children or the bruises.

"I'm going to be an Agent someday." Carmody looks at me as though I am looking right back, like I am a willing participant in his conversation. But his face is unclear and his words are fuzzy. It feels like I am encased in amber.

"You know why?" he continues, as though I care. "Because someone needs to put an end to these Underground bastards for good. And I'd love for it to be me."

"Yeah," I mutter, distant from Carmody, separate from everything, still eyeing the picket fence once occupied by blue feathers. "Underground bastards."

Carmody walks away. I wait for him to return the evidence to the Cleaners, who are still ridding the house of our presence, but he climbs into the passenger's seat of the car instead.

I'm about to follow him when the bluebird returns. It chirps at me, tilting its head like it has something important to say. I stand there staring at it for a long time, until my arm begins to move on its own accord, reaching outward. It flies away.

I climb into the car without another word and start the engine. Though we drive down the street and exit the neighborhood, I leave without leaving.

I am still on that green lawn, reaching for something I will never have again.

There is something numbing about the return to Headquarters.

I'm silent as I park the car in the lot, tuning out Carmody's distant chatter. He speaks of rebel conspiracies, shaking his head as he goes on and on about elaborate and nonexistent smuggling rings, mysterious disappearances, unexplained deaths, and the circulation of medicine from beyond our borders.

There are layers to my refusal to listen. I know that Carmody speaks of nothing but myth, exaggeration at best. I'm familiar with routines like this —the spattering of incoherent nonsense pro-Chaser families like to spit out when they see a fault in the system they cannot safely identify without risking Slander. So they blame every little problem on the rebels instead, on the rumored group of people living in the woods, waiting to make their move.

It's ridiculous.

My father knows the Undergrounders and works with them on a routine basis. There are no rebels in the woods. There are no complicated smuggling rings, no unseen political plots.

It is only the work of a few individuals living under the Presidency's nose, breaking the rules to survive—and helping others do the same. They find and share medicine for people who need it, that is all. There is simply nothing more to it.

But putting the invalidity of his conspiracy aside, I cannot wrap my head around the fact that Carmody has fresh blood on his hands—and he doesn't seem to care one bit.

And mostly, I just can't bring myself to feel a thing.

I'm mindless when we walk through the scanners in the lobby. The act is no longer something I think much about. We've all trained ourselves to ignore the buzzing in our heads, the reaction caused by the trackers located somewhere in our bodies, unseen. We look past the nauseating feeling that comes with knowing something so horrible lives inside you—and has done so since the moment you took your first breath. There is simply no point in fretting about something you cannot change.

Carmody and I enter the buttonless elevator. There are scanners here too, invisible ones crafted into the doors. The receptionists can reroute the machines as needed, but usually, the elevators identify our names and know exactly where we need to go.

"You're on edge," Carmody notes, pulling me away from my thoughts.

"Really?" I mumble. "I hadn't noticed."

"I get it, man. The Underground is a scary subject, and you're a sensitive guy. I'll save my ramblings for another day." Carmody gives me a demeaning pat on the back.

Yeah, that's what I'm bothered by. I swallow the urge to dish out an attitudinal reply when the elevator dings.

The second floor is nothing like the training basement. The interior is an imitation of the lobby, every surface that same seamless spread of glistening white. It is a big square with high ceilings, like two of my old school gyms stacked on top of each other, with balcony-like walkways circling around the perimeter above. All four walls are flat and empty, one belonging to the elevator and the other three holding separate entrances to long hallways.

I haven't been inside all the rooms that the corridors lead to, but I've seen a few of them. There are database rooms where one can access advanced versions of the computers on suit wrists. There are small libraries where one can find books on Chaser theory and combat techniques. There are bathrooms and break rooms and even a little cafe for those who can manage to have an appetite at all. I heard they serve organic juice.

And there are many locked doors, offices occupied by our superiors, the experienced Officers in charge of Floor 2's new recruits.

Carmody and I step away from the elevator and into the square. It's dotted with benches and potted plants—Nightjade, by the looks of it. We're all familiar with those succulent blue-green leaves, those purple-black berries sprinkled among little white flowers. It's a manipulative reminder of who we are, a subtle attack on our humanity disguised as an interior design choice.

A marble fountain rests in the center of the square, but instead of water, it spouts words. Thousands of little blue holograms fall like silent streams of liquid, shifting to an audio recording of soft running water.

I asked about it, once. It's a projector trick, an illusionary trick of the light. The words are not words, but names from our database.

They belong to every person who has ever been exterminated.

It is said to boost morale, to serve as a symbol of why it is we do what we do. We Chase to give water to all, to give new life.

But I know the real reason why it exists. Like the pots of nightshade, it's a reminder of what we have done. The guilt will keep us loyal; hypocrites cannot find fault in the Corps.

"McLellan. Carmody," a cheery voice calls to our right, and I turn my head to see Price walking toward us with a tablet in hand. We move to meet him halfway, the three of us stopping when we've formed a small circle in the middle of the busy square.

"I see you've successfully completed your assignment," Price says with a grin, gesturing toward his tablet. "It's refreshing to see such a clean first job. A lot of new Officers snap at this point. Refusing to exterminate, running away, falling victim to nervous breakdowns. Those expulsions are always the worst to handle." He shakes his head. "Most fresh recruits don't last a week past Orientation."

Orientation. The week we spent shadowing other experienced Officers, watching how they killed, expected to learn from their efficiency. They had several tips that still keep me awake at night.

We're only on our first day.

"Anyway, good job, you two." Price grins, giving the both of us a pat on the back before turning to my partner. "So Duke. Giving McLellan enough trouble?"

"As much as I can." Carmody chuckles.

I want to vomit.

"You never forget your first partner," Price says, flashing me a grin before turning to face Carmody again. "Friends for life, I'm telling ya."

"Or rivals," I say without thinking. Price and Carmody go dead quiet before erupting in laughter.

"The quiet ones are always the funniest, aren't they? Timid on the outside, but man, do they surprise you with what they're capable of," Price says. "That was definitely Ian. He and McLellan are a lot alike, don't you think?"

"Definitely," Carmody replies, giving me a smirk I cannot read.

"So how is he?" Price says. "I haven't heard much from him lately."

"Yeah, me neither," Carmody says, forcing a grin. "He's been pretty busy."

"Of course he's busy. He's an Agent." Price shakes his head. "We're lucky, you know. We Officers have it easy. Agents are the ones carrying the real burdens. Tracking down outliers and what not, taking orders directly from the Presidency itself."

Outliers? My brows furrow together.

Carmody nods. "It's tough work."

"Nothing you're not cut out for," Price chuckles. "You gonna follow in Ian's footsteps? Rise up the ranks and take out those damn rebels?"

My gut knots, and I swallow a nervous lump in my throat. "Rebels?"

Surely an Officer as experienced as Price can't believe those rumors. They're baseless, nothing but a collection of speculations, a scapegoat to target the civilians who dare question the system's validity.

Price grins. "Yep. Exciting work, isn't it?"

Carmody notices my discomfort and gives me yet another degrading pat on the back. "McLellan here's been dealing with some anxiety about the whole Undergrounder thing. Freaks him out, I think."

"Would you cut that out? It does not." I shoot him a glare.

Carmody laughs. "You think I don't remember the way you were in elementary school? Every time the subject came up you'd walk away. You were always so scared of everything. It was funny as shit."

My heart drops at the remembrance because he isn't wrong. Of course I left at any mention of an Undergrounder ghost story. I knew about my father's connections; I didn't want to give anything away.

Price shifts his attention to me. "Ah, McLellan. Playground urban legends do them too much justice. They're just a bunch of Runners and smugglers."

"An annoying lot of troublemakers," Carmody adds, tone bitter.

"They're a moronic group, really," Price continues. "And most Runners don't survive long enough to find the survivors. As long as we Officers are careful around the Pick, there isn't really much to worry about."

My heart is beating a mile a minute. "But... some do survive?"

Price nods. "It's rare, but some manage to escape and live to tell the tale. Not all of them are Underground material, though."

"But the Undergrounders are real?" I ask, eyes wide. "And the Corps knows this for a fact?"

All my life, I never thought the Undergrounders were anything to worry about. In my mind, they were people like my father, tired, desperate, and goodhearted.

But if they really are behind this so-called rebellion Carmody speaks of... what could this mean for Eddie? For my dad? How much does the Corps really know?

What have they gotten themselves into?

"Oh, they're real alright," Price replies, snapping me out of it. "They've been causing a bit of trouble for us recently, but it's not anything to dwell on too much. Nothing our good Officers and Agents can't handle."

"Trouble?" Carmody repeats.

Price nods, leaning closer in our circle and lowering his voice. "They're about to announce this in a bit, when everyone returns from their first task, but... rumor has it that the Underground has sent one of their own to infiltrate our most recent haul of cadets."

For once, Carmody and I are on the same page. We share the same peeled-open eyes, the same exchange of nervous, questioning glances.

"*A Double Agent?*" we say in unison.

Price nods again, expression grim. "A Double Agent."

A Double Agent.

I think of Eddie, about her new role, about the Underground details I know she is withholding. I recall the agreement we made after she discovered my acceptance letter, how I'm supposed to provide her with secrets she can trade in exchange for training as a healer.

Am I the Double Agent they're talking about?

The room spins, and the air tightens its grip around my throat. Heart racing, head light, gut whirling, I resist the urge to keel over and clutch my stomach. If it hadn't already emptied out its contents on the Birch lawn, I don't doubt it would have done so now.

Stay calm, I command myself. *Stay. Calm. You have to. There are people you care about—deeply—and their lives depend on your silence.*

I fix my posture and force myself to keep my face straight.

"A Double Agent..." Carmody says. "Do you have any idea who it might be?"

"As of right now, no." Price stretches his lips into a thin line, shaking his head. "But you two are the most trusted out of our recent trainees. You scored the highest because you performed with the most resilience. You're good Chasers, through and through."

They don't suspect me, I think to myself, trying my best to conceal the relief. *Not yet, at least.*

"So if either of you sees or hears anything suspicious..." Price leans even closer, tucking his tablet beneath his arm and placing a hand on either of our shoulders. "You know where to find me. And you better believe me when I tell you how substantially the Corps likes to reward their loyal players."

I swallow another set of nervous gulps.

Price pulls away, looking at my partner. "And who knows? Maybe Ian's footsteps aren't as hard to follow as you'd think."

Something flashes behind Carmody's eyes, like he's remembering something. "Oh, Price, there's something I wanted to show you and Pittman."

The Officer raises an eyebrow. "Really?"

Perplexed, I watch as Carmody presses a button on his wrist, opening the storage compartment in his suit. He pulls out the bottle of pills he took from the Birch scene. "I took this from the Cleaners. They're smuggled, obviously. I'm thinking the man we exterminated either bought this from another civilian or acquired this directly from the Undergrounders themselves. Thought it could be run for prints or something. Might be a good lead."

Price takes the bottle from Carmody with his free gloved hand, grinning from ear to ear. "You two are just full of surprises today, aren't you?"

Carmody smirks, too proud.

"I'll show this to Pittman and see what she thinks about it. I'll get back to you if we find any prints," Price says. He turns to walk away, but he stops himself, turning to face me. "Oh, and McLellan—there's no reason to be afraid of the Undergrounders."

Price gives me a dimpled grin that isn't as comforting as he intends it to be. "We'll take them down someday. I can promise you that."

And with that, the Chaser walks away, leaving Carmody and me alone in the square.

"I don't know about you, but I'm starving," Carmody tells me, stretching his arms over his head like he's just returned from a jog and not an extermination assignment. "Wanna get a smoothie or something? I hear the juice bar's really good."

"I'd rather drop dead."

"Suit yourself."

Carmody leaves, walking down one of the hallways to reach the cafeteria —and I am finally left alone.

I can barely breathe. I walk over to the fountain and take a seat on the edge, trying to absorb the reality of the conversation.

I can't believe the Corps knows this much. I always figured they knew the Undergrounders existed and let them live; that they viewed them as harmless pests, either too insignificant to be cared much about, or too small to be seen at all. But a rebellion? Even I wasn't aware of this.

And then I realize something. *Eddie knows.* She knows the Underground is bigger than it seems. They are organized, at least a little bit—they have to be. I get the feeling that Eddie knows they are involved in more than contraband trade and illegal healing too. *And she didn't tell me.*

I try to exhale, but it feels like there are rocks sitting in my lungs, weighing down my breath, preventing its escape. This is why Eddie hasn't asked me for any information yet—and why I haven't heard any information from her end either. She must be deeper in this than I thought.

Even after everything we've done, she still doesn't trust me enough to let me know.

There is something peculiar about the way the thought cuts me so. It shouldn't sting, but it does. It stings and I hate myself because of it.

Of course Eddie doesn't trust me. I've become a Chaser, after all. How can she not hate me for that?

Maybe she never stopped hating me—even after the fence. Even after the sand. Even after that night in the field, when I wrongly thought that maybe—just maybe—she wanted to lean a bit closer too.

I try to shake the thoughts away. There is no use in feeling disappointed. Eddie is doing what she thinks is best for her and her family. For Margot. If I were to leak any information to the Corps by accident, I'd incriminate myself and my father—and Eddie. We'd be exterminated for treason and Margot would be left alone.

I have to be careful. More than ever, I have to pretend to be loyal to this system or risk the price.

They don't suspect me yet, I remind myself. They still believe this charade of mine. But what does that say about me? About what I have become?

About the name I have lost?

I'm taken away from my thoughts when someone takes a seat to my left. I whip my head around, expecting more pestering from Carmody, but to my surprise, it is not my partner who sits next to me. It's Salazar.

She doesn't look at me. She stares straight ahead, face blank, a single tear falling down her cheek.

"Lori?"

She doesn't respond, and right away, I know she's just returned from her first assignment.

"Where's Hale?" I ask. Still, she doesn't say a word. My heart beats faster when I remember his reaction on our last day of training, the way he tumbled out of the elevator, so sick and broken. Price's words echo in my head. *A lot of new Officers snap at this point...*

"Lori?" I say her name again, trembling, begging for a response.

A few minutes fly by, and Salazar doesn't say a word. She only stares, frozen in time, eyes clouded with tears she tries so hard to hold inside.

And then, she finally speaks.

"He exterminated a child."

My heart stops completely. The room spins, my vision blurring as I try to take in her words.

"They're going to assign me a new partner soon." She stands up, wiping away the tears, unable to look at me.

"What?" My eyes widen. "What happened to Patrick?"

Salazar closes her eyes, shaking her head.

"Tell me, Lori," I beg. "Please."

Most fresh recruits don't last a week...

"I'll see you around, McLellan." She spares me the smallest of glances before walking away, vanishing behind a set of corridor doors.

And I am left so very, very alone.

I sit on the edge of the fountain for a long time, running my hand through the water that does not really exist. In all the hours I've spent throughout this last week, studying every lost name, trying to catch a glimpse of the quickly fleeting pieces, I have never been able to find my mother.

But I swear I see the name of Patrick Hale flash by.

EDDIE

Sunday, December 31
The Pick

♪ NEW LOW - MIDDLE CLASS RUT ♪

Everything is always hectic on the day of the Pick.

The streets are overcrowded and tumultuous. I'm glad I chose to walk today, because I would hate to be stuck in this sort of traffic—though the continuous stream of passing strangers splashing me with sidewalk puddles isn't particularly enjoyable either. A pedestrian is chaos incarnate, especially on December 31st.

Everyone is hurrying to make last minute preparations before New Year's Eve. The city is filled with people desperate to get groceries for their feasts or decor for the festivities. Although the holiday buzz is sweet with notes of nostalgia and togetherness, the true meaning behind the rush is grim. Every citizen in America will be celebrating one of two things.

To celebrate being spared from the Pick, or to celebrate one last time before they die.

But I've always celebrated something different. Today is the birthday of Ren and Margot McLellan, and I need to see them.

I wear my baggiest pair of deep-pocketed jeans and my most comfortable sweatshirt, which just so happens to be Ren's old crewneck. I don't feel so weird about wearing it anymore. He gave it to me, after it all, and was quite persistent about me keeping it. His loss, my gain, I suppose. But I do wish I wore something warmer.

I wrap my coat tighter around my body to avoid the rain, but it's no use. Of course, a storm decided to infect the city today of all days—the one day I thought it would be nice to take a walk and get some fresh air on my way to the McLellans'. *Joker's luck.*

I've been visiting the McLellans a lot over the last few months, but things are still unstable between Margot and me. Now, my trips to the McLellan house are different. I visit Ren, mostly, but part of me visits him just to have an excuse to be near Margot. Even if my lies have distanced her from me, the least I can do is be physically close to her.

We still hang out, of course, though not much, and our talks are never substantial. All we do is watch movies or read together—and Ren usually joins us. Ever since the cow field incident, things have been different between Margot and me. Like a candle has been dampened and we're savoring the last bit of fading smoke.

Ren and I feel different too. There isn't a better way to put it.

My neighborhood is up in the hills, surrounded by sopping trees and flooding creeks and custom-built houses that often display quite questionable architectural choices. The McLellans, however, are located about half an hour's walk away from mine. They live in a smaller house that's set on a street filled with dozens of others just like it, and my feet are thankful for the flat and easily navigated terrain.

When I walk up to the house, I see that Ren's car isn't there.

I curse myself for being so idiotic. *Of course he's at Headquarters today.* But he isn't the only reason why I walked all the way over here to begin with.

I don't want to walk back without doing what I came here to do, so I walk up to the door and invite myself in anyway. I hang my coat on the rack and take off my shoes to avoid leaving a muddy mess everywhere, and I look around the corner to see if anyone's downstairs.

"He's not here," Margot announces from the couch. She reads an old novel from the Yesterdays and fidgets with her necklace.

"Do you know where he is?" I ask.

"He said he was with you." She doesn't look up from her book.

Again, another stupid move on my part. He's Chasing—that's what he's doing.

It's customary for Chasers around the country to report to the closest Corps headquarters for the Pick—something about conflict of interest. They aren't told the Card results until they kill their first assignment. After all, it's harder to justify any hatred toward the Corps if you've just killed a person with the same pair of Cards as the person you're concerned about. It's a way to desensitize the Officers—to ensure the killing machines remain efficient.

The psychology behind it makes sense, but I'm still bothered by Ren's absence. There was something I wanted to tell him. I need to talk to him, while I still have the chance. *Just in case.*

But I need to talk to Margot too.

"Oh yeah. We were gonna meet up somewhere, but I forgot, I guess." I try to excuse my presence as well as Ren's absence. Margot doesn't say anything, and I can tell she knows I'm lying again. I need to tell her something true, because she deserves to hear it.

"I actually wanted to talk to you. You know, wish you a happy birthday and everything," I say, walking into the living room and sitting next to Margot on the couch. Her eyes remain glued to her book, but she hasn't turned a page for quite some time now.

"I brought it." I reach inside my pocket and pull out an old bottle of black nail polish. We've been sharing it for ages, and now, there is only a small bit of paint left, just enough for two. *I'll have to buy a new bottle next year.*

Margot doesn't look away from her book, but I can tell she isn't reading. Her eyes are slowed to a still, no longer flickering from side to side.

I wonder if she'll tell me to go, to leave her alone so she can enjoy reading her book in peace. I almost stand up and exit so she doesn't have to. But to my surprise, she sets the book down with a sigh and holds out her hand.

I can't help but smile.

I twist the lid off the bottle and take Margot's left hand in mine. With the other hand, I brush the polish onto her pinky finger.

"It smells weird," she says plainly, watching me paint.

"This one's non-toxic." I don't look up from my work.

"I remember," Margot says. "It just smells different this time."

It's quiet as I move to the next nail, her left ring finger. There is something soothing about the act of painting her nails, like I'm reliving a warm memory with every brush stroke. I suppose we both are, in a way.

"I can't believe we're still doing this." Margot sighs. She doesn't sound reminiscent.

"I know." I chuckle. There's another awkward pause.

"Are you going to make me say it?"

I scoff. "Are you kidding? Of course I am."

Margot leans her head back, eyes rolling. "It's so stupid."

"Every year, Margot," I remind her. "Every year on this day. We pinky promised, remember? That's an unbreakable oath. And tradition is tradition."

It's silent again. I move to her middle finger, trying not to get any paint on the sides and failing miserably. My hands are not as shaky as Margot's, but they're not exactly steady either. I paint her index finger and her thumb before taking her right hand in mine.

"*If our nails grow forever,*" I begin, still painting, "*even after we're dead...*"

I wait for her to repeat the line, but she says nothing. I finish it myself. "*Let this be a mark of you and me.*"

Margot's hand twitches violently, and a drop of nail polish stains the knuckle of her right index finger.

"Sorry," she mutters.

"Tic?"

She nods.

Without thinking, I use my sleeve to wipe the drop away. I pause when I remember what I'm wearing. I feel stupid for ruining the sleeve with paint, but even more idiotic for worrying about the mishap at all. *It's just a sweatshirt*, I tell myself. *It's nothing.*

Margot notices my hesitation, and to my surprise, she finishes our saying.

"*We're dressing up our own funeral,*" she says like clockwork as I finish painting her last finger. "*We hold our life and death in our hands.*"

I meet her gaze, locking her eyes with mine. We study each other in cricket silence until we cannot keep it in anymore, and we burst out in laughter.

"Oh God." Margot chuckles, wiping a tear. "We thought we were so edgy in fifth grade."

"Please don't remind me."

"We're so gross."

"We really are, aren't we?" I close the lid on the bottle and reach over to put it back in my pocket.

"What are you doing?" she asks, holding out her hand. "I'm supposed to do yours too, genius."

I look at her, and I hold back a grin.

Margot shakes the polish, twisting off the cap and brushing the excess paint on the edge of the bottle. Gently, she takes my fingers in hers, and she begins to work.

She paints a lot slower than me, her movements jagged and strained by her usual muscle weakness, but it's nothing new. I don't mind it, really, and there's a part of me that prefers it. Messiness is the truest form of authenticity.

I watch her paint. For a moment, I forget everything. What I've done, what I've hidden, what I'll become. I forget what a horrible day it is—and that we are no longer children. There is then, and it is now, and we share a solitude I would trade the world to hold on to, just for a little longer.

"*If our nails grow forever,*" Margot says quietly, her voice wavering to match her hands, "*even after we're dead...*"

I smile. "*Let this be a mark of you and me.*"

For some reason, my throat tightens, and I wonder if I might cry.

Margot finishes my right hand and moves to paint the left, brushing my nails with careful, meticulous strokes. I watch her as she works, treating something so frivolous with too much care for my sake, when I have been careless with hers.

"I'm really sorry, you know," I mutter.

Margot stops painting, but she keeps her eyes fixed on my nails. She continues. "For what?"

"You know." I look down at my jeans, thankful for the rips that give me something to fidget with, because I can't look her in the eye. "For—everything, really. For being such an awful friend and hiding things, and not spending as much time with you as I should."

"And for lying about taking a summer class at the junior college?"

The words hit me like a swerving truck. I cannot control the widening of my eyes, or the quickening of my heartbeat, or the burning fear in my gut that tells me she knows everything. *There's no way she knows the truth*, I try to reassure myself, desperate for something to cling to. *She can't know.*

Margot stops painting, leaving the last pinky-promise finger untouched. She closes the bottle, biting her lip. I wonder if she's angry, but when I look at her, I can see that I thought wrong.

She is hurting, but she is so far from knowing anger.

"I know that Chasers have to be somewhere the day before the Pick, Eddie. I'm..." She chokes on her words. "I'm not as dumb as you think I am. I know that."

No. This cannot be happening.

Keep painting, Margot, I want to tell her, but I cannot. *Forget about this and please just keep painting.*

"And I'm scared, Ed. Because you're here and Ren is not." A tear rolls down her cheek. "Ren's not here and I don't want to think about the possibility but..." She pauses, wiping her nose with her sleeve.

Everything around me comes to a complete pause. I knew this would happen someday. I knew everything would catch up to Ren and me, but my heart pounds anyway. My stomach does somersaults and I wonder if I might be sick. *I'm not ready for this.*

I don't want her to say the words, but I wait for her to say them.

"Ren's a Chaser, isn't he?"

And there they are.

Margot's eyes look like glass, glossed over and glistening. I still cannot find any anger behind them, only hurt. I'd like to think I would prefer the anger, because seeing the sadness in her gaze is the same as a knife to the heart.

Be mad at me, I want to scream. *Please be mad at me, because this hurts too much.*

How can I tell her the truth, even now? I take one look at the pain in her eyes as she awaits confirmation and I know that it will break her.

Someday, I will tell her the truth. But today is not the day I want to see Margot break.

I reach out and hold her hand in mine, rubbing my thumb against the back side of her palm. I am careful not to smear our paint.

"Of course not," I tell her. No matter how hard I try to contain myself, my eyes grow watery too.

"Then why won't you tell me what's really going on?" Her lip trembles, and I can't bear to see it.

There is a pause that remains for centuries.

I close my eyes and take a deep breath.

"You were right all along. From the very beginning." I exhale and open my eyes, avoiding her stare. I pull my hand away to pick at the strings that stretch between the tears in my jeans. I have to lie to her one more time.

Just once more.

"Ren and I—we've been... seeing each other."

I pause because the words taste sour and strange. They feel odd on my tongue, a lie so improbable I can barely make the words out at all.

"And you've always known, but I insisted on keeping it a secret," I explain. I wipe a tear with the back of my sleeve. "I thought it would be better for it to come from him."

I close my eyes, trying to focus on my breathing, but it trembles as Margot does. I open them again and I still cannot bear to meet her stare.

"So we came up with these lies to—I don't know, to keep things hidden until the right moment came along," I say. "But as we grew deeper, it only felt harder to tell you the truth."

Margot turns away from me as I speak, because she can't bear to look at me either.

"Please," I beg. "Be mad at me, not him."

Please be mad at me.

She doesn't say anything.

"Margot, I'm so sorry. I know I should have told you but—"

"Why didn't you just tell me from the beginning?" Her voice has increased in volume, and so has her frustration. "Why did you have to lie about it this whole time?"

"Margot..."

"I would have been happy, you know." Margot sniffles, her voice wavering. "I would have been so unbelievably happy for you two if this was what you really wanted."

I cannot find the right words.

"I can't even look at you right now," she says, closing her eyes. "I wish you would have told me the truth a long time ago."

Before I can say anything, she rises to her feet, setting the bottle down. Her voice cracks. "You're my everything, you know."

"And you're mine," I choke. I stand, slowly. "You always have been."

"Then why did you do it?"

I have the right words, and I still cannot say them.

Without another word, Margot turns around. She walks up the stairs and disappears into her room, closing the door behind her.

I stay on the couch for a while. I don't know how to do or be anything but still. I stare at the drying paint on my hands, every fingernail coated in black but the last on my left. My pinky finger, the one I used to make promises I would only end up breaking.

I don't want to leave but I know I shouldn't stay. A briar of thorns grows within me, devouring me in a guilt that never leaves. It only expands, growing, knotting, and twisting until it is all-consuming. I wonder how long it'll take until I'm nothing but a pile of bones on the floor.

The feeling remains as I walk up the stairs, marinating in my own culpability. As much as I want to listen to my anxiety and bolt out the door, I know I came here for more reasons than one, and I still intend to complete a task before I leave.

Being in Ren's room always reminds me of the day I was caught snooping —the day this all began. It still looks the same. His walls are painted that same desaturated navy blue, his shelves stacked with the same tattered books —even his school backpack is still in the same place.

It's strange to think about how much has changed since I stepped foot within these walls that day, even if the room itself hasn't shifted at all.

I don't know why I'm here. Ren is out of the house, and the whole point of coming over today was to tell him everything. To tell him how wrong I have been. To tell him how important he is, face to face. Just in case.

Everyone always seems to have a *Just in Case* before the Pick. You never really expect your Cards to be pulled during the draw, but the possibility is always there. With a *Just in Case*, it is always better to be safe.

It's surprising how so many lies and truths come out during the last few days leading up to December 31st. There are always a whole lot of weddings planned before New Year's and babies born in the beginning of October. The number of suicide attempts spike because people would rather take their lives into their own hands and die by their own terms. There's a routine increase in proposals, filed divorces, purchased lottery tickets, drug use, parties, petty crimes, elopements, murder, and just about everything in between. Some of it is desire, part of it is bravery—but most of it is fear.

It's like the end of the world, but if the end of the world was an annually occurring holiday.

I walk over to Ren's desk and sit down in his swivel chair. I search for something to write with and manage to find a dull pencil, but I don't see any paper lying around so I find myself searching through his backpack for a second time.

I pull out his old botany notebook and flip through the pages. His handwriting is the neat kind of messy, a script of intelligence. I stop leafing through the book when I reach a blank page in the back.

I write everything.

The pencil grows duller and duller with every word I spill, scratching against the lined paper as my thoughts become tangible. I write every word I didn't say, every truth I didn't articulate. I tell him all the things I wanted to tell him in the cow field when we were laying next to each other beneath the stars and the words were so close to coming out.

I tell him just how much I've grown to care about him. And I thank him for caring about me too, when I'm probably the person he should care about the least.

I close the notebook when I finish and leave it on his desk. I wonder if he'll even notice it's there.

If he doesn't see it before the Pick, I'll just have to tell him when this is all over.

It happens at 10:00 on the evening of December 31st.

Every television in the country is turned on, every voice hushed as the Presidency materializes before us.

My family and I are all in the same room for the first time in months, and I'm disheartened by the absence of the McLellans. I try not to think of last year, or the many years before that.

Before our parents realized their opposing political views, this holiday of death was a day for our families to come together and enjoy each other's company. We would watch the draw, experience the fear together, and celebrate our survival with ice cream sundaes and tender steaks.

Even after everything happened, even without Ren and Asa, Margot and I always made it a tradition to watch the draw together because of our matching Cards. We wanted to be near each other, *Just In Case*.

This year, she insisted on staying home. Milo asked about her whereabouts and I told him she was getting over a cold.

But I know the truth. She doesn't want to see me, even on the most terrifying night of the year. Even if it could very well be our last. Even if we really are dressing up for our own shared funeral.

We're all silent as the broadcast begins.

The Presidency appears on the screen, seven men and women in black suits sitting behind a long white table. Their faces are all edited out, but you can see just enough of them to know how real they are. As robotic as they are, as strange and unseen as their faces might appear, they are still human—as much as I wish they were not.

A member of the Presidency stands up in her seat and speaks into a microphone. Her hair is cut in a sleek black bob that bounces when she moves. She wears the same black suit as the rest of them, and a pair of large pearl earrings. I imagine her coming home from a long day of work to a family who doesn't suspect a thing. She will remove her earrings and sleep in a bed that doesn't know it holds a monster.

"We thank you all for playing your part and joining us today as we gather for this year's draw, the beginning of the national event known as the Pick," she says into the microphone. Her voice is deep, distorted beyond recognition. An applause track plays, and she claps along with it.

I think about her words and find it odd that we're being thanked for mandatory participation. She is expressing gratitude for millions of people who are willingly living out the beginning of their worst nightmare.

"Another President will now address the public," the stranger says, and she sits back down in her seat.

We all wait for the President to stand up and begin their speech.

It's the same speech every year, but we're obligated to listen, to digest this annual reminder that in the end, we are all reduced to nothing but a database of names and tattoos.

It's so quiet I'm convinced that if the man dropped a pin, I would hear it all the way over here in Northern Oregon without the help of a microphone. It would be earth-shaking, and we would all tremble at the sound.

And then he stands, and the world comes to a pause.

"Good evening, America."

His voice is heavily edited and it's nothing less than grotesque. His words are so deep, twisted, and horrifying, so perverted from the natural human sound that listening is painful. It scratches the inside of my ears and scrapes my core, and I am left with chills.

"Today is the day we all have been waiting for," he says, like a proud father of millions. "Today is the day we will all witness the official results for the New Year's Pick."

He pauses, like he expects us to cheer. A recording does.

"We all know the origins of this beloved event. The world was dying, but we were saved by Nightjade."

They play no applause track this time.

"With the production of Nightjade," he explains, "essential policies were put in place that allowed our country to become the only thriving nation left on the globe."

He pauses to let us absorb the grandeur.

"Our system has been unconventionally perfected to give us all food and water. To privilege us all with freedom from the pollution, the energy shortages, the crime, and the lack of necessary resources that haunted us. This order has given us life. Opportunity. Happiness.

"Everything you own, everything you do, everything you are—even the very air you breathe—is all made possible by this system."

He hesitates again, and my heart skips a beat.

"And now, to mark the beginning of yet another prosperous year, we will begin the draw."

He sits back down in his seat, and an Agent enters the scene to hand him a small box, no bigger than his palm. The Agent exits without a word, and I can hear her footsteps echo long after she's gone. The camera zooms in on the box as the President opens it on the table.

I know what lies inside, but every year it is just as mesmerizing.

The box contains a set of fifty-four playing cards, including two identical Jokers. I watch in awe as he removes the stack from its container, toying with it in his hands. I lean forward in my seat. Milo is uninterested and my parents have elsewhere minds, but I always like to get a good look at them. They could kill me, after all.

It's strange to think about what playing cards used to mean in the Yesterdays. They were used for games, of all things, to pass the time and bond with friends and family, to enjoy what it feels like to be alive.

Now, they are no longer a symbol of leisure, but death. A different kind of game is going on, and a playing card is the end of all things good.

They're weapons.

He pours the cards out of the box, spilling them out on the white table in front of him. He mixes them around with his wrinkled fingertips, slowly, like a cartoon witch brewing something in a cauldron. I watch as he stirs. He then collects them, one by one, arranging them into a neat stack in his hand.

All lips are sealed. Everyone sits on the edge of their seat, sweating, fidgeting, falling apart as he cuts the deck in two. Time slows like falling honey as he starts to shuffle the cards.

He takes both cuts in either hand, arching them with his thumbs inward. He shuffles it once, twice, three times. Each time the man halves the deck and riffles the cards together, he seems to move at a more leisurely speed. He swims through molasses, so unhurried it aches.

Millions of people lean forward in their seats. Nails are bitten to the bloody quick. We glue our eyes to the screen, and we watch the President play his slow, torturous game in solitude.

The Earth spins slower on its axis as he stacks the shuffled cards for a seventh time. We reside within a desktop globe approaching a complete halt, and the heart of every citizen seems to beat the same way. Because we all know that someone's world is going to end tonight. Thousands upon thousands of somebodies will perish for the good of the game.

The President closes his eyes. It is all so quiet that the microphone picks up the sound of the shuffling deck, the whisper of falling paper. We all listen as a single card is drawn.

"Joker."

A pause.

A blink.

I close my eyes. I try to remember how to breathe as the color slowly drains from my face. Now, the spinning has come to a true halt.

They live on my wrists as tattoos, but I haven't seen a real Joker card until now. For the past eighteen years, not a single one of my Cards has been drawn, from what I can remember. I've feared this moment my whole life. But now that it's here, I realize how small it looks on the screen. I wonder how something so seemingly insignificant, something so uncontrollable, could have such a fatal impact.

Milo chews on his nails as the President shuffles the deck once again, but there isn't much left to bite. My mother holds his other hand tightly, and my father leans forward to bring his face closer to the television.

The deck is shuffled a fourth time.

Five times.

Six.

Seven.

All is quiet. All is calm. I close my eyes, and I listen to the lull of a distant rainfall. I think about the coast of Port Keys, where I have been spending so much of my time playing pretend. I think about the breaks I've spent with my feet buried in the shore, staring at absolutely nothing at all. I hear the rain of now, and it sounds so much like the waves of then.

I imagine I am standing on that coast again, holding a shell to either ear, feeling every drop of mist so deeply in my bones. I feel every grain of sand, every calling gull, every breath of wind. In this dark living room, trying not to fall apart, I feel as much as I can.

And we all wait.

"Joker."

My mother is the first to scream. I am torn in two and fall back down to Earth when she shrieks something unrecognizable.

For a moment, Milo remains perfectly still. He is too shocked to move, to breathe, to blink. But the stillness breaks. From the corner of my eye, I can see Milo jump to his feet, shouting something inaudible to my father. He asks if this is true, if this is really happening. He wonders if it's some cruel idea of a joke. My mother joins in, yelling at my father, because there must be something he can do.

I am still.

Everyone is familiar with the odds, but you never really believe that it'll be you. You picture the possibility in your head a thousand times, over and over and over again until you're dizzy. And somehow, you never expect the Cards to have anything to do with your fate, and you separate yourself from the notion entirely. Because how could the odds turn on you so coldly?

And then it happens. Your Cards are drawn, and you realize you're going to die.

My Cards were pulled by two human hands.

One Joker. Two Jokers. Two fates converging.

I am going to die tonight.

"For God's sake, everyone calm down," my father shouts. His voice is thunderous, slicing through the chaos like a hot knife to butter. "She's Immune, remember?"

The yelling comes to a halt. My family exchanges glances as the man continues, softening his tone. "We all are."

This time, my father's the liar. But of course, he doesn't know that.

Something about his words makes my mother cry with a higher intensity than before. He holds her in his arms and strokes her back with a gentleness I've only witnessed a few times in my lifetime. Mom's tears soak his shirt like a pool of blood blooming against the fabric, and I see a tear drop down from another source. My father is crying too.

Milo comes up to my side to hug me tightly, and before I know it we're all interlocked in a miserable mass of wailing human beings. My family cries for my death, and though they think it won't happen, I know it will.

I let them cry with relief. From my own eyes, there are no tears, and I don't say a word. All I can think about is how badly I want this moment to stretch on for an eternity. Because this will be the last memory I have of my family, and I want to hold onto it for as long as I can. I can't let myself cry.

But everything comes to a stop when they knock on the door.

All is quiet as my family exchanges nervous glances. My father looks to my mom, and then to me, though I cannot bring myself to look him in the eye.

"What was that?" Milo is quiet when he asks the question, both voice and body wavering like the last leaf of a barren winter branch. Dad looks at my mother again, and then back to the entryway.

We can see the door from where we sit. It's tall and coated in a layer of black paint that matches my unfinished nails. It's only a few feet away, so near, but no one moves to see who waits beyond the barrier of wood.

"Someone's at the door, I think," Mom notes, though we all heard the knock.

And I know who.

"It's just the storm. Makes the house creak sometimes," my father argues, but I can tell he's just as concerned about the noise as everyone else.

The atmosphere shifts, turning heavy and grim when the knock repeats. It's louder than it was before, a repetitive slam of angry knuckles that will not stop echoing in my head.

"Open up," someone shouts from the other side.

My father's face pales, and I can practically see his heart cease to beat. He looks as if he knows exactly who our visitors are, but no matter how obvious it may be, he cannot come to terms with the truth.

"I'll handle this," he says.

We all watch with wide, burning eyes as the man stands up and walks toward the door. He pauses when he reaches his destination, reaching toward the knob, but hesitating. Something tells him not to open it. Something urges him to question his outreach. But he blinks the reluctance away.

The doorknob clicks as it opens. Drops of downpour force their way inside, along with two young men in high-tech suits of glistening white armor.

They're Chasers, and they've come here to kill me.

"We're here for Lavender Voclain," one of the Officers announces. He is a boy my age with light brown hair, more human than I thought he would look.

My father is so stunned he doesn't bother to close the door.

"You must be mistaken." He laughs nervously, but there isn't a drop of humor in his voice. "My daughter is a Chaser."

The Chasers exchange puzzled glances before turning back to face my father. I realize that this is the first time I've seen my dad display an emotion that resembles fear.

"She—she told me she didn't have to report for duty tonight. Something about policy and new trainees," he says, scrambling. "Was she mistaken? Are you here to retrieve her?"

"We're here because her name was assigned to us, and she needs to be exterminated. She isn't listed as a Chaser anywhere in our system," the other Officer says. He is a dark-haired, unshaven man, who can't be much younger than my mother. She starts to cry again, but this time she does so in silence. I see tears fall from Milo's face and land on his trembling hands.

"Dad—" I swallow my nerves, standing up to try and explain, but I'm cut off. He holds up a hand. *Let me handle this*, he says without speaking.

"No," my father says to the men in white, releasing another empty chuckle. "No no no. You're wrong. She's a Chaser. She went to training and brought home her uniform and everything."

They blink.

"You know," Dad says, gesturing with his hands, "those white cubes?"

"If she were a Chaser, we would know," the second Officer states coldly.

"This is outrageous," my dad says. His face turns beet red, and I can see the irrational fury boiling over inside him. "I can't believe that such a highly esteemed and technologically advanced operation would make such an elementary level mistake. I need to report this. This is—*horrifically* incorrect. Maddeningly so."

"Mr. Voclain," the first Chaser says aggressively, stepping forward. "Lavender Voclain is to be exterminated tonight, and that is final."

"Dad!" I shout this time, and my father whips his head around to yell at me.

"Not now, Lavender." His face is crimson with rage, and he turns around to stare at the Chasers once again. "I'll show you the uniform. It's here, I swear on my life."

The Chasers exchange suspecting glances. "There's a Chaser uniform in this household?"

"Yes," my father insists. "It's in my daughter's room, down the hall and to the right. You can see for yourselves."

The Officers give each other that look again, and the dark-haired one exits the room before I can say anything.

When the Chaser leaves, I run to where my father stands, tugging on his shirt. The remaining Officer glares.

"Dad, please, I need to—"

He turns to face me. "I need you to calm down."

"Will you just listen to me?" I beg, choking on the words as my eyes gloss over. "I'm trying to tell you, I—"

"Lavender," he interrupts again, but before I blow a fuse, I realize that his expression is not angry. For what feels like the first time in my life, he is not frustrated with me.

There is something protective about the way he looks at me. He gives me a sad grin, placing his hands on my shoulders. "Everything is going to be alright. I know you're a Chaser. We'll sort this out, don't you worry."

I feel like I'm going to scream.

"I'm not—"

Just then, the other Chaser returns. My father turns his head to watch, and so do I.

As expected, he comes back empty-handed. Ren is using his uniform tonight, and I don't have it with me.

But what I didn't expect is to find him holding up my hunting dagger instead.

"My sensors didn't detect any Chaser uniforms in the vicinity." The Officer glares. "But they did pick up on *this* in the girl's sock drawer."

My father is speechless.

"Are you aware that weapons of this variety have been outlawed?" the man questions, directing his scowl toward me. I open my mouth to speak, but the words don't come out.

"Oh for God's sake, it doesn't matter if she has a knife or not," my father throws his hands in the air. "She's a Chaser. She has Immunity."

The Officers don't buy it.

"I swear, I saw her uniform," my father argues. "She came home with this white cube, every day after training. She said it was her uniform."

"This is getting out of hand." The brown-haired Chaser says as he turns to face his partner. The other Officer whispers something into the ear of his partner.

All is quiet as they whisper. I turn to face my mother, to look at Milo, but they are both fixated on the Officers, watching carefully with red, dripping eyes.

And then they turn to face us all, scouring each and every one of us with their eyes before settling their gaze on my father.

"Mateo Voclain," one of them says, "by the instruction of the Presidency and in accordance with the Nightjade Order, the Chaser Corps is obligated to terminate your life."

My heart stops.

I cannot breathe. I think about the words and I am overcome with nausea, choking on a sour mix of bile and fear, trying not to topple over, fighting so hard to keep myself upright. My head pounds vigorously and I wonder if I might fall over after all.

"What?" Dad says softly, articulating our shared confusion.

"The Nightjade Order clearly states that any acts of protest against a Chaser and their duties will result in the death of the Picked assignment's immediate family," one of the men explains, but his expression has changed. There is a hint of eagerness in his voice, the sound of a man content with his work.

"I would also like to remind you that those who attempt to flee from being Picked will initiate the same lethal consequence."

His words don't feel real. They *can't* be real.

I was quick to accept my own death, but this is different. This is my family.

I'm the liar. I'm the one who brought them all into this mess. I'm the one whose Cards were pulled, and I deserve nothing less than the fate they want to force upon me. I am the one who needs to die, not them.

I want to scream. I want to cry and shout and claw at the Chasers until my throat bleeds, to tell them I'm the one they came to kill so they should just get on with it. But beyond my own control, my lips remain still, refusing to part.

Why can't I say anything? Why won't the screams come out?

Am I really this afraid?

Before I can do anything, one of the men pulls a Nightjade syringe somewhere out of his uniform. The Chaser to his left does the same, and I feel the color drain from my skin when I see what they hold.

These aren't like the syringes my father uses to cook and bake in the kitchen, or even the ones Cedar and I found in that treatment room. These are thick, brimming with a dark purple substance I can only assume to be Nightjade, and the tip gleams with sharpness.

These are not tools. These are clean, sadistic weapons used for one thing and one thing alone.

One of the Chasers looks at his partner, and for a moment, I can taste the malice in the air. The other returns the expression with a haunting grin that sends a shiver through me, icing the marrow in my bones and stopping my blood in its tracks.

I want to lunge at them and claw the skin right off their skeletons. I want to fight them, to roll out the door and tumble down the driveway and into the rain and lead them away from my family. I would do whatever it takes to pry that syringe from his cold, armored hands.

My instincts scream louder than they ever have before, urging me to move. To do something, anything at all. But I am still, frozen as my blood, grounded in place by this fear I never asked for. I have to move.

Why can't I move?

Before I can act or even blink, the brown-haired Chaser takes a step closer. He raises the syringe in the air. I almost scream, but there isn't enough time.

My father is stabbed in the neck.

I shriek as the world crumbles around me. I fall to my knees, and everything is suddenly nothing at all. There is only color, blended together in one horrible, inconceivable haze. My eyes are coated with salt. Everything is foggy. If I could move, I'd check my body for blood, because although I have no outer wound, I too have been stabbed.

My mother howls. My brother sobs, but I can't seem to hear a thing. Every sense of mine has been joined together into one indecipherable mess I can't unravel, no matter how hard I try. I am drowning in a pool of yarn.

The Chaser doesn't remove the syringe right away. He leaves it in as my father crumples to the ground, and the man stands over him once he's fallen.

"Not so high and mighty now, are you?" the Officer hisses. He twists the syringe around in Dad's neck. A stream of blood trickles from the wound, staining the floorboards red. I am too weak to vomit.

I yell something inaudible as the Chaser stabs my father again, this time in the chest. My dad has already stopped breathing, but the Chaser doesn't care. He stabs him again and again and again until I can no longer look. Because this is a game, and these Chasers know exactly who is in control.

There are no consequences for people like them.

I don't have time to fully register what's happening before my mother flies forward. She falls to my father's lifeless body and strokes his hair, smiling down at him with one last gesture of love before a syringe meets her shoulder. Nightjade invades her bloodstream, and she collapses instantly.

I'm in hysterics. I can't stop shrieking. My whole body shakes with anger, with sorrow and shock and every feeling I've ever felt before. It's too much, and my body cannot handle it. There is something wrong and I cannot move. My throat is raw and I taste blood, but the cries keep coming. The tears keep falling. I am falling. My mind tells my limbs to fight but nothing is working the way it should.

My words are not recognizable, but I beg the men in white to kill me. I scream as loud as my lungs will allow and beg them to murder me next, because I can't take any more of this. And I refuse to see my brother fall too. Not Milo. Not after all I've already witnessed.

Sobbing, I beg to no one. "Please."

Take me first.

I can't watch him leave me.

I tell the universe that I will die a thousand deaths after this. That I will willingly give myself to an eternity of pain if I can only have the privilege to stop breathing right now. Death hangs heavy in the air, thick and sweet like Nightjade syrup. I want to taste it.

But the Chasers don't have a chance to lay a hand on me.

Milo attacks the dark-haired Officer with a fury I've never seen before. He leaps at the man and knocks him to the ground, kneeling on his legs and taking the confiscated knife before he has a chance to react.

I am petrified as I watch my younger brother raise the blade up high.

I am breathless as I watch it fall.

And I am lost when I see it plunge into the man's neck.

Milo screams something indecipherable. He removes the knife from the Chaser's gurgling throat and lets it fall again as I scramble to my feet, taking steps back to avoid the spatter.

It falls again. And again, and again, and again. There is so much blood, more than I thought any human could contain. The Chaser is worse than dead, punctured and mauled, but my brother will not stop.

My brother. The reserved homeschool boy who wrote stories in secret, who tinkered with artifacts from another era in the dark to remain unseen.

And now I see him. I see him with a knife in his hand, kneeling over a mutilated corpse, soaking in a pool of blood.

Just then, the dead Chaser's brown-haired partner tackles my brother to the ground, knocking him off the dead Officer and sending the blade flying. The two of them scramble to grab the bloodied weapon, but the Chaser is quicker, grabbing it before my brother has the chance.

Milo lunges at the Officer. They are locked in a horrifying struggle for power as they both fight for the knife, an alligator rolling with a freshly caught gazelle. I cannot tell which one of them has the jaws.

"Run!" My brother's face is stained with tears and blood.

"I'm not leaving you!" The words are coarse and burn when I shout them. I shake my head, trembling uncontrollably.

"*Don't be an idiot*!" My brother grumbles, grunting as he and the Chaser clasp their hands together, trying so desperately to push the other back.

But I have to be an idiot. I have to stay with Milo because I can't leave him.

I gasp when the Chaser is finally able to push Milo off of him. But instead of going for my brother, the Officer gives him one look—and he lunges at me.

Something sharp slices into the upper flesh of my left arm, retracting crudely as a gnarled cry exits my mouth. Everything is on fire, but the burning is distant, because I have already been swallowed by greater pains. *At least it was me, and not him.*

I wait for the final blow as I soak in my own blood.

Before I can blink, Milo is on his feet again, giving all he has into keeping the man away from me. He tackles, he kicks, he flails, but he is no match for a trained Officer of the Chaser Corps.

My brother falls flat on his back, hitting his head on the hardwood, squeezing his eyes shut upon impact. The Chaser forgets about me and kneels on Milo's legs, raising the blade high in the air with both hands, ready to carve into his chest.

Get up, I want to scream. *Do something.*

But the words are gone again. My lips are frozen, my breath swept away by some invisible force I cannot name. Agony. Understanding. Fear, perhaps. Maybe even some sick, twisted combination of them all.

I cannot speak, but I scream when the Chaser lets the knife fall.

My eyes come to a close all on their own. I cannot look. I will not look, because if I do, that will be a fate far worse than death.

I fall to my knees, burying my head in my hands.

Please, I beg to no one, *why won't you take me?*

Just then, I hear something. Something small, something faint, almost like a cough, or a wince.

When I open my eyes, I expect the absolute worst. But what I see takes me by surprise, and I inhale sharply, covering my mouth with my hands.

My brother, sitting upright with his back against the couch with a knife in his hands—and a gaping wound in his abdomen.

He sits in a pool of his own blood, and that of the two dead Chasers to his left. I glance to his side and find the black-haired Chaser with a slit throat.

Milo's eyes flicker between half open and closed, and his breathing is shallow. I crawl to his side frantically, holding back tears to keep my vision clear and failing miserably.

"Milo..." I sob. "What did you do?"

He gives me a weak half smile, unable to keep his eyes open.

"Something really, really stupid," he mumbles, coughing.

"Yeah." I chuckle because he needs me to, wiping my nose with my sleeve. "You did."

"Dodged a stab to the heart and slit the monster's throat once he removed the knife." He coughs again, wincing as more blood pours out from the hole in his side.

"Stop talking. You're only making it worse," I tell him, leaning over to investigate the wound. It's much worse than I thought.

I close my eyes to think, biting my lip, trying not to cry any more than I already am. I don't want to scare him, but I have no idea what to do. There are procedures to follow for injuries like this, and because I haven't had much formal training yet, I know nothing about healing.

But when I open my eyes again, Milo can't open his.

"Milo?" My voice cracks, and I place a hand on his shoulder. "Milo, wake up."

My eyes burn with an onslaught of fresh tears. For a moment, I'm completely still, terrified of what I must do. I reach over to check for a pulse. His skin is clammy against my fingertips. I pause, praying to every good Yesterday deity I know that I will feel something, anything.

To my relief, I feel a heartbeat. But his pulse is faint, and I know he doesn't have much time. He needs medicine I don't have. Healthcare I can't give.

But the McLellans keep medicine hidden in their house for emergencies. Maybe they won't have exactly what he needs, but they'll have something to help, and anything is better than nothing.

"I'll be back," I whisper, giving my brother one last kiss on the forehead, plucking the bloody dagger from the ground. "I promise."

I cannot kiss my parents goodbye.

I pound on the door, and my sobs are drowned out by the rain. I can't tell where my cries end and the storm begins.

I slam my right against the wood a second time, but I have no luck. Clutching my shoulder, I don't know what else to do but open the door and run inside.

I want to call for help. I want to call for Margot, the last sister I have left on this earth. For Asa, the man who has been my second father all these years. For Ren.

They can help me, I reassure myself. *They'll know what I have to do.*

I run through the kitchen and living room, desperate to find somebody —*anybody*—but my efforts are fruitless. No one is here.

I crouch down below the sink and pull open a drawer of oven mitts. I throw them aside, lifting up the false bottom to find their emergency stash, because I cannot help anyone like this.

Among other items that are unfamiliar to me, I find a roll of bandages, a mint tin first-aid kit, and an orange bottle of pills. I recognize the name as a Yesterday antibiotic I learned about in school, but when I check the expiration date, I see that it's still fresh. *Smuggled from an outside connection,* I assume. *The Unseen can't be crossing borders, can they?*

I don't have the energy or the time to think about it any longer. I pop an antibiotic in my mouth and swallow, just in case, desperate to prevent infection. I shove the bottle and the first aid tin into my pocket. I grab the bandage roll and unravel a stretch of cloth, but before I snap it off with my teeth, I pause, remembering what I read in one of Asa's old books. My breathing is shaky and my whole body is on fire, but I take a deep breath, and I find the image in my mind.

I see the words, and I follow their guidance as I stand up and rinse off the wound in the sink. The bleeding has stopped, for the most part, maybe because I've been applying pressure to the injury.

Now I wrap my upper arm in a bandage, tying it sloppily before I put the drawer back in place. I turn the corner and make my way upstairs, drowning in my own hysteria and confusion as I search for just one familiar face. Someone has to be home.

But when I reach the second floor, I find not one, but two familiar faces.

"Milo's hurt," I choke. "I need help, please, I—"

Asa McLellan is on his knees, hunched over and sobbing violently. My arrival doesn't spark a single flinch from Asa, and I don't know if it's because he heard me walk in or if he doesn't want to acknowledge my presence. Slowly, I make my way closer to see what he's crying about, and I break when I do.

Margot is on the floor, and she is completely still.

Every part of me that was once good and whole shatters when I see the rope tangled below.

I cannot tell what I'm looking at, I cannot see what I'm seeing, and I cannot hear the cries I'm hearing. I have gone completely numb.

I fall to the ground beside her. My knees scrape the carpet through the tears in my jeans, but I don't care. I can't feel anything.

"Why isn't she moving?" My voice is stained with horror, still tainted by the fresh memory of what I've only just escaped. But with every second that melts away while I stare at the scene in front of me, I sink deeper and deeper into something else entirely.

Asa doesn't say anything. His head falls to his chest. He doesn't answer me, and instead, he continues to cry.

"Asa?" My lip quivers, voice quaking as it cuts through broken sobs. "Why isn't she moving?"

He waits, and then he speaks so quietly I can barely make out the words. "She's gone, Eddie."

"No." I grab Margot's hand. Her skin is cold to the touch. "She's right here."

"Eddie..."

"No—no no no no no. She can't be gone. She can't be. She's—she's right here. *She's right here!*"

I'm not breathing enough, or maybe I am breathing too much. I cannot tell.

"I didn't have time to tell her," Asa whimpers. "She heard the word *Joker* and I left the living room to grab the papers... to show her... but I couldn't find them." His eyes close. "When I returned, she had already locked herself in the room."

No. Don't say it.

Don't say it, Asa. Please.

I don't think I'm breathing at all.

"She took her own life before I could tell her about the Immunity." He holds his head in his hands. "I've been paying for it this whole time."

This is an impossibility. A fluke. A flaw. An illusion. A trick of the light.

It has to be. Because this is not the reality I fought for. This is not the reality I was willing to sacrifice everything for.

She's right here, I scream in silence.

"I was too late." The words sound like scratches coming from Asa's throat.

If this is what living will be like from now on, I don't think I want to live at all.

"You're wrong." I shake my head. "That's—no. She's here. She's breathing, right? I can feel it. I can feel her breathing."

"*She's gone.*" Asa's voice is cracked beneath the weight of what I cannot seem to accept, his words unstable. "She's dead."

"*She's not gone, she's right here! How many times do I have to say it?*"

I shout so loud my vocal cords burn. There is a rage scalding within me, so hot every part of myself has reached a boiling point. My wound throbs and my head pounds and my skin burns, but I move forward. I pull Margot close, and I hold her as tight as I can, because she cannot leave. She cannot. I stroke her hair, and she is just as here as she has ever been.

How can he not see? How can he not see her? She's right here. She's alive. She has to be, because Margot is everything, and I am nothing without that.

But if she isn't gone, then why do I weep? What is this blood-seasoned howl, this debilitating misery? This pain—like every bone has shattered within me, and the only structure I know is what it feels like.

I never knew a person could feel hurt like this. That a person could break into a thousand pieces, and remain all at once. I shouldn't be breathing. I shouldn't be alive.

"*She's gone, Eddie!*" Asa is not angry, but his voice roars before soothing to an empty, quiet calm. "She's gone."

The weeping stops. I sit there for what feels like an eternity, trying so hard to will my brain to convince my mouth to open, to force the words out, but I cannot find any. My body doesn't listen. My mind doesn't listen. All I can say is nothing at all, because deep down, I have finally learned the most cutting truth of all.

I have lost everything.

All I once knew is now a pile of sand. I try to sift through it, to search for the life I used to know—but everything slips. It falls through my fingers. Everything is either absent or left in parts, and there is nothing to hold on to.

I can't even remember what it feels like to be whole anymore.

Margot lived a life without control, with illness and Nightjade wrapped tightly around her throat. It barely left her any room to breathe. I can feel the fear she must have felt when her Cards were pulled. I can understand why she would want to take control in the very end.

But she didn't have to do this.

She should have known about her protection from the very beginning.

"Why?" I mutter, unmoving. "Why did you do it?"

Asa doesn't look at me, or maybe he can't.

"Answer me, Asa." I raise my voice, but it plummets pathetically. "Please."

He shifts his focus, only able to meet my eye for a moment. His gaze is gray and hollow. We wait.

"I've been paying for Margot's Immunity ever since I found out what was really going on with her." He shakes his head. A single tear falls, following the curve of his hollow cheekbones. "I couldn't afford any for Ren. And I just—I didn't have it in me to tell them."

His hands rest in his lap, upturned as he studies the paths in his palms. "I wasn't strong enough."

I feel like I am going to be sick.

The world spins even faster, and Asa's sentences echo in my head as I finally register the full weight of his words.

If he's been paying for her Immunity this whole time, then what was all of this for?

I clench my fingers into tremoring fists. I want to punch a wall until my knuckles bleed, to tear out my hair in handfuls and scream into the floor. If Ren and I had known the truth, none of this would have happened.

He wouldn't have become a Chaser. I wouldn't have pretended to be one. I would have been Picked and killed anyway, but at least my family would have been spared. They wouldn't have protested my death if they didn't believe my lies.

Why am I here, and not them?

I think about Margot, about the torture that was the simple act of living every day. I think of her pain, and I realize that I would have turned Unseen in every possible timeline, no matter her Immunity status. There is no version of myself that wouldn't want to fight to make this world a better place for Margot.

I'm not sure what is left to fight for without her.

I want to be angry at Asa, but when I look at the broken man in front of me, I cannot. I remember the blood I am soaked in and realize that I wasn't strong enough either, in more ways than I can count on all fingers. There is more blood on my hands than my own. I unclench my fists and my thoughts center around Milo.

Why did I Run? I should have stayed behind. I should have left this world by my brother's side. I should have pried a syringe from a Chaser's cold dead hands to complete the deed myself. Then I wouldn't have to know what it feels like to be a part of a world with so many holes.

I should have let myself die. Because I can't live without a reason, and all of my reasons are either dead or about to be.

"I need you to take this." Asa reaches out and drops something cold into my hand. *Margot's necklace.*

Horrified, I look up at him, eyes wide. "I can't."

"You need it more than I do." His gaze is red and watery. "Now go."

"What?" My brow furrows.

"They're coming. They'll be here soon. Now go," Asa commands.

I shake my head. "I can't go. Milo needs medicine and I don't know if he—" I choke, closing my eyes. "I don't know if he's breathing, Asa." I open them again, and they burn with hot, saline water. "I can't leave him."

"You must, Eddie. I'll find Milo. I can hide him in our basement and give him the help he needs, but you *must* Run."

I don't say anything.

"They're coming, Eddie. Please," he begs, voice cracking. "You need to live. Live for your brother. For Ren." He pauses. "Live for her."

Live for her.

His words echo in my head, and I wish I never heard them at all because I crave death.

All I want to do is let them come for me. All I want to do is give up, to taste the sweet bliss of a life discontinued. But is it wrong for me to just give up? Is it wrong for me to waste the life I've been allowed to keep living, when it's been gifted to me by the massacre of my family?

Will their deaths be in vain if I die tonight?

I clench Margot's necklace within my fist. The gold locket and its chain leave indents in my skin.

My brother put his life on the line to save me. After losing everything, he risked all he had left to ensure my escape.

I can't let his sacrifice be in vain. I can't let any of their lives go to waste. As undeserving as I am, what choice do I have?

Something brings me to my feet.

I am not in control of my own legs as I bolt downstairs and through the door. I can hear Milo's voice echo one last time before the remnants of his scream are devoured by the sound of the rain, and I wonder if I really heard a scream at all.

Run.

REN

Sunday, December 31
The Pick

♪ KILL OR BE KILLED - DIRTY SWEET ♪

We kill the man swiftly.

He is gray and frail, and he meets his maker at the age of ninety-two by the hand of Carmody and a Nightjade injection. He thanks us before he falls to the ground.

Carmody insisted that we take his own car instead of the Corps-issued vehicles we have access to. It's a refurbished sports car from the Yesterdays, and it's been subjected to so many upgrades that it runs smoother than any car I've been inside.

Though I know he's too focused on image and the fact that he's my Second, I let it be. I would rather have him hungry for control and handle all the killings than fight for my authority and have to participate in the dirty work.

I don't care that I'm using his car instead of my own. I'm just thankful that *he* insisted on killing the man tonight.

"That was painless." Carmody folds his arms behind his head and leans back in his seat. "Thought he'd put up a fight."

Painless. His words make my teeth grind together. For him, maybe, but certainly not for that man. Certainly not for me.

"Someone's in a bad mood tonight." He chuckles. "Did Eddie finally decide to dump your ass? Good for her."

I want to slam on the brakes and give him a piece of my mind, but I don't. Talking to him is the last thing I want to be doing right now, and my mind is too busy to focus on anything but Margot and Dad. And Eddie. God, how I hope she's okay.

This is my first draw spent away from home. In fact, I didn't watch the draw at all tonight. The results are kept secret from Officers until we complete our first task of the year, so we kill our first assignment without knowing which Cards they hold. The only information you have is their name and location, all to avoid conflicted interests and ensure maximum efficiency on the first night.

It makes sense, really, to think of the kill before the Cards. I wouldn't have been able to focus on getting the job done if I knew of a person who had been Picked.

The first night of the Pick is the easiest, they say. It's the stragglers that cause complications, the leftovers. *The Runners.*

There are always Runners. Every year without fail, a few people manage to escape their fate and live just a little bit longer before being hunted and exterminated. You never really hear of a Runner who survives longer than a few days after the draw, but people always try to flee nonetheless.

Then again, the trackers beneath our Card tattoos aren't exactly public knowledge. They're what makes this all possible. I doubt we would have much control without the use of microchips.

Attention, Officer.

A recorded voice speaks out from both of our uniforms. It startles me at first, but Carmody doesn't seem to be fazed by the announcements anymore. He doesn't seem to be affected by any of this, really, and it's unsettling.

> We congratulate you on exterminating your first assignment
> of the year. Listen carefully, as the results for this year's
> draw will be revealed to you momentarily.

The computers pause to load more data and I bite my lip. I know that my Chasing has allowed my family to be spared from the Pick entirely, but I can't imagine how afraid they must have been when they watched the event unfold, unsure if they would make it through the night. I think of Margot, of her physical and mental fragility, and I wonder just how much of a toll this night has had on her. Severe stress can quicken the reproduction pace of Lyme bacteria, from all I've read. I don't want her having any weird reactions to all of this.

Maybe I can take her out to juice when all the stores open up again. That always cheers her up.

> Clearance received. This year's draw will now be revealed.

I keep my left hand on the wheel and bite the nails of my right. A bead of sweat forms on my forehead and drips along the side of my face, tickling its way down my neck and disappearing before another drop takes its place.

I don't feel ready to hear this. But there is no such thing as ready. There is no way to prepare for the worst. If ready can never be, then I can never be ready for anything.

Breathe, I tell myself, but I cannot.

We wait in perfect silence until the silence is quiet no more.

> This year's Picked Cards are Joker and Joker.

The car swerves as everything goes numb.

I lose control of my limbs, and we drive off the side of the road, crashing through stalks of dead grass. Carmody reaches over to catch the wheel.

"What the hell, man?" he yells, steering us back to the pavement. "You scratch my car and I'll kill you."

I blink, taking hold of the steering wheel once again, but I can barely breathe as I tighten my grip. I shouldn't be driving anymore.

The world around me spins. It is vicious, I am dizzy, and I cannot seem to inhale.

Eddie's Cards have been pulled.

She's a Joker. Two, in fact. Her wrists are painted with the mark of bad luck, and the statistically inaccurate superstition I never believed in has finally caught up to her.

Nothing can happen to Eddie. I won't allow it. Not after everything. She will be okay, because I will make it okay. I have to make it all okay.

Because I can't lose Eddie.

I'm frantic. I press my foot on the gas, and the engine growls as our speed gradually increases. I'm driving well past the limit but I can't allow myself to go any slower. I have to find her before it's too late.

Cars honk aggressively as we fly deeper into the city, racing against the clock in a series of missed red lights and middle fingers protruding through rolled-down windows. Carmody is on edge.

"Seriously man, what is your *problem*?" he seethes rhetorically. "Are you *trying* to get us killed?"

"*Just shut the hell up, okay*?" I shout through gritted teeth.

"I can't just sit here and let you wreck my car."

"Well you're gonna have to."

I'm desperate for breath, starving for air, but no matter how hard I try, I can't seem to inhale. My lungs have shut down and I no longer have the ability to process the overwhelming abundance of oxygen around me. The entirety of my body seems to tremble as I try not to think of the unthinkable. Eddie was Picked. But I can't think about the odds, because no matter what the Presidency tells us, the odds don't like to be fair, and I don't know what I'll do with myself if they were unfair tonight.

I need to stop at my house first. It's closer than the Voclains', and my dad and Margot will have some idea of what's going on. I need to know what they've heard about Eddie.

And though my absence has told them enough, I need to tell my family the truth.

We pull into the driveway after what feels like an eternity. I leave the car running and don't bother closing the door behind me, abandoning Carmody in his vehicle as I hurry through the rain and into the entryway of the house. The door is unlocked, but I think nothing of it.

"Hello?" My voice cracks, water dripping off my armor as I run. I don't bother to close the door behind me. "Margot?"

I keep my uniform on and step inside. The basement door is open just a crack, a habit of old houses in the winter, and I shut it closed. No one answers my reply.

I run into the kitchen, scanning the area for a family member. Someone who can tell me something—anything at all.

"Dad?" I call, desperate for a reply that never comes.

But when I run into the living room, I can see him sitting alone on the couch. His head is hung low and he holds it in his hands. My eyes gloss over before my father says a word because I know this look all too well.

This is how he looks when he misses Mom.

I can feel the world stop spinning, but not much else. There is no more breath in my lungs. There is no stir in my soul, no beat in my heart. Every part of me trembles.

The world doesn't tell you the truth about grief. I have never been told what it feels like to melt into something else entirely, like wax exposed to flame. In all of my days, in all of my pain, I have never known what it is like to burn like this.

I imagine this is what it feels like to be on the other side of a Nightjade syringe, to stare my death in the eyes, to know my end is beginning. Maybe we really do know when we're about to die.

"Dad?" Beyond all odds, I speak again.

I wait for him to say something, anything at all, but this time, I'm not searching for an answer. I've already found it in his silence.

The beads of saltwater are acidic and I am burned by the creation of my eyes. The world fades, the lines blur, the syringe nears. With every moment of my father's hesitation, I am less, and less, and less. He cannot look at me when he says the words.

"It's Margot."

And I melt entirely.

They are soaked in blood.

Both of them, eyes shut but sleepless, still as still can be.

Despite what most would think, I'm not familiar with blood. I can wield a Nightjade syringe like a pencil, but when my assignments are exterminated, they never bleed. I know the color of blood, its makeup, the way it flows through the body—but not its persistence. I've never had the chance to realize that when there's so much of it all at once, you can almost taste it.

Not until I find the Voclains.

Only five fleeting minutes ago, I made my way toward the scene like a lamb to a slaughter that wasn't mine. Rain was falling in whispering curtains that covered my white uniform in little glass beads. I readied my fist to knock on the door as my partner and I walked up the front steps, clenching my fingers and unfurling them over and over again. I fidgeted to the rhythm of the downpour, hoping it would soothe the nerves I'd been dizzy with all evening.

It did not.

The house was dreadfully silent as we entered in search of our target. There was not a person in sight, but instincts and Chaser protocol urged us to search in caution, just in case our target was hiding nearby. I expected to hear the shuffle of evading sneakers, but the only audible sounds were the slow drum of our boots and the eerie percussion of rain. The same rain we carelessly tracked inside the house as though it belonged to strangers, and not a family I once knew so well.

The foyer showcased no evidence of the violence we would eventually find. Well-loved shoes lined the walls, all cloaked in the same thick coat of mud. If I didn't know any better, I would've believed they still had a purpose. My partner didn't pay any attention to the shoes as we walked inside, but to me, each one was a bleak symbol of a life once lived.

I couldn't bring myself to look him in the eye, but he seemed unaffected. Apathy allowed him to be separate, because it was a Chaser's job to be just that. Disconnected. You couldn't complete an assignment with guilt standing in the way.

But he didn't know the Voclains like I did.

The kitchen was cleaner, but it still displayed bits and pieces of the people the Voclains once were. A vague grocery list was scribbled on the back of a receipt left on the counter. Report cards and faded photographs of school athletic teams decorated the fridge like paintings. Grimy dishes were piled too high in the sink, a forgotten chore that no Voclain would ever be able to complete again.

I did not see their bodies until I entered the living room and found myself stepping in a thick pool of blood. It fanned behind Mr. and Mrs. Voclain like a crimson mirror, but it did not belong to them.

The Voclains were lucky. They got the syringe. But the two dead Chasers were the ones to suffer from knife wounds.

And now I stand here, looming over their still-warm bodies while I mentally replay the horrors that took place. There is so much blood. Its flavor rests on my tongue, sour and metallic, the seasoning of death. I wonder if its taste will ever leave.

I stare at the corpses, at the mutilated necks of the white-armored Officers, lifeless at my feet. I can tell they'd been punctured again and again by a hand that could have only belonged to our target. Who else could have done this but Eddie—the sole survivor of this occurrence?

She loves her family more than anything. She would have fought back, right?

My eyes flicker back to Eddie's parents. Mr. and Mrs. Voclain look so peaceful, so hollow. I assume her father, Mateo, was the first to go. Adele's body hovers over her husband's lifeless shell, somehow tending to him as she strokes his dark hair from beyond the grave.

I stare at Eddie's dead mother, whose eyes are still pried open. I watch her belly, waiting for it to rise and fall, waiting for some sign of life that never comes. *She really is dead.*

Dead because of people like me.

I reach out to close her eyes—but I can't.

The Voclains would still be breathing if it weren't for the system I devoted my life to when I became a Chaser, despite everything—*everyone*—it has taken away from me.

The same system Eddie cheated when she Ran away.

But of course she Ran. She couldn't have let this happen on purpose—I know Eddie better than that. After killing the Chasers for what they did to her parents, she must have fled.

My partner crouches down, running a finger through the blood of our fallen Officers. He inspects the stain on his gloved hand. "I know what happened."

My body trembles. I bite back a scream. *He doesn't know a damn thing.* But I can't open my mouth or peel my eyes away from the blood.

"It's written all over the scene." He stands up, wiping his finger on the back of the couch. "The Chasers came knocking, looking for Eddie, and when she tried to Run, they killed her family. Runner's penalty."

The Runner's penalty. It keeps us obedient, eager to accept our fates and let death come, because we all know the consequences of Running away. A Runner causes far more bloodshed than their own.

"Eddie didn't Run." I shake my head. My skull is filled with denial's cotton, my vision hazy. The frame of my sight lightens like someone has set the edges on fire. "She would never do that."

"It's the only explanation. They wouldn't have killed her parents for any other reason." He lets out a deep, frustrated sigh. "I don't care if you two had a history. She's your assignment now, and the evidence is all here."

He takes a few steps closer, walking over the dead Voclains without a second thought. He places a hand on my armored shoulder, gaze hollow. "You need to face the facts."

Face the facts.

Face the facts?

I can never face the facts, because these are not facts.

Something doesn't add up here. No one knows our target like I do. Although I can't verbalize my doubts without appearing disloyal to the Corps, I know that Eddie can't be at fault.

I need to find her. I need to save her, to figure out what really happened.

Even though I'm expected to kill her.

My partner urges us to move forward and continue to look for our target. His words are like the call of some faraway train, distant and meaningless.

I know I should cry, but grief is a luxury I can no longer afford. I sold that privilege for a white uniform.

Instead, I rise to my feet, remove my gloves, and wash the Voclains' dishes until the last plate is fully clean. But I can't stop. I keep scrubbing until the ceramic shatters under the pressure of my grip. I hold the shards as tightly as I can until more blood drips to the floor, staining the kitchen tile red.

But the sound of the drops is swallowed by the rain, and I can't bring myself to clean the mess. I fall to my knees and stare at the red dots until I can no longer keep my eyes open.

And before I know it, I am sobbing, and the sound of my cries is swallowed up too.

I freeze when I'm startled by my uniform's computer for a second time. I can barely hear the voice, because I am numb.

Attention, Officer.

There is a pause, almost conversational, until the machine continues.

You and your partner have been assigned to locate and exterminate a Runner. Please prepare to receive the name of said Runner.

The computer makes a noise to signal that it's loading, and the screen on the wrist of my uniform lights up with three moving dots. I watch them dance, twirling far too playfully to signify such a horrible wait. The dots come to a jarring halt when my wrist speaks up again.

The name of your assignment is Lavender Adele Voclain.

I am lifeless.

I have given every tear, to the point where I am no longer able to shed any at all. I stare at the drops of blood that decorate the kitchen floor. *My blood.*

I wish Eddie stayed. But I wish Margot stayed even more.

I don't realize how much time has passed until Carmody's voice appears over the radio in my uniform's wrist, sawing through the air in a way that makes my ears ring.

I've been waiting in the car for an hour. We're leaving.

The words sink in, but not fully. They are coated in thick layers of fog. My mouth is dry and sour and I keep it still.

Reaction is not a function I obtain when I am joined by the presence of footsteps. I don't need to look up beyond the pair of muddy white boots to know that it's Carmody. I cannot tell how much time has gone by since he radioed me.

"Ren." My partner pauses, waiting for a response until he lets out an exasperated sigh. "I don't think it's good for you to be in this house, man. Come on."

I stare at my glistening chrome refrigerator reflection. My back is pressed against the cabinetry below the sink, legs outstretched. The appliance stands near my toes, a blurred mirror that does not reciprocate my image with clarity.

"Ren."

How odd to be called a name that no longer belongs to you.

My eyelids are too heavy of a weight to bear and they fall shut, the way my father used to yank our shutters closed whenever a pair of Chasers patrolled the neighborhood. Perhaps my mind is doing the same thing.

I'm about to let myself drift away to some hopefully infinite slumber when something slams against the side of my face.

Molars grind against the side of my cheek upon the impact, drawing a metallic crimson liquid I spit out on the floor. Instincts tell my hand to comfort the side of my face, perhaps protect it with a palm, but all I have the energy to do is look up at Carmody, too empty to be angry at his backhanded slap.

He grabs me by the collar of my suit and pulls me to my feet, not kindly, but not the way he treated me on that playground either.

"I know tonight has been your hell. I know you might still be in that hell for a long time, maybe even from here on out. But listen, man." Carmody looks me dead in the eye. For the first time, I notice that his are a helpless gray like my father's, lost in some distant fog of a torment I will never understand.

"We can't waste any more time, not when we've got a target to find," the Chaser continues. "And if we don't—if we screw this up somehow—*we'll* be the ones facing extermination, not her."

My tongue remains paralyzed.

"Do you wanna let your life go to waste like that? All for some reckless maniac who never gave a damn about you or anyone else? She's a coward, Ren. And a Runner."

His breathing grows heavier and he lets out a sigh, placing his hands on his hips. He studies the blood on the floor and the cut on my hand, and then he folds his arms across his chest, staring me in the eye though I refuse to meet his gaze.

"Don't you wanna find justice for her family? For the Officers?"

He gestures toward the bodies in the living room. We both feel their presence, but neither of us is able to look at them. I observe the contorted reflection in my muddy white boots instead, barely able to recognize myself in its mirror.

Then Carmody leans closer, and his next words are almost a whisper. "Think about your sister."

Slowly, my chin lifts, and my gaze rises to meet his.

I don't trust Carmody. But there is something about his words I cannot ignore, something already present he just now triggered. Like he's twisted some giant brass toy key in my back and now, everything feels different. The color of the blood on the floor. The smell of iron in the air. The dry, metallic taste in my mouth that will never leave me behind. The tears that will no longer fall, no matter how badly I deserve to feel them.

And this boiling hatred has such a sweet flavor.

I lift my chin even higher. I take another look at the Voclains' mutilated bodies, and I vomit in the kitchen sink.

The bile stings on its way up. I wipe my lips, clutching the white porcelain edges of the sink, trembling beyond my control. Carmody said I've been rotting with these corpses for an hour, but I'd swear it's been a lifetime. And even still, I will never get used to their image.

I remember being on the debate team with Eddie our freshman year. They always said to look at every fact, to study every possible approach, to learn both sides of an argument inside and out. I spent the longest sixty minutes of my life in my own head, doing just that.

I want to believe in Eddie's innocence. I want to believe she's a better person than the picture Carmody painted with his observations. But I have laid out every fact. I have studied every possible approach. I learned both sides of this argument inside and out until I felt my gut turn the same way.

Maybe I understood her once, and maybe she understood me too. But I cannot deny the evidence.

Eddie ran. Her fate was served to her, simple and quick, but instead of taking it honorably, she tried to flee—and her family's death was her punishment.

There is no other explanation. The Officers who killed the Voclains wouldn't have had any reason to do so without Eddie's escape. The runner penalty is clear about the consequences of trying to evade extermination. Her parents wouldn't have protested her death or tried to fight off the Chasers either, because Mateo respected the Presidency above all else—and they have a living son to think about.

Had.

I've already checked for Milo. His tracker is disabled. He's deceased, reduced to nothing but a name in a database, just like his parents. The chip signaled death at this location, but the whereabouts of his body are another mystery we'll have to uncover later.

Remembering Milo, the boy I played with as a child and the young man I came to know at the river, makes me vomit all over again.

I stare at the sink for a while, clutching the sides with burning knuckles, blood rushing ceaselessly to my lowered head. I lift my chin, wipe the bile from my lips, and turn to stare at an old crayon drawing on the fridge. I take one look at a backwards, five-stemmed *E* and know it was Eddie who drew this image of her family long ago, every member labeled with green wax strokes.

I remove the magnet and take the paper in my hands. My grip leaves unforgiving crinkles on either edge as I hold it like a living thing. My breathing grows shallow and it falls from my hands, floating quietly until it hits the floor, soaking in the droplets of blood.

Nothing will ever be the same.

"I'm going back to the car." Carmody shoots me a dirty, pitiful look. "And this time, you're joining me whether you want to or not."

And with that, the Officer leaves, and I have no choice but to follow.

I step out into the rain, absorbing its unforgiving touch. The drops no longer feel cleansing. I am coated in a layer of filth that will never be washed away.

Eddie made the decision to Run. But why did she do it? Her memory is better than anyone's. She knows the punishment that comes as a result of running.

We all know. She just didn't care.

I know agony no more. Now, it is rage I have befriended. Because Margot didn't deserve her fate. I sacrificed everything—my values, my morals, my *humanity*—all so she could live. I thought I was protecting her by keeping her and my father in the dark, and Margot paid the price for my mistakes.

But Eddie chose her own path. She chose to defy the system, to refuse the option of Chasing and the Immunity that came with it. She chose to risk her own safety to fulfill some childish dream of rebellion. And even still, she Ran, knowing exactly what it would cost her.

And I hate her for it. I hate her so much I can barely breathe. Because she is the monster, not me. A person who would sacrifice their family's lives for their own safety is no hero.

I hate Eddie because I trusted her to be better.

I hate Eddie because Margot was too good to leave.

I hate Eddie because she is alive, and my sister is not.

I don't know what will happen if I refuse to give in to this sweet loathing —this burning, all-encompassing rage. If I let this flame die out, I know I will feel the weight of absence, because I am hollow without Margot, nothing but an empty shell of what used to be a human. A machine, programmed to fulfill a purpose without second thought.

Machine, I think, and I look down at the screen on my wrist. I open the map and select Eddie's name, waiting until a little blue dot appears beneath the glass, already a mile away.

Subject: Lavender Voclain has been located.

The little dot blinks.

Her name echoes in my mind until it loses all meaning, a word repeated so many times its definition is no longer a part of my vocabulary.

Lavender Voclain is no longer here. She has been replaced with a little blinking dot, a target on a map. She took her family's breath to keep her own. She deserves the fate she was supposed to take willingly.

I'll find her, not because I have been told to, but because I must. I have lost everything, and without this hatred, I will be left with nothing. And I don't want to know what nothing feels like.

I will let myself be consumed.

And just like that, something inside me switches off, and the last part of me that's human is devoured by the machine I have become.

PART TWO
TRUTH

EDDIE

Sunday, December 31
Day 0

The creek is overflowing.

The air feels thicker than the muddy stream of water. Every part of everything weighs down like bars of gold, slowing my movements. The rain feels heavy. The night feels heavy. The cold, the oxygen...

The knowing.

The water is spilling over, but it's shallow enough for me to wade through. Its levels are usually low, but with this storm, its depth flourishes. When I was younger, I used to beg for weather like this, for a full creek and plenty of dirt to play with. Now, I don't think I'll ever love the rain or mud again.

I'm not sure what brought me here. I know I wasn't thinking when I Ran, and I can barely think now. All I know is that for now, I am hidden, secluded between steep dirt banks and dampened flora. *You are safe, for now*, I tell myself. But I know how intertwined I am with the habit of lying.

The creek is tucked away between my neighborhood and the McLellans', and once served as the setting for many memories of my childhood. We used to go *creek walking*—which was our name for wading through the water in our rain boots until we got too tired to continue. We'd spot salamanders and catch little guppies in the cups of our palms, but we always made sure to let them go. And when we were finished, Margot would suggest that we go back to her house for a warm cup of peppermint hot cocoa.

It's strange to think that one day, Margot, Ren, and I tucked our feet into our boots and went for our last creek walk. And we never went back again, because we were simply too old. The activity had slipped our minds with the arrival of new interests. I wonder how many *lasts* I've unknowingly experienced.

How many unspoken goodbyes were said without my knowledge.

Though the water itself is thin, I feel like I'm walking in refrigerated maple syrup. But instead of immersing myself in a sweet amber liquid, I'm bathing in mud and filth. It reeks like the stench of a neglected aquarium.

I clutch the wound in my left shoulder with my right arm. Blood leaks from my open flesh, falling with the rain. But I have lost so much I can no longer tell that it's leaving, like saying the same word so many times you forget what it means.

Although my speed is compromised, there is a comforting advantage to being hidden. Though a little strategizing wouldn't have hurt, this might actually be the only way for me to leave the city without being detected by the abundance of Chasers that are active tonight, searching for people like me. *The kind of cowards who Run.*

My entirety is covered in mud and rain and tears as I make my way to the shelter of a small concrete overpass. The creek cuts through a quiet, distant suburb, where a road passes over the water to serve as a bridge topped with asphalt. A car driving over would think of it as just another road, sided with a small stone fence and trees. I can picture how it looks beneath an absent daylight; this is usually where Margot, Ren, and I would call it quits as children.

But things are different now, black and gray and desolate. I am all alone.

Every part of me has absorbed the cold like a sponge. No corner of myself is left untainted. My joints, fingers, and toes ache with a throbbing sort of numbness, and I know I need to rest. I'm lightheaded, too sapped of warmth and energy to go any farther.

I trudge under the overpass before wading out of the water, collapsing on the rocky dirt slopes that lie beneath the bridge. I see a flat rock at the top of one of the sides, fairly dry beneath this concrete ceiling.

The rock would be cold on any other day, but right now, anything but the water is warm. I set my knife down and curl up on the dirty stone, shivering violently. My teeth chatter and my bones rattle and I feel so close to shattering. Although my body won't stay still, I can't seem to move a muscle on my own. I am completely frozen.

Is this death? *Has it finally come for me?*

I imagine the Grim Reaper following me through the creek and sitting down on the rock next to me. "Alright," he says. "You've had one last adventure. It's time to go now."

And he takes my hand, and we go wherever the dead people go. Wherever Margot and the rest of my family are—because it makes no sense that they are gone while I am still alive. I can't live in a world without them, because with their absence, there is no world to dwell, no air to breathe, no life to live.

I'm the one who spent so much of my life lying and pretending to be things that I'm not. In my foolish attempts to play hero and assign meaning to this life I should never have been given, I have ruined everything.

How can I keep living when everyone I love is gone? And when the only person left undying happens to be a Chaser?

I want to drown in these tears of mine.

My mind wanders to Ren. I know he doesn't want to Chase. He's not a killing machine—he's a boy. A boy I cared about once, who I will never see again.

I think about his embrace. I remember the warmth of his touch, how safe I felt in his arms. What an easy feeling to forget in the midst of so much cold.

I really have lost everything, haven't I?

"Stop crying. I don't want to hear it."

I sit up as soon as I hear a new voice, whipping my head around.

I thought I was alone beneath this bridge, but an older woman with matted red hair sits on a rock similar to mine, wearing rags that fall right off her bony shoulder. For a moment I think her legs are crossed, but I correct myself. *One of them is missing.*

For a moment all I can do is stare, eyes swollen and puffed, until I bring myself to turn back around. I curl up on my rock and continue to soak up its imaginary warmth, wanting nothing more than to drift away and never open my eyes again. *What a wonderful thing it must be to disappear.*

"Ignoring me, are you?" The stranger scoffs. "Of course you are. Who am I kidding—just look at you. Healthy. Well-fed. You've run away from home, haven't you?"

I cannot afford to spare the strength it will require to reply, so I do not.

"It's only a matter of time before they come and get me," the woman says, and I assume she's referring to Chasers. "I've been out here for well over the allowed three months. And you know how it goes—they sure do love their penalties."

I sit up, turning to face her. She scoffs at me again. "You might be the last person I talk to before they take me, you know."

There is something about her words that invite more tears to fall.

"Oh, quit your crying. Look at you. You have nothing to be crying about." She shakes her head. "You've got two good legs. You have something to Run from—something to live for. That's more than I could ever dream of."

And with that, she turns away, closing her eyes and falling back to sleep.

Even after she goes quiet, her words ring in my ears, the stinging echo of a ceaseless bell.

Legs and a life to live. I think of all the people who have lost the right to live—all because of the choices I made.

"You can lie all you want," Mom had said, *"but every lie will come back to bite you someday. They always do."*

I should have told them all the truth, but I never did, and now I have to live with the consequences.

But there is no use in feeling sorry for myself—none at all. Because if I live I must do so to fulfill a use, to serve something beyond me, and I cannot do that with the restraints of self-pity. I planted this seed of misery by hand, and now I must eat the fruit that has grown in its place.

I have to bear this burden because I deserve to feel its weight. Death is a reward, and my punishment is the weight of remaining.

I have to live for Margot because she cannot, to live for my family because of their sacrifice. To live for my brother, who might be alive. To live for Ren, because he means something, even if he shouldn't in light of what he's become.

I have to live, if only to see a world without a single Chaser in it.

I have to Run.

I open my fist and put on Margot's locket before falling into a deep slumber.

REN

Monday, January 1
Day 1

♪ DEVIL YOU KNOW - PINBACK ♪

Eddie is traceable, but she's difficult to follow.

The screen on my uniform's left wrist displays a rough map of the area. The landscape is a plane of dark green, muddled with swirling topographical lines—and a tiny blue dot somewhere down this creek.

How strange it is that Eddie has been reduced to something so small and separate.

The air is thick with the taste of mud and pine. Everything is a sickening olive green, from the water I stand in to the blanket of sword fern and English ivy that covers both sloping dirt banks. A bluebird chirps overhead as it flies by, singing a silky tune of innocence. It has no idea why we are here.

It's sunny today, but the light doesn't suit the morning. It is too airy for the density of what I breathe, of this weight I feel all around me. I doubt that light will properly suit anything ever again. *Because the sun doesn't belong here*, I remind myself. *It has already left this world.*

I'm silent as Carmody and I trudge through the water, approaching the overpass in front of us. I haven't spoken a word or spared a single tear for hours. I feel like a breaker box; someone has cut me open and flipped a dozen switches I can't identify, because the names on the labels have worn away.

I cannot grieve. I cannot cry. All I can think about is Eddie, and how she willingly chose to Run, knowing that Chasers would be required to come after her family as punishment. She had everything, once, and she took it all for granted.

Lavender Voclain used to be the luckiest person alive, but she never had a clue. That is why she deserves this fate of hers.

And what was her mistake? She believed her life was worth more than her entire family's. She was always bound to fall, and I should have known she would take so many people down with her.

But in spite of it all, more than anything, I hate the person I used to be. Because I think I cared about her once. At least something close to that.

I look down at my wrist, nudging Carmody when the little blue dot begins to move. We pause our wading and he looks down at his own map, puzzled by Eddie's movements. She doesn't seem to be going in any particular direction, following only the curves of the creek.

"You think she's trying to leave town?" Carmody asks, brows furrowed.

"That's what I'm thinking," I say. There is no color in my voice anymore. "You see this line here? That's the creek, and by the looks of it, she's gonna keep walking through it."

"Where does it lead?"

"West."

"What's west?"

"The coastline. There's not much over there besides the ocean and a couple of..." My words trail off as it hits me. "Cow fields." I look at Carmody. "I know where she's going."

"So we can ditch the creek and just head west?"

"No, we should follow her trail as closely as we can, which should be easy enough with our suits. No car for now," I reason. "We would have to take quite a few twists and turns to get out of town by car to reach the dairy fields. And by the time we make it over there, she'll probably have left the creek." I pause. "She's weakened by now, from spending the night out here and the continuation of her trek this morning. It won't take long to catch up to her if we just keep to the creek."

Carmody stares at me for a moment, and then his lips curl. "I didn't expect you to be so good at this, McLellan."

I want to break his nose, but I cannot spare the energy. Not now. "If I'm good," I mutter, "it's only because I have to be."

Just then, a high-pitched beep emits from our armor, signifying that an assignment is within a nearby radius. We exchange glances and survey our surroundings, hoping to find Eddie somewhere near these rocks. *Maybe our trackers are off*, I wonder. *Could she be closer than we thought? Not a mile ahead, but right here?*

But it's not Eddie we find.

I've only heard of the homeless through history lessons about the Yesterdays, but they've become such a rarity that not many have ever seen one up close.

I remember asking my father about it, once. He said they aren't extinct; the system isn't that perfect. They wander from place to place in hopes of avoiding their fate, never staying in one place for longer than a week. They're simply exterminated before people have the chance to notice them.

The redheaded woman is dressed in rags, and she's missing a leg. She stares at us like prey to predator, an unblinking deer in headlights unable to avoid the metal carriage flying in its direction.

Carmody notices her too, and he gives me a look before whispering into the computer on his wrist. "Suit, how long has the nearest target been homeless?"

We pause, waiting for a response.

Four months.

I expect Carmody's eyes to widen, for him to show any outward reaction at all, but he expresses nothing. "They're only allowed three. Do we exterminate her?"

If he asked the same question a month ago, I doubt I would have been able to answer. In all my past assignments, the thought of ending another life was enough to make me sick. I know sleepless nights like the back of my hand.

But do I have the right to feel guilty? Do I deserve to feel human at all, after I've already killed a man?

The consequence of locating and ignoring an assignment in need of extermination is expulsion from the Corps—another frilled word for death.

Inside me, there is an undeniable desire for an ending, but it is no longer about what I want. I cannot die yet, not when there is a job I must complete. There are wrongs to make right—and a target to destroy. I will not be entranced by death and all its frills.

I look at Carmody, who stands still but restless, awaiting an answer.

There is a skill required to address something shattered. When you look at a pile of broken glass, there is no use in remembering what shape it used to be, because it will never take that form again. All one can really do is take a broom and sweep away the mess.

I will never be who I once was.

"Yeah." I turn to walk away, reflective boots muddied with water and algae. "Exterminate her."

There are so many messes to clean.

EDDIE

Monday, January 1
Day 1

♪ NARROW MARGINS - HALF MOON RUN ♪

My legs might be dissolving.

It feels as though I'm made of bath salt, like there won't be anything left of me if I stay in the water for any longer.

I've been walking through this creek for hours. My wound is on fire, my muscles cramped and sore from last night's sleeping arrangement upon the rocks. I place a hand on my upper left arm, tracing the puncture mark with a wince. *I need rest—and water*, I remind myself. *I need to keep this wound clean.*

The storm has broken away, leaving me vulnerable to the unforgiving glare of the sun. The rays burn uncomfortably at the back of my neck. I feel exposed without the shield of fog, rain, and the night—and I'm suddenly aware of how difficult it will be to hide from anyone, let alone a Chaser.

But I still have my knife, clutched in my right hand. I don't care who it is—I will be ready for anyone dressed in white.

Sunlight has brought sweat and thirst into the equation. My mouth is dry and tastes like dirt, but I know I can't drink the water around me, or even use it to clean the scalding wound in my arm. This water is filthy and unusable, filled with all sorts of bacteria and parasites—and probably enough animal waste to fertilize an entire field of crops.

As dehydrated as I am, I have to ignore the alluring idea of taking a sip. *But I need water.* I close my eyes and clutch my growling stomach. *And food.*

I can't remember the last time I sat down and had a full meal. Mouth watering, I imagine a dish of chicken and steamed veggies, salted and spiced to perfection, drizzled with a bit of hot sauce. I drool at the tangy thought of puya peppers and apple cider vinegar.

But really, I would be grateful for anything. Just something to soothe these hunger pains. Though I'm not sure I deserve the nourishment a full belly would bring.

The creek has led me far from the suburbs. Deep into the woods, I am surrounded by fronds of lush sword fern, slick, moss-coated rocks, and the desperate reach of evergreen branches. I can hear rushing water somewhere up ahead, but not much else.

It's peaceful out here. Quiet, without another human in sight. There is only me and the birds and the pine. *I really am all alone.*

I wonder if the rest of my life will be lived out in solitude. Not that it matters, anyway. I cannot bring myself to care.

As I walk, I wrap my arms around my body, trying to preserve whatever warmth I have left. I pause when I realize that I'm wearing Ren's sweatshirt —the same forest green crewneck he gave me months ago.

Ever since he let me keep it, it's become a part of my regular attire. I've gotten so used to wearing it that I often forget it isn't truly mine. I doubt he would want it back now.

It's a mess, stained with so much dirt and blood. I wonder if I'll ever be able to clean it. Maybe the stains will leave the fabric, but I don't think they will ever leave me. *Ren likes things to be clean.*

I keep walking.

I pause again when I pick up on a familiar scent—only a trace. Through the stench of murky creek water, I cannot smell much else, but there is something there. Something I know.

Focused, I take a deep breath. Immediately, I recognize the sharp aroma of freshly grazed grass and alfalfa hay and cringe at the earthy odor of cow manure. *I know exactly where I am.*

I drag myself along the muddy incline of the bank to my right, crouching when I reach the top. Squinting, I try to make out the shapes in the distance, relieved to see a cow pasture through the trees.

I've made it, I think to myself. *I'm out of town.*

I stand up and check my surroundings for unwanted visitors, but just as I suspected, I am completely alone.

I remove Ren's sweatshirt and wring out the water, eager to relieve some of the weight—a necessity if I want to increase my speed. Cloudy liquid drips from the fabric and onto the dirt below my feet. It's chilly against my bare skin as I put it back on. Still damp, but significantly lighter than it used to be.

My jeans are trickier to wring out, and even when I do, the denim still feels soaked. They're still heavy when I slip them back on, but the comfort is nothing compared to the horrible feeling of wet socks.

I take off my no-longer-white sneakers and pour out the puddles. I remove my socks to squeeze out the moisture, and when I reach down to put them on once more, I see that my feet are purple and blistered from the cold.

Grimacing, I walk through the pine trees that line the creek, coming to a pause behind a wide trunk to observe my surroundings again. The pasture beyond these last few trees is vast, a flat and expansive clearing in the woods, with a highway slicing through the middle.

A small one-story house rests at the edge of this field, with a red barn on the opposite end. Cows with hazelnut and creamy white hides dot the landscape as they chew mouthfuls of vibrant grass. I saw them as beautiful once, but now, the sight of them only hurts. I think about that night with Ren. In spite of everything I try to smile, but I cannot remember how to. I wonder if it is an act that can be relearned, or if, once lost, it is gone for good.

The sighting of a metal container in the distance yanks me away from my reminiscence. I can see it all the way from here, planted near the barn. *A water trough.*

My feet move with a mind of their own. I sprint as fast as I can across the pasture, avoiding piles of cow droppings and puddles of fresh rain. Every part of my body burns with fatigue, but in my desperation, I do not care.

I stumble when I reach the trough, falling to my knees. I peer over the edge of the bin to examine the water inside.

To my luck, it's not as contaminated as I expected it to be. The surface is speckled with a few blades of grass, but other than that, it looks clear.

I pause, remembering something I read in one of Asa's old books, debating whether I should risk drinking stagnant water.

But from the looks of it, the cows are well-fed, and the barn is bright with fresh red paint. Surely whoever runs this place must give them clean water too. I need hydration, and I cannot guarantee that my luck will lead me to a better source than this.

I set my knife down in the grass and scoop handfuls of water into my mouth. The liquid is sweet and earthy. Although it's a drastic improvement from what the creek held, it's still dirtier than what I'm used to. But it's water, and it flows down my throat like medicine. *I should get used to discomfort.*

I use my hands as a cup and rinse out my hair. I close my eyes and comb out the mud and leaves with the tips of my fingers, careful not to leave a mess in the trough. They deserve clean water more than I do.

But before I can brush through the mats in my hair, I am interrupted.

"What are you doing on my property?"

I open my eyes, jumping to my feet, spinning around to face the owner of the new voice.

And when I do, there is a person standing in front of me.

He's an older man with crossed arms and a glare that could slice me in half. His black hair is speckled with gray, and he wears a dusty pair of work pants and grimy boots that rise well past his shins. His gloves are caked in mud. *This must be the man who takes care of the cows.*

"Well?" he spits. "You gonna answer me or not?"

I open my mouth to reply but freeze. No words will come out. *Run,* I scream in silence, but my legs won't work either. All I can do is tremble.

"You in some kind of trouble?"

I shake my head no. If he's offering help, I don't want it—and I don't need it. Help will get me caught. *I just hope he'll let me leave.*

"Wait a minute..." His eyes widen. "You're a Runner, aren't you?"

Before I can say anything, he grabs both of my wrists, checking my Cards. My injured arm throbs with a jolt of pain as he examines them, and sure enough, he is met with two black Joker tattoos. He lets go as soon as he registers the images, like he'll catch some sort of disease if he touches my skin for any longer.

And then something else clicks in his mind. He looks like he's had an idea, and I know exactly what he's thinking.

This system loves enforcing penalties, but it loves rewarding good behavior even more. I know the prize for turning in a Runner is a year's worth of Immunity—and so does he.

"Come with me," the man says, pulling me by the arm and leading me across the grass.

I turn my head around, eyeing the knife that rests in the grass by the trough that grows smaller and smaller. I want to fight back, but I don't have the energy, let alone the will. I'm still so weak, in more ways than one.

I consider begging, but the thought of stooping so low makes my eyes gloss over. I don't deserve to beg for my life.

The Eddie Voclain of before would never beg. She would free her wrist from this pathetic man and kick him where it hurts, and she would run as far as she possibly could. She would rather fight than die.

But now, all I can do is wonder if it would really be so bad to get turned in.

No, I correct myself. *I can't think like that.* I clutch Margot's locket with my free hand and take a deep breath as Asa's words echo in my memory. *Live for her.*

He pulls me to an old storage shed near the barn, filled with ranching equipment I can't identify. It's dark in here, and everything is coated in dirt and cobwebs. He takes me to a corner and points to the ground.

"Wait here," he instructs, and I do as he says before he exits the building.

When he returns, there will be a Chaser by his side. I shudder at the thought.

I can't see much in here. A sliver of light filters in through a thin crack between the shed doors, but it doesn't reach me. I wish there was a window, or some other opening I could use to analyze what's going on outside the building, but there are none. I've quite literally been left in the dark.

The longer I wait, the more my eyes adjust. The shapes around me are nebulous and hard to make out, but I look around the room anyway, desperate to find something I can use as a weapon.

I rise to my feet, wincing as a jolt of pain courses through my veins. There is so much of it I can no longer feel the parts as separate from the whole. My feet throb, cold and numb and blistered. There is a twinge in my neck and a pounding in my head. The wound in my arm burns something horrible, and with my drenched clothes plastered to my gooseflesh skin, I'm barely able to keep myself from shivering. There are a thousand little pieces to this aching, and I cannot help but think of Margot.

This is a glimpse of what it felt like to be her, I tell myself. She was the perfect storm, a collection of countless symptoms that never really went away—and most of them were invisible, unable to be seen from the outside, impossible to be understood. She often told me how odd it was to her that most healthy people had an off switch for pain. She always joked about it of course, but I know her suffering was more unbearable than she ever let on.

I blink back a fresh round of tears I cannot afford to feel right now. *Stop thinking like that—or you'll never get out of here alive.*

Weapons, I remind myself, scanning my surroundings once again. There are shapes in the dark, outlines of dormant tractors, riding mowers, and about a dozen other pieces of equipment I cannot name. *He has to have a shovel in here, right?* I could definitely fight him off with a shovel.

Slowly, I walk forward, arms positioned in front of my body so I can feel my surroundings. I'm cautious as I move, careful not to trip over something.

But I do. I stub my toe against something heavy, swearing under my breath as I bring my foot up to meet my hand, grabbing it tenderly. I bite my lip and massage the injured toe, letting the irritation run its course.

This isn't working. I can't navigate in the dark, not without my vision. There are so many almosts, so many shapes that are closer or farther away than they seem. I cannot trust myself.

I let out a frustrated exhale and close my eyes. But when I do, it is like I am seeing the light again. Distractions fade away. I can smell the rust, the dirt, the cow fields outside—even the pine in the distance. I find the earthy aroma of creekwater, still clinging to my clothes. And somewhere, farther than all, I sense lemon and tea tree. *I will never use that shampoo again.*

Focus, I tell myself. I take a deep breath, and I move forward.

It is much easier to navigate the dark shed with my eyes closed. I can focus on the tap of my shoes against the floorboards, the way they stop creaking when I grow closer to something heavy. I can trust my arms to reach, to feel, to guide my legs through.

Before I know it, I am facing the back wall. I allow myself to open my eyes, and sure enough, I stand right before a wall of tools. Even in the dark, now that I am up close, I can see all of my options. Shovels and rakes are propped against the wall, large enough to do a lot of damage. But I'll need something more subtle, something I can hide and carry with me.

I shift my gaze upward and notice a collection of pegs that hold smaller variations of the tools. I reach out a hand to trace them, pausing over a particularly enticing two-prong handheld weeder with crisp, pointed tips. *Perfect.*

There is a noise outside, and I whip my head around, listening carefully to make out the sounds—footsteps against grass, and something like a metal bucket. The farmer must be coming back.

Now familiar with the twists and turns, I grab the weeder and hurry back to my initial spot with my eyes open.

I manage to sit down just as the man returns, holding a bucket of hot water and a handful of clean cloths.

The shed doors open, and the front half of the room is flooded with sunlight. At first, my pulse races at the sight of him, but the panic subsides when he dips one of the cloths in water. He wrings it out before pulling down my sleeve, tearing away my old bandage to clean the wound. It stings, and I bite my tongue.

"It's clotted a bit," he grumbles, eyeing me with a suspicion I cannot place. "You applied pressure to stop the bleeding."

My forehead wrinkles as I try to remember, and then I nod. I did. Subconsciously, on my way to the McLellan's, I made sure to apply pressure.

The weeder rests on the ground between my back and the wall. If I have to, I will reach for it.

"Not many would know to do that," the man says. "They don't teach advanced first aid anymore."

I shrug. "I read a lot of books."

He smiles. "As you should."

When the wound is clean, he wraps a scrap of thin fabric around my arm, securing it with a knot.

He's healing me. If it's his job to care for cattle, he must know a little bit about basic Yesterday veterinary care. The thought of being treated as an animal would make me shiver, because I know exactly why he's doing this.

It can't be out of kindness. People are not kind. If he wants the reward, I can't die before the Chasers get here. I am one with the cattle, prepared for slaughter.

He stands up with a sigh, wiping his hands on his shirt, staining it with my blood. "I should have some medicine back at my cottage. It isn't much —and it might be expired—but you don't want an infection. Always best to be proactive in these cases."

Medicine? Why would he offer me medicine, worried about infection, if he expects me to be exterminated? *And how could he have access to something like that?*

I think about the deliveries I made with Cedar, the homemade naturopathic tinctures and smuggled medicine we traded to people just like this stranger. If he has medicine, he does not believe in Chasing. *Maybe he won't turn me in after all.*

The man turns around to walk away, but I stop him. "Wait."

He pauses, turning back to face me.

"I think I have something in here." I reach into my pocket, pulling out the bottle of antibiotics I took from the McLellan's emergency drawer, thankful I'm wearing my baggiest pair of jeans—with pockets that can hold things like pill bottles and breath-mint first aid tins. "These will work, right?"

The man stares at the bottle, eyes wide. He looks at me and the bottle and then me again, his gaze flickering between the two for what feels like an eternity. I wonder if showing him the medicine was the wrong choice. *He could turn me in for having these too.*

Then he nods. "These will work." He takes the bottle, inspecting the label. "You're supposed to take two every twenty-four hours."

"I took one already."

"When?"

I freeze. My heart throbs, my gut knots. Everything around me grows thick with a numbing haze as I remember.

"Hello?" the man says, snapping me out of it.

"Last night," I reply, and he nods again.

"You should take another one now, just in case." He sets the bottle down next to him, resting it on the front of a rusty old lawn mower. "But not on an empty stomach or you'll be sick. I'll be back with some food and fresh water."

The man walks away again, leaving me alone with the bucket and bloodied cloths.

Food and fresh water. The thought alone is enough to make me salivate, but can I really stay here? Should I run now, while I have the chance? I still don't know if I can trust this man, and even if I can, every second I'm here is a moment I am putting him in harm's way. He could be killed for harboring a Runner.

I could use a meal. But at what cost?

Maybe if I wait for him to walk far enough, I can retrieve my knife and run into the woods. There's a high probability that he'll see me, but he won't be able to catch up if he's all the way across the field.

I don't know what I should do when I reach the woods. No one leaves the cities; they are clean, with pristine white architecture and the comforts of state-of-the-art technology. While smaller towns are old, with chipped paint and little access to urban luxuries, they are still preferable to nature.

No one has a reason to go into the woods anymore. No one dares to stray too far from the food and water.

I try not to imagine what lurks within the forest around me, now that it's been abandoned for so many years, along with every other remote expanse of landscape. I think about the secrets it must hold—and I wonder if I can survive long enough to find out what they are.

My plotting is interrupted when I hear voices.

My heartbeat and thoughts come to a pause. I can't make out the words through these walls of rotting wood, but I hear enough to know they exist only a few yards past the shed.

Fear knots my gut into an arthritic series of twists. Could the man really have summoned a pair of Chasers here so quickly? *They couldn't have arrived already*, I think to myself, *unless I'm being followed*. Chasers are efficient, but only human. Somewhat human.

I move from my spot in the corner and crawl, crouching near the entrance, tucking myself behind the large open door and pressing my back against the wall. The voices are clearer now, but not completely. I can't tell what's going on from listening alone; I have to take a look.

Slowly, I inch closer to the shed's opening. I try to inhale but my breathing is shaky. Hesitant, I steal a glance outside.

I'm too far to see exactly what they look like, and their backs are facing my way so I couldn't see their faces even if I were closer. But I'd be able to recognize those glistening white uniforms from anywhere.

The farmer is talking to a pair of Chasers.

I'm going to be sick.

This can't be happening. Not now. Not after everything. Everything I've done, everything I've seen, everything I've survived. *Everything I've lost.*

There is a clarity that arrives whenever death becomes an option. Now that it is close again, knocking on my door with its knowing knuckles, I realize how little I want it to meet me. Dying is not a feat I am ready to accomplish.

Something inside me switches, and I realize that I've got it all backwards.

I have to live because they are gone, don't I? I have to live because their lives were taken—and mine was not.

I can breathe. I can drink water. I can feel the grass beneath my feet, and I can Run. There are memories I need to carry and I cannot bear their weight as a corpse.

If the system wants me dead, I will stay alive long enough to spite it. And if Running is the only thing I can do to accomplish that, then so be it.

I take a deep breath and run out of the barn.

I hurry back to the water trough and crouch behind it, relieved to find my knife exactly where I dropped it. I rinse off the leftover blood and wipe it on the grass.

I'm close enough to the conversation to make out a few words, but far enough to convince myself that I'm unseen. I try to listen to what they're saying in case I really am being followed; I need to find out as much as I can.

"She'd be about this tall. Dark brown hair, curly, falls to her elbows."

The voice belongs to a young male, no older than twenty, maybe even younger than that. If this is a pair of new recruits, they are inexperienced and bound to make mistakes. *Maybe that will give me an advantage*, I hope.

But something about this voice sounds oddly familiar. I've heard it somewhere, though I can't seem to place my finger on it.

"A young girl, you say?" the farmer questions.

"She would have been covered in mud or water," the first Chaser notes.

And then, the Chaser's partner speaks. "If you've seen anyone who fits this description, you're obligated to let us know."

I choke on my own breath.

For a moment, I swear the world stops spinning. Because I know that voice better than my own. I know that voice like the one that snags you in a room crowded with people, the one that draws you in close and refuses to let you go. It's infested my mind in more ways than one. It has teased me, tortured me, trusted me—saved me. In a world full of so much noise, that voice has become the only sound I want to hear.

Ren is here. Ren is here, and I can breathe again.

But so is Duke Carmody.

My brows furrow as I try to piece together the puzzle in front of me. I had no idea Duke was a Chaser, let alone Ren's partner. Why did he feel the need to keep that a secret from me for so long?

A person like Duke should never be a Chaser. He's cruel, and cruel Chasers make sadistic Chasers.

I shake the thoughts away. I can't think about Duke right now.

Because Ren is here. Ren is here, alive and breathing, and he's come to find me.

It's odd to see him in his uniform, but I've seen worse things. And I know he isn't a Chaser, really; it's an act, a role he pretended to play for...

I stop the train of thought, swallowing a lump in my throat.

All I can think about is how relieved I am to see him.

I want to wave him over. I want Ren to find me and I want him to embrace me again, the way he held me when he cried into my shoulder. I need a shoulder. I need *his* shoulder. He is the only one who could ever understand. But I have to remain still as the conversation continues again.

"What's the occasion? She a Runner or something?" the farmer asks.

There is a pause as the two Chasers exchange glances. Ren turns to the man again, and he speaks. "She's wanted by the Presidency and must be exterminated."

Exterminated?

I cannot recognize his voice anymore.

That's not Ren. It *can't* be Ren. They must have done something to him. Someone else must be hiding inside that armor, wearing his skin as their own. He's a wolf in sheep's skin.

This is not the Ren I know; this is an entirely different creature.

This is a predator. A cold-blooded, shark-smile predator that has devoured the last person I had left.

I need to get away as soon as I can, because in a moment this will all sink in and I won't be able to move. If I don't make a run for it right now, I never will. Staying here means death—by the hand of a boy I once knew so well.

My story is bound to end someday, but I sure as hell won't let it become a tragedy.

I stand up slowly while their backs are still turned, careful not to make a sound. Knife in hand, I crouch, walking the length of the trough with my back arched, trying to avoid detection. But I'm not careful enough in my efforts, because the farmer looks directly at me.

Our eyes lock. There is something he sees in me that I cannot.

He doesn't outwardly express any feelings of surprise, but I know he sees me. Even still, he moves his eyes back toward the Chasers and begins to speak to them once again.

"You know, come to think of it—I saw something earlier," the farmer says. He places an arm over Ren's shoulder as he talks, and I swallow my heart as it tries to leap through my throat.

"Yeah?" Duke questions eagerly.

"There was a girl in that creek over there. I thought I was just seeing things, but—it just felt so real. She just kept walking through." The farmer points in the opposite direction, and while Ren and Duke are preoccupied, he shoots me a look.

Something about that look rattles my bones. I hear Milo's desperate voice in the back of my mind, yelling the very last thing he said to me with hands stained red by Chaser blood.

Run.

I swallow this unreadable hurricane of emotions and before I know it, I'm running north, deeper and deeper into a mouth with evergreen teeth, away from the monster who has been hiding beneath my bed this entire time.

A monster whose existence I must force myself to acknowledge if I want to survive.

REN

Monday, January 1
Day 1

The farmer seemed helpful at first, but we had to kill him eventually. He was a kind man. A bit rough around the edges, but ultimately goodhearted. Because kind people bring bread and water to hidden Runners on their property and try to cover it up by claiming they were the ones hungry and not the fugitive they're trying to help.

Unfortunately for him, caring for people in a world like this is a death sentence. He should have known that helping wounded animals would only stain his hands red.

His body falls, hitting the grass with a soft thud. Carmody kneels down to check the corpse for a heartbeat that doesn't exist, just to be sure.

I turn around and study the field. The cows keep grazing, unaware of what they have lost. I can't look at the dead farmer; I can't dwell on a death that shouldn't matter to me when a much more important task should be taking up my attention.

"Cleaners will be here in a bit," Carmody says, rising to his feet and wiping grass stains from his uniform. "They'll do a more thorough scan for anything unusual, but I think it'd be best if we took a look around first. Looked for anything suspicious."

"We need to look for Eddie."

"But if he's helping Runners, don't you think he could be—"

"Enough with the Undergrounder bullshit, man. We need to stay focused," I snap. "Her tracker said she was on the property and I doubt she could've slipped away from us unnoticed. We'll take a look around, but I want your attention on the Runner. Not the dead man."

Carmody nods, glaring without another word.

We scan the area around us, eyes peeled for any sign of movement. A light breeze toys with my hair, scattering strands across my vision, tracing my skin with salted breaths. I stare, spinning slowly to observe the pasture with my hands over my eyes to block the sun. Clouds inch past overhead, drenching the field with drastic light. A storm is coming. Slowly, but it will arrive soon enough.

Something catches my eye—a rusty metal water trough that stands a few yards away. I looked over it at first, taking it in as a part of the scenery, but I notice it now, and I urge Carmody to follow me.

We walk over to the trough, readying ourselves, just in case our target could be crouched behind it. We round its corner.

To my disappointment, Eddie is nowhere to be found. But something else snags my vision, and I crouch down to investigate.

A small patch of grass in front of the trough is coated in a thin layer of blood. There isn't much, but there's enough.

"You see this?" I say, pointing to the blood. "She must have been taking a drink here."

Carmody crouches down beside me, running his finger along the patch. It stains his armor a deep, dark crimson, almost brown.

"This is old," Carmody says, wiping the substance off of his glove and onto the grass.

"She's wounded," I add, remembering the farmer's blood-coated hands.

"Probably." Carmody shakes his head, rising to his feet. "But I don't think this blood is hers."

I stand up too. "Who else would it belong to?"

"The Officers."

My mind flashes with images of two dead Chasers, soaking in a pool of red.

"If the blood was coming from an open wound, wouldn't it have left more on the grass?" Carmody asks. "The farmer had some on his hands. That means he was probably helping her bandage it up or clean it or something before we got here. Eddie isn't skilled enough to know how to do that on her own."

You know nothing, I want to tell Carmody, but I can't without giving myself away. If I know she wants to be an Underground healer, then I'm just as much of a traitor as she is.

"She's full of surprises," I say. "I wouldn't put anything past her."

"Alright, fair." Carmody shrugs. "But I think this blood is from the murder weapon, not a wound."

I think back to forging that letter in my father's room with Eddie, and her questions about knives. Chasers don't carry weapons like that. I saw those dead Officers; only a knife could have torn them up that way. I picture the girl in my father's closet and realize she's probably had this weapon for a long time.

And she took it with her too.

Maybe she's deeper Underground than I thought.

"She'll be easy to kill, once we catch her—even if she's armed," Carmody says. "But if she's brought the knife with her..."

"... then she's still putting up a fight," I finish Carmody's sentence, staring at the blood on the grass. It looks like sealing wax. *She hasn't given up yet.*

"Yeah." My partner sighs. "And I have a feeling this whole Chasing part is going to be a major pain in the ass."

I don't tell him how much I agree.

We follow a path of broken grass to a run-down storage shed. Carmody slides open the doors, and we are immediately overwhelmed by the stench of rusting metal and gasoline. But Eddie is nowhere to be seen.

"Look," Carmody says, pointing to a run-down tractor. Set on top of the old machine is a neon orange bottle of pills, not unlike what we discovered in Todd Birch's home. "That man must have left these here for Eddie. Maybe she really is wounded."

Carmody grabs the bottle like a pot of gold, holding the label up to his face. "What are these?"

I take the container from him, inspecting it myself. Like the Birch bottle, this one must have been smuggled in from beyond our borders.

"Antibiotics," I say, recognizing the name—and then my heart stops.

I know this medicine, I realize, eyes wide and unblinking. My father managed to find some for our emergency drawer a while back, just in case Margot ever had another one of her ear infections. *Eddie must have taken it from our home.*

Which can only mean she knows what happened to Margot.

"You don't think she's... one of them, do you?" Carmody asks.

"You really think Eddie's smart enough to pull off something like that?" I scoff, opening the storage compartment in my suit and tucking the bottle away. "These belonged to the farmer."

My heart races. Carmody can never know Eddie is an Undergrounder. Wouldn't that lead him directly to my father? To me?

"You okay there, McLellan?" Carmody asks, yanking me back to Earth. "You look a little... unwell."

"I'm fine," I snap. I can't look at him.

"Got it." Carmody raises both hands, giving me a dirty look. "How'd you know they were antibiotics, anyway?"

I pause, forming a lie. "I did some research at HQ. After Birch."

Carmody smirks. "So you've taken an interest in the rebels then too."

"No. Not really," I say, irritated and a little too quickly. "I was just curious. They're nothing to worry about."

"Actually..." He looks around the room. "I think this case might have more to do with the Underground than we think."

My brows furrow together. "That's ridiculous."

"Just think about it, man," the Chaser says, eyes bright. "What are the odds of some lucky Runner stumbling across a hiding place like this—*and* a person who is willing to risk their life to help—being just a coincidence?"

"Slim."

"See?"

"Maybe she's just lucky," I argue. "And plenty of people bargain with Underground smugglers. Just because this farmer had a heart and a bit of contraband doesn't mean he was a rebel himself."

Carmody shakes his head. "I think there's something going on here. Undergrounders love taking in Runners, you know. That's how they bring in most of their people."

"Do you really think she's capable of something like this?" I force myself to laugh. "You really think *Eddie* has Underground connections?"

"Alright, maybe it is a long shot." Carmody glares. "But you said it yourself—she's full of surprises."

I shake my head and step away to continue our search. I scan the room, noticing a bucket and some bloody cloths in the corner by the shed doors. Curious, I walk over to investigate, crouching down to see a sharp handheld gardening tool on the ground nearby.

"Look at this," I say, picking up the pronged weeding device. I rise to my feet, turning around to face Carmody. "My guess is that she was planning on using this as a weapon of some sort. Which means she didn't trust the farmer at first—or didn't know him at all. Doesn't look like a previously established Underground connection to me."

Carmody doesn't reply. There is something about his expression that makes me nervous. *He doesn't like how adamant I'm being about my Undergrounder denial*, I realize. *It's making me look suspicious too.*

"Hey—whatever happened to that evidence we found from the Birch case?" I ask, changing the subject. "Did Price ever get back to you about that?"

Carmody nods, taking the weeder in his hand to study it curiously before sliding it into his storage compartment. I give him a look. "What? You can always benefit from another weapon."

Pick your battles carefully, I tell myself, shaking my head and letting it go. "Did they ever find any prints on the bottle?"

"No." Frustrated, Carmody shakes his head. "I mean, technically they did."

"That's good news, right?"

Hesitant, he lets out a heavy sigh. "The prints belong to a man who's been dead for over a decade."

My head flinches back. "What?"

"You heard me."

"But the pills were newly manufactured." I stare at a speck of dirt on the floorboards, brows furrowed. "That makes no sense."

"It does, if you think about it," Carmody says. "Price thinks this guy knew about the trackers and was somehow able to figure out where they're located. Cut it out and destroyed it or something, then joined the Underground after."

"You're marked as dead if your tracker's destroyed?" I ask, and Carmody nods.

"We learned about this in training, man."

"Sorry." I made an effort not to pay too much attention back then.

"When a person dies, so does their tracker. Makes it easier to keep track of who's really gone," Carmody explains. "But I guess extra complications arise when people learn the truth about them and destroy the trackers on purpose."

"So that's why the Corps is so paranoid about keeping the trackers a secret..." My words trail off as I try to think about what this could mean. *How did this man know where the tracker was located? Even us officers don't have access to that information—only the Agency.*

I shake the thoughts away. *You can't think about this now*, I tell myself. *Stay focused on finding Eddie. That is your job. That will make everything right again.*

"We're wasting time," I say.

"But Eddie—"

"The farmer is the one with the Underground connection—not Eddie. He's the one who provided her with first aid and medicine, he's the one who was going to help her hide. Until we intervened. And now, she's all on her own. No connections, no survival skills." I look Carmody in the eye. "We have nothing to worry about."

He gives me a glare, and I reciprocate the gesture.

"Eddie is not an Undergrounder," I say, as firm as I can be when my whole body is trembling. "She never was, never will be."

"You don't know her like you think you do, McLellan. You saw what happened to her family." He shakes his head. "She's dangerous."

"No. You're wrong." I stretch my lips into a thin line, nostrils flaring. "I know she's dangerous. I know her better than anybody."

I know exactly what she is capable of—and I always have.

Carmody opens his mouth like he's about to say something, but this time, he decides to bite his tongue. I am his One, after all. He has to pretend he believes I'm right.

"If Eddie's not in the cottage," I say, turning around to exit the shed, "we're leaving."

The farmer's house is surprisingly neat for a man who had such a messy occupation. His cottage is spotless; the only mess in his home is what Carmody and I are creating by searching the place.

Every room is a trip to the Yesterdays, detailed with pastel yellow paint, sun-faded floral drapes, ivory wainscoting, and crown molding—every piece a symbol of an aged house filled with warm memories.

Carmody and I check the two bedrooms first. One of them belongs to the farmer, simple and practical, with plain walls and no decoration. The other room appears to be for guests, though everything inside is coated in a thick layer of dust. Old photos and handmade trinkets rest on an ornate chestnut wardrobe, and flowery curtains block the windows. There is no light in this room.

Without any luck, Carmody and I circle back to the main room. In front of its brick fireplace rests two brown sofas, facing a scratched coffee table piled with a few tattered books.

"I think I found his reason," Carmody says, walking over to the fireplace to pluck a framed photo from the mantle. He holds it up to show me a picture of a woman with flowing brown hair, taken decades ago.

"Reason for what?" I question bitterly, scouring the living room for any clues. We need to find where Eddie might be hiding. The tracker on my uniform's map places her on this farm, but we still don't know her exact location. She could be anywhere.

"For helping her," Carmody says.

He puts the photo back incorrectly and leans against the wall, pulling a cigarette and a lighter from a hidden compartment in his uniform. I brace my throat for the burning as he takes a long drag, releasing a curl of smoke into the room like he owns the place.

"I don't know what you're talking about," I mutter, falling to the floor to squint under one of the couches.

"What are you doing?"

"What do you think?"

"I doubt she's under there, McLellan."

"Trapdoors. Loose floorboards hiding keys. You never know." I don't bother to look at him as I continue my task.

"You need to relax, alright? We've already checked every room in the house," Carmody grumbles.

"Relax? *Relax*?" I stand up and whip around to glare at him. "Eddie got her entire family killed, and you want me to *relax* when she could be hiding right beneath our noses? You want me to *relax* after"—I stop myself, choking on the words—"after everything that's happened?"

Carmody doesn't say a word.

I scoff, shaking my head in disbelief. "Grow the hell up, man. And never use that word again."

"Message received." He widens his eyes, holding the cigarette between his teeth so he can raise both hands in innocence.

"And put that thing out. It reeks," I snap. "That's an order."

"Aye, aye, captain," he mocks. He follows my instructions, muttering an irritated string of complaints under his breath.

We turn the house upside down without any luck. We've checked everywhere—the field, the shed, the entirety of the dead man's cottage—but we haven't found a single clue.

The whole house is pristine, almost untouched. I know Eddie isn't the kind of girl to clean up her messes. She left her medicine behind in that shed, after all. Everywhere she goes, she brings chaos without a second thought. Certainly, she would have left something else behind—some indicator to let us know where she's hiding. Some sort of clue. A mistake.

I check the map on my wrist once more, and when I do, I can barely believe what I'm seeing.

The blue dot has moved into the woods—and we were too busy searching the house to notice.

"Look at the map." I rub my forehead, shaking my head.

Carmody gives me a look, checking the screen on his wrist before closing his eyes and swearing under his breath. "How did we miss her?"

"She was *right here* and we didn't see her." I stare at the coffee table, falling to a seat on the couch.

"She couldn't have gone very far," Carmody says. "If we run now we'll be able to catch her."

"No," I argue. "We need rest. We should wait until she tires herself out."

Carmody gives me a puzzled look.

"Think about it," I continue. "She spent all night and morning walking through that creek, and now she's Running again. And from what we've gathered she's probably injured too. You're right about her not going very far but I think we should get some rest now and go after her at nightfall, when she's asleep."

"I think we should go now. Rest later."

I close my eyes, taking a deep, shaking breath. *I am so unbearably tired.*

"We're staying here," I say. "We need rest if we want to catch up to her. And if we move at night, we'll be able to find her in her sleep and get this over with."

"You're acting like she'll be hard to catch," Carmody says, pulling out another cigarette. "She's not as strong as she acts. I mean, if you hadn't shown up that night—"

In a blink, I'm on my feet, grabbing Carmody's wrist before he has the chance to light a second smoke. He lets the cigarette fall from his mouth with a delinquent smile, chuckling as he yanks his arm free.

"So set on killing her, but you still won't let me say anything bad about her, huh?" Carmody's voice is so hollow it sends prickles down my spine.

"Why protect her now?"

"I'm not protecting her." My hands tremble. *She doesn't need or deserve protection.*

"Are you sure?" His grin returns, chilling and empty. "You seem awfully set on giving her a head start."

My glare intensifies. "I'm just being logical."

"So am I."

"I think you've forgotten who's in charge of this whole operation," I say, voice low.

Carmody laughs again. "So you'd rather have control than be reasonable?"

"This has nothing to do with control," I seethe. "You're just bothered because you're the Second. It's immature and pathetic."

"Come on, McLellan. We both know that's not true." Carmody steps closer, a defective intimidation attempt.

I chuckle bitterly. "I'm not afraid of you."

"You should be," he says, inching even closer. "Have you forgotten our fun little history, Ren? Because I haven't. And Eddie's not here to save you this time."

I flinch at the sound of my name, glaring as my jaw tightens.

"The only reason you're still breathing right now is because I've chosen my career—my *life*—over the satisfaction I would get by kicking your ass," Carmody says.

"You think I care?" I stand still. I am numb to his tactics, to the fear he is trying to incite. "I could just blow a little sand in your eyes and you'll run off crying."

Carmody jerks forward, but I pin him against the wall before he can shove me. *"You're dead if you try anything like that again."*

He stares at me for a long time, inhaling deeply, jaw clenched and nostrils flaring. I wait for him to push me away, to start hitting me like he did at that playground.

And then he shakes free. I watch him walk over to the couch and sit down, crossing his arms, flexing and unflexing his fists.

I sigh when I see the old clock on the wall and notice its advancements, a sign of wasted time. I sit on the second sofa across from him and lean forward with my elbows on my knees.

"Look. We need to think about this objectively, alright?" I say emptily. "If we wanna get this done we have to get along. No more of—whatever this is."

He scoffs, but I think he agrees.

"We have a job to do, remember?" I point out. "And we could be killed if we don't do it right."

"Whatever." He unsuits before hauling his legs up on the sofa, resting on his back.

Eager to get some rest, I do the same, but I keep my uniform on.

It's been an exhausting couple of days. I think about how the last time I was asleep, I was in my own bed, and my life was in one piece. I close my eyes and brace myself for the nightmares that are bound to come.

"That night." Carmody speaks just as my eyes glue shut. I don't respond or turn to look at him, but he keeps talking. "You know why I was at the park?"

I refuse to reply. I don't want to initiate a conversation; I need sleep, and I couldn't care less about whatever Carmody has to say.

"My parents booked a trip to Napa instead of coming to my graduation, so they were gone. But they called me that night. I thought they were congratulating me or something." He laughs without warmth. "But you know what they called me for?"

He waits for a response I do not give.

"They called to tell me they stopped paying for my Immunity."

I turn around so my back faces him, but he continues to speak.

"They didn't even wish me a happy birthday. That night was my eighteenth, you know." He pauses before continuing. "It's funny, really. They always told me they'd stop paying for Immunity after I turned eighteen. I took the Chaser exam and everything to prepare for the day that happened." He hesitates again. "But they stopped making payments before I even got my letter."

Carmody's tone is comical, but the hurt it masks is painfully obvious. I know the things he speaks of must keep him awake at night; they mean more to him than he lets himself believe.

"Ian's an Agent and everything... but he opted out of shared Immunity. Didn't want our parents to have any. Because they're assholes, you know. And they can afford to pay for it anyway." He lets out a heavy sigh. "That means I don't get any from him either. But I get it, though. He thought our parents were already paying for it. And he always wanted me to Chase with him anyway."

I stretch my lips into a thin line, inhaling deeply. "Go to sleep."

"You know what else they told me? That night on the phone?"

"What?" I mumble, hoping my reply will hurry the story along so I can get some rest.

"They stopped paying for it when I was *twelve*." He laughs. "And I had no idea! Ian didn't know either."

I'm silent again, this time because I have no idea what to say. I can't laugh with him—it's not my place, and I have no laughter left to give. But I refuse to sympathize with him either, because I don't think he deserves it. I say nothing.

"So don't tell me to take this job seriously," Carmody says, lowering his voice. "'Cause I need it just as much as you do." I hear him shift, turning his back to face me before falling into a deep slumber.

I keep my eyes closed, but even after Carmody drifts off to sleep, I cannot bring myself to do the same thing. His words are stuck on repeat in my mind. Not his sob story, but what he said about Eddie.

How I still felt the need to protect her—even though my only purpose right now is to ensure her death.

I want to blame it all on old instincts, on the way my guilt has trained me to feel about her these past few months. Before the night of the draw, I probably would have done anything to keep her safe.

How can I hate her now when I used to care about her so much? How can I do my job right if there's a chance those old feelings will resurface?

I can't play pretend if I want to survive. If I want to get this job done, I have to learn to hate her. To truly, *truly* hate her.

I have to see her as the monster she's become—for my own sake.

EDDIE

Monday, January 1
Day 1

I run like the dirt is made of hot coals.

My lungs and feet are on fire. My head pounds, every muscle in my body aching just the way it should after running for an hour. I feel knotted, like taffy twisted and stretched into a misshapen pretzel. No part of me is spared.

I used to run in high school, but not like this. Never this fast, this persistent, this desperate. Nothing could have prepared me for what it feels like to run for my life—not even a little bit.

I don't know which direction I'm going, but I know it's far from the cow field and even farther from the city, and that's all that matters.

Logistics will come later, I tell myself, panting. *I just need to get as far away from my old world as possible.*

When I am far enough I will come up with a plan, something more concrete than surviving out in the wilderness as long as fate allows. There has to be more out there, more to the rumors of people disappearing in the woods, more to the Unseen.

Someday I will set my mind on finding them. But for now, I Run.

I've learned a lot since I fled the farm. It took me a while to realize that I can't think about what I'm doing. Distraction is key. I can't dwell on the wound in my arm. I can't think about my hammering head or my aching chest or the stitches in my side—or else the pain will be too heavy to bear.

But it is too easy to forget about the Running pain. Because there are worse pains to distract myself from, and I cannot seem to focus on anything else but their burning.

As I Run, all I can think about is the Pick. Images from the night of the draw never leave my mind. They are sewn into the very seams of my soul, woven into every fiber of my being. When I close my eyes, they only saturate, so vibrant in color I can smell the seeping red. They don't leave when I open them either.

I am never seeing anything else. *I will never forget what I have seen.*

That Chaser twisting a thick syringe into my father's neck. My mother falling victim to the same fate. Milo shredding the man's throat to a bloody pulp for what he did.

Milo, I remember, stopping dead in my tracks. I let out a heavy, trembling sigh, squeezing my eyes shut. I wonder if Asa was able to hide him, to give him the medicine he needs.

But I cannot forget that wound in his torso. I can never forget the pain in his eyes, the shaking of his breath, the color draining from his skin as he bled and bled and bled.

My shoulders tighten. I shove my hands under my arms, hugging my torso. There is a question I would give anything not to ask, but it rings in my mind nonetheless. *What if he did stop breathing after all?*

What if Milo was already gone when I said goodbye?

No, I tell myself, snapping out of it. *You can't think like that. Not now.*

I shake my head and wipe my eyes. If he really is okay—if Asa was able to get to him on time—I will be no good to my brother dead.

I start running again.

I tumble to the ground as the sun sets, not sure if my fall is the result of a warped root sticking out of the dirt or pure exhaustion. I sit up against a tree trunk, resting my head against the dampened bark as my lungs work overtime.

My breathing is violent and staggered, and now that I'm not moving, the thought of getting up ever again feels impossible.

I want to fall asleep but I know I can't, no matter how badly I might need it. I can't rest for too long with Ren and Duke on my trail. If I want to make decent progress, I'll need to get a head start tonight while they're sleeping. *But first, I need water.*

I stand up and scope the area in search of some sort of stream, pushing my way past clusters of sword fern and blackberry bushes turned barren by winter's icy touch. If only it was summer, when the bushes are rich with ripe, tangy fruits, the forest bursting at the seams with life. But there is no life here, not that I can see. Winter carries wastelands.

It takes me a while to find it, but I grin when I stumble upon a stream, letting out a shaky burst of laughter. It's small, calm, and clear, and the liquid trickles across a path of river stones. I assume the water is coming from a larger source.

I stumble toward the brook and fall to my knees at its bank. I cup my hands and drink the clean water in desperate gulps, so quickly it gives me a brain freeze.

I would have downed the entire rivulet if it weren't for the growling in my gut. I clutch my abdomen to soothe these hunger pains, but it does nothing. My limbs feel weak and heavy, and I realize how long it's been since I've had a full stomach.

I search for something edible, scouring the area for some kind of plant I might recognize from the McLellans' old botanical books. There are a few pages I can remember, but some of their images are constructed in parts, like puzzles without the last piece. No one is immune to forgetting, even me. *I wish I'd read more when I had the chance.*

I follow the brook's trail through shrubs and slopes, tripping on roots until I break through a wall of trees. I stop dead in my tracks.

My breaths deepen and slow as I take in the scenery. A river cuts through the woods like a railroad track, sided with fields of round river stones and tufts of grass that emerge from the rocks like patches of emerald hair. Beyond the rocks, the forest continues, all dirt, ferns, and mud.

My breath catches as I remember a Sunday in May. Laughter erupts from somewhere far, and I can hear the splashing of water, like I'm back at the river again, watching Milo and Margot jump off that bridge. I remember what it felt like to sink beneath the surface with Ren.

It was so cold down there.

Focus, I tell myself, swallowing fresh tears as the laughter fades away. *Don't think about that.*

I forage through the wooded areas along the perimeter of the river, hoping to find some edible greenery. I know better than to gamble with unfamiliar mushrooms or mysterious berries. One thing might look like another thing and before I know it, I'll be vomiting on the ground, regurgitating my own intestines.

Despite my inherently bad luck, I find something familiar and smile. *Miner's lettuce.* I recognize the cluster from the books. As a child, their leaves always reminded me of pirate ships, with little white flowers as their sails.

I fall to my knees, scrambling to inhale a crisp handful. They taste refreshing and sweet, like spinach without the bitterness. I grab as much as I can until the pains are somewhat soothed, but it doesn't do much to fill me up. I'll need more sustenance.

Raising my chin, I look up to the sky and watch the sun sink deeper beneath the horizon, leaving the world with less and less light. As darkness creeps closer, the sun's leaving paints the air a furious tangerine that looks too warm to suit the night. Shivering, I rub my arms with my hands. My clothes still feel wet. I need warmth, and I need to find it now before it gets too dark to see what I'm doing.

I'm no expert in building fires. The only knowledge I have is what I've collected from our own fireplace and a few old movies here and there. I know the basics, but everything beyond that is far past my limitations.

I gather a sad pile of sticks and a few decent-sized logs. They're all soaked from last night's storm, but they'll have to do. I throw them all on the rocks by the river, except for a good slab of wood and a small stick.

I kneel down and make a circle of rocks, and create a tent of sticks. When it's built, I grab the wooden slab and pat it dry with my sweatshirt. *Ren's sweatshirt.* I pretend not to notice the smeared black polish still clung to the sleeve, or my half-painted nails.

Closing my eyes, I try to think back to something I read, scanning my memories for the next step. The recollection is fuzzy, but I think I have to twist the stick against the slab.

The sky darkens quickly. I speed up my movements, palms blistering as I twist and twist. But no matter how hard I try, I can't seem to find a spark.

I drop the stick when my arms are too sore to go on, massaging my wrist. *This isn't working.*

And then I remember the first aid tin. Weren't there a few matches inside? Can't I use those to start a fire? I pat around in my pockets, looking for the breath mint container that held the McLellan's first aid supplies without any luck.

My breathing grows quick and shallow. I feel around my jeans again, and still, I cannot find the first aid kit—or the antibiotics.

My shoulders slump in defeat. I can't believe I left it all behind. I had medicine for my arm, bandages, and tools—and I left it all in that shed. I was too focused on escaping to remember to grab them. *Too focused on Ren's betrayal.*

I had everything and I left it all behind.

I grasp at the sides of my head, trying to regain control. There is no use dwelling on things I can't change. I have to keep trying.

Biting my lip, I pick up the stick once again, and I twist. I spin it between my palms until my skin grows red and irritated, until my wrists burn and my back aches.

And then I see them: little sparks of gold, dancing around the friction like moths to light. I cannot help but grin as the sparks meet the tinder, forming a beautiful vermillion flame.

Using my hands, I shield it from the light breeze, sheltering it with my own skin. Slowly but surely, the flame grows. I move the slab and burning timber inside the wooden tent I've made, adjusting the sticks until it all catches fire.

For a moment, I pause, breathing in the smoke as tendrils of amber light curl into the sky. The flames reach up and twirl in searching twists—until they fade into nothing but a few sparks that die out above my head.

I did that. And I cannot believe that it's true

I study the flames for a long time. It's strange when you think about what you're really capable of. A week ago I never would have believed that I could start a fire without the crutch of a lighter or match.

Though it's not very big, I think it's alright for my first try. But it's not as warm as I would like it to be. I feed the fire with more fuel.

I think about what the fire is made of. Not of burning sticks and smoking pine needles, but my choices. This fire wouldn't exist without my hand. Without the decision I made to start it. Without the horrible things that pushed me out here, in the middle of the woods.

I wonder what choices I could have made differently back then. Choices that would have made this moment an impossibility. As I watch the flames grow, I decide that I'd give anything to go back in time.

And then, something splashes in the water behind me.

I whip my head around. My hands shake as I pull out my knife, gripping it tightly, scanning shadowed scenery to see what caused the noise.

My gut cartwheels into a wall. It can't be Ren and Duke already; I haven't been paused for that long, have I?

I remember the smoke in Asa's room—when Ren and I were forging that phony letter—and then my eyes flicker to my own fire. Will this smoke lead them to me?

To my relief, I don't see a pair of Chasers, but I do see a fish breaking through the river's surface. I sigh, shoulders slouching as I watch the scaled creature leap in the air, flying in an elegant arc before landing with yet another splash.

Hunger propels me to my feet. Before I can stop myself, I'm wading through the water. More fish scurry away when I arrive, but they don't stray too far from where I'm standing.

Like a predator, I watch, waiting patiently for the right moment. I think about catching guppies with Margot and Ren during our childhood Creek Walks. *Wait for the prey to trust you,* I remember Ren saying. *When they start to nibble your toes, scoop them up with your hands.*

While they are much larger than the little ones I knew during my youth, these fish are not very different. One of them is easily fooled.

Its scales are sleeker than I thought, slippery like bar soap. But even as it flails in desperation, I manage to maintain my hold, because I am just as desperate. It whips back and forth in violent strokes. I watch it flail and flail and flail, fighting until the very end. The fish stops moving.

I put a stick in its mouth and position it between two larger river rocks to let the meat roast over the open flame. But the fire is too small, and I know I must feed it some more.

I grab an additional log and lean close, holding it over the heart of my growing creation, hesitant and strategic in my placement. I drop it instantly when the flame kisses the inside of my palm.

In a blink, my hand recoils. I press the burnt flesh against my chest, biting my lip and trying not to let myself cry. I rise to my feet and hurry to the edge of the creek.

Frantic, I dip my hand into the water. It soothes the pain for a fleeting moment that fades too soon. I take it out when the cold becomes too much to bear.

I turn my hand over to assess the damage and grimace at the sight of my red flesh. This will morph into a blister, and my skin will be scarred once it's healed. I chuckle bitterly. This burn scar will cover the one I earned with Ren after graduation, when we both found ourselves with splinters in our palms.

Now, the marks on our skin will no longer match. Soon enough his will change too, maybe heal over completely, and we'll both forget about who we used to be. *No one is immune to forgetting.*

The aroma of freshly roasted seafood pulls me out of my thoughts. For a moment, the thought of a hot meal is enough to make my heart race. But when I realize what my excitement means, I start to weep.

I've never even hurt an animal before. Not once. This is the first time I've killed a living thing. I sob until the flesh begins to burn.

The fire behind me brings light to my reflection in the water. I can't even recognize myself anymore. My hair is matted and tangled, my face is smeared with river grime. Maybe luck will be on my side for once, and Ren won't be able to recognize me either.

Or maybe this is no disguise, and maybe it really isn't all that lucky.

Maybe he expects to see a monster, and he'll spot me right away.

I turn away from the river to sit by the fire. I can't bear to look at myself anymore. I doubt I'll ever be able to see my reflection the same way again.

As I move, I feel Margot's locket tickle my neck. The charm hits my chest and I reach my fingers up to feel it close. Touching the jewelry seems to humanize me, and I need that now more than ever.

I take the necklace off to examine it closely. It reminds me of her—of what I'm surviving for. What I'm fighting for. I can't live for any reason other than to remember the people I've lost.

But survival isn't free. It comes at a price—and one of those costs is charred and roasting on a spit.

I wonder what would have happened if I told her everything from the beginning. Maybe if I'd mentioned something the day I found the letter, she would have told her dad and he would have come clean about his payments for Margot's Immunity. Maybe she wouldn't have thought she was getting Picked.

Sure, exposing Ren's secret would have caused some arguments, but they would have subsided eventually. Taking the exam is not Chasing; he would have been forgiven. Ren wouldn't have been forced to sign his life away to the system—and my family would have known the truth all along. They wouldn't have protested my extermination; they would have let me die when the Chasers came knocking.

There are about a thousand things I could have done differently, a thousand things that could have let the people I love keep breathing. But time only moves in one direction and it cannot be turned back. The only thing I can do now is stay alive.

I have to keep going. I have to keep Running. I'll repay these debts with my survival, and I'll do everything they cannot—because they deserve at least that much. It'd only be selfish of me to give up now.

I'll live for all of them, I tell myself. *And I'll fix every broken thing I can.*

I look up, staring at the canopy of leaves that shroud the sky. All around, mountainous pines loom above me, towering like gods from a different time. I think about how trees have lived to witness so much. They've faced fires and floods, diseases and storms. They've been scarred by humanity's touch, and yet they remain, lingering in spite of it all.

I don't think trees even have the ability to give up. They go on because they know nothing else.

Maybe they choose to live like this. Maybe they choose to be still and continuous.

My attention falls down to the locket again. I lift it over my head and let it fall into my left palm.

Against a backdrop of dying flame, the gold glistens, blinking to the rhythm of flickering sparks. For the first time I can recall, I wonder what lies inside its clamshell grasp—and I decide it needs to be opened.

There must be a photograph inside. If the subject isn't Margot, then at least it will be someone else. Any human face will be better than staring at a burning dead fish with popped eyes and crackling flesh. I need to see *someone.*

The locket doesn't budge. It's been glued shut with age, and I can tell it hasn't been opened for a long time—years, maybe. I try to pry it open again, but it makes the burn on my right palm sting.

I use my fingernails this time. The nail on my index finger breaks painfully, chipping away the remnants of Margot's polish. The gold shell falls open.

There is no photo inside.

I stare at a small compass instead, set within the bottom half of the locket. It's intricate, crafted with the vintage intricacy I always noticed in Milo's Yesterday trinkets.

Etched into the interior of its golden lid is a single letter, a slanted *N*— the initial for north. My eyes widen. Below the letter is a vertical line with serpentine curves that snake down like a river.

This can't be a coincidence, I tell myself. Asa is smarter than coincidences. Everything he does is intentional, and it's always been that way.

This is more than a reminder of Margot, more than a token of what I must keep breathing for.

Asa gave me a map—and he wants me to follow it.

REN

Tuesday, January 2
Day 2

When Carmody and I wake up the next morning, Eddie is already ten miles ahead of us.

I reload the map two times—three times—just to make sure the information is correct. And sure enough, the tiny blue dot is deep within the expanse of forest that lies north of this farm.

Carmody mutters something under his breath as he scrambles to suit up. "I told you we should have followed her last night. I knew she was gonna keep going. I *knew* it." He shakes his head. "I can't believe we forgot to set an alarm, man."

"None of that matters now," I snap. "Grab anything you think we'll need. I doubt we'll have access to much food for the next few days."

Carmody rolls his eyes, but I ignore it.

The dead rancher doesn't have much in his pantry, just a few jars of hand-canned goods and baking supplies. I'm lucky to find a few bags of some kind of jerky, and I take all of them from the cupboards before shoving the supplies in two old backpacks I managed to find around the house. We'll need them; the small storage compartments in our suits can only hold so much.

No one is here to protest this pantry raid, but it feels like we're robbing him. *Is it possible to rob a dead man?* I wonder, shoving changes of old clothing and nonperishable food inside the bags.

Maybe—but not this one. He was a criminal. He tried to help a Runner, and dying was simply his part to play. Everything he owned belongs to the Presidency now.

We start with a light jog as soon as we approach the woods. Carmody insists on moving at a faster speed, but I decide our priority is steadiness. The longer we move without stopping, the quicker we'll be able to get this job done.

Things don't get difficult until the ground is no longer flat. The forest floor is uneven, broken apart by arthritic roots and moss-coated rocks. I take extra caution to avoid tripping over fallen branches and blackberry brambles, which only becomes increasingly difficult as light exertion melts into heavy fatigue.

Carmody runs silently by my side. After about twenty minutes or so, he clears his throat.

"What?" I say, keeping my eyes fixed ahead of me.

"I was just thinking..." he says, doing the same. "We probably shouldn't underestimate her..."

"Who?" I ask blankly, though I already know the answer.

"Eddie," Carmody replies. I hate how he calls her that, like they knew each other. Like he has the right to call her by that name.

He doesn't know what it was like to know her, I think with a glare. He doesn't know what it's like to know someone who is capable of causing the death of their entire family, when you did everything in your power to protect the people you love and ended up failing anyway. Knowing a person like Eddie is the worst kind of punishment.

"Isn't that what you were doing yesterday?" I reply to Carmody's initial statement rudely. "And I already explained to you that my decision to *let us sleep* was not based on underestimation."

"And I already told you back then—I'm not underestimating her." He shakes his head as we jog. "I already underestimated her once before, and I'm not making that mistake again."

I shrug, but I'm surprised by his willingness to admit any kind of vulnerability, especially regarding Eddie.

"The sand was more than just a few grains, you know." Carmody's voice is somber. "It was like... two *handfuls*. And you know what she did?"

I don't say anything. Carmody continues again, refusing to look at me as we run. "It was more than just a light throw, more than what you experience on playgrounds as a kid."

"Tragic."

"I'm serious, dude. She rubbed it into my eyes." Carmody lets out a bitter laugh. "Couldn't see for days 'cause I didn't wash it out in time. Had to call someone from the party just to find my way home, but they were too drunk to lead me back quickly enough. My sight was still fuzzy by the time we started training."

"What's your point?"

"That she's smart." He chuckles again, just as hollow as before. "She's a pain in the ass, but... underestimation would be stupid on our part."

I keep my mouth shut, because I can't talk about Eddie anymore.

We take our first break at nightfall, using the spark feature in our uniforms to light a fire. It's easier than I thought it would be.

Carmody offers to let me use his personal lighter—the one he always carries with him—and he's visibly bothered when I decline. But he forgets about his annoyance soon enough as we sit around the flame and try to enjoy its warmth.

I sit on a log and command my suit to free my hands. With the armored gloves gone, I can feel the heat of the flames against my skin, the light sting of stray sparks. There is a comfort to knowing I am not entirely numb.

"Why are your gloves off?" Carmody asks, using his chin to gesture in my direction as I hold my palms above the fire. "Our suits have temperature settings, you know."

I don't look at him. "I know."

"What, is yours defective or something?"

"No."

"Okay…" His brows crease together. "Suit yourself, then."

Flickering flames break the silence, filling in the cracks with a symphony of pops and snaps. Burning pine needles send tendrils of sharp smoke into the sky that wrap around my neck and disappear into the night. I breathe in the aroma, and I watch the fire dance. The coals are so red, so enticing, like glowing rubies. *Are they really that hot?*

I notice a mark on my right palm, from the sliver of wood that cut my skin that night with Eddie. I remember the way her hands felt in mine, how soft they were—how glad I was to be holding them, no matter how fiercely I pretended to hate the girl they belonged to.

That was all pretend, I tell myself. Now, I know what it feels like to truly hate her. For her, I have so much rage, burning even hotter and brighter than the red coals I study so closely.

I look back down at my hand, disgusted by the presence of the scar. By this permanent reminder of Eddie and all we used to be. *I want it gone.*

I shift my gaze to observe the fire once again. I reach forward without thinking. I hold a ruby in my hand.

And I drop the coal immediately.

I curse under my breath as I pull my hand away, holding it close to my chest. The inside of my uniform is warm, but the sleek outer surface still feels cold against my skin. It soothes the burn for only a moment until the sting returns with a sharp throb.

Startled, Carmody rises to his feet. "*What were you thinking, McLellan?*"

"I wasn't," I mutter, brows creased. I stare at the fire for a moment longer, and then I pull my hand away, uncurling my fist to see a patch of raw red skin where my splinter scar used to be.

Carmody rolls his eyes before walking around the fire and finding a seat on the log to my right.

"Look," he says with a heavy sigh. "I'm… sorry."

I scoff. "For what?"

"I'm trying to be a good guy here, alright?"

"Fine, fine. Go ahead."

He sighs again before continuing. "I'm sorry. For giving you so much shit about her."

Her. I'm not sure if it's better to hear him call her Eddie or no name at all.

"I know you two had some kind of history or whatever. I mean, I'm the one who found you two on the playground. I'm not blind," he says.

I can't look at him. All I can see is the burn, bright red and blistering, right where mine and Eddie's scar used to be.

"And... I know it's probably pretty damn hard to be doing what we're doing." He swallows a lump in his throat, and I can hear it. "So. Sorry."

"There's nothing to apologize for," I tell him. Not to make him feel better—because he's Carmody, and I couldn't care less about that. I say it for myself.

He nods. "Alright."

It's quiet again until Carmody opens his uniform's storage compartment. He reaches inside and pulls out a tube of antiseptic cream, manufactured specifically for the Chaser Corps. Every suit comes with one, and I have my own, but I accept it when he offers it to me. It stings a little when I apply it to the burn, but after a few minutes, it's soothing. When I'm finished, I whisper a command to my suit and my hands are gloved again.

The two of us stare at the fire for a long time. We do nothing but listen to the flames whisper and crack, until I lift my gaze upward, turning to stare Carmody in the eye. "There's something I want you to know. Something I never want you to question again."

He raises an eyebrow. "Okay?"

"I hate her."

For a moment, he is still, brows creased. He looks at me like I'm a time bomb without a timer. And then he speaks, slowly, like he's treading on eggshells. "Can I ask why?"

I stare at the fire, studying its movements, how it consumes so much and leaves so little behind. "She's the reason her family is dead."

Carmody nods.

"Eddie was supposed to die." There is a lump in my throat I try so hard to swallow, but it remains. "My sister was supposed to live, and so were the Voclains."

I shake my head and stare at the sky. It's hard to see the stars through so much smoke, but I make out a few between the branches. "She never knew how lucky she was."

That is why I hate her.

"Good." Carmody's expression melts into a hollow, devilish grin. "Glad we're on the same page."

Are we? I hold the question back.

"You know what will make this all feel better?" Carmody asks. I give him a tired look, no longer in the mood for this conversation. "Exterminating her."

"Yeah." I stare at the fire again and watch the wood burn.

He gives me a pat on the back. "That will make everything alright."

I'm tired and all I want is to sleep, but Carmody is more energized than I've ever seen him. He is high on the thrill of the hunt, drooling with the desire to finish the job and put an end to Eddie's trail of chaos for good. He doesn't go to bed.

I don't respond as he begins to tell me stories. I nod, muttering a few empty replies in hopes that he'll tire himself out. But aside from that, I'm silent. I'm not in the mood to talk to him anymore—but I doubt I would feel different with anyone else.

Talking has become a chore, a nuisance that becomes unmistakably clear as Carmody tells me all about every party, hookup, and fistfight of his teenage career. His spirits are higher than they should be for a person whose one job is to be a killer.

"You have any good ghost stories?" he questions after finishing his last tall tale.

"No."

"I do."

I grit my teeth. "I don't care."

If he doesn't shut up, I think to myself, *I'm hitting him in the face.*

"You know that old urban legend?" Carmody says. "The one everyone was obsessed with back in elementary school?"

"No." I open my mouth to tell him to stop talking, but the words he says next bring me to a pause.

"The one about the people in the woods?"

I sit up and look at him with furrowed brows, because I know exactly what he's talking about.

Of course I remember. There are always rumors about people living out here in this massive expanse of evergreen, and people who disappear. There's even talk about a few myths from the Yesterdays that remained prevalent throughout the years, tales of frightening concepts like Bigfoot, moth men, and cults. But as a kid, I always thought the people were the scariest. Because people can be like monsters too; the only difference is that they're real.

"I don't know if these stories are related to the rebels," Carmody says. "But all legends agree there are people living in these very woods."

I roll my eyes. Whether the rumors have some truth to them or not, I know Carmody will blow things way out of proportion.

"Do you know the most famous one?"

"Look, dude, we have a busy day tomorrow—"

"The kidnapping that happened in Port Keys a few years ago?" he interrupts.

A kidnapping?

"I don't know what you're talking about," I say. I'm unfamiliar with this particular tale, but I'm not interested in hearing more about it.

"I can't believe you don't remember." He laughs, shaking his head. "But then again, you never really had any friends in school. No wonder you never heard it."

"Cool." I lie back down and turn away from him, ignoring his chatter and closing my eyes in an attempt to get some much-needed sleep. But as much as I would like to forget about Carmody and the rest of the world for a while, there is a small part of me that wants to know more.

"They call it an urban legend because they don't want people to think it really happened," Carmody says. "But it's true."

The Chaser pauses for a moment. Water trickles somewhere nearby. A stream, maybe. The fire crackles. There are crickets too, and the miserable croaking of some lonely toad who sounds like an old door being opened and shut a thousand times over. And if I listen carefully, I swear I can hear the pines breathe. How can there be so much sound in a forest that seems so empty?

"Some say there are no people in the woods. That these whisperings are only rumors," Carmody claims grimly, his voice low. "But these are no rumors, McLellan."

He picks up a stick and pokes at the fire, toying with the flames.

"I hear talk in the Corps about the possibility of Runners hiding somewhere in the woods. Or ghosts of Runners, maybe. 'Cause these people don't have microchips, and neither do ghosts." He chuckles. "Underground rebels, Runners, ghosts, whoever they are—these people aren't good people. They're criminals."

Carmody reaches into his bag and pops a handful of jerky in his mouth, chewing slowly before he resumes. "The boy was only a year older than us, you know."

I stare at the armor coating my legs, watching the fire dance in its reflection. I know where he's going with this.

"We would have been four at the time," Carmody continues. "This boy went to school in Port Keys, probably had a pretty normal life. Until someone broke in one night and took him right out of his bed."

His words send shivers down my spine. I don't turn around to look at him, but for once, I keep my ears tuned to his voice.

"But you wanna hear the weirdest part about the whole thing?" Carmody asks.

I pause. "What?"

"Part of his eye was left behind," he says. "Whoever took him *cut out part of his eye* and crushed it. They found it on his pillow." He shakes his head and stares at the sky. "He was marked dead that night."

I swallow a growing lump in my throat. "Did they ever..."

"Find the body?" Carmody asks, and I nod. "No. They never did." He sighs, poking at the fire again. "Probably dismembered him out here in these very woods."

He says goodnight, stomping out the fire without another word. The toad continues its lament. A coyote cries somewhere far.

Carmody falls asleep quickly, but my eyes do not close for a long, long time.

Monday, January 8
Day 8

Our days are lived out comfortably, thanks to our uniforms.

We use the map in our wrists to follow Eddie's trail as her Running leads her up the river. We construct and ignite fires easily thanks to the armor's lighter feature—though Carmody insists on using the one he carries with him—and we live on smoked jerky and canned peaches that taste like sunshine.

As much as I dislike both my partner and my target, being out here is more refreshing than I thought it would be. Away from the city, away from seeing the system at work—away from a house too empty to be lived in again. There is something detoxifying about solitude. It pushes away everything I can't bring myself to think about.

We catch up to Eddie quicker than I expected. It's a beautiful day when we stumble across her, but it's clear that her luck has not been as forgiving as ours. Her wavy hair is matted with leaves and her skin is painted with river grime. We see her through trees that stand like the bars of a cage. They trap her within these woods like a prisoner, but this prisoner doesn't know she's been caught; she's been caged this whole time and she has no idea.

When Carmody spots her, his face lights up like a child on a holiday morning. He stares at her through a break in the bramble, eyes wide, his face shadowed with leaf-shaped freckles, watching like a predator in wait. Before he runs forward to seize her, to finally bring an end to the operation, I stick my palm up, and he goes still.

"Why wait? She's right there," he whispers, crouching lower behind the wall of blackberry bushes we hide behind. I signal for him to shut it.

I want to wait. I want to take a moment to strategize and think of every possible outcome, to make plans in case something goes wrong. Because with Eddie, nothing ever seems to go right.

I inhale her image and try to digest it, but it gets caught on the way down. There is something surreal about the way she exists in front of me. She is a scene of oil pigments, so unbelievably close, but still a painting of somewhere far.

She crouches down by the water, cupping handfuls of water into her mouth. Every inch of her body is caked in blotches of mud and dirt. Her face is already carved by hunger, cheeks sharper and no longer as heart-shaped as they used to be.

I can see her weakness in the way she holds herself. Her exhaustion is so pathetic I almost pity her. She looks so different from the girl I used to know, and something within me aches. For what, I cannot say.

Silently, Carmody and I watch Eddie rise to her feet. When she stretches, I can see the shape of her ribs, the jutting sharpness of her hip bones. I try not to think about how hungry she must be—how badly she must ache.

Eddie yawns for a moment before reaching into her shirt, retrieving something I cannot see from my distance. She looks down at a small object in her hand and then lifts her chin to study her surroundings before moving forward.

"What is she doing?" Carmody asks quietly, brows furrowed.

I shrug, eyes plastered to our target.

Carmody squints. "Is that a compass?"

"I don't know," I say. "But it sure looks like one."

How could she possibly have access to a compass? I wonder. People have no need for compasses anymore. No one goes anywhere unless they have to. Yesterday devices like that are difficult to come by.

We lay low from afar, and I gesture for Carmody to stay hidden as we follow her down the river. We're careful to keep our space—to avoid setting off the audible alert in our uniforms that tells us an assignment is near—but we stay close enough to watch her every move. I study her like a book.

Once, she was hard to read. But I know better now. Eddie is a book I have memorized. Even from our distance, I can tell her movements are desperate and sloppy. She's not careful enough to hide her tracks or throw us off her trail, and she certainly doesn't know she's being watched.

And there is one thing I know for certain.

Soon, it becomes unmistakably clear that Lavender Voclain isn't just running away; she's going somewhere.

"Let's say she is using a compass, right?" I whisper. "On top of that, she's been following the river, when I'm sure there are easier routes out there. It's not fun to walk on river rocks."

"Right."

"So?" I ask, raising a brow. "What could that mean?"

"That she's going north?"

I nod. "She seems to be following the North Star too."

Carmody scoffs. "The North Star? What is that, a Yesterday band?"

I glare. "No, genius. It's a star."

My partner shrugs, looking back into his binoculars to study our target once again. "I won't ask how you know that."

"But why is she so insistent on going north?" I say. "There's nothing there anymore but a bunch of woods and abandoned Yesterday towns. She's not heading toward any major city or landmark either."

"That we know of," Carmody points out, and I give him a puzzled look. There is silence, until he speaks up again. "Remember what I told you last night?"

I give him another confused look.

"You know, the urban legends? Like when parents used to make their kids behave by saying things like *stop crying or I'll send you to live with the people in the woods—*"

"Okay, okay, I get it."

"Remember what else I told you?"

I let out a jagged sigh. "Carmody, we don't have time for this."

"I doubt it's related to the old ghost stories or anything, but I wasn't lying when I said there's talk in the Corps," he continues. "About Runners who have never been located. Their trackers turn off and they just vanish."

"How's that relevant to Eddie right now?" I say. "They probably just died. Death disables the trackers, you said it yourself."

"But that's the thing. No one has ever found their bodies—not once," he reasons. "Even though the Corps likes to keep it hidden from the public, you would think that at least *one* body would show up, right? With so many Runners going missing?"

I pause, chewing the inside of my lip. "I guess so."

I hate to agree with him, but his words are slowly starting to make more and more sense. Something in my gut tells me that as much as I would love to discount his ideas—to avoid seeing the rest of my father's Underground iceberg—there might be an ounce of truth in Carmody's words.

"You think there could really be people out in the woods?" I mutter.

Carmody nods, stretching his lips into a thin white line. He almost looks as unsure as I do. For a moment, I swear I see him tremble, just a little. "I think so."

I swallow the growing lump in my throat. Could he be right? Could there really be people living out here? People like Eddie, who find some way to survive, despite the unfavorable odds shoved down their throats?

My heart pounds louder in its cage. There is a sinking feeling in my gut that tells me I still haven't seen the rest of that iceberg.

Focus, I think to myself, pushing the thoughts down. I clear my throat. "Can we confirm it's a compass?"

"Did you forget about these?"

Carmody pulls a pair of binoculars out of one of the compartments in his suit, reminding me of our gear's intricate technology—and how little I paid attention during training.

I reach inside my own compartment and fish out a pair. It's compact at first, like a thick white chocolate bar, square and sleek. But once unfolded, the binoculars cover the span of both my eyes. I adjust a small dial and squint to make out Eddie's shape, and Carmody does the same.

We watch her carefully, noting her every step, her every blink, her every breath. She keeps walking farther away from our post, and we wait anxiously for her to do something of interest. Anything.

I tap my foot. *Don't be afraid, Eddie*, I want to say. *Use your compass.* I zoom in even more, enhancing my vision, moving closer and closer to the girl who feels so far away.

And when I see it, I drop the binoculars like a ruby-red coal.

Carmody turns his head to face me, brows angled downward. "What?"

"That's—"

I stop myself.

What questions would arise if I told him exactly what I saw?

What suspicions would fall on *me*?

I shake my head, picking up the binoculars again before holding them up to my face. My hands tremble as I try to regain focus. "It's a compass, alright."

It's not hers, I want to scream. I want to shout the words until my throat is scratched raw, until my words echo and bounce between every tree in sight. I want the whole world to know that what she holds does not belong to her. *She has no right.*

"Yeah, it is," Carmody says, his forehead still wrinkled with concern.

I force myself to breathe, and I shrug. "It's just... bizarre. That's all."

"What do we do?" my partner asks, and I pause. What *do* we do?

It's not like I can tell him about the necklace. If that compass is leading her somewhere and gets tied back to myself or my father, the consequences will be fatal.

They'd hold an investigation like they did with Todd Birch's pills, because they are more desperate to snuff out the Underground fire than they let on.

My father's undefined connection to the Undergrounders would finally be revealed, to both myself and the Corps. I would be put under a microscope too, and I wouldn't be able to lie my way out of that cage. We would both be killed for this simple connection, even with the protection of Immunity.

Because no one is Immune to the consequences of treason. Even those with the deepest pockets can never escape the punishment of directly betraying the Presidency.

And even if this strange compass is never tied back to me—even if we kill her right now before seeking further instruction, even if we forget all about Eddie and the rumors of the people in the woods—how will I get answers?

I need to know what my family has to do with this. I need to know why Eddie has Margot's locket, and why, all this time, it has held a compass inside. I need to figure it out, and I need to take it back.

Eddie doesn't deserve to hold something so precious. To use it as a tool to further her own unrighteous personal gain.

I put my binoculars away and turn to face Carmody. "We can't kill her."

Carmody shoots up, rising to his feet. "*What?*"

"*Listen,*" I say, pulling him back down before he's seen. "If she's leading us somewhere, we can't kill her. Not yet."

He turns to study Eddie, and then me once again. He releases a slow, strained sigh and flattens his tone. "Should I call Price? He and Pittman might have a procedure for us to—"

"*No,*" I snap. Carmody widens his eyes, and I shake my head, soothing my tone back to normal. "Whatever you do, do not call Headquarters."

"Why?"

"If they think Eddie has ties with some conspiracy, we'll be taken off the case and given a new assignment. We're too inexperienced for something like this. It'll be handled by our superiors or maybe even Agents," I explain. "Wouldn't you rather be the one to kill Eddie, after everything she did to you?"

He pauses to consider my question.

"She thinks you're stupid and weak," I claim. "Don't you wanna prove her wrong?"

My partner is still. He doesn't move a muscle, and for a moment, I worry that I've said the wrong thing. That he's caught wind of my manipulation and is debating whether or not to turn me into HQ for suspicious activity —or kill me for treason himself. I open my mouth to say something, to try and reassure him.

But before I get the chance, he laughs. He laughs a menacing laugh so grim and hollow it sends shivers up and down my spine. "I like the way you think, McLellan."

"She could lead us to vital information." I force a grin too, because I need to reach Carmody. I need to stoop to his level if I want to sway him in my direction. "Just think about it. If we exterminated an *entire group* of missing Runners—with your connections to Price and your brother—we would get promoted like *that.*" I snap my fingers for emphasis.

Carmody chuckles again before taking another look at Eddie through his binoculars, studying her with something that almost resembles desire. And then, he turns back to face me. "I have one condition."

"Yeah?"

"I wanna be the one to do it. To kill her."

He smiles like a predator who, instead of hunting to live, lives to hunt. His shark teeth drip with drooling anticipation, and I get the nauseating feeling that one day, I will see him put those teeth to good use.

I swallow my disgust and hold out a hand. "It's a deal."

He accepts.

"And one more thing," he says, pulling his hand away to study Eddie once again. "We won't kill her quickly."

"We won't?" I ask. His eyes are filled with something so grim it makes my stomach churn.

"No." He shakes his head. "She'll die a slow death—I'll make sure of it."

My jaw tightens as I clench my fingers into fists and stare at the ground. I try so hard to keep my hands from shaking, but I can't—because I was wrong before.

Carmody enjoys the hunt, but he enjoys the prey even more.

I force a chuckle and give him a pat on the back. "And I can't wait for that day to come."

In the corner of my eye, I notice him clenching his fist, like he's toying with something in his glove. I crease my brows together, studying his hand to see what's caged within his palm. And then I see it—a small emerald charm, dangling from his armored knuckles.

Eddie's bracelet.

"What is that?" I snap. The words are more aggressive than I intended.

"Oh, this little thing?" He holds the bracelet in the air by the end of the chain, letting it twirl and glisten in the light like wind chimes. "Just a little something I found at the park after that fun little fight of ours. Saw it in the sand and remembered seeing it on Eddie's wrist. She must have dropped it or something." He grins smugly, snatching it from the air and tucking it back into the storage compartment in his uniform. "I'll give it back to her when our job is done."

Nostrils flaring, I grind my teeth together, mustering all the strength in my body to keep from tearing the bracelet straight out of his suit. Carmody doesn't have permission to carry that. It's not his. It's not okay.

It's not right.

"You okay there, McLellan?"

Mateo Voclain's dead body appears in my mind, and I have to blink the image away.

Focus, I tell myself. *Choose your battles carefully. It's just a bracelet.* And I need Carmody to believe we're on the same page.

"I'm fine." I force a grin before shifting my gaze back to Eddie. "I'm just fine."

He doesn't see me clench my fists.

Stop protecting her.

I pay close attention to my partner as we continue to follow Eddie deeper and deeper into the woods.

It's just a matter of time before she realizes we've already caught her. We just have to wait. *Let the prey come to you, they say.*

Night falls slowly, and it weighs heavy on my shoulders. I wonder if Eddie knows how limited her days have become. For all she knows, this could be her last night alive.

When Eddie stops to rest for the night, Carmody and I do the same, yards away, hidden by a barrier of blackberry bushes. Carmody arranges a pile of sticks and pulls out his lighter, but I catch his arm, shaking my head. We are too close to our target to start a fire tonight. The smoke would blow our cover, and then we'd never know where Eddie is truly going. She would never agree to lead us to her destination—if there is a destination at all— and I wouldn't be able to keep Carmody from exterminating her right there.

No fire.

We set up camp for the night. Carmody pulls out a bag of the dead rancher's jerky and inhales a few handfuls before falling asleep. Our supply is running low; we'll be out in a few days.

Once I'm sure that Carmody is truly sleeping, I crouch down and walk closer to Eddie. My steps are light and quiet, conditioned from training, like I'm walking over hot coals.

I'm only a few yards away when a twig snaps beneath my boots. I fall to my knees, ducking behind the shelter of more blackberries. The cover of darkness lets me peek beyond the bush to watch her.

She shoots upward and whips her head around, spinning in circles to identify the sound.

But her movements are not as quick as I expect them to be. They are no longer keen and sharp, but tired and dull. She looks so frail I wonder if a strong wind could knock her over and keep her down. I notice the way she clutches her upper left arm, the way her mouth is twisted in something that almost looks like nausea. My eyes trace her cheek, her neck, her hands. Her skin is glistening and beaded beneath the moonlight.

Infection, I realize, remembering my first aid training. I touch the part of my armored chest where the uniform's storage compartment resides, imagining the antibiotics that rest inside—the very same ones Eddie left in that farmer's shed. *She needs these.*

What good will it do if she dies before I get my answers?

And who will I be after she is gone? When I can no longer fill this gaping hole in my chest with anger?

I close my eyes and try so hard to inhale, but my breathing feels strained. *Why am I shaking like this? What is this weakness? This pounding in my chest?*

When Eddie sees that no one is around, she makes herself a bed of dirt and falls asleep.

I don't know where I'm going when I rise to my feet. I walk back toward camp, but I don't stop. I step over Carmody's motionless body and I keep going, past the log I will lay my head upon when I am finished, past the circle of dead blackberry bushes. I walk over Eddie's old footsteps feeling more hollow than ever.

Many yards away from where Carmody sleeps and even farther from Eddie is a moss-coated boulder I've grown to know better than my own reflection. There are so many of them in these woods; too many to know each stone by name, or care what happens to it.

I do not know why I sit on that rock, or why I stay there for such a long time. My suit keeps me warm, but a light breeze still toys with my hair, chilling my skin. I remember what I thought back on that dairy farm.

That storm is still brewing; I can feel it.

A twig snaps. Something darts across the ground by my feet, coming to a jarring halt by a nearby rock. I whip my head around to see a little gray rabbit, nibbling on the shrubbery with its back facing me. I was sitting so still for so long I doubt it saw me as anything but another moss-covered stone, one among millions.

I am quiet as I open the storage compartment in my suit. The rabbit doesn't see the garden weeder I hold in my hands.

I am merciful, and it dies quickly.

The game rests five feet away from where Eddie sleeps.

In the dead rabbit's mouth are three antibiotic pills. It is no peace offering, no sign of my forgiveness. I will never forgive Eddie for running. But she can't die yet—because I need her alive. *I need answers.*

When she wakes up, and if she finds the medicine inside, I hope she doesn't question it too much. She will remember the teal capsules and the blocky string of numbers printed onto their sides. She will know exactly what they are.

Eddie has made a thousand bad choices in her lifetime, but she is smarter than she gives herself credit for. She can't know that I am the one assigned to her case, but she must know she's being Chased by *someone*, because her unexpected survival is why Chasers exist. If anything, she'll be foolish enough to see the medicine as some sort of peace offering.

I just hope it doesn't make her afraid to use that compass. *Maybe she won't think that far ahead.*

I sit behind that same blackberry bush, studying Eddie, waiting for the right moment to toss a small stone in her direction. Ideally, I would wait for her to find it in the morning, but I don't want to risk the corpse being discovered by whatever hungry creatures roam these woods. She needs the medicine, of course, but she needs the food too. She can't survive on foraged greens and small bony fish forever.

I need to wake her up so she can take the medicine before her infection gets worse, but I can't bring myself to move. *What if she sees me hiding? What if I am found?* Then she'll never use that compass again, in fear of leading me to whatever destination she targets. She'll run off as far as she can and kill herself with the exertion.

Before I gather the courage to make a sound, something else does the job for me.

In the dark, beyond this shield of blackberry bushes, something approaches the dead rabbit.

It's a small creature with red-brown fur and a thick, feathery tail. For a moment, I wonder if it could be some wild dog, but when I stick my head out from behind the bush to get a closer look, I realize it's too small. I take in its auburn fur and large, pointed ears and realize this must be a fox—and it's here to take the rabbit.

I toss the stone near the animal's feat, trying to ward it off. The fox jumps back a few paces and, to my surprise, lets out a startled yelp that sounds a little too close to a human scream.

Eddie jolts awake, torso unfolding as she scrambles to a seated position with bent knees, clutching the dirt beneath her like a comforter. I hide behind the bush, heart pounding, watching her through the breaks in the thorny bramble. She takes one look at the fox and it runs off, disappearing into the thick of the woods.

She clutches her chest, sighing with relief and hanging her head down low. But the relief is short-lived, fading just as quickly as it arrived when she sees the dead rabbit. *Good—she'll think the fox left it behind. Maybe she'll ingest the medicine by accident—then she won't question anything.*

Hidden, I watch her walk over to the dead rabbit. For a moment I worry her closeness will set off the alert system in my suit, but I am still too far for it to be triggered.

She crouches down by the corpse and gently strokes its fur with one hand, using the other to check its wounds. And when the rabbit twitches, I have to bite my tongue to keep from gasping.

It's still alive. How could I have missed that?

I think about how the creature must be suffering, all because of what I did. But I shake the thought away. I killed it—or thought I did—because

Eddie needs it. She needs the food, and I needed to find a way to give her those antibiotic pills. Because no matter how badly I hate her, I need her alive. I pray she has the courage to prioritize her own survival for once, and end the rabbit's suffering.

You are hungry, weak, and sick. You need it, Eddie.

The rabbit starts convulsing, twitching again, this time more violently —like it's coughing something up. *The pills*, I realize, heart racing. My eyes widen and I cover my mouth with my hands as jabs of nausea overwhelm me. *It must be choking.* But Eddie doesn't know that. She will try to save it, to cure its puncture wounds—and blame herself when it dies.

And she does. She examines the blood-stained hole in its abdomen, surrounded by red, matted fur. She presses the sleeves of her sweater against the wound, trying to stop the bleeding, careful not to press too hard in order to keep the animal breathing. From where I crouch behind these thorns of mine, I can see her eyes turn to glass, glistening beneath the moonlight as she tries, and fails, to save the rabbit.

I thought I knew Eddie better than anyone, but I was wrong before. Because the face she makes right now is something I will never be able to translate. It is so empty, so void of all emotion I cannot for the life of me tell what she is thinking. Is she startled? Tired? Scared? Broken so far beyond my ability to understand?

And then she moves, her motions robotic. When she pulls out her knife, I expect her to start carving the dead creature, to prepare a meal for herself. I have to blink a few times to realize it is not flesh she cuts, but the ground.

She is cutting the ground. She uses the blade to chip away at the hard layer of cold, frozen dirt until a mound of moist soil is revealed. There is a tightness in my chest that will not loosen as I watch her toss the knife aside, and use her bare hands to claw at the dirt.

No! I want to scream. *No no no. You can't be doing what I think you're doing.*

When Eddie's fingernails are covered in blood, raw from the clawing, there is a rabbit-sized hole in the ground. She crawls over to the corpse. Trembling, she picks up the poor, lifeless creature, walking on her knees to place it in its grave.

Don't do it, I beg without a sound, watching with lost breath as she uses her hands to scoop piles of dirt on top of the creature. *Don't do it, Eddie.*

She needs that rabbit because she needs food and medicine. She needs that rabbit because I need answers. *Can't you see?* I want to scream. *I'm protecting you.*

Eddie buries the body and marks its grave with the stone I threw at the fox. My jaw tightens and I close my eyes, hands shaking as I clench my fingers into fists. The rabbit's sacrifice was all for nothing.

My sacrifice was all for nothing.

She slumps back, staring off into the distance at something I cannot see. A tear falls, and then another and another until she is sobbing. I watch as she hugs her knees with muddy hands, shifting slowly back and forth like she is rocking herself to sleep. She is the only one left to soothe her pains. She is her own cradle.

"*He's gone,*" she whispers, so quietly I can barely hear the words at all.

It takes me a moment to realize she isn't talking about the animal she buried. My gut plummets when I remember the Voclains—the wounds in their bodies, so similar to the rabbit's, and all that blood on the floor. The pool whose reflection I saw myself in. It feels like I'm free-falling and I cannot seem to exhale.

After a while, Eddie goes still. She lays her head near the rabbit's grave, and she falls asleep muttering her dead brother's name. The boy whose body I never found. *How is she only realizing this now?*

I wonder if I really do have the whole picture of everything that happened that night. I wonder if the reason why I never found Milo's body on the scene of his death is because, like the rabbit, Eddie buried him before she ran.

Does she feel remorse for what she's done?

Does she regret choosing to Run—and everything it did to her family?

Don't think about it, I tell myself. I need to stay focused.

Careful not to make a sound, I rise to my feet. I walk back toward camp, pausing to give Eddie one last look before exiting the scene.

Carmody is still asleep. I walk past him and I lay my head on a log that smells like dirt. When I lie on my back and study the sky through a canopy of pine, I can see the North Star.

Eddie does not forget things easily. I know she remembers what I told her back in the cow field about following that star. I cannot help but wonder if she would go north, with or without Margot's locket to guide her.

The locket. I still don't understand why she has it, or why there has been a compass held inside all this time. I'm not even sure if Margot knew what her necklace held. Did my father know?

There is a quiet part of me that wonders what I would have done if we hadn't noticed the necklace. If Eddie didn't have Margot's locket—if she wasn't using the compass, right at that very moment—would I have killed her?

Would I have had the strength to bring out the Nightjade syringe myself, or would I have left Carmody to do the dirty work once again?

Would I have *let* him?

I think about how angry I was when I grabbed his wrist back at the dead farmer's cottage. I think about the pure, unadulterated disgust I feel every time Carmody mentions Eddie's eventual death, in spite of my hatred. I cannot help but question if I'm being logical by postponing her extermination—or if I am only stalling, because deep down, I know I could never really do it.

No—that can't be the case. She doesn't need to be protected. She doesn't *deserve* to be protected, and I don't think she wants to be. That witless burial was the perfect example of how little she desires to be saved. Eddie deserves the fate the system designed for her, because whether she likes it or not, that's how our world works. There is no use fighting against something you can never change.

Her family is dead because she Ran. Her family is dead because she was too selfish to stay and let death find her.

I have to hate her, because if I don't, what does that make me?

If I don't hate her, how is that fair to her dead family? To Margot? To anyone and everyone who has ever died an undeserving fate?

I can never stop hating her. It has to be this way if I want to make things right. Because how can I correct this world if I can't correct Lavender Voclain?

Eddie is an error. A flaw. A fluke. She must be exterminated to restore balance, to resolve the unjustness she's caused, to make things right again. She is a fracture in the bones of the world, and I will fix her break.

I see her in my mind when I close my eyes. We are both underwater again. Her dark hair fans above her head and her skin glows in the murk, floating with me in that brief forever. I reach out to touch her, but she swims away.

Before I can follow, something grabs me, and I am pulled under, deeper and deeper into some infinite sea as I drift into a restless slumber. I look down to see the monster who has me, but I see no talons. It is Eddie who has a hold on me.

The next morning, I wake up surrounded by snow.

EDDIE

Tuesday, January 9
Day 9

We're in the car.

My father is at the wheel, and I'm wearing the black wool coat he takes to work on colder days, because I left my own jacket at home.

It's one of the last days of school, and Dad wanted to give me a ride to class. I refused at first, but he insisted, so I decided to let it be. We even stopped at a drive-thru café, something we've only done once or twice before. He remembered my order from last time. I've transitioned from hot cocoa to black coffee over the years because I like its bitterness, but the sweetness of the beverage and its gesture are refreshing, and it makes me smile.

I feel warm. Warmed by the chocolate drink, warmed by the coat. Warmed by the presence of a loving father.

We sit in silence for a while until Dad clears his throat. "I wanted to say sorry."

I nearly choke on my drink. I avoid spitting the beverage across his pristine dashboard, but a bit of hot cocoa dribbles down my lip.

This has never happened to me before, not once. He never says sorry; he doesn't believe in saying sorry. He thinks it's a sign of weakness. By his definition, an apology is a waste of time.

On the rare occasion that he does try to resolve conflict, he always says the word apologize *instead, like he's above feeling sorry.*

"For what?" I say, my voice as bitter as the coffee I would have ordered without him, because I know exactly what he should be apologizing for.

I try to count it all on my fingers, but everything is not a number one can count to.

"For—you know," he mutters, struggling to articulate his feelings. I almost feel sorry for him. "Being a little harsh sometimes."

"It's okay," I lie. "I'm fine."

"No, it's not okay. I need to be—" He takes a deep breath. This is hard for him to say. "—a better father. To both of you."

My dad is too uncomfortable to look at me and he doesn't see me smile, but I can tell he senses my expression nonetheless. I feel guilty for smiling. He shouldn't be the only one apologizing.

I know his parenting is manipulative. I know he's toxic and approaches everything with such a stubborn mindset he can't always see things clearly.

But I haven't exactly been the easiest daughter either. I'm a liar. And no matter how hard I try, I can never get past my own pride and meet just one of his expectations.

I think back to every name I've called him in anger, every harsh truth I've embellished in rudeness, every unpleasant thing I've ever said to him. I have no idea what lies in front of me, but I have a feeling that someday, I will want to take it all back.

But I can't take it back, so I do the second best thing.

"I forgive you, and I'm sorry," I whisper.

But the words don't come out.

I hold back tears. "You have no idea how badly I want to say that to you."

It's a cold morning, but my father's love brings me warmth until his image fades into nothingness.

I wake up in the middle of the night, covered in snow.

There is no warmth. There is no hot cocoa.

There is no coat.

I'm too weak to sit up and check my surroundings, but I know I'm not in my father's car anymore, because I never was. That was no memory. The real memory involves me getting in the car with a boy I would learn to hate again—and a boy who would hate me back.

Now, I'm nowhere. I'm weak, a version of myself I despise more than anything else on the planet, because this version of me exists without the people I've lost.

Curling into a fetal position like a dying animal does little to soothe the burning cold. Snow falls around me in delicate sprinkles, each one so soft, so weightless, like kisses from the wind. It's funny to me, how such fragile flakes can pile up so subtly, until all of a sudden you're trapped by their weight and stilled by their coldness. I don't want to think about all the things that work the exact same way.

Instead, I try to wiggle my toes, but I can't tell if they move or not, because there isn't anything left for me to feel. The numbness has taken over. There is no life in my feet, or my legs, or my arms, or my fingers—or any part of me. My lashes collect snowflakes like dust and nearly weigh my lids down to closure. I can only see the world through a blurred fault—and it is so dark.

Beyond all odds, I muster up the strength to move my arms, just enough to pat my body and feel for that wool coat. But as numb as I am, I don't have to feel anything to know it's not there.

My father never gave me a ride that morning. We never had that conversation and I never got to say sorry, because I pushed him away. He never heard my words and I didn't get the chance to tell him how much I loved him. How much I *still* love him.

No. I correct my mistake. I had a chance. I had every chance in the world, and he died thinking I hated him, all because I distanced myself from everyone I cared about. I lied to my father, I lied to Margot, I lied to Ren —I lied to all of them.

I'm as foolish as they come. I was never unlucky, not even close. I had everything once, and it took losing it all for me to see that.

I try not to cry because I don't want my eyes to freeze over like the rest of my body already has, but I do. I sob with the last ounce of strength I have left, because I'm not wearing Dad's wool coat. I'm wearing the sweatshirt Ren gave me so long ago, and I'm too weak to take it off. I'm wearing the garment of a Chaser. It's soaked through and heavy with snow.

I wonder if the snow would be more bearable if I had taken my father's coat that day. If I had just gone with him instead, then I would be wearing wool instead of synthetic cotton. Warm, loving wool.

I hold my knife in my hands, clutching it close to my chest like funeral flowers. As more and more snow falls around me, I think of the rabbit because I see myself in her.

They say not to bite the hand that feeds you. But what do you do when the same hand that has been feeding you your whole life is the one that desires to carry out your demise?

What do you do when one day, you wake up and the food is now a gun and the hand is now your killer? Do you bite the hand then, or do you bite the bullet?

I feel the draining kiss of hypothermia. Only when the cold bites do I realize its fangs are filled with venom. The poison burns, and I feel the world around me start to drift away.

But somehow, despite it all, I find warmth.

It's so warm. So unbelievably, horribly warm. *Let me sleep.*

Maybe the hand was poisoning me the whole time. Bit by bit, little by little, not enough to kill me all at once.

Maybe the hand knew that one day, I would be fed one last time before the poison became too much for my body and mind to handle, and my life would

just

   simply

     end.

RE N

Tuesday, January 9
Day 9

A day after the snow comes, Carmody and I stumble upon the cabin. Eddie had stopped hiking to set up some sort of camp, and Carmody and I thought it would be a good idea if we did the same thing. We needed a place to park ourselves for a while, a spot far enough from our assignment to avoid detection, but close enough for us to take turns watching her every move.

The temperature control system in our uniforms gave us no need to start a fire and we didn't want to worry about the smoke exposing us, so our list of criteria for a hideout was small. We were to remain both unseen and unheard, and that was it.

The cabin is about a quarter mile away from Eddie's spot by the river. From where she resides, she cannot see the building's structure—only a blanket of white, pierced by the green peaks of evergreen trees. The cabin blends right in.

It's abandoned, by the looks of it. It's one of those log cabins that you might see on a Yesterday postcard, or maybe the cover of an old book. It's boxy with a pointed roof and decaying wood, and it smells like damp evergreen needles. Old sconces from the Yesterdays decorate the front porch, but their glass is discolored and broken. I doubt they've been lit for quite some time now.

I remember what my father told me about the Wandering Pandemic, about all the people who left their homes in search of water and died on their journey for survival. I can't help but wonder if this was once somebody's home.

I get the same feeling that I got days ago, back at the cow farm. It feels like we're stealing something important from a ghost.

"You know what's kind of funny to think about?" Carmody says as we approach the structure.

"What?" I reply, jaw clenched. My tone is sharper than I intend it to be, but I'm finding it harder to care about things like that anymore.

"That Eddie's over there struggling while we've found *this*." He chuckles to himself, shaking his head. "If she had strayed from the river—just a little bit—she would have found this."

I open my mouth to tell him he's being obnoxious, but I hold my tongue —because surprisingly, he makes an interesting point.

If Eddie's going to such extreme lengths to avoid straying from the river, then it must be for a reason. She would've had better luck finding cover from last night's snowstorm if she headed away from the river. And yet, she stays near the water, choosing to never leave its side. I can't help but wonder what she knows.

I am not prolonging her life by postponing her death, I remind myself. I just want answers.

But I can't think about her eventual death right now. I can hate her all I want, but right now, her extermination isn't a priority. We just have to figure out what she's up to first.

The cabin is unlocked, but it's been some time since the front door has been opened. Carmody has to use an excessive amount of force to push it open. But when he does, our noses are filled with the sweet aroma of old wood and yellowed paper. There are notes of cinnamon too.

We close the door behind us and inspect our new surroundings. There's not much to look at, really, but curiosity urges me to take a look around. The cabin is more like a studio apartment back in the city than a house— no bedroom, just one open space with a bed, a couch in front of the fireplace, and a black wood-burning stove in the corner. Though the fireplace hasn't been lit in ages, everything smells like flames are still burning. It's just as cozy as it is eerie.

Carmody crinkles his nose. "This place is a bit gross, don't you think?"

"Sure," I say, but the cabin isn't gross. For its age, the building is immaculate. It's actually a little bit strange. There is no rot, no visible water damage —and there isn't a pest in sight.

Carmody volunteers to take the first watch shift, presumably to avoid dealing with the responsibility in the evening, when things are cold, dark, and uninteresting to a person like him. He likes to see things happen. He likes to watch chaos unfold, so he watches whatever he can in hopes of catching a glimpse.

I know he likes to watch Eddie. I know he likes to see her suffer, to see her struggle and wither away in desperation. It almost excites him, and it sickens me.

He is the perfect product of his upbringing, a gross example of what comes out of a household that teaches its children to devalue human life by refusing to value his. I pity him and his weakness.

But I don't mind the evening shift. I prefer the quietude of doing my job while things are still. So I let it be, and I get some sleep while I can.

I start my shift right before the sun begins to set. The world is still as bright as midday, but I know the light will be leaving soon, and it's warm with age as it illuminates the scene in front of me.

I can see Eddie clearly through the snow-capped blackberry bushes. It takes my eyes a moment to adjust to her shape, but when I realize what's going on, it's painful to watch.

She stares face to face with a rabbit that looks so horribly similar to the one she buried. It's small, gray, and well-fed, and I watch her wait for the creature to inch closer. I wonder how delicious the animal must look to Eddie, who hasn't eaten anything substantial for days. She's growing thinner with every missed meal. I've seen it all unfold.

I've seen the way she moves, and she is growing weaker every day.

I've seen the way her arm is bandaged, covered in dried brown blood.

I've seen the way she starves, though she keeps a hunting knife close.

I've seen the way she clutches her stomach almost habitually, like she's gotten used to hunger.

I see her struggle, and as I do, I realize how little she knows of her fate. She has no idea she is simply waiting to die.

I watch her face the creature. I wait for her to make a move. I wait for her to show me that after all this time, she's learned to fight for herself.

But Eddie doesn't lunge for the rabbit. Instead, she holds out her hand, offering her share of greens to the creature. They're all she has left.

The rodent is hesitant at first, but eventually, it grabs the plants right out of her hand, nipping her flesh in the process. She pulls back instantly and winces as the animal hops away with a fresh meal, leaving behind a girl who just might starve to death.

I don't know why it makes me so angry, but I tremble, closing my eyes and inhaling sharply. *She feels guilty for not being able to save the rabbit from before, doesn't she?*

As she cradles her bitten hand, I notice a grotesque patch of red skin on her palm. It looks like a burn. It twists along her hand like warm-colored paint that just won't wash off, and I can't believe that after spending so many hours watching nothing but her, I missed it.

But when I observe it more closely, I notice the red isn't red alone, but marbled with yellow and green. My gut churns when I realize that her stab wound is not what's infected—it's the burn.

I look down at my own hands, protected by sturdy gloves of sleek white armor. I was burned too. But I had this uniform. I had ointment, and I was protected from the elements.

I feel something cold and gentle tickle the back of my neck and whip my head around, expecting to find someone standing behind me. But instead, all I see is white. I look up to the sky, feeling little flurries of frozen water bless my skin with kisses. The snow keeps falling as I watch Eddie with hidden eyes, witnessing the progression of her weakness, a downfall I expected from the beginning.

She's smart at first. She paces back and forth in the snow, hugging her own body tightly as she walks. She resists the urge to huddle up on the ground and fall victim to the cold by using light physical exertion to keep her body warm.

But the night falls with the snow, and it only grows colder as the moon makes itself known. The lower the temperature drops, the harder it is for her to keep moving.

Her pacing slows to a shivering trudge and the trudging eventually fades to a halt. She comes to a complete pause too frozen to move but too weak to stand. Even as she falls to her knees, she still refuses to lie down.

She sits like that for an hour. She wraps her arms around her torso, trembling furiously as the snow piles higher and higher. She's so still that her dark hair is painted with snowflakes as if the sky has mistaken her for a small tree. Each white dot is a star against her matted waves until the top of her head is no longer a night sky but a flowerless meadow in winter.

I imagine a thousand tiny white hands tugging at her body, urging her to curl up on the ground and fall asleep. And when she refuses, they pull at every part of her until she has no choice but to succumb.

I watch her fall. Behind these barren blackberry bushes, comfortable in my gear and fattened with stolen meals, I watch her lose. A human girl—who could have been victorious in another world—is no match for the punishing hands of the natural world.

Eddie is completely alone, and she drifts into the deepest sleep of all.

It is cutting to watch her grow so still, to watch the snow sap the love and anger and life from her veins. It tugs at something inside me, and I don't know why I ache.

I want to pity her, but I can't. I have to fight it. I have to resist every urge I have to help her, because I have a job to do, and it must be done. My life depends on it. My sister's memory depends on it—and the memory of the Voclains who died in a pool of blood red innocence.

But what if Eddie becomes a memory too?

We're on a mission to gather information. We need to figure out where she was going, and why she was using the necklace to do so. *She can't leave like this*, I tell myself. Not yet. Not when I have so many unanswered questions.

But as I watch her, motionless in the snow, I wonder if some questions are meant to go unanswered. I wonder if I will ever know the truth. I wonder if this is better—if freezing to death in the arms of some false warmth is a better death by Nightjade. Death by Chaser. Death by a monster of the worst possible kind. Maybe this is how Lavender Voclain was meant to go all along.

And even still, in spite of it all, I find myself asking the same question as before.

Who will I be when she is gone?

They say your life flashes before your eyes when you're about to die. But they don't tell you that witnessing the death of another—the death of someone you used to care so much about—invites the same result. Because I see her.

I see a child climbing the tree in my backyard to pick pine cones for my sister.

I see a girl lying on her stomach, kicking her legs in the air as she dips her nose into an open book.

I see a scholar with too much knowledge for her own good.

I see an illegal healer in the making.

I see a gaze I used to know found again underwater.

I see a face covered in mud because we both cared.

I see a protector nearly blind another to save my life.

I see a beautiful girl staring at the stars in an empty cow field.

I see her lips as she smiles and how I would like to forget them, because once, between blades of grass, I might have wanted to feel them against my own.

I hear her laugh. I smell her hair, lemon and tea tree. I feel her warmth.

I see a young woman asleep by my side, in the sand beneath a play struc-ture. And now, I see her fast asleep in the snow.

But most of all, I see Eddie. And I can't let her go.

Something brings me to my feet. I move without my own permission. Snow falls and the moon is there to help me see where I'm going. But it is still so dark as I stand above her.

I crouch down and touch her cold neck to search for a pulse, and my own heartbeat comes to a pause when I don't feel anything for a moment.

And then I feel it. A heartbeat, faint and fluttered and fading, but not gone. She is still breathing—but barely. With her starved self and infected wound, and now this hypothermia, she can't have much time.

A white blanket of snow covers her body and brings out the blue in her lips. They no longer look soft and full of fiery words, but chapped and drained of life. I look down at the screen on my uniform's wrist to enable the flashlight, but when I do, I notice the map has gone static. I no longer see Eddie's blue dot on the screen, or anything at all for that matter. This snowstorm is a fence between her tracker and my suit. That's why it doesn't alert me of her closeness, as it did with the woman under the bridge all those days ago.

The wind picks up speed, an unforgiving hiss I struggle to speak over. "Suit, unsuit." The words don't feel like my own.

I have to repeat myself for the armor to hear me, and then again. But eventually it obeys and folds into its cubic storage form.

Immediately, I am struck by the cold. It is infectious, seeping into my every pore, freezing the blood in my veins and the marrow in my bones. In only a few seconds of exposure, I am so much weaker than I was before. My body was used to the heated luxury of my suit, and now that I'm without it, I can barely move.

Instinctively, I wrap my arms around my body, hugging my torso, keeping my warmth close. But the warmth within me fades by the minute.

It feels like I'm swimming through drying cement as I crouch down again, carefully rolling over Eddie's nearly lifeless body until she's flat on her back. Trembling, I place the cube next to her frozen feet and step away.

"Suit," I call out through the sound of the blizzard that grows around us. The cube doesn't budge. "*Suit!*"

It hears me the second time, and sure enough, the armor wraps itself around Eddie, the panels unfolding in harmony with one another until she is fully embraced.

"Suit, warm." It listens, lights flashing to let me know. I hear it buzz as it begins to heat up Eddie's nearly lifeless body.

I notice her knife buried in the snow. I pick it up with shaking hands and place it between my chattering teeth, because she would want it with her. I force myself to stand, but this time, I'm holding Eddie on my back, carrying her with the strength I should be saving in this cold. I'm brought back to my training with Salazar, and I realize this situation is no different. New weight, new distance, new obstacles—but the concept is still the same.

You can do this, I reassure myself. *You have to.*

Alone, Eddie and the uniform are light, but the combination of both makes it difficult for me to walk forward. And in this cold, I am a thousand times weaker than I've ever been. After only the first step, I stumble—nearly dropping Eddie in the process—but I somehow manage to regain my balance.

I walk. Every step is pain, every inch a lifetime. I've only been without my uniform for a moment, and I can already feel myself growing weak. I don't know how Eddie managed to keep breathing for as long as she did.

Without the protection of my suit, I have no shoes. Although training ended months ago, my feet are still sensitive. They are still scarred from all the things they made us do when one of us spoke out of turn, said the wrong thing, or looked at Pittman in a way she didn't like.

They itch all the time. The first aid ointment helps, but scars are not a thing easily faded. The burning never really goes away.

I feel like I'm walking coals again. I think about that long white corridor and the white snow I'm surrounded by. For a moment, I feel like I'm back in that room, like I'm reliving that nightmare of mine for the thousandth time. I look down at the ground behind me, half expecting to see footprints of blood like my non-existent scarred-over wounds have opened up again, as they often used to do. There is no blood. There is nothing but white.

This is far worse than walking coals.

Five minutes pass, and I haven't moved more than fifty feet. The stretch of land between the riverbank and the cabin feels like a steep incline, as though I'm climbing a mountain in the middle of a storm. But it's completely flat.

The snow is furious. My fingers and toes are already numb and I know it can't be a good sign. I worry that if they get too cold, they'll freeze and snap off, like the double grape popsicles I used to scarf down as a child. Or maybe my entire body will snap in two.

I clench my chattering jaw. There is a part of me that is just as raging as this storm, because despite everything—despite all the chaos Eddie has caused—I am risking my life for her sake. What is this change? Why help her now? The prey has walked directly into my trap, and instead of letting nature do the job for me, I decided to cut the chains and set my target loose.

I tell myself I'm doing this for the good of the mission. I will guide her behind the scenes, watch her every move, gather the needed info—and when she is no longer needed, she will be exterminated. And if we happen to stumble across Carmody's fantasized Undergrounder base in the process, then so be it.

Exterminated. Again, as it always has, the word rings in my ears. Its echo makes me sick.

But the half of me that isn't angry is ashamed, and I don't know why. I turn my shoulder to steal a glance at Eddie's face, and immediately, the guilt is a blow that nearly knocks me over. Heavier than the physical weight I carry, it crushes me. Because she doesn't look like the monster I pictured in my head.

Why does she look so innocent?

And when I reach the cabin—tattered and broken and barely holding on by the thinnest of all threads—I realize something. I realize it as I remove my uniform from Eddie's limp body and lay her gently on the bed. I realize it as I tuck her beneath the quilt, sewn by hands that passed long before us. I realize it as I command a very confused Carmody to finally use his lighter, to put a flame in both the fireplace and the wood-burning stove, and fill a pot with snow to get some water boiling. I realize it as I place a pan of hot water at the edge of the bed, hiding it beneath the covers. I realize it as I place a warm rag on her forehead and tuck a strand of hair behind her ear before recoiling my hand in fear.

I realize that I never hated her. I hated the fact that I couldn't hate her, even if I wanted to.

I couldn't stop caring for Eddie if I tried.

EDDIE

Friday, January 12
Day 12

When I wake up in an empty cabin, I come to the conclusion that I'm dead.

I died. I felt myself fade into nothing. My soul seeped into the snow and disappeared for good, and I was gone. It was too cold, dark, and lonely to be a figment of my imagination.

But something about being here, right now, feels more real than even that.

I hold my hands in front of my face. My right palm is wrapped in a fresh bandage, clean and bright against the patchwork quilt that covers me. The burn is sealed, but the rest of the skin on both of my hands is covered in itching red blisters, perhaps a result of the cold snow exposure.

I look down to find myself in a clean set of dry and oversized clothing. I wear a retro Nordic sweater that has to be decades old, but it's still in good shape, and a lot warmer than my old sweatshirt. I pat my legs down. I've been dressed in a pair of men's jeans that don't fit right.

This isn't right. None of this is right. This isn't what I've been wearing for the past week. I am not covered in blood and dirt anymore.

A bundle of flickering flames even glows brightly in the fireplace. I peel a wet rag from my forehead, imagining that it was once warm. I feel a pan of water at the end of the bed by my feet, and a fresh bandage is wrapped around my punctured arm, where the Chaser stabbed me with my own knife so long ago.

None of this feels fake, but it doesn't feel real either. Have I done it? Have I walked through hell to reach heaven at last? I look down at my hands, studying the blisters they were given by the snow. I pinch myself to make sure I'm not dreaming, but nothing happens. I pinch myself again—and still, nothing. Maybe a regular pinch isn't enough.

Instead, I use my jagged fingernails to dig into the bandage that surrounds my green burn. I wince at the sensation, shaking my hand to get rid of the sting.

I wait for the scene around me to shift, to blend together and morph into the real world, a prison of white snow. But when everything stays the same, I jolt into a sitting position.

I'm not dead.

I'm not dead or even dreaming. I'm alive—I'm safe—and I have no idea how.

I can tell it's early in the day from the light that seeps in through the window. I turn my head to study it. The glass is old, thick, and warped, flanked by cinnamon-colored flannel curtains.

The soft glow of morning touches everything, from the wood-burning stove in the center of the room to the round beams of lumber that stretch across the ceiling. If it weren't for the morning's gentle sun, this room would be completely dark, save for the amber glow of the fire. I wonder who's been keeping it going, and I ponder the mystery with a nervous gulp.

I feel dizzy. My heartbeat quickens and my head grows so light I worry it'll pop off and float away. Because I realize that if I am here and not out there—if there is a fire, alive and burning like me—then someone must have saved me from the snow.

I turn to my side and notice a wooden nightstand next to my bed, where my knife rests. *That's odd.* It's polished and clean, no longer crusted in dried blood.

I try to get out of bed, but it's a greater challenge than I thought it'd be. I'm frail from the aftermath of everything and I don't have the strength to move as I normally would.

I sit upright, shifting my body sideways. I place my feet on a red rug that rests on the floor. When I shift my gaze downward, I can see they've been covered in fresh white socks.

Curious, I remove one of the socks and check on the condition of my toes. To my surprise, all ten of them remain; not a single one is frostbitten beyond saving. They're still a bit red and covered in glistening blisters like my fingers, but that will heal with time. I wiggle them just to see if I can, and to my luck, they obey the command perfectly. I can even feel the muscles twist and stretch, and the itchy burn of the blisters.

I turn my neck to inspect the rest of the room, trying to pinpoint my shoes. The sneakers rest in front of the fireplace like a sleeping cat, and I shiver. *Someone must have placed them there to dry.*

Slowly, I use my arms to force the rest of my body to stand. Blood rushes to my head and for a moment, my vision is completely black. The sudden movement makes me so lightheaded I can't help but wonder just how long I've been out.

Legs aching and head pounding, I limp over to the fireplace. The dizziness returns when I bend down to feel my sneakers. They're still wet, and while they're a lot cleaner than they used to be, they still leave a muddy residue on my fingertips.

I take a second look at the fireplace. My clothes have been scrubbed clean—save for the smudge of black nail polish on the sleeves of Ren's old sweatshirt—and now hang to dry above the crackling flames. My gut sinks when I realize what this means, and everything seems to sink in all at once.

I was dying. I should have died out there in the snow, but I was saved. The cabin's owner must have found me and carried me here. They tended to my wounds, they gave me a fresh set of clothes. They kept two fires going, one in the hearth and one in the wood-burning stove. They even saved my feet from frostbite with that pan of water I found in the bed.

This entire time, someone has been taking care of me—and I have no idea who they are.

For a brief, stupid moment, I wonder if it could have been Ren and Carmody. Did they finally catch up to me? Have they saved me, just so they can exterminate me?

The thought chills me before I fix my thinking. Because that can't be possible. They would have killed me on the spot, and they wouldn't have left me with my knife. If they hate me enough to follow me all the way out here—to hunt me like some wounded animal—they wouldn't have taken the time to clean my weapon and my clothes or to make sure I was warm and comfortable while I slept either.

I have to remind myself that I don't know Ren anymore. I have to remember that his grief has turned him into a ruthless killer—and me into his number one target.

Then who could it have been?

I don't have much strength, but I manage to walk around the room, slowly observing my surroundings for any clues. I peer over the sofa to check for any slept-in blankets, but the couch is neatly made. Its quilted throw pillows are neatly arranged on either side, and a knit blanket hangs neatly over the back like a cape.

I make my way toward the small table that sits on the other side of the room. I trace the chairs to check for warmth, but my fingers touch cold wood instead. No one has been sitting here—not for a long time, at least. I crouch down to peek for crumbs, sighing when I realize the floor is spotless. Whoever saved me left no evidence behind, and I can't shake the feeling that I'm alone again.

As I try to stand up, Margot's necklace falls to the floor. *Whoever saved me must have put it back on incorrectly*, I think to myself. I'm just glad I dropped it now and not earlier, because I'd quite literally be lost without it. But as I crawl to reach the fallen piece of jewelry, to my surprise, one of the floorboards feels loose beneath my bandaged hand.

When Margot's locket is secured, I observe the floorboard. I press it again, and sure enough, it wobbles. I lift it up from its place, half-expecting to find an empty compartment—and finding the opposite instead.

Inside, there is a letter placed on top of a book, surrounded by a collection of about a dozen glass bottles. Each container is filled with herb-stuffed vegetable glycerin capsules. I find it odd, but I ignore the bottles and the book for now, reaching for the letter instead.

The envelope is covered in a thin coat of dust. It's been sitting here for quite some time, but it's not as yellowed as I assume it should be. Confusingly enough, it almost looks *new*.

I pause for a moment, contemplating whether or not I should open it. Maybe this will give me some sort of clue so I can figure out where I am—and who saved me.

My curiosity gets the best of me. I open the envelope and pull out a piece of crinkled note paper. The letter is written in beautifully messy script that twists and turns on the page, refusing to sit still between the light blue lines. I unfold the rest of the letter and squint to read the writing.

A—

It's been a while.

Caution has been of the utmost importance lately, as you know. We've just implemented the riskiest and perhaps most crucial part of the plan. Mistakes cannot be afforded at the moment. You understand.

I didn't want to worry my messenger with much either; this particular part of the job is close to his heart, and you know how he can be. I can't be sending him on too many trips right now. He's already worrying himself to death. I'm sure I'll fill you in on all the details in person someday when you finally decide to take the kids up here.

It's quiet, you know. You'd like it. A lot quieter than you'd think, even with everything that's been going on. Maybe when M feels up to making the trip? Though I doubt she feels up to doing anything at all. I would feel the same way in her position, though she's a lot stronger than I could be—at least from what you've told me over the years.

Speaking of M, one of our healers found this book in our library and I thought it would serve a better purpose on your shelf than his. It's another one from the Yesterdays about natural healing strategies. Something about diet. I have yet to read it, but I'll have him summarize it for me. Again—we're all very busy up here.

How's R doing? Still quiet and serious like his father? I'm glad he's been spending more time with an old friend lately. I find it strange that she's so invested in our work at such a young age, but you shouldn't be so quick to dismiss the interest she expresses. We can't afford to pick and choose our fighters in this line of work, A. Even if you think it's too dangerous for her, we need all the eyes we can get.

I hope this letter finds you sooner this time, A. I love hearing from you. Not just about the kids, but you too. Your letters keep me going.

Everything I do is for them—but it's for you too. All three of you give me a reason to do what I do and to be who I am. I just wish they were able to know that. Someday they will.

Alright, it's getting late and there's so much work that needs to be done. People are hard to manage.

Remember what we talked about. When my messenger meets with our newest Double, he'll tell her to proceed with the plan. So be ready for her to come and retrieve you. The kids too, if they're okay with making the move.

That is all I can say for now.

You better stay safe, A. I mean it. I'll see you soon.

Always,
N

The letter falls from my hands.

It flutters to the ground like a flake of snow, too light to hold everything it carries.

In my core, it feels like the cold has returned. It expands and expands and expands, freezing all it touches, chilling every part of me until I am completely numb. My hands shiver.

I rise to my feet, holding onto the table for support, slumping into a chair as I stare at the wall. My gaze cannot seem to settle on any one thing, and my breaths are shaky and thin.

I bend over and snatch the letter from the ground so I can read it over again. I read it two times. Three times. Four, for good measure. And then I read it a fifth time because I still don't believe what I'm reading.

This is impossible.

A letter to *A* from *N*?

I open my locket again and study the map etched in the lid. My eyes snake up the river and read the familiar letter until the etching becomes fuzzy and my eyes begin to cross.

Is this where Asa wanted me to go? *N* for north? Or maybe *N*, for whoever wrote this letter?

By giving me Margot's necklace, this map, did he assume I would run into the woods where I once met with Cedar? That I would connect the dots and end up here in this cabin?

But why? What could possibly be so important about a musty old cottage in the woods?

Pieces of the letter echo in my mind. *N, A, M,* and *R.* Plans and people and interests and books and Doubles and messengers—and healers.

The Unseen. The phrase hits like a punch to the stomach, and I feel like I've swallowed a gallon of water in one gulp. The words weigh heavy in my gut and my heartbeat quickens its pace, pounding against my head and my chest like angry fists.

None of this makes any sense. I shouldn't jump to these conclusions so quickly; everything I'm thinking is too far of a stretch to be possible. I'm sure of it.

But what if I have it all wrong? What if it all makes *perfect* sense? What if this letter holds the answer to every single one of my questions?

Has Asa really led me to the Unseen? This camp Cedar spoke of, long ago?

Is this why his trips to get medicine used to take so long? He often left Ren and Margot home alone for days at a time, never giving them much information at all. But what if he'd been visiting this same cabin every time?

What if he kept it a secret from Ren and Margot for their own safety, because he knew their curiosity could lead to his children being killed for treason—or ruining the entire Unseen operation?

I examine the floorboard compartment once again. I see the book and the bottles of herb-stuffed capsules, and something in my gut tells me this is where it all began. This is where those botanical encyclopedias came from, and every other Yesterday book I devoured as a child. This is where Margot got her herbal supplements—how she was kept alive.

But where are the Unseen now? This can't be their only meeting point. The operation is too large to be reliant on a tiny wooden structure in the middle of an empty forest.

There has to be more, and I want to know it all. I still don't understand the truth behind Asa's connection to the Unseen, or why they were so set on helping Margot.

I need to figure out who N is, and I need to know what they're planning. I didn't run this far to turn around without getting any answers.

The world goes quiet. For a moment, there is a spark in my core, the smallest flicker of warmth. I think about the Unseen. And then there is a flame, and it melts the cold away—because I remember.

I remember who I was before. I remember why I've done any of this at all. I remember that I too am Unseen.

I have to prove that I deserve to be alive. I have to help fix this world somehow, and I will do it all for my family's sake. For Margot's—because she was and will always be a part of my family too.

I'm yanked away from my thoughts when there is a noise.

My heart beats faster and my eyes widen. I hold my breath to listen.

Someone is coming. Heavy footsteps knock against the porch, growing stronger as they approach the door, but my pulse feels even louder. I wait for what feels like an eternity until there's a pause. I inhale but I can't let the breath go. I squeeze my eyes shut and wait.

The door creaks, and someone walks into the cabin.

I open my eyes.

He's not the ax murderer I expected—or at least, he doesn't look like one. He's a thin but sturdy man with a pair of round glasses that rest upon a sharp nose. *Not a man*, I realize. Though his chin is scruffy with hints of facial hair, his youth is obvious. He can't be any older than nineteen.

He's tall and dressed in a rust-colored puffer jacket and light jeans, with a mess of dark brown hair that's almost black, but not quite. Every inch of his body is covered in snowflakes; he must have walked a long way to get here.

Wait a minute.

Wait a minute.

I open my mouth to say something, but I stutter in silence, unable to find the right words. My whole body is frozen, save for my hands, which cannot seem to stop shaking.

I see the hair. The leather satchel slung over his shoulder. In perfect daylight, I see him—without the shades.

One of his eyes is not brown like the other, but a cloudy white marbled with hints of honeydew green. It looks as though it rolled to the back of his head once, and has been stuck ever since. A familiar scar cuts through the surrounding skin like a jagged serpent of carved flesh.

Cedar.

Is he the one who saved me?

A lump forms in my throat. We both stare at each other for a long time, with about a thousand questions left unspoken. It's been so long—far too long—but slowly, he recognizes me. I'm so unbelievably happy to see his horrible, obnoxious face that I want to cry.

But I don't think he feels the same way—because he's pointing a hunting knife in my direction.

"What are you doing here?"

There's something different about his voice. He's not the Cedar I used to know, but cold and rigid, calculating and suspicious. I remember when I first saw him in the woods, when he thought I was there to turn him into the Corps. How angry he was that I was there at all.

This is a thousand times worse.

I drop the letter, standing up slowly and holding up my hands to prove my innocence. He steps forward, the knife still pointed toward me.

I swallow my shock and compose myself with a glare. "What are *you* doing here?"

He comes to a pause a foot away, glaring right back. "I asked first."

"I don't care. I want an answer." I want to fold my arms, to show him his threat doesn't scare me, but I can't bring myself to move.

"Hate to break it to you pal, but you're not the one holding the knife here." I sense a familiar trace of sarcasm in his voice, but it's more bitter than I remember. I cannot shake the feeling that he'll kill me if he has to, whether he wants to or not.

He is Unseen, after all.

"Cedar," I mutter. I stare him right in his good eye, desperate to reach him. "It's me. Eddie. Remember?"

Something behind his gaze flickers for a moment as it all comes back to him. The jobs, the hiding, the running around in the dark. Breaking into my room to threaten me—on several occasions. *He recognizes me. He remembers.*

But he doesn't drop the blade, and the glare remains. "I know exactly who you are."

Then why is he threatened by me? I study the weapon with an irritated frown. "Are you going to wave that knife in my face all day?"

He shrugs. "Depends."

"On what?"

"On why you're here, and why you were reading *that*." He points to the ground, where I dropped the letter.

He's definitely not the person who brought me to this cabin, but he acts as though he owns the place. And if he doesn't, then he must have a tight connection with the owner, at least.

If it wasn't him, then who saved me?

"I don't know," I reply, my voice low.

"What do you mean, you *don't know*? You're the intruder here." He inches closer, bringing the weapon closer to my face.

"I'm telling you, I don't know why I'm here." I raise my voice, just a little. For once, I'm telling the truth. "Someone brought me here."

"I don't believe you." He moves even closer.

My breathing grows shaky. "Why not?"

"You really expect me to believe this is all a coincidence?" He laughs, but darkly.

"Yeah?"

"You know, most people aren't exactly thrilled about the idea of leaving their whole world behind—of *risking their life*—to become fully Unseen." He paces back and forth, still pointing the knife in my direction.

I suppress a nod, back still pressed against the wall, gulping anxiously. All I can do is blink.

"So it's just some lucky little coincidence that you were in the right place at the right time, all those months ago? That you were able to substitute for a correspondence with a *very important* contact we haven't heard from in days? That you were *so* incredibly eager for me to show you the ropes? And now, you're here, on the most inconvenient of all days, ready to interrupt *another* vital rendezvous? With *another* vital contact who isn't here?" Now, his voice trembles more than mine. "My—"

Cedar stops pacing. He opens his mouth to speak again, but can't seem to articulate the words. He clears his throat, snapping out of it to glare at me like I've just threatened his entire family. "I just think it's a little suspicious, that's all."

Of course, I think to myself. The one time I'm telling the truth—the one time I'm not caught up in a lie—my words are not believed. I can't say my bad luck surprises me, but it's frustrating nonetheless.

Back at home, I worked so hard to gain his trust. It hurts to know that after everything that happened, I still don't have it. I wonder if I ever did.

"If I'm interrupting anything, I'm sorry. I didn't exactly plan this, you know," I say impatiently. I take a deep breath and let it go, smoothing the cracks in my voice. "Someone brought me here."

"And why would they do that?"

I laugh bitterly. "You think *I* know?" The faults in my voice reappear. "One moment I'm out there *freezing to death*, and the next thing I know I'm waking up in this cabin. I don't know who saved me or how long I've been out or why I'm even here, and I'm a little freaked out about it, okay?"

He remains silent, observing me like a hawk. I hold my breath as he looks me up and down and pray that I don't look like a liar—just this once.

He shakes his head. "I don't buy it."

"Keep your money." Now, I fold my arms. "I'm telling the truth."

"Oh please. Don't give me that." He scoffs. "We both know you're too smart to get lost in the woods. There's a reason you're out here."

I swallow the growing lump in my throat. I know exactly why I'm here, and he does not.

"Wait a minute." He speaks quickly. I can see the gears in his brain turn faster until something clicks into place. "You're one of them."

I give him a blank look. "What?"

"Drop the act, Voclain. You know what I'm talking about."

"There is no act!"

"Bullshit."

"I'm telling the truth, alright?" I snap before lowering my voice and releasing a sigh. I hug my chest tighter, shoulders tense. "You know me. Maybe not much, but enough to know I'm on your side."

He glowers coldly in my direction, and my face pales. I remember what he thought back in those woods—and after that night, when I thought he'd been killed.

Cedar really believes I'm a Chaser.

"If I were one of them," I tell him, voice low and unwavering, "you'd be dead right now, and we both know it."

Before I can blink, he steps forward, cornering me into the wall, knife against my throat. He's careful not to draw blood, but he could easily do so in an instant. "And if I weren't such a nice guy, you'd be dead too, Voclain."

I let out a hollow chuckle. "Nice?"

"Watch it."

I grit my teeth. "You don't scare me."

"Your mistake, not mine." He applies more pressure, and I know that if he moves it any closer my throat will be slit before I can blink. For a brief moment, it sends shivers down my spine. "Now tell me: where's your uniform?"

"I don't have a uniform."

"I don't have all day here," he seethes, but he doesn't yell. In fact, he hasn't yelled once. He's good at maintaining a calm composure, though I can tell he's more distressed than he wants me to know. Maybe even a little afraid.

"I still don't know what you're talking about." I lower my voice. He moves his face closer until his nose is inches away from mine.

"Name," he asks, quickly and quietly.

"Lavender Voclain." My remark is just as swift.

"Age."

"Eighteen."

"Birthday."

"April 1st."

"Division?"

His last question catches me off guard, and I stare at him with a puzzled look. I truly have no idea what he's talking about.

He flares his nostrils, staring at me for a long time before releasing an aggravated sigh. Relief floods through me when he lowers the knife, but he still grips it just as tightly.

"Chasers are brainwashed. They're trained to answer those questions like *that*." He snaps his fingers. "And especially that last one." His glare softens. "You're either a really good liar, or a really terrible Chaser."

"I'd die before becoming a Chaser," I hiss, disgusted by his accusation. "How could you think such a thing?"

"Then what are you?"

I pause, scowling, but then my glare melts away. He's asked me this question before, so very long ago. How unfortunate it is that I finally have the answer. "A Runner."

Cedar's glare fades too. For a moment, I recognize the smallest hint of concern in his eye, but it is quick to fade. He clears his throat.

"What's on your hand?" He holds his palm out, asking permission to investigate. I find it ironic that he would ask permission to touch my hands, and not to press a knife against my throat.

I nod, and Cedar takes my fingers in his. I watch as he analyzes the chilblains, evaluating the radish-colored blisters like an equation that needs to be solved.

"Let me see your feet."

"Okay, what the hell—"

"I'm not asking," he snaps.

Glowering, I pull off my fresh pair of socks, using the wall for balance. He crouches down and performs the same investigation for my toes. They're much darker than my fingers, and the damaged skin glistens in the morning light. He gestures for me to put my socks back on and stands up.

"You really were out in the cold, weren't you?" he asks, voice low.

I nod, staring at my feet.

He lets out a heavy sigh. "Seems to me you've suffered from some minor frostbite, but you were saved just in time by the looks of it. If you were out there for any longer you probably would have lost a toe or two." He sheathes his knife and places it in his pocket. "But that doesn't mean I trust you."

"I really am a"—I choke on the word—"a Runner."

He nods, unable to look me in the eye. "Can I see your Cards?"

I pull up my sleeves and reveal my tattoos. They rest on my wrists like life-sized Joker Cards, though the only basis I have for my comparison is what I've seen on TV during the Pick. The ink is black and crisp, and the edges are sharp, a cage that traps the laughing jester inside. Cedar gives me a look to ask if he can inspect them, and I nod.

Gently, he takes my wrists in his hands and reads the Cards. But he finds my stare again as soon as he sees my double Jokers. He looks at me with wide eyes, still holding my wrists. "Voclain..."

My throat and chest suddenly feel tight and I avert my gaze. I can't cry in front of him. I can't show Cedar my weakness.

He sees my reaction and studies me, trying to figure out what's wrong. After a while, he lets go to pull up his own sleeves. "I guess we have one thing in common."

I look at his wrists. Like me, Cedar has a Joker on one wrist, but the other is painted with a 2 of Spades. I notice that both Cards are crossed out with a crudely tattooed *X*, a subtle act of rebellion.

I give him an empty smile.

"Did you happen to see who brought you in?" he questions, changing the subject. But this time, his words aren't interrogative, but almost hopeful, like he wants me to say yes. I wonder if he came here to look for some*one*, not some*thing*.

"No," I mutter apologetically. That brief moment of hope fades away, and Cedar curses under his breath.

He walks over to the table before closing the floorboard compartment and picking the letter off the ground. He doesn't even bother to read it before folding it and placing it on the table, leading me to assume he knows exactly what it contains—or that the letter isn't meant for him.

He pauses, turning to look at me again. "How much of that letter did you read?"

"Is *all of it* an acceptable answer?"

"Dear God, Voclain." He sighs, taking a seat in one of the wooden chairs before rubbing his face in exhaustion. "Things are not looking good for you right now."

"What do you mean?" I scoff. "I haven't done anything wrong."

"You're here, and that's your first mistake." He shakes his head. "And you went and read that letter too."

"I don't get why any of this is such a big deal."

"This is more important than you could ever understand," he snaps, shaking his head and letting out a dry laugh. "You have no idea what you've interfered with by being here—today, especially."

I open and close my mouth, biting my lip, unsure of what to say.

"I can't let you go, and I won't kill you if you cooperate," the smuggler announces after a while, turning around to face me again. He takes a few slow steps toward me until we're standing only a foot away. "But I'll slit your throat if I have to."

"Understandable," I say with a nod, but I have a difficult time believing his threat.

He glares at me for a long moment. And then, to my surprise, he takes a step forward—and wraps his arms around me.

He buries his chin in my hair, his voice barely a whisper. "It's good to see you, Voclain."

My shoulders tense. I don't remember the last time I felt the touch of another human. Cedar is one of the last familiarities I have left, and soon enough, my shoulders relax, and I wrap my arms around him too. I hold him as tight as I can, squeezing my eyes shut and clutching the back of his jacket. "It's good to see you too."

For the first time in a long time, I feel like smiling. But I save it.

"I'm sorry," Cedar whispers, so quietly I almost miss it. He knows what must have happened to make me a Runner. *He knows what I have lost.*

After a long time, he clears his throat and pulls away, avoiding my gaze. He slings his worn leather satchel over his shoulder and walks over to a closet in the corner of the room, opening it to retrieve a pair of heavy-duty combat boots. He tosses them in my direction and I barely make the catch.

"You want me to *wear* these?" I raise an eyebrow at the suggestion. They're two sizes too big, not to mention ancient. I'm not intrigued by the idea of wearing what must be a dead man's pair of shoes.

He gives me a look. "Would you rather get *real* frostbite this time?"

I roll my eyes, but I don't say another word as I slip them on. He takes off his rust-orange puffer jacket and throws it at me. This time, I put it on without hesitation.

"Where are we going?" I ask, walking over to stand by his side.

He replies unenthusiastically. "To meet someone."

"Why?"

"Worry about it when we get there," he grumbles, making his way to the cabin's entryway and opening the door.

"But—"

"Can it," he says sharply. "You don't get to ask questions right now. It's dangerous."

"Just one?"

"No."

"Can you at least tell me your real name?"

Cedar pauses in the doorway, refusing to say a word for a moment or two. When he turns his head around, I almost expect an answer. But my expectations are wrong. He stares at me blankly before turning around once again, walking out the door without another word.

I grab my knife, but I forget to grab my old clothing. I abandon Ren's sweatshirt, my torn jeans, and my muddy sneakers, and with them, I leave behind the last pieces of a world I thought I knew so well.

Cedar walks much faster than I do.

Thankfully, the storm has passed. But there's still a lot of frozen ground to cover and it's not pleasant. This stretch of forest is astonishingly intricate, like a web of pine spun by some incomprehensible arachnid entity. I can't believe Cedar has managed to lead us a whole mile without checking a map. He trudges through the snow with experienced feet, navigating this vast expanse of evergreen like his own backyard.

I struggle to keep up with his strides. My night in the snow and the bedrest that followed must have taken a toll on my strength—not to mention all the time I've spent on the move. I've been Running for so long I no longer bother to keep track of the days.

The jacket helps. I feel less like a human girl and more like a pumpkin when I wear it, but it's warm and comfortable and built for this kind of weather. I can't help but wonder how much time Cedar spends outdoors.

I grit my teeth, frowning at him as he walks ahead of me. "I hate this."

"That's nice," he replies, refusing to look behind him as we labor through piles of snow.

"My feet are cold."

"Really?" he mocks.

"You realize I nearly froze to death, right?" I protest. "Don't you know what hypothermia is?"

"It'd be concerning if I didn't."

That's right, I remember. He's a healer too. "It really would be."

"If I give you some water, will you shut the hell up?" he murmurs, still refusing to spare a glance in my direction.

"No."

"What will it take for you to stop complaining, then?"

"Answers," I say. "I feel like a prisoner."

"You are. Technically."

"Oh, come on."

"Maybe I should ditch my knife and just let you go. Or you know what could do? I could just give *you* the knife, and *you* can take me somewhere instead. Wait, wait, I have a better idea: you can just kill me." He comes to a halt before finally looking in my direction. "Would you stop complaining then?"

"Yes, I would actually." I take my own knife from behind my back and lift it up to show him. "But I don't need your knife, I have my own."

He pauses, and for a moment, I wonder if he'll take it from me. I know it was a gift from him to begin with, but this blade has been in my possession through the worst moments of my life, and I don't want to lose it.

He stares at the knife, brows furrowed, and then looks back at me. "You've kept that with you this whole time?"

"Maybe."

But then, he surprises me. "I've taught you well, then."

"You didn't teach me anything."

His lips curl into something resembling a smirk. "Maybe."

He comes to a halt, opening his satchel and rummaging through its contents. He pulls out an empty leather sheath and tosses it to me.

"You just happen to have this on you?" I raise an eyebrow, catching the object quickly. I slide it over the blade and attach it to my belt loop.

"Yeah." He shrugs, and I give him a look. "I collect knives, big deal. And it goes with the one you have anyway. I just forgot to give you the sheath along with it."

I frown, remembering all the surgical blades he harvested from my dad's office in secret. "How many do you have on you right now?"

He grins before turning right back around. I shake my head, and we move on once again.

As much as I hate to admit it, I know I probably shouldn't be up and about yet. I still feel so weak after being trapped in that storm. I have no idea who saved me or how long I was out, and I'm beyond grateful for the rest, but I can't stop thinking about spending just one more moment in bed. One more moment without the burning touch of snow.

We hike a bit longer until we approach a clearing. There's another cabin up ahead, but this one isn't as clean as the one I woke up inside this morning, nor as warm and forgiving. The exterior is falling apart, the wood rotted and crumbling like it's been vacant for decades. It's gray and ominous and probably doesn't smell too pleasant.

Cedar comes to a stop when we reach the front door. He turns to look at me, face grim. "If you wanna get out of this alive, I'd watch what you say from here on out."

"I didn't say any—"

He pulls out the knife again before I can finish, threatening me into silence. "I mean it. If you wanna live another day, stay quiet." He puts the knife back in its place and places a hand on the doorknob. "I'm warning you."

I want to ask about a thousand different questions, but all I can do is nod in silence and swallow my nerves as he opens the door.

Overcome with the odor of decay, I peer inside, feet planted in the doorway. The smell of mildew and chimney soot burns on the way down. When I notice how small the building is, I decide it's less like a cabin and more like a storage shed. The only furniture that can fit inside is an aged wooden round table, a few chairs, and a rusting industrial work table with a sink in the back, coated in enough cobwebs to stuff a mattress.

My heart drops to my feet. There are two people sitting in those chairs, and they are glaring right in my direction.

One of them is a middle-aged man with broad shoulders and a brown mustache that looks like it belongs in the Yesterdays. Something about the way he holds himself seems too casual, almost humorous. I blink twice to make sure the left side of his face really is occupied by a black eye patch, an anomaly I've never seen before. He leans back in his chair, crossing his arms and staring at me like my captor has just dragged in a mythical creature.

The woman sitting across from him must be a decade older than me, but there's still a youthful fire to her nature—the kind that stays with you, even as you age. She has dark brown skin and a narrow chin she holds high with admirable sophistication. My appearance seems to have sparked a twinkle of curiosity that she blinks away in an instant.

She frowns, raising a single displeased brow. "*This* is her?"

"Doesn't look like much of a Chaser." The man chuckles. "Guess that's a good thing, huh?"

"She's not—" Cedar looks at me for a moment and sighs. He leans down to whisper in my ear. "Stay out here. And don't do anything stupid."

I open my mouth to protest, but the door shuts in my face before I can speak, locking me outside. I hurry closer and press my ear against the wood, hoping to make out some of their conversation.

Cedar's voice is muffled. "She's not my sister."

His sister? What is he talking about?

And then I remember the girl in Esmerelda's photographs and all the stories about her daughter—the one who decided to become a Chaser.

What is going on?

"What did you just say?" I hear the man ask, voice low.

"I said she's not my sister," Cedar repeats slowly, his tone grim. "That's not our Double out there."

For a moment, all is quiet. But the silence is quick to fade.

"*What the hell, Aaron!*" the woman seethes. Through this wood barrier, I can hear what sounds like chair legs scraping against the floor, and assume everyone is standing up now.

I should be worried by what I'm hearing. But for the first time in such a long, horrible time, I smile—because I have finally been given a name.

Not the ridiculous code name he came up with on the spot in the woods to protect his identity. Not the nickname I've been calling him this entire time. This is a real, solid name.

Aaron.

"Please tell me she's just some Runner and not—" The woman lowers her voice to finish the rest of her sentence, like she doesn't want me to hear through the door. "Not one of *them*."

"Is she chipped?" The man says.

Chipped? I remember Cedar using that word a few times over the summer. But there's no time to think about what it means, because the conversation continues.

"Yes, she's a Runner. I found her in the cabin." Cedar—no, Aaron whispers, but his whisper sounds more like a yell. Then his tone changes, and I can hear him sigh through the door. "She's chipped."

I don't see it in their expressions, but I can feel the atmosphere around me darken. I've ruined something by being here, and it's obvious that no one is happy about it. I want to burst through the door and tell these two strangers that I'm not a Chaser. I could never be a Chaser, and I would rather die than do such a thing.

But Aaron's words of warning echo in my memory, and I get the feeling that his threats held at least a little bit of significance. I have to keep my mouth shut.

"She's *chipped*?" the woman exclaims. "And you bring her *here*?"

"Do you have any idea what this means?" The man's attitude has transformed into something cold and frustrated. I can clearly picture the angry scowl that must be dominating his expression.

"*Yes*, I know what this means," Aaron hisses. *I'm not stupid*, he says without speaking.

"The cabin's been compromised," the man says. "We don't know who this girl is or what information she has. She could have told someone about what she found."

"She couldn't have. She doesn't have a radio," Aaron argues.

"Are you sure? You searched her and everything?"

"Yes," Aaron lies, and I wonder why. He didn't search me. Not in the way they're implying. *Maybe he does trust me—at least a little bit.*

"How do we know she's working alone?" the woman adds. "She could very well know about your sister."

"She's not one of them," Aaron states. "She's a Runner. Her Cards match—she's a double Joker. Apparently, she got caught in the snow, passed out, and woke up in the cabin. Shows signs of frostbite and everything."

"And we're supposed to just believe that? What else could she be except a damn Chaser?" the man exclaims.

"She can't be a Runner—not in this weather," the woman adds. "There's no way she could have survived in the snow for long."

"Look, I know you guys don't trust her. I didn't at first. But here's the thing." Aaron sighs. "I know her."

The woman scoffs. "What do you mean, you know her?"

"You've got to be shitting me." I picture the man placing his head in his hands. "As in, *know her* know her?"

I can practically hear Aaron's glare. "What's that supposed to mean?"

"Oh God, he's got a soft spot for her," the woman chimes in, clearly distressed.

"You're both a couple of idiots," Aaron snaps. "I did a few jobs with her back when I was in the city last summer. Asa vouched for her."

The room goes quiet at the mention of Asa's name, and my curiosity only grows. *These people know him too?*

"Asa vouched for her?" the man clarifies, his tone changed. I assume Aaron nods in response. "Well damn. That certainly complicates things."

"Look, you guys know I'm not stupid, alright?" Aaron says with a sigh. "If she were a real threat, I would have handled the situation a long time ago."

I don't want to know what he means by *handling it*, but for some reason, the statement eases my worries, just a little.

"Why would Asa vouch for her?" the woman questions.

"She knows the twins," Aaron responds, and it all goes quiet again. *They know about Margot*, I realize, feeling the weight of the air. My throat tightens. *They must know.*

"That doesn't mean we can trust her," the woman adds, although her tone is softer. "I think we need to be proactive here. This is a sensitive time for all of us, and we can't afford any loose ends. We can't be vulnerable right now."

"*Proactive?*" Aaron scorns, voice rising quickly. Things are said in silence, and his voice changes. "No."

"Aaron…"

He chuckles darkly. "No. I'm not doing that—"

"Aaron," the man interrupts.

"*I'm not doing that!*" Aaron shouts, going quiet for a moment until he lowers his voice. "She's innocent, alright? She's not a threat to anyone. She's hurt."

"What if she does turn out to be a spy? What then?" the woman argues.

"Even if she was," Aaron says between gritted teeth, "I don't think we should do *anything*"—he pauses, presumably to glare at his comrades—"without getting Noriko's input first."

My heart skips a beat. *Noriko?*

I know that name.

The sky is heavier than ever. It feels like the world is swallowing itself whole, like a snake with its own tail in its mouth. My breathing grows shaky, my hands tremble, and I find myself falling to my knees. I lean against the door, staring at nothing at all.

This is impossible.

But when I pause for a moment to think about it, all of the puzzle pieces start to make a little more sense. It's like putting on glasses for the first time and realizing there are details and textures you've never seen, grains in the floorboards you've been walking on your whole life.

I think back to the letter, scanning the words over and over again in my memory. I read those four names a dozen times just to make sure I have them right, because I don't want to believe what I'm thinking.

N. A. M. R.

Noriko.

Asa.

Margot.

Ren.

Suddenly, I'm not sure I remember how to breathe.

Who are these people? And why on earth did Asa want me to come here?

"Noriko would want this girl dealt with as soon as possible," the woman in the cabin mutters beyond the door, snapping me back into reality. I press my ear even closer to the wood.

"You can't know that, Viv," Aaron says, voice cracking. There must be more to his frustration than I realize. "None of us really know anything right now, which is why I think we should call her over."

"She's swamped. She can't make it down here," the man points out. "That's why she has messengers in the first place. To do things when she can't do them herself."

"I have a feeling she would come down pretty quick if we told her what's going on, Cecil," Aaron claims. "We have bigger problems than Eddie right now."

"Eddie?" the man—presumably Cecil—questions.

There's a sound, like he's been hit in the shoulder. "The girl," Viv seethes.

"Okay, okay. Got it."

"Look, Aaron. Calling her down here would be a waste of everyone's time," Viv explains. "We should just deal with the girl now and tell Noriko about it when we get back."

"Like hell you will," Aaron seethes.

"Woah, everyone just calm down," Cecil insists. I can hear him stand up. "No one's killing anybody yet. Alright?"

Kill? Nothing I read in that letter seems like information worth killing me for. Something else must be going on here, something I don't know.

I remove my ear from the door and study my surroundings. If I had enough energy, I could make a run for it. I could forget about the mystery of Aaron and the Unseen, the map in Margot's locket, the plot unfolding underfoot, and my mystery savior and just live the rest of my life in a cave somewhere. But for miles in every direction, all I see is snow.

I sigh, closing my eyes. Even if I wanted to escape, my body is too weak, and I know these people wouldn't think twice before coming after me. Aaron could hunt me down in the blink of an eye. And for some reason— even after all this talk of killing—my current situation feels a whole lot safer than being hunted by Ren and Duke. *I have to stay put.*

"Aaron's got a point," Cecil finally says. "I think Noriko would appreciate us letting her know what's going on. But I gotta agree with Viv—she'd be pissed if this all ended up being a waste of time."

"But she would be more upset if we didn't handle this right," Aaron adds.

"And this girl might know something about my sister's whereabouts. Maybe she saw some important detail or remembers something about whoever carried her to the cabin."

The conversation comes to a pause, and I can barely make out the sound of Aaron sighing. "We need to be really careful about this."

Cecil swears under his breath, and I can hear him collapse into his seat again. I picture him shaking his head. "I knew sending in another Double was a bad idea."

"I'll call Noriko over," Aaron says, followed by a beeping of some sort. It's not a phone, but the sound makes me wonder if it could be some sort of Yesterday communication device. I remember Milo toying around with them back at home, and it tugs at something in my chest.

I hear Aaron mutter into the device but I can't pick out the words. In a moment, there's another beep, and I hear him rummage through his satchel to put it away.

"Wait, why aren't we watching the girl?" Viv says. "She could be running for the hills right now."

"She's not going anywhere," Aaron says. "Like I said, she's hurt. Recovering from hypothermia and malnutrition and God knows what else."

"And you *left her out in the snow*?" Cecil asks.

"Thought she'd prefer a little snow to one of you two slicing her throat," Aaron retorts.

"I don't care who she is or what she has. We need to be keeping an eye on her." I hear footsteps that I assume to be Viv's, but they come to a pause.

"I'll handle this," Aaron says, stopping her. "My sister's *life* could be at risk here, remember? And she's been..." He trails off before clearing his throat. "We have to go about this carefully."

It's quiet for a moment until Aaron finally opens the front door. He stares at me blankly, reaching out an arm to help me up the step as Viv glares over his shoulder. "You can come in now."

I walk inside and he closes the door, gesturing for me to take a seat while everyone else stands. Aaron keeps himself next to me and the man leans against the wall to my right, and Viv stands by the door like she expects me to escape.

But escaping is no longer on my mind; all I can think about is the letter. Millions of questions buzz in my mind like a swarm of agitated bees, each sting burning more than the last.

We wait for a soundless eternity. No one mutters a single word as they all stare at me, studying me like a jigsaw puzzle with just one color, or a specimen they can't figure out how to dissect.

I lay my head on the table, using my elbows as a pillow and closing my eyes. I know I won't be able to truly rest with all these hushed stares prickling the back of my neck, but I can't hold my head up for any longer.

I'm not sure how much time has passed when the door opens. It fans the cold and bits of powdery snow inside the cabin, startling me upright. A woman with long black hair walks in, commanding the attention of every eye in the room as she closes the door and sits down at the table.

She's the same age as Cecil and has a missing left eye to match. But she doesn't cover it up with a patch or with the shades Aaron uses to conceal his scar and half-blindness. The part of her face where the organ should be is twisted and gnarled. I find it really odd that three people in this room have something wrong with the same eye, but I keep my lips pressed shut.

When she sets her arms on the table to further investigate my mystery, I realize that she has no left hand either. Instead, it's been replaced with a roughly made prosthetic, constructed entirely out of black metal and polymer. It doesn't look like our kind of technology back home, almost homemade in comparison. It doesn't seem to be less functional—just different.

The room is completely devoid of noise as we all hold our breath, like a vacuum no sound can travel through, not even a heartbeat. The woman studies me intently. She moves her arms from the table and crosses them together against her chest, raising an eyebrow, looking me up and down. I feel like a prisoner.

"I heard someone was found in the cabin where our Double was supposed to be," the woman finally says. She speaks to everyone else, but her gaze is glued to me. "Is this her?"

"She says someone *brought* her to the cabin." Viv fills the stranger in with a tightened jaw. "But we think she's one of them."

Aaron is quick to argue. "She's not a Chaser."

"A *Chaser*?" the woman questions skeptically, eyeing me up and down before looking back at Aaron and Viv. "What reason would a Chaser have to be out here alone? And in an old cabin too?"

"I think this has something to do with our new Double," Cecil says. He speaks respectfully, and I understand why. This stranger certainly knows how to command a room.

"My guess is that our Double leaked some sort of information, and they sent a pair to intervene with the rendezvous at the cabin. I doubt this girl's working alone." The man gestures his chin in my direction. I glare at him, biting my tongue and trying my hardest to follow Aaron's instructions. I have to keep quiet.

"She would never do that. This is just as important to her as it is to all of us," Aaron snaps, but I can tell he's not referring to me. "She gave up *everything* for this cause, and I swear if either of you you say one more—"

The woman holds up a hand to let him know he's been heard. He's reluctant to back down, but he stops talking with a frown.

"What do you have to say about all of this?" the stranger says, interrupting every angry staring contest in the room. At first, I assume she's talking to someone else, but then I realize it's me she's looking at. For some reason, she's the only person in the room without a glare.

"Me?" I point a finger at my own chest.

"Who else would I be referring to?" she asks rhetorically. Her voice sounds cold for a moment before she gives me a wry smile.

"Well, I..." Now that I finally have a chance to talk, I have no idea what to say. I don't know how much information *I* can trust these people with, but I get the feeling that I need to say the right thing if I want to get out of here alive.

I have to tell the truth—the whole truth. Lying has already done enough.

"It's okay," the woman says. "I know my comrades here don't always come off as very friendly, but we're not bad people. You can trust us."

"I'd tell her the truth if I were you," Viv threatens, and the woman signs for her to hush. Viv scoffs before leaning against the wall, folding her arms with attitude.

The truth. What is the truth, exactly? A moment ago, I thought I had it pinned down exactly. I'm a Runner. That was my truth.

But now, as every able eye in the room eagerly stares at me with expectations I need to correct, my tongue is tied in a knot, and I can't figure out how to straighten out my story. How can I start from the beginning when I have no idea where the beginning starts—and when everything I once saw as a beginning seems more like an end?

Aaron notices my distress and leans over to whisper in her ear. "There's something you should know, N. I—" Aaron begins to explain our connection, but she holds up a hand.

"Let her talk," she says, and to my surprise, he doesn't argue against it. "Go on."

I have to start simply.

"I was Picked." The words taste bitter in my mouth and it takes everything I have not to be sick.

The woman stares at me, waiting for me to continue. I take a deep breath and close my eyes for a moment, forcing myself to open them again when I'm flooded with unwanted memories.

I can't bear to see my loved ones lifeless again, or the bloodied wound that surely took Milo's life. But I swallow the lump in my throat and keep going anyway, because I must.

"I was Picked," I repeat slowly. My breath is shakier than my hands, and a bead of sweat forms around my brow. I almost feel feverish. "And when the Chasers came, my family... they were killed for protesting."

The woman nods almost empathetically as I speak, urging me to go on.

"But my brother fought the Chasers off long enough for me to escape." My eyes water and I forget how to breathe when I think about Milo. I try and fail to inhale, staring at a knot in the wood table, putting every ounce of my focus into that little imperfection to keep myself from crying. *I will not show them weakness.*

"I didn't want to leave him, but I needed to find help," I continue. "I sent someone to help him but I knew I'd be Chased and I couldn't go back home. So I Ran."

The stranger nods again. I get the sense that Viv and Cecil don't quite believe me yet, but the way this woman stares at me tells me that maybe—

just maybe—she sees just a little bit of truth in my words.

Aaron is no longer glaring, but I can tell his thoughts are elsewhere. He's pulled out one of his knives and fidgets with an unrecognizable wood carving, channeling his worries into smooth, precise strokes.

"So how exactly did you end up at the cabin?" the woman asks, breaking the silence and drawing my attention back to her one-eyed gaze. "Coincidence?"

"I was given a compass—well, a map, actually—before I left the city. And I followed it all the way here, but then I got stuck in the snowstorm. I woke up in the cabin and that's when I was found and *threatened* by him." I nod in Aaron's direction, shooting him a glare. He rolls his eyes before ignoring me, continuing to whittle away at the little piece of wood he holds.

"I thought I was found by whoever owned the cabin, but... I guess I was wrong. I have no idea who saved me." I stare at the knot in the table.

"Wait, rewind for a moment." The woman places her hands on the table again, leaning forward in both interest and concern. "You were given a map?"

"Yeah, this. It's a compass with some engravings inside." I pull out Margot's locket from beneath the protection of my sweater, and the stranger jumps like I've pulled out a bomb.

"Where did you get that?" she asks frantically. I hear a hint of desperation in her voice, maybe even anger.

"I told you, someone gave it to me," I reply, losing my patience.

For the first time since she walked in the room, she glares at me for what feels like eons until she speaks a sentence that chills me to my core.

"That's my daughter's necklace you're wearing."

REN

Friday, January 12
Day 12

When I first stumbled into the cabin carrying a dying girl on my back, Carmody was quick to protest.

He didn't see the point in setting up camp out in the snow to let Eddie take our place in the cabin. *We're the ones with power*, he'd said. We're the ones in uniforms.

But it was easy to convince him to cooperate. My proposal was simple. We would nurse our target back to life, and when she was back in good health, she'd be left on her own again, and we'd continue our investigation. She would never suspect Chasers to be the ones to save her. I argued that the mystery of who brought her to the cabin might increase Eddie's interest in the people in the woods, and the process would go by a lot quicker.

We'll be praised, I reminded him. *We'll be one step closer to a promotion to Agent.*

He wasn't happy about it, but to my relief, Carmody agreed to keep his hands off Eddie for the time being—and that is exactly what I want.

But that was two days ago, and Eddie still hasn't woken up.

Carmody and I have been keeping a close eye on her, but we've moved out of the cabin to remain hidden from Eddie in case she wakes up. Camping in the snow isn't comfortable, but our uniforms make it somewhat bearable. Survivable at the very least.

I feel like I'm grasping at straws. Carmody believes me when I tell him it is a plan I hold in my hands when it's only desperation in a mask. I know I'm walking on thin ice. His reserve for patience is unsubstantial at best, and it's only a matter of time before he cannot wait any longer.

Carmody's getting restless. He is tired of watching, tired of being quiet, tired of letting Eddie act as though she's free and not caged within the trap he thinks we've set. He's losing sight of the value of studying her for answers. He's a boy who likes control, and he can't handle a life without it.

I don't let him near her.

Every few hours, I've been walking back to the cabin to see if she's awake. And every time without fail, she remains fast asleep. I'll check her pulse and reheat the pan of water by her feet to make sure the purple in her toes will keep on fading away, and I'll tend to the fire too. But today is different.

I walk up to the house, carrying logs and bits of wood for the hearth. I watch the cabin as I approach, relieved to find the chimney offering a plume of smoke to a cold gray sky. *Good*, I think. *The fire's still going.*

I open the front door with one arm and step inside, but what I find makes the firewood fall to the ground with a thud. Because Eddie is nowhere to be seen. Not in the bed, not on the couch, not at the table—she has vanished into thin air.

And there is someone else in her place.

Something keeps me from breathing. My heart pounds against my chest at a mile a minute as I take in her short bob of sleek black hair, her familiar brown eyes—and a face it takes me too long to recognize, because it shouldn't be staring across from me.

Not here. Not now. Not like this.

In a blink, I pull out my Nightjade gun before I realize what I'm doing. She moves quickly, pulling her own weapon from her pocket and aiming it in my direction with trembling hands.

I study her angrily, questioning everything about her. Her tan skin is rosy from the cold and her dark hair is covered in delicate sprinkles of snow.

From the looks of it, she's been on quite the hike, all in vintage winter gear rather than a Chaser uniform.

She seems flustered and confused, but the more we examine each other, the more our mutual suspicion grows into bitterness. I glare at her with a passion so dark it surprises me.

I don't care who she is or how kind she was during training. I don't care if I called her a friend once, because that piece of information no longer has any value to me. I couldn't give a damn if I tried.

If Loretta Salazar has done something to Eddie, I will kill her.

"*Where is she?*" I seethe, pointing the gun in her direction with one arm.

"I don't know what you're talking about." She glares at me with a fury that matches my own. "Now why don't you tell me what you've done to my brother?"

Her brother? I have no idea what she's talking about, and it only makes my patience thinner.

"I don't know anything about your brother," I spit. "Now tell me where Eddie is, because I swear to all things good—I'll kill you if you don't."

"What do you mean, you don't know anything?"

"Stop playing around, Salazar." I move closer, holding the gun with both hands now, so tightly it burns. "What did you do to her?"

Salazar looks at me for a moment, studying me for a long time. And then, her gaze softens. She lowers her gun, but she keeps it in her hands, eyeing me with something that almost looks like pity.

But I'm still not convinced she's innocent in all of this. It can't be a coincidence that she is here and Eddie is gone.

"Ren," she says my name gently, and for some reason, it makes me angrier. "You're not a killer."

"You don't know that." I tremble. My mind flashes with images of the man who begged for a mercy I couldn't give him.

The man I killed, whose name I still haven't forgotten, no matter how hard I try.

"I do know," Salazar argues, her words calmer than they should be. "I was with you, Ren. I saw you during training. You're not meant to be a Chaser and you know it."

I open my mouth to argue, but I'm interrupted as Carmody's ghost stories begin to play in my head. The rumors of people in the woods, children being kidnapped and possibly dismembered, the whisperings in the Corps about the missing Runners and Double Agents and everything in between.

Something big is going on here, and it's playing out right before my eyes.

"It's you," I mutter, unable to believe the words tumbling out of my mouth. "You're the Double Agent they've been looking for."

Salazar doesn't say a word, and the world beneath my feet suddenly feels unsteady.

Once, I thought the system was invincible. Once, I thought the only way to survive was to play along. But now I wonder if I should know better.

No one can know everything, not even the Corps. There has to be something they don't know, or things they do know and what to keep hidden. Truths labeled as rumors, real stories turned tall, escaped Runners deemed as ghosts.

This cabin must be a meeting place of some sort, and Salazar is involved somehow. That's the only explanation I have.

"Drop the gun, Ren." Salazar's voice is a whisper. "This isn't you."

"You don't know anything about me." I want to scream, but the words come out broken instead.

"I know you more than you think."

"*You don't know anything about me.*" This time, I manage to yell. I feel like I'm going to explode. My heart beats so loudly that I hear it pounding in my head, desperate fists against my skull.

I move closer and place a shaky finger on the gun's trigger, trying not to let my fear shatter the authority I need to maintain. I speak slowly, pausing between each word. "Where is Eddie?"

Salazar doesn't say anything, and her silence brings my worst fears to life. A thousand different possibilities swarm my mind until I'm dizzy. Someone has taken Eddie—I feel, deep down in my bones. And the only person here is Salazar.

She's guilty—she has to be. She's the one standing here in Eddie's place. Slowly, my finger traces up and down the trigger and I close my eyes.

I can't look at Salazar when I shoot her, but if she's done something to Eddie, I have to do it. I have to right this wrong. I have to make this correction.

"Wait!" Salazar calls, and I open my eyes. Her kind face is twisted with fear. But for some inexplicable reason, I realize she is not afraid of me. She is afraid for me.

"Your mother," she blurts quietly. "I know where she is."

A pause. A heartbeat. Three, maybe more.

The gun falls from my hands and hits the floor.

"No," I mutter, shaking my head. I take a step back and close my eyes. I've gone mad. I'm hearing things. "My mother is dead."

"You've got it all wrong, Ren." Salazar's eyes are glossier than they were a moment ago, and she offers me an unexpected smile. "Your mother is still alive."

"That's impossible." I feel my voice crack like old pavement. I take another step backward, wanting to distance myself from this girl who won't stop spitting out lies. "She was Picked right after I was born. My father *saw her* die. He told me."

"She isn't dead, Ren," Salazar contends. "Your father lied to you. It was for your own good but he lied to you, and you need to trust me."

"He would never do that."

Would he?

I'm brought back to the night of the Pick. I try to block out the memory but his voice is so horribly clear. I remember him telling me that Margot's Immunity had been paid for the entire time.

I remember the way he looked at me, when he saw me standing there in my uniform for the first time, unable to speak or blink or even breathe. I remember the guilt in his eyes, the way he looked at me as though he understood why I had to do any of this at all.

If the mother of his children were truly killed, wouldn't he have felt something more than guilt? Wouldn't he hate me for who I've become?

No. I shake the thoughts from my mind. He lied about Margot's Immunity, but he would never lie to me about something like this. Not about my mother.

"I'm telling the truth, Ren," Salazar says, her voice soft. "She's waiting for you to join her."

I shake my head so violently it aches. "I don't know what you're talking about."

"Ren." She puts the gun in her pocket. Her tone is gentle, but her words hit me with incredible force. "She still loves you. She always has."

I collapse on my knees, falling to the floor like firewood. I'm too stunned to move. All I can do is stare at the walls like they're closing in on me and there's absolutely nothing I can do about it.

"I know you don't believe me, but please. I need you to tell me the truth," she says, trembling. "Have you seen my brother?"

I can barely hear her. She takes my silence as a no.

"Ren. Look at me." She crouches down in front of me, reaching out a finger to gently lift up my chin. She speaks so softly I struggle. "There's something really important I need to tell you."

All I can do is stare at the wall.

"If you happen to see my brother," she says, "tell him I'll do it myself. He'll know what that means. Can you do that for me?"

I still can't speak. Salazar studies me for a moment longer before nodding to herself and taking her exit, leaving me alone in the cabin before I have the chance to grab my gun again.

I sit there for a while, not knowing what to do or what to think or how to breathe. Everything feels numb, like I've been left in the snow overnight and my entire body has been bitten by frost.

Salazar couldn't have been telling the truth. Everything she said was a lie, just a bunch of meaningless words she strung together to throw me off and save her own skin. Because I know my dad would never lie to me like that.

I know why he lied to me about Margot's Immunity. He didn't want me to feel less valued, because he could only afford to pay for one child's survival and not the other, and Margot was at a higher risk.

My father lied to me once, and there's nothing I can do about it now but hope the lie was working alone.

But I wish he had told me the truth about Margot long ago, because I would have understood. I would have thanked him, and I would have lived the rest of my life in peace knowing my sister was safe. I wouldn't have become a Chaser and I wouldn't have lied to my family. I never would have met that white room where my feet burned and bled. I never would have touched that Nightjade syringe or plunged it into that man's throat.

And without any reason to lean on her, I would have continued to hate Eddie for that stupid mistake at the river, and I would have been spared from her devastating grasp.

Is that really all we were? The thought hits like a blow to the stomach, knocking the wind out of me.

I'm unsure if a minute or an hour or a year has passed by the time Carmody walks in, alarmed by my prolonged absence. He asks what happened and I tell him that Eddie left before I arrived.

I don't tell him that Eddie was still too sick to have walked up and left on her own. I know for a fact that she would have stayed here for a little while longer to get some rest before moving on. Someone took her, but Carmody cannot be trusted and I keep my mouth shut.

My mind is elsewhere as Carmody complains about Eddie's disappearance, upset that we didn't kill her when we had the chance. But I'm too absorbed in my rage and confusion to care about anything else.

I wasn't angry about my father's lie before this moment, but now I cannot help but wonder if the only thing that brought Eddie and I together was the game of pretend we played in our foolish attempts to save my sister from her eventual death. All we've done is rooted in that one lie—that one secret we kept so close.

Once, I hated Eddie because I was scared of her fire and her recklessness. Her foolish, burning fury.

Months ago, I hated Eddie for something completely different. In that river covered in mud, between that wooden fence, in the cow field beneath the stars, I hated her because I couldn't.

And then my hatred became a sick game of pretend because I too was sick. My grief had made me ill. Eddie was still breathing with red hands, and Margot, in all her innocence, was gone.

But now, I hate her more than ever. I cannot forget the way I hated her back when she was all I wanted, even if I don't understand what happened on that night we lost everything, even if the blood on her hands could perhaps be entirely her fault, as I initially thought. Maybe we are both monsters, but I don't care.

I hate Eddie more than I have hated anyone before, because no matter how hard I try to pull myself away, I am so hopelessly and helplessly lost without her.

And I need to find her, because I have to find myself again too.

EDDIE

Friday, January 12
Day 12

♪ AFTER TIME - HIMALAYAS ♪

"That's my daughter's necklace you're wearing."

The words stun me for a moment until I blink the shock away.

"Her mother is dead," I argue, angry that this stranger would ever make such a claim.

Even when that claim aligns with what I've been suspecting, deep down in the places where things I don't want to believe like to reside.

"Everyone out. I need to talk to her." The woman stands up to enforce her command. Aaron and the others exchange puzzled looks before their leader glares. "Alone."

The group is hesitant to leave me alone, especially Aaron, but they respect her wishes nonetheless and exit the cabin to give us some privacy. Aaron pauses to whisper something in her ear, and she gives him a nod before he leaves, closing the door behind him. She sits back down in the chair across from me.

She keeps her lips sealed for a while, observing me for what feels like hours.

She reads me through the lens of this new information, questioning everything I said before and reanalyzing it with the necklace in mind.

To her, I'm an impossibility. But she's an impossibility too.

"This cabin is pretty special, did you know that?" she says.

I shake my head no.

"We're miles from the closest town. No mics, no listeners. It's just you and me, kid." She pauses. "What's your name?"

"Eddie," I mutter, remembering what Aaron said so long ago about names. Identity is power, and despite all I pretend to be, I feel scared giving it away.

"I mean your full name, kiddo."

"Lavender Voclain," I answer, tapping my feet anxiously as I wait for a response on her part.

"I know who you are," she says out of the blue. "You're Ren and Margot's friend, aren't you? Asa's vouched? Aaron's partner in crime?"

Hearing Margot's name is a stab to the chest. I picture Aaron's hunting knife, and the memory of losing her whittles me like wood. It eats at every inch of my flesh and bone and mind and blood until I am nothing but a gory pile of grief.

The woman gives me a look as if to repeat her question and I nod, though I don't know how she has this information.

She shouldn't know this. This woman can't know Ren and Margot, and she most certainly cannot know me.

Their mother was Picked right after they were born, never to be seen or heard from again because she was killed. Exterminated. Murdered. *Dead.* This woman is either crazy or a liar, maybe even both.

"My name is Noriko Teshima," she informs me. "I'm their mother."

"That's impossible," I reply, choking on my own words as the image from Ren's torn out yearbook page surges through my mind. "She's been—"

"Dead for eighteen years?"

I'm speechless. Not because it's unbelievable, but because somehow, some way, it manages to be just that.

If it's true, everything would suddenly make sense. This impossibility could be the one piece of information I'm missing.

Of course Asa would have ties to the Unseen if Ren and Margot's mother is involved—and of course he would want to keep it a secret from everyone, including me.

But what I don't understand is why he lied to his children about her alleged death, and how they weren't all subjected to the Runner penalty.

No. I correct my thinking. There is no sense here. Whatever fraction of clarity this could bring is only overshadowed by more and more questions.

"Do you mind if I tell you a few things?" she asks, breaking my silence. "If that's okay with you."

I nod, because I don't have another choice.

"Their father and I... we were in love once," she explains, speaking slowly. Her eye drifts away from my gaze and fixes on the wall behind me. Her stare seems hazy, like she's reminiscing about a time she would give anything to travel back to.

"Asa and I were the textbook definition of young love," she continues with a bittersweet grin. "We never married, but we moved in together right out of high school. I studied history while he started his auto repair shop. It wasn't much, but it was enough. Fast forward a few years, and Ren and Margot were born."

It's hard to imagine grumpy old Asa in love, but the concept makes the corner of my lips twitch.

"But I was Picked before the twins were even tattooed," Noriko says, and her grin disappears in an instant. "Asa had to take them in alone, and they were never registered as mine. Wrote their mother down as *deceased.* No one in the Corps seemed to question it. They have greater worries during the aftermath of the Pick, I suppose."

That would explain why they were spared from the Runner penalty. If Asa and Noriko never married and the twins were never registered under a Runner's name, the system wouldn't be able to draw those connections. *This must be why he lied about her death*, I realize. To keep them safe.

"I don't know what I was thinking when I Ran," Noriko continues. "Irrationality and fear made me process everything differently. I thought I was saving my children by sparing them the burden of seeing their mother get killed before their eyes, even if they wouldn't remember it later on. So I

Ran away from everything I knew. I left Asa a letter but I never got to say goodbye, and it broke me."

She pauses, staring at the knot in the table. This is difficult for her to talk about, that's for sure.

"I told him I would start a new life, out in that cabin the two of us found when we were camping one day, something people used to do in the Yesterdays. Told him I wouldn't stop Running until this world was a world where I could be a mother to my children—and I was willing to do anything to get to that point."

She sighs with an empty sort of sadness, mourning a life lost. I can tell she wishes for things to be different because I feel the same way.

I hate myself for Running, for being a coward and refusing to die by my family's side as I should have. But at the same time, I know I have to keep going. I Run for them—I fight for them—even though they are gone. And something in Noriko's gaze tells me she understands exactly what it feels like.

Maybe—just maybe—there might be some truth to what she's saying.

"You and I are actually quite similar, you know," Noriko says. "I was once a Runner too, right here in these very same woods. I was surviving; I was getting by just fine. But I just couldn't shake the Chasers off my trail." She pauses, shaking her head, digging up memories that want to stay buried. "No matter where I turned, they were always so close behind me."

Noriko sighs. "I was exhausted and I knew I wouldn't be able to survive for much longer if I couldn't throw them off my trail somehow. I tried setting traps, or making dead animal parts look human to fake my own death. But nothing worked."

Her words chill me to the core because I know exactly what it feels like to be hunted. My gut gnarls as I wonder where Ren and Carmody are now. *I'll let her know about that problem later.*

"I Ran for nearly two months," Noriko says, clearing her throat. "It took me that long to realize I was being tracked."

Tracked? What could she possibly mean by that? Of course she was being tracked. Chasers are trained to Chase. They know how to follow footprints, how to read the land, how to analyze the mind of their prey. They are hunters, and Runners are their game.

"Tracked?" I articulate my confusion.

Noriko nods, pointing to my wrist with her good hand. "It was the only logical explanation to me at the time. I thought there must have been something more to these tattoos, something I was missing." She comes to a pause, and to my surprise, she grins. "That's when I came up with a theory."

"A theory?"

She nods. "I wondered if we could be microchipped."

Microchipped.

The word rings through my mind like a warning bell, every echo churning my stomach until I feel like throwing up what little food I have left in my gut. The color drains from my face and I can't even blink, because I'm afraid that if I do, this will all become real.

I grab my wrists, feeling each one with my hands, as if touching the tattoos will somehow get rid of the tracker that hides beneath my skin. Every part of myself feels so separate, like I'm sewn of scraps that were never mine to begin with.

All this time, I thought my body was my own, the one thing this system could never take away from me. But now I realize how faulty that line of thinking is. Our bodies have never been our own; from the moment we're born, we're branded and turned into machines whose only purpose is to serve a system that wants them dead. I'm nothing but an object they can program to their liking.

If my own body isn't even my own, then what do I have? I have nothing.

"There are simply no words to describe that kind of violation," Noriko says.

"Yeah," I mutter, hands shaking uncontrollably. I can't stop touching my wrists.

"I thought it was beneath the tattoos," she continues. "It would make sense, right? So much focus is put on these Cards of ours. They get so much attention—almost *too* much attention."

Wordless, she looks down at where her left hand used to be.

I gasp, covering my mouth with my sleeves. "You didn't…"

"I did." She boasts a proud smirk I can't understand. "I cut off my hand from the wrist down."

"Holy shit." My skin grows pale and clammy. Nausea cuts through the hunger and turns me inside out.

"When you're all alone with no human contact for weeks, you start to notice things about yourself," she explains. "I was the only interesting thing around for miles. I can't even tell you how many hours I spent just staring at the tattoos, desperate for answers.

"By the time an answer did come, I was desperate. I had everything and nothing to lose at the same time. I had to test my hypothesis, or risk the consequences."

"How did you—know which one to cut?" I fail to swallow a growing lump in my throat.

"I took a guess," she says with a shrug. "I'm right-handed, so I chose my left."

This is all just a coincidence, I try to reassure myself. *This is all some strange, twisted coincidence.* I force myself to speak through the block in my head. "That's... a pretty big gamble."

"Every day is a gamble, kid. The sooner you learn how to manipulate your odds, the better," Noriko says. "I knew there were a thousand other possibilities. Maybe we were microchipped in both wrists, I thought. Maybe they were in our brains. Or maybe we weren't being tracked at all.

"But we're talking about survival, here. I was ready to cut myself apart piece by piece if it meant getting an answer. I had already lost everything— what was one hand, when I was already convinced I'd eventually meet a Nightjade syringe?"

She pauses as if she expects me to reply, but I answer the question in silence. *Nothing.*

"I sharpened a rock—and I tested my guess," she says. "It took ages, but eventually my hand was gone. Used my clothes for bandages, applied pressure to the wound, and when I was physically able to do so, I dissected the severed limb."

She chuckles for a moment and speaks again before I have the chance to respond. "It's funny, really. How I thought it would work."

My left wrist aches at the thought, and I rub it tenderly, scratching an imaginary itch. "What do you mean?"

"I wouldn't say I did it for nothing, necessarily," she replies. "Proved a theory wrong, that's for sure. But the Chasers were still tracking me somehow."

I give her a puzzled look.

"There are no microchips in our wrists." Noriko sighs, her breath filled with regret. "And when I realized that, it felt as though the Presidency itself was mocking me—pointing a slimy finger in my face and laughing at me for being so foolish.

"Wasn't until I lost my eye that I realized the truth."

I gulp nervously again. "Truth?"

"I always had a fondness for old Yesterday books. My limited knowledge helped me keep my blood loss low—but I still lost a lot. I was weak and starving, struggling to adapt to the loss of my hand—and the hopelessness of it all.

"It got worse, until one day, I just... collapsed." She stares at the table. "It was a pretty bad fall. Face first in a bundle of dead branches."

Elaboration isn't necessary for me to picture the image perfectly in my mind. The room spins, and all I can do is bite my lip and try not to think about what that must have felt like.

"And that's when I saw it," Noriko says. "I was screaming and dizzy with pain, but I had to look at my eye. I had to confirm that it truly was gone." She hesitates. "And when I picked it up, I noticed there was something inside my lost eye. Something I wouldn't have caught if I hadn't chosen to take a look.

"That was one of the greatest moments of my life. Because that's when I discovered the one thing that will save us all."

"And what's that?" I ask softly.

"Truth, Eddie. I found the truth." I'm not sure how she's able to grin, but she does. And for a brief moment, I swear I see Margot in her smile.

"When we are born, we are tattooed. And then we are taken away to be microchipped twice in complete secrecy," Noriko explains. "The Corps has a made-up division of workers they call Chippers. But the real microchipping is done by Agents—the highest division in the Corps that works directly under the Presidency. Every Chaser knows they exist, but only Agents know *where* they are."

She waits for me to absorb it all. I can't, not yet, but I nod anyway, brows furrowed. "How does it go so unnoticed?"

"They use advanced surgical technology to place them in our eyes. They're so small they can't be felt, and since we are chipped from such a young age, we wouldn't know any different, even if we could feel them. Only the Agents and the Presidency have access to this truth."

"But I don't understand." I shake my head. "Why guard the location of these trackers so closely?"

"Because this is how we are controlled," she says. "And you can't break free from control unless you know where it originates, can you?"

"No, I guess not."

"The unfortunate thing is, it's a truth so easily hidden. People who lose eyes and limbs are deemed unproductive and killed by Nightjade laws or sentenced to work in the tombs. No one suspects that we're microchipped, and certainly not in the eye of all places," Noriko adds.

"But how is knowing this... truth... going to save anyone?" I ask, thinking back to her statement from earlier.

"This truth lets us see things we are not supposed to see. We are the unseeing Unseen, Eddie. We are physically blinded but our eyes are open to so much more because of it. This knowledge will let us break free from the hands wrapped around our throats."

"We?" I repeat. Noriko nods.

"I was so close to dying." She stares at the table again. "There were moments where I considered ending it all myself—that is, until I made a discovery."

My eyes widen. *There's more?*

"I stumbled across an abandoned religious compound from the Yesterdays, emptied of human life by the Wandering but stocked full of things that could sustain it," Noriko explains. "Survival kits. Military gear. A small hospital. Food storage. An old library. Arts and craft rooms. Ceramic and glassblowing and construction studios. Gardens and emptied livestock barns. Portable houses. A church. It even had its own sewage and hydro-electric system too.

"It might as well have been an entire town, separate from the eye of the Corps, and ready to be filled with Runners like me.

"I couldn't believe my luck." She laughs to herself, staring at the wall before shifting her gaze to meet mine. "Because of what I found, I was able to live."

I cannot keep my jaw closed as the world turns upside down.

I feel like everything has been turned inside out. All I've known—everything I once thought I knew for certain—is no longer applicable. I've been living with a puzzle I couldn't solve for so long, but now, the parts have all changed shape. Pieces are starting to fit together.

This is it. This is the place I've been looking for, long before Asa gave me that compass, long before I met Aaron all those months ago. This is what I have been searching for, longing for, praying for—and even still, I have found more than I could have ever hoped to uncover. I have found the Unseen, and Aaron is right.

This is so much bigger than anything I've ever known.

"I found someone else eventually," Noriko says. "Cecil Logan, the man you met earlier, was the first Runner I met."

I think back to the man with the mustache and eye patch with a nod.

"He was running from a different city to the east, and we found each other in the woods nearby the compound. I told him everything I knew, and he let me take out his eye. I didn't have the skills to remove the tracker another way."

So that explains Cecil's patch, I think to myself. But what about Aaron's eye? And Viv, the woman with perfect sight?

"From there, everything just kept growing," she continues. "We even started going out and *looking* for people. Every Runner we located became an important piece of something bigger than ourselves, and it was a beautiful thing to witness. It still is."

"But I don't understand," I say. "How did you and Asa find each other again?"

"Cecil and I were on a trip to find some livestock to bring back to the compound. Turkeys, wild pigs, Chip farms we could steal from—anything. We traveled pretty far, and by coincidence or my own subconscious instinct, we reached the cabin that I had once found with Asa."

She gives me a broken smile, but her stare is quick to avert. "I missed him terribly. It was killing me." She shakes her head, staring at that knot in the table once again. "That kind of love absolutely destroys you."

I try to keep my eyes from watering when I think back to Ren and Margot, remembering the way things used to be. Before Ren changed into someone else completely. Before Margot was taken from me for good. That was some kind of love. A vital part of myself was torn away—and it destroyed me.

"I don't know why I wrote a letter to Asa, but I did." Noriko looks me in the eye again, yanking me out of my thoughts. "I wrote something only he would understand, just to see if he ever came looking for me now and then. I left it on the table and when I came back the next year, searching for Runners instead of wild turkeys—I found his response." She chuckles. "I discovered the floorboard compartment and began to write him letters, explaining everything. We've been keeping in touch ever since then."

Noriko pauses to flash me a grin. "And that's how I found out about you, Eddie. Guess you were getting a little nosy about our little healer operation."

"Really?" I blush at the thought, flattered to be important enough to mention.

"Long story short, Asa couldn't make the trip with the kids, not with Margot's condition. But he still wanted to help us—so he became a middleman for lost people. He would escort those who wanted a new life to the cabin from the city, and from there, someone on our side would debug them and take them to the compound. We wanted our place in the woods to be a refuge, and the cabin plays a major role in the process."

She sighs. "Which is why your arrival had everyone so frightened. They thought you were an undercover Officer or a Corps informant sent to stop an extremely important rendezvous."

My eyebrows arch higher. "Plan?"

"A plan to spread the truth."

"But..." I say. "I just don't understand why you're telling me all of this. I mean I'm thankful and everything, but... why trust me?"

"Because Asa and my children trusted you," Noriko replies. "And we're in desperate need of allies. People like you, who know the system and how it works. People who have been wronged by it. People who know how brutally it tears everyone apart. People who carry a fire like the very one you burn." She pauses, tone grim. "We need you on our side, Eddie."

I stare at my hands. "I don't know if I can do anything to help."

"That's what they want you to think, kiddo." Noriko's grin returns. "Aaron told me a little bit about you when he returned from the city last summer. You seem pretty solid to me."

I blush, although I don't believe it.

"Either way," Noriko says, "you've got a brain, don't you?"

"I hope so."

"And you want things to change?"

"Of course I do," I answer, almost defensively.

"Then we need you," she says, reaching out with her good hand. Her touch is warm, and I'm reminded of my own mother.

For once, I feel needed. For once I feel like maybe—just maybe—I can escape the world I left behind, for good this time. But I want to help others do the same. I'm desperate for a purpose and the flicker in this woman's eye tells me I've stumbled upon exactly what I'm looking for.

This is what I've been searching for all my life, and it took losing everything to reach it.

"But we can't take you back to the compound," Noriko says, and all the hope I regained is shattered in an instant.

"Oh." I stare at my shoes.

"Not yet, at least."

I look up again. Part of my hope is bandaged, but I'm wary of what the future may hold.

Noriko leans back in her chair, crossing her arms. "If you want us to let you live, there's something that must be done before we can take you back to the compound."

"Yeah?" I whisper, terrified of what her next sentence will be.

"We need to debug you," she says. "Tonight."

JULIA ROSEMARY TURK

REN

Friday, January 12
Day 12

We're back to square one.

Carmody and I track Eddie using the maps on our wrists, just like we did from the beginning. We hike through a layer of hardened snow the color of our uniforms. I feel like a broken tap, drained by an endless outpouring of energy.

I still haven't told Carmody about Salazar or the reality behind Eddie's disappearance. He has no idea she's been taken from us, right beneath our noses.

Every crunching step I take is possessed by an anger I struggle to place. I can't tell where Salazar's loyalties lie. She is involved in all of this somehow, but I cannot for the life of me understand what part she plays, and the lies she spun about my mother make my blood boil.

The truth doesn't make sense anymore. As impossible as it is to believe, a small part of me wonders if something really could be unfolding behind the scenes, something I have yet to realize.

I feel like I'm back in that dead farmer's pasture, smelling the eventual onslaught of a storm looming in the distance. Logic is no longer something I can lean on. The world around me feels unstable, and I know it's only a matter of time before something structurally integral unravels completely.

I think about my mother and the yearbook photo I left at home, a place that is no longer mine. I try to picture what she would look like if she were still alive. But every time I close my eyes, all I see is Margot, and it's like I lost her all over again.

My legs stumble. Carmody turns around to give me a look and I keep walking, refusing to return his questioning stare.

I shake away all thoughts of my mother. Aimless speculation will do no good. I need to focus. If I want the truth, I need to find Eddie—and Salazar.

Slowing my steps, I watch Carmody gain a lead he doesn't notice. While he walks yards ahead of me, slowly, I whisper a new command to the screen on my wrist.

"Suit," I say, hands shaking. "Show me the location of Loretta Salazar."

Patiently, I wait. I expect her blue dot to show up close to Eddie's, but to my dismay, Salazar is going in the opposite direction, back toward the city. I scramble to change the tracker back to Eddie, my heart pounding in rib-shattering convulsions.

If Salazar didn't take her, then who did?

We catch up to Eddie's dot at nightfall.

The sky is darkened by the hour, but the moon provides just enough light for us to see our surroundings clearly. Her tracker led us to yet another wooden structure out in the woods, but this one is nothing like the last.

It almost looks haunted, quiet, and somber, darkened by a rot that tells me it's been around far longer than I have. I doubt it could fit more than a bed within its four walls. When I glance down at the map on my wrist, I know this is where Eddie must be.

We walk away from the cabin to set up camp, far enough to remain safely out of the structure's sight. We don't start a fire in fear of being seen, but we set our bags down and take a seat in the snow behind a large fallen tree trunk the size of two resting cows. I lean against the log and stretch my legs out.

"So what do we do now?" Carmody reaches into his bag, pulling out the last of our jerky. He pops a handful in his mouth and chews as he speaks. "We pretty much have her cornered."

"We still need to figure out where she's going," I tell him. "If HQ learned that we came close to finding valuable intel and screwed it all up by exterminating her right away, we would never hear the end of it. Mistakes mean death in the Corps."

"Yeah, but how would they know?" Carmody swallows his bite and pops another slice of jerky in his mouth.

He has a point. We haven't reported Eddie's potential rebel connection to Headquarters yet, and if we did, they would probably dismiss the speculation anyway. I hide a frustrated sigh and close my eyes. *You have to convince him. You need to hold him off, just a little bit longer.*

"That's not the point," I argue. "Remember the plan? We figure out where she's going. She leads us to the missing Runners, we exterminate a few lost assignments, and enjoy killing her afterward."

Carmody stretches his lips into a thin, frustrated line, shifting them back and forth like he wants to say something he shouldn't.

"Wouldn't you rather be rewarded for all this trouble?" I ask. "We've already waited this long; just imagine the kind of promotion we'd receive if we took down an *entire* encampment of lost Runners."

Carmody sighs, so obviously conflicted. Sure, the idea of praise intrigues him—but killing Eddie has a firmer grip on his desire, and he's tired of waiting. It's only a matter of time before he loses interest in the Underground and lets his sadistic side outweigh his rationality.

I'm running out of time.

"You think she could have been heading for that old shack over there?" Carmody asks.

"Why would she go through so much trouble to find a place like that?" I scoff. "You really think that dump could be a camp of Runners?"

"I guess not," Carmody grumbles in annoyance, slumping lower against the log.

Convince him, I remind myself. *Convince him you want to kill her as much as he does.*

"But hey." I push through my hollowness and force an empty smirk. "This will all be over soon. And when we're done letting her lead the way —she's all yours."

"I won't kill her with Nightjade, that's for sure." Carmody chuckles, tossing the last piece of jerky into his mouth before chewing slowly. "Nightjade's too easy. Too painless. She deserves to suffer more than that."

My hands instinctively clench into fists, but I uncurl them just as quickly, loosening my jaw and shoulders for the sake of the act. It takes all I have not to beat him to a bloody pulp.

But I have to keep my cool. I have to remain calm, and worst of all, I have to play along, at least while I come up with some sort of plan. I need to figure out how to rid myself of this pest.

"Yeah," I say, drawing patterns in the snow to busy my hands. "She does."

He shakes his head, staring at the scabrous trunk of a nearby pine. "I just hate all this damn waiting around."

Distract him, I tell myself.

"How are you gonna do it?" I force the words out like a belch. "You know, when it's time?"

Carmody turns to face me, lips curled. "Oh, there's plenty I want to do." He chuckles, staring straight ahead as he imagines things I don't want to picture. "I'll start with the eyes. A little sand, maybe."

"Good idea."

I brace myself for whatever horrors he'll speak of next, watching as Carmody pours the remaining crumbs into his mouth before tossing the plastic bag to the side. "We're all out of jerky."

An idea pops into my head.

"Go find something then," I suggest. "A deer or a rabbit or something."

"Gross."

I raise a brow, challenging his ego with an amused laugh. "You do know how to hunt, right?"

"Yeah." Carmody scoffs, face red. "Of course I do."

"Then it shouldn't be a problem."

"Why can't you do it?"

"Why can't you take orders?"

He grumbles a few profanities before rising to his feet, bending over to pull a white Corps-issued blade from his backpack. He gives me the finger before walking away. I watch him weave between trees until he vanishes out of sight.

He'll be gone for a long time, I think to myself. He has no idea how to hunt—and his pride won't let him return unsuccessfully.

Using the map on my wrist, I wait until Carmody's far enough before walking to the new cabin, hiding behind a distant rock to analyze the scene. I check the map again, but this time, I look for Eddie's dot. Sure enough, it's as I suspected—she's inside.

I think about her while I watch the rotting shack. I think about how innocent she looked in the snow, hushed to slumber by the cruel lullaby of a whistling blizzard. She looked too unknowing to be true, like she grew up in a bubble, sheltered and uncorrupt.

My throat tightens. How could a person so seemingly innocent leave so much death in their wake? How could a girl I once trusted more than anyone cause the death of her entire family?

There has to be more to what happened on the night of the draw. If there's more to the ghost stories about the people in the woods, there has to be more to Eddie's story too.

Because no matter how hard I tried to convince myself to believe the evidence, the Eddie of my yesterdays would never leave her family behind. She was the most loyal person I knew, and even in the end, as Margot pushed her away, Eddie still fought to stay by her side.

I close my eyes. *Please*, I beg to no one. *Let there be more to that night. Let there be truth to the innocence I saw in the snow.*

The cabin door opens, pulling me down to earth.

My heart does cartwheels when I see her, dressed in a dark rust puffer jacket that must be twice her size, practically draping over the spare clothes I'd given her at the first cabin. My only warm sweater, my favorite pair of jeans, my last clean pair of socks. It's strange to see her so full of life after spending so many hours wondering if she would ever wake up.

But she's not alone.

By her side is a tall young man who wears a pair of wire glasses and a black long sweater, the fabric too thin for someone who isn't used to this weather. His face is unshaven, giving him the illusion of age, but I know he can't be much older than I am. A few strands of hair fall in front of his forehead, almost concealing the jagged scar that cuts through his left eye. I notice a sheathed hunting knife attached to his belt and grind my teeth together. *This is the person who took her.*

I watch from afar as he and Eddie walk into the woods, turning their backs to the cabin and exiting my view. I make sure to stay close behind, watching them meticulously while maintaining a safe distance, hiding behind thick tree trunks and fallen logs to stay as unseen as possible. But what I witness puzzles me.

Eddie doesn't seem to be in much distress, and neither does he. I notice she has a matching sheath on her belt, holding the knife she's carried with her all along. If she were in a hostage situation, why would they leave her with her weapon, let alone provide her with a way to carry it?

At first, the only words exchanged are complaints from Eddie about the snow and her shoes and the boy's dry remarks. But as the minutes melt together, they start to converse with a strange kind of calmness that makes me uneasy. I still have no idea who this guy is, or what he could possibly be doing with her.

"Why don't you trust me?" Eddie asks out of the blue, looking up at the stranger while they walk. "You have *multiple* higher-ups who trust me."

Higher-ups? I think, crouching behind a shrub.

The stranger shrugs.

"Do you really think I'm some Chaser informant sent to spy on a few campers in the woods?"

"I like the spy theory," he says, and I can't tell if he's being serious or not. "But you're wrong about that last part, pal. We're more than a handful of campers, you know."

Eddie jabs her elbow into his arm. "What did I tell you about *pal?*"

"Sorry," he says. She gives him a look and he rolls his eyes with a sigh.

"My sincerest apologies, Your Darkness."

"Thank you." Eddie beams. It's quiet for a moment until she speaks again. "Hey—if you really think I'm a spy, you wouldn't have said that just now. About your numbers."

What numbers? My eyebrows pinch together. I move behind a rock this time, catching up to continue my eavesdropping.

"Does it matter?" the stranger responds. "If you were a decent spy, you'd already know about our numbers."

Eddie nods. "Good point."

I stop in my tracks, pressing my back against a large trunk and running a hand through my hair. My heart races a thousand miles a minute, my mind buzzing with questions. There is no doubt that these two know each other—their joking proves it. But what could this possibly mean? *Is he one of the Runners in the woods?*

Quietly, I crouch down, running to hide behind another bush. I need to figure out who this person is—and how they know each other.

"Okay, but what if I was a bad spy?" Eddie asks.

"If you were a bad spy we wouldn't be talking right now because I'd be able to escape. Find some peace and quiet in a tree or something."

Eddie grins. "So you think I'm a *good* spy?"

"No, I think you're absurd."

"I'll take that as a compliment."

"Please don't."

There's a pause. "In all seriousness," Eddie finally says, staring down at her shoes before looking up at him again. "You... trust me, right?"

It's quiet again as they continue to walk. The stranger puts his hands in his pockets and keeps his gaze fixed straight ahead. "Command must think you're pretty special if they want you to come back to the compound."

Eddie gives him a small grin, and I halt completely. The blood in my veins stops coursing, and everything suddenly feels so cold.

Compound?

All this time, I doubted the rumors. I couldn't bring myself to believe the word *Undergrounder* was anything more than a term used to label disjointed smugglers and lawbreakers. I never expected the Undergrounders to be unified enough to run an entire compound of people out here in the woods.

This guy must be an Undergrounder. That's the only explanation I have.

"Why do we have to come all the way out here?" Eddie asks after a while, pulling me out of my thoughts as I hurry to catch up.

"An alert will go out once you've been debugged, and your status in the Corps database will switch to *dead*, right?" the stranger explains.

"Right..."

"So if a bunch of people are *dying* in one location, don't you think it would be seen as a little odd?"

Eddie shrugs. "I guess."

"They'd send a few Officers to investigate the location, maybe even a few Agents. And bam. Compound exposed. A hundred missing Runners and their children will die."

"*A hundred*?" Eddie gawks in awe at the number, and so do I.

The young man laughs. "And that's rounding down."

My heart pounds against my chest because this is exactly the kind of information I've been looking for all along.

The realization settles within me like a sinking stone. If I wanted to, I could call Headquarters right now and let them know just what's lurking in the woods. This tip alone would be grounds for a promotion, with or without any action on my part. I could forget all about this whole ordeal and walk away with clean hands.

But I couldn't care less about the mission anymore. I don't care about gathering intel for the Corps or even exterminating Eddie. The only thing I can think about is saving her from whatever fate these strangers have paved out for her, because something about this situation doesn't sit right with me—and I would rather face a lifetime of unanswered questions than a lifetime without Eddie.

There is no one else I hate like her. But there is no one else I need like her either.

I need to figure out what's really going on so I can come up with a plan. All I can do for now is listen.

"Don't act so surprised," the stranger tells Eddie.

"And how do you guys even know so much about the Corps?" she asks. "I mean, even I never knew anything about divisions and trackers."

"Double Agents. Strategists and analysts at the compound too," he answers simply. "You actually interrupted a very important rendezvous with one of our Doubles today."

"With your sister?" Eddie asks.

I'm taken aback when the boy stops dead in his tracks, glaring. "Where did you hear that?"

I trace the compartment that holds my Nightjade gun, ready to pull it out in an instant.

"From you," Eddie says, and they keep walking. "You weren't very quiet when you were all talking in the cabin. You know, when you *locked me out in the snow.*"

"And you were what, gardening?"

But Eddie doesn't get the joke. Her exposure to Yesterday literature was limited to only what she could find in our house, and I don't think I ever saw her with anything but those botanical encyclopedias. Unlike this Undergrounder and me, she's never read anything about eavesdropping hobbits.

Eddie scrunches her nose. "I don't get it."

"Of course you don't." The stranger sighs, shaking his head. "You Chips are really uncultured."

"Don't call me Chip."

"Sure thing, Samwise."

"That's not my name." Eddie stops walking, folding her arms. "And speaking of names, I know *Cedar* isn't yours."

"No one told you?"

"That's confidential."

"Right," he snaps, pointing an index finger in her direction. "You're a spy."

"I'm serious, though," Eddie says, lowering her voice. "I want to know your full name and I want to hear it from you. Middle name and all. Trust should go both ways if we're going to do this, don't you think?"

He frowns, and Eddie gives him a broken smile.

What is she talking about? I think to myself, head low as I carefully move from the shelter of my current bush to that of a log. *What could they possibly be planning to accomplish all the way out here?*

"Here. I'll go first." Eddie clears her throat and holds out her hand, speaking with faux sophistication. "Lavender Adele Voclain." She raises a brow. "And you are?"

He studies her for a long moment, debating whether or not to play along. Eventually, he lets out a sigh, pulling out his hand to accept Eddie's invitation like they're greeting each other for the first time.

"The name's Aaron Lark Kabir," he says, joining Eddie's formal act with his chin raised high. He drops the voice before shoving his hand back into his pocket, lips curled at the corners. "It's very nice to meet you again, Voclain."

They continue to walk in silence for a while. I follow close behind, careful not to snap any twigs and give away my cover. The air is so cold and dark, so eerily quiet. Out here, this late, there is nothing but the sound of footsteps crunching in the snow.

"You mentioned trust," the Undergrounder—Aaron—says, keeping his gaze fixed straight ahead. "Whether you follow through with this or not, I don't see the point in keeping secrets anymore."

For a moment Eddie beams, but the excitement is quick to fade. When she looks down at her shoes, I realize what he means.

They're walking all the way out here for a reason. Maybe Eddie has to perform some sort of task, some Underground ritual to prove she's worth joining their ranks—and something about Aaron's words leads me to believe failure isn't an option.

My whole body trembles. If she doesn't follow through, what will they do to her?

Aaron looks at Eddie for a moment before staring at his shoes too. "There's something I need to tell you, because... I don't know. You might be able to help."

Eddie nods softly. "Alright."

"Back in the cabin..." He bites his lip like the words are hard to say before letting out a sigh. "I was supposed to meet with my sister."

Eddie stares at her boots. "But I was in your meeting spot."

Aaron nods, shoulders tense. He pushes his hands deeper inside his pockets. "She either saw you and got scared away or"—he chokes on the words—"or something happened to her."

"I didn't see anyone," Eddie mutters. "I'm really sorry."

"It's okay." The Undergrounder shrugs, but I can tell he's more worried than he lets on. "Either way, it's not your fault."

It's silent again until Eddie looks up at Aaron, giving him a half-hearted but comforting smile. "What's her name?"

His lips twitch, like he's trying to smile but can't. "Loretta Salazar."

I stumble over a root, twigs snapping like fractured bones. Eddie and Aaron stop dead in their tracks. Eddie's hand falls to her sheath. "What was that?"

Aaron already holds a knife. "I don't know."

I duck behind the shelter of a frozen blackberry bush, peering through the cracks. Aaron spins around, scouring his surroundings. He stares right at the bramble I hid behind before sheathing his knife. They keep walking.

I can barely breathe. A chill prickles the base of my neck, slithering down my spine and coating my arms in goosebumps. Even beneath the warmth of my suit, I shiver.

This is the brother Salazar was looking for at the cabin, the one she thought I'd hurt.

Salazar is the Double Agent the Corps was looking for.

As I think back to the cabin, guilt pinches my gut, pulling and tugging until I feel like I'm going to be sick. She was just as scared as I was, just as desperate. And I had the audacity to pull out my gun, while she only did so for defense.

But something else overrides the guilt, an unshakable gnawing in my center that aches unlike anything I've felt before.

If Salazar really was telling the truth about Eddie, then what about all the things she said about my mother?

Sweating, I shake the thoughts out of my head. I can't think about these things right now. *Focus*, I tell myself, catching up to Aaron and Eddie. I crouch behind a mossy stone.

"Loretta Salazar," Eddie repeats. "How old is she?"

"She's a year younger than me."

"So?"

"Eighteen."

Eddie smiles. "So my age, then."

Aaron nods.

"Half-sister?" she questions, pointing out their different surnames, and in the moonlight, I can see the Undergrounder shake his head no.

"My dad heard about the compound when I was really young," Aaron explains. "Told my mom that we should make the move out here, but she thought he was crazy. So he left without us. Said he'd come back and rescue me one day. He had no idea she was pregnant with my sister."

"Oh wow."

"Yeah." Aaron chuckles, almost bitterly. "My mom had Lori take her own last name. Guess she didn't want her to have any ties to my dad. It was safer that way."

"Makes sense."

"And that was that for a while." Aaron stares straight ahead. "I didn't remember much about my father when I was little. He was pretty much a stranger to me."

"I'm sorry to hear you never knew him," Eddie says. Her words are surprisingly gentle. "That must have been rough."

Aaron glares. "Maybe I wasn't finished with my story yet."

Eddie rolls her eyes. "Sorry."

"After my fifth birthday, he came in the middle of the night to debug me. Carried me screaming and crying to the compound." He comes to a halt, removing his glasses to reveal the rough scar that runs through his left eye. The eye is a cloudy white, and from the looks of it, probably blind.

"I wouldn't stop struggling while he did it. And my father was new to the art of debugging, so his technique was pretty rough." Aaron chuckles, putting his glasses back on. "I paid for it."

My hands tremble as I remember everything that Carmody said the other night by the fire. What I once thought was nothing more than an exaggerated urban legend now sounds far too close to Aaron's story to be a coincidence.

The kidnapping, the scarred eye, this *debugging* process Aaron speaks about—could this be the child from Port Keys? The one who was taken away and allegedly *dismembered*?

I feel like I've swallowed a handful of rocks. I can't help but wonder how many unexplained disappearances can be tied back to these people in the woods.

"That must have been..." Eddie begins, but her voice trails off as she tries to find the right words.

"Terrifying?"

"Yeah."

"It was. But, I would have done the same thing if I were him." Aaron leans against a tree with his hands in his pockets, looking up at the sky. "It's safer out here." He shifts his gaze back to Eddie. "Better out here."

Eddie stares at the canopy of leaves above her head. "I believe it."

"He's a good man, my father. Though a little anesthesia couldn't have hurt," Aaron says with a fleeting grin. "But now it's my mother I barely know."

Eddie leans against her own tree across from him. "I'm sorry."

The Undergrounder nods in thanks, and neither of them says anything for a few moments until Eddie reignites the conversation. "So how did you reconnect with your sister?"

"I was depressed without her," Aaron explains as the two of them start walking again. "Wouldn't sleep, wouldn't eat. She was my best friend, you know?"

Eddie nods sadly, staring down at her feet.

"So my father sent one of our middlemen to check up on Lori and my mother every once in a while. He eventually arranged visits for me and even delivered letters every now and then. It wasn't much, but it was something."

It's quiet again, and all I can hear is the crisp hum of frozen footsteps. A coyote laments in the distance.

"You know," Eddie says, looking up at Aaron, "your mom showed me photos of you as a kid. Back when I first met her."

Aaron's eyes widen. "What?"

"Nothing embarrassing. Don't worry." Eddie chuckles. "But I think she looks at them a lot. She has a whole photo album and everything.

"Huh." Aaron suppresses a grin in the dark. "I had no idea."

It's silent for the rest of the walk until they come to a pause. I duck behind the safety of a large boulder blanketed in snow and dead moss, peeking my head out to watch.

Aaron stops walking, letting his leather satchel fall to the snow. "This seems like a spot."

"Alright," Eddie mutters.

Immediately, I can tell the atmosphere has changed. Everything is solemn and gloomy, thick with an unsettling sort of anticipation I can feel in my bones.

"I don't like you very much and I know you're not very fond of me either." Aaron walks closer to Eddie, placing his hand on her shoulders. "But I'm still human, and I don't like seeing people suffer."

She nods, refusing to look him in the eye. What could she possibly be so afraid of?

"This is going to be uncomfortable for the both of us, but it'll hurt you more than it'll hurt me. Debugging isn't a painless process."

She nods again, staring at his scar.

I shudder at the thought of Aaron's story, clenching and uncurling my fists. *What is he going to do to her eye?*

Aaron bends over to rummage through his satchel for a moment until he pauses, feeling Eddie's eyes on him. He stands back up again. "You look worried."

"Of course I'm worried."

"My dad spent *years* developing a way to extract the chip without taking out the entire eye," Aaron explains. "Trust me, it's a lot safer than you'd think. You're lucky we're not in a hurry right now so I can perform the surgery instead of just removing the whole thing altogether."

Eddie glares. "That doesn't make me feel any better."

My stare widens. The word *debugging* plays over and over again in my mind until I realize what it must mean.

This Undergrounder knows about the trackers. He knows where they are too—and he's going to cut Eddie's right out of her eye.

My heart races. Does this guy really know what he's doing? How can a wood-dwelling rebel possibly be educated enough to know how to perform a surgery like this without consequence—and how can Eddie trust him to operate on her?

How can *I* trust him?

"Look. I still have the anesthetics we stole from your—" Aaron cuts himself off for a moment before continuing. "If it'll make you feel better, I can knock you out for a bit if you want, but it's the riskier option. Since you Chips aren't exactly exposed to doctors, we don't know how your body will react to general anesthesia. It's also pretty unnatural, if you care about that sort of thing."

Eddie pauses, thinking about it for a moment. "I don't want to use my dad's anesthetics."

"Are you sure?" Aaron looks at her with wide eyes, surprised.

"I want to be awake," Eddie insists.

"You might end up passing out from the pain anyway, depending on your tolerance. It's—quite shocking. And horrible, if I forgot to mention that little detail."

"That's very comforting to hear."

He frowns, folding his arms. "You wanted honesty, remember?"

She looks at a tree behind him. "I do."

It's quiet for a moment until Aaron sighs, shoving his hands in his pockets again. "Are you sure you want to do this?"

"I don't really have another choice, do I?" Eddie chuckles, but it doesn't mask her fear as well as she thought it would.

"You *do* have a choice," Aaron argues. "I won't force you to make this decision."

"I know." Eddie's voice is even softer now.

"You might want to lie down against that log right there," the stranger says, pointing to a fallen tree.

It's about the height of a house cat and stretches a few yards in either direction. Eddie walks over to the center. I watch as Aaron takes off his black sweater and lays it down on the ground near her feet. He seems comfortable in just a plain white tee, despite the cold. He offers a helping hand as she takes a seat on the sweater and leans against the log, but she doesn't take it.

A shrill rip echoes through the trees as Aaron tears off a small piece of his shirt. He rolls it into a cylinder, offering it to Eddie. "You're gonna need something to bite down on."

"I'm not putting your shirt in my mouth."

"We do laundry at the compound you know," Aaron says, unamused. "I'm probably cleaner than you are right now."

"I don't buy it."

"Would you rather lose your tongue?" he snaps.

Eddie takes the cylinder, shoving the fabric into her mouth without another complaint.

"Hold my hand if you need to. Don't want you biting off your tongue or anything." Aaron kneels in the snow beside her. He takes something out of his pocket, but it's too dark for me to see what it is. "Though you might be better off without it."

"Thanks." Eddie's voice is muffled by the fabric. "Jeez, how many knives do you *have*?"

"Okay, maybe I like to whittle and maybe I carry a surgical blade with me everywhere I go. But I don't see anything wrong with that."

Aaron takes the object—a surgical blade, I assume—and holds it between his teeth. I watch as he reaches into his satchel, pulling out supplies I don't recognize. When he's done, he stares at Eddie again, lowering his voice. "Are you sure you want to do this?"

"Again, I don't have much of a choice." Eddie gives him a smile, but I can tell it's all pretend. She's terrified right now.

I can't imagine how alone she must feel.

"That's a lie," Aaron says. "You always have a choice."

"*Every choice I had was taken from me,*" Eddie snaps, spitting out the fabric. "You think I wanted to Run? You think I wanted to leave my family behind after I saw what those Chasers did to them? You think I *chose* to survive? To get taken to that cabin and then dragged all the way out here?" Her voice cracks. "I thought I was going to die out there in the snow. I came to terms with it. Hell, giving up felt like the only real choice I've made in a really, *really* long time."

Her words feel like a knife to the chest. *What is she talking about?*

I thought I knew what happened that night. She Ran, and her family was killed because of it. Everyone knows about the Runner penalty.

Unless there truly is more to that night, and I've had it all backwards this entire time.

"The moment we're born into this world, every choice is taken away from us. We're told who we are and what we can and can't be until we no longer know what it means to be human at all. Sometimes the only way to survive is to play along." Eddie lowers her voice. "So I don't have a choice, Aaron. It's either this or death."

"Exactly," Aaron says, and Eddie shoots him a puzzled glare. "You always have a choice, Voclain. Even if you're making a choice to avoid the consequence that comes, it's still a choice. Yeah, certain things can take away our ability to make choices without consequences. And yeah, sometimes that can make you feel trapped.

"But I'm giving you the knife, Eddie," Aaron states, holding up the tool so she can see it. "And you're gonna choose when you want to give it to me."

He extends his hand, offering her the blade.

Eddie takes it gingerly, turning it over in her hands to study it closely. I can barely make out its shape in the dark, but I can tell that it's a small surgical knife, no larger than her palm. She studies it like it's familiar, as though it means something to her.

Aaron's tone turns grim. "You know what will happen if we don't debug you, right?"

"I know," Eddie mutters, keeping her gaze fixed on the surgical blade.

"You know too much now. The Command will order your execution, and I'll probably be the one to carry it out," Aaron says, swallowing some lump in his throat. "But that doesn't need to happen."

"I know."

Execution? The word is haunting, like the call of a bell. *I can't afford to panic right now*, I think to myself.

I won't let it escalate to that.

"Playing along isn't the only way to survive, you know." Aaron leans his back against the log, stretching out his legs. He stares at the sky for a moment before finding Eddie's face again.

"How so?" she whispers.

"You can choose to play your own game," he says. "You don't have to play by their rules. Even if it feels like you're playing all by yourself."

Something about his words makes Eddie's lips curl, almost mischievously. The more I watch these two interact, the less it feels like she needs to be saved.

But I have to intervene, I remind myself. I have no idea how this operation is going to go, or how much this guy can be trusted. I can't just sit back and watch someone hurt her—not again.

"What are you gonna choose?" Aaron sits upright on top of the log, leaning over with his arms resting against his knees. He laces his fingers together loosely. "Comfort or pain?"

I inch closer, shrouded by the bushes and trees that flank the boulder, desperate to hear every word.

Eddie thinks about her answer. "Pain."

"Life or death?"

"Life."

"Your game, or theirs?"

"*Mine.*"

"So what do you say, Lone Player?" Aaron's grin is crooked. "Are you ready?"

My heart beats faster. I listen closely for her reply.

But Eddie doesn't say a word. Instead, she places the knife back in Aaron's hands.

"You'll be okay," he says.

He offers her a hand to squeeze, and this time she takes it. She puts the fabric back in her mouth. And before I realize what's happening, the air is cut with a bone-chilling scream.

It curdles both blood and marrow, echoing throughout the woods and shattering all silence. Coyotes howl somewhere in the distance, and a flock of birds scatters from their roosts in the trees. The very forest itself seems to be crying right by Eddie's side—and for some reason, I am crying too.

I can't look. I hide behind the rock because I'm too weak to watch him cut her. Once again, I let her get hurt. I'm still behind that slide, still too frightened by the idea of making things worse to intervene.

It feels like I'm letting Carmody attack her all over again. As Eddie screams, I can see him on that playground. I can see the malice in his eyes.

I'm stilled by the sound. I'm too frozen to do anything but bury my head in my hands and weep. I weep for the person I used to be, for the person Eddie used to be, for the girl I'd forgotten about and learned to care for and forgot about all over again.

I cry for all we once were and the things we will be because of it. Because how can you unlearn hate? Is it even possible to go back to the way things were?

Deep down, I know the answer. There is no going back. There is no magic clock to turn, no high-tech button to press, no dream to wake up from. There's only here and now and tomorrow.

And even if she wants me to stay in her yesterdays, Eddie is the only tomorrow I have left. I have to do something to keep her alive.

But I'm too late. She's screamed herself unconscious. Everything is a deadly kind of silent, a chill that makes me forget about the cold. The forest has gone quiet again. I look beyond the rock to see that Eddie's body has gone limp. As Aaron continues the operation, she is completely still.

I need to get closer, I tell myself. *Just a bit closer.*

I move an inch—and I trigger the alarm.

In any other place, the beeping would be quiet. But in this vast expanse of wood and silence, it echoes, spinning through the trees like a dozen boomerangs that won't come back.

Frantic, I crouch behind a nearby bush, trying to disable the alarm. To my surprise, it wasn't my close proximity that triggered it.

The notification on my wrist tells me that Lavender Voclain is deceased.

Aaron stops what he's doing. He whips his head around and scrambles to his feet, now holding a second knife that looks a lot larger than the small surgical blade he'd been using a moment before.

"Hello?" He shouts. I duck lower behind the bush, covering my head with my hands.

I wait. Every second lasts an hour, and when it all goes quiet again, I lift my head up, expecting the coast to be clear.

But he's standing right above me.

Aaron grabs the collar of the undershirt beneath my suit, yanking me to my feet. In a blink, he pins me to the wall of the boulder, one hand holding my hair—and the other holding a knife to my throat. "Tell me one reason why I shouldn't kill you right now."

I reach for my Nightjade gun compartment, but he knees my fingers against the rock. "Watch it, pal," he says through gritted teeth. "Now tell me. Who are you, and why are you here?"

"I'm here for Eddie," I seethe, jaw tight.

"No shit."

"You don't understand. I—I know her. She's my..." My voice trails off. I can't find the right words to finish the sentence.

"Your target, yeah. Like hell I'm letting you exterminate her on my watch," he spits. "Now give me an answer before I *slit your goddamn throat.*"

"*Exterminate her?*" I push him off. He stumbles back, but he's quick to his feet.

"Don't act so surprised," he scoffs, pressing a finger against my armored chest. "You're the Chaser here, not me."

I ignore Aaron and push my way past him, jogging over to Eddie's motionless body. I command my suit to remove the gloves and place two fingers against her neck. A sigh of relief escapes my lips when I find a pulse, and I order the armor around my hand to return. *She's alright*, I conclude. It's just as I thought; her tracker was destroyed

"What the hell are you doing?" Aaron calls out, following me over to Eddie.

"Checking for a pulse." I don't bother to look up at him as he approaches. I keep my eyes fixed on Eddie, scanning her for any sign of movement. But she remains perfectly still, fast asleep in the snow once again.

"What, so you can make sure the job gets done if she's still breathing?" Aaron scoffs.

I stand up, whipping my head around to look him dead in the eye.

"You're the one who did this to her, not me. You're the one who should be explaining yourself."

"*Me?*" He laughs bitterly. "I'm not the one wearing white here, pal."

"I would never hurt her," I snap, but it doesn't come out as confidently as I want it to. *I already have.*

"Look, I'm done shitting around here." Before I can back away, Aaron yanks me by the collar, holding the knife to my throat once again. "Who are you, and why are you here?"

I can't give him an answer.

"I'm not asking again."

"My name is Ren," I say, trying to calm myself down. I know I could pull out my gun if I tried hard enough, but I can't afford a fight right now. I need answers, and I don't know how this guy would retaliate to an escalation like that. Judging by the way he holds a knife, he has far more experience than I do, even with my training.

But to my surprise, something in Aaron's face loosens. His brows curve downward in confusion. "What did you just say?"

"My name is Ren," I repeat. "Ren McLellan."

His expression hardens. "You're lying."

"*I'm not lying, okay?*" I hold my hands up defensively, annoyed by his refusal to accept the truth.

"No." Aaron shakes his head in disbelief. "There's no way you're Noriko's kid. Her Ren would never be one of *them*. Not in a million years."

The solid ground I'm standing on finally crumbles to dust.

Was Salazar telling the truth after all?

"You know my"—I choke on the words like I'm spitting out a brick— "my mom?"

For a moment, Aaron's gaze softens. His anger is replaced by a puzzled expression.

"You gotta believe me, man." My voice cracks. I know I'm not myself anymore, but I don't know how to convince this guy that my name is still my own.

"I think you're a liar," Aaron says, the frustration returning. "Why should I believe anyone in a uniform?"

I don't have an answer to give.

I don't know how to persuade him that I'm *good*, because I'm not. I stopped being one of the good guys a long time ago. I fell away from that part of me the moment I first picked up that Nightjade syringe.

And then, something pops into my head—and I think I know how to get Aaron to believe me.

"I know about Lori," I blurt out.

Shock drains the color from Aaron's expression, but instead of removing the knife, he presses it even deeper into my skin. The blade stings, and I know my next wrong word will truly be my last.

"I swear, if you did something to her I will *kill you*. Slowly. Do you understand?" He pushes me against a tree, and I let him. "*Do you understand?*"

"I never laid a hand on Lori."

"*Then where is she?*"

"I don't know. I was looking for Eddie and I found her in the cabin, okay?" I confess, hoping the ring of truth around my words will calm him down.

It doesn't. He grips my collar even tighter.

"At first she thought I did something to her brother, and I'm guessing that's you," I explain. "But she believed me when I said I was only looking for Eddie. And she told me something."

His nostrils flare. "What did she tell you?"

"That my mother is alive. That she needs me by her side." My voice wavers as I recall Salazar's words. I still don't want to believe them. "She also left a message. For you, just in case we crossed paths."

His eyes widen, hands trembling. "What?"

I nod. "She told me to tell you that she's doing it herself. She said you'd know what that means."

Aaron doesn't say a word. The anger has left his glare, but his brows remain furrowed. Reluctantly, he removes the knife from my throat and steps back. I rub my hands around my neck, trying to soothe the stinging.

"You really want me to believe you?" he asks after a moment. The intensity in his tone has decreased, and if I didn't know any better, he would almost seem calm.

"Yes."

"You really want to help Eddie?"

"Of course I do."

There's a pause. "Then your loyalties change today," Aaron says grimly. "Right here, right now."

I pause, unsure of what he means. I agree because I feel like I must. "Alright..."

"You are no longer an Officer. You're no longer a member of the Corps. From this day forward, you'll quit their game and play alone." He nods at my uniform. "Starting with *that*."

I shoot him a questioning look. Reluctantly, I unsuit, leaving myself in the dark green tee and jeans I mindlessly packed before Carmody and I left home so long ago. I'm thankful I left my black Chaser underclothes in the bags I made Carmody carry, because I don't want to wear anything that belongs to the Corps. *Never again.*

"Your suits have a self-destruct function, don't they?" Aaron asks, and I nod, remembering my training.

Self-destruction. It's a way to complete your own execution, create a minor blast, and protect the secrets of the Corps at the same time.

"You can't leak vital information if you're dead," Pittman had once said. *"And might as well take an enemy out with you."*

The Undergrounder gives me a look, and I know what he wants me to do. I hesitate for a moment before taking the cube and walking several yards away, setting it down in the snow. I place my palm on the side, letting it scan my handprint. Only I can be the one to initiate its self-destruction. I jog back to where Aaron stands.

"Suit," I call when I'm far enough. "Take me."

In an instant, the cube combusts in an orange glow the size of the boulder I hid behind earlier. We plug our ears and squeeze our eyes shut, dropping low to the ground. Ages pass before we open them again.

A serpent of smoke slips into the sky. The suit is nothing but a pile of scraps and a juvenile flame. Aaron runs over to stomp out the fire before it has a chance to grow. I stand in my place and wait for him to return.

"Now do you trust me?" I ask when he does, folding my arms.

"Of course not." He mirrors the gesture before nodding to the smoldering remains of my uniform. "You can just say that and take out a Chaser suit?"

I shake my head no. "It's fingerprint protected."

He nods, and we stand there in silence. He glares at me for a long time before letting out a sigh. "So..."

"So." I stare at my feet.

"You're Noriko's kid?"

I nod, and Aaron nods too. His eyes flash with a burst of sad remembrance, and he opens his mouth as if to apologize, but decides against it. He clears his throat and straightens his posture. "So, Ren. You really wanna join our side?"

I glance at Eddie's motionless body before looking at Aaron again. "I do."

I don't know much about the Undergrounders, and I don't know which side has the answer. I only know that I need to go where Eddie goes because I can't let her Run on her own again. *I can't be alone again.*

I stare at Eddie again as she lies there in the snow, her head resting against the log like a pillow. Beneath the moonlight, she looks like an illusion. I almost wonder if she's really here.

All this time, I thought I was protecting Eddie. But right now, as I stand here in the snow with this stranger, the truth is clearer than ever.

Eddie doesn't need me. She never has.

But I need her.

I can't hide behind slides and rocks anymore. I have to make a choice, and I need to make it now.

I meet Aaron's gaze. "What now?"

"Now?" He smirks. "We test that loyalty of yours."

"Anything," I respond, desperate not to lose her again.

"I need to cut something out of your eye."

The thought of a blade going anywhere near my eye makes me shudder. No wonder Eddie went unconscious. She must have passed out from the pain, and the idea of her suffering cuts me deeper than any knife could.

But I can't be afraid anymore.

And I need to meet my mother, because I've missed her more than I let myself believe.

"Okay," I say. I take a deep breath and walk closer to the stranger with the knife. "Cut me."

And in a single moment, the world burns.

EDDIE

Saturday, January 13
Day 13

♪ BLACK CREME - HRVRD ♪

I wake up to a world on fire.

The stench of rubbing alcohol that fills my lungs. The light shining in my eyes, so bright it's almost blinding. The hollow pit of nothingness in my stomach, the bark-like dryness of parched lips, the pounding ache in my skull. All of it burns as my senses come back to life.

My head feels like it's been stuffed full of cotton. The world is blurry until I blink it clear, absorbing my surroundings. From what I've seen in history textbooks and the occasional Yesterday film, it looks like a cheap hospital room, with cream walls and gray carpet for a floor. I'm greeted with unfriendly beeps and LED lights that worsen the throbbing behind my left eye, and it takes me a moment to realize how much pain I'm in.

I angle my chin downward to study my freshly bandaged injuries. The wound in my arm has healed better than I expected over these last couple of weeks, no longer anything but an itch, and I can barely feel the inflammation of my right palm's burn.

But nothing is healed completely. Although my eye hurts the worst, my entire body is a tangle of deep aches and sharp pangs.

I notice that something soft keeps my left eye shut, a bandage of some sort. Everything that happened last night floods back to me in an instant. I remember Aaron, the knife, and the fire in my eye before everything went black. My hand flies to the new bandage to make sure my eye is still there. The pressure of my touch hurts enough to tell me all I need to know.

"She's awake." I hear a voice, and I turn my head to the left to see Aaron sitting in a chair next to the bed where I lie.

He wears jeans and a dark blue knit sweater. His hair has been partially combed back, but with little effort, as it is still the same criss-cross mess it always seems to be.

"She is?" I reply to his statement, groggily pulling myself upright. Blood rushes to my head and the room spins enough to make me motion sick.

He raises a brow. "Is she?"

"I don't know. Doesn't feel like it," I tease, eager to distract myself from the gnawing migraine that chisels away at my skull. "Wait." I touch my eye's bandage once again. "Am I..."

"Yes," Aaron says. "You are quite hideous now." I frown, and he rolls his eyes. "Yes. You're debugged."

"Oh," I reply, unable to say much more. I have mixed feelings about my survival. "Did I..."

"You did not lose your eye." Aaron gives me a small but reassuring smile. "I was able to remove the tracker without damaging the organ. They're both present and accounted for."

I nod, and regret the action instantly. My head is buzzing like a swarm of bees.

"Your sight will be completely fine, by the way— as long as you keep your left eye protected with that bandage. Unless you somehow manage to injure yourself before the incision fully heals, you have nothing to worry about. Your vision will be as good as new." He leans back in his chair, hands on the back of his head. "And I'm an excellent surgeon, so, do with that information what you will."

"Whatever." I shake my head before my right eye widens. "Aaron?"

"Yeah?"

I pause. "Where are we?"

"We're home." With a crooked grin, he stretches his arms out wide before letting them fall into his lap. "This is the Cut."

My nose crinkles. "The Cut?"

"The compound. Camp. Home base. HQ. My secret lair—"

"Okay, I get it." I interrupt him. "But... why *the Cut*?"

"That's what we call this place," he says. "We've been communicating with a few sister compounds up north, but we're the only base like this for miles. The largest on the west coast too."

He pulls a deck of playing cards out of his pocket. I recoil instantly, like they'll hurt me if I get too close. I scoot as far away from the objects as possible, pressing my back against the headboard, heart pounding.

"Hey, hey. It's okay. They're just pieces of paper. They don't bite." Aaron holds up the deck for me to see. "Have you ever played a game of cards?"

I relax my shoulders. "No."

"Right—of course you haven't," he mutters, remembering that it's illegal to own a deck of cards where I come from. Only the Presidency has access to such sacred symbols.

"You see this?" He splits the deck in two before shuffling the cards. "How I had to cut the deck in order to shuffle it?"

"Yeah?"

The cards arch before falling back in place with a hiss. "And how it all comes back together after?"

I nod. He doesn't start a game, but he keeps the cards in his hands, cutting and shuffling over and over again, fidgeting like he might as well be whittling wood. Watching the shuffling of the deck is calming to me for a reason I can't pinpoint.

"There's this thing people like to say around here—that this place will cut the people in two. Like the deck." Now, he places the cards back in their box. "Good battles evil, truth battles deceit, knowledge battles the unknown, you get the gist. We've created a distinct split with two clear sides."

"Makes sense."

"But we won't be cut forever. They tell us that too." He puts the box away before leaning forward again. "How are you feeling?"

"Fantastic."

"Good." His wit falls away and he asks the next question more softly. "Really, how's the pain?"

"Excruciating."

"That's more like it." He grabs a tattered composition notebook from the side table to his right and takes note of something. "*Patient feels like absolute garbage*."

"Very good observational skills."

"Thank you. They did save your life, after all," he adds, closing the book and tossing it to the side. "Another day, another—heal, or whatever."

"Hey." I fold my arms. "Speaking of *healing*, you promised me training last summer. Remember?"

"Don't worry, I remember." He grins. "How are those plants doing?"

My eyes widen. I forgot all about those.

"I kept them alive, I swear." Aaron chuckles at my response and I give him a look. "What?"

"I was just messing with you," he says. "Even if you happened to be a plant killer, I would've taught you anyway. There's more to healing and herbalism than the actual growing of the plants, and I've pretty much got that covered. You'll see."

If I were closer, I would punch him in the shoulder. "You're horrible."

He laughs. "What, you thought I would *take you out* or something for letting a few plants die?"

"Actually, yes, I did." My face turns red and I hold my chin up higher. "You've threatened me on multiple occasions, so I think it's pretty justified."

And then the atmosphere shifts. "You wanna heal for her, don't you?" he asks gently, and something in his voice tells me exactly what he knows.

I feel a surge of nausea at the mention of Margot, and I do everything in my power to keep my eyes from watering at the thought of her.

"One of our messengers contacted Asa in the city after we heard about the double Joker draw," Aaron says slowly, pausing. His tone is apologetic, and I feel myself begin to choke up. "I'm so sorry about what happened to her."

I can't say anything. I can't tell him it's okay because I'm done lying. But I can't thank him for his apology either, because he has nothing to be sorry for —and I'm afraid that if I say another word I'll start crying.

There is a familiar guilt in Aaron's eyes that I recognize immediately, because I see it in my own reflection. He feels like he could have done more to save her too.

"How did you know Margot?" I ask, changing the subject.

"Noriko talks about her kids all the time," Aaron says. "It's sweet, really. My old man was the one in charge of delivering books from our library and herbal remedies to the cabin. But after he shattered his foot I took over."

My eyes widen. "He shattered his foot?"

"Got caught in a minor accident during one of his trips. Gained a few major fractures, but we were able to save his foot. He just can't do everything he used to do anymore—but don't tell him that."

"I'm sorry to hear that."

"He's fine now. Just bitter that he had to pass the torch down to me so soon." Aaron shrugs. "It's alright though. I've got most of the healing covered around here."

"You know what? I used to read those old herbalism encyclopedias. Back when I was a kid, at the McLellan's house." I sit up straighter in the bed, picking at a loose thread in the sheets in fond remembrance. "They're what made me so interested in healing in the first place."

"Oh really?"

"Well, as annoying as you are, I could really use an extra pair of hands around here," Aaron says. "Viv helps out sometimes, but she's a strategist at heart. Does a lot of big-picture planning with Noriko and Cecil and everyone else over at the church. So usually, I'm left to handle this job by myself."

"I wouldn't be much help."

"You can learn," Aaron says. "We need to train more people around here to be knowledgeable about first aid and trauma surgery. Especially with everything coming up."

"What do you mean?"

"The plan?" he clarifies, raising an eyebrow. "Doomsday?"

I shake my head to signify that he's lost me, and he sighs in frustration. "You've got to be kidding me. No one told you?"

"Sorry?"

"Well, you've got a lot to learn, Your Darkness." Aaron gets out of his chair and reaches out his hand. "Can you stand?"

"I think so." I grab his arm and move to the edge of the bed, and sure enough, I'm able to rise to my feet with his support.

The room spins as the blood rushes to my head. My vision goes dark for a moment, but he keeps me steady. "You alright?"

I nod. "Yeah."

"C'mon." He starts to walk out of the room once I'm no longer dizzy. "I promised to give you a tour of the Cut."

The cold bites as soon as we step outside. I realize that I'm wearing Aaron's jacket, but I still shiver.

I pause to observe the building we just exited. The *hospital* isn't much of a hospital, but rather a few portable rooms retrofitted to serve the purpose of one, with metal ramps for entrances. It's no longer snowing, but everything is blanketed in white. I just wish it would go ahead and melt away already.

We walk down what must be a dirt road, but I can't be sure. A few people hack away at the snow with shovels and wave at Aaron as we walk by. He returns the gestures casually, greeting every stranger by name.

The road cuts through a small neighborhood of modular rooms arranged like rows and building blocks. They all look the same on the outside, with beige paneling and metal walkway ramps. Doubting they're all makeshift hospitals, I can't help but wonder what must be hidden within their walls.

"We call this the Block." Aaron turns around to face me, walking backwards with his arms outstretched. He spins around again and points at things as he continues.

"Some of these portables are residential areas, homes for families with children and whatnot—although some of the families who have been here for a while have been here long enough to build their own permanent homes."

I nod, eyes wide as I study everything we walk past.

"Most of what you see here on the Block are actually shops, but we don't really have a form of currency here. Just ration slips, which aren't too official either. You can find clothes over there. Prepped meals over there, nonperishable goods there. School materials. You can check out tools for gardening and stuff way over there."

"How do you guys even have access to all of this?" I ask, grinning in awe.

"Most of it was left here. Other things we learn to make ourselves or sneak in from neighboring cities." Aaron shrugs. "This was the home of a religious commune back in the Yesterdays. We don't know whether it was abandoned from the Wandering or shut down by the government, but—they really were prepared for anything."

"Huh," I reply, struggling to keep up with his long strides. He slows down when he notices.

"It's clear they had a heavy focus on disaster prep and the concept of being independently sustainable," Aaron continues. "We're pretty lucky that Noriko stumbled upon all of this back in the day."

He looks around contently, and for once, he almost seems—*happy*, not like the grumpy rebel smuggler I thought I knew. By the way he holds himself and the grin plastered to his face, I can tell he's proud to be in a place like this, even if they don't have access to the luxuries we *Chips* are used to. People like me, who were born and raised as machinery cogs.

But here, no one seems to serve any one leader—not even Noriko, who commands them. The Cut serves the Cut, and I get the feeling that everyone here would die for the good of the group in a heartbeat.

"It's all so secluded too," I note as we approach the end of the Block.

"It really is." Aaron nods, and I think about the vastness of the woods I was trapped in for so long. "I doubt we'll be discovered any time soon."

I cross my arms against my chest to try and retain more body heat. "Are you guys prepared? You know, just in case it does happen?"

Aaron flashes me an arrogant smirk. "We're prepared, alright."

"Let's say some Chasers *do* stumble upon this place. How can you fight against Nightjade weaponry?"

"Oh, Sam," Aaron says, losing me with the reference once again.

"What?"

"There's so much you don't know," he adds, and I feel a twinge in my chest. Ren said the same thing to me, once.

I stop dead in my tracks. *Ren.*

What will he think when he realizes I'm legally dead? Will he find it strange? Will he keep looking for me?

What would he think about all of this?

Stop thinking about him, I tell myself, ejecting the questions from my mind. *He abandoned you. He betrayed you.*

"Everything alright there, Voclain?" Aaron asks, pulling me out of my thoughts.

"Yeah. I'm fine." I nod, and we keep walking. It feels like I'm lying all over again.

"We have a few Double Agents in the Corps who bring back samples of Nightjade for my father and me to study, both the plant itself and the occasional vial of serum," Aaron explains. "But my accident-prone dad broke a vial one day. The glass cut his hand and the Nightjade went straight into his system, and when I found him, I thought he was dead."

My brows pinch together. "And he wasn't?"

"Nope—but he mimicked death for a whole day."

"That can't be true." I shake my head. "There's no way he could have survived if the Nightjade got in his system."

"Your idea of what's impossible is a bit different than ours, don't you think?"

I pause. "I guess so."

"Impossibility is the biggest liar of them all, Voclain. You'll be better off once you learn that," he says, and I hide a smile.

"Anyway, my dad tested a couple of rats after that, and the results were the same. False death," Aaron continues. "He eventually got some human volunteers around the Cut and tested the theory on them too."

I meet Aaron's gaze, my good eye peeled open wide. "So... Nightjade isn't poisonous?"

"Not quite." Aaron shakes his head grimly. "All of our previous doubles tested this theory by watching Chasers out in the field, specifically Officers, who handle Nightjade regularly."

I stare down at my shoes. "They didn't wake up, did they?"

Aaron shakes his head no.

"So what was different with your dad?"

Aaron gives me a look. "I think you can answer that question yourself."

"Not the tracker, right?" I reply, blood running cold as Aaron nods. "That's..."

"Impossible? Yep," he says. "But you're absolutely right."

I close my eyes, shaking my head. "That doesn't make any sense."

"It does, when you understand how it works," Aaron argues. "This is something we've been studying for years now."

"What's your theory?"

"Nightjade was an extremely valuable development at the time," he explains. "It's a genetically modified hybrid of sleeping nightshade and some drought-tolerable species like jade, easy to farm because it thrives in dry and rocky soil."

I nod, letting him continue.

"It grows quickly and needs little to no water—and it just so happens to be extremely toxic," he claims. "Makes the body come very close to shutting down, putting you in this weird position somewhere between sleep and death."

"I don't like that."

"Me neither," he says. "Anyway, by the time Nightjade was developed, the government had already been planning to establish the Pick. They just needed a highly controllable way to kill people in mass quantities without using too many resources."

"So no bombs or Yesterday guns?"

He nods. "Exactly."

"And Nightjade allows them to have a controllable weapon without consuming too many resources during the manufacturing process?"

"Looks like someone's catching on." He grins. "So they leaped on the opportunity. Told the world they were close to developing a new era for weaponry, and used scare tactics to put the Nightjade Order into place."

"No other countries stepped in to intervene either. Part of it was their own weakness, of course. The rest of the world was and still is suffering pretty badly. But I think they were mostly afraid."

"I get why they were so interested in Nightjade," I say. "But... why is it only fatal to people with trackers?"

"Well…" Aaron sighs. "My dad's theory is that the microchips aren't just trackers."

My whole body shivers as we walk, skin crawling like I'm coated in a layer of invisible mites. "They aren't?"

"The trackers release a chemical into your bloodstream. A drug of sorts, so to speak." Aaron stares at his feet before looking me dead in the eye. "Depressants."

I stop walking. The world suddenly spins, like I'm standing up for the first time in years. More blood rushes to my head. I feel like I'm seeing the world through a dizzying haze, a suffocating mist I cannot step away from.

This can't be real. This can't be true, because if it is…

I think back to Margot. To my family. To Ren. To myself, and how broken I've felt for so very, very long.

"But…" I choke, looking up to meet Aaron's gaze again. "Why? Why do such a thing?"

"Weaken the mind," Aaron says softly, "and you weaken the body too."

There's a lump in my throat the size of a river rock, and I fail to swallow it down. "That's why Nightjade is fatal to people with trackers? And weaker against those who don't have them?"

"Yes," he says, and I still avert my gaze.

"And you've proven this?"

Aaron hesitates before nodding solemnly.

"Do you need to sit down?" he asks, voice low. "We can take a break if you want. I know this is a lot to take in."

Yes.

"No." I shake my head. "But why not just use real poison?" I turn to face him now, forcing the worries down. "Something that will just kill anyone right away?"

"Again, resources are a huge issue," Aaron explains. "Nightjade doesn't use a lot of space or water so it's really easy to farm, and it grows really quickly too. Faster than duckweed."

"Things would be a lot simpler if they could just push a button and release a bunch of toxins into someone's system."

"That's not as easy to control. And any malfunction could be fatal to those they want to keep alive," he answers. "But death isn't their only objective here."

I pause, afraid of what he might say.

"This is about fear, Voclain," Aaron says, voice somber. "The trackers, the depressants, Nightjade—all of it. Fear keeps people in place." He stares straight ahead, jaw clenched. "Fear keeps people controlled."

My stomach growls, churning in emptiness. I feel like I'm going to be sick. If I wasn't so hungry, I think I would be. "This is why nothing has changed?" I mutter, hugging my abdomen tighter. "This is why no one has tried to fix anything?"

Aaron gives me an empty smile that doesn't reassure either of us. "I think so."

In silence, we start walking again. I can't say a word as I soak everything in. I can't tell whether to feel angry or violated or everything at once. If I think about it too much right now, I don't think I'll be able to keep myself from breaking something.

Aaron and I turn a corner, exiting the Block and walking through a path lined by trees. We approach a group of larger buildings, all of them centered around a stone square. The buildings here are not portable like the Block, but constructed from ivy-laced and crumbling red bricks that have clearly been around since the Yesterdays. I spot an old church and something that looks like a library, but the purposes of the other buildings remain unknown.

I follow Aaron closely as we walk through the middle of the square. It's covered by a thick carpet of snow, and there's a stone fountain in the center that spews out icicles instead of flowing water. It's topped with a statue of a rabbit, but someone's attached wooden antlers to either side of its head. Immediately, I remember the image on Asa's sealing ring.

"Has that fountain always been here?" I ask as we walk by.

Aaron nods. "For as long as I can remember."

"The antlers look new."

"Someone added them years ago. We like to use the jackalope as a symbol," he says. "Some people in the Yesterdays used to believe that jackalopes were real, that they lived out in the woods unseen."

"And some say there are *people* living in the woods," I tease.

He flashes me a small, crooked smile. "Exactly."

My jaw drops as we approach the church. I've never been inside one before; they were all shut down by the Presidency long ago. But some still exist, empty but remaining, artifacts of a time lost.

A white steeple towers high above white wood walls and stained glass windows that look more like candy. Looking up for so long makes me dizzy, and I almost slip as we walk up the icy brick steps. Aaron grabs me before I split my head open.

"Woah, woah. Careful." He glares. "Remember what I said about your eye?"

I return the expression. "I'm not going to injure myself before it heals."

"There we go." He opens the door, and we walk inside.

The inside of the church looks nothing like I thought it would. The only reminder that this was once a religious meeting place is the collection of pews lined up in the back. Everything else has been completely modified.

The walls have been painted a desaturated navy blue that reminds me of Ren's room back home. Every wood surface is dark and detailed with age, and a massive television screen is mounted on the back wall, behind the steps that lead to a broad walnut pulpit platform.

To the platform's left is a black round table scattered with paper, notes, and closed laptops that lead me to believe this is not only a place for mingling, but a place to get work done.

The two side walls are both smothered in hundreds of pinned documents, photos, letters, and other pieces that create two expansive evidence boards. There's a pool table on one side of the room, and on the other side lies two different tables with wood models of what looks like the Cut and some building that's unfamiliar to me. A few people that I don't recognize look up from their game of pool and wave at Aaron.

"This is the church." He walks to the back of the building and opens his arms out wide before shoving his hands in his pockets. "Stuff happens here sometimes."

He leads me up the steps to stand behind the podium. Now that I'm up here, I can see every little detail. I take a moment to breathe it all in. There is something exhilarating about the air here, and I inhale everything.

I'm startled when the front doors burst open. Gray daylight floods the room as two people walk into the building. I squint to make out their faces through the brightness, but I don't realize who they are until the doors come to a close and the light fades away.

And when I see him, I nearly fall over.

I can't believe what I'm witnessing. My pulse hammers against my ribcage, every heartbeat bruising more than the last. I blink a dozen times and his image still doesn't fade away.

He walks inside like a mirage, side by side with his mother. She speaks to him softly, pointing and whispering things into his ear like he's just another freshly debugged Runner seeking refuge.

Like he didn't spend the last two weeks Chasing me.

I think about every painful day and haunting night I suffered out in those woods. He and Carmody hunted me like prey, and now he's here, pretending like nothing happened?

Why is he here? He betrayed me, and he did it in the worst possible way.

I can't picture him as the boy who once fought for me anymore. Now, all I can see is the boy who wanted me dead.

I turn to Aaron, my eyes throbbing with rage. "What is *he* doing here?" My voice cracks and I don't know why I feel like crying. "Don't you know who he is? *What* he is?"

Aaron gives me a puzzled stare. "You really don't remember anything from last night?"

"I don't," I whisper through clenched teeth. "How is that relevant?"

"He followed us into the woods," Aaron says softly. "He was convinced I was going to hurt you, so he stayed close behind and we got into a little... altercation, after you passed out."

"He wasn't wrong," I grumble. "I have the bandage on my eye to prove it."

"Not the point," he says. "I had a knife to his throat 'cause I thought he was assigned to your case—which I guess ended up being true—but he stood up to me, even with a blade against his neck. For you."

"No." I shake my head vigorously. "Ren wouldn't do that."

"Well he did," Aaron argues. "He was so set on coming with you and making sure you were safe that he let me debug him too. Though he didn't pass out like you did."

My heart drops, pulse rattling at a tempo that makes it hard to breathe. "What about Carmody? His partner?"

"You don't have to worry about him for now," Aaron assures me, surprisingly calm. "I talked to Ren about it, and none of us know his exact location. Guess he left on a short little hunting excursion or something while your buddy over there escaped."

"He's not my *buddy*," I grumble. "I just... I don't get why he followed me. Without—you know—wanting to *kill* me and all. It doesn't make any sense."

"Beats me. You're pretty difficult to be around."

"You're not any better." I glare. "I just don't—I don't mean anything to Ren. Not anymore."

"Not many things make sense, but I wouldn't overthink this if I were you," he tells me. "I'm gonna let the two of you work this out now."

He pats my good shoulder and starts to walk away, but I grab his arm to stop him.

"Don't you dare make me talk to him," I hiss.

"Look I get it, you're attached to me. It's understandable. I mean, we were lovers once, many moons ago," he teases.

"I hate you." I yank my arm away.

The humor fades from his voice. "You can't put off this conversation forever, you know."

"But—"

"I will say this though," Aaron interrupts, turning his body to face me and looking me straight in the eye. "He's the one that carried you here, not me." He shakes his head. "Poor guy got a chip carved out of his eye by a stranger so he could be the one to carry you on his back through the snow. No uniform. I offered to help of course, but he wouldn't let me."

My eye widens. "What?"

Aaron sighs, looking over at where Ren stands. "I'd say you mean something to him. Can't say what, but... something, at least."

And with that, he walks away to socialize at the pool table, leaving me alone to stare at Ren from my comfortable distance.

He looks so defeated from here. I can see the grief that eats him away, and I recognize it because I'm haunted by the same feeling.

He sees me staring and freezes.

But I don't look away. It's as if time has petrified the world for just the two of us, and all we can do is stand and watch each other from afar.

Even when I look away, his good eye remains glued to me. We are worlds away, but here we are, standing in the same room.

And then, he lifts up a hand, and he walks away.

REN

Friday, January 12
Day 12

I'm covered in dirt and snow when I meet my mother.

I used to think about this moment so often as a child. I was happy with my life and I loved my family more than anything, but there were times when I used to dream about the woman who brought me into this world —and weep over the fact that she was taken away before I got the chance to know her.

My father never told me much about her—only her name, and that she was Picked shortly after I was born. But that was all the information I needed. Because without anything else, she could be whoever I wanted her to be.

Some days I believed she had some sort of magic ability, and that one day, I would discover that I had it too. Sometimes I pictured her as a pirate. It was easier to believe she was at sea than underground.

She was a dragon-taming knight, the author of my current favorite book, a count on an adventure for revenge, and about a thousand other figures I sculpted in my head. Her shape was forever shifting, and that's how I coped with the fact that she really wasn't anything at all.

Everything is pitch black as Aaron leads me through what he calls the Block. We walk up a ramp and inside a small portable building, and when he flips on the light switch, I realize it's the Cut's version of a hospital. It would look brand new if it weren't so outdated; I can tell it isn't used much. He tells me to keep holding onto Eddie while he prepares the hospital bed for her.

The door opens as Aaron helps me lay Eddie's unconscious body down on the hospital bed, and I'm too focused on making sure she's alright that I don't even notice someone has entered the room. Not until I hear her speak to me.

"Ren?" a voice mutters, and I whip my head around.

And in an instant, I know exactly who she is.

She has no left eye or hand, scarred inside and out. She's sadder than I imagined, but she is my mother, and she is more than I ever dreamed she would be.

Because she is here, and she is alive.

My voice cracks. "Mom."

She stares at me like I'm the illusion and not her. We blink in united unbelieving, praying this isn't a dream. Her eye waters and mine does the same. Neither of us knows what to say. We stand in silence for a bittersweet eternity.

And then, she hugs me. She runs over to me and hugs me tighter than I've ever been hugged before, dirt and snow and all.

"Your father told me about her," she whispers painfully. I don't know what she's talking about for a moment, but when her words sink in, I freeze.

The world has been put on pause for so long. But now, it feels like everything is spinning, rewinding in a hazy blur of shapes and colors while I'm left standing still. I see my sister. I see her life, and I see her emptiness.

And for the first time since everything happened, I let myself cry for Margot.

I collapse. My mother is no longer a stranger when I find my embrace, when I feel her tears against my hair. We have both lost everything.

I weep until I have no more tears to give. Not for the Voclains, not for Eddie, not for myself—but for Margot.

My mother and I sit at a table on the far side of the room.

She tells me the truth. She tells me why she Ran, about the trackers, the true purpose of Nightjade—everything. In one long conversation, the veil I've been covered by my entire life is lifted. But my mother is an integral part of the Cut, and when duty calls, she is taken from me once again.

Aaron and I don't chat while he fixes me up. By now I know it must be the early hours of the morning, but he stays in this hospital nonetheless, checking for any wounds I must have acquired from my time spent in the woods.

I know he has other reasons for staying here so late. He doesn't trust me to be alone with Eddie, as though I'll exterminate her the second someone turns their back on me. It's laughable, really, because I don't trust him with her either—even if they have met before in some other life I never knew.

Aaron tells me he's a *healer*, but he can't do much to heal me other than clean the thin sliver of broken skin across my neck and cover my eye with a bandage.

I'm relieved when he begins to put his supplies away, but to my dismay, he still doesn't leave. He sits down in the chair across from me and clears his throat.

"Sorry for... you know." He nods to the scratch running across my neck. "That."

"It's nothing," I say plainly. "Feels like a paper cut."

"So." He clears his throat again, and the air in the room starts to weigh uncomfortably on the both of us. "We have a few empty portables. Noriko's busy, but I can make some arrangements for you. Find you somewhere to stay."

"Okay."

"She wants to show you around in the morning, but I can take you to a room now if you want," Aaron says, and I can tell he wants me to leave.

"I'm fine," I say, voice blank. "I'll sleep in here tonight."

"You sure?" Aaron raises an eyebrow. "You'd rather sleep on the floor? The portables have beds, you know."

I keep my face stone-cold. "I don't mind."

"A carpet is a gross place." He leans back in his chair with crossed arms, eyeing me with suspicion. "Lots of germs. Bacteria. Mold, even."

My nostrils flare as I try to suppress my disgust. "Like I said, I don't mind."

"Alright." We have a small staring contest for a moment before he speaks again. "Well, I'll be staying here too to keep her vitals in check. She's still pretty shaken up from the hypothermia and malnourishment, and Noriko wants me to keep a close eye on her. So we'll be sharing the floor."

"Fine by me."

"Great. Well let me just make things a bit cozier for you." He stands up and walks over to the room's one armchair, grabbing the small red throw pillow that rests upon it. He walks over to the corner of the room farthest away from Eddie and sets it down on the floor. "You can have the pillow, I don't need it."

"You sure?" I question, competing in plastic politeness. "It must be really uncomfortable to sleep on the floor without a pillow."

"Oh, I insist," Aaron replies overenthusiastically. "Please. Take it."

"Well if you *insist*, then I guess I must." I walk over to the pillow, plucking it from the floor and moving over to the area next to Eddie's hospital bed. I set it down on the ground and lie down, making sure I'm as close as possible.

Aaron switches off the light. I expect him to claim a spot on the opposite side, but instead, he settles down right next to me, flat on his back with his own palms for a pillow. After a moment, he beams, turning to look at me while propping his head up with his hand. "This sure is nice, isn't it?"

"Oh, yeah. Real cozy." I turn over on my side and mirror his faux grin.

Aaron moves his hands away from the back of his head and takes out his hunting knife, holding it in his arms like funeral flowers as he rests.

"You sleep with a knife?"

"Always."

"I'm not gonna lay a hand on her and you know that." I break the act with a frown. Aaron isn't so quick to let down his wall of mockery.

"We'll see." He smiles again, closing his eyes as he keeps his hands wrapped around the weapon. "Goodnight."

Aaron falls asleep first, and I can't seem to do the same. As much as I would like to sleep, my mind is too busy to let my body rest. All I can do is stare at the ceiling. It feels strange to be so close to Eddie and still so far away.

I think back to the girl she used to be, who led me by the hand to the park after graduation, who insisted that I join her on the slide we used to frequent as children.

I wish I had joined her all those months ago. I wish I went down that slide with her when I had the chance.

As I lay here with this burning wound in my eye, the most painful thing of all is knowing that nothing will be the same after tonight.

There is no real going back.

Saturday, January 13
Day 13

Morning light illuminates my mother's face as she takes me on her promised tour.

I'm a little disheartened that we left before Eddie woke up, and I still don't trust Aaron. But my mother insisted on showing me around, and I don't have much else of a choice. I'll have to talk to Eddie later.

We walk down a row of manufactured buildings my mother calls the Block. She says they serve as shops and residential spaces for the Unseen—the term they use for the people of the Cut. Turns out *Undergrounders* is Chip slang, and I am no longer a part of that world.

"Did you learn anything about the Broadcasting Centers during training?" my mother asks as we walk.

I shake my head. "No."

"I guess that makes sense. That's more of a NOT thing, right?"

"Yeah." I nod, thinking of Lori.

"Well, as you know, the Presidency always has complete control over what airs," my mother states. "Each state has a Broadcasting Center that receives and distributes area-specific information to every television and radio in its zone."

"Makes sense."

"Each of these centers also has the ability to initiate a nationwide broadcast, if they have clearance to do so."

I raise my eyebrows. "I never knew that."

"Most people don't, especially Chips." My mother shakes her head with a sigh. "They just turn on their devices and mindlessly accept everything they're fed."

There's a pause for a moment until I interrupt the silence. "So what do these Broadcasting Centers have to do with anything?"

She gives me a confident grin. "We've spent the last few years learning everything we possibly can about the Blurts."

"Blurts?"

"Sorry, that's what we've been calling the Broadcasting Centers," she clarifies, and I nod. "We've acquired a handful of Double Agents over time. Ideally, we want one in each Corps division, but that can be difficult because we can't always predict which field our people will be assigned to."

"Sounds like a gamble," I note, and she agrees.

"We've been in desperate need of a Double to feed us intel from the NOT Division," she says. "Thankfully, Loretta Salazar pulled us out of that rut."

My eyes widen. "Lori?"

My mother nods. "Aaron's little sister. She's our very first NOT."

"That's the most difficult division to get into. Aside from the Agency."

"Tell me about it," she continues. "We've been waiting for a Double like Lori for years. Thanks to her, we now have the access codes we need to move forward with our plan. If we manage to infiltrate the closest Blurt, we can use the codes to send a broadcast to every TV and radio in the country."

"A broadcast?" I ask. "About what?"

"We'll tell everyone the truth." She beams at me. "Maybe it won't be enough to save us all, but... it's a start."

And for the first time in what feels like ages, I smile too.

We exit the Block and approach the square, which is where the compound's most crucial buildings are located. The church, the library, the guarded armory, and the information center all sit around a frost-covered stone fountain of a jackalope. It's cheery for a place of such high importance—and I think it's the smell of change in the air.

As we walk up the steps of the church, my mother turns to me. "Ready to see the room where it happens?" I nod.

It takes a moment for my eyes to adjust, but when my vision settles and the setting seeps in, my jaw nearly drops.

It looks like an expansion of a detective's office from an old Yesterday book, covered from floor to ceiling in technology and information. The electronic equipment is advanced for such an outdated facility. I remember my mother mentioning something about how messengers often bring goods and intel back from the city, and I bet this room is a result of that.

"This is the church," my mother explains, gesturing with her hands. "This is where we like to hold meetings. And socialize, if we have the time."

But as I'm studying the room, something else catches my eye. Some*one*.

Eddie must have woken up shortly after my mother and I left, and Aaron probably led her along a different path through the Block than the one we traveled. Because she is here, wide awake, standing yards away.

I haven't felt her gaze against mine in a long, long time.

She stares with her visible eye, and when I look at her bandages, all I want to do is tell her just how okay it is for her to be small sometimes. Because she said the same thing to me once. She told me so many things that I wish I could tell her now.

But I see the way she looks at me. *She doesn't trust me anymore.*

I've let so many things happen to her. Maybe I never lifted a finger, but I've hurt her. I doubted the patterns of her character. I let my pain and rage and Duke goddamn Carmody get in the way of my trust for her. I let her suffer in solitude.

In more ways than I can count, I have been the source of so much of her pain—and I'll regret it for the rest of my life.

Aaron mutters something to Eddie before walking away to the pool table, and now she's left to stand alone by the podium.

My mother leans over to whisper to me. "You're lucky to have her, you know."

"I know," I mutter, still staring straight ahead. But I had no idea how lucky I was when it counted.

And with that, my mother walks away too, leaving Eddie and I to stare at each other from across the room. Neither of us moves a muscle, motionless mosquitoes trapped in amber.

But I'm tired of waiting for things to happen. I hold up my hand for Eddie to see, point to the scar on my palm, and leave the church without saying a word to anyone.

I walk down the steps and back through the square, praying that Eddie understood my sign. I make my way to a wooden fence around the bend and beyond the trees, where there's a green metal bench topped with snow.

I wipe the snow off the bench. I turn around, but I don't see Eddie walk out of the church.

I doubt she'll ever come. I realize how foolish it was of me to expect her to agree to talk after everything I've done. I might be waiting by this bench forever.

I don't sit down, but a few minutes pass and I begin to grow restless. My foot taps impatiently and I let out a sigh. I know it's wrong of me to feel disappointed, but I do anyway. All I can do is stand here and stare at the bench, waiting for a girl who will never come.

But my disappointment is short-lived.

"If you wanted help with your homework, you should have just said so."

I turn around to find Eddie standing behind me, holding up her bandaged hand and pointing to where her splinter scar used to be. I'm pleased to see that she's grinning, but her eyes are glossed with emotion. She is so horribly far from happy.

"Lavender Voclain is struggling with botany." I try my hardest to return her broken smile. "Who would have guessed?"

We both stand still for a moment. She almost looks disappointed, like it was easier to see me as a Chaser. But I am no longer protected by that armor, and I can't hide behind its weight. I can't use it to justify the things I do or say or think.

I'm just me. No suit, no weapons—just the shell of Ren.

Eddie surprises me when she takes a step forward. She climbs on top of the bench, using its height to hoist herself over the fence. I hear her land in the snow with a soft thud.

I walk over to the fence to see if she made it to the other side okay, but this time around, there are no gaps in the wood for me to peek through. This barrier is solid. We are separate.

I press my forehead against the fence. "Any plans for the day?" My voice almost breaks, like cracks in the hardened snow beneath me. It's so cold now. "Adventures to embark upon? People to meet?"

"None at all," Eddie whispers. I can't see her, but I know she isn't smiling.

I can sense that her back faces me now as she slides down the fence to sit on the ground. After a moment of quiet, I do the same. Our backs are touching through this wooden cage, but we are not close. We look in completely different directions, and we see things the other cannot.

How ironic it is that today is beautiful. The sun is muted by the gray, but I can see bits of light glimmer upon the snow in a way that's almost surreal. Everything feels so dream-like.

"You meant everything, once."

The sound of Eddie's voice makes my heart stop.

Once. It means the same thing as *not anymore.* It's a word designed for yesterdays, and it hurts far more than the burning in my eye ever could.

"Now I'm not so sure what I felt back then," Eddie mutters. *Or what I feel now,* she says without speaking.

I think it's easier for both of us to talk with the fence in the way, because she can't see the way I crumble beneath the weight of her sentences. And I can't see the way she's hurt by my silence.

I know there isn't anything I can say that will make this better. But I've been quiet for so long. I've spent so much of my life waiting for the right moments and the right words to find me. After everything that's happened, I know that time is a fleeting thing. I can't afford to live the rest of my life in silence, waiting for things that will never arrive.

Every moment is the right moment, because at any moment everything can be gone.

"I'm sorry, Eddie." There are faults in my voice again. "I'm so... so sorry. For everything."

She doesn't say a word.

This is pathetic. I close my eye. "I should have known you better."

Eddie doesn't respond, and I wonder whether or not she heard me. I wait a few moments until I hear her voice again. "But you didn't, Ren."

Hearing my name spoken with so much weight attached, so much pain, is more than I can bear.

"You were going to hurt me." She whispers so quietly I can barely hear her. "You were going to kill me."

"I was never going to hurt you." My voice cracks and I choke on the words. "I had everything backwards and I thought that hating you was the only way to survive. The only way to honor her memory. All of their memories."

I swallow the lump that forms in my throat. "I was lost, and I was wrong, Eddie. I was so wrong, and I was wrong in every worst way."

She keeps her mouth closed, and I wait for a response that doesn't come.

"I never wanted to hurt you," I say. "All along, I was in this constant battle with myself. My whole world turned upside down and I couldn't tell what was right anymore. I hated myself for trying so hard to hate you, and it tore me apart."

"But it tore me apart too, Ren," she says, trembling as she talks. "It tore both of us apart and I don't know if I can... I don't know if I can forgive you for that."

"Eddie—"

"*You wanted me dead,*" Eddie exclaims, her words so intense I see flashes of black in the sky as a single black crow escapes its branch. The words burn, but I can tell they hurt her more than they hurt me. "Whether you meant it or not, I thought you wanted me dead." She mutters so softly I almost miss it. "How can I forget that?"

I close my eye again, touching the back of my head to the fence, scraping through my mind and rummaging through every word I know. No matter how many times I rearrange the sentences in my head, nothing sounds like the right thing to say.

But I need to reach her. I need to tell the truth.

"Losing Margot broke me, Ed." Hot tears fall down my right cheek as I mention her name, and I wipe them with an icy hand. "It broke me."

"It broke me too." Eddie's voice breaks. "I never stop thinking about her, or my parents, or Milo, or the Chasers my brother stabbed to death for my sake, and whether or not your dad was able to get there in time after I ran to give him medicine, and I—" She chokes on the words. They are too much.

I want to say something but my mouth stays shut, and the tears fall faster than I can manage.

"That night never leaves me, you know." She's crying now; I can hear it in her voice. "Every time I close my eyes I see them. I see all of them. But they don't go away when I wake either." There's a pause, and I can hear sniffling from the other side of the fence.

"I wish I could, but I couldn't hate you. I tried, but I couldn't." She sobs, and it sounds like she's been waiting to tell me these words for a long time. "Even though you wore the same uniform I see in my nightmares. Even after all you did."

"I wanted to help you," I say. "I just didn't know how. And I'm sorry."

"*You left me out in the snow to die!*" There's a long, dreadful pause. Eddie lowers her voice to a near whisper. "You left me out in the snow, to die. And I hate that I don't hate you for that."

Her words are a slow death. She doesn't know the lengths I went to protect her. Even beneath my Chaser mask, I was always fighting to keep her alive, and she has no idea.

"I was saved by some Unseen *stranger* because you stopped caring about me." I can hear her wipe her face with the sleeve of Aaron's puffer jacket. "I knew you hated me, but I didn't know you hated me enough to let me die like that." She sniffles. "And that's what hurts the most, Ren. You stopped caring."

"Eddie..."

"*What?*" she yells, and it frightens me for a moment. In all the years I've spent knowing her, she has never sounded this angry before. I feel like everything inside me is being carved out.

We wait in silence as I try to piece together a response. I know I need to tell the truth. She needs to know that I never stopped caring, and I don't know how to convince her with anything but the truth. *Say it, Ren,* I tell myself. Now is the time.

"I carried you to that cabin."

"What?" she whispers, voice quivering.

I close my eyes again. I never wanted her to know. But now, I realize she needs to hear it. She needs to know I care.

There are no right moments.

"I told Carmody we should rest at that cow farm because deep down, I wanted you to get a head start. I grasped at straws and came up with an excuse to prolong your extermination. I kept him busy so he wouldn't hurt you." I hold back pitiful tears. "I was *always* fighting for you. But you didn't know it at the time, and I'm not sure I knew either."

I pause, inhaling slowly.

"That night in the snow—I gave you my suit and carried you on my back in the middle of the blizzard to bring you back to the cabin," I tell her, as soft as I possibly can. "I tended to your wounds. I gave you medicine and my last set of clean clothes. I kept the fires going and made sure you always had a warm pan of water at your feet. And I would do it all again if I had to. I would carry you on my back forever to keep you safe from harm."

Talking now feels more like spitting up rocks. "I know you don't need me. I know you are stronger than I'll ever be. I just... I want you to know that you were never alone."

All is silent, and I hear Eddie sniffle again.

"I'm not blind enough to expect you to forgive me. I'm not selfish enough to ask for that either." My voice wavers. "So I'm asking you to hate me. Hate me as long as you need to. Hate me forever, Eddie, because..." I sigh. Even now, I still can't say the words. "You can say that I've wronged you, because I have. But you can never say that I stopped caring because it's simply not true."

I never wanted this. I did not choose to burn for Eddie, but I do, and I have been for quite some time. Nothing is more maddening than that.

It has taken me so long to realize, but all this time, she was not falling alone. She did not jump, and she did not pull me down with her.

We were both falling, both of us at once, and she caught me.

I'm not angry at Eddie. I'm not angry at all. But after a long time, I leave anyway, because I can't bear to be in this snow for any longer.

EDDIE

Saturday, January 13
Day 13

Ren leaves me in the snow, again.

I sit against the fence for a long time. The ground is frozen and the cold burns my toes, but I'm too enraged to care.

Ren is infuriating in the worst sort of way. I'm angry at Ren for a dozen reasons I can explain and a thousand reasons I can't. He can't tell me so many world-changing things and just leave, and he certainly didn't let me say all I wanted to say. What does he know about caring anyway? He didn't even give me a chance to say thank you.

But why should I thank him? I never asked to be saved. Dying in the snow would have been a fitting end. It would have been peaceful, and it would have given me the illusion of warmth. I was so close to seeing everyone I love again and he took that away from me.

I was *this close* to meeting my perfect ending, and he ruined it all. But he did it for him, not for me. He saved me because he wouldn't have been able to handle the guilt of watching me die before his eyes. That's not caring for someone; that's selfishness.

I don't hate him because he stopped caring. I hate him because he didn't.

He never stopped caring, not even when I wanted him to. Not even once.

How can he not despise me, after everything *I've* done? None of this would have happened if I did as I was told, if I didn't question the world I was born into. I could have tried my best to be a good person without setting my sight on tearing this system apart.

I could have done better.

Ren's words echo in my mind for what feels like an eternity until someone knocks on the fence. I'm startled by the sound, but I don't have to think too hard about who it might be. "Come in."

I sniffle, and there's a pause before Aaron hops over the fence. He sits down beside me without a word. He watches me sulk with keen eyes until he can't sit still for any longer. He takes out a knife and begins to whittle away at one of the wood carvings he's been working on.

But this knife is different from his others, like it's been specifically designed for carving. It makes me wonder if this hobby might be more than a simple pastime to him. I steal a glance at the chunk of wood in his hands out of curiosity. It's the size of his palm and incredibly intricate, but I can't tell exactly what it is yet.

"It's a jackalope, if that's what you're wondering," Aaron says. "I carve one for every new Cut arrival."

I hug my knees, leaning my head in the opposite direction. I'm not in the mood to talk to him.

"Which means I gotta make one for Ren, unfortunately," Aaron grumbles. "But here." He holds out the now-finished carving, and I hesitate before reluctantly taking it from his hand.

Now that I'm holding it, the carving's identity is obvious. It's unmistakably a jackalope, but this one has been detailed with delicate engravings of some sort of flower, and when I look closer, I realize they must be tiny swirls of lavender.

The amount of care that went into carving this piece is apparent. It's not a chunk of wood anymore, but artwork, and the transformation astonishes me.

"My dad used to work with wood a lot," Aaron says. "It was the only memory I had of him as a kid, back when I was still living with my mother.

When I was old enough, I eventually developed a passion for it. Used rocks instead of knives and didn't make anything meaningful, just sheep. And cows."

He chuckles at the nostalgia. "But he doesn't do it anymore. I guess he lost that passion, you know?" Aaron shrugs, and I avoid his gaze. "Now he spends all his time glassblowing instead. False eyes for people who couldn't get the Chip surgery for whatever reason, lab equipment for him and me, just—functional stuff. Nothing artistic anymore."

I keep staring at the jackalope without a word.

"So if you were wondering why I even bother with any of this wood-carving nonsense, I guess that's why." He stretches and leans back against the fence, cushioning his head with his hands and crossing his legs like this is a green summer lawn and not frozen ground. "You better not give me any shit for this or I'm taking Harold back."

"Harold?" I turn to him, raising an eyebrow. "You gave it a name?"

"Of course I did. I'm sensible."

It's quiet for a moment as I turn the carving over in my hands. "I like cows, you know."

"Pardon?"

"You mentioned you used to carve cows," I reply, still staring at the jackalope. "They're my favorite."

"Noted." He smiles, but this smile is different. There is no arrogance. No sarcasm, no teasing—just a genuine grin.

I turn my head to the left and look up at him. I can't bring myself to smile like he is. "Why are you here, Aaron?"

"Damn, Voclain—I don't know. Didn't think we would get all existential or anything. I guess my mom and my dad—"

"You know what I mean." I glare. Although it's kind of him to try and lighten the mood, I don't think it can be lightened. I lower my voice. "Why are you here?"

He stares at his shoes. "Because I have to be."

Of course he does, I think. Noriko must want him to keep an eye on me. Even after everything, I still can't be trusted. I rise to my feet, chest tight and I don't know why.

"No, not like that." Aaron stands up too, hands in his pockets. "I just—" He struggles to say the words, like he's afraid to break down the cynical barrier he's grown comfortable behind. "I thought you could use a friend. Alright?"

I don't know what to say to that. I turn to face the fence, ready to climb over, but I stop myself, and I'm not sure why. "Aaron?"

"Yeah?"

I hesitate. "Do you ever..."

My voice trails off. I hug my abdomen tighter. I can't finish the sentence and I press my head against the fence, throat burning as everything I want to say festers inside of it. It feels like my chest is caving in on itself. My breaths arrive shorter, and I can't seem to catch them. Sweat pools in the palms of my trembling hands. Everything is suddenly too much all at once, and I have no idea what's wrong with me.

He walks closer, speaking quietly. "Do I ever what?"

I pull my head away from the fence, biting my lip and staring at a distant tree. I can't bring myself to look at him. "Do you ever feel like you could have done more?"

His shoulders slump in defeat like he's staring at a wounded animal. "Voclain."

My whole body feels like it's on fire. For a moment, breathing is the hardest thing, because my body will not do it, and I know I don't deserve another breath. My heart pounds faster, its rhythm extinguishing every other sound and blurring the shapes around me.

I feel like I'm back in that river with Milo and Margot and Ren. But instead of finding my way back to the surface, I can't for the life of me stop sinking.

Aaron's brows pinch together with concern. "Voclain?"

Breathing is the same as swimming through honey. I hunch over, one palm against the fence and the other clutching my chest. I squeeze my eyes shut, trying to swallow whatever this is, but it won't go away. It's like there's been something swelling inside me that's finally ready to burst.

"Hey, hey." Aaron is by my side. "Are you okay?"

No. "Yes."

"Can you breathe?"

Barely. "I can breathe just fine."

"Voclain," he says slowly. "I think you're having a panic attack."

"I'm fine, Aaron." I'm still unable to look at him. Still unable to breathe.

"How about we sit down, alright?" he says, tone calm. "There's a bluebird over there. Wanna take a look?"

"I said I'm *fine*, alright?" I snap without meaning to, something cracking in my voice. "*I'm okay.* I'm okay, I'm—"

Not okay.

I shake my head and try to turn away, but Aaron places a pair of gentle hands on my shoulders, anchoring me in place. Grounding me. "Eddie, please. Look at me."

When I do, I regret it instantly. The world stops spinning. I stop sinking. There is something in his eyes that makes everything so unbearably real.

I shiver. "I'm not okay."

I feel like I'm unraveling, and he stares at me like I'm wholly wound. "And that's perfectly okay."

Neither of us says anything for what feels like eons. Several yards away, the bluebird hops closer, head twitching from side to side before it flies off. Aaron shoves his hands in his pockets.

"Losing your family like that—losing Margot..." His bottom lip curls inward. He stares at his shoes momentarily before meeting my gaze once more. "I can never pretend to know what that must feel like. But I do know this."

I study the snow beneath our feet. Carefully, he places a single finger beneath my chin, urging me to look up again.

"You blame yourself for atrocities you didn't commit. You hold yourself accountable for actions you don't even have the right to claim."

Hot tears well up in the corners of my eyes, even with the bandage, and it stings. My nails dig into my palms. Who is he to talk about my rights? I should be talking about *his*. He has no right to tell me these things. He knows nothing.

"Margot's death was a result of an illness, and a world that wouldn't let her overcome it. A world that made her feel like the only choice she had was..." His voice cracks. He can't say the words. "And changing the world wasn't a battle she could win on her own."

I look up, only to find that Aaron's eyes are glossed over too. I've never seen him like this before. I think back to what I noticed in him earlier, realizing that he feels just as guilty as I do. He was the one providing the medicine—and even he couldn't heal her.

I clench my jaw as Aaron shakes his head. "What happened could have very well been possible with or without your influence. You can't place the blame on anyone's shoulders but theirs." He uses his hands to gesture in the distance. "The people in the suits who numb our minds and watch our every move and carve our skin with ink. The people who refuse to understand that living shouldn't be about who was born with the right goddamn lottery ticket."

He shakes his head and stares at the trees for a moment, tracing one of his tattoos, feeling the scarred lines of the crude X mark he put in place himself. He looks down at his hands. "You can't be angry at yourself for what happened, Voclain. There's no use. You just can't."

"Then who else am I supposed to direct this anger toward? This shame?" I feel like screaming, but the words come out soft and scratched. "Don't you get it? *My family would still be alive if it weren't for me.*"

Silence. I slide my back against the fence until I'm sitting on the ground again, tears streaming down my cheeks. I want to kick something. I want to tear something apart, to set the world on fire and burn right along with it. I can't stop trembling. There is so much rage that I am weakened by its weight.

Aaron takes a seat in front of me, hugging his knees loosely. He locks his gaze with mine. "That's not true."

"You know nothing about my truths." Without meaning to, my voice raises in volume, clawing at my throat.

Truth. It's such a horrible word. I think of Ren, about lying by his side in that cow field. We thought we knew what truth meant back then, but we were foolish to believe such a thing.

"And you know nothing about theirs," Aaron replies so calmly it's infuriating. "I didn't know your family, but I know you. They must have been good people to raise a girl like Lavender Voclain."

I scoff, observing a pebble stuck in the snow. "I'm not in the mood for jokes."

"I'm serious," Aaron snaps before lowering his voice back down to a near whisper. "They would have protested your death, with or without the lies."

My vision clouds, burning with salt. I want to argue with him, to tell him how wrong he is, but I can't. No matter how little I may have deserved it, deep down, I know he's right.

My mother and father would have protested my death until the very end.

And Milo, I think to myself, pressing my eyes shut.

"Eddie." Aaron lifts my chin up again, and I open my eyes. His hand falls and he keeps his knees close to his chest. "You may not think so, but your worth..." He swallows a lump in his throat. "Your worth can't even be quantified."

I want to look away, but his stare has me in a chokehold I despise him for.

"Your family loved you. Margot loved you."

"*I know they did*," I shout hoarsely, shaking my head. "They loved me and they were too good for doing it."

"No. Don't do that. It'll eat you alive, Voclain." Aaron's tone is firm. Not loud, but stern, like he knows what it's like to hate himself too. "The anger? Direct it inward and you'll drive yourself mad."

I wipe a tear with my sleeve, feeling more pathetic than ever. "I don't know how to be anything else but angry."

"I'm not asking you to be anything else." Aaron rises to his feet. He shoves one hand in his pocket, offering me the other. "Hell, I'm asking you to be angrier. Fuel your motivation with rage. Be angry at them, Voclain. Not yourself. Never that."

I stare at him, blinking. He stares right back, something flickering behind his gaze. "So what do you say, Your Darkness? Are you accepting my invitation or what?"

"Invitation?"

"To be absolutely wrathful, of course." Aaron grins.

I pause, staring at the scarred hand outstretched in front of me. And I take it.

I pull myself to my feet, dusting bits of snow from my pants once I find my balance. He gives me a pat on the back and moves on ahead.

"Aaron?"

He pauses, looking over his shoulder. "Yeah?"

Without thinking, I walk up behind him and fling my arms around his waist. He grows rigid, shoulders tense, still and stiff like a carved marble statue.

"Thank you," I whisper. He says nothing.

And then his posture softens. Slowly, carefully, he turns around to pull me into a real embrace.

I bury my face into his shirt, not wanting him to see my weakness. Because I am shattered, and I cry for every fractured piece.

Gently, Aaron sets his chin on the top of my head. One hand is pressed against my back, and the other holds my hair like I will fade away. "You're killing me, Voclain."

"I'm sorry." I can barely whisper the words.

"Never be." The words seep out fragile and faulted. "It's a grave I'll gladly dig."

For the smallest of moments, I wonder if he might be crying too.

We stand like that for a while until I pull my face free to wipe a tear. He wriggles out of my grip with a sniffle, swatting me away like he would a pest. "Alright, alright. Enough of that. You'll soften my edges."

I laugh half-heartedly, wiping the last tear. I wrap my arms around myself instead. "We can't have that now, can we?"

"No." He turns back around, looking over his shoulder one last time before walking ahead. "Absolutely wrathful, remember?"

I nod. "Always."

"Good," he says. "Oh, and Voclain?"

"Yeah?"

"The tour isn't over yet." His lips lift into a wry curl. "There's something I really think you need to see."

I thought I knew what it felt like to be small—but nothing could have prepared me for the greenhouse.

Aaron and I stand underneath an aventurine dome of glistening glass panels, warped with age and laced with ivy. With high ceilings and intricate water fixtures, it's unlike anything I've ever seen before. Split into different closed-off sections, each part of the building overflows with emerald-green leafery and dew-covered flowers that glint like gems. No matter where I turn, there are plants grabbing my ankles and brushing against the side of my cheek. I've never felt so breathless, privileged, and insignificant all at once.

"I call this the main room." Aaron pulls off his sweater to reveal a clean white tee. I remove my puffer jacket, and he walks our extra layers over to a hook by the door before returning to my side. "It's pretty miscellaneous, as you can tell. Doesn't have much of a purpose other than to look nice and grow stuff."

I nod, unable to give much more of a response. I'm stuck trying to scrape my jaw off the floor, spinning in small circles as I absorb everything around me. The room hums with the buzz of insects and the chirping of small songbirds. Unlike the frigid world outside, this air is warm and humid, dense with the sticky sweetness of floral perfumes and nectar. The moisture in the air teases my hair, curling it around my face in tighter ringlets than usual. An entire ecosystem seems to be flourishing in this sea glass palace, like a giant bioactive terrarium. It feels like I've taken a step into the Yester-days, when rainforests were still alive and lush, when the world wasn't so brittle and gray and dead.

An elegantly tiled pool of shallow water occupies the center, stretching across the room in one large rectangle. Flanked with lush potted greenery, it looks like a hidden secret. I walk along the edge of the pool, stopping to crouch down and trace my fingers along the surface of the water. Even in the room's warmth, the liquid feels cool against my fingertips.

For the first time in what feels like ages, I am met by my reflection. I see myself in a warped mirror image that pulsates every time a ring of ripples passes through it, waving like a mirage. I look so different than I thought I would. Like I'm an entirely new person. I splash the image and it contorts into something unrecognizable.

I rise to my feet, wiping the water on my jeans and inspecting the rest of my surroundings. The floor is a satin-polished concrete that announces my every step with a soft *click*. As I pace slowly, I notice that two separate staircases occupy either side of the room, with ornate stone steps that lead up to a balcony that curls around the interior of the dome. I can only imagine how many hours Aaron has spent up there, unreachable from every bad thing, just enjoying the beauty of it all.

I shift my gaze to the abundance of fruit trees that line the edges of the room in large blue ceramic pots, trying not to salivate. It's been a while since I've had anything to eat, and the sight of all this greenery makes me remember just how starved I really am. I clutch my growling abdomen to soothe the hunger pains but it does little to help.

"You must be starving," Aaron says, arms folded. "Why didn't you say anything earlier? We could have gotten you some breakfast."

I shrug. "It's easier to get used to hunger than to pay attention to it all the time."

He studies me, stretching his lips into a thin line before shaking his head and moving on. "Well, we grow a lot of food here. You see all these?" Aaron points to the fruit trees. "You can take your pick."

I point to a round tree, spotted with plump orange fruits that gleam in pools of warm afternoon light. The fruits are smooth and topped with curling leaves that look like stars.

Aaron leads me over to the tree without hesitation, plucking one of the orange oddities from its branch. He wipes it with the fabric of his shirt before handing it to me. Now that I hold it in my hands, I inspect the fruit with suspicion.

"Go on, try it."

Cautiously, I sink my teeth into its flesh and find myself overwhelmed by a bland rush of sweetness. I discover that I'm not a fan of the taste at all, but regardless, I devour it in a blink. Aaron hands me another one and I inhale it ravenously.

"We grow a lot of persimmons here," Aaron says. "I personally think they're gross, but the trees produce a lot of fruit and they're extremely nutritious. More bang for your buck, I guess."

"They're disgusting." I chuckle. But I jump up to grab a third one anyway, because I'm desperate to eat my fill.

For the first time in weeks, I feel nourished.

"This is where we'll be working most of the time," Aaron explains, walking in a circle and spreading his hands out wide. "It's the largest and most functional of the buildings here at the Cut—and it belongs exclusively to our herbalism department. *And* the botanical research department. Oh, and we can't forget the agricultural department either."

"Let me guess—that's all you?"

"Bingo." Aaron smirks. "Let me show you around."

But before we get the chance to leave, something materializes before me. For a moment, I think it's a piece of paper falling from the ceiling, but that wouldn't make any sense, and instead, I am left puzzled. It flutters like a falling leaf. Its patterns are irregular, almost *alive* in its movement. It's painted turquoise and black and it lands on my nose.

But when I look down, I see a pair of alien eyes looking right back at me.

"Aaron," I mutter, trembling in fear as my heart picks up its pace. I'm too afraid to make any sudden movements as he walks over to inspect this *thing* that rests on my nose. It opens and folds like a piece of machinery, displaying strangely beautiful artwork as it does so.

"Calm down, Voclain." Aaron laughs. "It's not gonna hurt you."

"*You don't know that.*"

"It's just a butterfly. They're harmless pollinators."

A butterfly? I've only ever read about those in books. I stay frozen as he scoops it up gently, careful not to touch its wings. The creature rests on his finger for a while before flying away, and when I look up, I realize the whole place is swarming with them.

"They used to be a lot more common in the Yesterdays, but they're extremely endangered now. Which is probably why you didn't see many of them in the city, if any at all," Aaron says. "They also hibernate, so you wouldn't have seen them when you were out in the woods either. At least not this time of year." He looks up at the ceiling, eyeing the creatures with fondness. "But they were all here when Noriko found the place."

Aaron leads me through a doorway and into a smaller room overstuffed with planter boxes. Shelves of herbs and medicinal plants line the walls, sorted and labeled meticulously. There must be enough plants in here to supply not only the Cut, but all of Aaron's smuggling contacts with a lifetime of medicine.

"Wow," I say, breathing it all in. "This is…"

"The most wonderful thing you've ever seen?" Aaron finishes my sentence for me. "How kind of you."

I turn around to face him, eyes wide. "Did you really do all of this yourself?"

"Oh, no." He shakes his head. "I can't take all the credit. A lot of this was already here when we found it. Still had a few functioning automatic sprinklers and everything."

"Really?"

Aaron nods. "It took a lot of work to get it into proper shape—it was pretty overgrown and everything—but I managed."

"How do you manage all of this alone?"

"I do get a lot of help," he explains. "The automatic irrigation system is a lifesaver. Lori has made a lot of improvements over the years. I also get a lot of volunteer assistance as needed."

"Where did Lori learn how to do all of that?"

"She grew up tinkering with a lot of things. Taking stuff apart and putting it back together again."

Aaron's words feel like salt to a gaping sore. I look down at my feet. "My brother was the same way."

He notices my discomfort and gives me a half-hearted smile. *Maybe Milo and Lori would have gotten along.*

"So," I clear my throat, "what about your dad? You mentioned he was a healer. Does he help out too?"

"When he can, definitely." Aaron shoves his hands in his pockets. "My dad isn't as invested in plants as he is in healing, though. He works on the more human side of it all. You know, focusing on how Nightjade affects the human body rather than researching the structure of the plant itself like I do. I'm usually the one left taking care of this place."

"So what you're saying is…"

He winks. "This greenhouse is all ours, Voclain."

I walk along the shelves, tracing the wood with my fingers and reading the names of all the plants. Every herb is organized in alphabetical order. The ones I recognize tug at my heart, and I feel like I'm back on the McLellan's floor with Yesterday encyclopedias spread out like blankets around me. Aaron follows me close behind, hands behind his back as I observe his work. I can't even imagine all the hours he must pour into making this place as functional as it is beautiful.

"Where did you learn all of this?" I turn my head around to look at him for a moment before returning my gaze to the herbs.

"My father."

"Will I get to meet him sometime?" I ask. "He sounds like a pretty cool guy."

"Sometime, yeah." Aaron nods, placing his hands behind his back. "A lot of this also came from old Yesterday books, actually."

I whip my head around. "Books?"

"There's a huge library on the square," he says after a while. "I could take you there sometime."

My eyes widen. "Really?"

He wiggles his eyebrows, and I take it as a yes.

"I use a lot of what I've learned there to do—well, this." He gestures with his hands. "Part of your job here—if you choose to accept—will be to help me prepare herbal remedies and supplements. Tinctures, teas, salves, stuff like that. To keep the Cut healthy, you know?"

"And you make medicine for people outside the Cut too, right?" I ask, remembering all of the medicine we traded over the summer.

"We do help quite a few people when we can. Mostly just distant relatives of people at the Cut, or friends of friends. That kind of thing."

I nod.

"But as I mentioned before, there are a few other places like us out there," he says. "We call them sister compounds, but some of them are located in abandoned rural communities or just secluded clearings out in the woods. I'm sure there are some other abandoned compounds like this too."

He plucks a basil leaf from a pot on one of the shelves, eating it raw.

He offers me one too, and I take a bite. The flavor is sharp but refreshing, and I grab another one. *In addition to having antibacterial and anti-inflammatory properties, regular consumption of basil helps detox your body, manage stress, fight anxiety, and soothe depression,* I think to myself, reciting one of the passages I read as a child. I look at the leaf in my hands and realize that Aaron probably knows what he's doing.

"My point is," Aaron says, "I'm sure there are many rebel groups doing the same thing that we do, all across the country."

Curious, I reach out to touch a potted plant, and he swats my arm away. I scowl. "You just—" I point to the half-bitten basil leaf in his hands.

"Hey. I'm an experienced leaf-picker, alright? It takes a certain finesse."

I give him an unamused look. "Finesse?"

"I'm serious, Voclain." Aaron swallows his last basil leaf and leads me to another doorway. "Look, don't touch. Especially in this next room."

We exit the room and enter another one about the size of a large janitor's closet. When I look around, I realize that it might actually *be* a closet. The walls are lined with hooks of strange tools and equipment I don't recognize. I notice that instead of having a back wall, this room has a transparent curtain that leads to a larger section of the greenhouse.

Aaron hands me a device he calls a respirator mask. He instructs me to put it on along with a pair of gloves, but he doesn't bother wearing one as he leads me into the next part of the greenhouse.

The section is a rectangular glass box attached to the dome building behind us like the front of an igloo. This part feels more like a traditional greenhouse, with dirt floors and less overgrown flora. The corner by the entrance seems to be a makeshift lab of industrial sinks and plastic folding tables covered in miscellaneous equipment. But the majority of the room's square footage is taken up by a grid of low planter boxes filled with a plant I don't recognize.

"What is all of this?" I ask, my voice muffled by the mask.

"It's just a little something I've been working on," Aaron says. "I call it Catnap."

I crinkle my nose. "Like catnip?"

"No, like a catnap. It means a quick sleep, more of a light doze than a nap," Aaron explains. "It's a hybrid version of Nightjade that works as a natural sedative."

"How is it different from Nightjade?"

"Nightjade is only a sedative for the debugged. It kills Chips, remember?"

"So this one isn't deadly?"

"Not at all," Aaron says. "And it only works on Chips, since they're weakened by the chemical released by the trackers. But instead of causing death, it only causes sleep—and we debugged folks are completely immune to it."

"Then why do you want me to wear a mask?" I ask.

"Because the drug's still in your system. The trigger, as my dad likes to call it," he says. "But in a week or two, you'll be trigger-free like the rest of us."

Detox, I think, remembering the basil.

I study the sea of plants for a moment before turning back to Aaron. "Why do you need so much of it? What's it for?"

"You'll see later," he says. "But for now, we should probably get out of here." He walks toward the curtain, parting it for me to walk through. "I have work to do. You can hang out with Ren and Noriko for a while."

"Umm, that's not happening." I remove the mask and gloves once I'm inside the closet-like room, handing the gear to Aaron, who puts it back in its proper place.

"As long as Noriko's with you, you'll be safe. You won't be alone with him."

My chest tightens. "That's not what I'm worried about."

We walk through the room with the herbs and back into the main room with the dome. "I don't know what to tell you, Voclain."

"What sort of work are you doing?"

"Foraging for mushrooms."

"Can I tag along?"

"No."

Part of me wants to know more about Aaron's work as a healer and botanist, but the stronger half of my reasoning wants to avoid Ren at all costs. The thought of spending another moment with Ren—even with someone else there—is enough to make me want to scream.

"Why not?" I argue. "I'm supposed to be helping you out around here, right? Shouldn't you be teaching me things like foraging if it's an important part of your work?"

"You're malnourished, exhausted from Running, have healing wounds, and had minor hypothermia. Remember that? Hypothermia? And how you wouldn't shut up about it?"

"Yeah."

"Not to mention the panic attack."

I frown, face red. "So?"

"I'm serious, Voclain." All wit has drained from his voice, and he glares at me like I'm being unwise. "Those are no joke."

I look down at my feet, shoving my hands in my pockets.

"You just got debugged too. Some people have withdrawal symptoms so you need to be taking it easy while the trigger leaves your system," Aaron insists. "And taking it easy does *not* mean going on a hike in the snow and physically exerting yourself more than you have to."

"Is it a long hike?"

"No, but—"

"Then I'll be okay."

"It's still a no."

"Aaron." I grab his arm and we stop walking. I can't be around Ren. Not when it hurts too much to even think about him. "Please."

When Aaron looks down at me, I can tell he hears the desperation in my voice. He sees it in my eyes, and he has to turn away for a moment before looking at me again with a frustrated sigh. "Fine."

I give him a small grin. "Thank you."

"But if I can't physically stop you, I will most certainly fight you verbally."

"I can handle it," I say. "What's the worst that can happen?"

"Death by poisonous mushrooms, probably," Aaron says. "But that sounds more like a rescue to me."

The woods are a lot more peaceful now that I'm not on the run for my life.

Aaron and I hike quietly, but it's a good kind of silence that lets us hear things we wouldn't have noticed before. Like the crunching of shoes against a thick shield of snow, or the sound of my own heartbeat's fleeting thumps. A bird whistles somewhere in the distance, and I nearly jump as a rabbit scurries past our feet, snapping fallen twigs as it vanishes just as quickly as it appeared. I try not to think about the rabbit too much.

Our breaths hang in the air like curls of smoke. Towering pines loom above us like mountains, their velvety emerald branches weighed down by thick clumps of white. The citrusy aroma of evergreen needles and snow-dampened earth steeps in my nose like brewing tea.

Aaron walks by my side with his satchel slung over his shoulder, matching his pace to mine. He stares straight ahead for a long time, keeping track of the path, until he turns to face me.

"So… how was your talk today?" he asks flatly. "I mean it's not my place, but you seem preoccupied."

"It was fine," I grumble, gaze fixed on the trees in front of us.

"You don't sound very fine."

"Well I am."

"Are you sure?" He speaks slower now, raising an eyebrow in concern.

I let out a sigh, knowing I can't avoid the topic forever. "No."

He pauses. "Is there anything you can do about it?"

"I don't think so."

"Well, the good thing is," Aaron says, "there's usually an answer to every problem."

"Not this." I shake my head. "I don't think I can fix this."

"I'm not saying that everything is fixable. Because that's not really true," he says. "Sometimes the answer is just… doing what feels right to you. Whether that's communicating something you've been wanting to say, or —I don't know. Taking steps to heal from something that's been hurting you." I avert his gaze. "You just have to know how to find—*here!*"

He interrupts his own train of thought as he runs to a fallen log, where a few mushrooms stick to the wood and fan out like feathers. They're covered in bits of frost that look more like clumps of granulated white sugar than snow, and he wipes it off with the sleeve of his jacket. I crouch down to sit beside him.

"Turkey tails," he explains. "Magical stuff. Full of antioxidants, helps balance bacteria in your gut. Strengthens the immune system."

My gut twists in remembrance. "Margot took turkey tail supplements."

"I know." He turns to me and grins. "I was the one preparing them, remember?"

I help Aaron wipe away the snow and excess dirt before he begins to cut the strange life forms from their place on the log. There's something so youthful about his enthusiasm for the natural world, and the concept makes me grin.

Aaron is a mystery, and I get the sense that he really isn't the open book he pretends to be. I could recite all the facts he told me about the Cut and have only one or two sentences about his person, even after spending so many days by his side. Beneath his cynical surface, there seems to be a darkness to him I can't help but be wary of.

But there is a light too, and the more time I spend with him, the more I see it shine through.

I watch as he inspects each mushroom, removing any crawling critters he discovers on the way. He sets them free in the snow.

"Here," Aaron says after a while, pulling a spare sheathed knife out of his satchel. "Use this."

"I'm guessing you bring a hunting knife and a surgery blade *and* a spare with you everywhere you go."

"Good observation, Voclain. But actually, it's yours. I forgot to give it back to you this morning."

I held onto it for you after everything that happened last night, he says without speaking, afraid to remind me of the debugging—and Ren.

"Thank you." I grab the knife and uncover it, storing the sheath within my boots.

I follow Aaron's technique and begin to remove the turkey tails from the log, remembering to be gentle to the little black beetles I find along the way. I pluck them carefully from their hideouts and set them down as softly as possible.

One of the beetles falls over. Flat on its back, it kicks frantically, unable to find its way upright. I watch it struggle. I watch it try so hard to get back up, but it fails after each attempt.

There's something chilling about its helplessness. Something familiar. I can't bear to watch it happen anymore, so I turn it over and watch it scurry away. I shudder as I return to the task at hand.

We've harvested nearly all of the turkey tails by now. When Aaron is satisfied with our findings, I place the knife back in its sheath, tucked away in my boots for now. I rise to my feet, dusting off dirt and snow as Aaron shoves our findings in a small cloth sack he pulled from his satchel.

But before he has a chance to place the last of the mushrooms in his bag, a twig snaps.

Aaron and I freeze. The atmosphere has shifted. I clench my fists, hands trembling. Goosebumps prickle the back of my neck, sending shivers up and down my spine. My lungs lock up and swallow the key, because I know we are not alone out here. The air is too heavy for me to believe it is only a rabbit. I turn around so slowly I can hear my muscles creak.

Aaron drops the mushrooms, and they hit the snow without a sound.

Duke Carmody is standing behind us—and I scream when he shoots Aaron in the arm with a Nightjade bullet.

I cry out when Aaron falls to the ground, like I have fallen too. Blood drips from his wound and into snow, staining the milky layer of frost a gruesome pink that makes me sick to my stomach. Although Nightjade isn't fatal to him, it really does seem like he's dead for good. I want to rush to his side and help him, but I can't.

Duke is pointing the gun at me.

My nails burrow so deep within the flesh of my palms that I wonder if they draw blood. It takes everything I have to stand still. Unlike Aaron, I still have the trigger in my system. The tracker is long gone but the chemical still runs through my blood. One wrong move, one mistake, and I will be dead in the blink of an eye.

"Don't move," Duke snarls.

My heart rattles in its cage, pounding against my chest like it's trying to escape.

All my life, I have pretended to be so unafraid—but Duke Carmody is one of the only human beings who can scare me to silence.

He is not like Ren. He Chases with a different kind of necessity, the very same kind I saw in the eyes of the Officers who took everything away from me. Duke will do anything to get what he wants, and he will not let me stand in the way of his desires.

Hands shaking, I watch as Duke shifts. Nightjade guns are small compared to their Yesterday counterparts, and he fits it between his teeth to free his hands. He ties my wrists together with a thin rope before grabbing me by the hair and forcing me to stand up. It burns, but I can't let him know that.

I keep my face emotionless because he wants me to be afraid of him. He wants me to fear the boy with the Nightjade, but I won't allow him to receive that gratification. I won't let him see the dread I tremble with.

He pulls the gun out of his mouth and holds it against my back with burning white knuckles, the other arm holding my shoulder to keep me from running away.

"Walk," he orders, pressing the gun deeper between my shoulder blades. "Now."

I have no choice but to follow his instructions and move forward.

I am the beetle.

This morning, I was so angry at Ren for playing savior, for keeping me from my perfect death in the snow. I think back to how I felt at the fence, and how hard it was to breathe after he left me with all of those truths. But now, with a gun pressed to my back, I can finally see things clearly.

I would rather live to see a better tomorrow than meet my end before things change. I can't let myself be killed—not now. Not after seeing all the hope the Cut can bring to people just like me. Not until every truth festering in my throat is expelled.

I've finally come closer to realizing my purpose, and I know there is so much more for me to do. People to help, memories to honor, loved ones to grieve—and a world split in two that is not yet whole.

It can't end yet, not when it feels like my life has only begun.

"Where are you taking me?" I ask, because I need to say something—anything to make me feel like I have at least an ounce of control. To help me pretend I am unafraid.

"*Walk*," Duke repeats with more malice, and I shut my mouth in an instant.

We journey through the woods for what seems like years. Ages go by, and I almost expect the snow to melt around me. But it remains, mocking me as it always seems to do when death is close.

The trees start to spread out as we approach a rugged gray coastline that reminds me of my days at Port Keys, of all the hours I spent at that coffee shop on the edge of the world. We reach a collection of jagged cliffs covered in wild grass that look over the water below. Waves scream violently, crashing against wet corroded stone the color of nightfall. My skin is freckled with mist, and I can smell the stench of dried kelp and salt in the breeze that tangles my hair.

Even after all the time I spent at Port Keys over the summer, I've never ventured this close to the shore. All I know of the ocean is what I've seen through windows. I never imagined I'd make my first real trip to the sea with a gun glued to my back.

Duke lowers the gun and moves his grip to my arm. For a moment I'm worried he'll toss me off the side of the cliff, but he doesn't. Instead, he drags me down a sandy trail, all the way down to the shore. I start to wonder if being thrown off the cliff would have been a more desirable fate.

The sand below my feet is not the same as the finely ground substance I weaponized after graduation, back on that playground with Ren and Carmody. This sand can barely be called sand at all. Instead, we walk upon an ocean of tiny black pebbles, sharp and slick with saltwater.

He brings me about five feet away from the reach of the waves before throwing me to the sand. The grains are solidified by the moisture from the waves, a hard surface that sends a numbing jolt through my nerves.

With my hands tied behind my back, I struggle to sit upright. The wind toils with my tangled hair, making it difficult to see. Spits of saltwater and stray hands of hair slice the surface of my exposed right eye. It waters, but I do not cry. I will not cry. I am too angry to show him any scrap of weakness.

"Eddie Voclain, at last," Duke says with a hollow laugh. But there is no humor to be found in his voice. "I've been dreaming of this moment for a long time."

He walks over to where I sit in the sand, crouching with the gun in one hand. He runs the other through his greased brown hair before letting it drop. "Do you have any idea how *difficult* you've made things for me?"

I glare. "I've been told I'm difficult, yeah."

"I had a hunch that you were still alive, even after your tracker was disabled," he says, studying his white gun like fine wine he wants to critique. "Guess my suspicions were correct."

"Aww, he's learning!"

He slaps me across the face. My mouth fills with the taste of iron, and I spit the results of his hit directly on his armor.

Disgusted, he takes the gun and presses it against my forehead, reminding me who has the power in this situation. Certainly not the girl with tied hands. "I'd watch it if I were you."

I glower, shaking with uncertain rage, but I keep my mouth shut tight.

"You know, I can't really say I'm surprised by all of this." Duke chuckles. "When McLellan first went missing, I thought he finally went in for the kill without me. But deep down, I knew he would never lay a hand on you, even if he wanted to. Poor kid doesn't have my guts."

My mouth turns dry, and it's difficult to swallow with the lump that forms in my throat.

"And then *his* tracker went off, so I had to find you the old-fashioned way. Following your footprints, watching from a distance," he says. "You're reckless, you know. I found you and your friend over there far too easily."

"What do you want, Duke?" I seethe, trying not to imagine Aaron bleeding in the snow. Trying not to imagine what the answer could be.

"Information," the Chaser answers, removing the gun to study it again. "I checked in with HQ earlier and filled them in on everything. Unfortunately for you, the extermination order on your head has been lifted, temporarily. The Corps wants more info on you and your new buddies."

Duke chuckles, but then his voice grows dark. "I personally think it's a waste of time, but I have orders. Orders I'm obligated to follow."

"Information?" I scoff. "That's ridiculous."

"I think you know exactly what I'm talking about." He points the gun to my face again, tracing my jawline before pressing it into my neck. But he doesn't stop there. Instead, he shifts his aim to my upper arm—exactly where my healing wound resides. "I want you to tell me all about that little compound of yours."

My heart somersaults as I stare at the weapon. Chills pour from my neck, drenching my shoulders and dripping down the rest of my body. I forgot Aaron's jacket back in the greenhouse, but I'm still wearing a long-sleeved sweater that covers my skin.

If Duke knows where my wound is—then how long had he been watching me out in those woods? How long has he been waiting, stalking me like a stranded deer leading him right back to the rest of the herd?

And if he can exhibit that much patience, then how far is he willing to go to get the information he wants?

Duke's threats are rattling, but my face remains stoic. I can't let him see my disbelief.

"But don't be so quick to think you're off the hook, Voclain. I know a thing or two about pain." He digs the gun deeper into my bandaged wound, and I bite my lip to keep from crying out. He leans in closer to whisper in my ear. "This will all be so much easier if we make this quick."

I clench my jaw, ignoring the fire in my arm. "I don't know what you're talking about."

"You can't play dumb with me, Eddie. We're both so much smarter than that." He chuckles. "You're foolish, but you're no idiot."

"It's Lavender," I correct him. He has no right to call me Eddie. He doesn't know me at all.

To my surprise, he pulls the gun away from my wound, still holding it tight. With the other hand, he pulls something out of the storage compartment in his suit. I furrow my brows while trying to make out its shape, and then my eyes widen.

It's a handheld garden weeder, like the one I'd found in the farmer's toolshed. It even has the same wooden handle and everything. My heart drops when I realize it's the exact same tool I'd left behind.

My chest tightens and I feel like I'm sinking again when I realize what this means. If I had a tracker inside of me, then of course they were able to follow my every move, including my dairy farm detour. All the way to that shed I was hiding in.

That means when the farmer lied about my whereabouts, they knew I was still on the property.

Duke would not have let him live for that.

I squeeze my good eye shut, trying to stay afloat. I can't think about what they did to that man, or how I played a role in his demise. Not now. I need to focus on getting out of this alive.

Duke keeps the gun in hand, a reminder that in spite of his orders, he will kill me if he has to. No matter how much information I hold, I am still a traitor, and even a low-ranking Chaser like him could get away with a death like mine. He is in charge here, and he wants me to know my fate is in his hands.

Now, he presses the forked tip of the weeder against my arm's wound instead. He applies no pressure, but I tremble anyway, because I know he could in a blink. He leans over to whisper in my ear. "I would start talking, if I were you."

"You're delusional."

"Am I?"

"I already told you," I mutter. "I don't know what you're talking about."

"You know a lot more than you think, Eddie." He grins a haunting shark smile I will never be able to erase from my memory. "And you're going to tell me all of it."

Once, I believed that knowledge would save me. I thought seeking it out would help me protect the people I love. I thought it could help me fix the world I've learned to hate so much.

But I know how foolish I was for believing it was as simple as that. What knowledge I have is just as much my greatest weakness as it is my deadliest weapon. Now, what I know could put not only myself but the entire Cut in danger.

"Even if I did know what you're referring to," I hiss, "why would I do that?"

"Don't worry, Eddie. I'm not gonna kill you. Not yet, at least."

"*Lavender.*"

"But I will get you to talk," Duke says, ignoring my correction. "And I can make the last moments of your pathetic little life very, *very* painful."

I force myself to laugh. I will not be weak. *I will not show him my fear.*

"I don't think you have the guts."

Duke and all the air around him come to a jarring freeze. Even the wind that tosses waves and grains of sand and pieces of our hair seems to slow to a halt. The world has been dampened to a low, spine-chilling whisper.

By questioning his authority, my verbal claws have scratched too close to his Achilles' heel.

Nostrils flaring, Duke presses his lips into a thin, twitching line. "I have more guts than you'll ever have, Voclain."

Before I can say another word, he grabs me by the arms, dragging me away from the shoreline. I kick and flail and try to break free, but his grip on my tethered wrists remains firm, and I am no match for his unbreakable armor.

The sand grows coarse as the distance between us and the shore expands, and it feels like I'm being dragged across millions of sharp teeth rather than tiny little rocks. He lets me go when we reach the point where the sand is thickest. The grains are still a lot smaller than pebbles here, but they feel like crushed shards of glass. I crawl back and scramble upright, trying to distance myself from Duke as much as possible, but find myself cornered against a barnacle-crusted boulder.

He crouches in front of me, kneeling on my shins to keep me from moving away. Under his weight, my boot-hidden blade presses through its leather sheath and digs into the skin of my ankle. I bite my lip and try not to wince as my sock absorbs the spreading blood.

"You won't talk?" he growls. "Fine. I'll make you talk."

I say nothing.

My heart pounds angry fists against my chest as Duke reaches for the white bandage taped around my eye. Instinctively, my arms twitch to stop it, but they're still tied behind my back. Unlike a bandaid, he rips it off slowly, making sure to take his time with the peel. When it is gone, I squeeze my left eye shut, desperate to protect my recent wound from the threat of salted air.

Duke sets the weeder in the sand, with his Nightjade gun still wrapped beneath his left fingers. "You remember that night at the park now, don't you?"

"Of course I remember," I snap, remembering everything he did to Ren—and trying not to think about what Duke would have done if I hadn't intervened.

"*I couldn't see for days!*" he yells, spitting as the words fall out. "Do you have any idea what that kind of burning feels like? That weakness? To be temporarily blinded in *both* eyes?"

My left eye throbs. "You know nothing about pain if you're hung up on a bit of sand."

"You think it's funny, don't you?" He chuckles with empty eyes. "You won't find it so funny after you feel it for yourself. Suit, arms."

In an instant, his suit folds into itself until it's sleeveless. I don't know why he would suddenly decide to expose these limbs, but I don't question it further. Any weakness is something I can exploit.

But before I have time to defend myself, Duke uses his hand to hold my left socket open. The air burns the surgical wound in my eye as it's exposed to the wind and salt. It's nowhere close to being healed, and I try not to wince as it's cut by the breeze and flyaway strands of hair.

And as I struggle to pry him off, I realize why he removed the armor around his arms.

He wanted to free his hands. He wants to be precise; he wants to feel the effect of the pain he inflicts, and he couldn't do that with those bulky metal Chaser gloves in the way. He grabs a mound of damp wet sand with his free hand, coarse grains drip down his pale arm like something rotten—and the air is stolen from my lungs.

"*No*," I protest, as though it will save me. Sweat dews on my forehead like beads of glass. "You don't have to do this, Duke."

"You see, here's the thing." He grins that sickening grin again. "I do."

Sand shreds my recovering eye with a thousand needle-sharp talons. I feel like I'm back in the woods with a knife to my cornea, only now, I have a reason to be afraid. A reason to struggle, to unintentionally increase the crudeness of the act with my kicking and clawing and screaming. But no matter what I do, he doesn't budge.

I am the beetle.

He presses his hand against my face, packing the sand inside. It burns like nothing I've felt before, a thousand individual daggers impaling my eye all at once. All I can manage to do is scream.

"Are you ready to start talking now?" Duke sneers, holding up another handful of wet sand. "Why don't you go ahead and tell me who's in charge of this whole operation, huh?"

I want the agony to end. I want him to leave me alone, to leave my life for good, and never come back to haunt me again. I'm so tired of fighting and I just wish he and the sand and the pain would disappear.

But giving up would hurt so many people. For once, I will keep my mouth shut when it counts. No matter what happens—I *will* not talk.

Aaron's words echo in my head. *This is bigger than me. Bigger than all of us.*

"Never," I mutter.

I expect Duke to keep toying with the wound, but he doesn't. For a foolish heartbeat, I catch a glimpse of false hope, and I wonder if he's had his fill, if he's finally given up on getting me to speak.

But that blissful ignorance is short-lived, and my blood turns to stone as his focus transitions from a sand-filled socket to my one good eye.

I quiver, trembling helplessly as he holds my right eyelid open, terrified of the inevitable. I flail, trying to kick him off, but he pushes me back. My ears ring as the back of my head slams into the barnacled rock behind me.

He uses the hand with the gun to hold my hair, to keep me in place. My vision spins and I can't fight it when everything goes dark with sand. Coarse, heavy, salty sand. I shriek with the gulls that fly above our heads.

It feels like someone has taken a lit match to my eyes, like every time I scream I am swallowing gravel dry. With the enhancement Duke's armor provides, my struggling does nothing but worsen the pain.

There is no part of me that doesn't shake with the weakness Aaron warned me about. He cautioned me not to push myself—and I didn't listen. Again, I was reckless. Again, I didn't stop to think, and now I am paying the price.

I'm trapped—and there's absolutely nothing I can do about it.

"You know what I should do? To get you to talk?" he asks rhetorically, still pressing the sand into my open eye. "I should do this to Ren."

I jerk forward, rope cutting into my wrists as I try to break free. There is nothing I would love more than to claw his eyes out myself, but he pushes me back again. "So you still have a soft spot for him, huh? Even after he wanted to hurt you so badly?"

I spit in his face. Instead of slapping me, he speaks, and I cannot tell which form of torture I prefer.

"Wow. That's so..." He pauses, trying to find the perfect word to torment me. "Pathetic."

He laughs that bitter, vacant laugh of his. Even without my sight, I can feel his bestial gaze cutting into me, chilling my every pore.

"I pity you, Eddie," the Chaser says. "You love a boy who will never love you back."

"That's not true." I protest every part of his sentence.

"He was so obsessed with killing you," he says. From the sound of his voice, I can practically hear him grinning from ear to ear. "But you already knew that, right?"

I squirm, but he pins down my shoulders with both hands, including the one that holds the gun. "It was almost annoying." Duke chuckles. "He just wouldn't shut up about it. Went on and on and on, fantasizing about all the ways he could end your life. All he wanted to do was hurt you."

"You're a liar," I hiss, but not as confidently as I would have liked.

"You're the liar, Eddie. Remember?" He leans in so close I can feel his breath paint my face like sea spray. "Remember what you did to your family?"

I freeze. I stare without seeing. The wind blows, but I can't feel it.

"They died because you're a coward," he says. "And they died because you could never accept that fact as truth."

"*You don't know what you're talking about!*" I shriek so loud I can taste blood in my throat. "You know nothing."

"I don't know what made Ren change his mind, really. What made him save your life that night in the snow. You wanna know what I think?"

He keeps his left forearm pressed against my neck, and with his right hand, I can hear him reach for the weeder in the sand. He lifts it to my chin, tracing my cheekbones. The snake-tongued blade stops once it touches the corner of my left eye.

"I think he wants to get close to you again so he can enjoy your extermination. So he can live out all those twisted, sadistic fantasies he told me about in the woods."

I quiver with rage, baring my teeth. "You're sick."

"You've got it all backwards," Duke argues. "I'm not the sick one here... it's you. You're all sick. Each and every one of you goddamn rebel cultists.

"You're a bad luck charm, Eddie." He leans so close his lips touch my ear. "From the moment you were born, you were designed to make the world worse."

Before I can do anything to protest, he rolls up my left sleeve and removes the bandage from my arm. The weeder carves horizontally, slicing along the line left by another Chaser so long ago. I cry out in pain, but I can't struggle, and even if I could, I'd be afraid to make it worse. *Just push through*, I tell myself. *It'll be over soon.*

My stomach knots itself into arthritic twists, tangling and untangling itself in an endless repeating motion. I realize that he is not only retracing the wound but adding to it, slicing in a shape that feels like a horseshoe turned over on its side.

But when he lifts the weeder and moves to the flesh below, I realize that was no horseshoe.

It was a *U*.

I pull against the binds that tie my wrists together, trying with all my might to break free, but I can't. All the strength I thought I had is gone, taken from me by the hunger I was devoured by in the woods, the infection in my hand I couldn't fix with forgotten medicine, the snow that tapped the life from my veins like syrup. Every moment of weakness I've collected weighs heavy on my shoulders. There is nothing I can do to keep him from carving something else into my skin—something that feels too similar to an *N*.

And an *L*.

Another *U* tells me exactly what he's writing.

Every symbol he carves—with the weeder I once selected as a weapon—

feels like my own mistake. Although it is his knuckles wrapped around the blade, I feel like I am only doing this to myself. Like I deserve this branding I can't even manage to fight off.

But the letters Duke carves are nothing compared to the words he's burned into my mind. They echo in my skull, more debilitating than the pain or even the blindness, because they cloud more than just my sight.

What if he's right about Ren? About all of us?

About me?

I think about every death I've caused in the wake of my path to defiance. I think of the woman in the creek, who I put in danger just from passing by. I think of the farmer, who tried to help me and paid the price. I think of my father's coworker, who was only caught because of my interference.

I remember my family. I remember Margot.

Why is it that, even after all that has happened, I still can't stop forcing myself in places I don't belong?

All my life I've been trying to find my place because I didn't want to accept the one I was given. To escape my father's expectations, I made the McLellans my family. I made rebellion my dream. And now, I want more than anything to become Unseen.

I think about my tour of the Cut, of how proud Aaron seemed to call this place home—a home that now, thanks to me, might be destroyed.

But more than anything, I wonder if I'm not fit to back the right cause.

What if Duke is right about my defiance? It's like I've thought all this time. I'm not fighting back because I'm brave. I'm fighting back because I'm afraid.

I can hear Ren's voice in my head.

"You just love falling off that ledge, but you never stop to think about who is taken with you."

Maybe the Unseen will be better off if I just let Duke win.

Maybe the world will be better off without me in it.

He finishes his *Y*, ending the word halfway down my arm. He pulls the weeder away, but I know he's not finished.

"Still not talking?" He chuckles, and I no longer have the energy to be angry. "I can fix that."

I made it this far. If I can keep my mouth shut for long enough—if I can withstand him tearing me to pieces without giving him the result he desires —his patience will run out. He will kill me, and the Cut will be safe. I will be free. I will find my death in the snow.

But something, lodged deep within the very core of all that I am, tells me no.

Everything goes quiet, and for the smallest moment, all I can hear is my brother's voice.

Run.

The world stops spinning. My heart stops beating. Everything goes quiet, and for the first time in a long time, I am no longer sinking.

Because I decide that I have lost too much to stop fighting back.

Letting Duke win would be a betrayal of everything I have ever known. To everything I believe. To everything I'm fighting for.

To everyone I love.

Letting Duke win is letting the system win. In his eyes, in his armored flesh, in the unseen blood that stains his hands in permanence, Duke is the perfect example of every flaw in our society. He is a disease, and he will not stop until his malice is spread to all.

No matter how badly I hurt—no matter how weak the world wants me to be—I can't just sit here and let him do this. I have to fight back.

Because this is bigger than me, and I finally know what that means.

I will always fight back.

My head pounds. My eyes burn. I cannot see a goddamn thing, but I can feel Duke's bare arm pressing against my throat—and I bite down as hard as I possibly can.

I sink my teeth into his flesh with all the hunger I can muster. He recoils instantly, removing his hands from my shoulders like I'm made of hot coals. I can taste iron. He swears under his breath and I can feel his rage beginning to boil over, like a pot that has been left unstirred for far too long.

I spit his blood in the sand. "That was for the Unseen, you bastard."

I cannot see him, but when the air around me shifts, I can feel the boiling in his blood. I can hear his patience snap. "You'll pay for that, Eddie."

I wait for the Nightjade bullet to dig into my skin, for the poison to enter my bloodstream and finally bring me to an end I no longer desire. I am a beetle trapped on my back, but at least I kept kicking.

But nothing happens. No gun is fired, no Nightjade courses through my veins. There is only the distant whispering of waves and the desperate cry of some forgotten gull.

And then the silence is broken.

"Put the gun down, Carmody."

There is a noise. Something clicks, and I hear a new voice in the air. It is muted by the sound of the sea, but I can still hear it, clearer than anything I've ever heard before. I don't need my sight to know who it belongs to.

I know Ren's voice better than I know my own.

REN

Saturday, January 13
Day 13

The mist is cold, but my blood runs colder.

My mother was still showing me around when she realized she hadn't heard from Aaron in a while. She tried contacting him with a communicative device from the Yesterdays called a *walkie-talkie*, but it was no use. He didn't respond, no matter how many times she tried to make a connection.

According to my mother, Aaron doesn't go radio silent, no matter how busy he might be. After a bit of asking around, we confirmed that he'd left to go foraging with Eddie.

Everything was suddenly chilled, but not from the snow. The world was suddenly too loud and too quiet all at once. It felt like something vital had snapped within me, a sudden imbalancing shift I couldn't place.

My mother handed me a spare Yesterday gun without a word. She walked away, and we both knew I was going to follow her into the woods.

I thought it was Aaron, at first. I didn't trust him, and I certainly didn't trust him with Eddie. It's easy to kill people in the woods and call it an *accident*.

But my theory changed when we found him with a Nightjade bullet in his arm.

It was then when I knew. I knew exactly what was going on, because this was my nightmare walking, real and breathing, here and there, far and close, and gone.

And now, as I stand in the sand, the nightmare is staring my gun in the face.

I stand a mere two yards away from the Chaser, my mother a few feet to my right. Carmody kneels on Eddie's shins. Her hands are tied behind her back as she leans against a large barnacle-infested rock, her face covered in wet, rocky sand. There's a bite mark on Carmody's exposed arm, and judging by the Nightjade gun in his hand, he's not too happy about it.

I study Eddie again and immediately, I'm brought back to graduation. Carmody may have hit her back then, but now, he's done so much worse. His hands are covered in the same sand that's smeared across both of her eyes. I notice the bloody weeder in the sand and Eddie's left arm. The sleeve has been rolled up all the way, and when I realize what I'm seeing, my heart plummets.

In crude, bright red letters, he's carved a word into her skin.

UNLUCKY

It takes all the strength I have not to shred him to pieces with my own bare hands.

You can't do that, I tell myself. He has a Nightjade gun, and if I make any sudden moves, there's no telling what he'll do—and a Nightjade bullet is something we can't afford. Eddie is still too weak to fight off the poison. Even with the tracker gone, the trigger is still in mine and Eddie's blood, as my mother explained—and that's not counting all of the injuries she's gathered on the run. A Nightjade gun is just as deadly to us as a Yesterday one.

I remember everything else my mother told me about the trackers. *"You will be weak for a while,"* she'd said. *"You've lived your whole life with the chemical trigger in your system. Now that your tracker is gone, so are the doses. Your body will experience withdrawal."*

She's right. A migraine has been chipping away at my skull all day. Nausea marbles my stomach. Even as I stand here clenching this gun with all my might, my whole body shakes like I've eaten nothing but air for a week, and feverish flashes of heat come and go in waves. I won't be able to beat Carmody in a hand-to-hand brawl.

I squeeze my jaw so tightly it aches. *But look at what he's done.*

He's hurt Eddie one too many times, and for that, he'll pay dearly.

"Put the gun down, Carmody."

The Chaser whips his head around, eyes widening when he notices our arrival. But the shock is quick to fade, replaced by a devilish smirk, as though he expected me to follow her here. Instead of obeying my command, he chuckles, like I'm the one being held at gunpoint and not him.

Moving closer with both hands on my weapon, I point it at his face, shouting between gritted teeth. "I said, put the gun down."

In a blink he is on his feet, turning his body to aim his weapon at me. "You first."

We stand six feet apart, but it feels like we're even closer as I dig my glare into his gaze like daggers. "We both know that'll never happen."

"And we both know that's a lie."

We hold our gaze in a brutal pause. The gaps in the silence are filled by the low hum of waves rolling against the shore, and the gulls that cry ballads above our heads.

Wind tangles my hair in all directions, covering my eyes with loose black strands. The breeze and the bandage over my wounded eye compromise my sight, but I can see everything so clearly.

Today is the day that, in one way or another, Duke Carmody will finally cease to exist.

"Step away from her," I command with all the force I can muster. Carmody doesn't budge. *"Now."*

He glares at me for a moment, unblinking. I see my mother pull out her gun in my peripheral vision, but I keep my glare fixed on Carmody. *She has a plan*, I realize. I just need to keep Carmody distracted—and I need to get him as far away from Eddie as possible.

Before I have the chance to formulate a plan of my own, he charges at me.

In a blink his body rams into my own, knocking me back with a blow that forces the wind from my lungs. We fall to the sand with a jolting thud.

My gun is a lot heavier than the lightweight Nightjade guns Chasers are trained to use, but it's light enough that I manage to keep my left fingers locked firmly around the weapon as we struggle. My grip is tight enough to blister. *I can't let Carmody have it.*

Once again we are at each other's throats, rolling around in the sand and making desperate grabs for power. And once again, I'm no match for his physical strength.

But the stakes are so much higher now. We are no longer the children we were on that playground. We are soldiers who have been conditioned and beaten and burned into believing we are monsters.

I can feel my training come back to me. I can feel the purpose the Corps instilled in my mind, etched like the carving in Eddie's skin. I can feel every other need fade to background noise. *Exterminate.*

As I lie flat on my back, I slam my knuckles into Carmody's nose and steal a glance at my mother. She has her gun, but judging by the look on her face, she can't get a clear shot in the middle of this altercation.

A fist cracks into my jaw. I try to push Carmody off of me, doing everything in my power to keep him from grabbing hold of the weapon. But my efforts are useless, because in a matter of seconds, he's able to snatch the gun from my hand.

I'm still on the ground when Carmody rises to his feet. He rushes over to Eddie, yanking her up from the ground and holding her close to his chest.

I ignite, burning with rage as I watch him drag Eddie away from the boulder and toward the shore. He keeps going until he stands in about three feet of foaming sea.

Carmody makes Eddie kneel down in the water, fist clenched on the back of her sweater as he holds the smaller Nightjade gun between his teeth. He stands next to her and points the Yesterday pistol against her neck, and it sends shivers of fear down my spine. She struggles to break free but it's no use.

"Look who's in charge now, McLellan." Carmody uses his mouth to toss the lightweight Nightjade gun into the distant sand, close enough for him to guard it and far enough to be just out of my reach.

I rise to my feet, knees wavering. "Let her go."

"You see, Ren, I don't really wanna do that," Carmody says. "Not until somebody talks."

I'm not daring enough to look at my mother or stupid enough to draw attention to her movements, but out of the corner of my eye, I watch her move. Slowly, she walks over to the boulder and crouches behind it. Carmody is so focused on Eddie and me that he doesn't seem to notice.

Judging by Eddie's injuries, Carmody's lost his patience with her. He knows she won't crack—and now, he'll use her as leverage to extract the information he wants from me instead.

My throat tightens at the thought. I know I can't talk. I can't give him anything to report back to HQ. But I can't let him hurt her anymore either.

Carmody gestures his chin toward me, holding Eddie close. "What do you know about the compound?"

"I don't know what you're talking about."

Carmody doesn't like that answer, and he forces Eddie's face into the waves. She writhes in pain as the water washes away the sand, but stings the fresh wounds with salt.

Against Carmody's wishes, Eddie manages to lift her head up on her own, elbowing his hand against the hard surface of his armored legs. He curses under his breath and holds the gun to her head again, reminding her who has the advantage in the situation.

I clench my fists so tightly I cut my own skin with my nails.

You have to stay calm, I tell myself. *Remember?*

"It's not too late to come back to the right side, Ren," Carmody says, almost desperately. "I have a plan, you know. But I can't do it alone."

My entire body tremors as I try to keep myself calm.

"We can put an end to this pathetic resistance. We can put all of this to rest and come back as heroes. *Heroes,* Ren. Remember?" Carmody chuckles.

"Just think about the promotion we'll get. The money, fame, a lifetime of Immunity for you and whoever else you desire. No more of this messy rebellion stuff. We could be *Agents*, Ren. *Agents*. Just like Ian."

His voice lowers, like he seriously expects me to consider the offer. "We'll finally be able to make things right in the world." He pauses. "We'll finally receive the respect we deserve."

Out of the corner of my eye, I can see my mother, still hidden behind the boulder with her gun. Carmody is so consumed by the conversation that he forgets all about her presence.

He doesn't see her aim her pistol, waiting for the right moment to shoot. *I need to keep him talking.*

"Why would I ever help you?" I shout.

"It's not about me. It's about *you*," he calls back. "You want all of that, right? A life of comfort? A life of justice?"

Stay calm. I tremble, trying so hard not to lose it. "Let her go, Carmody."

"You could save her, you know." The Chaser pulls Eddie up from the water until she is back on her feet again, still pressing the gun to her neck.

She is too close to him for my mother to make a good shot.

"No one knows what you've done. Not yet," he argues. "Come back to the Corps. We'll make up some excuse. We'll blame your dead tracker on the rebels. Come back to the Immunity, and we'll end this rebellion before it begins."

I shake my head.

"Don't you get it?" Carmody laughs. "You're a Chaser, Ren, and you're both eighteen. You know you can share your Immunity with her."

My heart feels like it's risen to my throat. That's not an option I've ever considered.

"Who cares about that complicated little history of yours? It's just a formality, really. A piece of paper." His tone softens, like he truly wants me to think about it. "You can still save her."

I clench my jaw, forcing my mouth to stay closed. *You're only distracting him. You're not actually considering this.*

"But she'll never be anyone's *assignment* ever again." Carmody pauses, glaring at Eddie and back at me again. "Isn't that something you want?"

My brow beads with sweat. As much as I'd love to pull him apart limb by limb for all he's done to Eddie, I cannot help but wonder.

There are a thousand awful words that couldn't describe Carmody with justice, but he's right. Taking down the Cut and returning as heroes would be the easiest way out of this mess—and it might be the only way to make it out alive at all.

Eddie and I could leave all of this behind. We would never have to think about Running or Chasing or the Unseen ever again. We could live simple lives as blissfully ignorant people, getting by in peace.

It would be the closest thing to turning back time.

But even if we could turn back time, can we ever truly go back? We can't bring back the people we lost, and there are some wounds that time can never heal. We can't rid ourselves of the hurt.

But can we go back to being who we used to be?

No, I remind myself. *There is no going back.*

"Don't listen to him," Eddie calls out. "He doesn't know anything. He just wants to use you; none of what he's saying would work."

For a moment, her eyes flicker to behind the boulder where my mother hides, and she looks away just as quickly.

"If we went back, we'd both be killed," she shouts, trying not to look at my mother. "They don't let traitors live."

"You see, then there's the matter of you *not* cooperating," Carmody says, ignoring Eddie's commentary. He presses the gun firmer against her head "Tell me what you know or I'll blow her brains out."

His fingers tremble with the itch to pull the trigger. He's been waiting so long for this, and now, her cards are in his hands. I know I need to keep his focus on me while my mother waits for the right moment to take him down, and I need to trust that she knows what she's doing.

I also know that Carmody's patience is fleeting at best. I glance into his empty gray eyes, and I can tell the itch burns deeper. He needs to hear me say something valuable soon.

But once again, I'm at a complete loss for words. I can't betray my parents and everything they've worked for, but I can't let Carmody hurt Eddie either. I'm stuck between two impossible decisions, and I can't say anything at all.

"So this is how it's gonna be, Ren?" Carmody traces the trigger with his finger. From where I stand, I can see how Eddie trembles, wanting so badly to fight back. I want to knock him down and beat him to bloody ribbons, but any sudden movements will only make him retaliate rashly.

I'm trapped.

"I guess you leave me with no choice," he says.

My heartbeat pounds against my chest. My lungs pinch shut, and suddenly, breathing is the hardest possible thing. *What can I do?*

What can I possibly do against a Chaser with a gun?

But to my surprise, Carmody moves his gun away from Eddie's head. For a moment, my eyes widen, and I wonder if he'll lower it completely.

And then, he raises his arm to the left—and he pulls the trigger before my mother can shoot first.

Just as Carmody promised, the sound of a lead bullet echoes all around. I fall to my knees, squeezing my good eye shut and pressing my hands against my ears. Gulls cry above our heads, shrieking as they flee the scene. And then, all is quiet, like the world has been put on pause. I open my eye.

My mother has been shot.

I move without thinking, rushing to her side. I have no words, like some invisible hand has reached into my throat and pulled out my tongue. Breathing is a forgotten practice when I fall to her side.

She lies peacefully in the sand, eyes open wide. On my knees, I cradle her in my arms, unable to scrape my eyes from the gaping wound in her side that stains my hands crimson. Frantic, I try to remember what they told us about gunshot wounds in training. But I can't for the life of me think of anything at all. All I know is the color red.

"Ren!" Eddie calls from her distance. "She'll be okay. You need to stay focused, alright? Keep applying pressure and *do not stop.* Alright? I—"

"You really think I'm that stupid, McLellan?" Carmody interrupts, laughing maniacally. I look up to see that he still holds onto Eddie, and the gun has returned to its place against her neck. "You really think I didn't see that coming?"

I can't focus on anything but the blood. There is so much of it, infecting the sand around us like a red illness. I can't keep my eyes from watering as I try to follow Eddie's commands. *Keep applying pressure.* Using both hands, I do just that. Tears cloud my vision and I try to ignore the parade of unwanted thoughts marching through my head.

She doesn't say a word as her eyes flutter to a close, but then they open again—as though she's been surprised by something. Her right hand begins to twitch ever so slightly, and when I look down, I see that she's still holding her pistol.

Her knuckles turn ghostly as she holds it with all her might. I give her a frightened look, begging her not to do what I think she's about to do. She needs to be saving her strength. She needs to stay still so I can pressurize the wound, because I can't lose the mother I only met a day ago. Not again.

She gives me one last smile before shooting Carmody in the leg.

The force of the shot knocks the gun out of her hands, and she's too weak to do anything else but let her eyes come to a close once more.

My heart races and my head spins as I check her neck for a pulse, and to my relief and surprise, I feel a faint beating beneath my fingertips. *She's still alive.* But I need to stay by her side.

Keep applying pressure.

I won't lose her again.

Carmody falls back like he's been struck by a freight train. Nightjade bullets are no match for a Chaser uniform, but Chaser uniforms are no match for lead. The bullet has cut right through his armor.

He drops Eddie and the stolen Yesterday gun in an instant, shrieking in pain as his hostage scurries away from him. Gentle waves of salted foam roll over his left leg and steal his blood as he lies in the water, and I can't do anything but watch in shock as the liquid gradually becomes saturated with more and more red.

Eddie acts quickly. No longer a hostage, she steps through her tied arms to bring her wrists in front of her. She reaches down and pulls something out of her boot, and I don't realize what it is until she uses it to cut the twine.

She holds the blade in one hand and scrambles for the gun with the other. The sand was washed out of her eyes when Carmody shoved her head beneath the surface, but her vision is clouded by the damage and she can't see clearly.

Frantically, she searches for the weapon. With her knife still gripped in one hand, she feels around the shallow water, making careless splashes of blood as Carmody sits upright, outstretching his arm to reach for the same thing. But Eddie is not fast enough. He locates the pistol before she has the chance to grab it, and before I know it, he aims the gun at me again.

His arms quake as he glares in my direction, and it chills me to my core. Not once have I ever witnessed such pure, perfect anger from Carmody. I refused his twisted idea of mercy, and he will do anything to ensure I regret that decision.

"*I'll kill you, McLellan,*" he shouts over the waves. His voice is a low growl, like an injured beast still trying to put up a fight he knows he can't win.

But before he has the chance to pull the trigger, Eddie lunges at him.

In near darkness, she wrestles with Carmody for the gun, relying on touch alone to fight. She can barely see a thing, but she's furious, scratching and kicking and biting with a feral drive I've never seen before. But Carmody fights her right back.

I wish I could reach for my mother's dropped gun and end this all right now, but I know I can't remove my hands from her wound. There is still so much blood. And even if I could, I've only fired a Nightjade gun once in my life, and that was months ago during training. If my mother couldn't shoot at Carmody while I was brawling with him—even with all of her experience—then surely I wouldn't be able to, and especially with a Yesterday gun. My interference would only cause more harm. *I could hurt Eddie.*

I need to trust Eddie's words. She told me to keep applying pressure. She told me not to stop.

My stomach churns as I watch her fight with Carmody. She is clawing and kicking like she's releasing a lifetime of rage all in one go. Even with all her injuries, even against an armored Chaser, she gives her everything.

It is now that I realize just how wrong I've been to think that Eddie needs protection. She's protecting *me.*

I just need to trust her to protect herself too.

The conflict drives them farther from the water and back to the sand. They attack each other's weaknesses in a way that curdles my blood. Carmody grabs at her eyes, but Eddie's instincts are almost stronger now that she can't see the world around her. She dodges his moves until his finger swiftly scratches against her wounded eye.

Eddie calls out in pain and digs her claws into the wound in his thigh, resulting in a howl of pitiful agony that makes me wince. She grabs at the sand around her and escalates her retaliation to his attack by filling the wound with a handful of tiny rocks, not unlike what he did to her eyes near the rock. He yelps at her attack and writhes in excruciating discomfort.

She holds the handle of her knife, swinging it back and forth blindly, but all it does is scratch against his armor as Carmody backs away like a crab. Even with his bare arms and head as weak spots, compared to the uniform, her blade may as well be a child's toy.

But somehow, Eddie does it. She fights the odds with all she has and grabs the Yesterday gun.

She backs away from Carmody like the ground is on fire, scrambling to her feet. She sheaths her knife back in its place within her boot and aims the gun into the dark nothingness before her.

Watching Eddie hold the weapon pulls me out of my trance. I find my voice again and I call out, voice cutting through the hissing breeze, trying to help her see even though she cannot.

"*Turn around!*"

She rotates—but aims the gun in my direction.

"Not at me, to your right!"

She turns again, and Carmody moves out of the way. With every direction I call—every attempt to help her put an end to all of this—the Chaser moves accordingly. Eddie spins in a jagged circle as Carmody crawls to both avoid the gun and attempt to take it at the same time.

It's no use, I think to myself, closing my eyes and biting the inside of my cheek, trying so hard not to expect the absolute worst. *She's all alone.*

I stop calling out when Eddie closes her eyes.

She blocks out everything now, no longer trying to squint through a smokescreen of scratched vision, but removing her own sight completely.

I can see her tremble as she inhales. She breathes in everything; the shrieking of the gulls, the breath of the wind, the hum of the waves. The mist that touches her skin, the stench of dead kelp and sodium that burns our noses, the sand that sprays around her feet with every sudden movement.

I watch her as she follows the grains. As Carmody moves, so does the sand—and so does Eddie.

"Drop the damn gun, Eddie," he growls, lunging for her legs as she dodges. Eddie doesn't give in to his threats and keeps her mouth shut. *"Drop it!"*

Watching her shake, I realize that she doesn't want to shoot him. Even after everything he's done, even though he wears the same white uniform she hates above all else—she doesn't want to end his life.

I cannot help her from here. She has to trust herself. She has to trust what *she* believes to be right. She has no choice but to define her own version of the word, right here, right now. Not what the system sees as just, not what I see as right—but what she sees.

It's getting harder and harder to watch, because I know that every second Eddie waits is a second that Carmody could snatch that gun from her hands and take her away from me for good.

The clock ticks. It can no longer be about what is right, but what must be done. For her. For me. For the Cut. For all of us.

For tomorrow's sake.

I have to say something, I tell myself. She has to make the choice on her own—but if I don't say anything, I know she'll never do it, even if she knows she must.

No right moments.

As I sit here in the sand, holding my unconscious mother in my arms, I think back to what I overheard Aaron saying to her in the woods.

"So what are you gonna choose?" I shout, words shaking, eyes watering. "Comfort or pain?"

Eddie's quiet for a moment. The waves and the gulls seem to reply for her until she opens her mouth. "Pain."

"Death or life?" I shout.

"Life."

"Your game, or theirs?"

"Mine." Tears fall from her closed eyes.

"Whose game?" I repeat.

"*Mine!*"

Carmody limps to a stand, weakened by the blood loss, but desperate to gain control one last time.

"I trust you, Eddie," I yell through the wind, hoping my cracked voice will reach her. I swallow the lump in my throat and force a broken, empty smile she can't even see. "You are trustworthy."

She is still. She lets out a sigh, squeezing her eyes shut and biting her lip with a nod.

Eddie takes a deep breath. She steps forward, and Carmody hobbles back until he is cornered against the sea. They stand in shallow water once again, and he waits for the perfect moment to take the pistol from her hands. The blood from before has washed away, and the waves are now a fresh canvas, watching in emptiness, waiting to be painted.

She listens. She feels.

She waits.

And she lowers the gun.

"I don't want to kill you, Duke," she mutters. "I'm not like you."

No. My eyes widen, and I feel like she's burying that rabbit in the woods all over again. *What is she thinking?*

"*Why not?*" Carmody shouts. "*You know what I am, Eddie!*" His voice cracks. "You've always known what I am."

"You're right. I know what you are." She steps closer. "You've always been human, Duke. Maybe even a little more than the rest of us."

She can't see him, but he looks up at her with a glossed, wavering glare.

"You told Ren it's not too late to make the right choice. To join the right side," she continues. "Well you were right. It's never too late to do the right thing."

I want to scream as she steps even closer.

"You can become Unseen," Eddie says softly. "You can give up the pressure, the expectations, the pain—all of it. You'll never have to hurt anyone, ever again. You won't have to fight so hard against the good in you anymore." She grins as much as she is able. "You can be free."

Carmody's lip quivers, his glassy eyes turning red as he watches Eddie like wounded prey.

But I notice something move, something so subtle Eddie cannot see it with her vision. Carmody's right arm is behind his back, hiding something. He brings his Nightjade gun forward.

"No one can be free," he mutters, and he points the gun.

I shout moments before Carmody has the chance to pull the trigger. "*Eddie!*"

I close my eyes and listen to the third gunshot of the evening.

And when the world is quiet again, they open.

Chaser uniforms are not built to defend against Yesterday weaponry, a costly underestimation that sent Duke Carmody falling to the ground with a lead bullet in his heart. I wait for him to stand back up and laugh, to flash that brutal shark smile and kill us both.

But he is perfectly still.

And with him dies every cruel intention, all of it leaving his body with the blood that soaks the sand and turns the sea foam pink.

EDDIE

Saturday, January 13
Day 13

♪ SATURNINE - MYSTERY JETS ♪

"We need to debug him." I open my eyes.

The words come out like an automation, something robotic I've been programmed to say against my will. They don't feel human at all.

Nearly half an hour ago, Ren used Noriko's walkie-talkie to contact Cecil. Even after he and two other Unseen made it to the scene and carried her away to Aaron's father, I still couldn't bring myself to move.

I thought Ren would run after them and leave me here to deal with the body while the Cut does everything in their power to save his mother. We both know she's in good hands, but I'm surprised that he isn't by her side. For some inexplicable reason, he chooses to stay here and stand next to a killer.

I wasn't myself when I shot the gun. I dropped it immediately, but even as I stand here holding nothing but my knife, it still feels like the gun is in my hands. It still feels like I'm possessed by whatever took over me when I pulled the trigger, and now I can't seem to find my way back to where I was a second ago. I completely lost myself in less than a fraction of a second.

I don't feel as ill as I thought I would. I don't fall to the ground and succumb to nausea, because there is no nausea to fall victim to. I don't collapse and cry, because there are no tears to give.

I can't even bring myself to feel angry. Not at Carmody, not at Ren, not at myself. There is only emptiness.

I can see the shape of Carmody's lifeless body through my flawed vision. It's like my eyes are open underwater, only I'm standing on dry land. *Carmody's the one in the water*, I remind myself. Because I killed him.

Because he was about to kill me.

"Eddie," Ren places a bloodied hand on my shoulder. *He's already dead*, he tells me without saying anything.

"I know." I don't look at him. My eyes are glued to what rests near my feet, even though I can barely see Carmody at all. Beneath the haze of my scratched vision, he is just a shape with blurred edges, undefined even in death.

His suit begins to beep, finally getting a signal and reading Carmody's disabled tracker. It beeps nonstop, a perfect alarm system that will keep alerting nobody in particular until one of us steps forward to turn it off.

I don't budge. I stand completely still. Something tickles my right hand and I realize I've been holding this knife by the blade, not the handle, and blood trickles down into my fingertips. But I don't bother to look. I *can't* look, because I can't rip my eyes from the shape they are sewn to.

Ren crouches down and presses a few buttons on the uniform's wrist to turn off the beeping. He stands up again and wipes his hands on his jeans, as though that could wipe them clean. His skin is soaked with his mother's blood, and mine is soaked with Carmody's—and my own. There is no cleaning up after this; there is no going back.

"The tracker is dead, but we need to destroy it," I explain apathetically. "To be safe."

Ren stares at me for a moment, giving me a concerned look before releasing a sigh. "Alright."

He holds out his hand, expecting me to hand him the knife. I don't. I ignore Ren as I step closer to Carmody, kneeling down in the sand to do the job myself.

I'm silenced by something I can't name as I remove the dead boy's eye without hesitation. I'm careless with my bad sight and it's gruesome, and I expect to feel sick after carving out the tracker and crushing the device between my fingers. But I don't. My face is stone as I toss the repulsive remains into the sea. I can't see the sliced eye as it's devoured by the horizon, but I see it when a hungry seagull swoops down and snatches the thing in its beak.

That's when the nausea arrives.

I fall over, expecting to vomit into the blood-stained waves at any moment, but nothing comes. Something inside me has switched. I'm no longer empty but far too full, overcome with a new awareness that shatters me. I am overwhelmed by nothing and everything at once and I feel as though I'm crushing beneath the weight of the entire sky.

Because today, I became a killer.

Nothing in my body is working. I can't move a muscle, and I can only lie on my side in the sand and watch as Ren commands the dead boy's suit to fold. The armor removes itself from Carmody's body, compressing itself into that familiar white cube.

Ren drags the body and the cube out into the sea. He walks so far he almost slips out of my vision entirely. I watch as he takes Carmody's bare palm, pressing it against the suit. The cube glows, like it's reading the dead boy's hand. Ren whispers a command to the cubed uniform, and then, he lets go. He wades away, and it doesn't take long before Carmody's lifeless shell is swept out to sea.

Ren comes to a pause a few yards before he reaches the shore. He turns back around to stare in the direction of the dead Chaser and his lost uniform and shouts something into the blue.

"Suit," Ren calls. "Take me."

He is far enough to be spared from the blast as the suit self-destructs, but it sends a wave that rolls over his head and pulls him under.

One second. Two seconds. Five seconds. Ten. I panic when I don't see him come back up for air, heart racing as I wonder whether or not the suit took his command too literally.

But the panic is short-lived. He stands up and slicks back the mop of sopping hair that sticks to his eyes. It's gotten so much longer than it once was, and it hurts me a little. We're both so different from who we used to be.

He washes off the blood and starts to wade back to shore, his dark gray shirt and jeans weighed down by saltwater, pressing against his skin. I know he must be freezing but he doesn't shiver. Perhaps he's more numb than cold.

Before he makes it too close to the sand, I force myself to stand up. I make my way to the shoreline and step into the waves, noting how much the water feels like snow through the skin of my boots.

I wash the blood from the knife and put it back in its sheath, silent as I tie it to a belt loop with the little bit of twine left over from Carmody's makeshift handcuffs. Ren has paused, and I can see him a few feet in front of me. He stands with his back to the horizon, black water up to his waist as he waits for me to move. I refuse to look at him as I approach.

And before I know it, he stands so close that I can feel him, though we aren't touching at all. I can feel the way he looks down at me, the way he studies me with sympathy I don't even want. I feel the way he lowers his neck to meet a damaged eye that refuses to meet his back. I feel the way he reaches, how his arms find their way to my shoulders to pull me close.

He doesn't say a word as he holds me; he just does. I close my eyes, and for a moment—just a blink—it feels like we're the only humans left.

But the moment doesn't last, and when reality drags me back, all I can manage to do is wrap my arms around his waist and cry into his chest.

There are so many words I need to say, and yet I can't manage to say anything at all. My voice is drowned by uncontrollable sobs and the lulling pull of the waves. I feel like any moment the tides will take me away, and I too will forever become a part of the sea.

But they don't. Ren holds me tighter, even as the waves crash against his back. He stands like a rock and he doesn't budge, and suddenly, I forget everything we've done to each other. Every lie, every betrayal, every false understanding of hatred.

He is no longer the Chaser assigned to kill me. He is wholly Ren and nobody else, and he is shelter. And I'm starting to believe he was never anything but exactly that.

"I didn't..." I mutter after a long time, but can't bring myself to finish the sentence. *I didn't want to do it.*

"I know," Ren says.

"But I had to," I cry. "I know we always have a choice, but... that was not a choice made by me."

He remains quiet, somehow holding me even closer. He rests his head on top of mine.

"He was gonna kill me, and if I let him, he would have gotten you too," I whisper. My words are almost inaudible against the hiss of the sea, but somehow I know he hears me. "He would have killed you. It was a choice between you and him and I—I chose you, Ren. I had to."

Ren is still silent, and I think back to graduation. I think about the way I was overtaken by this uncontrollable drive to protect him. I think of how I lost control of my own free will and turned the sand into a weapon on that playground, all for Ren's sake.

I chose him.

"And I just wish the waves would go ahead and take me." I weep. "I wish the gulls would just tear me apart. I hate myself because I know that I would choose you again if I had to. I wouldn't even have to think about it. I would choose you, again and again and again."

"Eddie—"

"No, Ren." I raise my voice because I don't want him to finish that sentence. "You can't tell me I did the right thing. You can't tell me I shouldn't cry for him, or that he got what he deserved. Because none of it is true."

"Eddie."

"I did everything wrong and I did every wrong thing. I did all of it because I'm too selfish to live in a world without you in it. Because I'm too selfish to hate you as I should." I lower my voice again, and I press my forehead against his chest. I pause my words and close my eyes and pray for the sea to sweep me away. "You're all I have left."

I wait for him to tell me I'm wrong. I wait for him to say things I don't want to hear. But he doesn't say a word. We stand there until my feet grow numb from the cold, and as my hands start to lose feeling too, he finally speaks up.

"You don't know what I was trying to say," Ren whispers.

I look down at the water that surrounds us.

"I would have done the same thing," he continues. "In fact, there were days when I almost did. I told myself I hated you. I was trying so hard to play pretend, but—the way he talked about you in those woods..." He shakes his head, not wanting to think about it. "I nearly ended him back then."

I'm silent, because I had no idea. It chills me to think about the things Carmody must have said, but the fact that Ren would have done the same thing in my shoes chills me even more.

"You're everlasting." He chokes on the words. "You have wrecked me. Shattered me, even. But no matter how hard I try, I can't seem to rid myself of your persistence."

I feel my eyes begin to water again, because I know I've hurt him; I know I've made too many unredeemable mistakes. I've told too many lies. I've kept too many truths. There's so much blood on my hands, even as it washes away.

I wait for him to say something worse.

"You have ruined me beyond repair." He holds me as close as he can. "And even still, I will choose you endlessly."

We stand in the water until we're completely numb. I wipe my eyes with the back of my sleeve before Ren leads me back to shore, but it's no use. I'm soaked from head to toe and I can't tell how much of that is from my tears and how much is from the sea.

Ren stops me when we're on dry land. He pulls something out of his pocket, and when he opens his fist I see something familiar resting upon his palm. It's a small emerald charm bracelet—the exact one my father had given me all those nights ago. The one I thought I lost.

I freeze. I look up with furrowed brows, and I can feel my eyes begin to water as the tears make their way back. Why does he have this? And why would he give it back to me now?

"I don't want it." I shake my head and close my eyes, pushing his hand away.

"Carmody had it. He stole it after the fight," Ren says. "I think you should keep it."

"I already told you." I open my eyes to glare at him. "I don't want it."

Ren takes my hand and gently opens my fist, pooling the bracelet inside my curled fingers. "But I think you need it."

"I never appreciated it when I had it," I mutter.

I don't deserve to have it now. I deserve to miss it.

I hold the bracelet in my hands, and I wonder how something so delicate could hold so much weight. When I retract my arm to hurl it into the sea, Ren places a gentle hand on my shoulder, stopping me. Slowly, he lowers my arm and eases my fist open. He is careful as he secures the bracelet around my wrist. This time, he does it right. "Then appreciate it now."

Neither of us says anything else on the matter.

White birds circle the sky and dance between the gray, singing us farewell as we walk back up the trail and into the woods. I used to love them once. Now, every gull will remind me of something I want to forget, and I hate them with all the hate I have left.

But I thank them anyway, because I would still be numb if that gull hadn't done what it did. It reminded me that I'm still alive. I'm still breathing, and I'm still human.

I'm still capable of feeling pain—for the worst and best of people.

Ren finds his mother as soon as we make it back to the compound, and for the first time during my short stay at the Cut, I find myself completely alone.

Everyone is taken aback by the news of Noriko's injury. I listen in on hushed conversations as I make my way through the Block. Snow hasn't fallen for the past couple of days, but it's cold enough so that the world remains frozen beneath sheets of white. It sends more than one kind of shiver down my spine.

I hear whispers that Ren's mother is in stable condition, and that Aaron's father was able to remove the bullet successfully. I'm glad she's alright, for Ren's sake as much as her own.

Now my thoughts are centered around Aaron, and I shudder when I picture how lifeless Aaron looked back in those woods. I pin my arms against my stomach, trying to ignore the tightness in my chest. Logic tells me he'll be okay by tomorrow, but I still want to make sure he's alright. I know he'd do the same for me.

I owe him this visit. After all, it's my fault he's knocked out in the first place.

And my fault that Noriko's been shot.

And my fault that Carmody is dead.

As I approach the hospital wing, I can tell it's completely vacant. Noriko had been taken back to her own home for the operation since it was closer, so I assume Aaron must be occupying the bed in that makeshift hospital room.

My eyes are on fire and they're still fuzzy from Carmody's wrath, but I make my way up the ramp and knock on the door. Nobody answers. I knock a second time, leaning my ear against the door as I wait for a response that never comes. I sigh and turn the door knob myself.

Sure enough, Aaron has been placed on top of the hospital bed. It looks as though someone carried him here and forgot about him, and something tells me that's exactly what happened. The Nightjade pellet has been removed from his arm, judging by the bandage. But no one is here checking his vitals. No one is here sitting by his side, hoping he wakes up. Not anybody. They didn't even bother to put a blanket over him.

I take a seat in the chair next to the bed. I find it strange how we're ending the day with reversed roles. I woke up in a hospital bed this morning, and now, the person who tended to my wounds is fast asleep in the same one.

He looks a lot different in his sleep. For a guy who puts on such an aggressive mask, he looks so calm, almost peaceful. It makes me wonder if my anger transfers over to my own slumber—or if I too am calmed when I rest.

I sit in this hospital chair for a while. I pull Carmody's lighter out of my pocket, flicking it open and close. I'm surprised to see that it still works, and a little orange glow appears every time the lid comes off. But as soon as it's shut, the flame disappears. It's chilling to me how life can come to an end so quickly.

I didn't tell Ren I took it. I found it in one of his suit's storage compartments when he was busy helping the responders load his mother onto a stretcher. I couldn't tell him, because then he'd ask me why, and I wouldn't be able to give him an answer.

Soon it becomes too much for me to think about, so I put it back in my pocket and stare at the wall until that becomes too much too.

I watch Aaron for a long time. He's comfortable to look at, a familiarity in a world full of so many unknowns. His words from the fence play over in my head. *"I thought you could use a friend."*

I laugh halfheartedly to myself. I never thought I'd have one of those again.

A friend. Looking at Aaron and the emptiness of the room pushes me to my feet. I notice his tattered composition book on the side table by the bed, and I pick it up to leaf through the crinkled pages. *His handwriting is worse than mine.*

I stop at the last written-in page, the one titled with my name. I scan through all of the notes, crinkling my brow at a section of calculations— and I spot a formula.

$$P6 = X \text{ bpm}$$
$$P = \text{pulse, 10 seconds}$$

I squint at the scribbles on the page and realize that Aaron was calculating my pulse. Next to the number, I read his other notes.

FAST PULSE: dehydrated/infection? Chapped lips, probably. Inflamed burn wound. Recovering. Applied salve, should help.

Note: Patient feels like absolute garbage.

Seeing his careful calculations tugs at something in my chest. I stare at the page, and then back at Aaron, sleeping in this room all alone while his father is busy with Noriko. Who heals the healer?

I look back down at the notebook. I can replicate this page. Monitoring his pulse should be simple enough, and I know how to make simple observations. I've gathered enough information from all of those Yesterday books to look out for him, right?

And so I do. I grab a nearby pen and I make him his own page. I place two fingers on his wrist and I calculate his pulse. *Slower than mine*, I note. *If mine was fast, is this normal?* I check on his injured left arm. The bandage is soaked in blood.

I lift it up to see a small, circular wound the size of a pea, and I sigh with relief. *It's not too bad.* The bleeding has stopped, and the wound already appears to be scabbing over. But whoever had removed the pellet apparently didn't have time to clean his arm.

I sigh, setting down the notebook and removing the bandage. I close my eyes and think back to what I've read in the McLellan's Yesterday books, and follow a careful procedure. I clean the skin around his wound, wiping away the blood stains. My eyes dart to the side table, where a small tin of what looks like hand cream resides, thinking back to what Aaron mentioned about the salve he applied to my own wounds. Curious, I pick the tin up from the table and read the messy label I recognize as Aaron's own handwriting. *Antiseptic.* I smile to myself. *This should work.*

I rummage through the cabinets in the room to find dressing supplies. Carefully, I apply the salve before bandaging him up again. I find a clean knit blanket as well, and I toss it over him.

My eyes throb, and when I remember the stinging of my own wounds, I realize that I can take care of myself too.

I monitor my own vitals. I rinse my eyes out with clean water in the sink. I put another fresh bandage over my left one to keep it safe from further harm, trying not to think about the warnings Aaron gave me after the debugging operation. I remove my sweater and use a sponge to wash away all of the dirt, sand, and blood from my skin. And I refuse to look at the letters carved into my left arm, because in all my life, I don't think I've ever forgotten that word.

But I trace the carvings with my skin, grimacing when I do. They are still so raw, so sore to the touch, although I'm glad they aren't as deep as I thought. Still, I know they will scar.

Aaron's antiseptic salve stings at first, but after a moment it is soothing. It smells like lavender and tea tree, with a hint of lemongrass, beeswax, and olive oil. *This will heal me*, I tell myself as I apply it to every letter with trembling fingers, staring straight ahead. *This will heal me. I will heal. I can heal myself. I will heal.*

I'm not sure how many times I repeat those words.

Next, I comb the blood and sand from my hair. I rummage through the cabinets and grab the first soap I can find. Bending over with my head in the sink, I wash out every speck of dirt, every smear of crimson, every tangle. I wash myself clean, and I part my hair down the middle to wrangle my curls into a messy set of double braids that I tie with a bit of scavenged medical thread.

I will be clean again.

I manage to find a simple white tee in the cabinets below the counter. It smells fresh, and I pull it over my head. When I wash off my hands in the sink and start to re-dress my burn wound, I notice an orange bottle sitting on the counter. I pinch my brows together, tying off the bandage before wiping my hands on my jeans and picking up the bottle to read it.

Someone has written my name on the label. I recognize the information on the label, but what makes my heart drop is Ren's handwriting.

I think back to the tool shed, where I left behind the medicine. Because I'd just seen Ren in his uniform, confronting the farmer about my whereabouts with Carmody, and I couldn't bring myself to think straight.

Ren must have found this back in the shed, I realize. He would have known it was mine. It came from his own emergency drawer, after all.

My throat tightens. Water clouds my vision and I don't know why something within me aches. What reason could he have possibly had to carry it with him all this time, other than the fact that I might need it?

He told me he never stopped caring, and I didn't believe him.

I cannot for the life of me tell whether believing it now is the smartest thing I've ever done—or the most foolish.

I take the very last antibiotic in the bottle with a handful of faucet water before putting away all of my supplies. I know I'm clean now, but it doesn't feel that way. I still feel like I'm covered in dirt. In sand. *In blood.* Every ache within me only seems to cut deeper with every passing second.

I walk back over to Aaron's hospital bed. After scrawling one last sentence, I close the notebook and set it on the nightstand.

Note: Patient <u>looks</u> like absolute garbage.

I give Aaron one more look before leaving the portable. "Thank you," I whisper, though I know he can't hear me.

EDDIE

Saturday, January 20
Day 20

♪ IMPLODE ALRIGHT - BUILT BY SNOW ♪

"**W**hen I agreed to come to the meeting, you never mentioned it'd be at sunrise."

I complain as Aaron and I walk down the Block, making our way to the church. The sun crests evergreen mountains in the distance, shrouding everything in a veil of winter-dulled amber. A little light peeks through the clouds, but everything is still so gray.

A cold breeze toys with my loose hair, painting my cheeks red. It's chilly, even as I wrap my jacket around me. *Aaron's* jacket. He still insists that I wear it. He has plenty of clothes, he says, but from the way he keeps looking at me, I get the feeling he's uncomfortable parting with it. He gets on my nerves more than anyone, but deep down, he might be a little too generous for his own good.

"You really think you would have agreed to come to a strategist meeting this early in the morning?"

I flatten my lips. "No."

"Exactly. And besides, time is of the essence here," Aaron says. "The meeting was already postponed long enough. Noriko might be in a coma, but that doesn't mean the Cut has to be in one too."

I scoff, only because I know he's right. Ever since word got out that a Chaser was killed on the beach, things have been hectic without the steady hand of the Cut's leader to guide everyone through the aftermath.

Cecil—the man I met in the cabin and Noriko's fiercely loyal number two—decided the plan must take place as soon as humanly possible. A search team of Chasers will most likely be sent out to look for Ren and Carmody now that both of their trackers have been disabled, and if we don't act fast, the Cut could be attacked before we have a chance to fulfill our mission.

In other words, two months of preparation will be squeezed into a handful of days.

I look up at Aaron as we walk. "Why was I invited again?"

"Your undying love for the art of espionage."

"I'll have you know my patience is very limited today, so do with that what you will."

"Fine, fine." He glances at me before raising an eyebrow. "You want a real answer?"

"That's why I asked."

Aaron sighs, shaking his head and looking back at the road in front of us. "Ren's refusing to help without your involvement. He says he won't leave you behind if the Cut's at risk of an attack."

I roll my eyes, but I regret it instantly. My left one is no longer bandaged, but both of them still burn after Carmody's attack. Although the right side of my vision has started to clear up, the left hasn't been so forgiving, and the world around me lives in a foggy haze.

"It's not like I'd be helpless in an attack on the Cut. I can fight." I glare at no one in particular. "And that's not his decision to make."

"Fair." Aaron nods. "But you should know that Ren isn't the only reason you were invited. Your experience and skill set have piqued the strategists' interest."

"Skills? That's funny."

"I'm serious, Voclain. Espionage is a valuable trait."

I elbow him in the arm. He widens his eyes, placing a hand over the spot where I'd touched him, looking down at me like a beaten puppy. I glare. "I know your wound is on the other arm, genius."

He chuckles when I hit him again.

Ren and I haven't spoken since the day at the beach. Even after all we said to each other in the water, things are still uncomfortable between us. Nothing feels the way it used to.

There is no doubt that in some twisted, confusing way, he cares about me. The antibiotics I found last week are enough to prove that, but I can't tell if knowing this truth makes matters better or worse. The larger half of me believes it's only complicated things. I still don't know what to make of the apology he made at the fence, and I certainly don't know what to make of my own emotions.

I have no clue where we stand with anything, really. I don't understand why I still feel so angry at him, or if the *anger* is really anger at all, and not a tangled mass of thorny bramble growing inside my chest.

Aaron checks a Yesterday watch on his wrist. "They're probably gonna start without us. You took forever to get out of bed."

I ignore the latter sentence. "They?"

"Cecil, Hugo, Viv—all of them. They work as strategists under Noriko's instruction," Aaron says. "We have our leader, as you already know. And then we have Cecil, second in command. I'd call him our diplomat."

"Diplomat?"

Aaron nods. "He's responsible for negotiating with other rebel groups and things like that. Always working closely with Noriko to figure out ways we can sway the public in secret, connect with other Unseen, etc."

"Got it."

"Hugo would be our hacker. Responsible for all things tech and sometimes infiltrating the enemy's computer systems to gather sensitive information. You haven't met him yet, but he's a pretty cool guy. I think you'll get along well."

I give Aaron a small smile, and he continues.

"Viv is our tactician. The glue of the strategists, if you will. She helps with the logistics side of planning missions and works closely with other members of the group to ensure that everyone is on the same page. If she seems a bit on edge sometimes, it's only because it's her job to look out for everyone's back—and put everyone in their place. But you two seem to have a lot in common so I think you'll win her over pretty quickly."

I swallow nervously. "I hope so."

"Beau is..." Aaron sighs. "Where to begin, I don't even know."

I raise a brow. "Oh?"

"He's our demolitions expert, essentially. He's in charge of the armory. A bit trigger-happy, if you will, and has a thing for explosives. He may act a bit dense sometimes, but he's certainly full of surprises every now and then. He's definitely capable of more than you'd think."

I nod, trying not to show how intimidated I am by the concept of new faces.

"And then there's Lori, our engineer and Corps tech expert." Aaron lets out a sigh. He shoves his hands in his pockets, staring at his feet and kicking a patch of snow. "But she still hasn't shown up yet."

"Do you have any idea why?"

Aaron looks up at the sky. He shifts his gaze back down at me. "She was supposed to show up at the cabin that day, as you know."

I nod, staring at my shoes. Even if it wasn't really my fault, I still feel guilty for ruining that.

"The plan was to finally have her integrate with the Cut once she finally showed up at the cabin with the NOT intel we need for the mission."

"Isn't it risky to have people show up at that cabin with trackers?" I ask. "I mean, *I* still had a functioning tracker when Ren was..." I swallow the words away. "When I was resting in there. But Ren and Carmody were there too, and they also had their trackers. Shouldn't we be worried?"

Aaron gives me a halfhearted smile. "You see, that wasn't a part of our plan."

I chew on the inside of my cheek.

"So far, Asa has been the only chipped person to show up at the cabin. He's been doing it for ages to communicate with the Cut and we never had any issues with it. And whenever he'd help other people join us, he'd always debug them in the city to be safe. Places like that abandoned parking garage we went to."

"Right."

"The plan was for Lori—and my mother—to meet up with Asa, so they could be debugged and escorted here together."

My eyes widen. "Your mom?"

Aaron nods. "She's... always been on our side, in a way. Still thinks us rebels are crazy though." He shrugs. "I guess she was just afraid to take the risk and make the move out here with Lori. But now that my sister's old enough to make choices for herself, Mom realized it's probably time. Lori convinced her to agree."

I grin, happy to hear I'll be seeing Esmerelda again. "I'm glad."

"But..." Aaron sighs again, folding his arms across his chest as we turn a corner and walk down the tree-lined path that leads to the square. "Asa's gone radio silent. Ever since... you know. Everything."

My heart beats faster, shoulders tense. I nod.

"Anyway, Ren found Lori in that cabin, as you know," Aaron continues. "She was supposed to show up with Asa and our mom, but she was all alone. And she wasn't debugged. I'm guessing she took a calculated risk and showed up to that cabin chipped to tell me she couldn't find Asa anywhere."

"But she's a Chaser. Or, ex-Chaser," I say. "Did she try locating Asa's tracker?"

Aaron gives me a grim look. "She did."

I stop dead in my tracks. I feel like I've just cartwheeled head-first into a wall. My hands shake, and I look up at Aaron with peeled eyes. "What?"

"Asa's tracker's been disabled," Aaron says. "I wouldn't panic if I were you. Maybe something happened and he was forced to debug himself sooner than planned. Cecil thinks he might even be on his way to the Cut."

I nod, trying to suppress the worry, but my heart still pounds loudly in my ears.

"From Ren's information, I'm guessing Lori went out to try and... do everything herself."

"What does that mean?"

"Debug herself on her own," he says, swallowing a lump in his throat. "Maybe try to escort my mother here by herself too. Or look for Asa." As we walk, he kicks more snow, tensing his shoulders. "All we can really do now is trust that she'll show up."

"From what you've told me, she sounds incredibly intelligent." I try my best to give him a good grin. "She'll show up. Just give it time."

He can't smile back, but he tries to.

"So," I say, clearing my throat to change the subject. "You never told me *your* role."

"You know my role."

"Okay, but you've never explained it officially."

"Fine." He rolls his eyes. "You're looking at the group's healer, as you know. And scout."

"Scout?"

He nods. "Since my dad still helps with healing when he can, I do scouting missions too. I basically serve as a courier for Noriko. Sometimes I gather... intelligence, here and there."

"So *you're* the one with the love for *espionage*."

He sighs wryly. "Guilty."

I smile, but it fades when another question pops into my head. "And Ren?"

Aaron gives me a sad look, like he can see my knotted ribcage bramble himself. "He'll be our Chaser specialist, essentially. Probably help with combat strategy too. And since he already knows Lori we think they'll work well together."

"Makes sense."

"It also helps that he's the son of the person in charge of the entire Cut. He's bound to be subjected to at least a little bit of favoritism, right?"

"And... what will I be doing?"

"We haven't decided yet," he says, and I hold my arms close to my chest. "But hey, don't take that the wrong way. You're a valuable asset. The group just wants to learn a bit more about you first before they make any decisions about your role."

"Valuable?" I scoff. "I can barely hold a gun. And aside from the basics you've taught me, all I really know how to do with my knife is throw it at trees when I'm bored."

"You mean *my* trees?" Aaron glares, referring to the time I've been spending in the greenhouse *helping* him out—time I've wasted with my short attention span.

The truth is, I've been practicing. I know next to nothing about how to use a knife for combat, but I managed to find a few books in the library and I've been testing out a few tricks—mostly throwing.

I'm tired of feeling so helpless. I'm tired of feeling like that helpless rabbit I fed in the woods, and I'm tired of letting other people take care of me. I don't need anyone's pity. And for some reason, holding that blade in my hands makes me believe that fact even more.

There's something exhilarating to it. Not adrenaline. Not a lust for power. Not fear-driven desperation. Not a thrill, but the feeling of being capable of something other than being a good student for once in my life. I need to learn to protect myself.

Maybe if I learned it a long time ago, Noriko would have never been shot. She wouldn't be in a coma right now and the Cut wouldn't be in such a vulnerable place. Carmody wouldn't be dead.

I can't be weak anymore.

"It's not all about your physical skill set, Eddie," Aaron says. "Though I gotta say—you're a pretty quick learner."

"I haven't done anything valuable," I reply. Aside from stealing from my father, I think to myself, toying with the bracelet on my wrist.

"You Ran, Eddie," Aaron tells me like it's obvious. "You had no idea what you were doing or where you were going, but you Ran anyway because you didn't want to let the system win." He gives me a small smile. "You're the only other person at the Cut with an experience so similar to Noriko's. Everyone else had a hand to guide them, and you didn't. You survived all on your own." He stops walking once we reach the church, and then he turns to look at me. "You *are* a guiding hand."

I smile sadly at Aaron, thanking him for his words in silence.

I reach into my pocket and trace the wooden jackalope he gave me. I've carried it with me all week. At first, I saw it as a symbol of my own weakness, a sign of the pity he must have for me. But maybe I was wrong to think that way. Aaron might be one of the only people on the planet who *doesn't* feel sorry for me.

Now the jackalope feels more like a symbol of hope. It's not about what I've been through or what I've lost; it's about what I can do with my future in spite of it all.

Today, the church is different than it was when I was first introduced to the building a week ago. The same place that once felt completely relaxed and recreational is now filled with frantic people stressing over the execution of a fragile plan they've been brewing for months.

The group huddles around the round table by the podium, eyes on a man I don't recognize. He's thickly built, with rich brown skin and a bit of stubble on his chin. He looks about five years my senior, but something about him seems as mature as Cecil.

I watch as he removes a pair of square glasses and sets them on the table, running a hand through a head of curly black hair in frustration. I can tell that he's one of the original members of the Cut from the glass optic prosthetic he wears in his left socket, a symbol of a time before Aaron's father developed a more efficient debugging surgery. It's interesting how you can tell time at the Cut through people's eyes.

"We cannot *bomb* the entrance, Beau," he says to the young man sitting next to him.

"Hugo's right. Why is he even here?" Viv folds her arms angrily, gesturing to the same young man with her chin. "We don't need his input, we just need a few guns."

I lean over to Aaron and whisper. "Who are these two?"

Aaron points. "The one with the red hair is Beau Hackney. Like I said he's—quite the character."

Beau seems to be another one of the younger folks at the Cut, no older than twenty. He has a shaggy mop of greasy, fox-red hair, and a splash of freckles across a crooked nose that looks like it's been broken one too many times. Judging by the fact that he has two good eyes, I assume he hasn't been here as long as some of the others. *He's been debugged the easy way— like me.*

"Hugo Burke is the one with the laptop about to have a nervous breakdown, courtesy of Beau," Aaron whispers to me.

"This *child* should not be allowed to handle weapons, Cecil," Hugo complains.

"Noriko wanted Beau present today for a reason. Before her coma, she specifically requested that he be here." Cecil speaks up before noticing Aaron and me as we approach the table. "Hey, look who's here. It's about time."

"My bad," Aaron says as he takes the empty chair next to Cecil. I flash him a small smile to thank him for taking the blame, but my smile quickly disappears when I realize that the only free seat is next to Ren.

Aaron doesn't look at me, though I can tell he suppresses a grin, and I frown. *He did this on purpose.*

Ren looks up at me and nods hello as I sit down, but neither of us utters a word to the other. I can feel him staring, waiting for me to spare him a glance. But I can't bring myself to look at him—not after what he saw at the beach. Not after the blood we washed away together. He saw a vulnerable side of me that I never wanted to show to anyone.

Maybe that's why I can't even spare him a look. I feel pathetic. Whatever feeling of hope I had on the way here has been diminished almost instantly. Even with a knife, I'm still as weak as ever.

"Can someone please make it extremely clear to Beau that we will not be using any bombs? We don't even have a single explosive in the entire compound," Hugo says dryly before glaring at the person in question. "And no, you're not making any either. Not after the *entire field* you burned down last year."

Cecil keeps his eyes fixed on his nails, picking out the grime beneath them. "Beau, you heard the man. Cut it out."

"I'm Beau," the kid says from across the table. He winks charismatically, and I raise an eyebrow before giving him a slight wave.

"Maybe I missed the part where she asked," Hugo says, gaze focused on the laptop in front of him. I smile; Aaron was right. I like this guy.

"I still don't understand how we're going to get past the entrance without alerting the entire building," Viv says, continuing the conversation Aaron and I interrupted. "We can't just waltz right in. We know they have alarms, but there could be Officers posted at the front. Scanners of some sort. We still have no idea what sort of security measures they have, but *we* have to come up with a solution either way."

"Has Lori figured out a way to disable the alarms yet?" Hugo wonders, looking at Aaron.

"Actually, in light of her... absence, we have something different in mind," Cecil says.

The strategists exchange puzzled glances.

"We won't need to disable the alarms at all. They won't even have the ability to be pulled," Cecil elaborates. "Why don't you tell them what you've been working on, Aaron?"

I look over to Aaron, who smirks and gives Cecil a nod before walking over to a rolling whiteboard that's been positioned behind the table for the group to use. He uncaps a pen and writes a single word on the board.

"Catnap?" Beau's forehead creases. "The hell is that?"

"Gee, I don't know. It's not like he's about to explain it or anything," Viv retorts.

"Beau, please." Cecil rubs his temples. "We've talked about this. There are no stupid questions here. Why is that?"

"Because stupid questions are a waste of time," Beau quotes, as though this is something he's been told many times before. I bite my lip to hold back a snicker.

"Thank you," Cecil adds, nodding for Aaron to continue.

"Catnap is a modified version of Nightjade that works as a heavy sedative, but it's only effective on Chips. It won't work on you if you're debugged," Aaron explains. "It reacts with the same chemical trigger that causes fatality with Nightjade, only Catnap is not fatal. All it does is induce sleep."

"Does it work?" Viv questions, raising an eyebrow. Aaron nods.

"I've sent a few samples to some of our Doubles out in the field, and their reports all state that it's highly effective," Aaron responds. "I've also successfully cultivated a very healthy crop, so we have a lot of it in stock right now."

"What kind of a name is *Catnap*?" Beau scoffs, and Hugo nudges him in the arm.

"And how is this gonna help us?" Cecil asks, although I can tell he already knows the answer.

"Because we can use it as a sleeping gas—one that will only work on our targets and not us," Aaron says. "If we somehow figure out a way to distribute it to the Chips throughout the building all at once, then everything else will be a breeze. We'll be in and out of there in no time."

"Unfortunately, this is the reasoning behind Beau's presence today," Cecil says wryly. "Beau, what's your take on this? Any gear that will help us distribute some kind of gas?"

Beau pauses. He puts a hand to his chin to stop and think for a moment before looking up again. "You're gonna hate me for saying this..."

"Just say it," Cecil says.

"A bomb."

Viv lowers her head into her hands. "Oh God."

"Wait, he could be onto something actually," Aaron says. "We don't really have any other options, do we?"

"A simple stink bomb should be relatively simple to make," Cecil says.

"There are plenty of books about homemade explosives in the armory," Beau says. "I've read some of them."

Viv raises a brow. "That's unpleasant."

"As much as I hate to say it, I agree with Beau," Hugo says. "And with everything Aaron said, of course. This is probably the best option we have, considering our current situation. We need things to go as smoothly as possible and I think this might be the answer we need."

"Can you guys come up with something in two days?" Cecil asks, eyeing Aaron and Beau.

"Definitely," Beau answers, nodding at Aaron as they both exchange youthful smirks.

"Alright, so that matter's settled." Cecil marks something off a notebook that lies in front of him. "What about an exit strategy? Or the layout of the building? Do we have any intel or ideas about either of these two subjects?"

Viv speaks up. "We're still waiting for Lori to come with more information. Photos, blueprints, etcetera. She'll be able to learn a lot more than we can about the Blurt's layout as well as the area surrounding it."

"Have you heard anything from Lori yet?" Cecil asks. Aaron shakes his head no, and I can tell it worries him.

"Well, let's hope to God that she shows up in time," Cecil mutters. "We needed that info yesterday. Otherwise this whole operation could fall to shambles."

"She'll show up," Aaron insists, though I'm not sure Cecil believes it as much as Aaron does.

"Now that we got all of that out of the way—Ren," Cecil says, pointing his pen in his direction. "I gotta job for you."

"Me?" he stammers.

"I want you to do a little demo for us," Cecil explains. "Show these guys how to do a little Chaser-grade hand-to-hand combat, you know? Let them know how a Chaser fights. Just in case there's ever a need."

"Why me?"

Cecil gives him a look. "You're a Chaser, Ren."

"Was."

"The things you learned in training can still be useful to us. But, before we start with that..." Cecil shifts his gaze to meet mine. "I wanna know what Eddie has to say."

I'm startled when I hear my name, face warm as all eyes settle on me.

"Got anything to add? Anything you think we should know?" Cecil asks.

"Uh..." I freeze up. I didn't expect to be anything but a fly on the wall, but I know I have to say something. *I can't be useless anymore.*

"What will we say when we get there?" I ask frantically. "You know, for the broadcast? Is there like a script or something?"

"Noriko had something in mind, but..." Cecil pauses, clearly pained by her absence. He and Ren stare at the table. "We don't exactly have access to her mind right now."

"Eddie can write," Ren blurts out. Everyone turns to look at him again and my face is immediately painted crimson.

"Really?" Aaron's tone is droll, and Cecil chuckles.

"No, like *really* write. She's always been at the top of her class and has plenty of public speaking experience." Ren looks at me with a small smile.

"She's good at knowing what to say."

That's a lie, I think to myself as I look down at the wood grains on the table. It feels like I never know what to say. Not anything that feels right, at least.

"Yeah, actually, the kid's right," Aaron says. "We dealt with some pretty sensitive jobs last summer. We've gotten caught before. *Twice*, and once by Chasers. She talked us out of it both times."

"A talker, eh?" Cecil leans forward in his seat, hands folded. "Now that is useful."

My face heats up. I don't know what to say.

"I didn't even mention her memory," Ren says. "She can practically remember everything she's ever read."

Cecil looks surprised. "Really?"

Ren nods. "Last summer, she was able to forge an entire letter—word for word—and she only looked at it once."

"Now that's impressive."

"Damn, Voclain." Aaron raises both eyebrows. "Even I didn't know *that*."

"I have a hard time believing this," Viv says. "True photographic memories don't actually exist, you know."

"Okay, well, maybe it's not that," Ren says. "But she's good at memorizing the things she's interested in, anyway. Here." He turns to me. "What's your favorite book?"

"*Pride and Prejudice*." The answer flies out of my mouth before I can stop it. Aaron snickers, and I turn to glare at him. "If you're laughing, then you've read it too."

"Hey, it's a great book. Just didn't expect *you* of all people to enjoy it so much."

"Cut it out, Aaron," Cecil says before turning to Ren. "Where are you going with this?"

"Eddie," Ren says. "Can't you like... recite it or something?"

Viv rolls her eyes. "Everyone knows the first line of *Pride and Prejudice*."

Beau raises a hand. "I don't."

"We know," Hugo and Aaron reply in unison.

"Quiet, guys. Let her talk," Cecil says. He turns to face me. "Well? Can you?"

My face heats up. My memory is helpful, sure, but Ren is exaggerating. I can memorize facts and speeches and other important texts, but I can't remember *entire books*.

Everyone is looking at me. I'd rather drink vinegar than be under this kind of spotlight, but having no other choice, I sigh—and I recite what I can remember.

"It is a truth universally acknowledged, that a single man in possession of a good fortune must be in want of a wife. However little known the feelings or views of such a man may be on his first entering a neighborhood, this truth is so well fixed—"

"Alright, alright, we get it," Viv interrupts. "You're good."

"So," Cecil says, meeting my stare once again. "Would you be willing to write something for us?"

I stutter with wide eyes, absolutely petrified. "No, no. Ren's exaggerating. I can't address millions of people—I can't do that. It's too important."

"From what Ren and Aaron just told all of us—*and* from what Noriko's told me about what you had to go through to get here—I don't think there's a single person in this group more qualified to be in charge of the speech than you are." Cecil gives me a grin so genuine that I muster the strength to smile back, no matter how little I want to.

The thought of being in charge of something so fragile sickens me. In the wrong hands, this kind of responsibility can be fatal—and my hands are certainly not capable of carrying such a weight.

"Alright, so Eddie will write the broadcast. Remember—the whole purpose of this operation is to spread the truth. I'm assuming you know what that truth is?"

I think back to everything Noriko and Aaron have told me, and I nod.

"Good." Cecil jots something down in a tattered notebook and then clicks his pen shut. "I'd like to get Ren's demo over with as soon as possible so we all have time to think about it throughout the day and practice if you feel like you need it. After that, our main focus is developing the Catnap bombs. Got it?"

Everyone nods in unison, including myself.

"Good, good." Cecil grins at Ren. "Carry on with it, kid."

For the next hour or so, Ren shows us the basics of self-defense as well as a few offensive strategies. He explains how important it is to use your opponent's own body against them—how to let gravity and exhaustion do the work for you.

I still can't manage to look at Ren during his demonstration. I know I should be paying closer attention, but it would be even harder to focus if I glanced at him. So I keep my eyes on my boots, refusing to meet a gaze I know will break me.

I can't tell why his eyes are so dangerous. I can't tell if I'm traumatized by the beach or ashamed by the vulnerability I showed, or if I'm still angry at Ren for what he said by the fence before he walked away.

My mind feels overgrown. I need to find the root of this chaos, but no matter how hard I search and slash through the thicket, I can't seem to locate it without meeting a thousand sharp thorns along the way. I can't untangle this mess of emotions that's balled up inside me.

We've been split up into groups to practice a few of the things Ren covered in his demonstration. Viv is paired with Beau, although neither of them is too happy about the partnership.

Hugo looks a lot sturdier than I am, and I know we wouldn't make an effective pairing. Unfortunately, this means my choices are narrowed down to Ren and Aaron.

I'm disappointed but not shocked when Aaron and Hugo are paired, leaving me with Ren by default. He looks at me and nods to the back corner of the church and I walk over without sparing him another glance.

I feel angry but I'm not entirely sure why. I'm grateful that he came to my rescue at the beach, but every time I think back to our conversation at the fence, it only frustrates me. Maybe I'm bothered by what he said before storming off.

But most of all, I wonder if I'm angry because he made me realize something.

I think beyond all of the things he's done since my world fell apart, remembering that bridge by the river. I think about the mud and all the things we said, and I wonder if maybe, just maybe, we never hated each other at all.

"We should start with some scenarios," Ren says, clearing his throat and pulling me out of my thoughts.

I nod. "Alright."

"You're outside of the Blurt and a Chaser sneaks up on you like this." Ren grabs my wrist, and I twist it around to break free almost instantly.

"Nice job. What about this?" He grabs both of my wrists and I do the same thing, twisting them in an outward circle and slipping free of his grasp.

"Okay, good. What if they come at you like this?" He grabs me and pulls my back against his chest, wrapping both arms around my neck and planting his hands onto his own shoulders. "What do you do?"

I can feel his breath against the back of my neck, and for a moment, I'm brought back to that day in the sea, the way he held me when I thought I was unreachable. It chills me for a moment and I almost have to force the anger to come back.

"Use my elbow." I jab him in the gut as hard as I can.

He laughs and lets go, rubbing his side. "Damn."

"Sorry," I lie.

"I'm not surprised that you're a natural at this," he says. "You were the queen of elementary school fistfights."

A blink. I remember them. Hazily, but still. I can't even count the number of petty altercations we experienced together as young children.

He waits for a moment, hand on his chin as he thinks of something else to test me on. I steal a look at him while he stares at his shoes, and I can see how tired he is. Something's been eating away at him too, and we both share the same dark circles that rest beneath our eyes. I almost feel guilty, like it's somehow my fault he can't sleep at night. I'm sure I did something. I've done many things.

"Punch me," he says out of the blue, meeting my eyes.

For the first time in days, our gazes lock together. My sight is still full of fog, but it feels like I can see him clearly.

"What?" I ask quietly, confused by his instructions. I'm not going to punch him. We're not children anymore.

Ren steps closer, each step slower than the last until his nose is inches away from mine. He looks down to meet my stare and holds his palms in front of his chest before repeating his sentence in a low whisper. "Punch me."

I give him a questioning look, brows creasing with concern. I curl my hand into a fist and throw a weak punch into his hand.

"That's not an authentic Lavender Voclain punch," he says.

"What's that supposed to mean?" I scoff.

"I know from experience you can hit harder than that," Ren says, and I throw another punch before he shakes his head again. "You can do better than that."

"I'm not gonna hurt you."

"You won't."

I take a deep breath—and I punch him as hard as I can, slamming into his palm so violently I recoil my own arm in pain to shake it out. My burn has healed for the most part, but Carmody's carvings still ache.

"That's what I'm talking about." He tries to grin. "Now do it again."

Reluctantly, I listen. I hit his hands over and over and over again, falling into a groove of strikes that get more intense by the second. I think about nothing and everything at once and put all of it into every blow.

I do this until every single one of these unidentifiable emotions boils over. My mind is still so overgrown and I cannot seem to understand why. My throws slow to a gradual halt, and when my fists rest in his palms, his fingers twitch, like they want to curl around my own.

He speaks so softly, his voice a near whisper. "Did that help?"

"No." I shake my head and close my eyes, feeling even worse than before. *I can't look at him.*

I can't handle this anymore. I can't handle *anything* right now, not until I figure out what's wrong with me. I turn away to go sit down in one of the pews, but before I get the chance to do so, the church doors open with a flood of early morning light.

A girl walks in, with a short bob of black hair and a bandage over her eye. Behind her walk in three figures, unidentifiable in the blinding light.

I squint to make out the details of their faces, and as the doors close, taking the white light with them, I nearly fall to my knees.

One of the faces belongs to Asa McLellan. He wears a bandage too, and he looks tired, like he's aged a decade over these past few weeks. His hair is grayer than ever.

The other face belongs to Esmerelda Salazar. She looks tired too, but when I squint, I realize how similar she looks to the girl I can't identify. I look back at the girl and wonder if she could be Lori.

Before I get a good look at the fourth figure, I turn around and steal a glance at Aaron. He's speechless, but behind his stillness, I can see a life ignite in his eyes, a flicker of hope and wonder and a dozen other emotions. He stares at the mother and sister he hasn't seen in so long, and I don't need clear vision to tell that he's crying.

But then, a voice calls my name.

"Eddie?"

It takes a few blinks for me to realize my name was called at all. And when the voice settles, I become completely still.

My hands shake. I can feel my face blanch as my heartbeat hammers faster than ever. I whip my head around, so certain that I'm hallucinating.

And when I finally observe the identity of the fourth person, something in me breaks.

There is a shell I've been trapped inside for so long, and when I stare Milo in the eyes, it shatters completely.

No. I step back and shake my head, bumping into a church pew and nearly tumbling over.

It can't be him.

I know it can't. He died with the rest of my family. He sacrificed himself to save me. He bled to death while I ran to get help.

He's gone.

He went through hell for his sacrifice, and that is why I Ran. I Ran for Milo. I Ran for all of them, but it was his sacrifice that devoured me. I Ran because he died to save me—and I owed him my life.

I never witnessed his death, but there's no way he could have survived, and I knew that when I buried that rabbit in the woods.

"Eddie," he repeats, his freshly debugged face lighting up when he sees me staring back at him.

His loose black curls are tangled and frizzy, and his face is smudged with dirt. He looks at me in my disbelief, and the only thing that either of us can manage to do is stand still, because we are both seeing ghosts.

But even through these untrustworthy eyes of mine, I know this is no hallucination.

This is my brother, and he is alive.

I trample the disbelief and run to him. I run faster than I ran when I was Running for my life out in those unforgiving woods, faster than my legs allow, nearly falling before I reach him.

But I do. I reach him and I jump up to reach his neck, wrapping my arms around him and holding him tighter than I ever have before. He smells like pine needles and dirt.

Once, I hated that scent because it was a constant reminder of my solitude. But now, I decide it's my favorite smell on this entire planet. I hold him tight and breathe in the forest. I keep him in this embrace of ours and I don't let go.

Hot tears burn past the dark circles under my eyes. "Milo."

There are so many things I want to tell him. So many questions to ask, so many cries to share, so many stories to relay. I can think of a million right things to say but I'm afraid that any one thing will ruin this moment. That if I open my mouth, everything will become real again, and he'll be taken away from me. I'll wake up from this daydream only to be dragged back to the nightmare that is a world without my brother.

But the next sentence slips out against my will.

"I'm glad to know it's you I've been living for all along."

REN

Wednesday, January 24
Day 24

♪ THE LENGTHS - THE BLACK KEYS ♪

It feels odd, being back in the woods again. But it feels even stranger to know exactly where we're going.

Everyone was in shock when the visitors arrived, including myself. When I saw Eddie and Milo's reunion, some broken part of me healed, just a little. But Lori brought not only people, but information too. We all listened as she explained the multiple impossibilities that stood behind her.

The plan was originally for Asa to escort Lori and Esmerelda to the cabin after debugging them—and himself—in the city. But when Aaron's sister and mother showed up at their designated meeting spot, he wasn't there. Lori couldn't even get a signal from his tracker.

She knew that something was wrong, so she decided to take a risk and meet Aaron in the cabin by herself instead, leaving her mother behind in the city to be safe. And that's when Eddie and I unknowingly interfered— and when she decided she had no choice but to escort her and her mother to the Cut alone, for the sake of time.

Lori hurried back to Port Keys. She and her mother drove for the majority of the trip on the way back to get a head start, but they decided that since cars are easily tracked, they'd abandon it in the woods and make the last of the trek on foot. It was then when Lori and Esmerelda bumped into my father and Milo, who were headed to the Cut on their own too.

According to Milo, he remained with his dead family for hours, soaking up the blood and pretending he had died with them. He didn't want to be alive. But against all odds, he was still breathing.

Sometime after Eddie and I had stopped by our house at separate times, my father showed up, sickened by grief but knowing Milo was in trouble after Eddie ran to our home for help. He did all he could for the wound, and because he was too afraid of the mics listening in, he wrote him a note on a piece of paper before tossing it into the fire, explaining that there was a way out of this.

Apparently my father had been trained by Aaron's dad in the art of debugging in his service as a mule for the Unseen. He was often the one to debug families wanting to move to the rumored place in the woods or Runners he found on his trips. Milo, desperate to reunite with his sister, agreed to lose his chip.

The timing was perfect; the Chaser's database software didn't immediately find anything suspicious about his tracker suddenly going dead, because the rest of his family was exterminated that same night at that same location. My dad took him back to our house to hide until Milo was healed enough to make the journey.

It was for this reason that my father had to change plans. While Milo's tracker suddenly going dead wouldn't cause any immediate attention, he knew the Cleaners would be suspicious about a missing body. For the safety of both my father and Milo, they had to leave as soon as possible. And when they ran into Lori and Esmerelda, my father was able to take out their chips too.

After the initial shock subsided, Lori presented us with more information. In addition to the expected access codes, she also had a single flash drive filled with detailed photographs she took of the Blurt, a regional map of the area, and blueprints.

Apparently, the Blurt is positioned rurally, neighboring the dairy fields Eddie and I once explored.

Though the location differs from the one Eddie and I visited so long ago, it still feels odd to be traveling back to where we started. As my feet leave cavities in the snow, I think about how different we were each time we found ourselves in a cow field. We were both innocent the first time, but the second time marked the beginning of what seemed to be our end. I wonder how different things will be now.

Thanks to the map that Lori provided, this trip will be a lot shorter than the one we took to get to the Cut. Instead of following the winding river for so long, we've been able to slice directly through the woods to reach the Blurt. And now, after our first twenty-four hours of hiking in the snow, Lori has calculated that we'll be approaching the port of call within the next few days.

The shadow of dusk rests upon us as we move. Although I walk alone, I'm thankful to have some peace before the operation begins. But to my surprise, the more solitude I receive, the more I find that peace slipping away. I'm left alone to worry about every possible thing that could go wrong, and I can't help but overanalyze the dynamic of the people walking in front of me.

Eddie and Aaron have been spending quite a bit of time together, talking about healing and botany and God knows what else. I watch as he helps her strengthen her knife-throwing skills and explains the best ways to use a blade against a person in combat. She almost seems to be enjoying it.

But now that Milo has joined the mix, their dynamic seems to have taken a level up. Eddie can smile again. She's lost so much over the past few weeks, and now that her brother has essentially come back to life, a weight has been lifted off her chest. She looks like she can finally breathe.

It makes me beyond happy to watch her laugh with Milo and Aaron. But another part of me can't help but feel saddened by it all, as selfish as it is, because she hasn't smiled around me in the longest time.

I think back to the girl in the cow field, how we sprawled out underneath the stars and stared at each other until we were dragged back into reality to face the consequences of one of our many lies.

I'd like to believe I made her happy once. And now, every time she looks at me, I can see how badly it hurts her to do so. Simply being near me seems to bring her so much pain.

"You don't look too well," Lori says, pulling me out of my thoughts. She jogs to catch up, walking by my side.

I look down at her and shrug before staring back at the path ahead of us. "I mean, we are about to initiate a plan that my father has been plotting with my long-lost mother for years in secret so we can start a revolt and begin the process of tearing down an entire governmental system. I'm allowed to be a little on edge, aren't I?"

I tease, though she's right. I'm nowhere near well.

"I'm nervous, but I don't look *murderous* or anything," Lori says.

"Murderous?" I raise a brow. "I look murderous?"

"You're not gonna kill my brother or anything, are you?" she jokes. "I mean, I don't really like him that much either, but I still want him to stay alive, ya know?"

"What makes you say that?"

"Well for starters he's an arrogant asshole—"

"The other part."

She sighs. "Ren, you're giving him your death stare."

"I have a death stare?" I crease my brows.

"Yes, and it's at a ten right now."

"Not true."

"It is," she argues. There's a pause, and she looks up at me. "Are you gonna tell me what's wrong or what?"

I look to the side. "Shouldn't we be thinking about the plan?"

"Yes," Lori says. "That's why I'm here. I don't want you to make some devastating slip-up just because you spent the entire trip stewing over something that can easily be fixed."

"I don't think this is something that can be fixed too easily." I scoff.

There's another pause, and I listen to the snow crunching beneath my feet. I used to love snow as a kid, but things are different now.

"You're in love with her, aren't you?" Lori questions, and I almost trip.

At first I mistake her words for mockery. But to my surprise, her face is soft and genuine. She really means it.

"I'm not," I insist.

"I saw the way you looked in the cabin, when you thought I'd something to her," Lori says. "Before I told you about your mom, before you made the switch—you still loved her." She sighs. "I thought you were going to kill me, and I honestly think that if I'd done something to hurt her... you would have."

"Sorry for that, by the way." I give her an apologetic smile, and she shakes her head with a grin.

"Hey, I'm not any less guilty than you are." She smiles. "I would have killed you too."

"Strangely, that makes me feel a bit better."

"Any time."

We keep moving forward, trudging along the soft snow in tandem. Dusk has started to melt into nightfall, and it's becoming harder to make out Eddie's shape in the absence of light—dark brown waves of hair, Aaron's jacket, knit sweater, the baggy jeans I gave her back at the cabin, those already-beaten combat boots. She is a strange combination of many different things.

She is gentle but she will protect those she loves in a heartbeat. She is loyal but she will betray anyone for the sake of the greater good. She is afraid of her own weakness but she surprises everyone with her inner strength. She makes me smile more than anyone else on this planet ever could, and yet, it is her that I mourn with an ache I'd do anything to be rid of. Because I don't make her smile anymore.

"Tell her," Lori says, so quietly I almost don't hear her.

I give her a look, and part of me wants to ignore her. But I know she's only trying to help. "I already have. Many times."

"Did you?" she questions. "I highly doubt she would be avoiding you if you told her all you have to say. Because I see the way she looks at you too."

I look at Eddie as she walks, and I look back down at Lori, shaking my head. "It'll only make things worse. I know Eddie, and I know anything I have to say will ruin everything. It'll split us apart even further."

"It couldn't."

"I don't want that to be the last..." I let out a sigh, the ache in my chest only worsening. "I won't tell her. You know, just in case."

"Ren." Lori puts her hand on my shoulder. "If this is about a *Just in Case*, I think you should tell her."

She sighs, looking at the night sky for a moment before staring down at her shoes, hands in her pockets.

"Look," she says. "There was someone I loved back home. Loved them for years, actually, though I thought I hated them for a time." She laughs softly. "They were a pain but they were so smart and talented and everything beautiful about this world. I was waiting for the perfect moment to tell them exactly how I felt, but... the moment never came, and they found someone else."

"I'm sorry to hear that, Lori," I say, giving her a sympathetic smile.

"I'm fine. I've healed." She grins sadly. "But my point is, you shouldn't live your life waiting for perfect chances to arrive, because they never will."

Cecil orders the group to stop for the night, and Lori gives me a pat on the back before walking away to help. I've been left to navigate this solitude all on my own again.

Cecil, Aaron, and Viv begin to unpack a large tarp from one of the bags and spread it out across the snow. Hugo and Beau join in as well, and I know I should probably help them set up camp for the night, but I don't get the chance. My father walks up to me and places a hand on my shoulder.

"Hey bud." He smiles, but nothing about him seems happy. Not anymore. Somehow, it's comforting to know I'm not the only one who feels the same way.

I glance to my side to meet his face and I realize that he's probably the only person who understands how I feel—even more than Eddie. Margot was our blood.

And I saw the way Cecil was around my mother before she got shot; something about their dynamic reminds me of the friendship between Aaron and Eddie, and I can't imagine how it must feel for my father. He's lived the majority of the last eighteen years separated from the one woman he loved more than anything, and all this time she was getting to know the people of the Cut instead of him.

It's not like either of them could have done anything differently. There was no way we could have made the trip to the Cut with Margot in her condition. But there's something so heartbreaking about growing distant from the people you once knew so well. About seeing the connection unravel right before your eyes, knowing that it will never truly disappear, but it will grow thinner and thinner until it is hidden by other things.

I expect my father to ask me how I'm feeling, but he doesn't. He already knows the answer. Instead, he takes a seat on a fallen log to our side, and I join him.

We haven't gotten the chance to talk about what happened the night of the draw. I'm not angry at him for what he hid from us, and I know he's not angry at me for becoming a Chaser either. We both did what we did out of necessity. We both kept secrets for Margot's sake, and in the end, we both paid the heaviest price.

There are just simply no words to say. There are no right moments, but sometimes there are no right words either.

"Here," my father says, pulling something out of his pocket. "I want you to have this."

He reaches out his upturned palm, where the jackalope sealing ring rests. Gingerly, I pluck it from his hand, turning it over in my fingers. When I remember the last time I saw it, it feels like someone is slotting a hot blade into every wound I've ever known.

The last time I saw this ring, Eddie and I were hiding from Margot in the closet.

"Why?" I ask, sliding the ring onto my right index finger. I spin it around, fidgeting with it because I can't bring myself to look my dad in the eye.

He shrugs. "I always meant to. I just never got around to it, I guess."

I nod, because I understand. Our life with Margot was unpredictable, especially with my father's Unseen involvement thrown into the mix. Sometimes it felt like I was getting left behind, but I always understood why. I still understand.

"Your mother gave that to me, you know. Back when we first started seeing each other," my father says with a fond grin. He blows a strand of stray, gray-brown hair out of his eyes. "She always loved jackalopes."

I smile, but it's fleeting. We sit there in silence for a long time, staring at the trees. Underneath their constant shadow, I feel so small.

"Ren?" my father says, turning to face me. "There's something I've been meaning to ask you. Something I never got the chance to say."

I swallow nervously. "Yeah?"

"Did you..." He sighs, averting his gaze. He stares at his hands. "Did you know?"

"What do you mean?"

He meets my gaze again. "Did you know about the Immunity?"

Of course not, I want to say. *I wouldn't have become a Chaser if I knew.* But I know I can't tell him that. He already knows. "No, I didn't."

His brows crease with concern. "Are you sure?"

I nod. "What makes you ask?"

"Well..." He trails off, trying to find the words. "The receipts for Margot's Immunity weren't where I usually keep them. They were just... gone." He sighs. "I thought you might have found them—before I had a chance to explain to you why they exist in the first place."

"Dad," I tell him, placing a hand on his shoulder. "You don't have to explain." My throat tightens. "I've always understood."

Everything he's done has only been for Margot and me. I want him to know how much I love him for that, but I think he already does. He gives me a broken smile, and I return it as much as I am able.

But my smile is quick to drop.

"She knew." I look up at my father, eyes peeled wide. "She knew she had the Immunity."

My father's brows crease. "What do you mean?"

I tell him about the letter, trying not to show the faults in my voice when I talk about Margot. I tell him about how Eddie and I hid in the closet because Margot had come in to look for some books. I tell him about the file she took. At the time, I couldn't think much of it—I was too worried about keeping my own secret. But maybe, Margot had her own.

When I finish my story, my father looks to the sky. His good eye glosses over. A dulled violet dusk sweeps over our heads like a blanket, clouds and dark branches of pine working together to hide the stars. But for some reason, he looks as though he can count every single one. I cannot tell if he's crushed or relieved or both.

I look up too. "Sometimes I wonder... maybe the Pick was just the tipping point." Ren chokes on his words. "Maybe there was nothing we could have done."

"There will never be any real way of knowing." My father wipes his tears and turns to face me. "But there are things to do tomorrow, aren't there?"

For the first time in a long time, I smile. It's sad and broken and smaller than it once was, but it is mine. "Yeah. There are."

"You're still my everything, Ren," he says, voice wavering. "Your mother and I—all we've done has always been for the two of you. It always will be."

He doesn't let me reply before he stands up to go assist with setting up camp.

After the tarps have been spread across the snow, I help Aaron and Cecil find firewood and haul it into a pile. When Aaron lights the fire, we all sit around its warmth on rocks or small logs, quenching our thirst and eating our fill of dried meat and bread.

Aaron sits cross-legged on top of a small rock, with Eddie sitting to his right. He sharpens his knife while she talks to Milo, and I assume he'll be the one to keep watch while the others get some rest. Our group is hushed, and it would almost be peaceful if it weren't for the looming fear we all share.

Now is your chance, I tell myself. *Pull Eddie aside. Go talk to her.*

Suddenly, my eyes are drawn to Cecil as he comes to his feet, stumbling as far away from the camp as he can before falling to his knees and hurling into a bush.

Aaron sets the knife down and rushes to Cecil's side as he heaves, and we all look away, concern furrowing our brows. It's bizarre to see how illness can make even the strongest people seem so small.

Aaron assists Cecil to his feet and leads him over to the tarp, helping the man get inside his sleeping bag. His skin has a sheen to it. He glistens, covered in sweat, trembling as he lies down.

"Parasites, probably. Most likely from our last water stop. That stream was questionable," Aaron grumbles, swearing under his breath. "Everyone dump out their water. Now."

We all do as he says, opening our canteens and pouring the remnants into the snow.

"From now on, boil your water and be careful about the source. No stagnant water," Aaron orders, and we all nod.

He reaches into one of the group bags and pulls out a large pot, walking over to the creek that runs along the side of our camp to fill it up with water. When he comes back, he sets the pot on the fire, letting it boil before dividing it among us evenly, refilling our canteens.

"Does anyone else feel sick?" Aaron questions, eyebrows arched in concern. I shake my head, and so does the rest of the group. "Are you positive?"

"We're fine." Eddie places a hand on his shoulder. "Worry about Cecil."

It's quiet as Aaron makes the man an antiparasitic tea. He uses anise, clove, lavender, and the smallest bit of wormwood, pouring the steaming beverage into a cup and helping Cecil down the liquid in small gulps.

"I'm gonna hand out a milder tea with a bit of honey for everyone else, just to be safe," Aaron announces, and Eddie helps him with the task.

All this talk of antiparasitics makes me think of Margot and her treatment. I miss her more than usual tonight.

She's on my mind when Aaron walks over with a cup of tea. He reaches out to hand me the beverage, and I take it quickly, giving him a quick nod of thanks. He turns, readying himself to walk away, but something urges him to take a seat on the log next to me instead.

He sighs, taking a sip of his own tea. The two of us are quiet as he looks up at the sky, at the ground, and then at me again. His gaze fixes to his shoes.

"I..." He struggles to form the words, which surprises me. He always seems so confident. A little too grumpy for my taste, but so put together and sure. "There's something I've been meaning to tell you."

"I just wanted you to know..." He swallows nervously. "I wish I could have done more."

I give him a puzzled look—and then I realize what he's talking about.

It didn't register until now that all this time, Aaron and his father have been the ones providing medicine for Margot. My father didn't have the ability to be consistent with his trips to go fetch her supplements, but Aaron did a decent job researching and supplying them.

"He wanted to bring you two over to the Cut once you were adults, to give you the choice," Aaron tells me, and I look down at my feet, taking a sip of the tea. It's sweet, but I don't like the flavor.

"If she were here—if I could have seen her in person or talked to her or really, truly gained an understanding of her symptoms—maybe I could have treated her better," he says, letting out another painful sigh. "More than just sporadic collections of whatever herbal supplements we could scrounge up for Asa at the time."

It's quiet for a moment, and while I prefer it that way, I feel like I should say something.

"You and Eddie have that in common," I finally manage to mutter. "Healing has been her dream for a long time."

Aaron forces a soft grin. "I know."

"She always tries so hard to fix everything for everyone around her. Even when we were kids," I say, staring at the fire. "But... some things can't be changed. Some people can't be saved, no matter how badly we try."

Aaron doesn't say anything.

"As long as we've done the best we can with what we've been given..." I stare at the reflection in my teacup. "Maybe we can call that enough."

I can't tell which one of us needed to hear that more.

It's silent as we watch plumes of smoke unfurl into the night sky, and the way the flickering amber firelight dances across Eddie's face. She looks beautiful here, laughing and smiling with her brother. I wish I could reach her.

"Look man, I'm sorry for—you know. Holding you at knifepoint and stuff," Aaron mutters, forcefully clearing his throat. "Your mother would never betray her people, and if she trusts her son"—he smiles again, softly —"then maybe I can trust you too."

I look up at him, smirking ever so slightly. "I don't think you're a bad guy, Aaron."

He returns the smile, for real this time. "Neither are you."

Aaron pats my shoulder and gets up to leave. He brings Eddie a cup of tea before sitting by her side, chatting again. She's brought her sleeping bag away from the tarps to stay warm next to the fire, and she wraps it around herself like a blanket. Lori and Milo seem to be having their own separate conversation, and aside from myself and the sibling sets, everyone else has gone to sleep.

Eventually, Eddie drifts into a deep slumber with her head on Aaron's shoulder, slumped over while he laughs in conversation with Milo and Lori. They stay up for longer than they should, talking late into the night like old friends, trying their best to enjoy what little happy moments they have left.

I pretend to be asleep, watching from my own bedroll. Eddie looks so peaceful, so innocent, as she did in the snow. I can't wake her while she's sleeping like that. I decide to talk to her tomorrow.

Milo and Lori eventually close their eyes, but Aaron stays up alone, watching out for us all. I feel vulnerable as I close my eyes to the ringing metallic sweeps of sharpening stone against the blade he holds like a lifeline.

I manage to fall asleep after a while, but not long after I drift into a deep slumber, I dream of a Nightjade gun. Only this gun was different from the ones we were all trained to use as Officers back at the Corps. The shape was the same—round, small, more like a toy than a deadly weapon. But this gun was all black. I can't recall the hand behind the trigger or the face in front of its muzzle, but there was definitely a hand to pull it.

The dream leaves a bad taste in my mouth. It feels dry, like I swallowed a handful of salted sand and now my body begs for water. I reach over to pull my canteen from my bag, careful not to wake anyone. But as my luck would allow, it's completely empty from being poured out in the snow. *I forgot to refill it earlier.*

I look over to see the fire still burning, diminished, but still alive enough to boil some water. I unzip my sleeping bag slowly, silenced with caution. I pull the hood of my black waterproof jacket over my head, but it doesn't do much in terms of warmth. I lace up my boots with a shiver before walking out into the woods.

I remember hearing a stream on the walk to our campsite, and I try to listen for it as I walk deeper into the trees. I pause for a moment to cease the crunching of shoes against snow, waiting to hear the trickle of running water not yet frozen over by winter's cruel touch. For a moment, all I manage to pick out is sheer silence. And then, I hear it. I look beyond the shrubs that lie in front of me and see the smallest of brooks running through a bed of river stones.

I walk beyond the bushes until my feet approach the edge of the stream. I crouch down and twist off the cap of my canteen, careful not to let the tips of my exposed fingers touch the icy water as I fill up the container. But it all falls out of my hands when I hear a twig snap behind me.

"Couldn't sleep?" Milo stands behind me, holding his own water canteen with a scowl. I shrug as the pace of my heartbeat slows back to a normal tempo.

"Not surprised," he mutters, crouching down next to me to fill his own bottle with the stream's clear liquid. "You're a Chaser."

I pick up my canteen and refill it. "I'm not a Chaser."

"Once a Chaser, always a Chaser." He closes the cap of his bottle. "At least in my eyes."

I want to question why he only feels that way about me and not Lori, but I know the answer. Eddie wasn't Lori's assignment.

"I'm not a Chaser," I repeat, this time more firmly.

"If that's what you tell yourself to sleep at night, then hey, fine by me." He raises his hands in innocence. "Though from the looks of it, that method hasn't been very effective, has it?"

I glare at Milo. "Look dude, I don't know what your problem is—"

"I don't have a problem," Milo interrupts with false sincerity, pointing to his chest before turning his finger in my direction. "Do you have a problem?"

"You're a bad liar," I retort.

"You see, you've got it all wrong." He stands up, and I do the same. "I think the only liar here is you."

I tower over Milo, but he doesn't seem to care. There's something different about him. Something almost sinister, like the night of the draw and everything that happened since has crushed any ounce of juvenility within him.

Part of it saddens me. I know this isn't the real him. The real Milo is a goofball, a sarcastic loner, a big thinker. He preferred homeschool over the in-person variety and spent his time scavenging for old Yesterday music and joking around with Eddie. I don't know where that Milo went.

But he's right. *Once a Chaser, always a Chaser.* Nothing can take away the weight of using human beings like bargaining chips. Nothing can take away the guilt I'll feel for every waking moment of my life.

"I know why you hate me," I say, and Milo scoffs before looking at a tree in the distance. I stare at the same tree as I continue to speak.

"You hate me for what I had to become," I say. "But I didn't do it for the reasons you suspect. I made the choice myself and I take full responsibility for it, but—I did it all for my sister."

Milo doesn't say a word. He glares at his shoes, fidgeting with the cap of his water bottle.

"Margot was sick, and if anyone found out she would have been killed. So I Chased to give her Immunity." I laugh bitterly. "But my father had been paying for it the entire time."

I look up at the sky. Milo does the same thing and we both stand there for a moment, staring at the alluring abyss above our heads.

"Wouldn't you do the same thing for Eddie?" I ask, turning my head back to face him.

"I would do anything for her," Milo snaps. "And I would never do anything to hurt her."

I know Milo's words are directed at me, and it hurts. He knows what I did, and he knows that for a brief moment in time, I genuinely believed that killing Eddie was the only right thing to do. I let my hatred overtake me. I selfishly succumbed to my own anger because I thought it'd hurt less than grieving, but I was wrong.

And for that, I have no words to give. We are both brothers to sisters, here or gone, and we both want Eddie to be safe. I just wish he realized how similar we are.

"Look, I want you to know something." He inches closer, looking up at me. He's not small for a seventeen-year-old, but he doesn't have my father's height. Even still, he's not afraid of me, and by the look in his uncovered eye, I can see that nothing scares him anymore. Nothing else but the fear of losing his sister.

"If for some reason I'm not around to protect her..." Milo's anger breaks before he can continue to threaten me. He is overtaken by an unmentioned fear and he shakes his head, voice cracking. "You'll be there, right?"

Milo looks at me, and I'm surprised to see something different in his eye. He's terrified, haunted by the fear of losing the one person we both care about the most, and I am too.

"I'll be there," I promise.

Friday, January 24
Day 24

The next two days blend together as we approach our destination.

Eddie hasn't said a word to me since the day her brother arrived, and I can't blame her. She wants to spend as much time with Milo as possible before the plan commences, and he seems to have connected with Aaron as well.

But I haven't been focusing on that. Now, all I can think about is talking to Eddie.

None of the words feel adequate and none of the moments feel right, but I know I need to tell her. I need to tell her how much she means to me, because if I don't do it soon, something warns me I'll never get another chance. *Just in case*, I tell myself.

But no matter how hard I try, I can't seem to catch her alone.

"According to Lori's maps, we should be arriving soon," Cecil announces as we hike. Aaron's tea certainly worked wonders, but he's still weak from last night, walking slower than most of us.

"Thank God," Beau complains, out of breath.

"Why is that something you're looking forward to?" Hugo questions plainly. "The odds of any of us making it out of this alive—no, specifically *you*—are probably about one in—"

"I'm exhausted, okay? I'm tired of holding all these damn Catnap bombs in my bag," Beau groans.

"We're all exhausted," Aaron mumbles.

"Can't a guy just complain?"

"Yes, we complain about you all the time," Viv says.

"And I don't see *you* carrying anything, pretty boy." Beau scowls at Aaron.

"Fine, give me the bag then." Aaron rolls his eyes and takes the duffel bag of Catnap grenades.

"Can it, before I silence all four of you," Cecil grumbles, and they all cease their banter with an exchange of glares.

We're well into the afternoon, and the snow has started to melt against the arrival of the sun's warmth. Once, we walked against solid ground, frozen and sharpened by winter's iced touch. Now we trudge through a miserable slush that soaks through my shoes and makes me wish for more snowfall.

I watch Eddie from afar. She wears her hair in a pair of messy braids today, her curls glistening in the sun as she jokes with Aaron and her brother. While I so desperately want to speak to her before our plan begins, I can't seem to step forward and ask for a second of her time. I don't want to be selfish.

But I ache, because the thought of something happening to Eddie in the Blurt twists my stomach into irreversible knots. I need to tell her everything, all I wanted to say in that river or in front of that fence or upon that cow field, and every day since then. Because Eddie is everything, and I won't be like my parents. I won't waste eighteen years letting this distance rot us away.

Tell her.

But I never get the chance to say a word.

Before I can take another breath, we're surrounded by six white suits of armor.

EDDIE

Friday, January 24
Day 24

Ren is avoiding me.

I can't say I blame him for it. After all, I've been doing the same thing to him. I can't bring myself to be around him because I'm terrified of what I might say.

He means too much to me, and I can't ruin that with the inevitable mistake of saying the wrong thing. The healing scars running up and down my arm itch, and I scratch them. *Especially with my reputation for ruining things.*

I'm not sure what time it is, but I can tell that it's definitely sometime after noon. The sun has broken through the gray and melts the snow around us, making our trek a lot more uncomfortable than I thought it'd be. Every step brings me back to that night in the snow, and the memories send more shivers down my spine than the temperature.

Aaron can tell I'm uneasy. Milo is chatting with Lori now, but he's close behind us as Aaron and I walk in what feels like solitude. We're separated from the back of the group but not too close to Cecil, who walks several yards away, leading us all in the correct direction.

"Something's wrong." Aaron poses his question like a statement.

"No," I lie, but my deception is weak.

Aaron pauses for a moment. "Are you worried about the broadcast?"

I curse under my breath. *The broadcast.* My mind was preoccupied with thoughts of Ren, but now that Aaron has reminded me of the much more daunting task ahead of me, I remember that I've made a vital mistake.

"Aaron?" I stop in my tracks, muttering nervously before looking up at him, petrified.

"What?" He stares at me for a moment, but it doesn't take long for him to come to the same realization that I have.

"God, Voclain." He rubs his temple with his hands, knowing what I've done before I have the chance to say it. "Please don't say it."

"I messed up."

He sighs, closing his eyes and placing his hands on his hips, looking down at his feet. "You left your speech at the Cut, didn't you?"

I nod, staring down at my shoes in shame as we resume our walk.

My face turns pale. I can't believe I've let everybody down. They trusted me with one task, and that task happened to be the most crucial one of them all.

I was supposed to write something that could change the course of history. And I did. I spent hours staring at a blank page, writing and rewriting until I was buried in a pile of crumpled notebook pages.

But I did it. After what felt like ages, I finally found the perfect collection of words. They felt so right. They flowed as naturally as the blood that runs through my veins, and they rushed out onto the page faster than my pencil could capture them. It was the speech I never got to write, the one I would have loved to scream to everyone at graduation—though I didn't know anything about the truth at the time.

But now, I'll never get the chance to read those words to anyone.

"It's gonna be alright. Okay?" Aaron places a hand on my shoulder as we walk. He doesn't seem frustrated anymore, and both his tone and his expression are out of character for the situation. "You don't need a script. You have an excellent memory, right?"

"Yeah, but... it's like Viv said. A perfect memory isn't possible." I swallow the lump in my throat. "What if I freeze up? What if I don't remember?"

"Then you don't remember," Aaron says. "That's when you just... I don't know. Speak from the heart."

"*Speak from the heart?*" I seethe. "Just because I talked us out of a few things here and there does *not* mean I can play something this important by ear."

"Well, I don't know what to tell you, Voclain." He sighs. "I still think you're the most qualified one here to give that speech, even if you have to give it without a guide."

I shake my head no.

"Look, you know how I have zero faith in anyone or anything—ever," he explains. "Sure, I follow orders. Sure, I'm loyal to the Cut's leadership. But that doesn't mean I'm familiar with hope."

Something about his words makes me sad, and I switch my stare from the snow to Aaron's eyes. There's something there I only saw once, beyond that fence in the snow.

"I expect the worst because that's what I've been given," he says. "For a while, I thought that no one could ever understand what it felt like. To be taken from everything you know—to be *mutilated* by your own father, as much as you love the guy—and be forced to adapt to an entirely different world. I was separated from the mother I loved more than anything and the sister I would die for in a heartbeat. I was just... *so lonely*, Voclain. I was the only child at the compound for years."

He pauses, shaking his head. "And it wasn't like I was raised to be familiar with that," he says. "I spent the first five years of my life *surrounded* by children and people I was familiar with. I had friends at school and a dream to pursue a career as an artist or a *plant store guy* or a dinosaur or whatever the hell I wanted to do. I had a mother who was kind and a sister I was used to having by my side. I lost everything in one night, and for years, it felt like I had nothing.

"But you..." He drifts off, staring at me with a vulnerability I've never seen in him before. "You're the first person I've met who knows what that feels like. Hell, you know what it feels like more than anyone else in the Cut. You walk with so much grief on your shoulders, and still, you choose to continue."

I look down at my feet.

"Sure, maybe you're not as great with a knife as you could be. And maybe you have trouble focusing when I try to explain greenhouse routines or the chemical makeup of Nightjade," he teases, but his voice sombers up quickly. "But you're a *survivor*, Voclain. And a selfless one at that. Don't you understand how special that is?"

I look away, pressing my lips into a thin line. For a moment I'm angry at Aaron for bringing up such a delicate subject. I'm frustrated at myself too, for forgetting such a crucial part of the plan. But when I feel my eyes start to water, I know it's not due to that frustration. His words have done something to me.

"I've been meaning to give this to you." Aaron reaches into his pocket and pulls out an object wrapped in a piece of lined paper and tape. The wrapping is ridiculous and it makes the corners of my mouth twitch into the smallest resemblance of a smile.

"What is this?" I ask, taking the object in my hands. It feels heavy as it rests in my palm.

"Garbage for the girl who feels like garbage," he teases, and he nods for me to open it.

I remove the paper carefully, worried that if I rip it off efficiently, I'll ruin whatever lies beneath. But the item doesn't feel delicate. It feels sturdy, almost like a small river stone. He takes the paper from my hands and shoves it in his pocket as I realize the identity of the gift.

It's a wooden highland cow, and she has flowers in her hair. *Lavender.*

The cow is far more intricate than the jackalope that I still hold in my pocket, one of the three things I carry with me at all times—knife, lighter, carving. It's been crafted with unimaginable detail. Each strand of hair is a slice in the wood, each flower rich in complexity. I'm amazed at the fact that he was able to achieve such fine details with something as unforgiving as a knife.

"How did you..." My smile is wide, and I trail off before I finish my sentence.

"You mentioned you like cows, so, I thought I would give you a little good luck charm. Though I don't think you need it." He smirks. "You're enough of a good luck charm yourself."

My throat tightens when I look up at Aaron. "Thank you."

He shrugs like he hasn't done a thing, and we keep walking. "You play by your own rules, remember?" Aaron places his hands in his pockets. "You give people hope."

But whatever hope Aaron gave me in return is lost.

Because in the blink of an eye, we are all completely surrounded.

I can't believe we didn't notice them.

The woods are still diseased by a haunting white plague of snow, and though it's beginning to melt away, the ground is still completely colorless. A piece of paper would be lost forever if it were to fall and rest on the forest floor, but a Chaser uniform blends in even better.

There are six of them and ten of us. They stand in a circle around our group, closing us in until we are no longer spread out. We turn our backs to each other and face the Officers as they point sleek white Nightjade guns in our faces.

Each one of the soldiers looks more menacing than the last, and while we outnumber our attackers, their presence is still so threatening it curdles my blood. One little Nightjade bullet could kill those of us who are freshly debugged and knock out the rest.

We are vulnerable, and we've been cornered.

"*Freeze!*" one of the Officers barks. We all come to a halt as instructed, but by the time we do, everyone has their hands on a weapon—except for me and Milo.

I curse myself for not reacting sooner. I am completely defenseless, and the only weapon I have is the knife stored in my boot, far out of reach.

"Drop your weapons," the same Officer commands, her voice stern.

No one moves a muscle.

"I said, drop your weapons," she shouts. "*Now.*"

We all exchange glances before the group reluctantly obeys. Aaron comfortably drops his current knife with a smirk, though I know his favorite one is hidden somewhere on his body, along with at least one surgical blade and two different carving tools that he could gouge anyone's eyes with in an instant. And those are just the ones he's told me about.

Everyone else but Milo and I carry a Yesterday gun. Those who do have vintage pistols set them down by their feet. One of the Officers walks up to collect the weapons and shoves them all in a bag, out of reach from us hostages.

"Well, well." One of the Chasers steps forward until she is only five feet away from Ren. She looks him up and down, analyzing his place in all of this. "If it isn't Officer McLellan."

How does she know him? I question her words before I realize that this must be someone he knew back in the Corps. She wears a tight bun on top of her head and a scowl that chills me to my core.

"Pittman," he says blankly.

"Believe it or not, we were actually on a mission to *rescue* you from the rebels when Carmody called HQ." She begins to pace, holding her gun out as she speaks. "He filled us in on everything. How you tricked him into postponing your target's extermination so you could follow her to the rebel base out in the woods. How you *betrayed* your own partner to sneak off and find her, abandoning your mission and breaking your contract."

So he really was lying to Ren, I think to myself. *He just wanted him to talk.* Not that it makes what we did any more justifiable.

The commanding Chaser walks even closer to Ren before spitting in his face. "You're nothing but a filthy, treasonous deserter."

I know Ren has a thing about germs, and I can see his blood boil as he uses the back of his sleeve to wipe the saliva from his face. I watch as he clenches his fists, wanting so badly to make a move but not knowing how to proceed. The tension is killing him.

It's killing us all, but Beau is the first one to break.

The young man punches the closest Chaser with such force it sends the

Officer flying back into the snow. He blends in at first, until the nosebleed that follows stains the ice red. But the next soldier is quick to react, and he shoots Beau with a Nightjade bullet that hits him right in the chest.

Chaos incites as Beau falls to the ground, fast asleep but presumed dead by the unknowing Chasers. *Not even they know the truth*, I remind myself. Only Agents and the Unseen have that privilege.

Everyone leaps to action as I stand still in the middle of it all. Aaron tackles the Chaser closest to me before he has a chance to shoot me with Nightjade, and he struggles to rip the gun from the Officer's armor-protected hands. Aaron is strong, but the Chaser both meets and surpasses his strength. The two of them roll in the snow in a desperate scramble for control.

I don't want to tear my eyes away from the fight between Aaron and the Officer, but fear spins me in a circle to inspect the other parts of the conflict. I look behind me and see Cecil punching an Officer with his bare hands, knuckles bloodied with the rage of a man who spent his whole life waiting to beat a Chaser to a pulp. I imagine it must hurt to punch the thick Corps armor, but Cecil doesn't seem to care.

Cecil is certainly our best and most experienced fighter, but he is weakened by illness, and he is not as strong as he would be under normal circumstances. The tables turn quickly, and things escalate to a wrestling match on the ground. He does not have the advantage.

Ren jumps in to help, and he restrains the Chaser with the same chokehold we practiced with. There's fury in his eyes that reminds me of his first fight with Carmody. Now the Chaser's uniform is splattered with three sources of blood, one his own broken nose, and the other two Unseen fists.

Past them, Lori gives a roundhouse kick to a man in white that sends him tumbling. Viv takes the opportunity to steal his Nightjade gun and shoot him in the neck with an inky bullet, but another Chaser comes up from behind and takes it from her as soon as the weapon is fired.

I turn around to see Milo and Asa trying to disarm an Officer not far from them. My gut lurches, twisting with fear as I see my brother fight a Chaser for the third time in his young life.

I'm frozen in the midst of this commotion as a familiar fear creeps over me. I'm standing in the snow, but in my mind I am standing on hardwood floor, trapped in the middle of my living room as Chasers do unthinkable things to the people I love. I can see Milo stab an officer in the neck, staining our home red. My clouded eyesight takes in one thing but my mind registers it as something else entirely.

I can't move. I'm stuck in such a vulnerable position, trapped in a night that no longer exists.

This will be it, won't it?

Why can't I at least die fighting?

I know I pretend to be strong—but why can't I live up to my own standards? Why is it that every time my strength matters, I underestimate myself, just like everyone else? *What's standing in my way?*

Am I really this unlucky?

I whip around when I hear Ren cry out in pain. The leading Chaser has obtained Aaron's confiscated knife, and the fabric around Ren's knee is sliced open, blood dripping down into the snow.

She takes advantage of his weakness, pinning his back against a tree and positioning her stolen knife against his throat eagerly.

"I'm not going to kill you, McLellan." She chuckles, shaking her head. "But I will kill everyone else, and you'll be sent straight to the tombs. You will pay your debt and work yourself to a slow, painful death."

He struggles to move, but he is no match for a woman in a Chaser uniform. I watch in horror as he meets my gaze across the chaos before closing his eyes, bracing himself for the blade to come.

My body moves with a will of its own. Before I realize what I'm doing, I've unsheathed my hidden knife. I watch the Officer, studying her carefully, remembering the persimmon trees in Aaron's greenhouse.

But things are different now. My eyesight is not what it once was, and it's impossible to get a precise aim. I can't overthink it. I'm brought back to that beach with Carmody, and how helpless I felt with the fog in my vision—and how powerful I felt with closed eyes.

Fight back.

I look at her exposed neck one last time.

I shut my eyes, taking a deep breath before throwing the knife with all my might.

And when I open them, to the surprise of both myself and Ren, the Chaser crumples to the ground, folding over like paper stained with blood.

She isn't dead yet, and Ren leans over, eyes red as he whispers something to her. She whispers back, and her eyes close. Whatever she says leaves Ren petrified.

I have no time to register what I've just done before I am tackled by a Chaser, hitting my left arm on a rock. Something pops as I fall to the ground, and my shoulder burns as I cry out in pain. My knife is still in Pittman's neck, and I am completely defenseless.

But not a second goes by until Aaron lunges at him, bringing the Officer to the ground instead. I'm frantic as I crawl backwards, trying and failing to scramble to my feet. The pain in my shoulder is excruciating, and I'm unable to stand until Ren appears behind me, pulling me up from the snow and slinging my right arm around his shoulder.

"Eddie!" Aaron screams my name as he struggles with the same Chaser, his voice cracking with desperation. "*Run!*"

"*No way!*" I scream over the commotion of the brawl. I won't leave him behind, not after everything. I can't leave my brother either. I can't leave any of them.

"*Take the bag and go!*" He cries out louder as he and the Chaser grunt over the control of a Nightjade gun. "Lori and I will meet you there."

"I can't," I sob.

"You're the only one capable of finishing the job right now," Aaron shouts. "I promise, Lori and I will follow you. But you have to go."

"But—"

"*Go!*"

I look at Aaron and the bag on the ground and back at Aaron again. I can tell this isn't about me. This is about all of them. I trace the cow carving that rests in my pocket.

If living another day means that I can spread hope to just one more person, doesn't that make it worth it? Even if I can't see that hope myself?

I spin in circles as the fights around me continue. Everyone I've ever loved and every stranger I've grown to care about is here, battling in this snow while I have the chance to escape.

Right now, I am the only one who can keep this operation from dying out. They need someone to continue our job before it's too late. A Chaser will call for backup soon, and our time is more limited now than it ever has been. I need to start the broadcast as soon as possible.

They need me to survive. They need me to run.

I retrieve my knife, grab the bag of Catnap bombs with my right arm, and I make a run for it.

My legs burn with a familiar flame as I sprint, but the pain in my left shoulder is so excruciating that none of it matters. I race faster than I ever have before, and I'm brought back to that night in the creek, the night I thought my whole world had come to a tragic end.

But now, everything has changed. I am no longer running away from something but toward something. I have two good legs and I've given both of them a purpose. I've paved my own path. I've written my own game.

To my surprise, Ren is playing right alongside me. "Hand me the bag."

I toss it to him without hesitation, wincing as I hold my injured arm.

"Do we have a plan?" I'm panting as I speak, already out of breath from our sprint.

"Nope."

"Should we make one?"

"Put on the respirators, gas the first level, and make our way to the top. Work quickly so they don't set off any alarms. We'll wait for assistance from there," Ren suggests. "Yeah?"

"Yeah, I think that's all we've got."

If the situation weren't so dire, I'd find it humorous that Ren and I are speaking now as if nothing has happened. It took a state of crisis to bring us together, but when I think about it, isn't that how things have always been?

Right from the start, we were thrown into situations that forced our paths to intertwine, but we grow apart when our lives are no longer in danger. It's as if we don't know how to be around each other unless we must for the sake of our own survival.

Is that all this is? I ask myself. *Survival?*

We run for about a quarter mile, but the stretch feels three times its size as we try not to slip in slushed snow. I look behind us after a few minutes have passed, and to my surprise, there's not a single Chaser on our tail. There are only trees and rocks and thorny shrubs in our wake.

We come to a sliding halt once we reach a barbed-wire fence. This time, we're on the wooded side, a part of the landscape that looks out across the grass and the cows and the chipping coats of paint that blanket the barns far beyond, secluded within the very same scenery I remember admiring so long ago.

But now, the Blurt is standing right in front of me.

It's a lot smaller than I expected it to be. Its design is the same as the training center, a neat white cube with polished windows that reflect the sky. But rather than ten floors, this one has a measly three. It's so... simple. I conclude that the building's inability to stand out is intentional.

Ren and I crouch behind the fence to observe our surroundings. The parking lot is a gravel patch connected to a dirt road that leads out to the same winding highway we drove on months ago. A few polished vehicles are lined up in a neat row in front of the sidewalk, letting us know the building is definitely inhabited by quite a handful of Corps workers. We survey the area for signs of life, and to our luck, the entire lot is completely emptied of people. Not one person is outside.

"No one's out here," Ren whispers. I nod as he pulls out two respirator masks from Aaron's bag, and we put them on in silence.

The masks are heavy and obscure my vision even more than my recovering injuries do, but I know we must wear them nonetheless. I feel slightly isolated without the comfort of seeing Ren's facial expressions as he talks. He can be hard to read, and I doubt it'll be any easier to understand him with one of these in the way.

"Remember how these work?" He gestures to the bag of Catnap bombs. "Aaron went over it back at the Cut."

"I don't," I confess. I've memorized more book pages than I can count, but when it comes to verbal instructions, things go in one ear and out the other.

"Okay, I'll handle these then," he concludes. "Stay close and don't use your bad arm. Our goal is to get you to the top as soon as possible so you can begin the broadcast."

"Got it."

I hear him take a deep breath before he continues to speak. "Are you ready?"

I close my eyes and try to inhale, but my breath is shaky. "Yeah."

"Be prepared for anything, alright?" he says, and I nod my head in agreement.

We hop over the fence and sprint through the dead pasture as silently as we can. The grass whistles as we flee through its dry blades, but it's nothing like running on melting snow. We barely make a sound as we cut through the field and make our way toward the property.

Ren and I are swift, approaching the building's front door in a hurry. Like the training center, there seems to be only one way in and out.

Ren pulls open the door and we enter as casually as possible. We act natural for a moment, and surprisingly enough, everyone in the lobby seems too preoccupied to notice the pair of strangely masked people who just waltzed inside.

The building's interior is gloriously white. It glimmers as rays of midday light seep in through the modern glass windows, illuminating the lobby with an ironically angelic glow. It's filled with multiple reception desks and an abundance of NOT workers and Sitters going about their daily routines. I assume they'll be sent home soon, judging by the determined demeanor of their workflow. Little do they know, they'll be sleeping in the office tonight.

Ren reaches into the bag to pull out the first Catnap bomb, but to my horror, we are stopped before we get the chance to use it.

Two Officers stand in front of us, a man and a woman, towering like giants. The man has tawny hair pulled back into a bun, and the woman to his left wears an auburn braid. They both look too normal to be Chasers.

"Do you two have a reason for being here?" the woman questions, eyeing us with suspicion. I'm sure our masks must be disturbing to look at.

"Yeah, we do." Ren gives me a look. I nod, grinning, just before he punches the man in the face.

The Officer falls to the ground, pulling Ren down with him. As the woman tries to pull the two of them apart, I move as silently as possible, reaching into Aaron's bag to grab one of the Catnap bombs before the female Chaser grabs my left arm. I wince in so much pain it forces me to shut my eyes and bite my tongue.

She tightens her grip on my arm. "What do you think you're doing?"

"This." I throw the bomb.

Every worker on the first floor gasps in unison as the bomb hisses on the ground, releasing an invisible gas that not a single employee can see. Petrified, they wait for an explosion that never comes. I begin to wonder if this particular bomb is defective.

Suddenly, every floor one worker hits the polished ground with an eerie thud—including the Chasers. My gut churns as I stare in shock at the slumbering group of people in white clothing. They all look dead.

I crouch down and press my fingers against one of the fallen Chaser's necks, and as Aaron told us to expect, the pulse is so faint it almost feels gone. But their bodies are warm, and I can tell they are still alive.

"We need to check that they're all asleep," Ren says. "Hurry."

I nod and stay close to him as we scramble to check each person. There are about a dozen seemingly lifeless bodies scattered all around, and we're quick to ensure that each one of them is truly knocked out.

While the sight is terrifying to say the least, I can't help but let a grin spread across my face. I thank Aaron internally for working so hard over the past couple of days—no, *years*—to create something so effective.

We hurry over to a sleek white elevator as soon as we can. It looks so new it could have been installed the day before. Everything in this entire building seems so spotless, so in order, and we ruin it all.

Anything can change in a second.

The elevator opens and we hurry inside. It's filled with an abundance of white buttons, each one labeled neatly enough for Ren to press the correct one and send us on our journey to the second floor.

"There were no buttons at the training center's elevator," Ren points out. "Controlled by the receptionists, I guess."

"Really?" I ask, and he nods. "So elevator buttons are an earned privilege, huh?"

I question it lightheartedly, but I don't feel the way I talk. It's safe to say I'm terrified of what's to come. But I have to admit, the concept of the buttons is interesting. The system thrives on making it seem impossible to make decisions for yourself. It's as if these tiny elevator buttons are a mocking gift from the Presidency. *Here*, they say. *You can make one choice today. It's all yours.*

Ren and I choose to go up.

"Should we have grabbed the Officer's guns?" I ask, turning to Ren as the metal box moves.

"There's no time to go back for them." He shakes his head. "But don't worry. I don't think we'll need them."

The elevator ride takes years. I try not to think about the pain in my arm or the gash that snakes across Ren's knee, but we're both too miserable to ignore either factor.

Right before we come to a halt, Ren drops one of the Catnap bombs onto the floor of our tiny little room. I jump back. It begins to hiss violently, writhing as it releases that invisible but brutal substance we cannot see.

I glare at Ren. "What was that for?"

"So the gas will release from the elevator the moment it opens," he explains. "It'll leave less time for anyone to make last-second emergency calls before it kicks into their system. Or stop any additional Chasers before they get too close."

I nod. "Smart move."

The elevator comes to a halt and the doors spread open like the jaws of a metal beast. The second floor is jam-packed with white cubicles, each one manned by an employee surrounded by computers and tablets. I can't smell a thing with this mask on, but I imagine it rings with the scent of stale coffee and microwave lunches.

Our presence goes unseen for a moment, but not for long. The gas begins to knock out a few of the employees before Ren tosses an additional bomb in the center of the room for good measure. I hear notes of auditory surprise escape the lips of the workers as heads fall against desks, each one landing with a painful thud. We wait for the rest of the employees to fall asleep, but one man catches on and pulls his shirt over his mouth.

He rises to his feet. "What the hell is going on?"

"Nothing that concerns you," Ren calls through the mask. We wait for him to fall asleep, but he grabs a phone from his desk and begins to dial a number.

Ren calls out as I run over to the man. I don't realize what I'm doing until I've tackled him, and we wrestle for the phone for a moment as he calls into the device for help.

Borrowing Aaron's favorite scare tactic, I pull the knife from my boot and use my good arm to pin it against his throat. Horrified, he drops the communicator before finally falling asleep.

As soon as his eyes come to a close, I rise to my feet. I crush the phone with the heel of my boot until it crumbles to pieces beneath the soles of my feet.

"*Shit*," Ren mutters to himself as I meet him outside the elevator. "He's called the damn Corps."

"We'll be fine," I reassure him. "We still have time. There's no way they can analyze that call *and* send Officers to the scene before we're done with the broadcast. I'd say we have about half an hour, at the very least."

Ren sighs, pressing the *UP* button on the wall as we wait for the doors to open again. "You're probably right."

The elevator dings and the jaws open up once again, letting us inside. Ren pushes the button for the third floor.

This ride seems to take twice as long as the last one. I have a feeling the next floor will pose a smaller threat than the bottom two, but there's a churning in my gut that makes me more anxious than ever.

I reach into my pocket and feel the carving of the cow Aaron gave to me. *A good luck charm.* I smile at the words he told me, but I'm still not sure that I can do this. The fate of the entire operation lies entirely in my hands, and I cannot fail, because the consequences could be fatal at worst. I need to say the right thing but I don't know if I can.

Ren doesn't drop a bomb in the elevator this time. He's preoccupied like I am, and we have no time to prepare before the elevator door opens once again.

But the third floor is different. We step out of the transportation machine before it comes to an instant close, looking around the room to scan it for any signs of life. To our dismay, this story is entirely vacant.

We hesitate before walking into the strange place. The room is covered with a coat of rich black paint, and the entire back wall is covered from desktop to ceiling in computer screens that make up the Blurt's main control panels.

It's so dark I can barely see Ren as he stands close to me. The only illumination is the purple and pink-hued lights that bleed from the abundance of monitors and buttons along the back wall, and within that light and color, he almost glows.

The room is completely silent, save for the hum of computer fans and the beeping of devices I cannot name. They blink a soft melody like distant wind chimes. Even though the entire room is robotically inhuman, everything feels alive.

We've done all we can to move the mission along, and now, all that's left is to wait for Lori and Aaron to arrive with the access codes. Yet somehow, this feels like the most challenging part.

Ren and I stand in the middle of the room. My right shoulder touches his as we stare at the control panel, our views blocked by these ridiculous respirator masks.

I turn my head to look up at Ren, and he rotates his down to look at me. He seems so much taller than he used to. He stopped growing years ago, but he still looks changed. Maybe I feel smaller.

He turns the rest of his body to face me, and I mimic his movements. It's strange to face him this way. I imagine that this is what things would have been like at the fence after graduation, if we didn't have a physical barrier in the way. Now the only things keeping us apart are these masks.

"We made it," he says. His voice is muffled, but I can hear the contentment in his tone nonetheless.

"We did," I say. We stand in surprisingly painless silence for a few more moments until Ren takes off his mask.

I panic. "What are you doing?"

"There's no gas up here," he says. He places the mask back in Aaron's bag before reaching over to take mine. Slowly, gently, he lifts it from my face before storing it in its proper place. Now, there really isn't anything keeping us apart.

But we still feel so separate.

"I was worried about you," he says, inching closer to me. There's a sadness in his voice I can't unravel. "I thought—I don't know. That something would go wrong as it usually does and we'd be apart again."

Apart.

I look down at my boots. They're no longer leather, really, but an unclean collection of mud and dirt that serves as a permanent reminder of the places they've taken me.

Ren places a hand on my cheek, and I shiver. "I planned a *Just In Case.*" I give him a puzzled look. "I was going to tell you everything. All of the things I wanted to say but never could."

He hesitates for a moment and I speak up, gluing my eyes to these dirtied boots. "Why didn't you?"

"The Chasers came."

There's a pause. "And now here we are."

"So here we are," he agrees.

Neither of us says another word for what feels like a little eternity. He stands there with his hand on my cheek, neck craned down to look at a pair of eyes that refuse to meet his. His hair is a mess and it hangs over his forehead as he tries to steal a glance that I cannot seem to give.

"Will you hear me out?" he says quietly.

I nod, and he comes closer.

"Remember that night in the cow field?" he asks.

I nod again, too afraid to ruin whatever this is with the wrong words. Of course I remember that night. I remember it far more than I want to.

"Remember what we talked about?"

My breathing wavers. "All the truths I didn't know."

"I left some truths out," he says softly. "And then the opportunity to say them was gone. Or at least, I thought it was. But I know now that there are no real right moments. I know now that the right thing to say will never truly feel right, even if it's the rightest thing you've ever done."

I keep my gaze attached to the ground. I want to look up at him, but for some reason, I can't. I can't meet his eyes and it hurts me more than it hurts him.

"What truths?" I mutter, so quietly I can barely hear myself over the low rhythm of the controls that now lie to our left.

"There's something I never told you." A pause. "Something from before."

Before our world fell apart. I bite my lip, bracing myself. "You can tell me." The whisper is paper thin.

"After the river incident. When we were younger." He swallows deeply, like the words are hard to say. "Do you remember how we pretended to be strangers?"

I nod, because I do.

Following the split, I acted like he didn't even exist. Even when I went to the McLellans' house, I only spent time with Margot. I avoided Ren like the plague because I thought he hated me, and it was easier to convince myself that I hated him, too. It hurt less.

When we had classes together in school, we'd sit on opposite sides of the room. We'd avert our stares like our lives depended on it. After our separation, we interacted only when it was absolutely necessary. We forced ourselves to become strangers, even though we knew each other so well.

It was a cold, cruel distance.

"We were so close when we were kids. And you were the girl who scared me like no one else." He hesitates. "Do you know why?"

He was afraid of me?

I don't move, and I don't say a thing.

"I was scared of you because I knew what you could do to me."

My lungs constrict, like clay squeezed between the fingers of a clenched fist.

But then he continues.

"Because you had my whole heart." His words sound unbearably fragile. "You felt like the rightest thing, and that terrified me." He shakes his head. "And I spent years trying to find a way to reach you, to tell you that I never hated you. But so much time passed. I thought I was too late. Convincing myself we were better apart was..."

I finish the sentence for him. "Easier?"

He nods.

"You're Ren." I hold back the urge to reach my hand out, to trace my finger along his cheek. "It's impossible for you to be too late."

"There's something else I should have told you."

I nod, urging him to go on.

His voice falls to a whisper. "I wanted to kiss you."

I freeze.

That is an incredible impossibility. A horrendous, appalling, horrible impossibility I hate myself for ignoring. I can't even bring myself to blink. There is only me and the ground I stare at, and the knots that keep on unraveling in my stomach.

"Back in that field, next to the cow and under the moon," he says. "When you were covered in mud at the river. At the playground, when I woke up in the middle of the night and saw you asleep against my shoulder."

"You didn't wake me?"

"I couldn't." He shakes his head. "But there were moments long before that." He steps even closer. "Long before that."

I don't know what to say. My mouth falls open, and all I can do is tremble. Because I had no idea.

"I had a Just In Case plan too. Before the draw," I finally confess, my face flushed rosy. "I went over to your house but you weren't there. So I placed a letter in the back of your botany notebook and... left."

"Oh really?" He chuckles. "Are you going to tell me what it says?"

I swallow the bramble in my throat. "That I don't hate being around you."

"You're not so bad yourself, you know." He looks down at my hand, and our fingers intertwine. He presses his forehead against my own and I can feel his breath tickle my nose.

"I will never hurt you, Eddie," he says solemnly. I close my eyes because I so badly want to meet his stare, but I can't bring myself to do it. I'll break if I see the way he looks at me. "Never again."

The only thing I can hear is the whirring of computers in the background, the wind chime lullaby of their heartbeat. And Ren's full, vibrant pulse, finally in tune with my own. *Not slow*, I note.

"Why didn't you kiss me?" I ask so suddenly we're both surprised. "Back when you said you wanted to, you could have kissed me."

"There was always a fence in the way."

There is a pause as the background hum composes some melancholy tune, just for the two of us. I whisper to him. "Is the fence still here?"

He shakes his head no, tucking a loose curl behind my ear. He holds my face with both hands now, his touch so soft it fills my gut with light-hungry moths and makes my entire body go numb. He looks me in the eye as I finally find his gaze, and he brings my face even closer to his.

"Is the fence still here?" he whispers back, our noses touching. His mouth is so close to my own.

"I think the fence was in our heads the entire time."

All the bad things around us seem to melt away when Ren's lips discover mine. He tastes like blood but I do not care, and I breathe him in.

Every clock in the world ceases to tick. There is only him and me, standing alone under a makeshift electronic moon in the light of day. The lights from the monitors continue to flash around us as he pulls me closer, hands on my waist now as I wrap my arms around his neck.

I find every beautiful truth in his touch.

He has been here all along, and I was so foolish not to see that before. I mistook his fear for hatred and my heart for the same thing. It was so hard for me to be around him because being around him was the one thing I wanted most, and I refused to let myself believe that to be true. We were both terrified of wanting the wrong people.

But how stupid I am to love him more than all there is, because loving is dangerous. Loving is vulnerability. It is a weakness, something to either keep you Running or lead you straight down the path of self-sacrifice.

Love is the most dangerous game of all, and it's the one thing this system is built to destroy. It's programmed to fight against the lengths we will go for those we want to carry.

But I don't feel unsafe anymore. Not even a little bit. Because we've burned down that fence. I have reached him and he has reached me, and in Ren, I am no longer lost.

I have found him, and I have found myself too.

His lips part from mine and he pulls me into an embrace I never want to end. I let myself feel safe in his arms. I let myself feel protected from anything that could ever pull me away from him again.

"You have ruined me beyond repair," he whispers, and it feels like we're standing in the sea once again. "And even still, I will choose you endlessly."

I pull away, looking him in the eye again as he holds my face in his palms. I reach my hands up to meet his. "I will always choose you, Ren."

I realize how right I was not so long ago. This has always been about survival.

Because Ren is my one constant, and I cannot live without him. There is no one without the other. There is no I without him. In him, the world is there waiting, and it is unending.

And then the elevator opens.

REN

Friday, January 24
Day 24

Eddie pulls away from me when the elevator opens.

I step in front of her instinctively, but I lower my guard as soon as I realize that Lori and Aaron are the ones stepping out, and not a swarm of Officers coming to exterminate us. Lori is still in her respirator mask and takes it off once the elevator closes.

"We don't have much time," she says, shoving past us and making her way to the control panel. She takes a seat at the desk as comfortably as one of the workers we just put to sleep. "They'll send Agents over soon if the entire building isn't responding. We have to get this done quickly."

She presses a few buttons across the control panel, and the black screensaver of every monitor in sight switches off immediately, revealing one giant login screen that Lori gets past in a breeze. What was once just a small amount of light now feels like an explosion of brightness as every screen turns on and begins to run its designated software, a brightness so overwhelming I have to blink a few times to properly adjust my eyes to its glaring presence.

Eddie runs over to Aaron and wraps her arms around him. The gesture tugs at something in my gut, but while I still don't trust the guy, he doesn't seem as intimidating anymore. He pulls her off of him and begins to look her up and down frantically, spinning her around and inspecting her for wounds.

"You two okay? Any injuries?" he asks, though the question seems to be directed at Eddie more than myself. I shake my head no and I watch as Eddie does the same.

"I'm fine," she says.

"Did she hit her head? Her pupils are very dilated," Aaron questions without looking as he grabs her face to study it closely, checking for a concussion that isn't there.

"No." My face turns red as I think back to the kiss they nearly walked in on.

"Oh." He lets her go and clears his throat. "It's dark in here. That must be it."

"She did injure her shoulder though." I cross my arms, nodding in Eddie's direction. "I think it's dislocated."

Aaron glares at Eddie. "Why didn't you say anything?"

She shrugs, and it only makes her wince.

"I need to see it," Aaron says, and Eddie nods, removing her puffer jacket and pulling down her sleeve.

I gasp when I see her shoulder. Her arm looks more like that of a toy than a human, twisted and out of socket.

Without another word, Aaron pops it into place.

Eddie cries out in pain, closing her eye and leaning over, clutching her arm. She remains that way for a few more moments before standing up straight, glaring at Aaron. "Thanks for the warning."

"You're welcome," he grumbles. "Next time be honest about your injuries."

"Ren," she blurts, turning around to point at my knee. "A Chaser slashed him during the brawl."

"Really? You too?" Aaron swears under his breath, walking over to where

I stand. He crouches down to inspect the gash in my knee, visible through my torn jeans. "Next time you lie about an injury I'm kicking your ass, McLellan."

"What happened after we left?" Eddie asks. "Is everyone alright?"

"They're on their way," Aaron explains. He pulls a clean cloth from his satchel and smothers it with water from his canteen. He doesn't give me a warning either when he starts cleaning the wound of blood and debris, and it stings. "Once a few of the Chasers were knocked out, Lori and I ran here as fast as we could. I assume they're all fighting over who's gonna carry Beau back."

"Did anyone else get knocked out?" Eddie asks, with the thought of Milo in her eyes.

Aaron rubs a salve on my knee before covering the wound with a bandage and packing up his supplies. "No."

"Alright you guys," Lori calls out from the control panel, and we all pause. She turns the swivel chair around to face us with a grin. "You ready?"

Eddie nods, but I can see how nervous she is. She doesn't feel ready in the slightest. She has such a heavy burden to bear, and it pains me to know that I can't help her carry its weight. This is something she has to do all on her own. *I trust her.*

She turns to walk toward the control panel to meet Lori, but Aaron stops her. He puts a hand on her good shoulder and looks at her without an ounce of satire in his expression.

"Remember what I told you," he whispers and gives her a half smile. "You have a way with words, Voclain."

She smiles humorously and pulls out a wooden cow carving from her pocket. "None of that matters if I have my good luck charm."

"Who needs luck, anyway?" He winks, and Eddie puts the object back in its place. Aaron nods at the control panel. "Go get 'em, Lone Player."

"Eddie," I call out before she walks away. She turns to face me, and when she does, I want to be at a loss for words again. I want to wait for the right moment and the right things to tell her, but I know I can't do that anymore. *No right moments.*

I smile at her, and she comes over to give me a hug.

"You know more than you think you do," I whisper.

Her voice breaks when she whispers back. "Thank you."

She pulls away from me. I want to lose myself in her eyes again, but I know she has to go. I reach my arm out, lacing my fingers between hers as she turns to walk away. She gives them one last squeeze before our hands fall apart.

And with that she walks to the rainbow wall of monitors, staring up at them like a mountain she has to climb. I take one look at her as the light paints her face and know in an instant that this is what she was born to do.

She wasn't born unlucky, double Jokers and all.

Lavender Voclain was born to give people hope, and with that, she is the luckiest girl alive.

"Do you remember what you need to say?" Lori asks, and Eddie nods.

"Good." Lori turns back around and types something into the system.

We wait in silence until the monitors all come to the same collective change. A huge box appears on the screen, reflecting a camera image of Lori and letting us know that a recording will begin in thirty seconds.

Lori gestures for Eddie to come and take her place in the swivel chair, and when she does, the screen fills with Eddie's face instead. Lori gives her good shoulder a gentle squeeze before walking away.

All alone now, Eddie holds the microphone in her hand—and we all wait for the clock to tick.

Thirty seconds turn into twenty, and before I know it, I'm counting down from five. The world ages eons with every passing millisecond. *Four. Three. Two.*

One.

Eddie takes a deep, terrified breath.

And then it begins.

"Hello," she says into the screen, her voice echoing around us. Lori has successfully set up the broadcast to reach every able device across the country, but as we stand secluded in this empty room, it feels like we're completely alone.

"My name is Lavender," Eddie begins, and she pauses.

I wish I could carry this load for her—no, I wish I could carry *her* through it all—but I know that I cannot. I stand back and wait next to Aaron and Lori as we exchange glances.

But our looks are not nervous. We are confident in Eddie. Aaron gives me a proud grin, and I mirror it right back. She can do this. She's so much more capable than she thinks she is.

"And if I were you, I'd listen carefully—because everything you know is a lie." Eddie pauses again and blinks slowly. I can see her tremble as I stand across the room, and I wish I could hold her hand. I wish I could speak these difficult words for her.

"I was just like you once. Like all of you," she continues, voice wavering. "I grew up in a world where everything was one way, and anything opposing that way was automatically perceived as something bad. Something evil. A threat."

Eddie gulps nervously, and Aaron pulls his water canteen out of his bag to hand to Lori. She walks over and passes the bottle to Eddie, who nods and takes a sip. "But I'm here to tell you that we cannot think this way anymore."

Eddie's voice grows louder as she speaks, her confidence an inch higher than it was at the start. But she is still petrified, so afraid of making a mistake.

"The system is not for the good of humanity," she says. "It is for the good of a handful of people who will let humanity fall in the name of a system that serves them."

God, I love her.

"The Presidency is not what it used to be," Eddie continues. "A long time ago, we used to run as a democracy. Everyone had a piece of the crown until we slowly lost sight of how things should be.

"And now, it is run by a few people in black suits, who seek to profit from this game they call life and this death they call a game.

"How have we become so jaded?" She pauses. "We no longer value human life. We let so many innocent people fall victim to the way things are—and for what?" She laughs without humor. "This—this is wrong. This is twisted. Nothing we do can be for the sake of humanity if we no longer know what it means to be human.

"We are told that we will be saved if the odds allow and exterminated if they don't. We are told the game is just, that it is fairer than all other games known to man. But that's not true. It is not fair to pit person against person in this bloodbath we call a country. It is not fair to kill the families of Runners or offer Immunity as a reward to those who turn them in. It is not fair to end a person's life over petty crimes and human error. It is not fair to slaughter our country's brightest minds simply because they are too ill to run or walk or live like everyone else."

Eddie's voice cracks, and I can feel myself choking on her words too.

"My best friend had chronic Lyme disease," the girl continues. "She lived her life in fear. She was so good at pretending to be okay, but she was fading away, and her brother had to stop it by becoming a Chaser to give her Immunity. He thought that the only way to survive—the only way for his *sister* to survive—was to play along."

Eddie shakes her head. "Don't you see how terrible that is?"

There is a pause.

"To force someone into making choices they never wanted to make, choices that make you slowly lose sight of your own humanity." She shakes her head again, swallowing tears before they come. "He is not a monster. He Chased because he had to, and I bet there are many more people like him.

"But he couldn't save her." Eddie chokes up again as she speaks, and I feel my own eyes start to water as tears begin to form in the corners of her eyes. "None of us could, because this system is broken. It's broken because it works to break people. It broke *me*."

Eddie is crying now, but she is no longer shaking. There is no waver to her words. She stands firm, trying to show the world that she is not weak. She cries but she is strong because of it. "It broke me. Hell, it shattered me beyond repair. Because you see?"

Eddie sets down the microphone, lifting her sleeves to show the world her Joker tattoos before picking the mic back up again.

"I was Picked, and my family was slaughtered by Chasers for protesting my death." Eddie weeps, and I realize that I have tears too. I want to hold her like I did in the sea, with no one else around but the waves and the sand and the tide that wanted to pull us away.

But she must do this on her own.

"My brother put his own life on the line to save me. He tackled one of the Officers and fought back long enough for me to Run. I didn't want to leave him behind, but I didn't want my family's sacrifice to go in vain. I Ran because I had to honor their memory.

"But before I knew it, I stumbled upon the truth. And now I realize I Ran because I was meant to tell you all this very truth, right now. I was meant to bring you hope."

Eddie takes a deep breath before taking an additional gulp from Aaron's water bottle. She continues, her voice no longer terrified but commanding. She has finally transformed into Eddie Voclain, and the entire country is watching her overcome her worst fears.

"We need to learn to value the individual. Because once we stop valuing a human as an individual, we stop valuing the whole.

"There is so much more to life than just surviving. But if we continue this pattern of hatred and violence, we will bring about our own end.

"We are all told from the moment we are born to play our part. But times have changed. We need to change the game completely. We need to write our own rules, and we need to play alone."

There is another pause.

"If you don't believe that the Presidency has been lying to you this entire time, then check your own bodies," she says, hesitating. "We are microchipped and tracked. We are dosed with depressants. We have no privacy, no freedom. We are watched and listened to and tested like lab rats who don't even know they've been caged." She takes a deep breath. "The trackers are located in our left—"

The screen goes static, interrupting Eddie's speech.

"—eyes."

Lori hurries back to the control panel to assess the problem. After a moment, she turns around to stare at us grimly, her good eye peeled open with fear.

"There's nothing I can do, guys," she mutters. "It's been overridden."

But before any of us can say another word, the elevator doors open.

Two men I've never seen before this day walk in, but they walk in like they know us. They walk in as though they know us all, and by the looks of their black formal suits and the pair of shades covering their eyes, I wouldn't be surprised if they did.

We are all frozen in a dread unlike any other. We know nothing about them, but at the same time, we know everything.

They say you know an Agent when you see one, and it's true. We all know these two men must be Agents from the one Corps division no one is allowed to know anything about. A higher-up. A Presidential grunt, sent to implement a fatal penalty with the jet black Nightjade gun he holds in his hands. It glistens like hot coals.

Wordless, one of the men points his gun at Eddie.

Not one of us has a gun. They were all taken by the Chasers who fought us in the snow. Aaron and Eddie have knives, but this is no knife fight. We can't fight two armed Agents—not like this.

They must have been sent here to exterminate her, to end this measly rebellion before it has the chance to truly begin. He will kill this new symbol of hope. They will call her every name in the book. A fraud, a criminal, a murderer, a Runner. *A filthy traitor.*

They are here to take everything away from me, only minutes after I realized that I have it.

I do have everything. I have Eddie, and she's more than enough. She's more than I could ever ask for. She's more than I could ever deserve.

I think back to what Milo said to me last night by that stream, how we stared into the sky and remembered how we would do anything for our sisters. I think about how frightened he was to lose Eddie, and the promise I made to him. That I will be there. I will carry her.

The man holds the gun with two hands now. His long bony fingers trace the trigger, and every breath has been sucked out of the room.

We are all frozen in amber, unable to make a move because there is no right moment to do so. All heartbeats come to a complete stop as we wait for the inevitable to unfold before our eyes.

I will choose her endlessly.

All the things around me—Eddie's screams, the light from the control panel, the smell of wood in her hair—all of it melts away. I seem to have jumped in front of her.

But I'm smiling when the world goes black, because Eddie is holding my hand.

Eddie is everything, and I swear I see stars as everything fades into nothing at all.

EDDIE

Friday, January 24
Day 24

When Ren falls, everything goes numb.

I can't hear myself scream as I run to his side, and I can't see a single thing as my eyes burn with salt.

I am underwater again. Ren and I have jumped off that bridge by the river, and it is just him and I beneath the surface where nothing else can get through. I wish I could breathe down here. I wish Ren could breathe down here.

There is background noise from above the surface. I hear one of the Agents call out to his partner, noticing our strange left eyes and informing him we are rebels, that we have no chips. But the voices don't last long.

In his rage, Aaron is quick to react to the Nightjade bullet, grabbing the gun before slitting the Agent's throat in the blink of an eye. The other Agent is met with a roundhouse kick from Lori that knocks the gun from his hands. She grabs it before he has the chance, taking the dead Agent's gun from Aaron as well.

The last Agent, still alive, thinks quickly. Before I realize what's going on, he drags Ren up with both arms, using his limp body for a shield. He holds a finger against his shades—a communication device, perhaps—and he calls for backup. With Ren's proximity to the Agent and the current state of her healing vision, Lori can't make a good shot with her stolen Nightjade gun.

My mind is switched off again, and all I can manage to do is weep, screaming out as Aaron holds me back. I try so hard to get to the Agent, to reach him, to take Ren's empty shell from the man in the black suit. But I cannot. Aaron won't let me.

Aaron has armed himself with his knives, and Lori holds both Nightjade guns, one in either hand—and I am feral. The Agent knows he cannot take on three ravenous Unseen on his own, and no matter how loud I scream, I cannot keep him from leaving.

And the Agent takes Ren with him.

I can't hear Aaron's voice as he tries to calm me down from my hysterics. But I can feel something sharp in my neck, and in a blink, the world around me fades away.

Everything is cold. The ground beneath me, the air around me, the blood in my veins—all of it is chilled, and I wonder if this is another blizzard. I wonder if I really am back in that snow, if I'm only waking up from a dream.

But no snowflake touches me. There are no stars falling from the sky and painting everything white. The ground is frozen, but it's not ice. *Metal?*

Frantic, I pull myself upright and absorb my unfamiliar surroundings. I feel the ground around me to check again for snow, just to be sure, but my hands only find a metallic surface that quakes beneath me. It feels like the ground is moving.

"Where are we?" I ask no one at all as my vision begins to clear. I blink once, twice, five times before I'm able to realize that I'm in the back of a truck.

We're in the back of a truck.

It's a refrigerated semi-truck, by the looks of it. It's lined with metal bench-like ledges on either side that we all seem to be using as a seat. I see Viv and Hugo sitting with Milo across from me, and Beau is lying fast asleep on the ground by my feet. I wonder where Cecil is, and then I realize that he's probably the only person who knows how to drive a truck in the entire group, no matter how sick he may be.

But I don't see Ren anywhere. *Or Asa.*

"She's awake." I hear Lori's voice and turn to my left to see her sitting next to me, holding my hand. I assume she's been doing so while I slept here on this bench.

"There she is," Aaron replies with an empty smile. He's sitting to my right, and he seems saddened when he looks at me. "How are you feeling?"

I don't say anything, because he already knows the answer to my question. I don't feel anything at all.

"What is this?" I ask, observing the truck an additional time. In the corner, I see stacks of plastic crates, filled with what seem to be glass bottles of white liquid.

"We stole an industrial milk truck from the dairy farm next to the Blurt," Hugo says with a sigh, rubbing his temple. "The most *idiotic and predictable move!*"

He shouts the last part, looking at the head of the truck where the driver must be positioned beyond the barrier of a cold gray wall. Cecil is definitely at the wheel.

"Where are we going?" I question softly, but I don't really care to know the answer.

"End Harbor," Hugo answers as he sits across from me.

"End Harbor?"

"A sister compound up north, in Washington state," he explains slowly. "It's a small island that used to be occupied by a town in the Yesterdays, but the Wandering drove people out—and kept them out. It's been presumed abandoned ever since."

I don't want to nod, and I don't want to say anything.

"We can't go back to the Cut without putting everyone else in danger. All of us heading back at once just wasn't a good idea, so we sent Asa to fill

Noriko in once she wakes up."

I get the feeling that he's only answering my questions to comfort me. It's painfully obvious that this whole damn truck pities me, and it's not comforting in the slightest. It reminds me that I have a reason to be pitied.

"We'll get him back, Eddie." Lori rubs my hand as she holds it. "We'll get him back."

When I don't respond, her eyes sadden. "Do you remember what happened?"

I don't want to. I shake my head. *I can't remember. I won't.*

Lori gives Aaron a concerned look, and he nods. I'm frightened by their need to communicate through exchanged glances, as though I'm not sitting right in front of them. It makes me more uneasy than words spoken aloud. I watch as Lori takes a deep breath and closes her eyes, preparing herself for what she has to say. She speaks when she opens them again.

"Ren..." She sighs again, like the words are too painful for a person full of so much kindness to say. She drops my hand to put her head in her palms and begins to cry. "I'm sorry, I can't."

Aaron gives his sister that saddened look again before turning his body to face me. I stare up at him with wide eyes, praying that he won't say what I know he's going to say.

"A pair of Agents was dispatched to the Blurt. We think a call may have been made by one of the workers," Aaron explains, his words gentle, soft, and slow. His hands meet mine, but I'm too numb to feel them.

"They walked into the control room and one of them—he pointed his gun at you," Aaron continues, like this is just as hard for him to say as it is for me to hear.

"Why didn't he shoot?" I avert my gaze to stare at the wall across from me. I can't handle looking at Aaron anymore, because he can't bear to see me like this and I can tell.

I feel Aaron take another deep breath. "Because Ren took the Nightjade bullet for you."

"No." I shake my head, laughing coldly. "No. That didn't happen."

"The Agent realized he couldn't fight us alone. We also think he realized who we are, and what we know. He realized that Ren was debugged and must have thought there was a chance that he could still be alive, even after he took that Nightjade bullet for you.

"So he took him away and called for backup to deal with us. I had to... sedate you, because you wouldn't leave." Aaron mutters. "You were in hysterics and we had to get you out of there alive."

My eyes sting with hot tears, and I stare at the floor when even the wall becomes too much to look at. I shake my head. None of this is true. I won't allow it to be.

"Eddie." Aaron holds my hand tighter and closes his eyes as he speaks. "They have Ren, and we don't know if he's alive."

"Statistically speaking, the chances of his survival are pretty low," Hugo announces from across the room. "There's a high probability that the trigger wasn't completely out of his system when the Nightjade hit, so—"

"Dude, shut the hell up!" Aaron snaps.

"She's not an idiot, Aaron." Hugo defends himself, voice stern. "She has the right to know."

"I agree," Aaron glares with a chilling fury. "But not now."

"Eddie," Lori says, wiping tears from her eyes and holding my other hand in hers once again. She speaks so gently I want to fall asleep and never open my eyes again. "We don't know how much his body has healed from the tracker. If the trigger is no longer in his system, there's a good chance he survived that Nightjade bullet. And we're all going to do everything in our power to find him, alright?"

"But you have to understand that the odds of that are lower than—" Hugo pipes up, and I interrupt him.

"No," I retort aggressively. Everyone turns to look at me, and I keep my eyes glued to the ground. "He's alive."

He has to be alive. He has to be alive, or I cannot keep going. I can't keep Running anymore. I'm not strong enough to go on without him. I can't keep going if I can't keep choosing Ren.

Lori opens her mouth to say something, but she never gets the chance. She jumps in her seat when the truck's radio goes fuzzy. We plug our ears as static floods from the speakers, and Lori and Hugo exchange terrified glances. The two of them simultaneously open their laptops and prepare to watch what they both know is coming.

Lori stares at her computer screen for a moment before looking at Aaron with a panic that sends my gut in spirals. "There's another broadcast."

> Attention citizens.

The voice is heavily distorted, the same kind of distortion from the night of the draw.

> This is a member of the Presidency speaking. I am calling your attention to address a matter of utmost importance.

Everyone in the truck goes dead quiet. I move my hands away from Lori and Aaron and wrap my arms around my torso, trembling violently. I know what's coming can't be good and I struggle to breathe. But Aaron wraps an arm around me, and I'm calmed by a fraction of a degree.

> This is a national emergency.

The voice begins again, and we all listen in fear.

> We would like to inform you all of a particular individual who has caused our country a great amount of distress. We believe that you as citizens have a right to know about this new danger, and our main objective is to warn you all. To keep our people safe and united, even as the unimaginable becomes a reality.

> Lavender Adele Voclain is a wanted criminal who slaughtered her entire family before going on a killing spree. She brutally murdered four honorable Chasers in cold blood: Officers Jeffery Becker, Virgil Caldwell, Duke Carmody, and Ren McLellan.

I close my eyes at the sound of Ren's name. Aaron holds me tighter, and Lori wraps an arm around me too. They hold me close but I feel so empty, like a hollowed out shell of a person.

But... Jeffery Becker? Virgil Caldwell? The names are unfamiliar until I realize that they must be referring to the Chasers that Milo killed. The Chasers he *protected* me from.

The voice behind this broadcast is wrong. Ren is not dead. He's alive. He's still breathing somewhere, and we'll find him. We have to.

We believe that her motives are backed by her ties to an anti-Chaser conspiracist cult that obsesses over removing the eyes as a testament to each member's devotion. We believe that Voclain plays a leadership role in said cult, and wants to spread a major conspiracy to the public to incite fear, cause panic, and ultimately create chaos to confuse us all.

We've been looking for her quite some time now. Getting her into government custody alive is absolutely necessary; we need to extract valuable information from her in order to put an end to the Opticultist movement before it begins. We have reason to believe that in addition to their invasive broadcast, they have been planning physical attacks against innocent citizens. She is a dangerous individual who wants nothing but to take down our society and everyone in it. No one is safe as long as she roams free.

We ask you to please disregard her previous broadcast. Voclain broke into one of our Broadcasting Centers to spread her lies. She will do anything to gain power, including the murder of her innocent family. For listeners who have screens in front of them, we will now show photo evidence of the atrocities this woman has committed against her own flesh and blood.

A pause sends a chill coursing through me that freezes the marrow in my bones. I look down at Lori's laptop to see what the broadcast is showing to the public but Aaron covers my eyes with his hands. I fail, trying to squirm free. But he keeps my eyes covered. He doesn't want me to see what's on the screen, and I am overwhelmed with rage.

I know what they're showing. They're showing my family. They're showing the photographs the Cleaners must have taken of my dead mother and father before taking their bodies to be buried.

I don't care what they look like. I need to see them again, but Aaron won't let me. The broadcast continues as I give up, sobbing. I clutch his shirt in my hands and weep because I know there must have been a reason for him to keep me blind. I cry, because even after they took everything from me, they won't even let my family rest in peace.

> We are asking those of you with any information to come forward immediately. Anyone thought to be withholding information will be subjected to the necessary means to extract that information before being exterminated without exceptions. We would also like to announce that we are placing a bounty on Voclain's head for ten lifetimes of Immunity. I repeat, ten lifetimes of Immunity for you and your loved ones.

> We ask everyone to be vigilant. We ask you all to do what is necessary to protect this country and the system we value so much. We ask you all to play your part for the sake of humanity's protection and advancement.

> Before we end this broadcast, we would like to share proof with you all that details one of the atrocities Voclain committed against one of our very own Chasers.

> Here is video evidence of her shooting our beloved Officer Ren McLellan with illegally obtained Yesterday weaponry.

"What?" I scream. I jump up from my seat, the road rocking me back and forth as I stand.

Ren was never shot with Yesterday weaponry. What video are they talking about?

"Eddie, sit down. You'll hurt yourself." Lori tugs at my hand gently but I pull it away.

I listen, only because I need to see this new lie for myself.

I look over at Lori's computer screen to watch the broadcast. Aaron doesn't cover my eyes this time.

My eyes are still scratched and cloudy from the tears that have been forming within their corners, but I can see the screen clearly.

The video shows Ren, awake and alive, standing in the middle of a white room with his hands behind his back. He glares at whoever holds the camera, and he doesn't say a word.

If he's awake, that must mean Agents have an antidote for Nightjade. But why would they heal him? Did they wake him up just to record this video? There are a thousand questions swarming my mind, and all of them begin with *why*.

I reach out to touch the screen.

The broadcast sends a noise cracking through the speakers. Not the soft whisper of a Nightjade bullet, but something explosive, something metal.

It's the sound of a Yesterday pistol, the same unmistakable roll of thunder I heard at the beach that day with Carmody and Noriko.

But before I can blink again, I see it.

A red flower of blood blooms from Ren's abdomen. His back hits the wall. I watch him slide down slowly until he reaches the ground—and crumples. His eyes come to a close, and the video ends.

My ears ring, and I think I start to scream but I can't be sure. The truck rocks back and forth as it rolls across the road, but I rise to my feet again.

"Eddie, please. Sit down. You'll fall." Lori tries to grab my hand again but I don't let her.

"Not every wound is fatal, Eddie. Remember?" Aaron attempts to soothe my fear with reasoning, but it doesn't work. Nothing works.

Everything goes quiet except for the pounding in my chest. I'm too dizzy to see straight. My mind filters out all sound, and the world around me spins. It spins and spins and spins until all I can see is a pinwheel of colors and shapes.

The truck drives over a pothole and I let myself lose balance. I fall backward, crashing into the stack of milk bottles Lori warned me about. The glass shatters around me as the crates and I fall together, landing with a painless thud.

After I hit the floor, I am perfectly still. I stare at the ceiling as a stream of blood trickles from the back of my head, cutting through the puddle of milk that begins to spread around me. It's only glass, it's only falling, but it feels like I have been shot.

Because Ren is dead, and that is a bullet of the realest lead.

Get Lost. in bonus content for
Lone Player

Explore deleted scenes, author interviews, artwork, and more

LOSTISLANDPRESS.COM

"I have no shortage of uncertainties,
but there's one thing I know for a fact:
the Vermillion Keep is definitely haunted."

— Eddie Voclain

Acknowledgments

LONE PLAYER is an odd combination of many things, and it wouldn't be here today if it weren't for the help, support, and influence of some very fantastic people.

First, I want to thank Mel, who ended up as my publisher but began as a friend. Thank you for reaching out to me during quarantine and giving me some needed conversation. And thank you for all of your hard work with this book. You're an inspiration to so many young creatives, and you truly helped me shape *Lone Player* into something I never thought it would be.

I want to thank the Lost Island team for working so hard to get this book out there and ready for people to read. Thank you Katie, for your insightful notes and careful editing work. I'd also like to thank MAD Book Covers for giving me the gift of my debut novel's cover art, which was truly a dream come true. And thank you Amanda, the other 2021 contest winner, for all of your kindness, positivity, inspiration—and awesome music taste on Instagram.

The greatest of thanks to each and every one of my beta readers! I'm so grateful for your feedback. You guys were so fun to work with and gave me all the support, inspiration, and insight I needed.

And thank you, Raina. Thanks for holding my hand through difficult things, exchanging lore with me, sending me fan edits of our favorite enemies-to-lovers ships, and giving me life advice I didn't know I needed. May our lord Rye Wheat be with you in spirit wherever you go.

And, of course, to all of my supportive teachers—you know who you are—thank you for believing in me throughout the years. I highly doubt I'd be where I am today without your much-needed kindness and influence. If you had my brothers too, I hope you made it out okay. But thanks for taking care of them.

Lastly, I want to thank my family. Without your support, I wouldn't have had the strength, persistence, and desire to finish my first book.

I wrote this book after graduating early from high school, right smack in the middle of the worst parts of my health battle with chronic Lyme disease and co-infections. I was also recovering from my most-recent leg surgery (that involved the chopping-in-half of femurs and some pretty wild cyborg enhancements), living at home, surviving on nothing but tea and dragon-fruit oatmeal like some iMac gremlin while trying to draft *Lone Player* in twenty-eight days so I could submit it in time for the Lost Island contest. Thanks to you, I was able to do just that.

I know it can be a challenge to have an anxious author (goblin) as a daughter and sister—so thank you for always putting up with my shenanigans. Learning how to love being alive was not an easy climb, but you guys made it so possible.

Fender and Cricket, you make every day a joyous one.

Mom—thank you for working so hard to take care of me. I adore our laughs, our drives, and our random late-night talks. You're a trooper for enduring all of my car-ride ramblings about book ideas and writing anxiety. I know it's not always easy to be my mom, but you make it so easy to be your daughter.

I want to thank my Dad and Hollie, who are always there to support me, no matter how difficult I am. Dad—thank you for reading a very chaotic early draft of *Lone Player* and helping me come up with solutions I wouldn't have thought of on my own. Hollie—thank you for our bookstore trips, our conversations, and for listening to the silly stories I wrote as a kid. You and Dad have done so much for me, and truly helped shape my love for storytelling.

To Mason and Kaleb, who were such important parts of my childhood. We've had so many fun family vacations and silly memories together, and it's so wild to think about how much you guys have grown. Thanks for putting up with me during my chaotic elementary and middle school years. I hope life brings you guys all the goodness you deserve.

And to Michael and Ben. You guys are my best friends, my lifetime partners-in-mischief. You're always there for me to make sure I remember to eat, laugh, and breathe. You make me drink water even though it's gross. You pick me up when I fall down, and you always know what songs to play or jokes to tell when I'm freaking out about something. Our brainstorming sessions have become a necessity for all of my writing projects. I love being your older sister—and I can't wait to see where your stories take you. Night mush.

ABOUT THE AUTHOR

JULIA ROSEMARY TURK is the debut author of *Lone Player* and winner of the 2021 Lost Island Writing Contest. Born and raised in Northern California's wine country, Julia currently lives with her family (and two adorable dogs) as a writer, English major, and avid indie music enthusiast. She also has chronic Lyme disease and co-infections and is passionate about raising awareness. When she's not working on her next novel, Julia enjoys spending time outside, going on long drives, and brainstorming book ideas with her brothers.

JULIAROSEMARYTURK.CARRD.CO

Learn more about Lyme and how you can make a difference

ALSO FROM LOST ISLAND

NIGHTSHADE ACADEMY
MEL TORREFRANCA

Twenty teenagers are selected for an elite military boarding school, but only five will emerge as guardians—destined for a life of glamour and brutality.

THE MEMORY JUMPER
AMANDA MICHELLE BROWN

Adelaide, an illegal Memory Jumper, lives in an underground safe house with a narcissistic mother who secretly exploits her mind-altering powers for money.

MY BROTHER'S SPARE
SHIRA BEHORE

Valeria's secret investigation to find her mother's murderer pulls her into an alliance with Alias Black, the most infamous hitman in the kingdom.

ABOUT THE PUBLISHER

LOST ISLAND PRESS publishes dystopian, sci-fi, and fantasy books. Unlike mainstream presses, we don't publish everything for everyone. We publish for *you*. Our catalog offers grounded, character-driven stories that linger long after the last page. The kind you get lost in, that keep you up at night. And because our books have the same vibe, if you enjoy one, you'll enjoy them all.

LOSTISLANDPRESS.COM

Join our newsletter to claim a free ebook